HEAT
OF THE EVERFLAME

THE KINDRED'S CURSE SAGA, BOOK THREE

PENN COLE

Cover Design by Maria Spada

Editing by Kelly Helmick at Dog Star Creative Co

Map by Paulina Czaplińska

THE REALMS OF EMARION

LUMNOS, REALM OF LIGHT AND SHADOW

A light which burns, while shadows bite
Their eyes of blue haunt day and night

FORTOS, REALM OF FORCE AND VALOR

With eyes and swords enrobed in red
They'll mend you whole or strike you dead

FAUNOS, REALM OF BEAST AND BRUTE

Fur and feathers, beasts that crawl
Their yellow eyes control them all

ARBOROS, REALM OF ROOT AND THORN

Eyes of moss bring nature's scorn
The prettiest flowers have poison thorns

IGNIOS, REALM OF SAND AND FLAME

Flame in spirit, flame in sight
The desert holds their fiery might

UMBROS, REALM OF MIND AND SECRET

Irises black, with hearts to match
A kiss, and soon your mind they'll snatch

MEROS, REALM OF SEA AND SKY

A gaze to match the vengeful seas
In water deep, they'll drown your pleas

SOPHOS, REALM OF THOUGHT AND SPARK

The cunning spark of wisdom true
Rose eyes will be the death of you

MONTIOS, REALM OF STONE AND ICE

Violet stone to match their gaze
Beware their ice at end of days

For all those caught in the flames,
remember that the hottest fires
forge the strongest swords.

PART ONE

CHAPTER
ONE

S *hit.*
    I'm drowning.

Consciousness rolled into me like a cresting wave. Its current dragged me up from the black depths of my groggy mind, only to curl inward and slam me back under without warning.

My eyelids felt weighted by anchors. I tried to pry them open, but the slivers of light peeking through were too watery, too shapeless to catch hold of.

For a long, confusing moment, I flirted with lucidity, not quite sure if I was awake or dreaming, until a growing fire in my chest heaved me into the present.

I'm drowning, I thought again, the realization more urgent.

I screamed for help, and the sound came out gurgled and weak. Something clamped over my nose and mouth with bruising force.

My throat closed up in a struggle to keep the liquid out despite the desperate urge of my lungs to fill with air. An enormous pressure crushed my thrashing limbs and held them still.

"Stop struggling and swallow."

I stilled at the command. A cool breeze sent a chill prickling over my skin, which I began to realize was mostly dry and definitely not submerged.

My eyes fluttered open, and the hazy world sharpened on an unfamiliar face—a woman with dark brown skin and chestnut eyes, rows of thin braids swept into a knot atop her head.

"Swallow it, and we'll let you breathe." Though her tone was calm, her features were hard as stone and equally unrelenting.

I made a weak attempt at a struggle, but I could barely think past the inferno in my chest, and the woman's unconcerned stare suggested she was perfectly content to let me drown myself out of spite.

I forced the liquid down, and the hand pinching my nose closed fell away, allowing a burst of air to pump into my lungs and cool the fiery grip of panic.

"Good," the woman said, nodding.

She slowly peeled her palm from my lips, allowing me to suck in more air through my clenched teeth, but a quick dart of her eyes to someone I couldn't see had a muscled arm locking tightly around my jaw.

She lifted a mug to my lips. "Again," she commanded.

Liquid sloshed messily across my face. Fluid filled my nostrils, and the panicked sensation of drowning roared back to the surface.

"You'll be fine," she said calmly. "Drink up."

With little choice otherwise, I reluctantly swallowed another mouthful, then another.

My thoughts hitched on the taste coating my mouth. There was something vaguely familiar about it—harsh, almost metallic, but with a tangy bite of citrus smothered under the chalky taste of smoke and ash.

Dread seeped into my bones. I knew that flavor—I'd started every day with a cup of it for nearly ten years.

Flameroot.

"How much of this mixture are we supposed to make them drink?" the woman called over her shoulder.

"I put in three spoonfuls per cup," a voice answered. "Auralie's instructions only called for one, but with this girl being a Crown, I thought she might need a stronger dose."

My mother's name tore through me and hauled me back to the memory of my last moment of consciousness.

I'd been on the dais at the Kindred's Temple, surrounded by the other Crowns of Emarion's nine realms. After surviving the Challenging to earn my place as Queen, my Rite of Coronation had gone horribly wrong. Drops of my blood had summoned a bolt of energy that fractured the heartstone and sent tremors rippling across the sacred island of Coeurîle.

You are not the Queen of Lumnos, the Sophos Crown had accused. *You are an imposter.*

Before I'd been able to defend myself, my mother—the woman whose disappearance eight months ago had unlocked a coffer of secrets that forever changed my life—had emerged from the bushes, screaming my name and warning me to run.

And then everything had detonated into darkness.

"Where is she?" With my jaw still clamped, the words came out as a hiss. "Is Auralie here?"

The woman held my gaze as she slid a weapon from her side and dangled it precariously over my face. The blade was black, and it glittered under the patchy sunlight trickling through the trees.

My eyes went wide.

Godstone. Having been raised as a mortal, I knew very little about the rare material. Until visiting the Kindred's Temple, which was made entirely of the shimmering dark rock, I wasn't sure I'd ever even seen it.

But the one thing I did know was that the godstone's cut was toxic, usually fatal, to those with Descended blood.

"If you know what this is," the woman said, "then you know what I'm capable of doing to you if you get any wild ideas about trying to escape."

The arm around my jaw loosened, and I gave a slight nod. She studied me, her stern expression reinforcing the sincerity of her threat.

"Let her go," she said finally.

The pressure holding my body in place loosened, then disappeared. As I sat up, a ring of burly men scurried backward in a rush to get away. The woman remained at my side, though she took a wide step back and kept her blade tilted toward my chest.

I looked around. I was in some kind of forest, though these trees were not the familiar oak and pine of Lumnos. The thick trunks were as wide as a horse, covered in ropey vines, and stretched mile-high into the sky. Lush ferns and rainbow-hued flowers dotted the landscape.

This was nothing like the tall grass and wild-grown brush I'd seen on the island of Coeurîle. This looked more like Emarion's mainland—one of the southernmost realms, judging by the verdant vegetation.

A crowd stood in a circle around me with weapons drawn. Though a few other blades were also carved from godstone, most were forged from the telltale dark grey metal of Fortosian steel, which—unlike most mortal weapons—would slice easily through my fortified Descended skin.

5

Their expressions ranged from curiosity to wariness to outright hatred, but they all shared one common trait: brown eyes.

Mortal eyes.

The woman lowered her blade slightly. "My name is Cordellia. I'm the leader of our group."

"I'm Diem Bellator," I said. "I wish I could say it's nice to meet you, but I presume I'm not exactly an honored guest."

She shook her head. "Your presence here is not *welcome,* nor are you a *guest*."

My defensive instincts kicked in. I assessed the threats around me as my father had trained me to do. The reminder of him had a stab of grief needling at my heart, his recent murder still too fresh, but I quickly locked it away. I'd already learned how despair could consume me, if allowed to fester. I could not afford to make the same mistake twice.

There were at least forty mortals gathered around me, all armed. The faint sound of voices suggested more were nearby, and whispers drew my eyes to archers tucked high into the trees.

I had no weapons of my own. I tried to pull magic to my palms, but the effort was futile. My chest had hollowed out and my emotions had dulled to a blunt edge, signs that the flameroot had already taken effect.

I was trapped—and unnervingly vulnerable.

"Where is Auralie?" I asked again.

Cordellia's features pinched. "She's unavailable." I couldn't tell if the disapproval radiating from her expression was meant for me or my mother.

"I have no desire to hurt you," I said truthfully. "I'm not like the other Crowns. If I can just speak with Auralie, she'll explain. She's my—"

"Your mother. We know. That's why you're still alive."

Even with the flameroot dampening my emotions, my blood chilled.

I chose my next words carefully. "You must be close friends. My mother would not share the details of the flameroot if she did not trust you."

Cordellia's brows furrowed deeper. "If only she had been as forthcoming about her Descended offspring."

Ah—the disapproval was for us both.

My smile was wry and edged with bitterness. "If it's any consolation, she did not deem either of us worthy of that secret."

Surprised murmurs scuttled through the crowd.

Cordellia frowned. "You did not know you were Descended?"

"Not until I inherited the Crown." I hoped the honesty of my frustra-

6

tion slipped through in my sigh. "There is much I'm still learning myself—including how I came to be here with you now."

She looked me over for a moment, then signaled to two large men, who walked toward me carrying a pair of iron shackles connected by a thick, heavy chain. They puffed out their chests as they approached, though the intimidation tactic did little to hide the nerves in their big eyes and quivering hands.

"Up," Cordellia commanded. "Hands out, wrists together."

It cut against everything in my nature to give in, but I was out of alternatives. I stood and clasped my hands in front of me like a prayer. As one of the men secured the shackles to my wrists, I flashed a sweet smile at the other.

"Blessed is the Everflame, Brother," I said, batting my lashes with mock piety.

Both men froze, staring at me, then turned to Cordellia. She gestured for them to continue, but their reactions told me everything I needed to know.

These were not just any mortals.

"Is this how the Guardians of the Everflame treat a fellow Sister?" I asked, jingling the chunky metal chains.

"You're no Guardian," one of the men growled.

I clicked my tongue. "Wrong answer, Brother. I believe the proper response to the code words is '*Emarion soil, we shall reclaim.*' Though I confess, it has been a few weeks since my last meeting."

The man clacked the lock into place on my wrists and gave me a hard shove backward, sending me flailing ungracefully to the leaf-blanketed ground.

Cordellia barked an order that had the two men walking away with a snicker, then extended a hand to me. I shot her a distrustful look of my own, but I took her hand and let her help me back to my feet. At this close range, I towered over her by several inches. In fact, I stood taller than almost every mortal gathered in the clearing, man or woman.

I had become used to that growing up, believing myself unusually long-limbed for a mortal. Then my surprise fate as Queen had dragged me into the world of the naturally tall, muscled Descended, and I'd gone from being one of the biggest people in every room to one of the most petite—all while going from near-anonymity to the most powerful person in my realm.

It was a visible symbol of what my life had become. I lived with a foot in two worlds, each a mirror image of the other, never fitting quite right into either one. In a world of black and white, I was trying to find my place in shades of grey.

"I see you're familiar with our group," Cordellia said blandly.

Her restraint was impressive. Discovering that a Descended Queen had intimate knowledge of the forbidden rebel network should have been cause for alarm. Her expression showed only a placid apathy.

"Before I became Queen, I was a member of the Lumnos cell," I explained.

Cordellia's eyes shifted over my shoulder and narrowed. "Then it seems your mother was not the only one withholding information."

I started to follow her line of sight, but flickers of movement from the archers froze me in place.

"And after you became Queen?" she pushed. "Did your involvement continue?"

My shoulders tensed. Cordellia's shrewd eyes noted the movement.

"The relationship became... strained," I hedged. "But I spoke the truth when I said I have no desire to hurt you. I am no enemy to the Guardians."

"You're no friend of ours, either," a male voice rang out from behind me.

A man with pale skin and a thick, overgrown beard circled around and stepped into view. I recognized him immediately as the leader of the Lumnos cell and the man who had initiated me as a Guardian.

And the man who had branded me a traitor after I'd refused to obey his orders.

"Vance," I said in greeting, though it came out like a snarl. "I recall being a *friend* when I gave you access to the royal boat."

"Was that loyalty?" he shot back. "Or was it a woman desperate to win back her betrothed after she betrayed him and locked him in her dungeon?"

My stomach twisted at the mention of Henri. I wouldn't give Vance the satisfaction of admitting it, but he was right—I'd helped the Guardians in a last-ditch attempt to repair the broken trust between myself and my childhood love.

It had been immeasurably reckless considering what I knew the Guardians were capable of, but I had been so lost over my father's death, so consumed with rage at the Descended over his murder, I had naively convinced myself that I could find a way to help Henri while keeping the Guardians from taking things too far.

I should have known the Guardians would *always* take things too far.

Cordellia glanced between the two of us. "You never told me she helped with the planning for our attack on the island, Vance. And you certainly never mentioned she was a member of your cell."

"Attack?" I repeated. "What attack?"

Vance shrugged lightly. "Her membership was so brief, I barely remember it. And I did tell you she has been useful, even if she isn't trustworthy."

"*I'm* not trustworthy?" I took a few steps toward him. Cordellia wheeled her knife back in my direction to keep me at a distance. "I kept your secrets, didn't I? And I saved your life the night of the ball. *And* when the guards spotted us in the canal."

"And now I've returned the favor," he snapped. "You were spared from the attack. Consider my debt to you and your mother repaid in full."

"What debt to my mother?" I stormed closer to Vance, even as Cordellia's godstone blade came within inches of my skin. "Where is she? And what happened on the island?"

"Step back," Cordellia warned as she pushed herself between us.

My focus shifted to her, my voice rising with my anger. "You try to drown me, forcibly drug me, refuse to explain anything, and throw me in chains." I raised my fists, jolting the shackles with a loud clink. "I'll '*step back*' when one of you starts giving me answers."

One of the archers loosed an arrow, the edge of it whizzing past my ear as it barely missed my head. A few severed strands of my snow-white hair floated to the ground.

I held my glare in refusal to back down, channeling my father's lessons as his voice whispered guidance in my ear.

Never give in to a warning shot, or they'll only learn to shoot more often. Don't provoke a fight unless you intend to see it through.

I locked eyes with Cordellia and leaned in until the point of her dagger sat against my throat. A dare to act—and a very dangerous gamble.

"You know my mother, so you must also know my father," I rumbled. "And if you know anything about *him*, then you know I don't need magic or weapons to defend myself if I have to."

"See?" Vance sniped. "She's already threatening us. I told you she couldn't be trusted."

I slid my gaze to Vance and held his stare until he huffed and looked away.

"Step back, Miss Bellator," Cordellia said evenly. "Cooperate, and I'll give you answers."

Vance struck up his protests again, this time walking close to Cordellia and whispering his complaints too quietly for me to decipher. I watched a spark of irritation flip across her face before she reined it back in. She did not seem like a woman who let her frustration show easily—the fact Vance had pushed her this far told me there was a crack in the bond between the two Guardian leaders.

A crack I needed to widen.

I lowered my hands and took a slow step back as I dipped my chin in deference. "Forgive my anger," I said to Cordellia. "Where he is involved, I have a difficult time giving my trust. Like you, I've found Vance has a habit of withholding critical details. From women, at least." I gave her a loaded, knowing look. "Only his male colleagues were fully informed."

Vance scoffed. "I worked with your mother for years. *She* never had a problem with me."

"Really?" I cocked my head and frowned. "That's strange. She and I often discussed who in Lumnos she trusted with sensitive information, and she never once mentioned you."

He jabbed a finger in my direction. "You're just trying t—"

"That's enough, Brother Vance," Cordellia scolded. "I can handle this."

He stiffened and turned his glare on her. "I think you mean *Father* Vance."

"Only in Lumnos. Here in Arboros, you are a Brother, same as any other man."

Arboros, Realm of Root and Thorn.

I should have known. During my time as a Guardian, I'd heard the Lumnos and Arboros cells were working together on a mission, and Henri and my former healer colleague Lana, both Guardians, had left for Arboros days before the Rite of Coronation.

Vance crossed his arms. "I'm a realm leader just like you, *Mother* Cordellia. I've earned my title."

"Did you?" I cut in. "Henri told me you were just borrowing the title until the woman in charge returned."

Cordellia nodded. "She's right, Vance. You're only the Lumnos Father until Auralie can resume her post as the leader of the Guardians."

Leader of the Guardians.

Blood rushed from my head.

"What did you say?" I croaked. "Auralie—my mother... she's..."

Cordellia's brows rose. "You didn't know that, either? She's led us for nearly a decade."

The memories of my life somersaulted around me, reframed by an impossible new reality. My mother, Auralie Bellator, was the leader of the ruthless, violent rebels preparing to raise a bloody war against the Descended. Against *me*.

My mother, who had made her career working for the Descended as a healer in the Emarion Army.

My mother, who must have slept with a Descended man to become pregnant with me.

My mother, who had negotiated to send her son, Teller, to the Descended academy to grow up among Lumnos's elite.

All my cherished mental images of her suddenly felt warped and misshapen, the colors all wrong, like a painting left outside to wilt in the sun and rain. How could those choices have come from the same woman? Had my father known the truth about her? Did Teller know?

Did *Luther* know—was that why he had secretly helped her?

My chest squeezed painfully taut at the thought of him. He would be wondering where I was, fretting over whether I was safe, blaming himself for my capture. He had barely been willing to let me leave the palace without a small militia of guards—if he knew I was being held in chains in a rebel camp, he would stop at nothing to storm in and save me.

Just like he would have rushed in when he noticed the rebels attacking Coeurîle.

My heart leapt into my throat. "The attack—was anyone hurt? Were there any casualties?"

Cordellia's expression softened with a touch of sympathy. "Your mother survived. She wasn't hurt, but she—"

"Were any of the Descended killed?"

The question spilled out in a rush. I tried and failed miserably at feigning indifference, but there was a flurry of movement as mouths tightened and eyes narrowed, suspicion spreading like wildfire across the mortals' faces.

"There was a man who came with me to the island. He—he was a friend to my mother. And to me." My pulse picked up speed as the prospect of losing him grew too large and too real. "He's a good man. He helped the mortals. He—"

"You were the only Descended we were instructed to spare," Cordellia said curtly. All lingering warmth cooled from her tone. "There were casualties on both sides. I cannot offer you any more information than that."

My knees felt made of sawdust, ready to collapse at the slightest gust. If

Luther had been killed trying to protect me—and from an attack I might have played a part in bringing about...

I would never forgive myself, if that was the case. And I would never forgive my mother.

"Please," I begged, my anger giving way to desperation. "Tell me what happened. Why was my mother there? Why am I here?"

Cordellia sighed. "When it became clear the King of Lumnos would die soon, your mother knew the Crowns would have to meet to coronate his heir. She proposed that, during the ritual, we launch an attack to capture the island. She had an associate that was able to smuggle her onto Coeurîle this past Forging Day to set up explosives and light them once the Crowns arrived." She paused. "I don't think she anticipated her *daughter* would be the one coronated."

"Nor did we realize it would be eight months until we could strike," Vance muttered.

Scattered details from the last year began to slot into place.

Luther must have been the *associate* to bring her to the island. Only the Crowns were permitted access to Coeurîle, and even then only for specific occasions, but perhaps Luther had been permitted to go in the King's place, given his illness.

No wonder Luther had been so certain she would still be alive. With my mother's background, she would know how to forage on the island for safe food and water, and as long as she wasn't spotted by the army boats who patrolled the nearby waters, she would have been entirely undisturbed.

And that's why he had promised to recover her by year end—he knew she would be there for my Rite of Coronation.

Warring emotions played tug-of-war with my heart. Frustration with Luther for not telling me, but terror that something might have happened to him. Resentment at my mother for setting this all in motion with her secrets, and a desperate need to see her again and know she was safe.

"Auralie asked that we spare the next Lumnos Crown only if it was a man with dark hair and a scar," Cordellia continued. "You're lucky Vance was able to get to you in time. After you were knocked unconscious by the explosions, he dragged you to safety and got you off the island while the Descended were distracted."

Vance shot me a pointed look, his brows sky-high in expectation of my groveling thanks, but I couldn't tear my eyes from Cordellia. "The man with the scar—did you see him there? Did he survive?"

"I cannot say, and there's no way to know now. The bodies of the

Descended were burned to prevent their healing abilities from taking effect."

I swayed on unsteady legs as bile rose in my throat. It was the night of the armory fire all over again. Descended guards, dead and burning, for an attack I unwittingly brought about. Their blood on my hands, their corpses at my feet.

Only this time, the dead might not be strangers.

"Where is my mother? I need to see her."

"I told you, she's not here."

"Take me to her."

"I cannot do that."

"Why? Is she still on the island? Just release me, I'll find a way there myself." I tore at the metal cuffs on my wrists as nervous men edged toward me with weapons raised. One of them got too close, and I swung my chains at him, sending the men shuffling backward.

Cordellia raised a hand and took a hesitant step toward me. "You need to calm down."

"Is she in Lumnos?" I was becoming frantic, my words tripping over my tongue. "Let me go, let me get her—it's not safe for her there. You don't have to take me, I—I can make my way back on my own. Please, I need to leave."

She shook her head. "Diem—"

"*Let me go to her!*" I shouted.

"You can't," Vance interrupted. "She's in a prison cell in Fortos, awaiting execution. She was captured trying to protect *you*."

His words reverberated ominously through the chasm of my thoughts. I blinked at Cordellia and searched her face for some evidence that Vance was only riling me up out of petty revenge, but she pursed her lips and nodded.

"We're working on a rescue mission," she said. "We have allies in Fortos who may be able to help her."

Though her expression was confident, all I could focus on was the slight catch in her voice. My short time as Queen had taught me something about wearing a mask of assurance when failure was all but certain, and I knew it when I saw it.

"I'll go back to my realm and negotiate for her," I said. "I can speak with the King of Fortos. Now that I've been coronated, he might listen to me."

"You're a brand new queen with ties to the mortal world. You have no leverage and nothing to offer in exchange."

"And you do?" I shot back.

"*Yes*," she clipped. "We have the island now. The Crowns will need access to it to complete their rituals. They can't hold out for long—our sources tell us the longer they delay their ceremonies, the more unstable their magic becomes." She gave me a hard look. "And we have something else they'll need, too."

I frowned. "What?"

"You," Vance answered with a smirk. "They need all nine Crowns to complete the rituals. We're not giving them back the island, not even for Auralie. But we can give them you."

"Good," I said sharply, nodding. "I'll do it. Whatever you need."

Surprise dashed over both their faces.

"You'll cooperate?" Cordellia asked.

"She's my mother. Do you really think I will not do whatever it takes to save her?"

A crack of uncertainty broke through her expression. "You're a Descended. And a Crown. Your kind have never been loyal to ours."

"I'm part mortal, too. Your kind *are* my kind. As for my Crown, I'll tell you the same thing I told the Descended of Lumnos." I lifted my chin defiantly. "I intend to be a Queen that works for the good of *all* her people, regardless of their blood."

Her eyes narrowed. "You will not take the mortals' side, even though you have seen how we are treated?"

"I will do everything in my power to right the wrongs that have been done to the mortals, but I will not stand for violence against innocent people—mortal *or* Descended." I shot a glare at Vance, who grunted and rolled his eyes.

Cordelia's gaze roved slowly over me as she studied me more closely. I understood her prejudice—I had held the very same perception of the Descended mere weeks ago. I believed them all cruel, soulless, and incapable of compassion. I still might, had I not been forced into becoming one of them myself.

Although... something in the way she finished her assessment of me with a subtle nod, some quiet strength and certainty of conviction that glowed behind her deep russet eyes, left me hoping I might have more of an ally in her than I had thought.

"You have a mortal brother, correct?" she asked, and I nodded. "I can have the Lumnos Guardians get him from your realm and bring him here. He'll be safe with my people."

For a moment, I genuinely considered it. As a full-blooded mortal, Teller would be welcomed here, even if I wasn't. And though a rebel camp wasn't exactly a *safe* place to be, neither was the palace, especially with our father's killer still at large.

But bringing Teller here would mean ending his education—and his relationship with Lily—and if the Descended discovered he was being sheltered by the Guardians, it would put a target on his head I could never remove.

No. Teller had already lost too much. I could not take away what little of his happiness remained. I would have to trust my new Corbois friends to keep him safe.

"Leave him be," I answered finally. "I have allies there who will watch over him until I return."

"It may be quite some time," she warned. "We've sent messages to the Crowns, but we may not receive a response for months."

I stiffened. "I don't have months. The Descended in my realm were already itching to attack the mortals. If I don't return soon..." I thought of Aemonn and his appointment as executioner and head of the Royal Guard, and a chill crept over my skin. "I need to get back and stop them before things get worse."

"My men will take care of things in Lumnos," Vance interjected.

"No, your men will start a war in Lumnos," I protested. "Your approach is only going to get people killed."

"The war has already started, *Your Majesty*." He said the title like a curse, spitting on the ground and resting a hand on the hilt of his blade. "Unlike you, we're not afraid to fight—and die, if we must."

Cordellia raised a palm to cut me off before I could argue. "You said you would do whatever it takes—well, this is what it takes. Patience. And trust in us to handle our side."

I swallowed my protest, the taste of it bitter as it stuck in my throat. Too many swords hung precariously over my head. I needed to find Luther and make sure he was unhurt, rescue my mother and get answers from her about who and what I was, and return to Lumnos to take my throne before Remis and his allies could wreak havoc that I couldn't undo.

For now, I had no choice. I would have to wait and pray that when the blades came tumbling down, I had my own defenses in order.

CHAPTER

TWO

"Were you not listening when I said I agreed to help?"

The angry, neckless man grunted in response, then shoved me further into the trees.

Any hopes I had that my cooperation would earn me better treatment than a prisoner of war had been quickly dispelled when Cordellia ordered a Guardian to "chain her up with the other one"—a description I was equal parts eager and anxious to investigate.

"You could at least remove the shackles," I grumbled as I struggled to stay on my feet against his harsh jerking and pushing. "I'm not going to run. I gave my word that I would stay."

"You're a Descended," he sneered. "Your word means nothing."

"*Half*-Descended. We're not so different. I was raised mortal. I was treated like scum by them, too."

"You're all selfish at heart. It's in your blood, no upbringing's gonna change it."

I abruptly planted my feet, forcing us both to a stop. "You can't really believe that."

He sneered. "Lady, there's nothing I believe more."

"We both know there are good and bad mortals. Why can't there be good and bad Descended, too?"

He glared at me in a way that said he knew I was making sense and it pissed him off. "If you were raised like us, how can you defend them?"

"I can't. The shit they've put us through—" His eyes narrowed accusingly, and I rolled mine. "—fine, put *the mortals* through... it's unforgivable. But no matter how this war goes, we still have to live together when it ends. We can't do that if we refuse to see any good in each other."

I offered him a hopeful smile. His curled upper lip softened into more of a bark than a bite. There were cogs churning in his head, slogging through a toxic muck of earned prejudice I knew all too well.

As he worked his jaw, chewing on my words, my eyes drifted over his shoulder. Nestled in a circle of dense brush that obscured it almost entirely from view, I caught a glimpse of something that sent fear crackling down my veins.

Explosives. The favorite tool of the mortal rebels. Stacks upon stacks of them in an array of sizes and materials. Enough to level an entire town—or a Descended palace.

I took in a sharp breath, and the man followed my stare to the hoard of homemade bombs. His features gnarled into a scowl as any ground I might have earned with him eroded away.

"Planning your attack on us already?" He yanked me forward again. "Mother Dell might be willing to work with some of you, but that don't mean I have to trust you. I know what you are. Save your pretty words for some other fool."

We stalked along in silence until we reached a thinly forested area with tents scattered throughout. Chained to the trunk of a small tree was a woman on her knees, her hands similarly shackled, a glowing Crown of foliage and continuously blooming flowers hovering over her head.

"Arboros?" I gasped.

Her emerald eyes locked with mine and widened. "Lumnos!"

I turned my shocked expression on my escort. "You captured the Queen of the realm you're hiding in? Are all of you out of *your gods-damned minds?*"

He didn't respond, staring doggedly ahead as we approached her.

"Thank the Kindred you're alive," she said breathlessly. "I thought you'd been killed in the explosion."

The man began to secure my shackles to a chain woven around the base of the tree, and I felt a burst of relief that she and I would be close enough to talk—and for me to learn what had happened on the island.

My heart skipped a beat. If she had seen the attack, perhaps she had seen Luther get away safely. The question rose up in my throat and hung there, trapped in place by the terrifying prospect of discovering the answer.

"Are you hurt?" I asked instead.

Though the moss-lined cape I'd last seen her in now hung in singed tatters over her shoulders, she looked otherwise unscathed. She shook her head and climbed to her feet. "Did you see any of the others?"

"No—I thought I was the only one."

I frowned, thinking back over Cordellia and Vance's words. Why had they spoken as if I was the Guardians' only bargaining chip? If they already had the Arboros Queen to exchange for my mother's freedom, why keep me from returning to Lumnos?

Unless they didn't plan to let the Arboros Queen live that long.

"You're up next," the man barked at her. He waved over a few more Guardians to join him. They boxed us in against the base of the tree, several with knives out, another swinging a wooden club.

"What are you going to do with her?" I demanded, my hackles rising.

"Choosing to protect *them*, eh?" He snorted. "Just like I thought. Get out of the way, lady. She's coming with us."

I shimmied in front of her as much as the chains would allow, using myself as a shield. "Not until you swear she'll be brought back unharmed."

"I don't answer to you, half-breed. We're in charge here, and we'll do whatever we want."

I returned his scowl. "You sound just like the Descended."

A furious red flushed across his face. He jerked his chin at the others. "Grab her."

The Guardians launched forward. Before I could react, strong hands clamped around my arms and waist and dragged me out of the way. The lock on the Arboros Queen's chains clicked open, her panicked pleas for help sending my heart sprinting.

"No!" I shouted, thrashing against their grip. I swung my shackles over my head and connected with the solid flesh of a skull. A voice swore as the arms caging me loosened.

"We've got her," someone announced. The others released me and hurriedly ran out of my reach. One of them clutched a bloody gash at his temple, the promise of retribution burning in his glare.

I watched in horror as the Arboros Queen was dragged further away. "Lumnos!" she pleaded, her bright green eyes bulging wide.

I tried to rush toward her, but the hefty chains snapped me backward. "Arboros!" I cried helplessly.

A few men in the group lingered beside me and chuckled at my panic.

18

One of them spat at my feet. "Say goodbye to your pretty friend, Descended scum."

Boiling adrenaline surged through my veins. I pulled at my chains, straining against their hold as my feet clawed divots into the earth.

Having not been raised as a Descended or given the benefit of their in-depth education, I had no clue how far I could go before my body snapped. My very skin and bones were an enigma.

And what about the flameroot—did it dampen strength and healing like it affected magic? In my years under its influence, I had never attempted to push myself beyond what I believed a mortal could realistically do.

But what if I wasn't as weak as a mortal—what if I was capable of so much more?

At first, the men watched me in haughty amusement. Even as a Queen, in their eyes I was just a frail, pathetic woman, struggling pointlessly against the superiority of nature and of men.

But I had almost given up once before, and it had nearly cost me everything. Since then, I'd sworn to never be weak again. With or without my magic, I would not stop fighting—not now, not ever.

I strained forward against my chains. Mud curled around the soles of my impractical silk slippers as the balls of my feet sank deeper into the rain-softened soil. The iron shackles bit painfully into my skin, their metal joints squealing under the force of my tugging.

A crackling sound reverberated through the forest. The men's laughter abruptly stopped.

I grunted and pulled again at the manacles until the chain links began to groan and warp.

Behind me, the crackling grew louder, and I gained a step.

"What in the glaciers of hell," one of the men mumbled, his face blanching.

"The tree," another breathed.

I spared a glance over my shoulder. The trunk of the tree was cocked at an angle, roots dangling in the air and dripping clumps of freshly turned sod.

Even the Arboros Queen stared in disbelief.

I wasted no time, burrowing a new foothold and lurching forward in short, powerful bursts. With every yank, the tree tilted further, more and more roots springing free from the earth. The mortals began shouting, swarming, calling for help, surrounding the trunk.

With a liberating *clink*, the chain holding my right arm snapped apart.

Chaos broke out. Some Guardians fled, while others called for help. A few clawed onto the remaining chain that kept my left arm tethered.

"You can't hold me forever," I growled at the man who'd escorted me. "Let her stay here safely with me."

A split second of indecision wavered over his face. He squared his shoulders and snatched the wooden club from his colleague's hand. "Get the other one to Mother Dell," he ordered, then turned toward me. "I'll handle her."

I heaved forward with every ounce of remaining strength. The tree crunched and swayed, threatening to fall, as a crowd of Guardians pushed against the trunk to counter my efforts.

Their fight was as useless as a flower striking a nail. Despite the flame-root's effect, I was strong—*incredibly* strong. Stronger than I ever would have imagined. I wasn't sure the throng of mortals could have made a dent against me even if they were triple in number.

The thought was as exhilarating as it was worrying. Were all Descended this strong—and this difficult to contain?

I might have taken a moment to fret over what that would mean in the coming war, had the final chain not snapped free just as a club came barreling at my skull.

My momentum launched me forward not a second too soon, the weapon whizzing past the tip of my nose. I darted around the man before he could make a second attempt and sprinted for the horrified-looking Queen of Arboros.

And I might have made it, had my newfound finery not caught up with me. The long, silky blue-grey gown I had chosen for my coronation—*because it reminded me of Luther's eyes, and I'd wanted to feel like he was watching over me*, I remembered with a sharp pang in my chest—tangled around my legs and sent me sprawling. I scrambled to get back to my feet.

"Lumnos," the Arboros Queen screamed. "*Behind you!*"

I twisted around. The last thing I saw was a pair of thin brown eyes, smoldering with hatred, and the blur of a swinging club.

CHAPTER

THREE

I awoke with a groan and a headache from hell.

My eyelids flickered open to a star-flecked midnight sky. The drooping eye of the pale crescent moon gazed down at me with bland curiosity, leaving me with the feeling she was distinctly unimpressed.

I reached to rub at the sore spot near my temple, but my arm could barely move. In fact, almost none of me could move.

The Guardians had chained me up again, this time in a broad, grassy meadow with a single tree at its center. The trunk was massive, at least three times the width of the tree I'd nearly uprooted before, with tangled roots as thick as my thigh. A pair of shackles had been added to my ankles, and several heavy new chains were latched to each set of cuffs with barely enough slack to allow me to sit up.

Even with my Descended strength, there would be no escaping this.

Though there wasn't a soul in sight—including the Arboros Queen, I realized with sinking dread—I knew from the faint hum of voices and the smoky scent of a campfire that the Guardians weren't far away, and I was all but certain the wall of trees circling the clearing concealed archers ready to take me down if I somehow managed to get free.

I managed to gingerly press a hand to the wound on my head and sucked in air as soreness lanced across my scalp. It hurt like mad, but the ache was dull and widespread, the swelling only mild. It felt like it had been healing for days rather than hours.

It seemed the flameroot hadn't stopped my swift Descended healing. If I could avoid their godstone weapons, I might actually make it out of this place alive.

The sound of footsteps stole my attention. On the far side of the meadow, the lean form of a man emerged from the shadows.

My muscles tensed as his lanky silhouette sauntered closer. As my eyes adjusted to the dim moonlight, a gasp burst from my lips.

"Brecke?" I called out.

A cautious smile peeked through the overgrown mess of his beard. "You know, when I told Henri Albanon to make sure he held on to you, this wasn't the method I had in mind."

I choked out a laugh, the warmth in his tone having an unexpected impact. I hadn't realized how much I needed to know there was at least one person here who wasn't itching to kill me at the first opportunity.

He crouched in front of me and set down a tray with a bowl of stew and a mug full of steaming liquid. His hair had grown out, no longer shorn in the tight military style now that he'd abandoned his post as a bladesmith in the Emarion Army. It added a roughshod gravitas to his deceivingly youthful features.

His eyes rose to my Crown, its bright glow curiously unaffected by the flameroot. "Your situation has much changed since I last saw you, Diem Bellator."

I smiled grimly and jostled the chains binding my arms. "In more ways than one."

"I should have taken you up on the offer to test you for Descended skin when I met you in Fortos."

"I didn't know, Brecke. I swear it."

"I know." He sat on the patch of soil beside me. "I spoke to Henri just before the attack. He told me Auralie lied to you."

I stiffened. "Henri was on the island?"

Brecke nodded. "He asked me to keep an eye on you once the attack began."

Guilt weighed on my chest. I hadn't given Henri much more than a passing thought since regaining consciousness. My thoughts had been focused on my mother—and on Luther.

"Did he..." I swallowed. "Is—is he...?"

"Alive and well." Brecke gave me a bright smile, misreading my inner turmoil as mere concern. "He and the other Lumnos Guardians rushed home to avoid provoking suspicion. Only Vance stayed behind."

I let out a long, relieved sigh. Though my complicated feelings for Henri had become painful in a way I was still coming to terms with, he was my oldest friend. His life would always be precious to me—even if, soon, he might not want me in it ever again.

Brecke's grin widened. "I hear you two are getting married. A Descended Queen marrying a Guardian—that wedding will have one hell of a guest list." He nudged my leg with his knee. "Think I'll make the cut? I'm not above begging."

My forced smile must have looked as miserable as it felt. Brecke's smirk abruptly dropped away.

"You are still betrothed, aren't you?" he asked.

Henri's last words to me floated into my thoughts—the note he'd arranged for his father to deliver on the eve of my Challenging.

Good luck tomorrow. I'll see you soon. Remember, whatever it may look like, we are on the same side.

I hadn't understood at the time, but now...

"Brecke," I said slowly, "did Henri know Vance's plan was to capture me and keep me as a prisoner?"

He shifted his weight, looking deeply uncomfortable. "Vance and Cordellia planned the attack. The rest of us just do as we're told. We may not like the plan, but we—"

"*Did he know?*"

Brecke didn't respond. That was answer enough.

"Unbelievable," I growled.

"Oh, come on," he teased, "what's a little hostage-taking between future spouses?"

My jaw clenched.

He chuckled nervously. "It'll make a great story for the wedding toast. I'll tell it myself, I—"

"There's not going to be a wedding," I snapped.

He frowned. "Don't say that. I know you're upset, but you two can work through this."

I glanced off into the darkness, wishing I could slip into the foliage and disappear. I couldn't tell Brecke the real truth—that Henri and I had been done long before the attack. And deep down, I think we'd both known it, even if neither of us had been able to admit it to the other.

Henri had chosen the Guardians over me, and I had chosen Luther over him. Though I would always care for him, some gulfs were too deep, too broad, too laden with sharp objects to overcome.

Brecke let out a heavy sigh, scratching at the back of his neck. "The life of a Guardian isn't an easy one, you know. None of us want to keep secrets from the people we care about, but sometimes we have no choice. Some Guardians don't even tell their own spouses what we do to protect them."

I recoiled. "*Protect them?* Do you have any idea what the Lumnos Descended demanded for the attack on the Benette armory? Punishing the Guardians wasn't nearly enough. They wanted me to round up their friends and family and execute them just to send a message. And that was over a few carts of stolen weapons. What do you think they'll expect now that you've taken Coeurîle?" I gave a bitter, humorless laugh. "Your secrets aren't protecting anyone. Once this war starts, it won't matter who is and isn't a Guardian. No mortal will be safe from the violence."

Brecke's face paled, though an angry fire burned behind his gaze. "All the more reason our work is necessary. Henri is doing this for your future. That boy loves you."

I rolled my eyes. "Love requires honesty, Brecke."

"Your mother keeps it from your father. She made it clear to all of us that he is never to be told. Do you really believe she does not love him?"

"My father is *dead*," I shouted, my voice echoing across the moonlit clearing. "He's dead because of me. Because I was not prepared to be Queen. That chance was stolen from me by her lies." I leaned forward, pulling the chains on my arms taut. "And thanks to the Guardians, she wasn't even there to comfort her children as they mourned his death. So don't you dare lecture me on my mother's love—or her secrets."

His face softened with pity. Normally, the sight of it would only further provoke me, but with the flameroot muffling my temper and rendering the *voice* silent, I found my rising emotions quickly giving way to a terrible numbness. It took me back to all those years as a teenager, being reckless and picking fights just to feel *something* that might cut through the scarlet fog.

"I shouldn't have said anything," he murmured. "Apologies. It wasn't my place."

I slumped back against the tree trunk, tired and empty. "What *is* your place? What are you doing for the Guardians?"

"I used my position as Master Bladesmith in the army to redirect weapons to the rebels when I could. Often my orders to produce and ship weapons to certain areas would reveal the army's movements, and I would pass that information to the Guardians so they could intercept the shipment or clear their people out before reinforcements arrived."

"Sounds like a useful position."

"It was."

"So why did you quit?"

He raised an eyebrow. "How did you know I quit?"

"Oh, the King of Fortos might have mentioned to me that you disappeared with a large shipment of weapons—right after I told him you were a *'good family friend.'*"

Brecke sucked in air between his teeth. "Oh. That's bad."

I gave him a wry smile. "I'm sure he and my mother are having a nice long chat about it in her prison cell as we speak."

"I'm sorry," he said quietly.

A long silence passed in the darkness as my heart strained against its own set of shackles. It was hard to reconcile my simmering anger at my mother with my desperate fear that I might not be able to free her before the Descended took their revenge.

"I have to save her, Brecke," I whispered. I looked at him, my expression pleading. "I have to get her out of Fortos, and I have to get back to Lumnos before the Descended there go after the mortals. Help me. *Please.*"

"I wish I could, Diem, but it's not my call. Now that I'm a wanted man in Fortos, the Arboros cell has been kind enough to take me in, but I have no authority here. You'll have to trust in—"

"Cordellia and Vance," I finished glumly. "Vance made it very clear he's willing to sacrifice anyone to hurt the Descended. If my mother's life depends on him, she's as good as dead."

"I'll admit, Vance's methods are... controversial. But Dell is a thoughtful leader, and a damn smart one. If she thinks this is the way to save Auralie, give her a chance."

I hung my head, staring at the mass of thick chains leashing me in place while the people I loved were miles away, danger closing in on them from every side.

"Can you at least tell me what happened on the island?" I asked.

"When your mother went to Coeurîle, she was only able to smuggle in a few bombs. The plan was for her to place one on the north shore of the island as a diversion to attract the army boats so we could load in from Arboros in the south, then set off the rest at the Kindred's Temple. We were able to get a small group of Guardians in just before the attack to help light the fuses, but—"

"How did you manage that?"

"I can't tell you."

"Why not? I'm a Guardian, aren't I?" I raised my shackled wrists. "I'm cooperating."

Brecke threw me a sympathetic wince, but he didn't offer more.

I thought back to the morning of the attack, when Luther and I had departed from the canal beneath the palace. I hadn't mustered the courage to admit to him that I had given the Guardians access to the boat, but I had made him swear that he thoroughly checked it before we left.

But Luther had helped my mother spy on the late King—a mission for the Guardians, I now realized—and he'd helped her get to Coeurîle. He'd admitted to me before that he knew about the Guardians. Perhaps he'd even known my mother's role among them.

Was it possible he was helping the Guardians, too? Gods... had he known about the attack, too?

A part of me wanted it to be true, if only because it might mean that he had avoided the violence, leaving him alive and safe.

But I knew Luther too well now. In my heart, I knew he wouldn't condone such an attack—and he would *never* put me in harm's way.

My chest squeezed painfully.

"Fine," I muttered. "Continue."

"We'd hoped the bombs might bring down the Temple, but we underestimated the strength of the godstone. The explosions didn't even make a crack. Plan B was to take the stone at the center, but the Descended must have secured it in some way. It wouldn't move, and it burned us when we tried to touch it. So we went with Plan C—commandeer the entire Temple. I wasn't sure we'd really be able to do it, but the Descended can't use their magic on the island, and they're not used to relying on weapons alone. With our explosives and our godstone weapons, we had the upper hand."

I shot him a hard look. "That won't last forever. The Crowns will stop at nothing to take it back."

His answering stare was grim. "I know. But if we can hold it long enough for their Forging spell to break down, they may get desperate enough to make a deal. And if we can figure out how to get that rock out of the Temple, we'll have leverage even if they take back the island. They seem to care a great deal about protecting that stone, whatever it is." He studied me carefully. "Do you know anything about it?"

I swallowed. *The heartstone*—the source of the Forging magic.

This is our most precious secret, the Sophos Crown had said, *the truth that each of us guards with our lives. For if the heartstone is destroyed, so too shall our realms crumble and fall.*

26

Controlling the heartstone could indeed be the key to changing the tides in the coming war—but I had learned my lesson about entrusting the Guardians with dangerous information.

"No," I lied, covering my deceit with an irritated smirk. "The Crowns were just about to tell me all their dirty little secrets when a bomb interrupted us."

Brecke gave a halfhearted laugh and shrugged. "Ah, well. It was damaged in the attack—the initial explosion split a crack right through it. We've planted a ring of bombs around it so we can threaten to blow it to pieces if they try to take back the island by force."

What he didn't know was that the Guardians' bombs hadn't cracked the heartstone. It was the drops of my blood that had spilled onto its surface during the Rite of Coronation, sending a bolt of lightning into the stone, a tremor rolling through the earth, and a look of pure fear striking across the faces of the Descended Crowns.

What would the Guardians do with me if they knew *that?*

"Were you there during the attack?" I asked.

"Only for part of it."

"Did you see..." I paused to steady myself as my heart thundered in my chest. "Was there a Descended man there with long, dark hair and a scar down his face?"

Brecke frowned. "Was he one of the army soldiers?"

"No, he was my—"

I stopped short. I didn't even really know what Luther was to me yet. I only knew that if he was gone, it would destroy me.

"He was waiting for me at the Lumnos port," I said. "He would have run in to find me once the fighting began."

Brecke shook his head. "After the explosions, it was chaos. There was smoke everywhere, it was impossible to see much. You were knocked out by the initial blast, and then your mother ran right into the midst of it and dragged you out. She told me if I didn't get you off the island, she'd have my ass, and I know better than to ignore a threat from Auralie Bellator. I took you to Vance, and he and I got on a boat back to Arboros."

I leaned back against the tree, the rough bark biting into my skin through the tattered remains of my thin silk gown. My eyes rose to the midnight moon watching over me in her silent, secret way. Was Luther out there somewhere, staring at her too, wondering where I was?

The thought of it was a balm on my soul. If he was out there, he would keep my brother safe, and he would do everything he could to save my mother, if only because he knew how much it would mean to me. And if the Twenty Houses did try to take their revenge on the mortals of Lumnos, I had faith Luther would put his own life on the line to stop them, just as I would.

I might be without any true allies in this Guardian camp, but I wasn't alone in this war. That knowledge filled me with a quiet strength that I clung to as fiercely as I could.

"I'll visit again when I can." Brecke rose, nudging the forgotten tray of food with the toe of his boot. "You should eat."

My stomach growled its agreement. I hadn't eaten since the morning of the coronation—which, for all I knew, could have been a day ago or a *week* ago.

Could Descended die of hunger, or would my healing abilities keep me alive indefinitely? I added that question to the painfully long list of things I should know about my own body—but didn't, thanks to my mother.

Brecke turned to walk away, and I called out to him. "The Arboros Queen... did the Guardians kill her?"

He glanced at me over his shoulder, his expression unusually solemn. "Forget you saw her here, Diem. Forget everything you see here."

Without another word, he turned and walked away.

His answer hardly eased my concerns, but my stomach rumbled again and drew my attention back to the tray of food. I picked up the bowl of stew and raised it to my nose, inhaling deeply.

I stilled.

Buried deep beneath the delicious aromas of roasted meat and fragrant vegetables lay a faint trace of a too-familiar smell.

Citrus and smoke.

A small sip of the gravy and a whiff of the tea confirmed my suspicions. The Guardians had drugged it all with flameroot, intending to keep me weakened and powerless indefinitely.

I mimed eating for a few minutes, mindful of spying eyes in the surrounding forest. As I moved to place the dishes back on the tray, I pretended to clumsily drop the bowl and mug, then quickly concealed the spilled food with fallen leaves.

For the first time, a genuine smile spread across my face. Let them believe I was accepting their tainted food without complaint. Soon the flameroot would wear off, and my magic would return.

And when it did, there would be hell to pay.

CHAPTER

FOUR

L ife at the rebel camp—for me, at least—meant long hours of waiting, wondering, and imagining the worst-case scenarios that my loved ones might be enduring.

Though I rarely saw the mortals emerge from the circle of trees, I knew their camp must be close. I had expected to face interrogations—some effort to wrench from me what little information I had been given. Instead, I was left alone to simmer in my gloomy thoughts.

Each day brought a delivery of a flameroot-infused meal that I ignored until sunset, then carefully disposed of under cover of darkness.

I knew from my training as a healer that I could survive for weeks without food, but the lack of access to water was a fast-growing concern. Though my Descended healing was slowing the process, my dry, cracked lips and pounding headache warned me that the consequences were setting in. I was locked in a race between my magic and my death, wondering which one would catch up to me first.

Growing up, my mother had claimed that missing even a single day's dose of flameroot might bring my "visions" roaring back. I was learning the hard way that her warnings had been grossly exaggerated. After several days, I was still unable to summon a single spark.

I could feel *something*, though. As dawn rose over a brisk winter morning, dragging me from sleep into a woozy fog of thirst, hunger, and exhaustion, the hollow void in my chest tingled with a whisper of energy.

I didn't dare test it. Being chained to the lone tree in a meadow bathed in sunlight left me far too exposed, especially in my weakened state. I would have to wait until sundown, when I could more safely call on the shadows under cover of darkness.

I had nearly dozed off under the midday sun when a group of men, led by Vance, emerged from the foliage and headed my direction. Each of them carried glittering black blades and crossbows notched with black-tipped arrows that had my spine straightening.

"Up," one of the men barked. "You're coming with us."

I eyed them warily. "Coming where?"

He flashed me an acidic smirk. "Don't you want to relieve yourself in private?"

This was... unusual.

The only *relief* they'd been willing to give me thus far was a dirty bucket that my short chains forced me to keep only a foot or two away—a choice that I suspected was humiliating by design.

"Up," he snapped again. He reached down and grabbed my wrist, hauling me to my feet.

I swallowed down a yelp of pain as my stiff joints screamed at the harsh movement. After days without food or water and little opportunity to stretch my muscles, it was all I could do to stay upright.

Two men went to work unlatching my shackles from the chains. The others raised their weapons, their brown eyes loaded with trepidation.

I should probably have been more scared, but lightheadedness had the world tilting and turning. My legs were one strong breeze from collapsing, and the effects of dehydration made me feel like I'd drunk a barrel of wine. I woozily giggled at how absurdly *un*intimidated of me these men should really be.

From the nervy glances they threw each other and the way their hands tightened on their weapons, my laughter seemed to be having the opposite effect.

My chains unlocked and dropped to the ground. Vance leaned in with a glare. "No running from me this time. Try anything, and you're dead."

I didn't give him the satisfaction of an acknowledgment—mostly because I was struggling to focus my dizzied vision on his face—and he didn't bother waiting for it. He grabbed my shackles and began tugging me toward the forest.

I staggered behind him, nearly tripping over my soiled gown in an effort to keep up. Ten Guardians accompanied him—all of them male, several tall and laden with muscles. Each carried a godstone weapon and watched me like I was the incarnation of evil itself.

This was not the kind of group you sent for a simple escort to the latrine.

I dug my heels into the ground, trying to force Vance to a stop, but my energy was too drained. One quick yank from him sent me tumbling down to my knees.

"Get up," he ordered.

"Where are you really taking me?" I croaked through a bone-dry throat.

He smiled. "I guess you'll have to wait and find out."

A chuckle rippled through the group of men, setting alarm bells ringing in my head.

I was fairly sure Cordellia didn't want me dead—not yet, anyway. But if Vance got me alone and claimed that I'd lashed out and attacked him, that he'd had no choice but to put me down to save himself...

Deep inside my soul, the godhood stirred from its forced slumber.

"Get up," Vance repeated.

"No," I said quietly.

His smile vanished. "I said *get up*."

"No," I said again, stronger this time. I raised my chin and returned his scowl. "If you want to kill me, you'll have to do it right here, where everyone can see it."

Vance snatched a godstone dagger from the hands of one of the men and held the blade out, mere inches from my throat. "Get up now, or that's exactly what I'll do."

I swallowed my panic and forced myself to arch my neck toward the weapon. "Then do it."

It was a pathetically empty challenge. His men could toss me over their shoulder and carry me off wherever they wanted, and I'd be far too weak to fight them off. I prayed they were all too afraid of me to test that theory.

Vance's knuckles turned white where his grip squeezed the dagger's handle. He had been warm and welcoming—*kind*, even—when I had first met him, desperate for his approval as a novice Guardian. The second I'd challenged his authority, he had become a different person entirely. Even when he believed me a mortal, his compassion had always been contingent on my obedience to his control.

But I was the Queen of Lumnos.

And I would be controlled by no man.

"Better hurry up, Vance," I taunted him. "Wouldn't want Mother Cordellia showing up and putting you back in your place."

His nostrils flared. "Fine," he seethed between gritted teeth. "We'll do it here."

For a moment, terror swept through me as I wondered whether my mouth had really, truly gotten me killed this time.

But instead of jabbing the godstone knife into my neck and silencing me for good, he handed it back to the man he'd stolen it from and pulled a penknife from his pocket.

"Who's got the vials?" he asked.

One of the group stepped forward and pulled out a handful of empty glass jars. He was young, perhaps a year or two behind Teller, and though he was trying to mimic the same look of revulsion the other men wore, I could spot the waver of uncertainty on his face.

Vance turned back to me with a bone-chilling smile. "The rest of you, hold her in place."

The men rushed in to surround me. They pulled me back to my feet, their hands grabbing at my arms, my shoulders, my waist. My attempts to fight them off went nowhere, my energy reserves too low and my movements too sluggish. Within seconds, they had me pinned in place.

Fight.

The *voice's* call was barely more than a breath. I could feel it now, twitching and trembling as it strained to overcome the flameroot's lingering effects.

I wanted to answer. *Gods*, did I want to.

But there were too many mortals around me, too many glittering black weapons inches from my face. Without knowing how quickly or strongly my weakened magic could react, one miscalculation and I would be riddled with godstone arrowheads that even my Descended healing couldn't overcome.

And, despite it all, I did not want these men dead. Their hatred for me was born of an oppression I understood too well. I knew firsthand the injustices and the tragedies that had driven them here, and I could not blame them for craving vengeance for all the loved ones the Descended had taken from them. If my father's killer were standing in front of me, I wasn't sure I could hold myself back from taking my revenge, either.

Two of the men gripped my wrists and held them out to Vance. He flipped out the blade of the penknife, the dark grey metal marking it as Fortosian steel.

32

"This is probably going to hurt," he said.

He reached forward and slashed the blade's edge across both of my palms. I flinched at the sharp bite of pain as a line of dark red blood sprung up on my skin.

"What are you doing?" I demanded.

Vance ignored me and jerked his chin toward the Guardian with the vials. "Start filling them."

The boy's moon-round eyes jumped nervously between my face and my bleeding wounds as he uncorked two vials and held them beneath my palms to catch the falling liquid. His hands began shaking, and a few droplets of my blood missed the vials and spilled onto his own skin.

He violently recoiled, yanking his hands back with a yelp and dropping the jars. From the frantic way he scrubbed at the red liquid, I almost wondered if my blood had burned him.

After all, a few drops had cracked the supposedly indestructible heart-stone—who knew what else it was capable of destroying?

Vance smacked the back of the boy's head. "It's blood, you fool, not poison. It's not going to hurt you. In fact..." He turned his eerie smile back on me. "...it seems her blood is quite the useful substance."

I tried in vain to jerk my wrists away. "Why do you want my blood?"

The boy whimpered, his face flushing pink. He picked up the fallen jars and hesitantly moved them back in place, though with the tremble in his hands and my own struggling against the Guardians' grip, very little blood was making it inside.

Another of the men grunted in irritation and snatched the jars from the boy's hands. "I'll do it," he sneered. "I've got no problem painting myself red with Descended blood."

Instead of holding the jars low to catch the falling droplets, he shoved them up against my wounds, pushing the gashes open further. I cried out at the sharp spear of pain that bolted up my arms as several men chuckled smugly.

Fight, the *voice* begged, its hushed tone growing louder.

No, I warned it. *Not yet*.

"Why do you want my blood, Vance?" I said again through gritted teeth.

He shrugged. "You said it so well yourself. The Descended of Lumnos are already plotting to kill the mortals, and we don't have the luxury of waiting months for you to stop them. I'm simply collecting what I need to take matters into my own hands."

"How is my blood going to help you with that?"

"When we tried to sneak into the palace the night of the Ascension Ball, we discovered that *someone*—" His eyes sharpened on me. "—had tipped off the guards to close up the hidden entrance in the gardens."

I breathed out a thankful exhale. I had learned about the secret entrance on my first visit to the palace as a healer, and revealing it to the Guardians had meant breaking my sacred vows of secrecy. My regret over that bad decision had weighed heavily on me these past months. Discovering that no harm would ever come of it was a much-needed solace.

"Thankfully," Vance continued, "the priceless information you provided gave us a second path into the palace. There's just one small obstacle."

Every shred of relief I'd just felt rushed out of me as I realized what was coming next—and why he wanted my blood.

"No," I breathed.

"The bloodlocks in the hidden canal," Vance finished. "You were so kind to tell me that they only open for your blood. Now that won't be a problem."

"Vance, please," I begged. "There are children in that palace. Innocent people. Good people who want to help the mortals. My brother—"

"Then let's hope for their sakes that the other Crowns respond to our letter soon."

"No—don't do this. I'll help you. I'll do whatever you want, just don't—"

"Cut her again," the man with the vials interrupted. "The wounds are already closing up."

Vance flipped his switchblade back open.

Fight, the *voice* hissed.

I looked around frantically, taking in the men, their weapons, the archers in the trees, the distance to the forest.

If I unleashed my magic, could I run away faster than their godstone weapons could find me? Vance already had my blood—could I beat him back to Lumnos before he attacked the palace?

The painful prick of Vance's blade sent panic searing through me. All my conflicted thoughts burned away, and I reacted on pure instinct.

But I was not some full-blooded Descended elite, trained from infancy to wield lethal magic at a moment's notice. I was raised as a mortal, trained by the great war hero Andrei Bellator.

When pushed to my limit, it wasn't Lumnos's burns and barbs I turned to—it was blades and brawls.

With a burst of adrenaline-fueled strength, I yanked my hands free and threw my elbows into the faces of the men clutching my arms. I let my body go slack, becoming dead weight in the hold of the man whose arms crisscrossed my ribcage. He grunted and stumbled forward at the sudden shift, and I used his momentum against him, twisting my body until he was tumbling toward the ground.

I heard the twang of a crossbow, and a flash of black whizzed past my face. I froze for a split second, panting at the near-miss, then a lunge from another man had me moving again to avoid his godstone dagger's direct course for my chest.

"Don't kill her," Vance snapped, shoving the man away. "We need her alive for the blood to work."

Any relief his words gave me faded fast as four of his men sheathed their blades and launched at me. As I turned to run, a man with a crossbow stepped into my path. Two heavy bodies crashed into my back and pinned me down with their weight. Then the rest of the group was on me, crushing my spine with their knees and shoving my face into the cold soil until I could barely breathe, let alone move.

"Flip her over," Vance ordered.

The men roughly hauled me onto my back and sat on my limbs to hold me in place. My vision went wobbly and unfocused as the days without food and water finally caught up with me.

Vance squatted at my side. "I tried to do this the nice way, but you just can't seem to do what you're told." He leaned forward until his knee dug low into my ribs. "You have only yourself to blame."

I whimpered in between gasps for air. "Please—Vance, no—don't—"

He picked up an empty vial that had fallen during the scuffle and pulled out the cork stopper with his teeth. "Auralie told me once that head wounds bleed fastest. I hope those Descended healing abilities of yours work quickly."

I screamed as his blade sank into the flesh of my cheek. Rivulets of warm liquid gushed across my face and down my neck. As Vance pressed the vials into the wounds and filled them one by one, a trickle of blood spilled into my eyes and tinged the world in a crimson haze.

For a moment, my mind flashed back to Forging Day, the ominous blood sun blanketing the dark alleys of Paradise Row in its scarlet glow while Luther and my mother argued over a choice that would change my life in unimaginable ways.

"What's going on here?" a voice called out.

Vance jerked upright. "Cordellia—I... uh..."

"Vance, is that the Bellator girl?"

"*Help!*" I screamed. "Cordellia, help m—"

Vance clamped a hand over my mouth. "Everything's fine," he rushed out. "I had some business to address with her. Lumnos business—nothing for you to worry about."

Cordellia came into view as she approached. "We've discussed this, Vance. You're not in Lumnos, you're in Arboros. I gave orders not to remove her from that tree for any reason." She peered down at me with a deep frown. "Why is she covered in blood?"

I caught Cordellia's eyes and let out a muffled shriek against the suffocating clinch of Vance's hand, hoping she could see the desperation in my face, praying she would intervene.

Vance shifted his weight so his knee dropped sharply into my chest, punching the air from my lungs and silencing my protests. "I need her blood for a mission in Lumnos. When I'm done collecting it, you can do whatever you like with her."

"She's *my* prisoner," Cordellia said archly. "I'll do whatever I like with her right now."

Their bickering faded to the recesses of my mind as a different *voice* stole my focus.

Fight.

The urge to use my magic was steadily growing to a pull that I now had to struggle to hold back. After days without release, my godhood was restless and angry, made worse by the fear throbbing through my pounding heart and the pain splintering across my wounded body.

Still, I resisted. If I used my magic now, there would be no turning back. I had to wait until just the right moment, until I was absolutely certain that I—

The blare of distant horns rolled through the clearing. The mortals froze in unison, their eyes turning skyward.

Another horn blast rang out, this one nearer.

"*Incoming*," an archer shouted from high in a nearby tree. "Man your posts!"

Cordellia pointed at Vance. "Get her back to the tree and chain her up."

She shot him an uncompromising glare, then walked away as she began barking a stream of orders at the growing crowd of Guardians.

One of the men began to rise from where he kneeled on my arm. Vance raised a hand to stop him. "Stay there."

"But, sir... Mother Dell said to take her—"

"I'm almost done here. I'll chain her up when I'm finished."

The men shared unsure looks, but Vance gave them no time for debate. He slashed two more gashes on my wrists, then nudged the vials toward the men. "Fill those up."

As the horns grew louder and the meadow filled with a swarm of armed Guardians, the men exchanged a glance, then hurried to finish the deed.

Vance cut a fresh slice along my jaw, alarmingly close to where I knew crucial veins lay beneath the delicate skin. He muttered to himself as the ruby red liquid spilled out into a vial. "Come on, come on, fill up already..." His own hand had begun to quiver, his eyes darting to the sky.

"Incoming," the archers cried in an echoing chorus. "Attack incoming!"

The clearing devolved into a cacophony of shouting voices, running footsteps, weapons sliding from their sheaths, and the creak of catapults wheeling into place. Though I was still trapped in place, the *voice* inside me had joined in the frenzied orchestra, humming with excitement over the promise of violence.

In the midst of the chaos, my ears caught on a very different noise. A soft, rhythmic beat—far away, but quickly approaching. Familiar in a way that went deeper than memory.

Thump, thump, thump.

Wings.

My heart sang.

"Oh gods," one of the men at my side breathed. "Is that a...?"

"Incoming," the archers screamed. "*Gryvern incoming!*"

CHAPTER

FIVE

I almost laughed—I might have, had Vance's grimy hand not been jammed against my mouth.

This wasn't just any gryvern.

Our bond swelled and strengthened with every wingbeat. *Thump*—her fear for my safety. *Thump*—her rage at my pain. *Thump*—her ravenous hunger to destroy those who had brought me harm.

My gryvern, my beautiful Sorae, had come for me.

Cordellia's calm voice cut through the melee. "Everyone, get to your posts. Remember your training. We've prepared for this."

My joyful relief faltered at the steadiness of Cordellia's confidence. This was a *gryvern*, a legendary immortal beast that was part dragon, part eagle, and part lion. They were unbeatable by almost any weapon and nearly impossible to kill.

Cordellia should be panicking. They *all* should be panicking.

So why weren't they?

"Finally," Vance muttered, shoving the cork in his vial and tucking it away with the jars he snatched from the other men. But instead of rising, he held his position on top of me, his gaze fixed on the sky.

Sorae's piercing snarl ripped through the air. She was close—even with the flameroot's lingering effects, I could feel her presence so strongly across our bond.

Thank the gods I'd saved my weakened magic instead of wasting it on

Vance's paltry threats. I would need every ounce of it to fight off the Guardians long enough to mount Sorae and ride away with her to safety.

Any minute now she would find me, rescue me, take me home. If I could just get free of these men and get to her...

Fight, the *voice* demanded.

Soon, I promised.

Vance released his hand from my mouth to fumble for his larger weapons, allowing me to crane my head for a better look.

At first, all I saw was a mighty winged shadow silhouetted against the blinding sun. She tilted downward in a ferocious trajectory for the clearing, the sunlight illuminating her back.

And my joy became *bliss*.

Nestled between her wings, his dark hair unbound and whipping against his olive skin, a jeweled sword clenched in one hand and a shield of Fortosian steel in the other, was Prince Luther Corbois.

My Luther.

Even with a mile between us, his eyes found me in an instant. He took me in—pinned to the ground, my dress soiled with dirt, wet blood coating my body, Vance's knee lodged into my ribs.

The rage on his face could have leveled the continent.

Happy tears sprang to my eyes, and an ecstatic laugh bubbled out. Luther was alive—and he had come for me.

I had little faith in gods or men, but I believed in the fearsome dedication of Luther Corbois with every fiber of my being. He had proven that he would give anything, even his own life, to protect me. He would stop at nothing to take me home, help me rescue my mother, and stand by me to stop this war. Together, we could do this.

Everything was going to be okay.

"Prepare the ballista," Cordellia shouted. "Wait until the beast is close. The aim has to be perfect."

I turned my head toward her voice. At the edge of the treeline, a group of mortals stood around a tall structure that resembled a massive crossbow. Loaded into its grooved arm was a bolt as large as a person, its sharpened tip dotted with hunks of glittering black stone.

"By the Flames," I whispered. "No... *no!*"

Cordellia marched toward it. "Remember, the godstone has to pierce the beast's heart to kill it. We only have two bolts, so don't fire unless you're certain." She glanced at me, then scowled at Vance. "I told you to get her chained up. We need her under tree cover so the gryvern is forced to land."

Vance and his men finally climbed off me and yanked me to my knees, dragging me along the dirt toward the tree in the clearing's center.

I screamed again, thrashing against their hold. "Cordellia, don't do this—she's loyal to me. I won't let her hurt the mortals, I swear it!"

"She's loyal to the Descended Crown," Cordellia shouted back. "If you die, she'll turn on the mortals and kill us all. We can't take that risk."

Sorae roared a deafening war cry as she passed over our heads, flying so low that the downdraft from her wings sent a breeze fluttering through my hair. A stream of sapphire dragonfyre poured from her mouth and seared a line of scorched earth across the meadow.

The horde of mortals fled in terror. A few moved too slowly, and their flame-engulfed corpses staggered, then fell, lifeless and still.

Fight, the *voice* purred, galvanized by the slaughter.

No. This was not what I wanted. Death and bloodshed, Descended against mortal. It didn't matter that these rebels would slit my throat, given the chance—I was meant to be a better Queen with a higher purpose.

If carnage was the price of my freedom, the cost was too high.

I clutched desperately at Vance's tunic. "I can call her off. Let me go, and I'll stop the attack. No one else has to die."

He grabbed my arm and yanked me closer. "Why do you think we put you out here in the first place?" he snarled in my face.

Blood rushed from my head, my vision spinning as quickly as my thoughts.

Bait.

They hadn't placed me in the wide-open clearing to keep me out of trouble or to spy on me from a distance. They'd done it to show me off—to lure my protectors here and take them out, one by one.

Starting with Sorae.

Vance shoved me to the ground at the foot of the tree. "One of these days, you will finally accept that unlike you coward Descended, the Guardians are not afraid to die for our cause."

He gestured to his men to chain me up, and I scrambled to get away. My fingers clawed at the hard soil in a futile effort to clutch onto something, anything, to drag myself out of their grasp.

I had to stay out of those chains. If they managed to lock me up, I would be trapped, with no way to get to Sorae, and she would be a sitting duck for their godstone bolt. The thrum of my magic was stronger now, giving me confidence that I could use it if I had to, but it was still merely embers of its full strength. One miscalculation and I could drain myself dry.

One of the men caught hold of my ankle and jerked it backward. My movements were still too sluggish, and I couldn't react quickly enough to stop my body from collapsing.

With a nauseating *crack*, my head slammed onto a knobby, rock-hard root at the base of the tree, and my vision went watery.

Across the bond, Sorae felt my pain, and her fury exploded. She circled back toward me, her nostrils glowing as sapphire flames licked at her sharp-fanged jaws.

"Hurry up," Vance barked. "Get the chains on her."

The boy who had carried the vials for Vance latched a chain onto my shackles and rushed to secure it. With his hands still shaking, he struggled to thread the thick iron lock into place.

I tried to push him away, though my protests were pitifully feeble. Between my exhaustion, my dehydration, and my throbbing new head wound, I was barely clinging to consciousness.

A piercing shriek pulled my eyes to the sky, and Sorae's golden eyes locked with mine. A pulse of emotion washed across the bond as she made her intentions clear.

A promise—to protect me at all costs.

I grabbed the boy's wrist. "Go," I warned him. "She's coming. Run —now!"

His bulging eyes mirrored mine. He looked over his shoulder at the gryvern shooting toward him at lightning speed. "By the Undying Fire," he whimpered. "Gods protect me."

He dropped the chains and scrambled to get away. The other men in the group took one look at the fearsome beast spearing our direction, and they abandoned their posts and followed suit.

Only Vance remained. He unleashed a string of swears at his men, demanding in vain that they return.

"Vance, get out of here," I yelled at him. "She'll kill you."

"No," he spat out. "I'm not a coward."

"Better a coward than a corpse," I shot back. "If you're so determined to die, save it for a more important battle—I am not worth your life."

On that, at least, we seemed to agree.

Vance dared a glance behind him. Sorae was already surging over the clearing, her dragonfyre plume mere seconds away.

He gave me one final look, the side of his face slowly illuminating from the approaching inferno.

"*Run!*" I screamed.

I turned my face up to my gryvern and shut my eyes as the world went blue.

Even behind my eyelids, I was blinded by the sun-bright azure glow of Sorae's fire. It engulfed me, swallowed me up like the depths of the sea, but I felt no burns, no wounds, no pain—only a comforting warmth that, for one fleeting moment, left me entirely at peace.

But when I opened my eyes, I saw *war*.

A blackened line in the earth ran straight between my feet, scattered soft blue flames flickering in the surrounding grass. Behind me, the mammoth tree I'd been chained to was now a pile of ash. Only a few charred pieces of wood remained, along with a red-hot pool of molten metal that had once been my chains and shackles.

I looked around for bodies, relieved to see the mortals had escaped—all except Vance.

One second more and he might have been spared, but his ill-conceived bravery had cost him. He lay in a heap a few feet away, screaming and clutching a bloody, steaming mess of burnt flesh where his arm had once been.

I started toward him, my healer's instincts to *mend* and *save* kicking in, when a tremor rumbled through the earth.

Across the clearing, Sorae had landed in a patch of scorched soil. She threw her head back with an enraged roar that set the forest leaves trembling, then flooded the woods around her in a blazing firestorm, warning the mortals to keep their distance.

This was it—my chance to escape.

Sorae crouched down to her haunches as Luther slid from her back, his boots hitting the soil with a menacing thump. The wall of lingering flames and thick smoke made his form hazy, like the mirage of an oasis in the hot Ignios sands.

I was suddenly desperate to have his arms around me. Even when we had barely known each other, something about his embrace had always felt safe and impenetrable and inexplicably right.

His quiet strength had been my calm amidst the chaos. The faintest brush of his hand could center me when I was lost and catch me when I was falling. Somehow I just knew that if I could get to him, if I could just *touch* him, we would find a way out.

Exhaustion and relief tugged me staggering forward. My clothes had burned away under Sorae's flames, but the purifying blaze had also stripped me of the caked-on dirt and blood, leaving my skin cleansed and my soul feeling strangely renewed.

Luther's gaze traveled over my bare flesh, but there was none of the heated desire in it that normally sent my stomach fluttering. Instead, his features hardened to a sword-sharp edge.

I could imagine why—my pallid skin, my sunken, dark-rimmed eyes, my fresh bruises and still-bleeding wounds.

"How many times do I have to tell you—eyes up here, Corbois," I yelled out to him, forcing a teasing lilt into my hoarse voice. "We really have to stop meeting like this."

His gaze rose to mine, and we might as well have been the only two people left in the world.

Though I yearned to see that brilliant smile he reserved only for me, he was too far gone in his rage for my banter. Instead, in the crystal pools of his eyes, I saw the profound depth of his devotion. The intensity of it nearly brought me to my knees.

He had sworn that no force this side of death would keep him from my side, and Luther Corbois was a man of his word.

A warning tickled at the back of my mind. Over our months together, I had become so used to the heavy, enrobing aura of Luther's power I'd almost stopped noticing it.

But now it was the absence of that feeling that snagged my focus. Though he couldn't have been more than thirty yards away, there was a cold, empty nothingness in the air between us that, in Luther's presence, felt unmistakably wrong.

"Archers, take him down," Cordellia ordered.

A blur of black shot across the clearing and stopped me in my tracks. Luther raised his shield to his chest with no time to spare before an arrow collided into it and bounced away with a clang, leaving behind a tiny hole in the metal.

Another arrow followed, then another, and another. Luther crouched low beneath the shield's protection as a volley rained down on him and forced him to sink back against Sorae's side. Deflected arrows piled at his feet, and though most were tipped with the dull grey of Fortosian steel, a few bore that awful, telltale glittering black. Each godstone arrow left its mark in his shield, the slower ones making only dents, while others nearly pierced straight through.

If just one of them landed, if it even got close enough to cut a scratch on his skin...

Luther's frustrated glare peered out from behind his shield. Every time he made a move to advance, another volley pinned him back.

Why wasn't he using his magic? One flick of his wrist could flood this entire clearing and bring the mortals to their knees—yet he did nothing of the sort. Was he worried I would be angry because I'd asked him to spare the Guardians the night of the Ascension Ball?

Was he willing to go that far—sacrificing himself not just to protect me, but to avoid spilling mortal blood just to honor my wishes?

I was too scared to ask myself if that was a trade I was willing to make.

Sorae seemed to sense my growing worry. She flared her wings out protectively over Luther and arched her long, scaled neck, unleashing another stream of dragonfyre along the treetops. Leafy branches lit up in blue flame, and screams and groans became sickening thumps as charred bodies dropped out of the branches.

"No, Sorae," I shouted. "Don't hurt th—"

"*Launch the ballista!*"

For a moment, everything went silent. Then—the creak of a lever. The twang of an overwound rope. The whistle of a flying bolt.

I had no time to think. No luxury of debating the moral highs and lows of mortal bloodshed. No chance to weigh the cost of using the small spark of my magic that had emerged from the flameroot's suffocating fog.

As I watched the godstone-studded spear rip through the air on a certain course for my gryvern's beating heart, I had no time to do anything at all. Except...

Fight.

Just as I had that night in the forest with the direwolf, and again at the Challenging against Rhon Ghislaine, I managed only a whisper of a thought—an instinctual, ephemeral plea for salvation—and with a flare of silvery light, the bolt was gone. In its place, a cloud of ash floated away on the winter breeze.

I collapsed to my knees as my vision tunneled to near-blackness. Consciousness had become a fleeting concept. Whatever I had done, it had cost me dearly, both in magic and in energy.

I heard Luther shouting my name, then his boots striking the soil as he ran toward me.

Then the pluck of bowstrings and the patter of falling arrows, and his soft swears as he was pushed back once more.

It struck me then why I hadn't felt the aura of his deep well of power. He was a Lumnos Descended—and we were in Arboros. Outside of the borders of his *terremère*, without a Crown on his head to free him from the Forging spell's limits, Luther had no magic. He was nearly as defenseless as an ordinary mortal.

And he had come for me anyway.

"Load the second bolt," Cordellia commanded. "Quickly!"

"No," I whimpered. I tried to push to my feet and found myself collapsing onto my side instead. My heartbeat stuttered in a quick, uneven rhythm—a worrying sign.

I was suddenly so tired. So very, very tired.

"*Diem!*" Luther's voice was strained and desperate. "Diem—hold on, I'm coming!"

The world wobbled and dimmed. To my right, the Guardians slipped another shimmering black bolt into the ballista's arm. I knew I couldn't stop it a second time—my magic was too frazzled, too faint.

My head rolled groggily to the left. Luther had abandoned all sanity, braving a lethal hailstorm in a sprint for my side. My heart wrenched as one arrow sank into the flesh of his shoulder, then another lodged in his thigh.

Our eyes met.

"I'm sorry," I mouthed.

Take him home, and don't come back.

Sorae snarled a protest at the silent order I sent across our bond, but she was powerless to ignore it. No matter how fierce her desire to protect me, her free will was leashed to my command. She would obey me—even if that obedience cost me my life.

With two thundering steps, she was airborne again, the powerful downdraft of her wings sending the rest of the arrows off course. Luther looked up, then back at me, his eyes darkening near-black with rage.

"Don't you dare," he snarled. "Diem—"

His furious words cut short as Sorae's talons encircled his chest and plucked him into the air.

"Launch the ballista!" Cordellia shouted.

Save them, I pleaded with the *voice*.

It didn't answer.

My godhood was spent, and so was I.

My head fell back against the soil as my glassy eyes unfocused. The last thing I saw was the shimmer of sunlight on godstone as the second bolt raced toward a fleeing gryvern and an arrow-struck man.

CHAPTER
SIX

I was drowning again.

Just like before, I was pinned in place, my arms and legs trapped at my side. Liquid splashed across my face, then my nose pinched shut and a hand clamped across my lips to keep them closed.

"Swallow," a familiar voice commanded.

My eyes flew open. I instinctively jerked against my restraints as every thought washed from my mind except the fight-or-flight of looming death. As I strained to get free, I heard the jangle of chains and felt the cold bite of metal against my wrists.

"We've been through this before," the voice said. "Stop fighting and swallow."

My eyes darted to its owner. A few inches away, Cordellia watched with impassive resolve.

"You need the liquids, Diem," she said bluntly. "If you don't drink, you're going to pass out again, and next time, you might not wake up."

Perhaps knowing her words were too close to the truth, my throat involuntary forced the bitter, flameroot-tainted liquid down. The thrum of magic in my chest sputtered and disappeared, leaving me hollow once more.

Cordellia nodded, and the hands covering my face released me.

"Was that really necessary?" I rasped in between gasps for air to relieve my aching lungs.

"Yes," she snapped, giving me a hard look that challenged me to deny it. "Are you going to take the next drink willingly, or do we need to go for round two?"

I laid in silence for a moment, panting and giving my overwhelmed mind a moment to recognize that I was not, in fact, drowning to death at the bottom of the Sacred Sea.

Last I could remember, I was in the clearing, fighting Vance as he tried to steal my blood. Then Sorae had arrived with Luther and fighting had broken out, and then...

The ballista.

My heart began to pound in my ears.

"Did you kill them?" I whispered. "My gryvern and my..." I trailed off, still unable to find the words to describe what Luther had become to me.

"Eight of my people died. Another twenty have serious burns." Disdain dripped from Cordellia's voice. "I should keep the answer from you and let you suffer the way their families are suffering."

"I begged you to stop that attack. And when you refused, I called off my gryvern and sent away the deadliest Descended in Emarion before he cut you all to shreds." I rolled my head toward her with a harsh, bitter laugh. "Your people aren't dead because of me, Cordellia. They're dead because of *you*."

One of her men rammed a foot into my ribs, knocking me off the log I was sprawled on and sending me tumbling face-first into the ground.

I groaned and clutched my side, sharp pain rocketing through me with every inhale. None of the Guardians made any effort to help me. Even Cordellia remained still as she watched me writhe in pain on the forest floor, arms crossed over her chest.

I flopped onto my back, hacking and wincing. "White asterberry," I croaked out.

Cordellia cocked her head. "What?"

"Grind the stems into a paste and spread it on the burns." I coughed again and swore at the burst of pain, then forced the rest out through clenched teeth. "Speeds healing and wards off infection. It's a five-petaled flower with a purplish center. Usually grows on riverbanks."

She said nothing at first, watching me with an unreadable look while I scowled back. Finally, she glanced at a clump of three Guardians and jerked her chin. "Go, but don't give it to the wounded until I test it on myself first."

They nodded and scurried off.

I looked her over. "You were burned in the attack?"

"No." I arched a brow at her response, and she narrowed her eyes. "I'll give myself a burn on the campfire and test it."

I didn't know whether to laugh or scream. "You really distrust me that much?"

She didn't answer.

With considerable effort and several grunts of pain, I pushed myself upright and gingerly leaned back against the log. Cordellia crouched at my side and held out a large flask. "Drink."

I stared down at her hand, then glared back up at her, locking my jaw.

Cordellia sighed. "I guess we'll do this the hard way." She gestured for her people to grab me.

"No—stop," I shouted, snatching the flask from her hands. "Fine. I'll drink it."

"All of it," she ordered. "Spill even a drop, and I'll have you held down again so fast your head will spin."

I bit back a slew of snide comments and started to raise the flask to my lips, but my hands were shaking uncontrollably from a combination of my pitiful physical condition and my terror over Sorae and Luther's fates. I genuinely wasn't sure I could drink without making a mess of myself, and I wasn't willing to bet that her threat had been an empty one.

I squeezed my fingers around the flask and willed them to steady, desperately trying to conceal just how weak I had become. The effort was futile—my head lolled, and my vision began to blur and darken as I fought to stay conscious.

The sounds of movement followed, and I felt the warmth of a body sit beside me. Cordellia plucked the flask from my quivering hands and raised it to my lips.

I was too mortified to look her in the eyes as I tilted my head back and took a long drink. She looked amused as my face twisted at the acrid taste. Even after ten years of daily doses, I had never quite grown used to the flameroot's flavor, like drinking liquid ash.

She brought the flask up again, and I pressed my lips shut. She shot me a hard look. "Diem..."

"Did you kill them?"

Her expression gave away nothing, her face cold and unmoved.

My eyes began to burn with the spring of fresh tears, and I blinked furiously to fight them back. I could not allow these people the satisfaction of seeing me break.

"Did you kill them?" I hissed.

"No," she admitted. "Our bolt missed, and they both got away."

My head fell back against the log, relief overwhelming my senses. I still couldn't be certain Luther was safe. I'd watched two arrows pierce his flesh —if either of them were godstone, he could be dead already.

But there was hope. And hope was worth cherishing until the very last breath.

"Drink, Diem."

My hands steadied with a bit of renewed strength, and I took the flask and began to drink.

As I did, I stole a few glances at my new surroundings. There were tents in every direction and a ring of stones that I presumed to be a sparring circle. A large campfire burned nearby, and a row of firepits held bubbling pots and skewers of small game roasting on spits. The air was full of voices talking, weapons clanking, and the general sounds of life. A handful of Guardians stood around me, but countless more milled about in the background, their brown eyes casting furtive, hate-filled glances my way as they passed.

Mercifully, I was no longer naked, now dressed in plain mortal garb. The simple leather breeches and linen tunic were so similar to the clothes I'd worn every day before becoming Queen. The familiarity of it was unexpectedly comforting—a reminder of who I was and what I was fighting for.

They had moved me deeper into the forest, the meadow nowhere in sight. The vegetation was far denser and overgrown, shrouded from any spying gryverns that might fly overhead and likely far enough from any road so we wouldn't be stumbled on by hunters or passing travelers.

The perfect location for a rebel settlement.

When I'd emptied the flask, Cordellia clasped her hands together and leaned forward, forearms resting on her knees. "You used your magic. That wasn't supposed to be possible."

"I'm full of unexpected surprises," I said dryly.

Like still being alive, I thought to myself.

"We found several days' worth of food buried in holes at the tree you were chained to." She raised her eyebrows. "I'm guessing that soil has been watered with a few mugs of flameroot tea, as well?"

I glared at her in response.

She chuckled softly. "You're definitely Auralie's daughter."

The comment flooded me with a jumble of pride, anger, resentment, and worry, a reflection of the complicated feelings I'd developed toward my mother during her long absence.

Cordellia waved over a woman who stood nearby with a large burlap pouch.

The woman held the satchel to her chest in obvious reluctance to turn it over. "With all due respect Mother Dell, she wasted food our people needed. Our stocks are hard enough to maintain. If she wants to starve herself, we should let her."

The others murmured their agreement.

Cordellia gave me a heavy stare that said she wasn't entirely opposed, then shook her head and looked up at the mortals. "This woman assisted with the attack on the island, and a mission she helped with in Lumnos is the reason many of you have fine Descended weapons right now."

I flinched at her description. I didn't want credit for either attack, and had I known the whole truth, I wouldn't have gone along with any of it—but I supposed now wasn't the time for semantics.

"She's also a Descended Queen who can give Guardians safe harbor in her realm," Cordellia continued. "Shall we let her die for spite, or shall we remember our mission and do everything we can to save the lives of our people?"

The woman's face flushed. "Yes, of course, Mother Dell. Anything for our people." She shot me a fleeting scowl and chucked the sack at my feet, then spun on her heel and walked off.

"Thanks *so* much, Sister," I called out to her with exaggerated sweetness. The woman responded with a middle finger raised over her shoulder that had me unexpectedly smirking. "I like her."

"I don't think the feeling is mutual," Cordellia muttered.

I grabbed the pouch and opened it to find a loaf of hard bread along with several strips of dried meat. It was cold, simple fare, but after nearly a week without eating, even a plate of boot leather would have had my mouth watering. I raised the pouch to my nose, pleased to find no trace of the flameroot's distinctive odor. My stomach growled its approval, and I tore into the food with a fervor that was borderline embarrassing.

"No more drugged food?" I asked between bites.

"No. But from now on, I'm going to sit and personally watch while you drink each dose. You're a little old to need a nursemaid, but apparently, I have no choice."

"Looking forward to it. Feel free to take up my bad manners with my mother when you see her."

Her mouth tightened at my sarcastic bite. "Am I right to assume from the way that man looked like he was ready to cut down the gods themselves that he and the gryvern will be back very soon?"

"The gryvern won't. I commanded her to stay away. The man..." My appetite faltered, and my hands lowered to my lap. "He will."

"And I suppose he won't come alone next time, will he?"

I debated my answer. Perhaps in her mind, she envisioned him returning with the entire Emarion Army at his back. That wasn't Luther's style, and I had to hope he would know me well enough not to bring the wrath of the Fortos King down on a group of mortals for my benefit. But I also feared the trap she might set if she expected him to return alone.

"He'll do whatever it takes to free me," I said carefully. Let her take from that what she would.

She gave a weary sigh and looked up at the remaining Guardians. "We'll need to move the camp. Start spreading the word, and have everyone begin packing things up." They nodded and dispersed.

We sat alone together in silence for several minutes while I devoured the rest of the food. When I finished, Cordellia secured a second set of chains through the shackles at my wrists and wrapped them tightly around the fallen log.

"You'll have to find a new place to tie me up so you can lure in the people I care about and murder them," I said bitterly.

She took a seat on the grass in front of me. "You've only just been coronated, and you already care that deeply about a Descended man and the Crown's gryvern?"

The snap of disapproval in her voice suggested she couldn't imagine ever caring for anyone from the Descended world. I'd felt that way myself not that long ago—and likely still would, had a Crown not appeared from thin air above my head.

"You're the leader here," I said. "Do you have people who are loyal to you beyond all reason? Who believe in you so much they would take on certain death merely because you asked?"

She nodded solemnly. "Yes, I do."

"Then how would you feel if I chained you up, waited until they came to save you, then butchered them while making you watch?"

She shifted her weight, visibly uncomfortable at my insinuation. "That gryvern is a beast, not a person."

"*That gryvern* has more humanity in her heart than most humans I've met, including some Guardians. Which reminds me—" I smirked. "—how is Vance?"

A strange expression flickered across her face, there and gone too quickly for me to decipher. "He's recovering. His arm is in bad shape. I'm not sure how much use he'll have of it when it heals."

I expected to feel some righteous justice at that news. After all, Vance had hardly bat an eye at slicing me open and watching me bleed.

But I was Descended—I would heal, while Vance would carry the scars of this wound for the rest of his life. I could not bring myself to find happiness at a mortal's suffering. Even his.

"I can examine him," I offered. "I'm a healer. My mother trained me herself. I'll tend to him and the other wounded, if you'd like."

She looked startled at the offer. "I don't think that's a good idea, Diem. It's going to be hard enough as it is to keep my people from trying to take their revenge on you. If any of them die under your care, even if it's beyond your control, I fear there will be a mob even I cannot stop."

I bristled. "Revenge on *me?* I didn't wound them. I sent my gryvern away."

"Be that as it may, you're the only Descended in this camp, and my people were killed by a Descended beast. They want their pound of flesh, and they've no one else to take it from."

I drooped back against the log. I'd agreed to cooperate in the hopes that I might earn the mortals' trust. Instead, I'd made enemies of them simply by existing.

"What happened between you and Vance back in Lumnos?" she asked. "I can tell there's no love lost there."

"He didn't tell you?"

"He told me his side." She tilted her head. "I want to hear yours."

I studied her for a long moment, weighing the wisdom of giving her the full truth. After watching her lead the siege against Luther and Sorae, I had a hard time believing I could trust her, as Brecke had urged me to do. Then again, she was a friend of my mother. That had to count for *something*, and there was an earnestness in her expression that gave me a flicker of hope.

So I told her—about the murder of the boy and his mother that had driven me to join the Guardians, about my missions for Vance, and about my reservations about his merciless methods that treated everyone, even children, as expendable sacrifices. I told her how I'd fled from him the night of the armory attack, and how it had earned me his ire before I took my Crown—and how I'd cemented that hatred when I'd thwarted his attack at the Ascension Ball by sending the mortals home without bloodshed.

"But even before I joined the Guardians," I said once I'd finished, "Vance and his men were suspicious of me. I think he never trusted me because of who my father was."

"More likely because of who your mother is," she mumbled, almost too quietly to hear.

"My mother?" I frowned. "I thought she and Vance were friends."

There it was again—that fleeting, curious look on Cordellia's face.

She schooled her features back to disinterest. "They worked very closely. He's been a member of the Guardians nearly as long as she has, and his loyalty to the cause is beyond question. It's why she chose him as her second. They were... *are*... dedicated colleagues."

She stopped abruptly, and it seemed as if there was more she wanted to say. Perhaps out of wariness of me or loyalty to my mother, she held her tongue, and I decided not to push further. I knew well the burden of carrying my mother's secrets. I could not fault her for staying silent when I still guarded so many of them myself.

"Diem," she said after a moment, "do you still consider yourself a Guardian?"

I shrugged. "It hardly matters. We both know the Guardians will never welcome me now."

"That's not what I asked," she said curtly. "I heard you call yourself a Sister when you first arrived. Did you mean that?"

I looked down, chewing on my lip. Though I wanted to answer her honestly, the truth was a complex thing.

"I agree with the Guardians' mission—helping the mortals, ending the injustices," I began slowly, choosing my words with care. "I'd happily shatter this Crown, if it meant the end of Descended rule. Whatever good intentions the Kindred might have had in giving control of the continent to their children, their experiment did not work. Power has corrupted them."

She nodded approvingly. I took a deep breath before rushing through my next words.

"But I don't agree that we should imitate the Descended to defeat them. We shouldn't slaughter innocents or punish people because of their blood. The truly guilty must pay, of course, but..." I paused and looked back up at her. "I expected the Descended to be soulless and incapable of kindness, because that's what I was taught. I never imagined I would discover good people. *Compassionate* people. People who disagree with the mortals' treatment. As I got to know them, some have become my friends, my advisors..."

I choked on my words as I thought of what Luther, Taran, Alixe, Eleanor, Lily, and even Perthe had come to mean to me. The loyalty they had shown, even when I'd returned it with distrust. The faith they had in my vision for a new, better world.

"It's easy to condemn injustice when you're safe behind palace walls," Cordellia clipped. "Without action, their compassion might as well be indifference. Good intentions don't save lives."

"They should have done more," I agreed. "And we are right to demand they do more now. But is that a crime worthy of death? Some Guardians will never be satisfied until every last Descended is in a grave. I refuse to accept that as our solution."

Cordellia ran a hand over the long, thin braids cascading over her shoulders, her expression turning thoughtful. "I admit, I have seen potential for our kind to make peace. You're not the first Descended that has helped us. There are... *others*. Some in surprisingly high positions."

"Higher than a Queen?" I teased.

She didn't respond, staring off into the forest, lost in her thoughts.

Eventually she rose to leave. I reached out a hand to stop her, though my wrist jerked back as my chains came up short. "I need to get back to Lumnos, Cordellia."

"If you're seen there, our attempts to trade you for your mother will be ruined." She shot me a disapproving stare. "I thought you were willing to do whatever it takes to save her?"

"Of course I am. But..." I scrubbed my hands over my face and sighed, feeling suddenly unsure.

"The palace in Lumnos is secured with bloodlocks that can only be opened by the blood of the Crown and their—" I caught myself before the full truth slipped out—that my brother's blood would have the same effect. "Vance now has my blood, and he wants them all dead. He'll sneak in and kill them while they sleep." I scowled. "*You* might not take issue with that, but—"

"I am not Vance," she cut in. "I do not target innocent people."

"You were happy to target the two who came to save me."

"That gryvern has murdered countless mortals over the centuries."

"Not by choice," I shot back. "The Crowns ordered those deaths."

She cocked her head. "Was it not her choice to kill my people today—or did you order those deaths yourself?"

The words struck like a blow. Luther had warned me of this once.

Gryverns are loyal to their Crown, but they can act of their own will. If you fear someone, or even dislike them strongly, she might take their life in an effort to please you.

Despite the blame I'd hung on Cordellia's shoulders earlier, Sorae had killed those mortals for me—to protect me, to avenge me, to *please* me. All of them would be alive now, if not for me.

More blood to repay, more corpses to bury.

I clenched my jaw as frustration rose. "And what of the Descended man who came for me? Was he not innocent?"

"You mean Prince Luther?" Cordellia's expression soured. "Oh yes, I know who he is. The late King's favorite disciple, the man responsible for executing the half-mortal children. His apparent fondness for you does not erase his many crimes."

I started to defend him, then my lips snapped shut. Luther's secrets were his to share, not mine, and if my mother had not seen fit to tell Cordellia that she and Luther were working together to protect those children, perhaps there was a reason.

"*The point,*" I growled, "is that the royals may be spoiled, but most of them are no killers. There are only a few who deserve Vance's brand of justice."

In truth, I wasn't sure *any* of them did. Though I despised Garath and Remis for good reason, they'd known of my desires to protect the mortals, and they'd stood by me—begrudgingly, and out of self-interest, but they'd done it. I had not yet witnessed them turn their savagery on anyone but me, and I was not so petty that I was ready to see them butchered in their sleep for it. Not yet, anyway.

And Aemonn... I had seen both kindness and cruelty in him. His appointment by Remis as Keeper of the Laws put him at a crossroads between the hatefulness of his father and the good I believed him capable of. I couldn't be certain which path he was going to choose.

There were certainly Descended whose deaths would lose me no sleep —namely, the leaders of House Hanoverre—but among House Corbois, I could not fairly condemn any of them to execution at Vance's hand.

I raised my chin higher. "I am the Queen of Lumnos. The Guardians may think me a fake queen on an unearned throne, but I take my duty to protect my people seriously. I have to get back before anyone is slaughtered —mortal or Descended."

Cordellia gave me a sober look. "Even if doing so costs your mother her life?"

My shoulders sagged. I had no answer. I could only pray I wouldn't be forced to make that choice.

Her eyes roved over me in solemn silence, and then she turned to walk away. "I'll think on it."

"Cordellia, please—"

"I said I'll think on it," she called out without stopping. "Vance is still recovering here, so for now, your people are safe. I only wish I could say the same for mine."

CHAPTER
SEVEN

The next morning, we set off for a new camp.

The damage I'd done to my body must have been more severe than I thought, because even though Cordellia had allowed me fresh water, a hot meal, and even a bedroll for the night, I was still barely able to keep up with the mortals as we marched several hours through the wilderness.

It didn't help that she insisted I be blindfolded. I assured her I had no way of communicating my location—the flameroot had severed my connection to Sorae—but my promises went unheard, and I was left to stumble aimlessly over every rock and fallen limb in our path.

I had some idea of where we might be. The sound of distant waves and seagulls hinted that a coastline was nearby. Despite the winter season, the air was getting warmer and drier, suggesting we were closer to the desert climate of Ignios, Realm of Sand and Flame, rather than the humid jungles of Arboros's western neighbor, Faunos, Realm of Beast and Brute.

Eventually we arrived, and the mortals set about rebuilding their makeshift city. My frequent offers to assist were either outright ignored or met with colorful descriptions of where exactly I could shove my help.

The mortals were efficient, leading me to suspect moving was a frequent occurrence. By nightfall on the first day, the camp looked as if it had been there for weeks rather than hours.

Unlike the Guardians of Lumnos, these mortals had no lives outside of the rebel camp. They could not escape to the normalcy of a home shielded from their illicit rebellion, the way my mother had done for so many years. There were children and elderly here, entire family units living among the tents.

There would be no isolating any compromised members or mitigating the fallout. If their work here was discovered by the Descended, every last one of them was doomed.

I yearned to know more about what had brought them to this point. Arboros had a Mortal City of its own near the Ring Road—my mother and I had stayed there during our annual trips to Arboros's massive medicinal herb market. So why had these mortals chosen to live a nomadic life hiding deep within the forest?

Were they fugitives like Brecke, wanted for crimes in other realms? Had they been run out of town by other mortals for fear the rebel efforts would bring the Descended's wrath down on all their heads? Or perhaps they were true believers, dedicated enough to give over their entire lives to the cause.

If any of them had been willing to share their stories, Cordellia made sure they never got the chance. Over the next week that passed, two Guardians kept watch at all times, and their orders seemed to be keeping other mortals out as much as keeping me in.

My guards had little interest in talking—in fact, my interest only made them look at me with more suspicion. After a few days of one-sided efforts, I learned that if I pretended to sleep, they would eventually begin to chat. Following this discovery, I conveniently developed a mysterious case of narcolepsy that had me "napping" around the clock.

My persistence paid off late one night, when most of the mortals had gone to sleep and the camp was quiet. The man and woman guarding me turned from the usual camp gossip and Descended bashing to a discussion of Guardian activity in other realms.

"I hear the army hasn't even tried to take back the island," the man said. "They surrounded it with warships so we can't get in or out, but they haven't sent any soldiers to fight."

"Those bastards and their long lives," the woman answered. "They probably plan to wait it out and let the mortals on the island die of old age."

"Mother Dell says they have to take it back by Forging Day or their magic will start going wrong."

"'Going wrong'? What in the Flames does that mean?"

"I don't fuckin' know, do I look like an expert on Descended magical hoo-ha to you? I just know it means we could have some more action real soon."

"Forging Day is three months away. Can our people hold out that long?"

"Dunno. Let's hope they don't have to."

"We're gonna need reinforcements. Even with the Lumnos cell, we barely took the island. Could the Meros cell help?"

"They need to keep up what they're doing. They already blew up half the docks at the port, and they set up blockades on the waterways leading off the continent. It's keeping the army distracted, which is good for our guys on the island."

"What about the cells up north?"

"There's some real interesting rumors going 'round up there. A bunch of messenger hawks came this morning, and one of 'em was from the Montios base. Apparently some Descended showed up out of nowhere, claiming he hates his own kind and wants 'em dead as bad as we do."

"And they took his word for it?"

"He musta done something to prove himself, I guess. They say he's real powerful."

"I don't care. We shouldn't be working with them. It's bad enough that we have to play nice with two false Quee—"

"Shift's over, folks. Me and Herkin have got it from here."

My eyes opened in surprise at the familiar voice. Brecke was standing nearby, staring at me, his expression uncharacteristically hardened. A second Guardian stood next to him—a short, gangly twenty-something whose boyish features and patchy beard looked as if puberty had skipped right over him.

The two mortals guarding me glared at Brecke. There was a venom in their sneers I didn't quite understand, one usually reserved only for me.

"You're too early, army boy," the man grunted. "Our shift doesn't end 'til dawn."

Brecke shrugged, unbothered by the demeaning tone. "They just opened a casket of wine. Me and Herkin here are the newest to camp, and Mother Dell said we haven't earned wine privileges yet. She sent us to relieve you two for the night."

The guards looked at each other and grinned. I sat upright, watching the interaction with curiosity.

Brecke grabbed Herkin's arm and started to leave. "If you'd rather stay here and babysit, I guess we can—"

"Not so fast." The male guard hopped to his feet. "If Mother Dell gave you an order, you don't get to change it. That's not how we do things in Arboros."

Brecke raised his palms in surrender. "Lesson learned. We'll take over here."

The two didn't put up any further argument as they slapped each other excitedly on the arms and jogged off toward the sea of tents.

Brecke remained still and watched them walk away. His too-intense focus had my instincts prickling. When they were finally out of sight, he turned back to me.

"Get up. Mother Dell said to take you to the river to bathe. You're stinking up the camp."

His voice was biting and aloof. This wasn't the Brecke I knew. He'd brought me my daily meals since we'd moved camps, and though we kept our discussions minimal in light of the Guardians in constant earshot, he'd always at least been courteous.

"Now?" I asked. "It's the middle of the night."

"This isn't your fancy palace, princess. You do what you're told, when you're told."

I bristled. "Brecke, what's going on?"

He rolled his eyes. "Get her chains off, Herkin."

The man at his side stumbled a step. "Me? But—but I... she's a... maybe you should—"

"*Do it.*"

Herkin jumped a mile. He practically quivered as he shuffled toward me and unwound my chains with wobbling hands. I seriously considered shouting *boo!* at him and shaving a few years off of his life from sheer panic.

Brecke's stare locked with mine, and my brows creased in a questioning frown. He quickly looked away.

Once Herkin had the chains unlatched, he looked at me and gulped, then tried tugging me to my feet with laughably light pressure. I felt bad enough for him that I complied without argument.

"Brecke," I started again.

"No talking, Descended." He looked at Herkin and pointed to the forest. "You lead her, I'll keep watch from behind."

Herkin gave the faintest rattle of my chains, then whooshed out a giant sigh of relief when I obediently fell into step beside him.

We left the warm glow of the firelit camp and marched into the surrounding forest. With the leafy canopy blocking all moonlight, the area was nearly pitch black, lit only by the soft glow of my Crown.

"Did Mother Dell really tell you we should do this?" Herkin called out meekly over his shoulder. "I thought she said to keep the prisoner in the camp at all times."

"Are you accusing me of lying?" Brecke rumbled, low and lethal.

"No, I just—"

"You're calling me a traitor who would betray the Guardians to help a Descended Queen? Because if so, I will defend my honor. *To the death*, if necessary."

"No!" Herkin squeaked. "No, no—no death necessary. Forget I said anything."

"Good. Keep walking."

As we continued on, the light of camp became a dot in the distance, though the burbling sounds of the nearby stream were getting further away, rather than closer. Hair rose on the back of my neck.

Something about this wasn't right.

Something was—

I froze at a sudden flash of movement, followed by the sickening sound of metal crushing into flesh and bone. Herkin's limp body collapsed to the ground.

Brecke towered above him, the blood-flecked hilt of a rapier in his hands. "Sorry, kiddo." He reached down and laid a finger against Herkin's throat. "Ah, he's fine. He'll have a hell of a headache tomorrow, though."

"Brecke," I hissed, "what in the Undying Fire is going on?"

"Keep your voice down, Bellator." He sheathed his blade, then pulled a key from his pocket. He unlocked the shackles from my wrists and let them fall to the soil with a soft thump. As I gaped at him, his expression brightened into a wry grin. "I'll explain later. Come on, help me drag him over there."

We pulled Herkin's unconscious body to a nearby tree, where a pile of supplies had been stashed in a knot of gnarled roots. Brecke got to work tying Herkin up and gagging him with a long strip of fabric. He unlatched the dagger at Herkin's hip and started to hand it to me, then seemed to think better of it. He shot me an apologetic look as he nestled it in his own belt.

"Follow me," he whispered.

I trailed him as we doubled back to the rebel camp, though we kept a safe distance while creeping around the perimeter to the other side. I caught

fleeting glances at parts of the camp I hadn't seen before—a makeshift infirmary where several bodies were laid out on cots, a corral with a handful of
horses and small livestock, and several wooden carts laden with the rebels'
trademark bombs.

Voices broke the silence. Brecke grabbed my arm and yanked me down
beneath a patch of brush. He scowled at my Crown, his face illuminated in
a wash of pale blue light. "Can't you turn that thing off?"

"Oh, *now* you want me to use my magic," I muttered.

"Just put it away before it gets us killed."

I frowned. Lily had told me once that late King Ulther rarely wore his,
so I knew it was possible to conceal it, though all my attempts to will it
away thus far had failed. But that had been before I learned to control my
godhood.

I reached down inside myself, searching for some magical lightswitch
I'd never been able to find before, but I found only the vacant gulf left
behind by the flameroot.

Then again, maybe the Crown wasn't like my godhood. After all, it was
a creation of the Kindred's Forging spell, not my own magic. Maybe it
didn't live *inside* me at all.

I closed my eyes and pushed my consciousness outside my own body,
then sharpened my focus onto the space above my head.

I felt... *something*. It wasn't like anything I'd experienced before. It
didn't feel like its own living thing, the way the godhood did, nor was it a
connection to something else, like my bond with Sorae.

This felt like a glowing ember escaped from its hearth, a twinkling star
plucked from the midnight sky and entrusted to me for safekeeping. Its
energy felt entirely *other*—something that did not belong to me and would
one day return to the source from which it came.

I could sense instinctively that I had no real control over it. I could not
change it or destroy it or give it away. I could only hold it—on my head or
in my heart.

So I tugged it down, deep into my soul. A warm sensation followed its
path through my head and neck until it nestled in a pocket of my chest, a
pair of flames flickering in the void.

"Did it work?" I asked.

I opened my eyes, surprised to see only darkness. I blinked a few times
until my vision adjusted and focused in on Brecke's face.

Wariness crept onto his shadowed features as he took a slow step back.
"Does this mean the flameroot wore off?"

"I'll answer that if you tell me what we're doing."

"I'm helping you escape."

A ball of guilt knotted in my belly. "Is this Henri's doing? Did he come to break me out?"

"No," Brecke said simply. "And I'd appreciate it if you never tell him I had any part in this."

I shuffled my feet. I wanted to escape—I'd *begged* for it—but Cordellia had not yet heard back from the Crowns on her offer to trade me for my mother. Leaving now could seal her fate.

"Your turn," Brecke said. "Is your magic back?"

"No," I admitted. "It's still gone. The flameroot doesn't affect the Crown, I guess."

"Why not?"

"Well, again, the Crowns were just about to tell me how everything works when *somebody* decided to detonate a bunch of bombs, and now—"

"Forget I asked. Let's go, we don't have much time before someone notices you're missing."

We continued slinking through the forest, the sound of rolling waves growing louder. When the trees gave way to a sandy beach, Brecke held out an arm to hold me back. He craned his neck, peering through the night in search of something.

I nervously drummed my fingers on my thigh. "Brecke, I can't believe I'm saying this, but maybe I should go back. Cordellia said—"

"There," he whispered, pointing.

Further down the beach, a cloaked figure crouched alongside a small sailing dinghy. Brecke let out a soft whistle that sounded like birdsong, and the figure turned our direction. A second later, the same whistle came echoing back.

Brecke stepped onto the beach and gestured for me to follow. As we neared the boat, the moon cast its silvery light on the figure's face. I froze in place.

"Cordellia?" I asked, glancing between the two of them. "What's going on?"

"A response from Fortos arrived this morning," she said. "They rejected any trade for your return. I believe their exact words were '*Do with her what you will. All those who are guilty will face their consequences in due course.*'"

I clenched my jaw. "In other words, *go ahead and kill her so we don't have to do it ourselves.*"

She nodded. "Now that they know your mother is a Guardian, they must suspect you were involved in the attack on the island."

I looked out over the inky waters of the Sacred Sea. The lights of the army warships surrounding Coeurîle bobbed in the distance, barely visible on the horizon.

"What does this mean for rescuing my mother?" I asked. "Vance said you're not willing to give the island up in exchange for her."

"He's right. It's too valuable to sacrifice for any one person, even your mother."

My whole body sagged with the weight of hopelessness.

"But," she continued, "I've let them think we're still considering it. Perhaps they'll keep her alive long enough to see if she can be useful in getting the island back."

I let out a long, relieved sigh. "Thank you, Cordellia."

"Don't thank me yet. I'm letting you return to Lumnos, but if the Crowns believe you're working with us, your life may be in very real danger, even in your own realm."

"My life has been in danger since the second I became Queen. If the Crowns want me dead, they'll have to get in line."

She flashed a smirk, though it faded fast. "I don't know how long our people can hold Coeurîle. You need to get to your mother and free her yourself—soon."

I nodded grimly. "I'll find a way."

"I'm sorry for the secrecy in sneaking you out, but my people would not have stood by and let you walk away. It's better for us both if they believe you escaped."

I looked at Brecke. "What about you? When Herkin wakes up…"

He gave a casual shrug. "My time here is over, too. Dell was kind enough to take me in, but the others never really took to me. My army service will always make me a Descended sympathizer to them."

That was a sentiment I understood well—one I'd battled in my own way over my father's legacy.

"Where will you go now?" I asked.

"A cell up north, I think. Things there are heating up. As long as I'm willing to fight, I doubt they'll ask too many questions."

Guilt nipped at my heels. Brecke had risked his life and his reputation to help me, and now he was being forced into a warzone to escape the fallout.

"You could come to Lumnos instead," I offered. "The boat is small, but perhaps we could both fit. I can conceal you in the palace, or Henri—"

Brecke shook his head. "It's too dangerous for me there. Lumnos is swarming with army soldiers. If any of them recognized me, they'd kill me on the spot."

I frowned. "Why are Emarion Army soldiers in my realm?"

"A missing queen means an empty throne," Cordellia answered for him. "Power won't tolerate a void for long—it must always be filled by someone."

Brecke nodded. "You should get back and begin your reign before someone else does it for you." He winked. "*Your Majesty.*"

I smiled and reached out a hand. "Thank you for helping me, Brecke. I won't forget it."

He clasped my wrist. "Don't think I've forgotten about that favor you owe me for the blade I gave you when we met. I'll call it in one of these days."

I swallowed down the painful memory of how I'd burned the knife away in my meltdown after my father's death. Perhaps someday Brecke and I would share a drink while I told him the story of the blade's demise—but not today.

Cordellia stepped in my path. "I have one condition before you go."

She held out a flask, and I knew instantly what it contained.

"Haven't I taken enough? My magic is already gone, and we just agreed that I'm going back to a realm where people want me dead."

Cordellia's hard stare left no room for debate. "I have to ensure your magic doesn't return before I've had time to move my people to a new campsite. There are weapons in the boat. That's all we get as mortals, so it will have to be enough for you."

I snatched the flask from her hand, shooting them both unhappy looks as I forced down gulp after gulp of the disgusting liquid. I peered into the boat, noting a pair of dull grey metal blades, a bow, and a quiver of arrows.

"No godstone?" I asked wryly between sips.

"It took us centuries to collect the godstone weapons we have. They'll be crucial in the coming war. We can't afford to lose even a single piece." Her eyes narrowed. "You already destroyed a gryvern bolt that dated back to the Blood War."

"And I'll destroy the second one, if you try to kill Sorae again," I warned. I held up the flask. "You have your conditions, and I have mine."

She brushed back the edge of her overcoat, revealing the glittering blade of a godstone dagger. A subtle threat—but, judging from her silence, not enough to change her mind about helping me.

I handed back the empty flask, then walked over to the boat and climbed inside. Next to the weapons was a pack of food and a water gourd, as well as a heavy hooded cloak.

I looked back up. "Why are you helping me, Cordellia?"

She considered me for a moment. "What you said the other day about there being good people among the Descended—it reminded me of Auralie."

I frowned, confused. Never in my life had I heard my mother speak kindly about the Descended. All she would ever tell me is that they were dangerous, and I had to stay far away.

"She had similar ideas about trying to work with them," she continued. "It frequently caused issues with Vance. He was always pushing for more bloodshed. She and I spoke often about the difficulties we faced leading people like him."

My heart ached to hear her describe my mother in a way that was so foreign. She and I had always been close, spending most of every day together, either at home or the healer's center. Though I'd known she had her secrets, I thought I knew her better than anyone, even my father—but the Auralie that Cordellia was describing might as well be a stranger.

"Beyond her desire for peace," Cordellia went on, "your mother was strategic. If she had planned that attack on the armory, she would have done it quietly, with no bombs and little bloodshed, and she would have framed a Descended to leave them fighting each other for blame. Vance's approach was reckless. It put a target on all the mortals, and it nearly ruined the mission on Coeurîle that we've been planning for years.

"Vance is a loyal Guardian, I don't deny that, but if your mother had known she would be gone for this long, I don't believe she would have left him in control of the Lumnos cell. He plans to return to Lumnos tomorrow, and I admit, I share your concern at what he might do. I would feel better if you were there to temper him. Perhaps you can find a way to target his hatred on the people who deserve it."

I nodded. "I'll do my best."

She smiled, the first genuine one she'd ever offered me. "I suppose we're allies now, so you might as well call me Dell."

She beckoned to Brecke and they stepped forward to the water's edge, shoving the boat off the sand. Brecke gave me a final salute and turned back to the forest, but Cordellia lingered.

"There's a large camp in Montios," she called out. "Your mother knows where it is. If you're able to free her, get her there, and she'll be safe. So will your brother."

"But not me?"

She gave me a sympathetic look, but didn't bother to deny it.

I swallowed. "Thank you, Dell. I'm truly sorry for your people that died. If I could, I would prevent even a drop of mortal blood from spilling."

"I believe that you mean that, Diem, and I believe you have a good heart. But I fear you've not yet come to terms with the sacrifices this war will require before it's over—from everyone involved."

I had no answer to offer her, only an ominous suspicion her words might prove even truer than I could imagine.

I took the oars in my hands and began my long journey home.

"I'm trusting you," Cordellia shouted with a quick wave. "Don't make me regret it."

CHAPTER

EIGHT

As the Arboros shore faded, I relished in the peacefulness of the
midnight darkness. The water was a mirror beneath the watchful
moon, reflecting a smattering of bright, twinkling stars.

An eerie quiet hovered in the air. I expected to hear the high-pitched
orchestra of chirping insects or the caw of nocturnal seabirds, but the only
break in the silence was the soft, rhythmic lapping of my oars.

I hadn't been this alone since becoming Queen. The Crown had
brought with it a torrent of vigilant guards, sycophantic Corbois courtiers,
meetings with pompous House leaders, and the companionship of my new
Descended friends. Even in the rare moments without company, Sorae had
been a constant presence through our bond.

But here, adrift in the sea with the flameroot severing my link to the
magical world, I was well and truly on my own.

Though the solitude was a welcome respite, I was also overwhelmed by
a desire to be *home*. What happened at the coronation—and everything I'd
learned since—had rattled me. I needed to wrap my brother up in my arms
and finally tell him the truth about our mother, and then I needed to be
wrapped up in Luther's arms and hear his stoic assurance that no matter
how bleak things seemed, we would face it, and defeat it, together.

I gazed out toward home, my chest warming as I imagined the relief
those reunions would bring.

But they would not come soon. The distance to Lumnos was significant, and I could only row so fast on my own. I would need a strong wind to come along to catch my sail. Even then, I would have to risk pulling my boat to shore to rest and sleep.

That would be the most dangerous part of my trip. A visit by a Crown without invitation was a severe act of aggression. Setting even a foot onto the soil of another realm could earn my execution.

I weighed the risk of stopping in Faunos. Its Queen had been friendly when we'd met on Coeurîle. Perhaps with the flameroot muffling my magic, she wouldn't see my presence as a threat—but after my disastrous coronation and the Crowns' decision not to negotiate for my release, betting on goodwill from any of them was a dangerous wager.

My journey by sea would have to suffice.

I wondered, with a twinge of worry, how Brecke would make his own escape. He could purchase safe passage to the north at the port in Umbros, but to get there, he would have to bypass the vast deserts of Ignios.

Mortals were entirely forbidden within the Ignios borders, even on the Ring Road. Brecke would have to sail past its coast, a dangerous proposition when one wrong gust could bring him within the reach of their infamously ruthless Descended.

I sent out a silent prayer for his safe journey. His kindness despite my revelation as a Descended gave me hope that the peaceful future I dreamed of might not be so impossible after all.

The beginnings of a breeze kissed my cheeks, so I pulled in the oars and unfurled the flaxen sail wrapped around the center mast. Thankfully, my father had built a similar vessel for fishing and taught Teller and I to maneuver it, though my energetic spirit had never taken to the long, tranquil hours on the water like my brother. I had been all too happy to let it become their father-son bonding ritual while my own sailing skills rusted.

I forced myself to wade through that painful vault of memories, latching onto the sound of my father's voice barking instructions at me one afternoon as our little boat wobbled.

Your sail is flapping, Diem—tighten the mainsheet. Good, see how much faster we're moving? Now mind the boom, the wind is shifting. Your head, Diem, watch your head!

I grinned at the memory. The wind that day had been strong, and I'd been so exhilarated by our speed that I hadn't noticed when the changing breeze had sent the sail swinging back across the boat—and taking me with it.

That's a mistake you only make once, my father had teased as he'd hauled me out of the water, soaked and sputtering.

I fought the bittersweet grief that accompanied every thought of him as I pulled on the ropes. The wind quickly filled the sail and dragged me into a brisk pace.

Arboros faded away, and I nudged the boat's tiller to follow the shoreline. It would be faster to venture out into the open sea and straight for Lumnos, but without a compass to guide me, I could easily end up lost.

Suddenly, the wind shifted. The sail flapped loudly, then filled again from the other direction. I ducked just in time to miss the wooden beam flying over the top of my head. The boat began to rotate as the bow swung in a wide circle back toward the shore.

That was *odd*. Changing winds were normal, but I'd never felt a shift like that—never so extreme, so abrupt.

I scrambled to reset my course. By the time I'd managed to turn the boat and reset my ropes, I was nearly back to Arboros.

The breeze slowed, then stilled. The water turned glassy, and my dinghy bobbed in place. I sighed irritably and debated returning to oars, but no sooner had I reached for them than the wind picked back up, gusting so fiercely that my unbound hair swirled in my face.

I brushed it back with one hand and wrestled the ropes with the other in an awkward attempt to set the boat back on a path for deeper waters.

Before I could finish, the wind switched again. The sail went flying, and I couldn't adjust in time to avoid the thick wooden pole of the boom smacking against the side of my head.

"By the Flames," I hissed. I slumped into the floor of the boat and rubbed at my scalp until the stars stopped swimming in my vision. "*Fine.* No sailing tonight."

I carefully stood and lowered the sail, then began securing it to the mast. I was so focused on my task that I nearly toppled overboard when the boat struck land. I looked back to discover that I'd already run ashore on the Arboros coast.

I frowned down at the waves lapping along the shoreline. "Impossible," I murmured to myself. "The water wasn't moving that quickly."

I pushed off the sandy beach, then started rowing back out to sea. Rather than cutting smoothly through the water, my oars shuddered as if being dragged through mud. I grunted and threw my strength into fighting through it, winning a small bit of distance, but the second I stopped to catch my breath, the current swept me back toward land.

I looked around, at a loss for words. Powerful rip currents could indeed drag you out to sea in seconds, but I hadn't imagined one could pull you so forcefully to shore, especially in such calm waters.

I shoved off land once more and turned my boat crossways, attempting to row myself out of whatever bizarre current was determined to keep me from the sea. With considerable effort, I managed to put some distance between myself and the shore.

I let out a winded breath, laughing to myself at the absurdity of the situation. Nature seemed to have pit itself against me. It was almost as if some supernatural force was telling me to—

Thunk.

Splash.

Without warning, the dinghy tipped, dumping me into the freezing water. The cold stole the breath from my lungs, and I gasped for air as all my supplies sank into the water and disappeared.

"*Damn it,*" I shouted. "What in the tundras of hell am I supposed to do now?"

Seething, I dragged the boat back into shallow water. Weapons I could maybe survive without, but no food or fresh water? That would require constant trips to the mainland to hunt and forage, putting me at even higher risk of being caught and cutting my sailing time down to slivers.

I'd be lucky to make it home in a month, if I survived the trip at all.

I waded back to shore and collapsed onto the sand, panting for breath. If I returned to the Guardians, Brecke's sacrifice would have been for nothing, and Cordellia might not risk helping me a second time.

She'd mentioned moving her camp—if I could stay hidden long enough for them to leave, I could bide my time until the flameroot wore off enough to summon Sorae to take me home.

But the Guardians had a second godstone bolt. If the new campsite was close enough to see Sorae arrive, could I trust Dell not to use it?

Was that a risk I was willing to take?

Rustling in the trees caught my ear, then voices. I scrambled to my feet and bolted for the tree line, diving into the foliage just as a group emerged onto the beach.

"They didn't take it," one of them yelled. "The boat's still here."

"They must have gone inland instead," another said.

"Wait—why is the sail dripping?"

The group walked closer to the boat. I edged behind a nearby tree trunk, crouching lower as they approached.

"The ropes are wet."

"There's water in the floor. Maybe they capsized trying to get away."

"If so, they can't be far. You—go tell Mother Dell. Everyone else, spread out in pairs and start searching. Remember what the Mother said—take her alive if you can, but kill her if you must."

Well, *shit*. This complicated matters. I needed to get out of here fast.

I paused. Brecke and I had passed horses tied up on the outskirts of camp. If I could free one while everyone was distracted with the search, I could ride away before the Guardians had time to catch up.

That, at least, gave me a much-needed burst of confidence. I'd grown up sneaking through the woodlands of Lumnos. I'd learned how to conceal myself to hunt with my father and creep up on Henri or Teller unseen.

The forest had been my playground, and though these were not the familiar trees of Lumnos, I felt at ease among them all the same.

My eyes narrowed in on the woman who'd been tasked with returning to camp. On featherlight feet, I crawled out from my hiding place and followed her into the forest.

It was almost too easy. Though my seawater-drenched clothes made me slow and noisy, the woman's single-minded focus had her distracted, and her hurried thrashing through the foliage was loud enough to conceal my squelching footsteps from the other Guardians we passed.

The glow of the camp grew nearer. I was surprised at how few mortals I saw. With a rogue Guardian and a Descended prisoner gone missing, I expected the woods to be swarming, but there was hardly a soul in sight.

Perhaps the gods were looking out for me, after all.

As the woman sprinted through the tents, I broke away and headed for the horses. To my dismay, they were already in the process of being saddled, no doubt to aid in the search.

I needed a head start on my escape to avoid a fight with the mortals that might turn bloody. If I could get my hands on a sharp blade, I could slice the straps on the other saddles to sabotage the horses.

Beside the corral, two mortals stood together with heads stooped, talking excitedly. I crept along a row of small hay bales until their whispers grew into words.

"That is good news, but how does it change the plan?" one asked. "Should I keep readying the horses?"

"Hold for now," the other said, "Mother Dell says we're not leaving until we decide what to do."

"But if the other two got away, shouldn't we be moving? They know where we are. If that Queen comes back here—"

"Dell thinks she won't. I have to get back—you stay with the horses."

"Wait, I want to go see the—"

One of the figures jogged away. "Stay there!"

The other followed behind a few steps, crossing their arms and craning their neck for a better view. Just beyond their silhouette, a large crowd of Guardians had gathered around the central fire, shouting and cheering.

I swore as a quick glance around the corral revealed nothing helpful. I would have to go scavenging for a blade in the tents.

With the Guardian on watch still preoccupied by the commotion at the campfire, I slipped past them into the heart of the camp.

Nearby, pained cries hooked my attention. At the infirmary I'd seen earlier, several mortals lay sprawled on bedrolls, their bodies coated in layers of gauze that I knew concealed dragonfyre-scorched flesh.

At the center, a man sat on a large boulder with his head drooping low. His left arm was almost entirely gone.

My stomach twisted. I'd been the cause of these wounds. Even if I hadn't meant to, even if I'd done nothing to provoke it and could never have stopped it, I would always blame myself.

And so would they.

Heart heavy, I ducked into a darkened tent and rummaged quietly among the scattered belongings. My shoulders sank—no weapons.

I stole a long woolen cape and draped it over me, then tugged the hood low to shroud my distinctive hair and eyes. In these mortal clothes, soaked as they were, I just might be able to pass as a Guardian.

I held my breath and strutted out of the tent. I kept my head low, though there were hardly any mortals to avoid. Whatever was happening at the campfire, it had captured everyone's focus.

Needing the extra firelight—and perhaps losing a battle to my curiosity —I skulked closer to the crowd.

"Mother Dell, I have news," a woman's voice rang out above the clamor.

"Not now, Sister."

"But Mother, the boat... the prisoner must have found it and taken it to sea, but—"

"Thank you for letting me know, Sister. Let me address this matter first, then I'll hear your news."

Perfect—Dell was distracted.

I spied another vacant tent closer to the fire. I tucked my chin and marched toward it with a faux-confident swagger. A few eyes glanced my way, and I forced myself not to falter as I stooped beneath the open flap.

A grin burst across my face. Laying on the bedroll, its dark grey metal reflecting the glint of the firelight, lay an abandoned broadsword. It was bigger and heavier than I'd normally choose, but it was also intimidating as hell. Perhaps that would work in my favor.

With no weapons belt, I'd have to carry it by hand. I pulled the blade free of its scabbard and gave it a few light swings to test its balance.

Behind me, the sounds of shouting fell to a hush. Cordellia's voice drifted into the tent.

"You're too far from home," she said, her tone grave with warning. "You should not have come here."

"Where is she?"

I froze.

I knew that voice. That low timbre, that rumbling pitch. The dark, lethal calm lacing power in every syllable.

"You've only made the situation worse," Cordellia said.

"*Where is my Queen?*"

My heart seized in my chest.

"Luther," I breathed.

My grip tightened on the broadsword's hilt. All my plans evaporated from my mind, my focus now on the only thing that mattered—rescuing Luther from the mortals' wrath. I steeled my shoulders and turned to leave.

A hand clamped over my mouth.

My muscles locked up as I was hauled back into the stout wall of a chest. Whoever it was, he was tall, broad, and inhumanly strong. He single-handedly pinned my head in place against him as I squirmed to get free.

I swung the broadsword in an arc over my shoulder, hoping to catch his skull. His free hand caught my wrist and forced it down until the point of the blade sank into the soil, then he wrenched my fingers free of its hilt.

My other elbow jammed back into his ribs. He grunted and jerked forward, but his grip on me held firm. He released my wrist and snaked his arm around my torso.

I flailed and thrashed, kicking my legs and heaving my body in every direction. I used every trick my father had taught me, but the man was impossibly tough. Nothing I did could shake his hold.

Finally, I fell still, my heart galloping in my chest. The hand over my mouth pulled my face to the side as he lowered his lips to my ear.

"Blessed Kindred, Queenie. You sure know how to put up a fight."

CHAPTER
NINE

I sucked in a sharp breath through my nose and tapped my pinned hand against the man's legs in a show of surrender, and his arms fell away.

"You almost took me out with that sword," he chuckled, tugging down the hood of his cloak. "I know I promised to give my life for you, but that wasn't really what I had in m—"

"Taran!" I whisper-shouted. I turned and threw my arms around his neck, burying my face in his shoulder. "*Gods,* am I glad to see you."

His arms looped around me and squeezed, his own relief showing in the crushing force of his embrace. "You scared the hell out of us, going missing like that. Lu's about ready to burst a vein."

I pulled back and stared up at him, unable to keep the smile off my face. He was wearing his trademark grin, his ruggedly handsome features framed by messy dark blonde waves.

When I'd first met him at the palace, Taran had been the only Corbois cousin to treat me not as a Queen or a lowly half-breed, but as an equal. Our mutual love of sparring, dirty jokes, and teasing Luther had quickly earned him a place as one of my dearest friends.

He'd also proven himself willing to tell me the hard, unflattering truths I needed to hear, and that had made him a valuable ally.

"How did you find me?" I asked.

He snorted. "If I tell you that, Luther might slice off my balls. You'll have to pry the truth out of him, if you can."

My smile fell away. "I heard him out there. I think the mortals caught him."

"Oh, he walked right up and turned himself over. We were hoping they would chain him up next to you so I could find you and break you both out. By the time I saw you sneaking around out in the trees, it was too late to stop him."

I groaned. "I really need that man to stop putting his life at risk for me."

"Don't hold your breath."

"These mortals have godstone weapons, Taran. A lot of them. If Luther tries to fight them..." I shook my head to clear the dark thoughts of how badly this could go. "What was your plan to get us out?"

"Well, I... uh..." He scratched the back of his head. "I hadn't really made it that far. I'm not usually the brains of the operation."

"*Taran!* You let Luther give himself up with no plan to get him out?"

"He's High General. He didn't exactly ask permission. Besides, it was better than what *he* wanted to do, which was shove swords through their eye sockets until they gave you up." My mouth hung open, and Taran nodded somberly. "Luther's always been a little terrifying, but when it comes to you, Queenie..." He shuddered.

I walked to the tent's entrance and pulled the flap closed all but an inch so I could peer out unseen. Luther was on his knees, his hands bound behind his back, surrounded by a throng of mortals several heads deep. The Sword of Corbois lay in the grass a few feet away. Cordellia stood in front of him, talking too quietly for me to hear. Whatever they were discussing, it had Luther glaring at her with poison in his eyes.

Taran came up behind me and squeezed my shoulders.

"We'll get him out," he assured me. "And we have help. Look."

He pointed to the woods on the far end of camp. At first, I only saw a dark swath of foliage, but slowly the face of a woman edged out from behind a tree, her myriad piercings glittering under the moonlight.

"Alixe!" I gasped.

Taran pulled the flap open wider and waved at her, then pointed excitedly at me and grinned. Alixe rolled her eyes at her cousin's antics, but she flashed me a smile and a deferential nod.

My tension eased enormously. As Luther's right hand in the Royal Guard—and my newly minted military advisor—Alixe was a clever strategist and a fierce, capable warrior. She was exactly who I would have chosen to find a way out of a problem like this.

But my burgeoning hope was dampened by the glittering black points aimed at Luther's chest. The mortals could be jumpy around Descended, not to mention their willingness to take their vengeance on whichever one of us they could.

I sank back into the darkness of the tent, chewing my lip as my mind raced for a solution. Alixe would surely have a plan, but could we get to her without being seen—and before the mortals took their anger over my escape out on Luther?

Taran cocked his head. "How did you get out of the camp? And why were you sneaking back in?" He looked me over, eyebrows furrowing. "And why are you soaking wet?"

"Long story," I sighed. "We need a distraction. One that won't end with them turning us into pincushions with godstone arrows."

"How did they get so much godstone, anyway? I thought the Crowns destroyed it all. It's bad enough that we have to worry about rebel bombs."

"Bombs!" I cried. "That's it! There's a stockpile near the horses. We'll set one off and disorient them, then we can sneak Luther out."

"Using their own tricks against them. Ruthless, Queenie." He smirked. "I like it."

"There's just one problem—how to light the fuses."

"You're a Crown, your light magic works here."

"Not anymore. They've been drugging me with flameroot. It nullifies Descended magic."

Taran's face blanched. "Mortals can nullify our magic?"

"It wears off after a few days, but for now, I have nothing. I'm guessing you don't, either?"

"Well... I *shouldn't*..." He stretched out his palms and stared down at them. His muscles tensed as if he were straining against some invisible force. "I felt my magic go dark when we stepped over the Lumnos border, but on the journey here, every now and then, it almost felt like..." His forehead wrinkled as he strained again, fingers flexing and curling. After a moment, he grunted and shook his head. "No. Nothing here, either."

I grabbed the broadsword, then pulled my hood over my head. "I'll have to get a flame from one of the firepits."

"Let me do it. You're the Queen, you should get someplace safe and hide."

I shot him a lighthearted glare. "Don't insult me, Taran. I'm not that kind of Queen. Keep an eye on Luther, and wait for me near the horses. There are a few already saddled—if we're fast, we can grab them when we escape."

Taran sidestepped to block my path and frowned down at me. "Luther's not going to like this. Between the two of you, I'm not sure who I'm more scared to cross."

He pulled a thick leather baldric from his shoulder, then grabbed my broadsword's discarded scabbard and swapped it for his own. "Take this, at least," he insisted, securing it across my chest. He pulled a sheathed dagger from his boot and tucked it into my waistband. "And this. Oh, and take—"

I put my hand on his chest to still him. "I'll be fine, Taran. I'll meet you at the horses."

He blew out a breath and raked a hand down his face. "Lu's going to kill me."

I grinned and gave him a final swat on the arm, then turned and slowly crept out of the tent. The crowd had tightened around Luther, blocking him from view, but I could still hear the deep pitch of his voice arguing with Cordellia. The sound of it, the knowledge it gave me that he was alive and close by, rekindled my courage as I wove through the tents.

A few mortals scurried by, their shoulders brushing mine as they gossiped excitedly about the new hostage. Despite the late hour, half the camp had been roused after my disappearance, and the other half was now being awoken by the commotion. If we didn't get out soon, there would be more mortals than even four strong Descended could realistically take on. As it was, I was struggling with the looming possibility that I might soon have to choose between my Descended friends' lives or a mortal's.

My pulse picked up speed as I neared the edge of the tents. The crowd spilled into the pathway, forcing me to tuck my chin and murmur *pardon me* and *just passing through.*

When I finally emerged, my heart sank. A long line of darkened firepits lay extinguished for the night. There wasn't a single glowing red coal, let alone a flame to be found.

I wandered in search of an untended lantern or forgotten flint, finding nothing of use. One quick, simple option rose into the sky behind me— but it was also the biggest risk.

With a deep breath, I pivoted on my heel. I kept to the edges of the crowd and craned my neck in pretend interest in the hostage while sidestepping closer to the roaring bonfire.

Cordellia stood with her back to the flames, and with the intense heat of the blaze, few of the Guardians had gathered behind her. By the time I made it to the stone perimeter circling the logs, I was almost entirely exposed.

As slow as I dared, I made a show of stoking the fire. Sweat beaded my brow and trickled down the column of my throat. A partially unburnt branch lay just inside the wall of flames. I reached for it with a trembling hand.

My body locked up as memories of the armory attack surfaced. I felt it all over again—a heat so thick I couldn't breathe, flames so close they blistered my skin. I'd almost died there, among the smoke and the collapsing wreckage.

For a moment, I'd *wanted* to die there.

But, like a phoenix, the sigil of House Corbois, I had arisen from the ashes of that fire different than the woman who'd gone in.

We're not reborn in the flames, Eleanor had told me. *We're revealed.*

That night had opened my eyes to the true path of my life. I could not live with the Guardians' brand of justice-through-bloodshed, but neither could I do nothing while my people withered under Descended rule. Though it took the gauntlet of the Challenging for me to finally accept it, the flames of that inferno had not changed my fate, they'd *illuminated* it.

I stilled the quivering of my hand and removed the branch, a bright flame flickering at its tip. With a leisurely pace that bordered on excruciating, I strolled along the ring of stones.

As I passed behind Cordellia's back, I couldn't stop my face from turning to Luther. He'd always been a magnetic force I could never seem to resist.

When my eyes hit him, his gaze was already waiting for me. Though he showed no flicker of surprise or recognition, I'd long since learned to read the invisible signs of his heart. I knew the turmoil churning in his mind at knowing I was safe yet incredibly at risk. I felt the unbearable restraint it took him not to launch himself forward and shield my body with his own.

Instead, he did the next best thing.

Luther threw his head back and roared into the night. His shoulders arched behind him as he unleashed a long, crazed snarl at the moon. The crowd of mortals seized in fright, a number of them scrambling for their weapons as others stumbled into each other to back away. Even Cordellia flinched and shifted to a fighting stance.

It was a gift—a distraction to give me a chance to flee. I pursed my lips to hide my smile and scurried away, making a mental note to tease—and thank—him later.

Mercifully, the path to the corral was clear. The man I'd overheard earlier was still on watch, but like the others, he was entranced by Luther and his bizarre display. Just beyond the mortal, Taran's delighted grin shone from the shadows.

I dipped my chin and hurried past. The man abruptly spun to face me. "You there—what are you doing?"

"Nothing," I blurted. "I'm going to help with the search. It's dark, so..." I wiggled the makeshift torch, hoping that was explanation enough.

"You can't take an open flame this way—if the hay doesn't catch fire, the bombs will. You'll get us all killed."

I took a step back. "Right. I'll just... um..."

"Wait a minute..." The man walked closer, squinting down at my hip. "How did you get my sword?"

Shit.

He lunged forward. I darted just out of his reach, but the movement jostled my hood, revealing my face and stray wisps from my milk-white braid in the moonlight.

His eyes bulged, and he stumbled back a step. "I found her!" he shouted. "I found the Qu—"

Taran's hand slammed down over his mouth as he came up from behind and dragged the man off his feet. "Go light the bomb," he hissed. "Hurry!"

"Don't hurt him," I pleaded, provoking an incredulous look from Taran as he fought to keep the thrashing man contained. "They're *mortals*, Taran."

He groaned in exasperation. "Fine. *Go!*"

I bolted toward the bombs, my heart stumbling each time the flame sputtered and threatened to die. Shouting rang out behind me, though I couldn't tell whether it came from a friendly voice or a hostile one.

I skidded to a stop in front of the wooden cart and threw off the waxed canvas sheeting. There were containers of all sizes and shapes, some with thick liquids visible through clear glass bottles, others made of welded metal boxes that rattled when shook.

During my time in the Lumnos cell, I'd never been privy to the secrets of the Guardians' homemade bombs. I only knew they were extremely powerful—and extremely deadly.

I grabbed two at random and tucked them under my arm, then sprinted back for the campfire. I couldn't risk setting them off near the tents where the children might be sleeping, but I had to get close enough to send the mortals into chaos.

"Why do you have those?" a voice shouted as I bolted past. "You there, stop!"

"Old Gods, Lumnos, Kindred," I mumbled as the sound of running boots thundered behind me, "I could really use a favor from one of you right now."

I darted into the tree line at the edge of camp, then grabbed the larger of the vessels and held it up to the flame-tipped branch.

"What are you doing?"

A woman approached, gaping at me in horror. Her eyes locked on the bomb's fuse as it sparked and caught fire.

"Run," she screamed. "She's got a bomb!"

As she fled back into camp, I gingerly set the vessel on the soil, my heartbeat racing faster with each burnt inch of the fuse.

I followed the woman's path. "Bomb," I repeated, keeping my hood low and the unlit explosive tucked beneath my cloak. "Take cover!"

A wave of brown eyes, centered by a pair of blue-grey, snapped my direction.

"Bomb!" I yelled again. "*Everyone, r—*"

The forest exploded before they got the chance.

The fiery burst sent me flying face-first into the soil. Muffled ringing filled my ears while shrapnel of charred bark shot through the air. A fog of smoke and burning embers rolled into the clearing.

The Guardians scattered like ants. Some fled into the forest, others ran for their tents, and a few brave souls pulled their weapons and charged toward the site of the explosion.

Cordellia's authoritative voice cut through the commotion. "Round up the children and injured, get them to the beach. Archers, to the trees. Prepare the ballista—if the gryvern is back, let's be ready."

I clenched my jaw at her order, thankful Sorae was far away in Lumnos. On hands and knees, I crawled toward Luther as boots scurried in frantic circles and blocked him from my view.

A woman crouched at my side and put a gentle hand on my arm. "Are you alright?"

I swatted her away. "You should go."

She kneeled and reached for my hood. "Were you injured in the blast? I can h—"

"*Diem!*"

I jerked upright at the sound of Luther's shout. Through a break in the swarm, I spied four Guardians dragging him away, their blades inches from his skin.

"Y-you..." the woman stammered, scrambling backward.

"I won't hurt you," I promised. I raised my palms in innocence, but as I did, the second bomb dropped from under my arm and tumbled to the grass in front of me.

She let out a blood-curdling scream. "Bomb! *The Queen has a bomb!*"

I swore and snatched the explosive, then shot to my feet. With her shouts at my back, I ran to the campfire and lit the second fuse, then reared my arm back and prepared to throw.

My gaze crossed with Cordellia's. Her brown eyes flared wide with recognition of who I was and what I had done.

"Diem," she warned. "Don't."

But the fuse was short, and there was no time left for apologies. I hurled the bomb toward the tree line and ran.

CHAPTER

TEN

I made it to Luther just in time for the second explosion.

The Guardians dropped him and dove for cover, while Luther threw himself on top of me to shield my body from the blast. Streams of fiery wood rained down on a field of flaming debris.

I wriggled out from beneath his weight, then pulled the dagger Taran had given me and slashed through the ropes binding Luther's wrists. He growled as his hands fell free, a vicious predator uncaged at last.

My breath caught as he pulled me into his arms. Our lips came together like a surging wave on a rocky break, two unstoppable forces undeterred by the violence closing in on all sides.

It was a reckless kiss, a *dangerous* kiss—and I never wanted it to end.

He tasted of the spice of his fury and the sweetness of his relief. His urgent grip slid to the back of my neck, the burn of his skin against mine searing straight to my core.

"My Queen," he murmured, the words rumbling against my lips.

"Hello, Prince," I gasped. "I missed you, too."

An arrow whizzed past our heads, freezing us both in place.

"Respectfully, Your Majesty," Alixe shouted from nearby, "perhaps the reunion can wait?"

At her feet, a mortal lay dead with a throwing dagger lodged in his neck. She had stolen his bow and quiver and was firing off arrows at the other archers in the surrounding trees to give us cover.

My gut clenched at the man's lifeless face. More blood on my hands. More corpses at my feet.

"Are you hurt?" Luther asked, pulling me to my feet.

I swallowed and forced myself to rip my eyes from the dead mortal. I shook my head. "We need to get to the horses."

He nodded. "Your magic...?"

"Gone. They forced me to take flameroot."

He glowered and ran for the Sword of Corbois while I sheathed my dagger, pulling the broadsword from its scabbard. Around us, Guardians staggered through the smoke, shouting warnings both at us and about us.

"Alixe," I yelled. "This way!"

As the evening breeze cleared the haze from the air, the clang of clashing metal took its place. We moved as a trio through the melee, a three-backed beast fighting a burgeoning mob with hate smoldering in every brown eye.

Luther tried to push me between him and Alixe, but I shoved him off. I pounced forward to smash the flat side of my blade against a Guardian's arm before it could ram a spear through Alixe's side.

"Don't kill them," I begged. "They're mortals. They're just angry, they don't realize—"

"It's them or us, Your Majesty," Alixe gritted out. She had a shortsword in each hand that swung in elegant, precise strokes, almost artistic in their refinement. She was the deadliest kind of dancer, each movement choreographed to leave her audience in ribbons.

What Alixe displayed in grace, Luther matched in savagery. His blows were thunderous, shattering bone with every swing. I'd known Luther's strength went far beyond his magic, but even without the sparks and shadows at his command, he was a fearsome thing to behold.

"We can't save them all," he warned. His voice was as gentle as his rage would allow, sensitive to how deeply he knew this mattered to me. "Not if we plan to get out alive."

"I know, but—"

I yelped and ducked below the swing of a wooden club, then shoved my boot into its wielder's chest.

"We are not enemies," I shouted, unsure which of them I was really telling.

Amid a flurry of swings and jabs, Cordellia strode toward us, sword in hand.

"Call them off, Dell," I warned. "Let us leave here. No one else needs to get hurt."

"You know I can't do that," she yelled back, unspoken words riding her tone.

I knew she was right. Even if she wanted to help me—and the glare on her face left that very much in question—her people would mutiny before they let us walk away. We were too outnumbered, too penned in. They had the upper hand, and Cordellia could not cede it now.

"Give yourselves up," she warned, "before one of us is forced to do something we'll regret."

But that, I could not do. I was willing to put my own life in her care and risk the wrath of her people, but I would not ask the same of my Descended friends—my *family*.

A club connected with Luther's hip, knocking him down to a knee. The mortals had correctly pegged him as their biggest threat, and three of them were raining down blows in quick succession, giving him little time to defend and no time to recover.

A fourth man came tearing through the crowd with a long, glittering black blade raised above his head. His scowl fixed on Luther as he brought the sword plummeting down.

Without thinking, I lunged.

I hurled my body into the attacking Guardian. With a violent collision, we tumbled across the soil, Luther and Alixe shouting my name, until the mortal collapsed on top of me.

I froze stone-still, waiting to feel the consequences of his godstone blade. There was no pain, only the slowly growing warmth of hot liquid oozing across my belly.

The man and I gaped at each other. Our expressions were a mirror image of shock—and regret.

I didn't understand at first. Then he coughed, and a trickle of red leaked from the corner of his lips.

Luther roared and grabbed the man by his back. As his body lifted away, my broadsword slid from his gut with a sickening slurp. His blade fell from his limp hand, its edge bloodless and pristine.

"Are you wounded?" Luther barked.

I couldn't answer.

Luther and Alixe shifted to fight off the encroaching mob while I lay paralyzed by my horror.

I had killed a mortal—to save a Descended.

It didn't matter that the mortal was a stranger who wanted us dead, or that the Descended was becoming so dear to me, a blade through his heart would have cut as deeply as a blade through my own.

I had spilled the blood of my people.

For *them*.

"Diem, *are you hurt?*" Luther demanded again, his voice strained. The terror in it pulled me back to my senses.

"No," I croaked, blinking rapidly. "I... I'm..."

"Hey mortals!" a booming voice cried out over the cacophony. "*Incoming!*"

Three large vessels sailed overhead, instantly recognizable by the unlit fuses trailing behind them.

Clever Taran, I thought briefly. *A ruse to help us get away.*

And then my eyes moved to the end of their trajectory—straight into the blazing campfire.

A chorus of screams erupted. Luther grabbed Alixe and shoved her to the ground at my side, then fell on top of us just as the campsite exploded into a ball of flame.

Chunks of firewood became burning arrows that sliced through the air, piercing through bodies and tents and foliage as a rainstorm of embers fluttered and swirled. The patter of falling debris mixed with the moans of the injured, the whinnies of startled horses, and the cries of frightened children.

My heart crumbled. This wasn't what I wanted. All this violence and destruction was because of me, to *save* me.

Luther's eyes connected with mine, and I knew he saw me breaking. His hand brushed against my arm and lingered, a simple gesture that offered so much.

He wrapped an arm around Alixe's waist and another on mine, dragging us to our feet at his side, and together, we ran for the edge of camp.

Taran waved us over, barely visible through the smoky fog. He had the reins of one horse in his hand, the others nowhere to be found.

"The explosion spooked the rest away," he grumbled. "One of you can take Diem, I'll follow with the other on foot."

"You take her," Luther ordered. "Stay near the coast. Alixe and I will find you at dawn."

"We're not splitting up," I protested, my voice still hoarse from the shock of my kill.

Luther gave me a hard look. "This is the best way to keep you safe. If they catch you—"

"They won't kill me. I can't say the same for the three of you, and I will not spend another night wondering if the people I care about are dead." I steadied myself and raised my chin. "We stay together."

"Perhaps she's right," Alixe said hesitantly. "Without our magic, we may fare better if we keep our numbers strong."

I gave a sharp nod and set off for the woods. "Good. It's decided."

"Diem," Luther growled, reaching for my arm.

"That's a command from your Queen," I snapped.

He worked his jaw, his grip tightening around me. Obedience to the Crown—to *me*—ran as deeply in his blood as Sorae's, but unlike my gryvern, Luther could defy me. He just hadn't done it yet.

"Um, cousins?" Taran started, frowning over my shoulder. "Maybe we should—"

"I found them!" a voice shouted. "Over here!"

A line of dark figures emerged from the firelit haze, silhouetted swords and crossbows dangling from their hands. I knew without looking that Luther was about to toss me over the saddle and send the horse galloping into the woods, so I moved before he got the chance.

I ripped my arm from his grasp and bolted into the forest, away from the campsite, sheathing my broadsword as I wove my way through the trees. I didn't dare glance back, trusting in the others to follow me, but the thunder of too many footsteps warned me we weren't alone.

The forest canopy blotted out the moon, making it nearly impossible to avoid anything more than the largest of trees. Low branches and hanging vines smacked across my face while my feet stumbled over tangled roots and fallen logs. Too frequently I found myself tripping and sprawling onto the ground, but each time, a firm hand grabbed me by the waist and pulled me back up.

Every now and then an arrow would whistle through the air, and my heart would hold its breath. At each crack of an arrowhead splitting through wood, my tension eased, but every so often I heard a softer sound —a wet *thunk* that I could not distinguish as soil or flesh—and my soul would scream with fear at what price might be paid before this night ended.

We ran without ceasing, pushing our bodies to our limits. We ran so long that I lost any sense of time or location, ran so hard that my aching limbs turned from throbbing to numb.

We were outnumbered and outmatched. The Guardians lived among these trees, they knew them like old friends. There was no telling what secrets the forest held that might spell our doom. Any minute, we might run directly into a new rebel camp, tumble into an unexpected ravine, or find ourselves trapped by an uncrossable river.

Only one factor weighed in our favor: they were mortal, and we were Descended. And not just any Descended—*warrior* Descended.

Well... three warriors, at least, and whatever strange mortal-raised, Crown-wearing, grey-eyed *thing* I could claim to be.

After what felt like a lifetime, the footsteps behind us thinned out, then fell distant, then turned to silence. We kept going nevertheless, continuing on for what might have been minutes or hours, until our pace slowed and it was no longer roots or rocks but our own fatigue causing us to stumble.

"Cousins—*here*," Alixe's voice hissed nearby.

A hand reached out of the darkness and slid into mine, jerking me toward a massive tree whose rope-like roots stretched ten feet in all directions. A wide crack in its side gave way to a hollow center large enough for the four of us to slip inside.

Luther pulled me to one side of the opening. He pressed his body against mine, crushing me into the rough wall, then gestured for Taran and Alixe to take the opposite side. Uncomfortable as it was, it concealed us well within the trunk's inner shadows and out of sight from any passing Guardians that might glance inside.

"We'll wait here to see if they catch up," Luther whispered. Taran and Alixe murmured in agreement.

I set my head against his shoulder as we both fought to catch our breath. Our chests heaved in rapid rhythm until they fell in sync, rising and falling together as adrenaline gave way to tentative relief. His hands flattened against the bark on either side of me, a cage of the most exhilarating creation.

There was barely any light in the forest and none at all within the hollow of the tree. Blanketed in darkness, my palms glided over his arms, his chest, his shoulders, blindly searching for any sign of a wound.

"Were you hurt?" I asked. "The godstone—did any of it...?" I couldn't bear to finish.

He hesitated. Every second he didn't answer was an endless, torturous nightmare.

"I took a few cuts," he said finally, my heart stilling in my chest, "but none from godstone."

Had he not been pinning me upright with the force of his body, I might have collapsed. I threw my arms around his waist, clawing my fingers into his back and wishing I could somehow pull him even closer still.

His hands pressed to my face, gently tilting it up. I felt the press of his forehead and the brush of his nose. His hot breath rolled in like a summer storm across my skin.

"And you?" His lips grazed mine as he spoke. "When I last saw you, your body... your wounds..."

"Nothing serious," I rushed out. "Already healed."

Air flooded out of him, his shoulders going slack. He pulled me in for a long, languid kiss that felt desperate, yet exquisitely tender.

As the kiss deepened, he arched against me, his hard muscles rippling beneath my palms. The press of him ground my back against the bark, the rough friction sending fire through my blood.

"You sent me back to Lumnos," he said gruffly.

"You might have died if I hadn't."

"And you jumped in front of a blade meant for me."

"You might have died then, too."

His fingers slid beneath my jaw and twitched at my throat, curling in against my skin. "Neither of those things can happen again. *Ever.*"

I didn't respond, grateful for the darkness that concealed my eyeroll.

"Promise me," he demanded.

"I can't. And I won't."

He said nothing for a long moment, but with his chest pressed so close to mine, I felt his heartbeat speed its pace. One hand slid into my hair, still soaked from being dumped into the sea by a wayward boat. His fingers fisted in the long white strands with a tug that forced my face up further toward his.

"I require a promise, Your Majesty," he growled.

"I promise you I'll do anything to protect my people." My palm moved to his chest and settled over his heart. "That includes you, Luther Corbois, whether you like it or not."

He let out an unhappy sigh, and I smirked at my small victory. In the darkness, I pictured the muscles feathering along his jaw, his glacial eyes narrowing.

"Why are your clothes wet?" he asked.

I pulled my cloak tighter and laid my temple against his cheek, relishing the warmth of his flesh. "I have so much to tell you."

"So do I. Your brother is safe. I left my best guards on his watch, and Perthe has fixed himself to Teller's side until you return. But your mother—"

"—is in prison in Fortos." I sighed heavily. "I know. Cordellia, the woman in charge of the rebel camp, told me everything. I know my mother is a Guardian." I paused. "And I know how she got to the island."

His muscles tensed. "Are you angry with me for not telling you?"

I didn't answer at first—not because I was mad, but because I was ashamed. I had been such a hypocrite, giving him hell over his secrets, all the while hiding truths about my own involvement in the Guardians that had put him and his family at risk.

"I expected her to return with us at the coronation," he rushed out. "I wanted to give her the chance to tell you herself. I thought you both deserved that chance. But if she hadn't, I would have. I wasn't going to leave you in the dark. Diem, I swear—"

"I'm not angry," I said softly. "There are things I kept from you, too."

I stared across the shadows, where Taran and Alixe waited nearby. I trusted that Luther's feelings for me were strong enough to overcome my deceit, but I could not say the same for them. Selfishly, I could not bear it if I lost their faith.

I dropped my voice low. "We'll speak later. I want to know everything —and I want you to know everything, too."

He laid a light kiss below my ear, a sweet gesture of confirmation. This was one vow I had every intention of keeping. Whatever lies we once told, from this point forward, we couldn't let them divide us.

Our lives might end up depending on it.

CHAPTER
ELEVEN

W e waited in silence, holding each other in the dark and listening for any sign of approaching Guardians. The air hummed with a steady trill of insects and the rustle of wind-blown leaves—but no footsteps.

Eventually, Alixe emerged from the shadows and slipped out into the woods, and we held our breath in wait. After many tense minutes, she reappeared in the opening.

"No sign of them," she announced. "They should have come through by now. They must have given up the search."

"Or they went back to regroup and wait for daylight," Taran muttered.

"Either way, we'll be safe here for the night," Luther said.

I almost whimpered in protest as he released me and stepped into the dim sliver of light spilling in from the opening. The heat from his body disappeared, the chill winter air taking its place, and the wet clothing plastered to my skin turned frigid.

"Maybe we should keep going and put more distance between us and the camp," Taran suggested.

Luther shook his head. "We already have a long journey back to Arboros City to fetch our horses. I'd prefer not to make it any longer." He glanced in my direction, frowning. "If we don't rest, we might not outrun them a second time."

I knew his words were for my benefit. I started to step forward and argue, but my muscles had gone stiff in the cold. I had to grip the tree to keep from falling as my eyelids drooped.

Living in constant unease, being chained in place for days, my doomed attempt to sail away, the battle at the campsite—it had all worn on me far more than I'd realized.

My need to get to Luther had been a dam forcing me to stay collected. Now that we were together and I could see he was safe, my feeble walls had broken, sending a deluge of exhaustion and emotion coursing through me at a devastating pace.

My teeth began to chatter as the icy chill from my clothes seeped into my bones.

"Rest is good," I admitted. "We can decide our next steps in the morning."

Alixe nodded. "You all get some sleep. I'll take first watch outside." She gave me a shallow bow, then walked out of the hollow.

I winced at my aching muscles as I gathered what little strength I had and trailed her into the forest. "Alixe," I called out, shuffling to her side. "Thank you for coming to my aid today. You're an incredible fighter."

She dipped her chin. "It's an honor to fight in your service, Your Majesty." She gave me an appraising once over, her lips curving with a half-smile. "You fought well yourself—better than many of my soldiers in the Royal Guard. And very bravely, risking yourself the way you did."

I smirked. "Could you repeat that last part again—a little louder, so Luther can hear you?"

She laughed. "If it were anyone but you, Luther would commend them for being so selfless in battle. You're a credit to your father."

My heart swelled, her words as sweet as they were excruciating. When my thoughts turned their darkest, I often replayed that final conversation with my father—how disappointed in me he'd seemed, and how deeply that wound had cut.

I hoped that, wherever he was, he was proud of what I'd done in the Challenging—and I was determined to live a life that would make him even prouder still.

My throat burned with emotion, my energy too depleted to fight it off. I looked down to hide my watering eyes.

Alixe stiffened. "I'm sorry, I didn't mean to upset you. I won't bring him up again."

"Gods, no," I rushed out. "Please don't say that. I don't ever want him to be forgotten. Your words mean a great deal to me, that's all." I smiled as I brushed away an escaped tear. "You showed such respect to him at the palace. I won't ever forget that."

"It was my honor. I only wish I'd had more time to get to know him."

I could not answer without losing my composure, so I took a shaky breath and shifted my weight. "You must think me foolish for asking you not to kill the mortals earlier when they were trying so hard to kill us."

"It's not foolish. I understand. And I agree."

My eyebrows flew up. "You do?"

"I've been giving a lot of thought to that night before the Challenging, when you took me and Taran through Mortal City." Her eyes lowered as she tucked her short blue-black hair behind her ear, her expression unusually troubled. "As Vice General, that city is under my protection. For me to know so little of it, and to see how many are suffering there, some in ways I had the power to prevent..." Genuine pain filled her expression. "I cannot tell you how ashamed I was that night—and still am. I've thought about it every day since."

She frowned. "We Descended have isolated ourselves in our schools and our cities. Even in the army, the mortal units live and train separately. It's no excuse, but because I never *saw* the mortals, it was easy for me to convince myself they were doing fine."

"You cannot solve a problem you refuse to look at," I said.

"No, you cannot," she agreed. "So I wanted to say thank you—for making me look. And I'm sorry I was not brave enough to do so on my own."

"The mortals don't need your apologies, Alixe. Or your shame. They need your action."

It was a stern command, but I knew Alixe would understand. She was a woman of deeds, not words. She thrived in battle, and I had faith that a call to action would bring out the very best in her.

"I will," she vowed, and I believed her.

She gazed off into the woods with brows furrowed, seeming to be working through a dilemma in her mind. After a moment, she stood taller.

"I'd like to integrate the Royal Guard," she declared. "The mortals should have a hand in governing their own community. And they should be patrolling Lumnos City, too. It wouldn't hurt for the Descended to see them in positions of authority."

I nodded slowly, thinking. "It would give mortals more opportunities to work in Lumnos instead of being forced off to Fortos to join the army."

"Yes. We should be keeping our strongest in the realm, not sending them away."

"Your Descended guards won't like it," I warned. "There will be plenty of challenges."

"I suppose I'll just have to follow my Queen's lead. Challenges didn't stop you."

I grinned, puffing up at her compliment. "I think it's a brilliant idea. Have you discussed it with Luther?"

"Not yet. I was waiting until you were home safe and he wasn't so..." She pursed her lips. "...preoccupied."

Her loaded tone had me arching a brow, but I didn't press further. "Let's discuss it more when we're back in Lumnos. I suspect Luther will agree—and if he doesn't, I can be *very* persuasive."

I winked, drawing a laugh from Alixe that had Taran and Luther craning their necks from where they whispered near the hollow's entrance.

Alixe tilted her head in Luther's direction. "You know, he may say he doesn't want you to pick up a sword and face danger head-on, but it's also why he respects you. It's why we all do."

"He'll have to get used to it. I fear our days of facing danger head-on are only just beginning."

"Good." She cocked a hip and flexed her fingers around the hilt of her shortsword, her expression positively devilish. "I wouldn't have it any other way, Your Majesty."

I grinned and pulled my cloak tighter as I began to shiver. "You really don't have to use titles with me, Alixe. I'd like to think we're friends."

She hesitated, then grimaced. "We are friends. And I know how you feel about titles, but... I confess, I agree with Luther. They're more important than they seem. And you should use yours."

"I understand why *you* feel that way. Your titles are earned. I did nothing to earn this Crown."

"The Blessed Mother might disagree. She did not choose you for nothing. And you've already fought for it in the Challenging." She tilted her head at me and frowned. "I've spent my life trying to escape the Corbois name. I never wanted anything to be handed to me—I wanted to get there myself, through my own hard work. On that, I think you and I are very similar."

I nodded in agreement.

"But there are some whose respect I will never earn. For them, nothing I do will ever be enough. So I've learned to wield my titles without mercy.

They don't have to respect me, but they do have to salute me, obey me, and address me correctly. I don't need their support—just their submission.

"You, Your Majesty, will face the same thing. You have many detractors who do not like your background or who disagree with your vision... but they are still bound to obey you as Queen. That Crown, and the title that comes with it, is a weapon. Don't be afraid to use it."

I thought over her words. I'd been quick to ask the multitude of Corbois cousins to call me Diem, rather than using my title—and they'd been just as quick to treat me with open skepticism and contempt.

Perhaps she had a point.

"You really think it's that important?" I asked.

She nodded gravely. "On a battlefield, obedience to the chain of command can be the difference between victory or defeat. And, as you said, there may be many more battles in our future."

My heart lurched—she sounded so much like my father.

I smiled. "Your point is well taken. I'll think it over. Though I hope before this is all over, you and I can grab a pint and simply be Diem and Alixe for at least one night."

She gave me a final bow. "I'll be looking forward to it, Your Majesty."

I trudged back toward the hollow. Luther was leaning against the trunk with arms crossed, wearing that brilliant, elusive smile that had caught my heart and refused to let it go. Even in the gloomy dark of the wee hours, it was bright enough to light up the realm.

"Why do you look so happy?" I teased. "Did Taran agree to cuddle with you all night to keep you warm?"

"He is my cousin, you know."

"Since when has that stopped a Corbois?"

He grunted and pushed off the tree, reaching for me. "I'm happy because you're safe, and I'm at your side, and—" He stopped abruptly as his fingers curled around mine. His smile vanished. "Why are your hands so cold?"

"Well, it *is* winter."

"You're a block of ice." His tone had gone short and displeased. He reached up and brushed a thumb across my mouth. "Your lips are blue."

"You're fussing."

"You're *freezing*."

"I'm f-fine." I cringed as my chattering teeth gave me away. His fingertips grazed my throat and an intense shiver rocked through my body. It was as much from the effect of his touch as the cold, but it was too late to argue.

His eyes turned dark. "Get out of those wet clothes," he barked, reaching for the clasp of my cloak and yanking it from my shoulders. "We'll hang them to dry for tomorrow."

"I have no others to wear," I protested. "I can't—"

My voice hitched as I looked down at myself. My tunic was soaked—not just in seawater, but in dark crimson blood.

The blood of the man I'd slain at the camp.

Mortal blood.

In the chaos of fleeing, I'd blocked it out, forced myself to ignore what I'd done. Now, the evidence was inescapable.

The breath rushed out of me, then came back in short, panicked gulps. I threw off Taran's baldric and tried wiping the blood away, scrubbing my hands against the thin linen fabric, the scarlet stain spreading further onto my skin.

Blood on my hands, I thought, staring in horror at my trembling palms. *Corpses at my feet.*

"He was a m-mortal," I rasped out, my voice hoarse. "He was just trying to protect his people... *my* people..."

"It was an accident," Luther said gently. "You were only trying to stop his attack."

"I swore to use this Crown to protect them, and then I *killed* them."

He reached for me and I flinched away, feeling unworthy of his touch. I clutched my hands to my chest and squeezed my eyes closed, unable to bear the kindness on his face.

"You did everything you could. More of them might be dead if not for you."

"None of them would be dead if not for me," I shouted. My voice reverberated through the forest, hanging among the swaying branches. "Sorae killed some of them, too, and disfigured gods only know how many more—all because of *me*, Luther!"

"Look at me."

I staggered back. "Who even knows how many might have been hurt by the bombs, or burned by the fires, or—"

"*Diem*," he growled. "Look at me."

I forced my eyes open. Luther stood in front of me, his hands hovering a few inches from my face.

"May I touch you?"

His expression was calm, his voice steady—no longer gentle, but not harsh, either. My mountain in the windstorm, my island in a turbulent sea. I didn't answer, and he waited patiently, not moving any closer.

"Let me touch you," he urged again, quieter.

I gave the slightest nod, and his hands carefully came to rest on the sides of my face, holding my gaze to his.

"The war isn't just coming," he said, "it's here. The battles have already begun. People are going to die—that's unavoidable."

"I know," I whispered. "I just don't want them to die because of me."

"But they will, Diem. There will be blood spilled by every side. Some of it will be at your command, some may be by your own hand. And you can mourn them—you *should* mourn them—but you cannot carry their deaths on your shoulders."

"You did," I shot back weakly. "I've seen how you blamed yourself for the half-mortals you couldn't save."

Pain shadowed his features. "Yes. And it ate me alive. It turned me angry and hollow for a very long time." His fingers grazed my cheek. "I will not watch that happen to you."

My despair over the mortal's death mixed with the bone-rattling chill of hypothermia's early stages. The cold, the fatigue, the despair—it had all become one jumbled fog I couldn't see my way out of.

A violent shudder worked its way through my limbs, and Luther's jaw clenched. He took my hand and tugged me into the hollow of the tree. Taran was already asleep and snoring softly, but he'd folded his cloak and set it by the opening.

Luther pulled me into the dark blindness of the shadows. He slipped his hands beneath the hem of my tunic, his fingertips pausing on my icy skin. "May I undress you?" he whispered.

I managed out a quiet *yes*, and he wasted no time. He peeled the drenched linen over my head, then used the clean side to swipe my bloody palms. He removed my footwear, then loosened my waistband and slid the scratchy trousers down my legs. His touch turned even lighter as he tugged away my undergarments, taking care to keep his movements brief and deliberate.

When I was naked in the darkness, he came around behind me and unbraided my hair, tenderly combing it with his fingers to loosen the strands.

After a few moments of rustling, to my surprise, a thick sweater dropped over my head, hanging loosely off my frigid bones. The fibers were exquisitely soft, like no knit I'd ever felt before. It was already warmed with body heat, and it filled my nose with Luther's woodsy, peppery musk of cedar and moss.

More rustling followed, then Luther's hand brushed against my ankle, guiding it up and through a ring of gathered fabric, and again with the other leg. His knuckles grazed along my thighs and hips as he pulled up a pair of breeches, the supple leather like velvet against my skin. A pair of warm socks covered my feet, and a heavy overcoat settled on my shoulders.

"Luther," I said softly. "You can't give me all your clothes. You'll freeze."

"I have Taran's cloak. I'll be fine." He ran a hand up my arm and over my shoulder, clasping around the back of my neck. He pulled me in and pressed a kiss to my temple. "Lay down. I'll be back soon."

I wanted to argue, but my legs had other plans. I barely made it gracefully to the soil before collapsing on my side, curling into a ball, and letting my eyes flutter closed. At the edge of my consciousness, I caught Luther and Alixe whispering just outside, but the steady rumble of Taran's snoring was a strange lullaby that dragged me into sleep's depths.

Sometime later, I was roused by a warm body curling up behind me. A heavy arm draped protectively over my side, and I clutched onto it, groggily pulling it tighter. A second arm looped beneath me, then around me, until I was enfolded into a hard wall of muscle.

He spoke quiet words in my ear. Though I was half-asleep and too drowsy to retain them, they pushed my fears to the fringes of my mind and filled me with calm.

His heat seeped into mine, and mine into his. For the first time since my coronation, I was warm, and safe, and content.

CHAPTER

TWELVE

"Come on Alixe, let's wake them up."

My eyes cracked open to the thump of a heartbeat beneath my ear and two familiar voices arguing in hushed tones.

"Leave them be, Taran. The past two weeks have been hell on them both. You know Luther's barely slept."

"It's nearly midday. I want to talk to Queenie and hear what happened."

"*Her Majesty* will tell us when she wakes up."

I heard Taran's low grumbles. "Why do you get to decide?"

"When the Queen is asleep, Luther's in charge. When they're both asleep, I'm in charge. When all three of us are asleep, you're in charge."

"If the three of you are asleep, then there's no one left for me to be in charge *of*."

"Exactly."

I buried my face in Luther's chest to hide my laughter. I had turned to him in the night and curled into his side, my head resting on his shoulder. His hand had burrowed beneath my sweater, his flesh hot against mine where it lay in the curve of my waist. The other was joined with my hand atop his bare chest, our fingers intertwined.

"You're awake," he said, yawning. "How do you feel?"

"Better," I said honestly. I nestled in closer. "Warmer, at least."

His arm tightened around me, and I let out a comfortable hum. It was strange how *natural* it felt to wake up beside him in the woods, limbs draped over each other's bodies, unhurried and at peace despite the danger that nipped at our heels.

I gazed up at him sleepily. "I could have done a shift on night watch, you know. I may be Queen, but I don't need to be protected at all times."

His wry smirk told me exactly what he thought of *that* claim. Wisely, he kept it to himself.

"You'll have to take it up with Alixe and Taran," he said instead. "They let me sleep through my shift, too." His expression warmed as he brushed away a strand of hair that had fallen into my eyes. "Though I confess, I'm finding it hard to be angry."

Taran's voice drifted into the hollow again.

"Alixe, I'm *bored*."

I could almost see her eyes rolling in response.

"Go kill something then. Preferably something edible."

I grinned. "Perhaps we should go put them out of their misery."

"Perhaps," Luther answered.

Neither of us moved.

I trailed my finger along his scar where it emerged from the makeshift blanket we'd made of Taran's cloak, and Luther's muscles tensed. I tried to catch his eyes, but he was staring up, his smile gone, his expression now guarded.

My heart splintered. I knew Luther had a complicated relationship with his scars. They were a reminder of his greatest tragedy—his father's brutal murder of his secret mortal mother—and a source of his people's scorn. He'd been mocked for them by family, even by lovers. Yet he'd chosen to keep them, rather than have them healed away.

I still didn't fully understand why, but I was grateful for it. I was covered in scars of my own, on my skin and in my heart. In a Descended world that demanded perfection, it was our imperfections that had bonded us together.

"Now might be our only chance to speak alone," he said quietly.

I glanced at the large crack in the tree that opened up to the forest. My stolen cloak hung over it like a curtain, held up by two daggers stabbed into the bark, a thoughtful gesture to give us both darkness and privacy.

I looked back at Luther and nodded. "Tell me what you know about my mother."

He took a deep breath and sat upright, then grabbed me by the hips and pulled me into his lap until I was facing him, my legs straddling him on either side. He gave me a flat look at my attempts to drape Taran's cloak over his bare shoulders, snatching it from my hands and wrapping it around me instead.

"I first met her when she became the palace healer," he began. "I'd been watching the Guardians, so I knew she was their leader, but I also knew she was the best healer in the realm. For the children, that was more important. I let her work, but I kept a close eye on her."

I smiled. "That sounds familiar."

"Well, *she* didn't attack my guards or threaten to cut off my hand."

"Pity. It worked out so well for me."

"For us both." His arms looped low on my back, nudging me closer.

"One day," he went on, "I went to Mortal City for a half-mortal child that had been discovered. The girl was alive but had been gravely wounded by her Descended parent."

I laid a hand on his arm and squeezed gently, knowing the similarities to his own story and the brutal memories that must have evoked.

"I took the child to your mother and begged her to save the girl's life. She did—but she also realized the girl was half-mortal. She knew my duty as Keeper of the Laws was to execute them, not save them. She suspected what I was doing, and she said she wanted to help. She told me she had ways to transport people out of sight of the Descended. I knew her involvement with the Guardians, so I knew she was telling the truth.

"We started working together. She helped me with the children, and I helped with conditions in Mortal City—food and medicine for poor families or supplies for the healers, whatever she requested. Your mother and I were never friends, or even *friendly*, but together, we saved many people."

The thought of Luther and my mother working so closely provoked a web of conflicting emotions. I couldn't resist a pang of jealousy that he knew a side of her I'd never seen. And what had she thought of him? What would she think of my decision to give him my heart?

"As I began to trust her, I gave her freedom to move around the palace unescorted. That turned out to be a mistake. She took advantage and spied on the family—including me. When I found out and confronted her, she told me she had overheard me admit I was a half-mortal in an argument with my father. She threatened to tell everyone the truth and have me executed if I got in her way."

I swallowed hard. It was difficult to imagine the mother I knew spying on patients and threatening something so vicious. Then again, I was beginning to see that "*the mother I knew*" had only ever been half of the story.

"Wouldn't King Ulther have pardoned you?" I asked.

His eyes wandered as his expression turned pensive. "Perhaps. I wonder, sometimes, if he knew the truth. If that wasn't the very reason he made me Keeper of the Laws..." He went silent for a moment, then shook his head. "It didn't matter. Even if he had, the Twenty Houses would have demanded someone else be put in charge of the half-mortal executions. I couldn't risk that."

He hesitated again. "And, to be honest, I didn't entirely object to what your mother was doing. Under her leadership, the Guardians weren't violent. They stole food from the palace we could afford to replace. They intercepted shipments of silks to the wealthiest houses, then ruined them to make a point. When a mortal was accused of frivolous charges, they often snuck them out of Lumnos before they could be caught. I couldn't take issue with any of those acts."

My heart wrenched. That was what I'd hoped for when I joined the Guardians, not Vance's quest for violence. I wished so badly I could have joined under my mother's leadership. Had she kept it from me to protect me because she knew I was Descended—or because she didn't trust me?

Luther let out a long sigh. "I had been fighting in secret for so long, trying to use what influence I had to make a difference. Taran and Alixe knew some of it, but I kept them at a distance to protect them if I was caught. When I saw what your mother was doing, and how she wasn't afraid to put herself at risk..."

"You weren't alone anymore," I finished.

He nodded. "So I gave in to her demands. Sometimes she would tell me what she was up to, other times she wouldn't, like when she got your brother into the Descended school."

"Did she ever mention me?"

"Only once. She said if I came anywhere near you, if I even looked into you or had you followed, she would have me destroyed. There were times when I knew her threats were bluster, but on this, I believed her. She took protecting you very seriously."

"And you never wondered why?"

He hesitated, shoulders tensing. "It's not... uncommon that Descended men and mortal women..." He rubbed the back of his neck. "That is, as the presumed heir, sometimes... I found that some women... not that *you* would ever, of course, but..."

I grinned. "You thought she was worried we might sleep together if we met?"

Faint color rose to his cheeks. Luther Corbois, the mighty and terrifying Prince of Lumnos, was *blushing*. Over *me*.

"Gods forbid that ever happen," I said, my smile growing as I snaked my arms around him and pressed my chest to his.

He grunted, then leaned in and kissed the curve of my neck. "You laugh now, but I might be a dead man when we get her out of that prison."

If we get her out, I thought, my smile fading. Saving my mother from the wrath of the Crowns was a mountain even Luther Corbois might not be able to climb.

"How did you get her to the island?" I asked.

"The King was too sick to attend the Forging Day ritual, so the Crowns asked me to bring a vial of his blood. Your mother found out and demanded to come with me. She claimed there was a rare medicine only available on the island, and she wanted time to harvest a large supply. I hadn't yet learned about flameroot, or I would have said no. She believed the King would die soon and planned to return at my coronation. I warned her there was no guarantee that would happen, but she was willing to take that risk."

"So you had no idea what she and the Guardians planned to do?"

A shadow of hurt built in his eyes. "Many people were killed that day. *You* could have been killed. I would never contribute to that."

I dipped my chin to hide my face and the shame it would reveal. The weight of this secret had been burying me alive for so long. Though I was anxious to be free of it, I feared what it might cost me.

"I did," I said softly.

"You did what?"

I leaned away, feeling undeserving of his embrace. "I contributed. I helped them."

A long, unbearable silence stretched on.

"You knew they were going to attack?"

"No, but..." I took a deep breath and forced myself to look at him. "I was a Guardian, Luther. I helped them gather information. They used it for the armory attack and—"

"I know."

I sat straighter. "You do?"

"I've known for a while. When you took over your mother's role at the palace, I began to suspect. Then I saw you entering their meetings. When I heard you'd begun treating patients in Lumnos City, I assumed it was to spy. And besides—" His lips curved as he tilted my chin up. "—you're terrible at hiding your emotions. Every time the Guardians came up, you'd get that same tortured, guilty expression you're wearing now."

He brushed his thumb over my forehead, smoothing away the crease between my brows.

"You're not angry?" I asked.

"No. I've always known how much the mortals mean to you. It's hardly a shock you would join the rebel effort."

My body sagged as weeks of bottled tension melted away in an instant, replaced by a stunning kind of awe.

Luther had known. *He'd known.*

And he'd sworn to serve anyway.

His loyalty to me had always left me breathless, but this was something more, a faith that went beyond all sense and reason. I tried to tell myself it wasn't *me* he had believed in so strongly, but rather the goddess Lumnos. He'd devote himself as fiercely to any Crown she picked.

But my heart didn't quite believe it.

"I thought I would be helping people," I said, sighing. "I didn't realize how far the Guardians were willing to go."

"When your mother left for the island, she assured me they wouldn't cause trouble. I was a fool to believe her. I should have seen the armory attack coming—and the attack at the Ascension Ball."

I thought back on what Cordellia had told me and frowned. "I don't think my mother ordered those attacks. The man in charge of the Lumnos cell now, Vance, he—" My back stiffened. I sucked in a sharp breath, my eyes going wide. "Luther, *my blood.*"

His hands tightened on my hips, but I jerked away and scrambled to my feet. "We have to go—we have to get back to Lumnos right now. We can't wait—we can't let him—"

"Diem," Luther cut in, standing and clamping his hands on my shoulders to hold me in place. "Explain."

"Vance—he took my blood. The day you came with Sorae, he was stealing it to use on the palace bloodlocks." I clutched at Luther's arms. "He's going to sneak in and kill everyone. We have to get back before he does or... or—"

"Did you give your blood to him, or did he take it?"

"We need to get back. Teller, Lily—they're in danger!"

"Did you give it to him?"

I blinked at him, not understanding. "I... he..."

"Did you *want* him to have it?" Luther cocked his head, his expression more curious than concerned. "Did you give it of your own free will?"

"Of course not," I gasped. "He and his men held me down and cut me open."

His eyes turned stormy. "Then it's useless. Bloodlocks only work with blood that is willingly given."

Air rushed from my lungs. I slumped against him as my hammering heart slowed its rhythm.

"Tell me what you know about this *Vance*." He hissed the name like venom, the promise of vengeance rolling like thunder in his tone.

"He's dangerous, Luther. I'm not sure there's any line he won't cross. And he's not afraid to die."

"Good. I'll make sure he gets his wish."

A shiver crept up my spine, and I looked away.

Luther said nothing for a moment, and then his hand rose to my face, his knuckles grazing my cheekbone. "You don't want him hurt," he said slowly, sounding surprised. "Even after what he's done—you would spare his life."

"I honestly don't know," I admitted. "When my temper flares, I feel ready to slay the world. But when the sword is in my hand and the moment of truth comes... I worry I'm not strong enough to do what must be done." My head drooped low. "A Queen should have more courage than this."

Luther's broad hands settled firmly beneath my jaw. "Diem Bellator."

His use of my name—my *real* name, and not Diem Corbois or Her Majesty, as I was known to the Descended world—won back my gaze.

His jaw was set, his eyes narrow, his dark brows crowded in tight. If I didn't know better, I would think he was furious with me.

But what I saw in his eyes wasn't anger—it was a sense of wonder, enrobed in a boundless, eternal fidelity.

"Don't you dare mistake compassion for lack of courage," he growled. "Anyone can slaughter their enemies. Hate is easy—it's mercy that requires the greater strength. I'll be damned if I let you believe that beautiful heart of yours is a weakness. Trust your instincts, my Queen—above all else, trust *yourself*."

His mouth met mine with a fiery passion that burned of his faith. Every press of his lips was a confession, every stroke of his tongue a fervent prayer. It lit me up from within, coursing through my blood and filling my chest with an emotion so strong I dared not name it.

He had always believed in me. Not in a blind, oblivious way—he, perhaps more than anyone, knew I could falter. He'd been the one to pick up the pieces after so many of my mistakes.

He believed in who I was and what I could do. He saw my vision for what Emarion could be, and the strength that his conviction gave me was incalculable.

With Luther at my side, I felt invincible. And we would need that in the days to come.

I placed my palm above his heart on the curious patch of smooth, unmarred skin that interrupted the line of his scar. "I was so scared I'd lost you," I whispered. "After the attack, I thought..."

"Never." He placed his palm over my heart in a mirror image of my gesture. "I'm with you until the very end."

"Promise?" I asked, knowing the solemn weight that word carried with him.

He smiled back at me, earnest and without reserve. "I promise."

"*That's it,*" Taran's voice shouted. "*I'm going in!*"

The cloak over the opening flapped loudly as Taran flung it away and stomped inside, a bundle of cloth tucked beneath his arm. Sunny rays of light streamed in and illuminated our unusual embrace, Luther wearing only his undergarments while I drowned in layer upon layer of his oversized clothes.

Taran halted in place, perching his hands on his hips as he slowly looked us over. A suggestive grin spread across his face.

"Am I interrupting?" he asked, his eyebrows dancing.

"No," I said innocently.

"Yes," Luther muttered.

"You know, Queenie, it's a lot easier to—" Taran made an obscene gesture with his hands. "—if you both take your clothes *off*, instead of putting each other's clothes *on*."

"Get out, Taran," Luther ordered.

"But I have a present for Her Majesty." He tossed me the bundle, which I recognized as my clothes, now dried—and somehow cleaned of the dead mortal's blood.

I shot him a questioning look, and he shrugged, smiling sheepishly. "Alixe found a stream nearby. The shirt was already wet, so we thought a quick rinse couldn't hurt."

A lump formed in my throat at the thoughtfulness of the gesture. I walked over and gave him a kiss on his cheek. "Thank you, Taran."

He swung an arm around my waist and hauled me into his side, then grinned at Luther. "You know cousin, if you ever need a third—"

"*Out*," Luther barked.

"Fine, but if you two don't get out here soon, I'm making Lu wear Alixe's clothes next." Taran backed out of the hollow, winking at me before he pulled the cloak back into place.

I set the bundle down and began to remove Luther's clothes, first slipping off his overcoat, then tugging his socks free of my feet.

Luther stood nearby to collect each discarded item, politely averting his eyes. "I can leave, if you'd like some privacy."

I shot him a coy smile and shrugged. "It's nothing you haven't seen already."

With a fair amount of reluctance, I pulled off his sweater, already missing the way the warm, luxurious fabric had cocooned me in his scent. As I handed it off to him, his eyes stayed locked with mine, and it was the profound affection in his eyes, not my bare upper body, that had my cheeks flushing.

I turned my back to him and quickly shimmied out of his pants, tossing them over my shoulder with a nervous laugh, then hurried to put on my own undergarments.

"You know," I teased as I struggled to secure my bandeau, "you've seen me unclothed so many times, when we finally get a night alone together, there's hardly going to be anything worth looking at."

I stilled at the brush of his fingers against my skin. He pulled the straps from my hands and deftly secured the clasp. My back arched as his knuckles ran a slow trail up my spine.

I held my breath as he brushed the hair away from my ear and leaned in close.

"Diem, when you and I finally get a night alone together, looking will be the *least* of what I do to you."

AFTER DISCUSSING OUR OPTIONS, we decided to stay put for the day. We were well situated, with a stream nearby and overgrowth for easy hiding if the Guardians came searching. If there was no sign of them by dawn, we would set off for Arboros City to gather supplies for the long trip home.

With hours to kill, and against Luther's ardent insistence that we stay hidden, I'd taken the three of them out foraging for food. Being reunited with my friends and unburdened of the secrets I'd kept from Luther had me in high spirits, and I jumped eagerly at the opportunity to show them a bit of the forest lifestyle I'd grown up in.

I first taught them how to scavenge for wild berries, avoiding poisonous white and yellow types in favor of blues and blacks, and how to test the juices against the skin to ensure they were safe to eat.

I showed them tricks to distinguish edible mushrooms from those that would leave you drooling and seeing fae—and talked Taran out of trying the latter *"just for fun."*

They watched with shock as I nimbly scurried up trees to pluck eggs from unattended nests, then whittled a spear from a fallen branch and spiked a handful of trout from the nearby stream.

I taught them how to make basic medicines—a salve for burns, a tincture for clotting, and a boiled root that could be chewed to ease swelling or pain. Though we were all hale and in no need of healing, I had no idea what the months ahead would bring. If I could give them any extra advantage at surviving, I would take it.

By the time the sun set and we made our way back to the hollow, our arms were full with a hearty bounty.

"Is this really how you lived in Mortal City?" Taran asked. "Running around the woods stealing eggs and stabbing fish?"

"In a way," I said. "Most mortals couldn't afford to pay for the work we did as healers. Foraging helped us keep the healers' center stocked, and hunting kept food on our dinner table. My father sold the extra meat and hides at the market so we could afford the Crown's taxes."

The three cousins exchanged uncomfortable looks. Those taxes had funded their privileged lives at the palace and purchased the fancy blades and fine clothes they now wore on their bodies.

"I never enforced the penalties for unpaid taxes," Luther murmured. "If a mortal couldn't pay, I made sure the funds became *available* to them in other ways."

Taran and Alixe stared at him in surprise, evidently unaware of this part of his efforts.

"I'm glad to hear it," I said, "but it does not relieve the extreme lengths many mortals were forced to go to avoid that risk altogether."

Their faces looked so patently ashamed that I took pity on them and shrugged it off.

"It wasn't just necessity. The forest was *fun.*" I grinned at the wealth of memories that surfaced. "Teller and I would explore and imagine grand adventures of life outside Mortal City. It's where I bonded with my father while hunting and began learning my trade from my mother. It's where I had most of my... um... *romantic* activities."

Luther growled, and Taran cackled loudly and punched him in the arm.

I shot him a sympathetic smile. "I could spend a lifetime in the palace, and I think I'll still always feel the most *me* out among the trees."

Taran nudged my side. "I'm glad we got to see this side of you, even if we did nearly die in the process. When we get back to Lumnos, we'll have to raze the royal lodge and build a campsite instead."

"Don't go that far." My gaze caught Luther's. "I have a fond memory or two at the lodge, as well."

His eyes gleamed behind his stoic veneer. "Once we're back in Lumnos, you could spend more time there, if you'd like. Many Crowns ruled from the lodge when they wished to be alone."

"Or *almost* alone," Taran quipped, poking Luther with the end of my spear.

Luther grabbed a fish off its tip and whipped it toward Taran, who yelped as it slapped his cheek with a wet *smack*, but the heated look Luther shot me said he wasn't opposed to Taran's suggestion.

"Cousins, please stop playing with our dinner," Alixe scolded.

Taran handed off the spear to Alixe and unceremoniously dumped the bushel of berries he'd gathered into my arms. "Sorry, Queenie. Lu's gotta pay for that one."

Taran threw his head back and let out a wild roar. Alixe groaned and rolled her eyes, but Luther's expression turned exhilaratingly savage. He barely had time to shrug off his overcoat, its pockets bursting with mushrooms and eggs, before Taran came barreling into him.

"There's no magic out here, Princess," Taran yelled triumphantly, ramming a fist into Luther's ribs. "You might have a fair fight for once in your life."

"I've never needed magic to put you on your ass," Luther grunted back as he drove a shoulder into Taran's torso.

They tumbled to the ground in a flurry of blows and swears. This was no doubt a regular occurrence, as they paused in unison just long enough to rip their shirts off and set aside their weapons before clashing again. The glow of the sun's final rays turned their skin into liquid gold as their muscular bodies rippled and flexed with effort.

I sauntered up to Alixe's side, humming in appreciation. "A lot of mortal women would pay their life savings to watch this. *And* men."

She crossed her arms, looking significantly less enthralled. "A lot of Descended would, too."

Luther pinned Taran to the ground and glanced up at me with a wild-eyed smirk that had my stomach dancing.

"Think I can tell a few more sad stories and guilt them into oiling up and wrestling for the good of the realm?" I asked Alixe. "I could probably make enough to replace the Crown's taxes entirely."

"Taran will do it," she said. "Just bribe him with a cask of good wine."

"And Luther? What do I bribe him with?"

She glanced at me and dragged her eyes up and down my body pointedly in response.

She turned back to our campsite and I reluctantly followed with one final look at the free show. When we got to the hollow, we dumped the bounty we'd collected into a pile and set about separating the items and brushing away the stray dirt.

Eventually, Luther and Taran joined us, arms draped around each other's shoulders, sweating and panting and looking distracting enough to make my cheeks hot.

"Who won?" I asked.

"Me," they both answered.

Alixe frowned at the spear of fish. "We could build a fire to roast them, but I'm not sure how we would get it alight. I lost my flint during the battle."

"I can manage that," I answered.

"Your magic is back?" Taran asked, and I shook my head. "Then how?"

It was an effort not to roll my eyes. As formidable as they were, with the best education and training gold could buy, I sometimes forgot just how magic-dependent their upbringing had been.

"Have you learned nothing from me today?" I said. "The forest always provides."

I set about gathering the items I would need while the others collected wood. When I finally crouched at our makeshift firepit to generate the glowing embers, Alixe watched with rapt fascination. Once the fire was lit and roaring, she made me repeat the process again and again, then she pulled together her own supplies to practice until she'd done it successfully several times.

"I'm surprised they didn't teach you in the guard," I said as we turned our skewered fish over the flames. "It's one of the first survival skills I learned."

The three Corbois glanced awkwardly at each other.

"Descended have little need for survival skills," Alixe answered after a long silence. "If we leave the cities, we bring a caravan of supplies. If there's anything we run out of or forget..." She hesitated.

"You simply take it from the first mortal you find," I answered for her, and she winced and nodded.

I knew well the laws permitting Descended soldiers to seize any possession from a mortal without repayment "*in instances of urgent need.*" My father had lost many a haul of freshly caught game when hunting near them in the woods. It seemed *urgent need* more often translated to *passing fancy*.

I bit back a snide retort, reminding myself that these Descended, at least, were trying.

But it was times like these where I understood the Guardians the most. Though I adored the three Descended sitting beside me, when confronted so plainly with their obliviousness, the urge to unleash all my anger at them for years of injustice from their kind could be difficult to withstand.

Luther's knee nudged mine. "Things will change," he said quietly. "We will change them."

My jaw tightened. "Yes. We will."

CHAPTER

THIRTEEN

Over the next hours, we gorged ourselves on flaky fish and flame-roasted mushrooms, tucking the eggs away until morning. We laughed as we tossed berries into each other's mouths across the fire, and Taran was heartbroken to discover I had no survival trick for brewing ale or wine from scratch.

Eventually, the talk turned to more serious matters. I recounted most of what had transpired at the Guardians' camp, leaving out that I had once been a member myself. When I retold the story of my doomed attempt to sail home, Taran was practically rolling with laughter. Even Alixe struggled to contain her amusement at my misfortune. But Luther's expression was serene, almost reverent, and when I'd finished, he stared for a long time at the sky, murmuring words too softly for anyone to hear.

They were stunned to learn the rebels had taken the island. An official statement from the Crowns had declared the attack a "failed attempt" and claimed the Guardians involved were imprisoned or dead.

No one knew of the Arboros Queen's fate—nor, for that matter, had many known of mine. Other than the Crowns, as far as anyone in Lumnos had been told, I was safe at home, recovering from the bedlam of my coronation.

Despite the claims of failure, rebel cells had been bolstered by the invasion on Coeurîle. Violence had increased dramatically in nearly every realm. When I shared the rumor of a powerful Descended helping the rebels in the north, Taran and Alixe had looked startled and a little betrayed. It hurt my heart to wonder what they might think if they knew a powerful Descended Queen had helped the rebels in their own realm.

"What of Lumnos?" I asked finally. "How are things at home?"

"Largely unchanged," Alixe said. "Your show of force at the Challenging scared everyone enough to not risk provoking your temper. The Twenty Houses are operating as they did under Ulther's reign but pushing it no further."

"I heard the army sent soldiers to Lumnos. Did Remis request them?"

She and Luther exchanged a tense glance.

"Fortos has sent troops to every realm," Alixe answered slowly. "They say it's to discourage further violence."

The group fell silent.

"But?" I pushed.

"*But* those two think Remis is up to something," Taran cut in.

My eyes went straight to Luther. "What do you suspect?"

He exhaled deeply. "I don't know. He's not keeping any of us informed of his decisions anymore." Muscles ticked along his jaw. "But I don't like it."

"The number of soldiers sent to Lumnos is high compared to the other realms," Alixe added. "Very high."

"Too high," Luther muttered.

"Can't Eleanor overrule him?" I asked. The night after the Challenging, I'd chosen Eleanor—my first Corbois friend and my advisor on matters of court—to replace Remis as my Regent, giving her the authority to rule as Queen in my absence.

"He said he will not honor your decision until he hears it from you himself," Alixe said.

I swore beneath my breath. I'd kept the news from Remis, fearing he might do something rash to interrupt my coronation. Little did I know the Guardians would beat him to it.

"What of Aemonn?" I asked. "He has Remis's ear—has he said anything?"

Taran spat on the ground. "Nothing that rat says is worth hearing. All he's good for is worm food."

I shot him a stern look. "He's your brother."

"I don't care. He can rot."

"What happened with you two? I have a brother too, I know siblings can fight sometimes, but—"

"Aemonn is not Teller. You insult your brother by even mentioning them in the same sentence. Aemonn is exactly like my father, and we'd all be better off if they were both burning on a pyre."

"*Taran*," I scolded.

He gaped at me. "You're defending him? *Him?*"

Ever the mediator, Alixe interjected. "Aemonn is still the acting High General of the Royal Guard. He didn't follow through on his threat to send us away to the coast—"

"Yet," Taran grumbled.

"—and he gave us leave to come here. He hasn't helped us, but he hasn't gotten in our way, either."

My frown deepened. I still didn't know what to think of Aemonn. Though he'd been an ally to me at times, he was a man of many faces, each of them calculated for his personal benefit. Every interaction with him felt dangerous—and not in the fun way.

"I tried to convince my father to restore my titles," Luther growled. "He said I was too *distracted* searching for you to handle anything else."

Alixe and Taran's shared look suggested they didn't entirely disagree.

"So Aemonn is still Keeper of the Laws?" I locked eyes with Luther, my expression loaded. He nodded and said nothing more.

I let out a long sigh, scrubbing at my face. "And my brother—does he know about our mother?"

"He knows she's alive," Luther answered.

My brows rose. "Does he know anything else?"

"He knows she was arrested on Coeurîle and is in prison in Fortos." His face turned solemn. "Nothing more."

"Is there more to know?" Taran asked, glancing between us.

Neither of us answered.

"How did he take the news?" I asked.

Luther hesitated. Before he could respond, I saw the truth of it in his eyes—the pain he felt on my brother's behalf.

When I had withheld the truth from Teller about our mother's disappearance, this was exactly what I'd been trying to avoid—giving him hope she would return home safely, only to lose her all over again.

I buried my head in my hands. "First Mother, then Father, then me, now Mother again. He must be worried sick."

Luther moved to sit beside me, then took my hand and folded it into his. "I told him I'd seen you when I came with Sorae. I said you looked healthy and in good spirits. It was a lie, but I hoped it would calm his worries."

"I don't think he believed you," Taran mumbled.

Alixe smacked Taran's arm.

"What?" he protested, glaring at her. She shot him a pointed look, and he rolled his eyes. "You saw Luther when he got back. That wasn't a man who just saw the woman he loves '*healthy and in good spirits.*' We all knew she was in big trouble."

Luther's fingers tightened around mine.

"Stop talking," he snapped.

"Not helping, Taran," Alixe mouthed.

Taran ignored them both and looked at me. "Teller's a strong kid, Queenie. He's made out of the same stock you are. He'll get through this."

Surprisingly, Taran's words did ease my spirit. He was right—Teller was strong. He'd been the one to pull me from my dark grief and remind me to *fight* after our father's death. And, with Lily at his side and our newfound Corbois friends surrounding him in support, he wasn't alone. I knew first-hand what a difference that could make.

"We'll send a messenger hawk from Arboros City to let him know you're safe," Luther offered. His pale eyes almost seemed to glow from within as he watched me in his quiet, steady way.

I gazed up at him, Taran's words still ringing in my ears.

The woman he loves.

The weight of it hung in the air between us, its presence heady and thick. It surrounded me—holding me, comforting me, terrifying me, thrilling me. It was a living thing, whispering of a mighty force, almost like—

"*Luther,*" I gasped in realization. "Your magic."

I'd been so distracted by my emotions I'd almost missed the return of his powerful aura, a trait only the strongest Descended could sense—but there it was now, hovering protectively around me like a warm, heavy cloak.

He looked down as twin cords of light and shadow wove into a knot around our joined hands. I sucked in a sharp breath at the brush of his magic across my skin, each caress thrumming with a crackling energy. A deep, rumbling hum reverberated in my ears, hinting at his boundless well of power—but something about it felt stunted, almost unfinished, like a note missing its harmony.

"Impossible," Luther said, frowning down at his own creation. "I shouldn't have magic outside of Lumnos."

"I thought I felt mine return last night," Alixe said. "Before I could use it, it was gone again."

We all gaped in captivated confusion as Luther's magic twined its way up my arm. After a few moments, it wavered and vanished into mist, and the air again felt hollow, empty of his presence.

Luther's brows furrowed tighter. "Perhaps it has something to do with being near the Crown."

"I don't think so," Taran said. "When we passed through Faunos, my magic came back for a moment, too."

"Why didn't you say anything?" Luther demanded.

"Do you not remember the journey here, cousin?" Taran shot him a look. "You were on the warpath. Alixe and I were doing our best just to stay out of your way."

"You should have told me."

"You weren't interested in *chatting*. All you wanted to do was murder everyone and stare at that damn magic compass—"

"*Taran*," Alixe hissed.

Luther stiffened.

Taran grimaced.

"Magic compass?" I asked.

Luther's glare narrowed on Taran. His fingers crushed around mine, his shoulders pulled tight as a bowstring.

Taran's eyes went wide.

Alixe sighed and tugged him to his feet. "Come, cousin. Let's take a walk before you end up skewered over the fire next."

They both avoided our eyes and backed away from the campsite, shuffling into the shadows of the surrounding woods.

"What was *that* about?" I asked.

"Nothing," Luther snapped.

His cold veneer slipped into place, his bearing turning stony and indifferent. I frowned as I studied his face. I was used to seeing this side of him around others, but not alone—not with *me*.

I slid my other hand along his jaw, brushing my fingers through the dark stubble that had begun to grow. Though he leaned into my touch, his features softening for the briefest moment, he resisted as I tried to nudge his face toward me.

"Luther," I said gently.

I waited without pushing, sensing that some vulnerability had yanked him back behind his carefully built defenses. As much as I wanted to pull him out into the open, or at least tuck myself behind them at his side, I also knew this mask had grown out of tragedy and loss. Hiding his emotions had kept him and his loved ones alive in a dangerous world, and I couldn't fault him for doing so again, when the danger was closer than ever.

I squeezed his hand in wordless support and laid my head on his shoulder. I felt his chest rise and fall in a deep sigh.

Finally, he spoke.

"I saw them take you on the island. Your mother had wounded me, so I couldn't walk. But I tried—Blessed Kindred, I *tried*. I clawed my way through the dirt, screaming your name. Before I could get to you, a man came and carried you away." His throat bobbed as he swallowed. "Your body was so still. So terribly still."

He winced and looked down. "When I healed enough to walk, I ran through the fighting to the Lumnos pier, hoping to chase after you. I found Henri on the boat, attempting to stow some flameroot your mother had hidden nearby, and I confronted him. I could tell he knew where they had taken you, but he refused to tell me, even when things became... heated."

I held my breath. "Did you hurt him?"

Veins popped on Luther's forearm as his muscles tensed.

"No. Once I realized he wouldn't give in, I brought him and some other mortals back to Lumnos. I knew it's what you would want."

I sat up in surprise and stared at him, but still, he refused to meet my gaze.

"Sorae was frantic. She could sense you were in danger, but unless you summon her, her ability to find you takes time. I hoped, perhaps... if I could just get close enough..." He trailed off, then pulled my hand closer. "I'd seen the rebel boats going south, so we started there. For days, she and I flew in circles, hoping for some sign of you. And then..."

He closed his eyes.

"And then you found me," I murmured.

"Yes. And then you sent me away."

His harsh facade was still in place, but it was fractured, his dark fears oozing from within the cracks. When he finally looked up, I saw the imagined loss of me in his eyes and the wound it had left behind.

He dropped my hand and stood, turning his back to me as he paced around the fire.

"You would have done the same for me," I protested, rising to my feet.

"It's not the same. You're my Queen. It's my duty to protect you."

"And if I were not your Queen, would you have abandoned me? Left me to die?"

He whipped back around. "Never," he snarled.

"No, you wouldn't," I agreed. I walked up and pressed my hands to his chest. "I don't need some *duty* to protect you, Luther, because we both know the Crown isn't why you protect me."

We glared at each other in silence, neither of us truly angry but both of us too stubborn to give in. He reached up and seized my wrists as if he might pull them away. After a moment, his shoulders drooped.

"No," he said, sighing. "It isn't."

He dipped a hand into a pouch on his belt and pulled out a small object, then tightened his fist around it before I could see what it was.

"Sorae refused to fly, and I didn't know if I could find you again by foot. A search like that could take weeks, if you were even still in Arboros."

His voice picked up speed as his anxiety and fear came pouring out.

"I went to see the Guardians and threatened them within an inch of their lives. To their credit, few of them broke, and those that did knew nothing useful. Taran had to talk me out of breaking into the prison in Fortos to get your mother, in case *she* knew where you were. I might have done it anyway, and then I heard the rebels were trying to barter you, and I wondered if I should stay at the palace, in case you were returned. I didn't know what to do. You were missing, and I... I was..."

He laid his forehead against mine.

"I was lost," he whispered.

My heart clenched at the agony in his roughened voice. "And yet you found me," I said, and he gave a tight nod. "How?"

For a long time, he didn't move, didn't speak. Then he pulled back until my hands fell away. He slowly raised his fist in front of him and flicked the object in his hand open.

I arched my neck forward to peer at the small gold disc. At its center, a red arrow whirred softly as it spun against an ivory dial, then stopped with a *click*.

Suddenly, I knew what he held—and what it meant. I'd turned to the very same object when I was lost in my own darkness and desperate for a way out.

A compass—a gift from the Crown of Meros, given to me at my Ascension Ball—spelled with Kindred magic to lead to whatever one's heart most desires.

I took a hesitant step forward, and my breath caught as the arrow juddered in parallel with my movement. I raised my hand to cup it beneath his palm. The second my skin touched his, the arrow disappeared, and the dial glowed bright.

"I found you," he murmured.

My heartbeat thundered so loudly I thought he might hear it, or at least feel it in the pulse of charged silence that hummed between us. His gaze rose tentatively to my face, and mine to his.

There was no more mask, no facade or armor to shield his heart. It lay open before me, raw and vulnerable, mine to take—or to wound.

The woman he loves, Taran had called me.

When Henri had spoken that word to me for the first time, it had sent me into a panic. It had made me pull away and question everything. I'd loved Henri, but—did I love him *enough*? Did he truly understand me? Could I be the woman he wanted, and could he be the man I needed? Did we share the same dreams, the same goals, were we walking the same path— were we even walking the same direction?

I'd run from those questions, and from Henri, because deep in my heart, I'd already known the answer was *no*. Even before I knew I was Descended, before he and I were pushed apart by a Crown and a war, something between us had always been a little bit wrong.

But the man before me now was not Henri. And I was not running.

And when I stared at the proof of his affection glowing before me in tangible, irrefutable form, everything about it felt *right*.

I laid my hand on top of his and snapped the compass shut, then slid it back into the pouch on his belt and pulled the drawstring closed. My palms flattened against his waist, then slid over the hard planes of his muscled torso, pausing over his chest until I felt the steady beat beneath his skin.

"My heart desires you too, Luther Corbois."

There was one perfect, beautiful moment of stillness as my words sank into him.

Then he grinned, and I was in his arms. He hauled me into the air and wrapped my legs around his waist, both of us unable to restrain our smiles even as our lips met in a joyous dance.

"How long do you think we have until they return?" I breathed between kisses.

"Not long enough," he mumbled, though his broad hands clenched around my thighs as he carried me toward the hollow.

The crack of a twig snapping beneath a boot cut through the silence. I broke the kiss and groaned. "Back already?"

"Keep walking, Taran," Luther called out loudly. "I'm still considering roasting you on a spit."

His mouth worked its way to my neck, drawing a soft moan from me as my eyes fluttered closed and my fingers snaked into his hair.

Another sound rang out—dried leaves crunching under heavy footsteps.

Several footsteps.

Too many footsteps.

"Cousin."

Taran's voice had none of its usual mirth. It was quiet. Strained.

Luther went still, and my eyes flew open. Near the fire, Taran stood with his hands in the air, surrounded by a circle of brown-eyed men. Their spears were tipped in glittering black points that hovered inches from his chest.

My blood ran cold as Vance emerged from the shadows.

"Shameful, Your Majesty." His tongue clicked disapprovingly. "What will your betrothed think?"

CHAPTER

FOURTEEN

Vance smiled at the terror spreading across my face. The left arm of his tunic hung mostly empty, tied off at the elbow, and angry red skin peeked out from the bandages coating his neck. His features twisted in a cruel glare that radiated raw hatred.

Luther didn't move, his back still to the campfire. "Guardians?" he whispered in my ear. I nodded subtly. "Alixe?"

My eyes darted around the woods. More men had emerged from the trees, a few of them carrying godstone blades or crossbows.

"Missing," I mumbled back.

"Put her down," Vance ordered.

Luther slid me over his body until I was standing on my own. "Stay behind me," he mouthed with a grave look, then turned to face the group.

"Separate," Vance said. "Weapons off. Hands in the air."

I tugged off the baldric holding my broadsword and tossed it aside. "Did Cordellia send you to do this?"

Vance scowled. "I don't answer to her."

"You're in Arboros, and she's the Mother of the Arboros cell," I shot back. "Or are you all traitors who put the Guardians below your own interests?"

Some of the men exchanged hesitant looks.

Vance glanced at his men and frowned. "Dell is too soft on the

Descended. She's weak—just like your mother. If they're not strong enough to do what must be done in this war, me and my men will."

Luther pulled the Sword of Corbois from its scabbard and stabbed it forcefully into the soil in front of him. Instead of stepping away from me, he took a step back, pressing me further into his body.

"I said *separate*," Vance barked. "And I know you have more weapons than that."

I used Luther's body to shield my hands as I reached into my waistband and pulled a small dagger I'd borrowed from Alixe, then tucked it beneath Luther's sweater at his back. His low rumble told me he understood what I had done, and he didn't approve of me disarming myself for his benefit.

"That was my only one," I called out. I shifted to the side and lifted my tunic to show my bare waist as proof.

Luther pulled two more blades from the front of his belt and kneeled to unstrap one from his boot, then tossed them into a heap at his feet.

Vance gestured with his good arm. "Step away from each other."

I started to move, and Luther sidestepped to block me. "No," he said calmly.

"*Now*," Vance demanded.

"I'm not letting you anywhere near her. You have our weapons, and you have us surrounded. That's good enough."

Vance's eyes narrowed. He jabbed a finger toward Taran. "If I have to say it one more time, your friend here gets a spear to the belly. And we all know what that godstone can do to Descended scum."

Taran's eyes locked with Luther's. Some silent discussion passed between them, and when it was over, each of them gave a short nod. Taran's jaw pulled tight as his chin rose.

"No," I whispered. "Vance, please..."

"Go on then," Taran said. "You'll have to kill both of us to get to her. Might as well start with me."

Vance raised his eyebrows, looking between the two men, then at me. "Well, if she's willing to let them die, so am I." He shrugged. "Gut him."

"*Wait!*" I screamed, throwing myself forward. Luther reached for me, but I stumbled out of his grasp. "Stop—I'll do it. Whatever you want. Please, just don't hurt them."

The men with the spears looked at Vance for confirmation, and he smiled wide. "Good. At least one of you hasn't had your brain rotted away by toxic Descended blood."

He motioned for his men to collect our weapons, then turned to a man holding a crossbow and gestured to Luther. "If *he* moves—" He pointed at me. "—shoot *her*." The man nodded and raised the crossbow to my chest, the black-tipped arrow gleaming beneath the moonlight.

Luther's eyes turned dark with rage. His stance went preternaturally still, though his gaze followed Vance with predatory focus.

"I tried to warn Henri this would happen," Vance chided. "I told him Descended women think they're too good for us, but he said you weren't like that, because you were raised as a mortal."

He strolled closer, chuckling as Luther growled a low warning. "Then I told him that was even worse, because I've yet to meet a mortal woman who won't get on her knees when a Descended man comes calling." He stopped in front of me and sneered. "You're proof enough of that. Your mother was supposed to be our leader, and she spread her legs for one of them instead."

Fury exploded in my chest, turning my blood to boiling hot oil. Every muscle strained against my skin to launch at him and tear his tongue from his mouth. The only thing holding me back were the spears at Taran's side and the voice of my father in my ear.

Giving in to your emotions is the fastest way to lose a battle, he'd scolded. *Your temper has always been your weakness.*

I gritted my teeth and held my silence.

"But poor Henri insisted on standing by you. He swore you could be trusted. He thought your love for him could endure it all." Vance shot me a simpering look. "Love can be such a deceitful thing."

My stomach twisted with the heavy weight of guilt. Buried in Vance's vitriol was a small kernel of truth. I had asked Henri to trust me, to *love* me —and he had. But in the end, it hadn't been enough.

"What do you want, Vance?"

"My arm back, to start," he snapped.

"You're lucky that's all you lost. My gryvern would have killed you if I hadn't intervened."

"And if the gryvern hadn't, I would have," Luther rumbled.

"What I want," Vance snarled, "is my homeland. I want the Descended to leave—or die. Preferably the latter. *What I want* is for the mortals to rule over Emarion as we always should have."

"You know I'm an ally to the mortals," I protested. "We should be working together."

"We tried working together. I inducted you as a Guardian. I let you work on the Benette armory attack, the missions at the palace, even the preparation for the invasion of Coeurîle. And how well did all that go?"

Taran's back straightened. He frowned at me, surprised betrayal written on his features. I shot him a pleading look, silently begging his forgiveness. He shook his head and looked away.

Vance walked closer and tapped his blade on my cheek. "You say you want to help us, but when the blood starts flowing, you protect *them*."

"I won't stand by while you kill innocent people, no matter what blood they have," I said. "The mortals are my priority, but—"

"Your priority?" His brows jumped upward. "Really? A moment ago, it looked like your *priority* was whoring yourself out to a Descended while your mortal betrothed waits at home for your return."

"Oh shut up," Taran groaned. "Get to the point old man, or let's start stabbing each other already."

Even in Taran's banter, a hint of bitterness persisted. I tried to catch his eye, but still he refused to look at me.

"I'm trying to get back to Lumnos, Vance. You're the one stopping me." My eyes narrowed. "And stop pretending like you care about Henri. You'd happily sacrifice him—or any of these men—to spill a little Descended blood."

I looked past Vance to the men in his cadre, glancing at each of them in turn. "You all have every right to be angry with how the mortals have been mistreated. I understand your rage, and I swear to you, I am with you in this fight. All three of us are."

I gestured to Luther and Taran, and Vance's men eyed them with flagrant doubt. A few of their weapons lowered ever so slightly.

I pointed accusingly at Vance. "This man doesn't care if any of you live or die, as long as he gets his war. I'm trying to find a better way. I don't want one more drop of mortal blood spilled."

Vance let out a vicious laugh. "Tell that to the dead mortal you ran through with your sword."

I flinched. Any ground I had won with the men instantly eroded away as they nodded and murmured, their features hardening.

"That... that was an accident," I stammered. "I didn't want... I—I didn't mean to hurt him."

"I'm sure that will be a great comfort to his family." He turned to one of the men near Taran. "Tell me, Soritt, does it ease your grief to know your brother's murderer '*didn't mean to hurt him*'?"

The man's knuckles whitened where he gripped his spear. He glowered at me and spat. "Hell no, it doesn't."

"I'm so sorry," I said to him, shaking my head. "I never wanted that to happen. He was going to hurt my friend, and I—"

"Hurt your friend?" the man hissed. "Like this?" He jabbed his spear forward—straight into Taran's ribs.

I screamed in horror as the glittering black point lodged in Taran's flesh. His eyes went wide, his face going slack with shock.

I ran for him, but Vance stepped in my way. "Watch it," he warned. "Or your other *friend* gets the same treatment."

"You can stick me with all the godstone you have," Luther snarled. He was quivering with coiled fury, scorching wrath oozing from his every pore. "I'm still going to rip your lungs from your chest before I die."

Vance chuckled—though he subtly leaned a step back.

The mortal jerked his spear free, and Taran grunted and sank to his knees. My heart shattered at the trickles of red flowing through his fingers where he clutched his side.

"Put pressure on the wound, Taran," I said hoarsely, hot tears brimming in my eyes. "You're going to be fine."

"Is he?" Vance mocked. "I hear that godstone toxin is a nasty death. Slow and painful."

Sorrow overtook me, turning my legs weak and my vision watery. Taran had been an unexpected blessing, a rare source of joy even in the bleakest moments. He'd survived a hard life of his own under his father's cruelty, yet he'd found a way to come out smiling. I'd never told him how much that had inspired me. How much the gift of his friendship had meant.

"Cousin," Luther said softly, and their eyes met again.

I looked away, unable to bear the devastation carved on Luther's face. Taran was his dearest friend, loyal without exception and fiercely protective of Luther's happiness. Luther trusted so few and loved even fewer—to lose Taran would be unendurable.

"Why are you doing this, Vance?" I asked, my voice broken and defeated.

"I tried to work with you, Diem. I gave you chance after chance to prove yourself. You chose to protect them every time. For that, you have to pay."

He whispered something to the man with the crossbow, who suddenly turned his weapon on Luther.

Vance sighed. "Unfortunately, I can't kill you. Your blood is too valuable. So I'm taking you with me, and I'm making these two pay instead." He waved his hand at the other men. "Kill them both."

I didn't even have time to scream before the crossbow fired. Its metallic twang was an ominous chime, a death knell for my heart.

At the last second, the crossbow tipped up as if knocked from below. The arrow sliced through the air toward Luther—and missed him by inches.

"Diem, *run*," he growled.

I did run—but not away.

I lowered my shoulder and launched myself into Vance's wounded arm. He screamed in pain, staggering back into the men surrounding Taran.

Bedlam broke out as the crowd jumped into action. Men were moving, blades swinging, arrows flying. A hand gripped my arm and jerked me out of the way seconds before a godstone dagger swung at my face, but when I looked to see who had saved me, no one was there.

"If I'm dying anyway, let's make it fun, boys," Taran said, hurling himself into the wall of men. He moved like an animal, cracking skulls and snapping spears like twigs, completely uncaring of the godstone flying at him from every angle. Another black blade lodged into his shoulder and stopped my heart still. Taran simply laughed and yanked it free, then stabbed it back into its owner's eye.

My despair hardened to rage as a trio of men stalked toward me. Though I was without weapons or magic, I didn't care—my wrath was sharper than any blade. I launched off my heels to meet them, but an invisible hand looped around my waist and jerked me back.

"Get her out of here," Luther snarled, looking past me. "I'll get Taran." Seconds later, he was surrounded by men with swords and spears, swinging the tiny dagger I'd given him in a brutally outnumbered fight for his life.

The faceless force dragged me away. I screamed my protest and thrashed like a mindless, rabid creature.

"Let me go," I screeched.

"Forgive me, Your Majesty," Alixe's tense voice whispered in my ear. "We have to go now. I don't know how much longer my magic can hide us."

I froze in shock, then looked down at my feet—or where my feet *should* have been. In their place was empty air and fallen leaves.

Understanding hit me like a brick wall. I'd seen Alixe create illusions before, when she and my father had seemingly disappeared into thin air so he could sneak out of the palace unseen.

"We have to go back," I roared, still fighting her hold. "Taran, he's—"

"I know. I was too slow to stop it." Her tone was anguished and hollow. "But I can save you."

"No Alixe, we can help them, you can slip back in and—"

Her face flickered in front of me, then appeared in full. We both looked down at our bodies, once again visible.

Alixe swore. "My magic's gone. We have to go before they—"

"*Found them,*" a voice shouted. "*They're over here!*"

She grabbed my arm and ran.

We moved at a blistering place, Alixe flying over the terrain with impossible agility while I stumbled and lurched to keep up. Even in pitch dark, her athleticism was superhuman. She leapt over roots and branches with ease, even managing to gently push or pull me to keep me on a flatter path at her side.

Our pursuers had no chance of catching up, and the footsteps behind us faded quickly—but Alixe did not. She only pushed harder, sprinting onward like they might appear again at any second.

Each thump of our boots on the soil was a grim reminder of the two precious hearts we'd left behind. The urge burned in me to scream at her to stop, to turn back, to wait for some sign of our friends, but I forced myself to hold back for fear my voice would give us away.

Eventually the terrain began to change beneath my feet. The hard-packed soil turned softer and gritty. Each footstep sank into the ground and became harder and harder to pull free. Small, scratchy granules kicked up against my skin and worked their way into my boots.

Sand.

"Alixe," I hissed. "I think we're almost to—"

Without warning, the forest ended. Alixe grunted in pain as we emerged into a vast, open expanse of lifeless desert and tumbled to the ground.

I crawled over to where Alixe had collapsed in the sand. "Are you hurt?"

She winced and rubbed her arms. "It's just those damn borders. We should keep going until we find a place to hide."

"Hide?" I surveyed the new landscape. With the exception of the forest at our backs, we were surrounded by miles and miles of infinite dunes. There were no roads, no buildings, no vegetation, no water—only desert as far as the eye could see.

Alixe frowned as she took in the same reality. She sighed, then nudged me forward. "Let's at least get out of arrow range."

I recoiled from her hand. "We shouldn't have left them," I snapped.

"Taran was hurt. They needed our help, and we just *abandoned* them." My voice cracked on the final words, remembering Luther's impassioned vow.

"Luther ordered me to get you to safety," she insisted.

"And I ordered you to go back. You spoke to me of titles and chains of command—do I not outrank him as Queen? Is your oath to him or to me?"

She bristled at my accusation. "My oath is to keep you safe."

I made a low, disgusted noise and turned away from her, staring back toward the stark line of trees marking the border and the pockets of black that wove between them. The memory of the Meros compass gave me a small spark of hope—wherever he was, Luther could find his way back to me.

If he survived.

"Have faith in them, Your Majesty," Alixe said gently. "I would bet on Taran and Luther against a far more capable enemy than that."

"Even without their magic?"

"Yes, even so." She placed a hand on my shoulder. "We're trained to fight without our magic when we must. They can handle this."

My chest tightened. "But Taran..."

Alixe said nothing, though the tense squeeze of her fingers said she shared my anxious thoughts.

She turned away, gesturing for me to follow her, and I hesitated. "Perhaps we should go back into Arboros where we're not so exposed. We can find another hollow or climb a tree and wait."

"We're safer on this side of the border. The mortals won't follow us into Ignios."

"How do you know?"

She shot a grave look over her shoulder into the woods. "Trust me."

THE WAIT WAS PURE AGONY.

Alixe and I sat in the sand in dead silence, our attention fixed on the wall of trees we'd just escaped. Every time a bird rustled a branch or a creature skittered through the brush, my heart would stop, my lungs would still, and a flush of adrenaline would pulse through my veins.

In the inevitable stillness that followed, my body would shake until I forced myself to calm, and the vicious cycle would begin all over again.

When neither of us could take it any longer, Alixe broke the silence. "Did you ever learn anything about godstone as a healer?"

I smirked grimly at the irony. Godstone had been one of the many topics my mother forbid me to learn in her effort to shield me from the Descended world. Had her disappearance not prompted me to take over her work at the palace and pore over her notes on Descended ailments, I might not know about it even now.

"The small wounds aren't always fatal," I answered. "As long as the toxin doesn't spread, they heal. Slowly, but they heal."

"And if it does spread—is there any treatment?"

I clenched my jaw. "None that I know of."

She pulled her knees to her chest and wrapped her arms around them, dipping her head low. Almost too quietly to hear, she began whispering, offering up a prayer to the Blessed Mother Lumnos—to watch over Taran and Luther and return them to us, to guide Taran's healing from his wounds, and to carry us safely back to our *terremère*.

I felt suddenly out of place, a heathen intruder into a sacred rite.

When she finished, she gazed up to the sky. "I have no offering, Blessed Mother, but I hope you hear me all the same."

"Offering?" I asked.

Alixe looked at me. "When we pray to the Kindred, we give an offering of magic. Just a small drop, something to honor the gifts they bestowed. They say the magic given up in prayer is lost forever. In theory, that is—no one really knows for sure."

"If that's true, I'm surprised anyone prays at all. Aren't the Descended a bit, um, *obsessive* about keeping their magic strong?"

She cracked a small smile. "That's why the Kindred give the strongest magic to their most faithful servants. *'An ember given is a flame received.'*" She smiled. "At least that's what my mother yelled while chasing me around the palace as a child, trying to get me to say my prayers instead of sparring with my cousins."

I laughed at the thought of a tiny hellraising Alixe fleeing her exasperated parents. I imagined it looked quite a bit like my own childhood, a few miles away but an entire world apart.

"That explains Luther's power," I said. "I've never seen a man more devout."

Alixe nodded in agreement.

"But what about me? I've never prayed to her." I looked up at the stars and squinted as if I might come eye-to-eye with the divine old bird herself.

"I've made fun of her a fair bit. Cussed her out a few times. I asked her for a favor once, and I'm pretty sure she laughed in my face."

"Faith isn't always about prayer. Sometimes it's about sacrifice."

Her somber look sent a chill climbing up my spine. I didn't ask what she meant, and I wasn't sure I really wanted to know.

Her head turned toward Arboros, and she sucked in a breath.

My eyes shot to the trees. From the shadows, two figures appeared. One was staring at a small object in his hand, and the second was limping, his arm draped around the other's shoulders.

I started toward them, but Alixe grabbed me and pushed me back. "I'll go. You stay here."

"This is absurd," I hissed. "Stop treating me like a liability."

"You *are* a liability," she clipped, uncharacteristically losing her usual calm. "The three of us will always put your life first. If you wish to protect us, let us do our jobs to protect you."

Heated arguments swirled in my throat. "Fine," I gritted out. "Go."

I fumed at my involuntary helplessness as I watched her run to their side and take Taran's other arm over her shoulders.

Moments later, faces began to appear among the trees. I started to shout a warning, then paused as I realized the mortals had stopped their pursuit at the edge of the forest.

"I'm fine," Taran muttered when they approached. "Let me go already. I've had worse wounds from a bar fight."

They ignored his complaints, which only made him grumble louder, and laid him out on the sand. I kneeled at his side and gently peeled away his vest and the thick tunic underneath. The two gashes were already red and swelling, with fresh blood still seeping from the wounds.

"Are there any more?" I asked, looking up at Luther.

He stared at me with a pale, shellshocked expression. He didn't answer. From the empty glaze of his eyes, I wasn't sure he'd even heard me.

I leaned over and laid my palm on Luther's cheek. He seemed startled for a moment, then he pressed his hand against mine, clutching it with icy fingers that gripped mine like a lifeline.

My heart ached at seeing him so unraveled. His leaden features betrayed a loss he was already beginning to grieve.

"Just the two," Taran huffed. "Can't believe I got taken out by a bunch of mortals. It's a good thing I'm dying, I'd never live this down at home."

No one laughed.

Luther's eyelids squeezed shut. Alixe looked away, blinking rapidly as the moonlight gleamed off the wetness in her eyes.

I stared at Taran's injuries. The gravity of what he faced was overwhelming. The heft of it crushed me down, threatening to drag me back into the gloom of sorrow.

But before I was a prisoner of war or a Queen, I was a healer—and a damn good one. I did not fear wounds or sickness, I saw them as a puzzle to be solved. I might never have the courage to take lives, but I could save them.

At the very least, I could fight for them.

I took a deep breath, packing my panic and terror and heartbreak into a tiny box for another day, then shot Taran an irritated look.

"Don't be so dramatic. You're not dying."

He blinked at me. "I'm not?"

"Of course not." I ripped off the hem of my tunic and folded it into two squares, then pressed one to the cut on his rib. "I was just telling Alixe these small cuts usually heal on their own."

"They do?" Luther asked.

I couldn't risk looking at him and letting his grief crack my facade, so I put him to work instead. I grabbed his hand and laid it on the makeshift bandage. "Here, hold this in place. Firm pressure, but not too much. Alixe, take the one at his shoulder."

They shuffled closer to Taran to follow my instructions. I made small adjustments until I was satisfied, then I leaned over and plucked a dagger from one of Alixe's many sheaths. I pulled my tunic off completely and set about cutting it into a pile of long strips.

"Do you need more?" Alixe asked. "You can take mine, too."

"Or my coat," Luther added.

"No, those fancy Descended fabrics will irritate the wound. The linen is better." I grinned at Taran. "You know, if you wanted to get me topless, there were far easier ways to go about it." I winked. "Just ask Luther."

Taran winced through his laughter. "I would, but I don't want another blade in my side."

I risked a smile up at Luther. His vacant gaze was trained on Taran's wound.

"Look," Taran said, jerking his chin toward the forest.

At the edge of the woods, one of the mortal men had begun to shuffle forward beyond the tree line. He was walking haltingly, pausing after each step, his hands quivering at his side.

"Are they scared of the border?" I asked.

"If not, they should be," Taran muttered.

The man's progress made him braver. He took larger steps, his back straightening. He scowled up at the three of us and raised a finger. "You can't run from us forever, Descended sc—"

His voice turned to screams as a fire exploded at his feet, engulfing his body and consuming him in an instant. He fell to his knees, then collapsed forward with a guttural moan. Seconds later, the flames died to a flicker and extinguished. Where once there'd been a man, there was now only a charred, motionless husk.

"*Fucking Ignios*," Taran said. "I'd heard the rumors, but I didn't think it was true."

"What the hell was that?" I gasped.

"Ignios border defense," Alixe said darkly. "They put it in place after expelling all their mortals to ensure none of them came back."

Nausea rose in my throat. The sound of the dead man's screams were still echoing across the dunes. There wasn't even an Ignios Descended around to claim their kill—just another mortal death added to the tally.

"At least we know the mortals won't be coming after us here," Alixe said. "We're safe for now."

Taran sunk back against the sand. He lolled his head to the side and stared at me, his eyes jumping around my face in search of the truth. "You really think I'll survive this, Queenie?"

It was the lie of my life as I swallowed down my horror and plastered on a dazzling smile. I lifted a shoulder in a light, unbothered shrug. "Of course I do. We just need to keep the cuts clean. Think you can handle resting and giving them time to heal?"

His body sagged with a visceral sigh of relief. "Think you can stay out of trouble for a few days?"

I glanced over to the hateful brown eyes watching us from the darkness. "We'll see."

CHAPTER

FIFTEEN

When I rose with the dawn, Luther was already awake. He was in the same spot I'd last seen him, sitting out atop a large dune with his back to the rest of us.

While he stood watch, Alixe and I had taken Taran duty. We'd entertained him with laughter and teasing until he fell asleep, then curled into him on each side to keep his injured body warm through the frigid desert night.

I'd crept away to Luther once in the hopes of getting him to talk through what he was feeling, but he'd quickly brushed me off after forcing me to take his overcoat in lieu of my ruined shirt.

I'm fine, he'd insisted. *Just worried. Get some rest.*

Something in the tightness of his voice had warned me that he needed space, so I'd reluctantly agreed, though his shattered expression had stuck with me all night, haunting my troubled dreams.

"Did you get any sleep at all?" I asked as I plowed through the sand and knelt beside him.

"Some."

I snorted. "Liar."

"You're one to talk. That was quite a show you put on last night."

I raised an eyebrow at his curt tone. "Oh?"

"It was very convincing. I even believed it myself for a moment." He gazed off into the trees, the muscles along his throat flexing. "But I know a bit about godstone, too. Years ago, I planned to use it to poison my father, so I researched its effects. I know how unsurvivable it really is."

I steeled my face to disguise my shock. It was hardly a surprise that his relationship with his father was strained, but I hadn't realized Luther's hatred for Remis ran so deep—or so dark.

"If brewed into a poison, it is unsurvivable," I agreed, "but cuts from a blade are different. The small ones can heal."

"A quarter of them heal. The rest are fatal."

Again, I clutched at indifference despite the sinking weight in my chest. My mother's notes hadn't been quite so specific on the grim odds. And with Taran having two wounds...

"A quarter is not none," I chirped with false brightness. "Taran is strong and in good health, and he has his own personal healer to tend his wounds. His chances are surely better than most."

For a very long time, Luther said nothing. His dark, unbound hair fluttered in the morning breeze, a light dusting of pale sand clinging to his ribs where Taran's blood had soaked through the fine knit of his sweater the night before. His features gave away nothing, his walls too high for even me to see over.

"Is it right to lie to someone you love when you know death is coming?" he asked finally. "To let them believe the future might stretch on forever, when you know your time left together is far shorter? Or is that adding cruelty to tragedy?"

I shuffled closer to him until our shoulders touched. Though he made no move to embrace me, after a moment, I felt the faint press of him leaning into my side.

"There are many kinds of medicines," I said gently. "Some of them are easier to understand, like herbs and salves, but others are unexplainable. Faith. Happiness and laughter. Confidence in a positive outcome. Skin contact with loved ones. I've seen these things make a difference in patients that I thought were lost forever." I laid a palm on his arm. "I want to give Taran the best chance I can. If my lie could keep him alive, isn't that worth it in the end?"

Luther let out a long sigh. "Yes. Of course." He raked his hair back, then took my hand and pressed it to his lips. "You're an incredible healer. If anyone can save him, it's you."

I forced out an approving smile. "Come and sit with us. Taran needs you, too."

He nodded and stood, then reached down to help me up. Once I was on my feet, he grabbed me by the waist, pulling me in for a sudden hard, passionate kiss that left me breathless.

As much as I thrilled at the rush of fiery pleasure his touch always brought, there was a taste of sorrow on his lips that left my heart aching rather than racing.

"Are you alright?" I asked. I cringed as the words came out—how foolish that question seemed in light of all we now faced.

Out of kindness, or perhaps exhaustion, he didn't call me on it. "I'm fine," he said with a smile that felt even less genuine than mine. He tucked me under his arm and started toward the others. "Now I need you to hurry up and get Taran healed so I can stab him again for ruining my favorite sweater."

Though my worries were far from soothed, he left me no time to push further. A moment later, we were back at Taran's side, Luther arguing with him over who had fought better against the mortals while I gingerly changed the dressing on Taran's wounds.

"How do they look?" Alixe asked quietly as she leaned in and watched me work.

I peered beneath the gauze. The wound itself looked normal, similar enough to the hundreds of mortal cuts I'd treated over the years. What twisted the knife in my ribs were the tiny black veins webbing out from where the skin had split.

"Hard to say," I rushed out, quickly covering them up with fresh linen. "I really need water to clean them. Some of those herbs we saw in Arboros would be helpful, too."

I glanced at the forest boundary, and my heart sank. Faces still lingered in the trees, watching and waiting.

"If my magic returns, I'll sneak back over and get what we need," she offered.

"We're all going to need water soon enough. Food and shelter, too. If they're planning to wait us out indefinitely..."

She nodded in bleak understanding. "How long until the flameroot wears off and your magic returns?"

"A few more days, maybe longer."

"Can we..." She dropped her voice to a whisper. "Can he make it that long?"

We shared a grave look. "I'd rather not find out."

"We can hear you, you know." I looked over to see Taran frowning at me. "I knew that whole 'You're gonna be fine' act was a lie."

I swore internally and flipped the switch on my cheery facade. "It wasn't a lie. I just want to get you food and water so your body can heal." I made a show of rolling my eyes. "By the Flames, Taran, I've treated newborn babes that needed less coddling than this."

"I don't think we should be calling for any *Flames* when we're in *fucking Ignios*," he grumbled. "And isn't that saying forbidden?"

I smirked. "I'm the Queen. I'm un-forbidding it. The Everflame was here long before Lumnos was. If the Descended and the mortals have to learn to play nice, the Old Gods and the Kindred do, too."

He groaned and squinted up at the morning sky. "Blessed Mother Lumnos, I am your devoted servant. Please don't punish me for her blasphemy."

"My blasphemy? Taran, I've heard you say 'Lumnos's tits' at least ten times."

"Yes. *Devotedly*."

"If you two are done," Luther interjected, "I think I have a solution." He gazed off to the north. "I've seen old maps of Ignios from before they expelled the mortals. Their Mortal City was by the sea, near the Arboros border."

"We can't be far from there now," I said. "The rebel camp was close to the coast."

He nodded. "There could still be a freshwater source nearby, and we may be able to find shelter and scavenge for other supplies. The journey will be a hard one, though..." He glanced at Taran, then back at me, a question in his eyes.

"It's just a few hours of walking," Taran groused before I could answer. "I can handle it."

"Are you sure?" Alixe asked him, though her eyes were fixed on me.

Taran shoved our hands away and grunted as he stiffly climbed to his feet. He grabbed his discarded clothing and marched off into the sand. "Let me earn my manhood back before Her Majesty calls me a newborn babe again."

As it turned out, none of us were prepared for what *a few hours of walking* would demand in the desert.

Despite the winter season, the climate was unrelenting. Our faces turned pink and tender under the blazing sun, and even the chill in the air could not stop the sweat from pouring down our backs. Combined with the brutal aridity and lack of water to drink, the signs of dehydration set in alarmingly fast. By midday, we were all sporting cracked lips and throbbing, woozy heads.

I learned quickly that although our fortified Descended skin was difficult to *pierce*, it was not difficult to *irritate*. Fine granules of sand worked their way into our boots and clothes, grating painfully against our flesh.

The walk itself was torturously slow. The powdery terrain sucked down our heels and refused to let go, making every step a battle. We stayed near enough to the Arboros border to avoid getting lost in the open desert, but our desire to stay out of arrow range forced us to stay in the steep, hilly dunes.

The worst of it was the sandstorms. Every so often the wind would pick up, surrounding us in a blinding cyclone of grit. Each time, in terror of what the whirling sand might do to Taran's wounds, I would rip off the overcoat and fling it onto his chest, prompting Alixe and Luther to throw themselves on me to protect my bare flesh. Together, we would huddle and pray we came out alive.

Perhaps the most rattling aspect of the journey was that we weren't alone. In the harsh light of the sun, the Guardians' vigil was on full display as they marched easily through the woods at our side. It was a constant reminder that we were trapped, with death chasing us from the left, from the right, and in Taran's case, from within.

We kept a slow pace for his benefit—a fact he griped about for at least half the journey, though he endured it well. When the sun disappeared with neither a sea nor a city in sight, and we were forced to settle in for another night among the dunes, Taran was panting the least of us all. Despite my fatigue, it put a true smile on my face, my first real glimmer of hope that he might truly make it through.

But when I peeked beneath his bandages and saw that the mass of black veins had grown by an inch, my glimmer darkened to shadow.

While the battle raged on in his body, a different battle was taking place in my heart. I spent the evening telling my wildest stories, teaching Taran mortal drinking songs, and trading lighthearted ribbing about their very privileged upbringing and my very unrefined one. When eyelids finally began drooping, I jumped to volunteer for first watch, climbed over the nearest dune and out of sight, and collapsed into tears.

Or what passed for tears, when your eyes were too dried out to weep.

Every smile I shared with Taran was a nail lodged in my heart. I'd meant what I'd told Luther about joy being its own kind of medicine, and even if it did nothing, I wanted Taran's final days to be happy ones. He deserved to go out laughing.

But it had a cost. The constant effort to conceal my true feelings was eating me alive, and when I dared to look Alixe or Luther in the eye and see past our shared mask, I could tell it was killing them, too.

I *despised* Vance for what he'd done. I wasn't proud to admit that I'd spent half the journey recalling his screams when Sorae's dragonfyre had burned him or imagining all the gruesome ways I might make him pay. I both relished and feared what I might do if he was still in those woods when my magic returned.

And if we lost Taran... I wasn't sure I would be able to wait on my godhood to avenge him.

But I also knew my loathing was a mirror of what festered in the hearts of those mortal men, the same hate that had driven them to attack us in the first place. After all, how many of them had watched a loved one take their last breath at the tip of a Descended blade?

For at least one of them, that blade had been mine.

They had taken their revenge on Taran, and it had birthed a new hatred in me. If I took my revenge in return, it would only create new grudges, new blood feuds. Around and around we would go, hating and killing until no one was left standing. There was no good that could be borne of it.

And yet I hated them nevertheless.

I'd been fretting over how to convince the mortals and the Descended to choose peace over vengeance. But how could I stop a war between them when I couldn't even stop it in my own heart?

I reclined back onto the soft sand, gazing up into the inky, star-flecked blanket of night.

"Listen, Grandma Lumnos," I muttered, "I see what you were trying to do here. A Descended raised as a mortal, a Queen who doesn't want her throne. It's all very poetic. But you might have mucked it on this one. I really think you've got the wrong girl."

My nose wrinkled. "Why not Luther? He knows how to avoid making an enemy out of every Descended on the continent, which I seem entirely incapable of doing. If peace is your goal, surely he would be a better choice to wear your Crown."

I narrowed my eyes, head cocking. "Do you even choose *anyone?* Maybe all this talk of you choosing someone *worthy* is a lie made up by greedy men to convince the world they have divine permission for all their evil deeds. Maybe you're not handing out blessings at all, and it's up to us to decide whether we become villains or heroes."

Groaning, I rubbed my face. "Why am I talking to some dead lady who doesn't care? The desert is drying out my brain." I climbed to my feet and began plodding back to wake Alixe for her turn on watch. As I climbed up the dune, I paused and looked skyward one last time. "You don't get my prayers yet. Save Taran and get us home. Then we'll talk."

CHAPTER
SIXTEEN

We arrived at Mortal City early the next day.

Well, we arrived at the *ghost* of Mortal City.

From a distance, it looked as if it might still be a sleepy little hamlet, a place where humble, hardy people created lives of beautiful simplicity in their own quiet corner of the world.

The town was built around an oasis, a tiny fleck of blue and green on a canvas of boundless beige. Rows of buildings made of dark red clay sat in neat lines dotted with clusters of palm trees and overgrown citrus plants.

When we crested the final dune and spotted the glittering aqua spring still active at the center, we embraced with a round of grins. It looked like such a lush haven that I wondered for a moment if the sun hadn't cracked our brains and sent us into joint delusion.

But as we neared, it became clear this place was anything but idyllic.

It started with the skeletons. Hundreds of them half-buried in sand, picked clean by animals and bleached white by the sun. Most lay on the outskirts of the village, trailing up the sides of the surrounding dunes as if struck dead in the midst of escape. Icy fingers crawled up the back of my neck as I wondered what could drive someone out of this sanctuary and into the certain death of open desert.

Inside the town, the homes had been abandoned in a hurry. Pots hung over long-dead hearths, books sat open on desks, and children's toys lay scattered and forgotten. The wardrobes were still stocked full of clothes, and though we were all happy for the chance to exchange our ripped, soiled rags for breezy linens and soft wool, it felt a bit like vultures pecking meat off an old carcass.

Weapons were strangely plentiful. Many had been left sitting out on countertops, with a few even dropped in the streets. Whatever had chased these mortals away, apparently they had not believed their blades or bows would save them.

Though most were of mortal make, we scavenged some Fortosian steel blades to restock our arsenal, as nearly all our weapons had been taken in the skirmish with the Guardians—including the Sword of Corbois. Luther swore he was glad to be rid of its burden, but I ached at the void over his shoulder where the jeweled handle had once risen. With its loss, a piece of him seemed missing, too.

Our one disappointment, and now our greatest dilemma, was a lack of food. Everything in the buildings had long since rotted to dust, and though there were a handful of ripe kumquat trees that soothed the bite of our hunger, the other plants were months from harvest. Hardier desert-dwellers might know the tricks for finding hidden nutrition, but those secrets had died out on the dunes. We were foreign intruders on a hostile land, and unlike the forest, the desert did not provide.

"We could keep going to the coast," Alixe suggested, cupping her hands into the cool water of the spring and splashing it across her face. "We could catch some fish there, perhaps even wave down a passing boat and ask for help."

"No," Luther said immediately. "We're too exposed on the coast."

He was lounging in the shade of a nearby palm tree and watching the three of us wash away the crust of sand that coated our skin.

He looked at me. "You're an uninvited Crown. If you're caught here, the King of Ignios has the right to kill you on sight."

I dipped my rag in the spring and dabbed it to the wound on Taran's ribs. I was relieved to see that the dark veins had spread only slightly, and a thin scab was beginning to form over the cut.

"He knows I was kidnapped by the Guardians," I said. "Perhaps he'll hear me out and understand."

Luther's hand tightened around the bone hilt of the long, curved scimitar he'd found in one of the homes. "You met him. Did he seem like an understanding man to you?"

I thought back on my Rite of Coronation. My only exchange with the prickly Ignios King had been his sneer of disgust when he had discovered I was a "*half-breed*."

I frowned. "Not quite."

Taran smirked at me and folded his arms behind his head. After I'd refused to let him dive head-first and naked into the spring, he was getting far too much enjoyment out of the sponge bath I was giving him as a compromise.

"I agree with Luther," he said. "I wouldn't put it past them to kill us all if they spot us. They're mean, ruthless bastards, and they hate outsiders."

Alixe dipped a jug into the water and poured it through her cropped hair. "It wasn't always that way," she mused. "Ignios used to be famous for its hospitality. The Ring Road was packed with shops and inns welcoming travelers. They even had patrols to help anyone lost out in the dunes. They had the least resources of all nine realms, but they were the first to offer them up to anyone passing through."

"What happened?" I asked.

"The Blood War," Luther answered. "They tried to stay neutral and keep out of the fighting, but neither side would let them."

Alixe nodded. "Oases started getting poisoned. The springs are crucial to life here, so everyone suspected it was outsiders, but the Descended and mortals each blamed it on the other. The army refused to send soldiers to help unless Ignios joined the war effort. Eventually their Crown had to give in before the entire realm became uninhabitable, and the rebels hit them hard for it. By the end of the war, there was hardly anyone from Ignios left."

"Those who did survive never let go of their anger," Luther added. "They stopped welcoming outsiders, and when the current Crown took his throne, he banished all the mortals."

"He didn't banish them," I muttered, remembering what Henri had told me. "He killed them. He drove them into the dunes and let them roast to death under the sun."

"Where did you hear that?" Luther asked.

"From a friend, I think," I said, shrugging. The last thing I needed was Luther setting his sights on Henri again.

"Let me guess, one of your Guardian friends?" Taran said bitterly. His eyes narrowed, sparking with betrayal. "You know they spread lies about the Descended to trick people into joining, don't you?"

I clenched my jaw as I dried off his wound, then reached for a new batch of linen to wrap it. "The Guardians don't need to lie to do that,

Taran. The Descended give them plenty of recruiting material on their own."

"Taran has a point," Luther said gently. My eyes shot to his, and he gave me a meaningful stare. "We both know they can be... less than honest."

"And what do you suppose happened to them?" I snapped, pointing to the lines of white bones stretching up into the dunes. "What made all those mortals drop their weapons and run for their lives? What lie do the Guardians need to explain *that?*" I glared between the two of them. "I watched a man burn alive for the crime of stepping over their border. I don't care if what I heard was '*less than honest.*' It's no worse than what I've seen with my own eyes."

The others fell silent. I sniffed irritably and reached for the dressing at Taran's shoulder, ripping it away.

My heart stopped.

Unlike the cut on his ribs, this wound oozed with blood and a foul-smelling black liquid. The web of dark veins around it had thickened and grown, pulsing in time with his heartbeat.

The first signs of infection.

I quickly slammed the linen back down to conceal it. Taran winced and pull away. "I take it back, I believe you. You don't have to take it out on my body."

"Sorry," I mumbled. I dipped my chin and pretended to rummage in my pile of fabric to conceal my face and the terror racing across it.

My breathing came faster and shallower. I needed to disinfect the cut, but water would only do so much—he needed medicine. All the supplies I'd found here were spoiled. I'd seen herbs in Arboros that might help, but...

"You were really one of them?" Taran asked me. "You were a Guardian?"

I looked up at him in surprise. "What? I... I—"

His dark blonde brows pulled in tight, his features lined with hurt. "Was it only before you met us?"

I looked away and grabbed my wet cloth. Though my hands were shaking, I carefully wiped the wound as clean as I could, using my other hand to shield it from his view.

"Some of it was after," I admitted, too ashamed to look at him.

"The Guardians murder Descended." Taran's voice was angrier now, more accusing. "I've lost friends to their attacks."

"I never supported any of that. I only helped them gather information."

"But you still helped them. You got to know us, you became our friend, and you worked with them?"

"So did I," Luther said.

All our eyes cut to him. His expression was dark. "I've been helping the Guardians for years. I knew what they were capable of, and I did far more for them than Diem ever did. I even helped them after the attack on Coeurîle."

Alixe's jaw went slack. "Luther, I knew you were surveilling them, but... *helping* them?"

"Yes. And while Diem might regret her decision, I do not. I'd do it again, so if you're going to be mad at anyone, be mad at me, not her." He slowly pushed to his feet with a low grunt, then stalked off toward the city.

We sat in silence for a long minute. I couldn't take the awkward tension, so I reached for Taran's wound again. He shoved my hands away, then started to stand.

"Wait," I insisted. "At least let me put a fresh bandage on."

He blew out a harsh breath and sat, fuming silently while I rushed to wrap the injury in fresh linen before he or Alixe noticed its condition.

"I was going to let it go," he gritted out after a moment. "I didn't want to die angry at you. But if you're so convinced I'll live, then I'm gonna go ahead and be mad. At *both* of you, I guess."

A burning lump lodged in my throat. I raised my hands to show him I was finished, and he shot to his feet, but at the last minute, he stumbled to the side, nearly collapsing into the sand. Alixe and I both jumped forward to help him.

"I'm fine," he grumbled, though his eyes turned glassy as he hovered in place, swaying slightly on his feet. Alixe looked at me in alarm.

I avoided her stare. When Taran finally steadied, he yanked his arms back from us, then lurched off in Luther's direction.

On the ground, I spotted the discarded bandage, the white fabric stained with black. I dropped to my knees and hurriedly stuffed it into my pile of linen strips.

Alixe ran a hand down her face. She walked back to the water and stripped off her clothes, then grabbed a cloth and began scrubbing at her skin. We stayed like that for a while, the uncomfortable silence growing thicker by the minute, until finally I tossed the fabric aside and rose to face her.

"If you no longer wish to serve me, I understand." I forced my shoulders to straighten. "Of course, I don't want to lose you, but if you don't—"

"I gave you my vow, Your Majesty," she cut in. "I have every intention of fulfilling it. Nothing has changed for me."

I eyed her carefully. "Nothing?"

"Nothing."

I slowly removed my own clothes and joined her at her side. My gaze lingered on her face as I took the pitcher and poured water over my dry, reddened skin. "You're not angry with me?"

She looked out over the blue-green pool. "A few weeks ago, I might have been. But since I've learned about the violence the guards in Mortal City have caused and how bad the conditions are there..." She frowned. "You had every right to hate me for being in the Royal Guard. More, perhaps, given my position. But you never held it against me."

"I did at first," I admitted. "I held it against all of you. But you showed me there are good people within the guard, just as there are in the Guardians. I'd hoped we could find those people on both sides and bring them together somehow. Maybe I'm too naive, but I still do."

She walked over and took the cloth from my hand to rinse off the spots on my back I'd missed. "It's not naive. I'm not sure we stand a chance at winning this war if we don't."

I sighed heavily. "You said you came to respect me because of my actions the night of the armory fire. That wasn't courage, Alixe—that was guilt."

"Many people have reasons to feel guilty. Few are willing to sacrifice themselves to make it right." She laid a hand on my shoulder. "It does not change how I feel."

I closed my eyes, overwhelmed by her forgiveness. "Thank you," I murmured.

"Taran will understand, too. Give him some time, if—"

She stopped herself, but we both knew the words that came next.

If he has time left to give.

We helped each other finish washing and changed into the fresh clothing we'd found. The wide, billowing pants and cropped tunics were a much-needed change from the heavy fabrics we'd arrived in, and the colorful wool shawls would give a welcome respite when the temperature made its dramatic plummet into the frosty evening.

Alixe sat to lace her boots. "Is that how you and Luther first met—in the Guardians?"

"Not exactly," I said, laughing. "I was as shocked as you when I found out." I walked over and sat beside her, resting my elbows on my knees. "Luther has his reasons for helping them. It's not my place to share them, but I hope you'll extend him the same grace you've shown me."

"I will. I've learned to trust him, even when I don't understand him." She glanced in the direction he had stormed off, her features turning contemplative. "I'm glad he told you. It's so rare that he opens up to anyone. I've never seen—" She paused, frowning up at the sky. "Do you hear that?"

I followed her gaze to the wide blue expanse, where the afternoon sun was blazing in all its glory. There wasn't a cloud in the sky, let alone anything else. "Hear what?"

"It sounds like... pounding. Like a drum."

And then I heard it.

Thump, thump, thump.

Wings.

I leapt to my feet, a smile springing to my face for a fleeting moment—until I remembered the command I'd given.

A command that couldn't be broken.

"Alixe... shit, that's—"

She grabbed my arm. "Did you call Sorae?"

I shook my head. "No. And it can't be her."

Her face paled. "Hide. *Hurry.*"

We scrambled to gather our things and ran for the nearest structure, a small outdoor storage pen that must have been used to store firewood, judging from the decaying logs that cracked under our feet as we jumped inside and pulled the cover closed.

"What about Luther and Taran?" I whispered. "We have to warn them."

"We can't risk it. If that's who I think it is, and he finds you..."

She trailed off as we both peered through the cracks in the lashed bamboo that made up the walls of the enclosure. My pulse raced in time with the steady beat of the approaching wings. The sand whipped into a dusty cloud, forcing us to close our eyes and cover our noses with our scarves.

Paws crunched on dry sand, followed by the piercing scream of a gryvern's cry. When I looked again through the slim openings, I had to clamp a hand over my mouth to muffle my gasp.

The Ignios gryvern was an enormous beast. It was nearly twice Sorae's size, with golden feathers on its wings and scales of shimmering tan that seemed forged from the desert itself. A line of horns, each filed to a spear-sharp tip, ran up its snout and down its long neck.

Anger seeped from the beast like a foul smell, infecting the air with its hateful rancor. As its slitted eyes narrowed and scanned the oasis, the thick cords of muscle lining its powerful body bunched, looking ready to strike at any moment. Flames curled around its nostrils with every rumbling breath.

A man and two women dismounted from a saddle strapped to its back. The man was dressed in flowing white robes, his head swathed in a ginger-colored silk scarf that covered all but his dark orange eyes.

Though he appeared to have no weapons, the women were laden with them. A strappy leather harness wrapped around each of their midsections, bearing a small armory of thin, sharp throwing knives. Much like the gryvern, their tanned bodies were toned and curved with muscles that seemed permanently tensed for battle.

"Search the buildings," the man said. "If she's here, bring her to me. Kill the others."

The gryvern arched its neck toward the sky and released an ear-splitting snarl. Its body rippled as its clawed talons curled into the sand.

The women nodded and ran for the city. My pulse rattled watching them disappear into the streets. I prayed Luther and Taran were well hidden among the maze of clay walls.

The man pulled his headscarf down to his neck, revealing a familiar face, its leathery, sun-worn skin the same dark red hue as the buildings around us.

"The King?" Alixe mouthed at me, arching an eyebrow. I nodded, and her mouth set into a thin, grim frown.

"Where are you, Lumnos?" he bellowed. His booming voice startled me backward, causing the rotted wood to snap beneath my knees.

The Ignios King's head swiveled in our direction. Alixe grabbed my arm to still me, both of us holding our breath as we waited, frozen, staring in terror through the slatted bamboo.

He clasped his hands behind his back and strolled toward us, his long, dark beard swaying in the wind as his gaze swept across the oasis.

Everything fell deathly silent, save for the rustle of sand shifting under his sandaled heels. As quietly as we could manage, Alixe and I pulled small blades from our sheaths. If we were discovered, we had only a split second to react before he incinerated us into a pile of ash.

And if his fire magic worked anything like my destructive silvery light, even a split second might not be enough.

"I know you're here somewhere," he taunted.

A dark silhouette passed in front of the slivers of light leaking into the enclosure, then stopped. I dared to lean in for a closer look—and nearly came face to face with him as he dropped to one knee.

Had he been staring through the bamboo planks, he would have spotted me instantly, but his focus was elsewhere—on the terrain beneath his feet.

He ran his fingers leisurely through the sand as if it were water, then cupped it into his palm, letting the tiny granules sift through the air.

"The sand tells me its secrets," he hissed. He clenched his hand into a fist and raised it to his ear. "It whispers to me that there are three in my dunes who do not belong. But you're not one of them, are you?" His chin rose. "You're something else."

I nearly crumpled when he stood and began pacing the other direction. I should have known he would be able to sense our presence through the Forging magic that ran through Emarion's realms. I'd felt it myself the night of my Ascension Ball.

But when I had reached into the Lumnos soil that night and felt the anomalies of the Umbros Descended among my people, I hadn't been able to see their location. I only knew they were somewhere in my realm and they were not of Lumnos descent.

Which meant the Ignios King knew we were here—but not *where*.

"I've had a Crown on my lands before," he said loudly. "I know how the Forging magic bends around them and shimmers at their feet. Tell me, Lumnos, why do you not feel like one of them?" He spun around, eyes narrowing. "Why do you feel like one of *mine*?"

He sauntered forward, again passing in front of the storage pen. "One of mine, and yet not. You're something different. Something new. Even the sand doesn't know what to think of you. Where you walk, the Forging magic doesn't bend. It *shatters*." He glanced up at the sky. "Perhaps Sophos was right, and you are an imposter."

I saw Alixe's face turn to me in question, but I didn't return her stare. I hadn't told any of them, not even Luther, about the calamitous Rite of Coronation and the Sophos Crown's accusations. Not because I was ashamed—I knew I was no imposter. I'd done nothing to seize the throne, and my ability to command Sorae was proof enough that the Crown's authority had passed to me in earnest.

In part, I'd withheld the story because my catalogue of problems was growing longer by the day, and unpacking the petty insults of the Sophos Crown was low on my list.

But telling that story would also require explaining the heartstone and its vital importance to the Descended world. Some quiet intuition urged me that that secret was best left unspoken for now.

The Ignios King's dark gaze roamed across the turquoise water. "Where are you hiding, Lumnos?"

He strode closer to the shoreline, pausing near the palm tree where we'd all been gathered earlier. His attention caught on something near its base, and he kneeled closer, scooping up a clump of sand and rubbing his fingers together. He cocked his head, staring at his palm and frowning.

He walked back to his gryvern, staring into its golden eyes. "Can you sense them?"

The beast didn't react, though I knew firsthand the communication between a Crown and their gryvern went beyond words or gestures.

Whatever response he received, the King nodded curtly. "Good. Where are they?"

After a moment, his lip curled into a sneer. "*Nearby* is not helpful, Tybold. Take me to them."

The gryvern gave an indignant-sounding snort and flicked its tail into the sand.

"If you can't find where they're hiding, what good are you to me?" the King growled. "Tell me why they're in my realm."

Tybold's feathered wings puffed outward, then snapped in against its body. Its reptilian head shrunk back as if in anticipation.

"I don't care that they don't wish to hurt me, *I* wish to hurt *them*," the King roared. "Why are they here?" He slammed his fist into the soft, fleshy patch beneath the gryvern's mouth. "I command you to *answer me!*"

Trickles of blood dribbled from the beast's jaw, the same sensitive place my Sorae so dearly loved to be scratched. The gryvern hissed its fury, baring rows of vicious fangs. A ball of dragonfyre erupted from its throat with an enraged snarl, shooting across the sand before evaporating into smoke.

"Worthless creature," the King muttered. On each finger of his hand, the sharp spikes protruding from his metal rings were coated in red.

I ground my teeth together to keep from launching myself out into the open. "Gryverns read intentions, asshole, not minds," I mumbled.

The gryvern went preternaturally still. Its ochre pupils slid in a slow arc toward our pen and stopped.

Shit.

CHAPTER

SEVENTEEN

In my outburst, I'd overlooked one crucial fact—gryverns had hypersensitive hearing.

I stared through the slats, knowing with certainty Tybold had found us.

My foolish, stupid temper. I'd given us away and possibly cost us everything. Perhaps I could throw myself at the King's feet, swear that I'd come alone, and beg for his mercy.

My stare shot back and forth between man and beast, waiting for the moment of reckoning—but when the King turned and walked toward the city, the gryvern only sat, tilting its head, watching me in silence.

Twin flames grew from the center of the King's palms, then twined around his fingers. They swirled and expanded until his skin glowed red and fire consumed his arms from the elbows down. With a snap of his wrist, an ember jumped to his forehead and seemed to catch alight, igniting the fiery Crown above his head.

"Where are you, Lumnos?" the King said, his voice low and menacing. "If you will not come out on your own, you leave me no choice."

He thrust a hand out, sending a churning ball of fire shooting for a small granary. It exploded into an inferno that swelled through the inside and up to its thatched roof, turning it to cinders in a matter of seconds.

He flung his other arm toward a merchant's kiosk next, and a red-hot spear sliced through the air. It lodged into the canvas walls, sending them curling and blackening as the fire consumed it whole.

"Surely you desire a better fate than to burn alive?" the King taunted. "Think of your poor family. They'll never know how you died. They won't even have a body to bury."

His words stung more than he could possibly know. It wasn't death I feared, but the prospect of abandoning my mother to her fate in a Fortos prison and leaving my little brother with yet another family member whose loss he couldn't explain.

The air filled with the stench of smoke and char as the King continued his fiery pursuit. Structure after structure disappeared beneath crackling flame, the city lighting up in a series of impromptu bonfires.

My thrashing heart roasted alongside them. What if Taran and Luther were inside one of those buildings? What if the man I cherished burned for my cowardice?

I looked to Alixe, my defeat written plainly on my face. She shook her head. "Wait," she mouthed.

I spied between the slats. The gryvern was still staring at our hideaway, its scaly head cocked to one side.

With a twitch of his fingers, the King's blaze stretched its fiery arms toward a collection of nearby wooden carts, turning them into instant kindling. The fire was so close I could feel its heat through the planks concealing us from sight.

The King laughed and looked around in search of another target for his carnage. His focus landed on our storage pen, his mouth curling into a smirk.

A jarring, high-pitched screech stole his attention. His gaze darted to his gryvern, his thick brows pulling inward. "Into the dunes? Are you certain?"

"Your Majesty," a voice called out. From the streets of the city, the two women came jogging toward him. "We've searched the buildings. It doesn't seem like anyone's been here for years."

"They must have been here recently. There's fresh blood by the palm, and this is the only oasis for miles. Tybold thinks they fled." He looked at the other woman. "How soon can our riders get here?"

"If we return now to give the order, they'll arrive midday tomorrow," she answered.

"Let's do a final scout by air," the other woman suggested. "We'll have the guards start combing the dunes when they arrive."

"I want her found," the King snarled. Both women gave stiff nods and saluted.

They stalked to the gryvern and loaded onto its saddle. The King slammed his fist into the side of its neck. "Fly," he barked.

The gryvern's amber gaze lingered on me one last time. Then, with a few galloping steps, Tybold was airborne, and the King of Ignios was gone.

I barely lasted until the wingbeats had faded before I threw off the pen's cover and bolted for the city.

"Diem, we should wait," Alixe called, chasing behind me. She could no more have stopped me than halted the setting sun.

"*Luther*," I screamed, my feet slamming into the hard-packed sand of the town's roads. "*Taran!*"

Alixe followed, nervously scanning the sky. "I'll take the other streets," she offered, then sprinted in the other direction.

"Luther, Taran—where are you?" I yelled. I stopped at every unburnt building, throwing open every door. Again and again, I found empty rooms and the unanswered echo of my voice against the clay.

Columns of black smoke rose from the remains of the Ignios King's fiery attacks. My legs carried me toward them against my will. *What if...?*

When I got to the first of them, I stood in the threshold, staring blankly at the carnage. An army of tiny flames was scattered among the bits of still-burning debris. The Ignios fire had worked quickly, invading and destroying with savage precision, driven by the rage of its hateful commander.

I shuffled forward and scoured the blackened remains. *What if...?*

Movement in the corner caught my attention as the burnt husk of a large wooden wardrobe collapsed inward, sending a flurry of glowing embers floating into the air and something metal clattering to the floor, When I dug the toe of my boot into the pile that remained, a curved blade protruded from the ashes.

A scimitar, just like the one Luther had been carrying, inside a wardrobe—a perfect place to hide.

The world stopped turning.

The distant sound of Alixe calling my name grew louder as my trembling hand stretched toward the blade. Had it been his? Had it been *him?*

"Diem," Alixe hissed, skidding to a stop behind me. "What are you doing in here?"

"Alixe," I croaked. "I think..."

"Come with me," she interrupted. She jerked her head for me to follow, then took off running. I stood in a stupor for a moment, then slowly followed behind her.

She disappeared through the door of a large house on the outermost street. When I got there, a rug in the center of the room had been shoved aside to reveal a wooden trapdoor laying ajar. As I crept around its edge, I saw a staircase leading down into a shadowy abyss—and Taran, his arm slung around Luther's shoulder, slowly climbing their way back into the light.

"We found this cellar just in time," Luther said, helping Taran into a nearby chair. "A few more seconds and they—"

He grunted loudly as I hurled myself into his side and wrapped my arms around him, burying my face against his chest.

He hunched forward, then slid his hands to my shoulders and gently pried us apart. "What happened? Did the King see you?"

I gazed up at him, my throat too tight to answer, and soaked in every line and curve of his face. His features were strained and creased with worry, but so perfectly, gloriously *alive*.

He grazed the tips of his fingers along my cheek, and I leaned into his palm, letting his touch ground me. "What's wrong?" he asked.

"He burned some of the buildings," I managed to choke out. "I thought you were inside. I thought..."

Luther stilled, and for a moment, his expression turned as bleak as my own dark fears had been. It disappeared in a heartbeat, replaced by the steady calm of the Prince. "I'm here now," he said, kissing my temple.

"The Ignios King didn't see us, but he knows we're close," Alixe answered for me. "He's returning with his Royal Guard tomorrow."

"Let's go back to Arboros," Taran said. "I'd rather take my chances with the mortals."

Luther's jaw ticked. "I agree. Taran and I can distract them while you two slip back across. We'll push through their lines once you're both safe."

"With all their godstone, that's a death sentence," Alixe said.

"I already have one of those," Taran joked as he gestured to his chest, though his grin didn't quite make it to his eyes.

"We're not going to Arboros," I said firmly.

"What other choice do we have?" Taran asked.

As the others bickered over which of our many terrible options to choose from, I reluctantly pulled away from Luther and walked to the open doorway, chewing anxiously on my lip.

The dunes rose high around us on every side, their endless brown expanse stained by the haunting white flecks of the dead mortals' bones. The mortals had been lured to this valley by its life-giving water, only to be condemned to some brutal, unknown end.

In those final moments, the mortals had known their only chance at survival was to risk everything and run. Many had died—but perhaps some had not. Perhaps some had made it beyond the dunes and escaped the others' gruesome fate.

One thing was certain—none who stayed put had lived to tell the tale.

If you are outnumbered or overwhelmed, or if all seems lost, just keep moving. Onward, until the very last breath.

The memory of my father's teachings hovered around me as an idea took shape in my mind. It was a crazy idea, reckless, doomed to near-certain failure—in other words, the only kind I ever had.

But if we had any chance of the four of us surviving this together, we had to try.

I turned back to the others and perched my hands on my hips.

"We're going to Umbros," I announced.

"No," they answered in unison.

"Yes," I shot back. "The Ignios coastline is short. If we leave at dawn and stay near the water where the sand is more firm, we can move quickly. We'll be in Umbros by nightfall."

"There's no cover by the water," Alixe said. "If we're spotted, we're sitting ducks."

"It's a risk," I agreed. "But if we stay here, they could do the same thing to us they did to the mortals. We have to get out of Ignios."

"The Umbros Queen is even scarier than the Ignios King," Taran said. "At least the worst *he* can do is kill us."

I swallowed my unease and conjured a mocking grin. "What's wrong Taran, afraid of a little old Queen?"

He glared at me. "Yes. And you should be, too."

I shrugged. "We won't be there long. We'll go straight to the port and get the first boat to Lumnos."

Luther shook his head. "I don't like it. We should wait here. The flame-root will wear off soon. Once it does, you can call for Sorae."

"We might not live that long. Besides, the Guardians have a bolt that can shoot her out of the sky, and they're waiting just over those dunes. I can't risk bringing her this close to them."

"Diem," he said, his tone heavy with warning, "I don't have to tell you there is a particular reason why Umbros is dangerous for us."

He didn't offer more, but I caught his meaning. At the Ascension Ball, I'd opened up our minds to the Umbros representatives for the taking. Any

154

secret we guarded, they had no doubt shared with their Queen. If she found us, she could bring down our entire realm.

"We'll be careful," I said uneasily. "Straight to the port."

"If we're going, we should leave tonight," Alixe said. "I'd rather get a head start."

I struggled to flatten my expression. This part of my plan was the riskiest—and also the part I didn't dare reveal.

"Taran needs rest." He jumped from his seat to argue, and I grabbed his uninjured shoulder and shoved him back down. "And so do I. Let's take today to gather supplies and get as much sleep as we can. We'll leave at first light—that's an order from your Queen."

"MY TURN FOR WATCH?" Alixe asked groggily, rubbing at her eyes as she rolled over.

I nodded and shot her an apologetic look. "I tried to hold out longer, but I can barely stay awake. Mind taking over?"

"Of course." She slid out of bed and reached for her weapons belt. "Anything to report?"

"Not a thing," I lied, looking away. I crept over to where Taran slept nearby, gingerly laying a palm to his forehead. His skin was worryingly warm, and thin black lines were creeping out from beneath the bandage at his shoulder.

"How is he?" she whispered.

"Fine," I lied again.

I followed her out the front door and into the open air. Set amid an audience of twinkling stars, the full moon shone like a spotlight on the small village, illuminating it in a silvery glow.

Just my luck.

"Luther's sleeping next door, if you want to..." She trailed off, a smirk playing at her lips.

"Tempting," I said with a grin. "But I think he and I both need some rest tonight."

It was alarming how easy the lies and false emotions were becoming.

"I set up over there," I added, gesturing to the southern edge of town. "I left some fresh water and a few kumquats, in case you get hungry. I'll be in the next house over, if you need anything."

She nodded and gave me a low bow. "Goodnight, Your Majesty."

I made a show of yawning and headed for one of the empty houses. I strolled inside and closed the door all but a sliver, then hurried to change into the clothes I'd prepared. When I peered back out, Alixe was gone.

I grabbed my supplies, checked that the items I'd set up were still in place, and slipped out through a back door I'd scouted earlier.

The sand was soft and silent under my bare feet as I crept across the city. I needed to be on the northern border before the trap I'd laid set into motion. I came to the city's wide main road and stopped short with a swear.

Though Alixe was out of sight, at the far end, Luther's silhouette was outlined against the glittering surface of the spring. He kept his back to the city as he dipped a cloth into the water and dabbed it across his skin. He'd been asleep when I'd checked on him earlier in the night. At some point he must have awoken and gone to bathe alone.

My chest squeezed as I watched him. When he hadn't joined in with the rest of us in cleaning off earlier by the water, I'd chalked it up to discomfort over showing off his scar. I hadn't realized his desire to hide them ran quite this deep.

I wished he could see them the way I did, as a trophy of his strength in body and in spirit. I yearned to go to him, run my hands along their lines, graze my lips down every jagged mark until he had a much happier, much more *indecent* memory to associate them with—but it would have to wait.

We would have time for that once we were home safe in Lumnos.

With his back to me, I darted across the main road and wove my way through the buildings. I was almost in the clear when a loud clang reverberated through the midnight silence. I scurried up to a nearby roof just in time to spy Alixe running into the large home with the hidden cellar. Moments later, a hastily dressed Luther ran in behind her with his blade drawn.

I blew out a breath and bolted for the dunes, climbing as hard and fast as my bare feet would carry me. When I reached the crest, I threw myself across it, collapsing into the sand to catch my breath. I dared a quick peek back down onto the city to confirm Alixe and Luther were still inside the home, investigating the mysterious noise.

Though I'd escaped their notice, a long trail of footprints followed me through the sand, the one detail I hadn't planned for. I sighed and gathered my things. There was nothing I could do about it now.

By the time anyone saw them, it would already be too late.

CHAPTER
EIGHTEEN

"Where have you been?" Luther thundered.

I didn't answer at first, too winded from running for my life and scaling the steep dunes with an overloaded rucksack.

"Getting dinner," I wheezed out, strolling down the village road to where Alixe and Taran stood beside an absolutely apoplectic-looking Luther. My nose wrinkled as I looked up at the pinkish-purple sky. "More like breakfast now."

I set down my pack and a fish-laden spear, then unlaced the rabbit carcasses I'd hung around my neck.

Luther took the rabbits and glared at them like he might raise them from the dead just to have something to kill. "Where did you get these?"

I leaned forward to rest my hands on my knees and panted to catch my breath. "I went hunting."

"Where?"

I didn't answer.

His voice went low and soft. "Diem, tell me you did not go back to Arboros alone."

"I didn't go alone." I straightened and laid a hand over my heart. "Blessed Mother Lumnos was right here with me the entire time."

Taran edged away from Luther. Alixe sighed and rubbed her temples.

"What were you thinking?" Veins throbbed along Luther's arms, his eyes simmering. "We've been looking everywhere. We thought you'd been captured—or worse."

"I left a note."

Taran waved the scrap of paper I'd left folded on my pillow. "Believe it or not, '*If I'm not back by dawn, go to Umbros without me*' didn't ease a lot of concerns."

"And you took the compass," Luther snapped.

"If I hadn't, you would have come running across the border after me."

"*You're fucking right I would have!*"

Alixe eyed him with a frown, then looked at me. "How did you get there without being seen?"

"I figured they'd only have a man or two on watch at this hour, and they'd likely be focused on the dunes, so I went to the coast and swam in by sea." I shrugged. "They never even knew I was there."

The tiniest little lie. Insignificant, really. A fib too trivial to even be worth correcting.

"Why didn't you take one of us with you?" she asked. "We could have helped."

"You were on watch. Taran can't get in the seawater or it will infect his wounds." I tipped my head toward Luther. "And he would have said no."

"*I* should have been the one to go," he growled. "Alone."

I leaned over and grabbed my pack to hide my rolling eyes, then brushed past them as I strode toward one of the larger houses. "I needed some hard-to-find items," I called out over my shoulder. "It would have been too difficult to explain."

They followed me in and crowded behind me, watching as I dumped the contents of my bag onto a table and began sorting the food from the herbs.

"Besides, I work faster and quieter in the forest on my own." I flashed what I hoped was a reassuring smile. "Trust me, I was safer going alone."

"You shouldn't have gone at all." He slammed his fist into the table with such force it split a crack up the center of the wood. "*It should have been me.*"

I jumped at his outburst. His body was quivering, his shoulders high and tight. His features could have sliced bone with how sharply their edges were honed.

I'd known Luther would be upset, but this—this was something more than anger. This was something primal, something desolate. The darkness shadowing his face was unlike anything I'd ever seen in him.

Judging from the apprehensive looks on Taran and Alixe, neither had they.

I took a step back. He flinched, regret peppering his features.

He leaned his palms on the table and closed his eyes, hanging his head low. His shoulders rose up and down in a slowing pace until he spoke again, his voice quieter. "I'm sorry. I'm not angry—not with you. But you should not put yourself in danger like that. You are the Queen."

"Yes, Luther, I am the Queen," I clipped. "If I want to risk my life, that's my decision to make. I'm sick of being treated like a flower to be fenced off from any stomping feet. That's not who I am, and it's not the kind of Queen I want to be. I'm not planning to sit on a throne and look pretty, I'm planning to fight. I thought you of all people understood that. I thought..." I swallowed. "I thought you believed in me."

"I do," he said, almost inaudibly. "I always will." He took a slow, trembling breath, still refusing to meet my gaze. "I was supposed to be around to protect you."

I grabbed a mortar and pestle from the kitchen. "Things are only going to get more dangerous for me, and it won't stop when we're back in Lumnos. The Guardians want me dead, the Twenty Houses want me dead. Maybe even the Crowns, too. Every day will be a new threat to my life. You can't shield me from that, Luther. You won't always be there to—"

Luther shoved off the table and pushed past Alixe and Taran, throwing the door open and disappearing into the street.

The three of us stood in silence and stared after him, the swinging door still creaking on its hinges.

Taran scratched his neck. "I'll go talk to him."

"No," I said firmly. Our narrowed eyes locked in a battle of wills. I pointed at a chair by the table. "Sit. Queen's orders."

He grumbled and slumped into the chair.

"Alixe, do you mind cooking the meat?" I asked. "We don't have much time before we need to leave."

"As you wish, Your Majesty."

The cold formality in her tone wounded me, though I couldn't fault her for it. Concealing my plans from her had been a show of distrust. It would take time to earn back the inroads we'd made as friends.

I'd known my choice would have consequences with all of them. I just hoped the payoff was worth it.

Alixe left, and I busied myself grinding the herbs I'd collected and mashing them into a paste.

"Tunic off," I ordered to Taran.

He huffed and ripped his shirt over his head, stuffing it into a ball and flinging it across the room.

"Now remove your bandages. *Gently.*"

As he pulled away the bindings, I walked to a closet and grabbed a clean linen robe, then laid it out on the table and began cutting it into strips.

I shot him a glance. "I said gently, Taran, or you'll make them wor —*shit.*" I sucked in a breath as my blade slipped and sliced through my palm. Bits of crimson blood dripped into my bowl.

"Wonderful," I muttered. I hadn't gathered enough of the herbs to waste them remaking the batch. I knotted a strip of linen around my cut, then did my best to scoop out the blood-tainted sections.

"This might hurt," I warned as I pulled up a chair in front of Taran and began to spread the poultice across his wound. He gritted his teeth, staring straight ahead with no response.

Was this better than Alixe's distance? Worse than Luther's fury? Taran already felt like I'd betrayed him with the Guardians—what if this destroyed any chance at mending our bond?

I drooped at the thought as I took another handful and smoothed it over his inflamed skin.

"You did it for me, didn't you?" he mumbled.

I looked up at him, but his gaze was still fixed in the distance, guarded and unhappy.

He jerked his chin toward the wound. "You did it because that's getting worse."

I grabbed a fresh batch of linen and packed it on top of the poultice, then wrapped it around his shoulder to hold it in place.

"We needed supplies for the journey," I said.

"*Bullshit.* Even mortals can survive without food for a few days. If it wasn't for this, what did you get that was so important?"

I had no answer to give him. I reached for his second cut.

"Tell me the full story," he demanded. "The *real* one. Not the lie you gave them about how easy it was."

When it came to Taran, I had nothing left to lose. With our friendship so fractured and his life on the line, perhaps truth was the balm we both needed.

So I told him—how I'd tied up a stack of metal plates, with a candle burning beneath the rope, and how the eventual clattering fall had distracted Alixe and Luther long enough for me to escape unseen.

How I'd buried my clothes in the sand and waded so far out into the frigid sea that the shore nearly disappeared.

How I'd swam an hour down the beach, then hunted in the woods, naked and shivering, too afraid that dripping clothes would give me away. How I'd been forced to come back over land to avoid ruining the herbs with saltwater.

How I almost made it past the Guardians unseen—until a poorly timed sneeze forced me to run for my life while black arrows rained down on my head.

Though he gave no response, I noted the softening of his features and the small twitches of his lips at each absurd predicament or ballsy risk.

When his wounds were fully tended, I slouched back in my chair. "Well? Are you going to forgive me, or should I threaten to tell Luther you gave me the idea to go alone?"

His azure gaze thinned. "You wouldn't dare."

I crossed my arms with a savage smile.

"Fine. I forgive you. But I'm not sure Lu will. He got that *I'm-going-to-murder-someone* look again. It was even worse than after the island."

"He worries too much."

Taran snorted. "Have you met yourself? There's a lot to worry about."

I smirked. "Just get better, will you? Making him mad was a lot more fun when we did it together."

Despite my smile, a gnawing regret warned that I might have finally pushed Luther too far. He'd been stormy and withdrawn since leaving Arboros, and I'd been so focused on Taran's injuries that we'd hardly spoken. With his dearest friend's life in the balance, perhaps he was nursing wounds of his own—wounds I'd just poured salt right into.

I sighed guiltily and scooped the remaining herbs back into a dry pouch. Luther needed me, and he needed to know I was safe. There was little I could do to give him that comfort—especially here, especially now—but for him, I had to try.

As I turned to go check on Alixe, Taran grabbed my wrist, and our eyes met.

"Thank you, Diem. I'm too selfish to say I wish you hadn't done it. I hope you know I would have done it for you, too."

"Then prove it," I said, a spark of challenge in my tone. "I faced death for you and *lived*." I gestured to his wounds. "Time to return the favor."

His face gave way to a feral grin, that inveterate cheekiness I adored returning once more. "Anything for you, Queenie."

CHAPTER
NINETEEN

"*Are we there yet?*"

Alixe and I groaned in unison.

"Look around, Taran," she said. "Do you see anything other than sea or desert?"

"No."

"Then the answer is the same as the last fifteen times you asked."

"And if you ask again, I'm feeding you to Sorae when we get home," I added.

Taran nudged me with his elbow. "After all the trouble you went to last night to keep me alive?"

"Oh, I'll let you live. I'll just let Sorae nibble off an arm or two."

"I'd rather you tell her to take another one off that guy Vance."

"So would I," Alixe agreed.

"So would I."

I glanced over my shoulder at the sound of Luther's low voice. I tried to catch his eye, but he was staring off across the sea, his expression murky.

He'd been avoiding me all day. He had insisted we walk in formation with Alixe taking point, Taran at my side, and himself at the rear. Every time I tried to slow my pace to join him, he fell back even further, determined to maintain our distance.

I pulled at my top, ruffling it to waft a breeze over my skin. "I thought it would be cooler near the water. It's hotter here than in the dunes."

Alixe and Taran shot me quizzical stares.

"You're hot?" Taran rubbed his hands along his arms and shivered. "Queenie, it's freezing."

Alixe's thick cloak flapped loudly in a sudden gust as if to prove his point.

I frowned up at the sky. A quilt of clouds had rolled in, casting a gloomy pallor over the beach. Being so near to the sea brought a constant breeze, but while the others had burrowed deeper into their wools, I felt more like I was roasting in front of a hearth. I'd stripped down hours ago to my thinnest linen layer, though it had done little to stop pearls of sweat from forming like a necklace along my throat.

Taran's toe caught in the sand, and he stumbled. I jumped forward to catch his arm. "Do you need to sit?"

He swatted me away. "I'm clumsy, not weak."

"Maybe you should rest anyway."

"Let's stop," Luther cut in. "Just in case."

Taran threw his head back and whined. "We've rested enough. I'm ready to get to Umbros and see what trouble Her Majesty's going to get us all into this time."

"Don't test me today, Taran," Luther growled.

Taran shot me a look and pointed a thumb behind us. "*This is your fault,*" he mouthed.

"*Sorae's getting that thumb,*" I mouthed back.

We veered off the beach to a cluster of rocks, each of us taking the chance to shake out the windblown sand that had gathered in our clothes.

"Let me see your wounds," I insisted as I moved to Taran's side. The urge to check on the poultice had been nagging at me all day, though I was as nervous as I was eager. The herbs I'd collected in Arboros made up the strongest drawing salve I knew. If this didn't work to stop the godstone's spread, I wasn't sure what else I could do.

I cajoled Taran through his gripes about disrobing in the chilly weather and reached for the bandage on his ribs. His flesh felt ice cold under my palms. I convinced myself it was a positive omen—heat meant infection. Infection meant death.

My hands went still as I lifted the gauze.

I felt the weight of Taran's eyes watching me.

"What is it?" he asked. "Is it... is it bad?"

In the past, each new glimpse had revealed further spread of the poison, more ground lost to the dark invasion beneath his skin. I'd grown used to bracing for it, to throwing on a smile to distract him—and myself—from the slow defeat.

Nothing could have braced me for this.

"*Lumnos's tits*," Taran swore. "Is that...?"

Alixe and Luther rushed to my side, craning their necks to see.

I pulled off the gauze completely and stared at it, dumbstruck. The poultice had turned firm and black, resting like a lump of tar on the white linen.

And his skin...

"It's *healing*," Alixe breathed.

I struggled to find words. The gash in his side had slimmed to a thin cut surrounded by a patch of shiny pink flesh. The black veins that once splintered like lightning had receded and faded to a muted grey.

Taran sat up and tore off the bandage at his shoulder, contorting himself to get a better look. It, too, had improved remarkably. Though the wound was still large, the dark discharge had dried, and the poisonous web of veins had scaled back by half.

"This is good, isn't it? It's getting better?" Taran's face was bright, pleading for permission to give in to dormant hope.

"I don't know," I admitted. "I've never seen a salve work like this."

Luther crouched beside me and took the bandage from my hand to examine it. Tingles rippled where his skin brushed against mine, his nearness pulling me from my shock.

"Can you make more?" he asked.

I nodded and pulled off my rucksack to rummage for my supplies, then set to work preparing a new batch.

"It's not over yet," I warned, swiping away the sweat on my forehead. "The poultice is drawing out the infection, but it could spread again."

Taran gripped Luther by the shoulder as his grin spread from ear to ear. "She's not pretending everything's fine. That has to be a good sign."

Luther didn't answer, his focus consumed by my hands, engrossed in their every move. When I turned to clean off Taran's chest, Luther picked up the bowl to inspect it. "The Crowns have searched for a cure to godstone for centuries. If this is it—"

"It's not," I said. "My mother's notes said the toxin doesn't always respond." I balled some of the mixture in my hands to warm it and winked up at Taran. "Perhaps the Blessed Mother granted me a favor after all."

"The heathen repents!" he shouted gleefully.

"We are trying to stay hidden, Taran," Alixe scolded, but even she couldn't keep from smiling.

As my palm pressed to his chest, Taran sucked in air and winced. "Is it supposed to burn this time?"

"Burn?" I looked down at my hands. The liquid along the edges of the mixture had begun to bubble, and a light trail of steam rose from the top.

I frowned. "The water must have overheated in the canteen." I set that portion down to cool and reached for a fresh handful, taking it straight to Taran's chest.

Though he didn't pull away this time, his head cocked as he studied me. "Are *you* feeling alright?"

Luther's attention finally tore from the poultice. His eyes darted between me and Taran.

"I feel fine," I said. "Why do you ask?"

Taran wrapped his hand around my forearm. After a moment, he let go and shook out his palm. "It wasn't that slop that was burning. It's you."

Luther's back went rod straight. He reached for my arm. His face immediately twisted into a deep frown, then his palm moved to the side of my neck.

I leaned into it with a soft sigh. His skin was deliciously cold, a refreshing reprieve from the claustrophobic heat I'd been languishing in all day.

"You're burning up," he said gruffly.

"First you scold me for being too cold, now I'm too warm?" I joked.

He didn't laugh. None of them did.

Luther turned me to face him and cupped my face in his palms. He scowled at my skin like it had personally wronged him. "When did this start?"

"I'm fine. Just a bit overheated. Maybe I picked up a cold from my dip in the sea last night." I laughed awkwardly, shrinking a bit at his scrutiny. "I didn't know Descended could get fevers."

"We don't," Alixe answered. "Unless..." She stopped herself, eying Luther.

"Unless you were poisoned," Taran finished.

Luther's fingers tightened around me. "What have you eaten? Was your canteen filled from the spring? The berries you brought back, were they—"

"I'm not *poisoned*." I shot them all a stern look. "I am a healer you know, I do know what to look out for. I'm not achy or nauseous or light-headed. I'm just *hot*."

I reluctantly pulled Luther's hands away and gave them a squeeze. "I'm fine, truly. If I start to feel ill, I'll say something so we can rest. I promise."

His eyes roved over me. He was plainly unconvinced, but there was little he could do.

When I moved to pull back, he gave the faintest grip of resistance, not quite ready to let me go. The moment my fingers finally slid away, his emotions retreated back behind his mask, and the stoic Prince returned.

He took my mortar and pestle to wash in the seawater, and Alixe strolled further down the beach to scout, leaving Taran and I alone.

"You're going to put that man in an early grave from worrying over you," he said.

"Has he always been like this?"

"Overprotective?" Taran barked a laugh. "You have no idea. He thinks anything bad that happens to someone he cares about is *his* failure."

Atoning for his mother's death, I thought sadly. *He couldn't save her, so he's trying to save all of us.*

Taran leaned back on his hands as I shifted to bandage his ribs. "But the way he is with you? I've never seen him like that with anyone but Lily. We always said any boy who wanted Lil's heart would have to have a death wish." He grinned and flexed his abs under my hand. "Turned out he just needed a pretty older sister."

I rolled my eyes. "All Descended are pretty."

"Fine. A *feisty* older sister." He stared up at the sky. "Blessed Mother, you have one hell of a sense of humor putting those two couples together."

I flopped down beside Taran and stared out at Luther, who was still hunched over the water giving my tools a thorough scrub.

There were no words to explain the darkness that had consumed me in those brief, desolate moments when I'd believed he might be dead. The possibility of life without him had been a suffocating fate. Finding him alive was like learning how to breathe again.

"Do you really believe that?" I asked Taran. "You think the gods decide who we're meant to be with?"

"What's wrong with that?"

"I thought your mating bond ritual was about choosing the person you want to be with forever. If the gods have already paired us up, that's hardly a meaningful choice."

"The Kindred offer us gifts, but we don't have to accept them." He nudged me with his leg. "You almost chose someone else."

"So did he," I muttered, remembering how Luther had nearly sold his life away to Iléana to protect me from House Hanoverre.

"If he died tomorrow, who's to say Lumnos wouldn't bring someone else into your life who cares for you just as deeply as Lu does?"

"That seems unlikely," I murmured. My heart lurched at the thought.

"Maybe so." Taran's voice turned quiet. "But we don't always get to keep the people we love forever, so let's hope it's true."

Far in the distance, the rumble of thunder rolled through the air. The clouds above had darkened, the heavy air a portent of a coming storm.

Taran slapped his hand on my leg and rose to his feet. "This conversation is depressing. You got back safely from Arboros, I'm healing, and we're almost out of *fucking Ignios*. Today is a day for celebrating. And look..."

A hazy black shape hovered over his open palm. It was cut like a gemstone, but instead of sparkling under the light, within its facets the darkness seemed to rebound forever.

"Your magic is back again?" Alixe asked, walking up. "You had it once already this morning."

Taran wiggled his fingers and the gem shifted into a miniature shadowy gryvern. It wove in circles around me, nipping its dark fangs at my thumbs.

I grinned and scratched the tiny creature beneath its jaw. It gave a happy wiggle of its haunches then flew up to perch on my shoulder.

When I touched Taran's magic, I could feel the hum of his power over my skin—not the vast, dominant aria Luther's had been, but formidable nonetheless. I could also sense its friendly intentions, so much like its bearer.

I wondered what Taran's godhood demanded of him. Did it insist that he *fight*, like mine usually did? Or did it tell him to *tease?* To *grin?* To *drink?*

"It's coming back more frequently," Alixe said to Luther as he returned. Hers had appeared earlier as well, providing temporary safety while we walked under the cloak of her illusions. "Any sign of yours?"

"Not since the other day," he answered.

He looked at me in question, and I shook my head. I'd been waiting all day for some whisper of the *voice's* call. With my luck, the flameroot would wear off the very moment the danger had ended.

We resumed our trek, our pace brisker thanks to our new confidence in Taran's health. He kept Alixe and I entertained with shadow magic creations that grew increasingly obscene, while Luther fell further and further behind.

The storm continued its foreboding approach to land, bringing stronger winds and a darker sky. With the sun obscured by the clouds, it was nearly impossible to know how close we were to nightfall—and, thus, how close we were to Umbros.

Every turn along the coast had us stretching our necks for a glimpse of the realm's infamous black rock canyons, only to be greeted with more Ignios sand.

I second-guessed everything about my plan. What if the King flew overhead on his gryvern or his guard came riding over the dunes? What if they were already waiting for us at the border?

Worse—what if Taran's fear had been right, and Umbros brought even more danger than Ignios?

We'd been safe enough in the abandoned Mortal City, but I, in my infinite wisdom, had thrown around the weight of my Crown and forced us to go, all on some hunch that *onward* lay our salvation.

I looked back at Luther. He'd been staring at the ground, his hood pulled low, but his eyes rose to mine in an instant.

Trust your instincts, my Queen, he'd told me. *Above all else, trust yourself.*

After what I'd done last night, did he still believe those words? Did he still believe in *me*?

I laid a palm across my chest. Seconds later, I got my answer: with a slow nod, he did the same.

"Wait," Alixe hissed from up ahead.

We'd approached a rocky outcrop where she crouched at the point, peering down the beach.

"Three guards," she whispered. "They don't look like they're searching."

"Might be a watchpoint to look for anyone crossing the border off the Ring Road," Taran said.

"Can they kill us just for that?" I asked.

"Not unless they realize who you are," Luther said.

"We could wait here and hope my magic returns to hide us," Alixe suggested. "But the longer we wait, the more we risk being caught."

Taran pushed his shirt up his forearms, an excited gleam in his eyes. "There are three of them and four of us. If we strike first and I use my shield to stop their flames, we can take them down."

"An unprovoked attack on Ignios soil might start an entirely different war," Alixe warned.

Luther nodded. "There's no good option." He turned to me. "It's your decision, my Queen."

I stiffened.

Right... Authority. Control. Deference.

This was what I'd demanded from them.

Though the Crown was hidden away inside me, I felt its weight on my head more than I ever had.

I looked at Taran. "Do you still have your magic?" He conjured a shadow spear in response, and my insides knotted. "Then we go now—but we don't attack. Not unless we have no other choice."

"Yes, Your Majesty," they answered in unison.

They began moving like clockwork, their years of training together now acutely apparent. Luther issued commands about formation, attack strategy, what to say, when and how to retreat. Alixe and Taran acknowledged each order, their faces hard and battle-ready, adjusting their weapons.

Luther came behind me and pulled my cloak from my pack, then laid it across my shoulders. Despite the hard line of his mouth, his hands moved tenderly as he swept my hair over my shoulder and tucked it behind my ears to hide it from sight.

He wrapped a thick scarf around my neck and pulled my hood low over my head. "Keep your face down when we pass." He brushed a thumb along my cheekbone below my eyes. "Save these for me."

His palms skimmed over my hips and thighs to check each of my weapons. His touch left a trail of heat that set my already overwarm body ablaze.

Instinctively, I arched toward him. It was a biological imperative, this eternal craving to be closer, closer, and closer to him still.

My mind went to wildly inappropriate places as I wondered if that need would ever feel sated, even if his body was on me, *inside me.* He might have read those thoughts, with the way his mouth lingered near mine and his eyes burned with hunger.

But a moment later, he was gone, standing with Taran and debating the best non-magical defenses.

Still, the heat remained. My core was boiling, provoked by his protective touches and the mountain of heavy fabric suffocating me in my textile coffin.

"Alixe," I whispered, pulling her to the side. "If things go badly, I want you to take Taran and run to Umbros without me."

"You expect me to abandon my Queen to the enemy?" She looked offended I would even ask.

"You heard the King back in Mortal City. He wants me alive, but he told his guards to kill all of you. If it looks like we'll be captured, we're better off separating. You can go to Umbros and get Taran a healer, then send for help."

Though conflict was scrawled all over her face, she lowered her chin. "Yes, Your Majesty, if that's your order—but Luther will never agree."

I took a deep breath. "I know."

We gathered in a cluster, Alixe in front and the men close at my sides, and made the turn around the corner into view.

The distant chatter of the Ignios guards fell silent.

We walked on, my chin tucked and eyes lowered. I nervously fidgeted with my scarf, fighting the growing urge to rip it off my inflamed skin.

"*Shit*," Taran said under his breath. He flexed his hand. "My magic's gone."

My heart sank. I'd made the wrong call. Without Taran's magic, we were entirely defenseless from the Ignios guards' fire magic.

"Doesn't matter," Luther mumbled. "No turning back now."

"Halt," a voice barked from ahead. I didn't dare look up at the sound of boots approaching. "What's your business here?"

"Just passing through," Alixe answered. "We're on our way to the port in Umbros."

"You're supposed to stay on the Ring Road."

"We heard the beaches of Ignios were too beautiful to miss," Taran said. He let out a low whistle. "They do not disappoint. I love all your... uh... sand. And rocks. And... water. I think I even saw a tree somewhere—"

"You can't be here," the guard snapped. "Without an invitation from His Majesty the King, foreigners are to remain on the Ring Road."

"Our apologies," Alixe said. "The border is just ahead. Perhaps you might let us by this once so we can exit your realm with haste?"

A long silence followed, then quiet whispering and the crunch of footsteps on sand. Luther's hand pressed lightly against my back as my three companions pushed in closer to me.

"When did you leave Arboros?"

"Just this morning," Taran answered, giving me a suggestive elbow to the ribs.

"What were you doing there?"

"Hunting mortals." He said it so happily, so eagerly. I would have shivered, if my skin wasn't currently imitating the sun's surface. "A family friend was hurt in the attack on Coeurîle. We heard the Guardians responsible might be there, and we wanted to find 'em and make 'em pay."

"And did you?"

Taran bounced on his toes, his elbow prodding me again. "Let's just say the guy won't be *clapping* the next time he sees us."

Movement caught my eye. One of the guards had come up behind me. Their gloved hand reached for my hood.

Luther's arm curled around my waist and yanked me close to his chest. "Keep your hands off my mate," he snarled.

The sound of blades sliding from their sheaths rang out, followed by the hiss of fire. Warmth bloomed through me and set my mind reeling. At first I thought I'd been hit by the Ignios magic, but Luther's heartbeat was steady, his body still.

Perhaps it was the press of him against me—or the words he'd just spoken.

"You don't tell us what to do, *foreigner*," the guard behind me spat.

"We're not here to cause any trouble," Alixe soothed. "Our friend meant no harm by it. They're newly mated and still adjusting to the bond."

"You think that was bad, try sharing a camp with them," Taran joked. "None of us are getting any sleep."

One of the other guards chuckled.

"They're relentless, those two. All night long. Like rabbits."

More laughter.

"I tried to join in last night and he stabbed me right in the balls. Me, his own flesh and blood! It's still healing, wanna see the wound? Here, let me just take off—"

"Keep your pants on," the guard behind me muttered. "You can continue to the border, but stay near the water. No wandering into the dunes."

"We'll head straight out," Alixe agreed.

We immediately hurried past. Luther remained at my side, his arm locked around my waist.

I dared a glance forward, relieved to see an abrupt wall of black on the horizon—Umbros was finally within sight.

We might make it through this after all.

Once we were out of the guards' earshot, Luther ordered Alixe and

Taran to fall back, giving us a small window of privacy.

"Are you alright?" he asked. "I can feel the heat through your cloak."

"I'm fine," I said tightly.

I was not fine. My heart was racing, my blood pounding, my skin broiling. My hair was stuck to my face with sweat, my clothing soaked in it. The adrenaline brought on by the confrontation with the guards wasn't fading —it was *building*, as if preparing for some greater fight.

"What I said back there, about you being my..." He cleared his throat. "I was only trying to scare the guard off. If it made you uncomfortable—"

"It didn't," I rushed out. "It's fine. I'm fine."

That was also not *fine*.

Even though I knew it was an act, hearing the word "mate" from his mouth, hearing him claim me in that profound, irrevocable way was...

Confusing, maybe. Surprising, definitely.

Breath-stealing. Heart-whirling. World-shifting.

I was never a woman who had dreamed of commitment. I'd always met any attempt to contain me with a stubborn resolve to push back harder. Henri's marriage proposal had sent me running, and even when I'd eventually accepted, it had been with the grim awareness that his mortal life was short, and eventually I would be on my own again.

So to hear Luther call me mate, a bond that would permanently bind us through this life and beyond...

I should have been panicking. Shutting down, raising my walls. Fleeing for the hills.

And yet... I wasn't.

I dabbed at my flushed, sweat-soaked face with the corner of my scarf. Gods, why was it so unbearably *hot?*

"Are the guards out of sight yet?" I asked.

"Not yet. Are you sure you're feeling well?"

I turned my face up to him, trying to conjure up some semblance of a reassuring smile.

He stopped. "Diem, your eyes—they're *glowing*."

"They are? I mean, uh... good. My magic must be coming back." I tugged the scarf loose from my neck. It was getting hard to breathe in this heat, let alone think.

Luther didn't look convinced. "I've never seen them like that." He squinted and leaned in. "That doesn't look like Blessed Lumnos's light."

A slow rumble of thunder sounded across the sea, nearer this time. The telltale haze of approaching rain was visible on the horizon.

"Come on," I urged, tugging on his cloak. "We're almost to Umbros."

"You promised you would say something if you started to feel worse."

I clenched my jaw. I really needed to leave the promise-making to Luther.

"I do need a break," I grudgingly admitted. "But not until we're out of sight of the guards."

"The beach is straight until the border. I'm not sure we'll have a chance until we cross."

"I can make it."

Now even I was unconvinced.

Luther frowned. "At least have some water." He grabbed his canteen and twisted off the cap. I reached for it and our hands collided, sending water sloshing over the top.

The second the drops hit my skin, they sizzled and disappeared.

We both stopped. We looked at each other, then down at my hand.

He tilted the canteen over my wrist. The streams of liquid hissed against my skin, then evaporated in a tiny white wisp of steam.

"Impossible," he breathed.

"Is something wrong?" Alixe asked as she and Taran caught up to us.

"No," I blurted out, snatching my wrist back. "Let's keep going. We're almost to Umbros."

I turned before they could see me and walked as fast as I could for the border, the urge to escape Ignios becoming unbearable. I couldn't shake the feeling that if I stayed on this beach much longer, I was going to combust.

Something scratched at the back of my neck, and I yanked my scarf off completely. There were holes along the fabric, their edges blackened and curled. It looked as if someone had held it over a candle, just to let it—

Burn.

My breath hitched. The *voice* was back. The godhood was still weak from the flameroot, only a fragment of my full reservoir, but my magic was unmistakably there.

A relieved laugh almost bubbled out of me, though one gnawing worry held me back.

I had never heard that command.

The *voice* had told me to do a lot of things—to *fight*, to *destroy*, even to *kill*. It had talked to me, taunted me, pushed me, challenged me.

But it had never told me to *burn*.

The others' voices grew behind me. I could barely hear them over the crackle of a roaring fire building in my ears.

Burn.

"No," I whispered. "Not here. Not yet."

My sweat boiled away as quickly as it fell. I needed air, water, ice, relief, *something* to stop this torturous, inescapable heat.

The border was close, but still too far. Maybe if we ran—the guards would be suspicious, they might pursue us, but if we were faster...

I looked over my shoulder to gauge the distance.

"*Shit*, Queenie," Taran swore.

"You're glowing," Alixe gasped.

"My eyes, I know."

"No, Diem, your hands," Luther said.

I held up my palms and choked out a surprised cry. Every inch of my skin was bright red. Not just flushed or irritated—glowing, molten *red*.

I looked at the border, then the guards, then the border. The roaring grew in my ears, my vision tinging orange.

Burn.

"It's too far," I mumbled. "I... can't make it." I shoved off my ruck-sack and fumbled with the clasp on my cloak.

Luther's face filled with alarm. "What are you doing?"

"I need to cool off. It can't wait."

"The guards will see you," Alixe hissed.

Burn.

With a frustrated cry, I yanked a dagger from my hip to slice through the cloak's fastening. The heavy fabric fell from my shoulders, giving a flicker of sweet relief as the sea breeze gusted over my skin.

It lasted only a second as the suffocating, consuming heat roared back to life. I ripped off my weapons and staggered toward the shore, desperate to cool the inferno inside me.

Burn.

The moment I hit the sea, I collapsed to my knees. The water bubbled and steamed where it pooled around my skin.

Luther ran to my side and reached for me, and I scrambled to get away. "Stop—I don't want to hurt you."

He moved closer, undeterred. "Let me help you."

"No! Luther, I—"

BURN.

I couldn't take it anymore.

My control snapped. With hardly a choice, I surrendered.

And I *burned.*

CHAPTER

TWENTY

Everything was fire.

The glowing destruction was an infinite expanse. My skin, my clothes, my breath, my vision, my heart—all of it transformed into a searing, oppressive blaze that flooded the world in orange and red. The crackle of the flames turned deafening as I spun in search of a way out, finding only more fire, more fire, *more fire*.

It was as much inside me as on me and around me. My soul was smoldering, my spirit scorched. There was no "burning" and "not burning." There was only the fire.

Everywhere, the fire.

And the strangest part was that it felt *incredible*.

There was no pain, no welts or blisters—only the most exquisite sensation of release. The flames burned away the tension in my muscles and melted the fear clutching my heart. I felt lightweight, liberated, unleashed from some long dormant cage. It was a carnal kind of pleasure that had me laughing, then gasping, then moaning.

I was a creature of the embers, fire incarnate, a living flame. If this was what it meant to burn, I wanted to burn forever.

Maybe I would. This was how I'd always envisioned eternity in the Everflame of the mortal religions. Perhaps I had died on that beach—a surprise attack by the Ignios King, thrusting me into the afterlife without warning. Perhaps the great sacred tree had found my soul worthy and was welcoming me into the warmth of the Undying Fire.

Perhaps my father would be here. He would wrap me into one of his loving hugs and tell me he had been watching me. That he was *proud* of me. Dying wouldn't be so bad then. I missed him so much. So very, very much.

But when I walked deeper into the flames and gazed into my forever, a different man's face stared back. One look at those blue-grey eyes, so aglow with concern, and I knew it was not my time.

Not yet.

He called out my name, the sound of it resonating deep inside me. He was so close...

Too close.

"I'll burn you," I protested. I backed away and moved deeper into the sea. The rolling tide rose to my chest, the flames gurgling beneath the water.

Luther didn't relent, slowly following me into the waves, though his features twisted in pain.

"Go back," I pleaded. "I don't want to hurt you."

"It's not—" He locked up, his body shuddering.

"Luther, *please*, stop, the flames are burning you!"

"They're not. They won't." His voice was unwavering despite the discomfort written all over his face. He stretched out his hand. "Let me touch you."

He was so confident, so staunchly certain. And he had never led me astray before.

Tentative, terrified, I walked toward him.

My fingers trembled as they curled around his. I scoured his reaction for any sign of pain, but my touch seemed to have the opposite effect. The tightness in his jaw, the strain in his muscles—it melted away the moment he folded me into his arms.

"Deep breaths," he urged. "I've got you."

I realized I was gasping with panic, heaving for air. I slumped against him and forced my lungs to slow until each breath matched the soft, steady rise of his chest.

"You're mastering it so quickly," he murmured into my hair, his tone full of pride. "Our clothes aren't even burning."

I glanced down. The fabric enrobing both our bodies was intact, soaked beneath the water but dry where it touched the flames.

"I—I don't understand," I stammered. "I shouldn't be able to do this. I *can't* be doing this."

A vicious tremor rolled down my back. Luther slipped a hand behind my legs and lifted me, cradling me in his arms. I clung to his shoulders, head buried in his neck.

"What's happening to me?" I whispered.

He hesitated, then turned toward the beach. "We'll find answers later. Right now, let's go home."

The Ignios guards had indeed seen us, but they had not run to confront us. Instead, they were waiting, watching—and casting a column of fire into the sky.

The flames reignited across my body as we emerged from the sea. The water had tempered the fire's effects, but on dry land, it threatened to devour me whole.

I closed my eyes and wrestled against the urge to give in to its decadent release as Alixe and Taran joined us, their voices swirling in a flurry.

"What happened?"

"Is she being attacked? Is she hurt?"

"How is it not burning her? And why isn't it burning you?"

"Her magic's returning. She could be shielding."

"Why aren't the guards coming?"

"I don't like the look of that fire pillar."

"Neither do I."

"We need to get to the border. Fast."

"I'll get her bag—you three go ahead."

"I can walk," I tried to protest, but it came out all flames.

I didn't actually know if I could walk—or talk, or breathe, or do anything but *burn*.

Luther clutched me to his chest as they hurried down the beach. His muscles twitched beneath my touch, small grunts of effort catching in his throat.

"I can walk," I said again, louder. I poured my focus into willing the combustion to subside, and the flames dimmed to a flickering halo.

Luther's grip on me tightened. "Not yet," he whispered into my ear. His throat bobbed. "I'm not ready to let you go."

Shouting struck up in the distance behind us, then bootsteps, loud and steady. But not running—more like a march. Left, right, left, right. Growing louder and louder, nearer and nearer.

Thump, thump, thump.

No—not bootsteps.

Wings.

"Put me down," I shouted. "*Put me down!*"

Luther set me on my feet, though his hands stayed fixed on my hips. I twisted in his arms to face Alixe.

"Go," I yelled at her. "You have to go!"

Her eyes went wide. She looked up, scanning the sky, and I lunged forward to grab her arm. She flinched, then relaxed as my flames licked harmlessly around her.

"Remember what I said, Alixe. This is a battlefield, and I gave you a command." My tone went hoarse and desperate. "Obey your Queen."

She sagged, her expression tortured.

"What's going on?" Luther demanded. His eyes darted between us. "What command?"

Taran caught up to us carrying my bag and my weapons. I turned to him with a fierce stare.

"The King is coming, but Alixe and I have a plan. I need you to trust me and go with her, Taran. She'll tell you what to do when you're there."

He frowned but nodded, handing off my broadsword. Alixe gave me a hard look, then jerked her head toward the border, and the two of them took off running.

"Diem—" Luther started.

I faced him and curved a palm beneath his jaw. "Go with them. Please, Luther. Do this for me, I'm begging you."

"Do what? Where are they going?"

"To Umbros. I ordered Alixe to save herself and Taran." Fury tore across his features. I pressed a finger to his lips before he could protest. "They'll only die if they stay. They can't help me without magic, and neither can you. Luther, please, let the King take me—"

"Never," he snarled, clutching my hand. "*Never.*"

I knew my pleas were futile. As long as he drew breath, Luther would fight the gods themselves to stay at my side.

It didn't matter—our time was up.

The King of Ignios had arrived.

THE IGNIOS GRYVERN'S massive shadow passed over us as it flew low across the beach, the flames engulfing me fluttering in its wake. I gritted my teeth and pushed against the strange fiery urges, managing to win my body back and contain them in a circle at my feet.

Luther pulled his scimitar as we watched the King's descent. Four guards sat behind him on the gryvern's back, while the three from the watchpoint ran to join them.

Dismal odds. Deadly odds.

The gryvern slammed onto the beach with a spray of sand and seafoam. It whipped its dark-scaled head toward the sky, sending the golden chain at its neck jangling before it released an ear-splitting howl.

Its yellow eyes cut to me. The glow of dragonfyre built in its throat, smoke unfurling between its fangs as a rumble rolled from its chest.

It was a terrifying display—and a warning.

That it would defend its King. That it *had* to defend its King. Whether it wanted to or not.

And that was... curious.

The King leapt off the gryvern's back, followed by his guards. Luther and I raised our blades.

"I've been looking for you," the King drawled. "Many people have been looking for you."

"I was captured by the Guardians during the attack on the island," I called out. "I escaped, and they chased me into your realm. I assure you, I'm not here by choice."

"What a dreadful story. How lucky that you *escaped*." There was a serpentine edge to his voice, like poison given sound. "Why did you not ask for my assistance?"

"Under normal circumstances, a visit from another Crown would be unwelcome."

"Indeed. But these are not normal circumstances." His gaze lowered to the flames at my feet. "And you're not just another Crown, are you?"

I swallowed.

He stroked a hand along his dark beard. "Why don't you return with me to my palace, and we can discuss this further?"

Luther moved closer, his shoulder edging just slightly in front of mine.

"I need to get home," I said. "My family must be worried."

"Ah, yes... a mortal brother, isn't that right? And a mortal mother who is now sitting in a Fortos prison for having planned that attack."

I swallowed again.

"I'm sure it was all a misunderstanding. My mother would never... that is, once I'm home in Lumnos, I can—"

"You're not going anywhere."

Luther moved further in front of me. "You don't give her orders. This may be your realm, but she is still a Queen."

The King's eyes narrowed. "A Queen who is wanted for questioning by the Crowns of Emarion. An edict has been issued for her capture until those questions have been answered."

Oh, that was *bad*.

My fiery corona flared in tandem with my apprehension. The King's gaze snapped to me.

"I have questions of my own," he said. "Beginning with how you're wielding *my* flames."

"She isn't," Luther answered. I looked at him in surprise. "One of your people is attacking her. She's merely shielding herself in defense."

The King cocked his head. "Oh? Is she shielding you, too?"

His hand whipped forward and launched a churning knot of flame at Luther's chest. We both raised our palms in reflex, but only my shield appeared, shimmering in front of him a heartbeat before impact.

The King looked amused, his growing smile sending a prickle down the back of my neck.

"Luther, get behind me," I warned.

He ignored my pleas, steeling his shoulders at the King. "You're wasting your time, Ignios. You cannot defeat her. Your magic is a glimmer—hers is the sun."

Normally Luther's faith in me would send my heart careening, but the flameroot had only just begun to wear off. It could be hours, even days, before my magic grew to its full strength.

More concerningly, it wasn't *growing* at all. Something was draining it at the source, shrinking it as quickly as it swelled. If this came down to a true firefight, I'd be extinguished in seconds. Even the quick burst of my shield had left me feeling unnervingly spent.

Perhaps the King saw the doubt on my face, because he advanced a few more steps and settled his gaze on me. "Come with me peacefully, and I'll let your friend here live."

I laid a hand on Luther's back.

"Don't even think about it," he growled.

"He won't kill me—I think," I said quietly. "You can find me again with the compass. Come back with more soldiers."

"There's not enough time. I don't..." His jaw ticked. "I'm not leaving you. Not until you're safe."

His fingers clenched around the hilt of his blade as he lifted it higher. "She's not going anywhere," he yelled across the beach. "And neither am I."

"Very well." Dark flames danced in the King's orange-hued eyes. He waved a dismissive hand at his guards. "Take her. Kill him."

My shouts of protest were lost in the arsenal that ensued. Spears, bolts, blades, balls—all of them forged in fire and tearing toward us without mercy. My shield flew up with a grunt of effort that pushed me back a step.

The attacks kept coming, round after round. Black curls of smoke wafted up as each volley dissolved, though fissures were already appearing in my glimmering dome.

"*Harder*," the King demanded. "It's seven of you against one half-breed. This should be done already."

His guards intensified their efforts, their attacks turning shapeless and raw. Their aim moved up and down, left and right, a deadly dance of flame that forced me to build my shield wider, then taller, then thicker. Every change required more effort, more magic, that I simply didn't have. The godhood thrashed inside me, desperate to escape the flameroot's suffocating red haze.

I let out a cry as my chest began to hollow out. Luther pressed his forehead to my temple. "Dig deeper," he said fiercely. "You're more powerful than you know."

The flames at my feet sputtered like a candle fighting a breeze. I clung to him as a web of cracks splintered across my shield. "It's still too weak. I—I can't..."

Luther's fingers dug into my skin. "Haven't I given enough?" he roared up at the sky, muscles trembling. "At least return my magic. Let me save *her*."

The Ignios guards changed their attack, hammering their efforts on a single point in my shield. Their grueling assault felt as if it were burrowing past my defenses and worming beneath my very skin.

I had a minute—seconds, maybe.

There was one hope left. A lark, a prayer, a shot in the dark, an insane instinct that could be the final one I ever had.

I gazed up at Luther. My fingers trailed the white ridges of the scar from his temple, down his sculpted cheeks, across his lips. If this was where it all ended, I wanted *him* to be my final memory.

"Do you trust me?" I asked softly.

"With everything I am," he vowed.

I gripped him by the shoulders and twisted until my back was to the guards. Luther's eyes went round in dissent, but a squeeze of my hand stopped him still. I held his stare, and with a sigh, my shield crumpled and collapsed.

Luther's face illuminated in a kaleidoscope of red and orange as the guards' lethal attacks found their target. The flickering glow of the Ignios fire played along his furrowed brows, gleamed in his icy eyes, cast dancing shadows in the curve of his throat. It was terrifying, and yet more beautiful than words could honor. It burned the air from my lungs and left me gasping and breathless.

Tingling spread across my back. Scorch and snow, heat and hoarfrost, inferno and ice. It was neither painful nor pleasurable, yet both all at once —and somehow invigorating. Reenergizing.

My magic sparked back to life, burning brighter with every blow. As I turned, careful to keep Luther behind me, I no longer bothered to raise my shield. Though the guards' strikes were still coming, they absorbed harmlessly into my skin.

The King looked *deeply* unsettled.

With a swing of his hand, a tidal wave of fire rose and crested a head above me. I threw out my arms and accepted its crushing fall with a smile.

He tried again with a cannon of flame shot directly into my chest. I laughed.

I *laughed*.

"What kind of shield is that?" he spat.

Honestly, his guess was as good as mine. It didn't even feel like I was using my magic at all.

I had no idea how this was possible, but that had become my baseline state these days. My eyes, my body, my magic—none of it conformed to the Descended's neat little rules. All I knew was that it was my best hope of getting us out alive.

"It's the kind of shield you can't destroy," I crowed. "Let us leave, Ignios—while you still can."

His lip curled back over his teeth. "You're not leaving my realm, half-breed. If you refuse to fight like a Descended, then we'll kill you like a mortal."

A chorus of metal sang across the beach as weapons unleashed from the guards' restraints.

I lifted my broadsword. "Ready, my Prince?"

Luther shifted to my side. "Always, my Queen."

First came the long blades.

Though my father had trained me for all manner of battles, a sword was my weapon of choice. I preferred the distance it gave me from my opponent —the space to study their moves and read their tells. In a duel of long blades, the real adversary was my opponent's mind. No matter their size or strength, if I could outwit them, I could outwin them.

We fought well together, Luther and I. He also favored a sword, and unlike me, he was used to fighting in a scrum. He adeptly swerved and sidestepped each attack, then cut them off as they tried to surround us. Through all of it, he never strayed far from my side, his watchful eyes always guarding my back.

But I was doing just fine. The fighting exhilarated me, galvanized me. It mended the cracks in my broken spirit. Were our lives not on the line, I dare say I might have been having fun.

Then came the short blades.

Here, the stakes were higher. Short blades required speed, dexterity, clever footwork, familiarity on the terrain—all areas where Luther and I were at a disadvantage in our worn-down state.

The Ignios guards were mostly women. Small and lithe, quick on their feet. They darted across the sand with ease while we staggered and slowed.

They began to land small blows. A cut here, a slice there. Nothing grave enough to bring us down, but enough to leave us bleeding and off-kilter.

They were coordinated, well-trained, efficient.

We were exhausted, injured, outnumbered.

But we had one thing in our favor. We wanted to *live*—and we fought like it, every swing of our swords fueled by a desperate will to survive.

And as it turned out, they wanted to live, too. They took few risks, retreated too quickly. I saw it in the annoyed glances they cast at their King, who lounged at his gryvern's side, far from the melee. Whatever squabble he had with us, it was clear his guards did not deem it worth *their* deaths.

I needed some way to end this. The trickle of my returning magic had built to a shallow pool. If I used it wisely...

A break in the fighting dawned. I fell to my knees and slammed my palms to the sand, casting a barrier of blinding, silvery light.

Without saying a word, Luther understood my plan. He grabbed my hand, and we sprinted for the border.

"I'm almost drained," I panted in warning. "I can't hold them back much long—"

A shocked cry choked off my words as a wall of flame shot up at our feet. Though I felt only a tingle, Luther swore as the fire singed his sleeve, leaving a long red welt running up his arm.

The gryvern launched into the air behind us and flew overhead, setting down a few wingbeats later on the opposite end of the fire. The King sat tall on its back, smirking.

"Go," Luther barked at me. "His magic can't stop you, and he's too much of a coward to fight you by hand. If you run, you can make it."

My grip tightened on him. "I'm not leaving you."

He looked at me, a dark defeat already carved into his features. "It's too late for me. You have a world to lead, Diem. You have to go." He pulled me in and pressed a hard, lingering kiss to my lips.

A kiss that felt a lot like a goodbye.

I shoved him off. "Not without you," I hissed. "Together until the end, remember?"

His expression turned anguished, provoking a heavy knot of disquiet in my gut. "I believe in you, Diem. Don't ever forget that."

I shook my head, tears burning my eyes. "No, Luther, we can still fight—"

"Let me do this one last thing for you." He caressed my cheek. "Go, my Queen. *Live*."

"What's the matter, Lumnos?" the King yelled mockingly. "Can't your shield protect you?"

His smile curved wider and crueler, his eyes gleaming with the excitement of someone who had just unlocked a tricky riddle.

"Or is the problem—" He paused and raised a finger toward me as I braced for another assault. "—that it can't protect *him?*"

His finger twitched toward Luther, and a spear of flame lurched for my Prince's heart.

"No," I cried, throwing myself in its path. I gasped in relief as icy heat spread throughout my shoulder.

"I see," the King chuckled. "Don't bother with her. Set your blades on him."

I tried to raise another flare of light to blind them. My magic guttered and went dark—along with the mysterious flames coating my body.

The King's wall of fire began rolling forward. It licked at Luther's back, forcing him closer to the guards. He was surrounded—and there was nothing I could do to help.

Luther looked at me, a farewell in his eyes. "I will always be with you, Diem. I—"

A blur of grey flashed in front of his face. We both froze—then another blur flew at his thigh and struck.

Luther grunted and clutched at his leg. A dark red stain bloomed around the handle of a throwing knife jutting from his flesh.

"Stop!" I yelled at the King. "I'll give myself up. Spare him and take me!"

"Don't you dare," Luther snarled. He staggered toward me and shoved me hard just as another blade tore through his arm.

I careened through the King's flames, the disorienting cold-hot sensation flushing through me as I fell to the sand. When my vision steadied, the King's gryvern had arched its neck toward me. It watched me, blinking slowly.

Something stirred in my chest. A forgotten intuition, a memory you know exists but can't quite recall. In the depths of the creature's dark golden eyes, there was... not a message, exactly. Almost an emotion, as if—

Lightning splintered down from the darkening clouds, followed by a booming crack of thunder. Rain began to patter as the storm made landfall.

The sound of Luther's pained growls stole my attention. The King's fiery wall blocked him from my view, but the trail of blood in the sand told me enough.

"Call the guards off," I pleaded with the King. "Let him pass safely into Umbros, and I'll answer your questions."

The King calmly surveyed Luther from his spot high atop the gryvern. "He's fighting very hard for you. I don't think he's going to let you go without a fight."

"Don't do this. I'll surrender, I'll do anyth—"

"And even if I did, what's to stop him from returning to save you? He'll bring more of his friends to cause trouble in my realm."

"Please, *please*, I'm begging you—"

"As long as he lives, he's going to be a thorn in my side." He gave a drawn-out sigh that dripped with feigned sympathy. "This is better, in the end. A nice, quick death, so you and I can talk undisturbed."

He raised a palm toward Luther. I launched off the sand, hurling myself through the fire and praying I wasn't too late.

The flames blinded me for a moment—then Luther was there, his head turning toward me as I screamed his name.

He had no time to notice the Fortosian steel dagger spearing straight for his heart.

CHAPTER
TWENTY-ONE

W hat happened next was a blur.

There was movement and shouting. Fire and metal. Pain, then blood.

More shouting. More blood.

So much blood.

I laid on my back in the sand, fat raindrops splattering across my face, and a warm sense of acceptance spread through me. I couldn't help but smile.

What I'd done was reckless.

Irrational.

Irresponsible.

Desperate.

Possibly pointless.

And I didn't regret it for a second.

"Diem," Luther choked out at my side. His voice sounded hoarse. Pained. "What have you done?"

A strong arm slid beneath me and lifted me from the ground. Another hand brushed across my chest—and stopped.

Stopped on the gleaming hilt of a dagger, rising from the center of my chest.

Two blue-grey eyes moved into my vision. They were sad, so very sad, but filled with the most breathtaking sea of twinkling sparks and inky depths. The evening sky and the daylight, colliding together into a cloud of broken, glittering shards.

I wanted to tell those eyes something. Something important. But when I tried to speak, a coppery tang flooded my throat.

"It should have been me," he said roughly. "I should have told you." He pulled me into his body, hunching over me.

"Magic," I managed to gasp out.

He looked at me, confused, distraught. Not understanding. Rain soaked through his long, dark hair, matting it to his blood-flecked olive skin.

"You idiots," the King snarled in the background. "I said to kill *him*, not her."

A weighty presence spread across my body, squeezing me, holding me, caressing me, consuming me. It was immensely strong, its fierce grip impossible to fight. It dragged me in and held me close, refusing to let me go.

"Now I have a mess to clean up," the King grumbled. "I don't need Sophos sniffing around looking for her body to run their tests on."

"M-magic," I stammered again. My eyelids drooped. The strange sensation was warm, inviting. It felt safe. It felt like *home*. I wanted so badly to stop fighting and surrender to it forever.

Luther laid me out on the sand and yanked a scarf from around his shoulders, hurriedly folding it into a square. With quivering hands and tortured eyes, he pulled the blade free, and hot liquid spilled across my chest. He covered the wound with the fabric, leaning his weight into it.

"Firm pressure, right?" he asked, his eyes frantically searching mine. "But not too much?"

I wanted to nod, but there was something else I needed to say. Something so crucial, so vitally urgent, even more important than my own life.

A chill swept across my skin, and the orange glow around us disappeared. The King had dropped his wall of flames.

He sighed loudly. "We'll kill them both and incinerate the bodies with dragonfyre. If anyone asks, they were never in our realm, understood?"

Luther's eyes darted up, then back at me. He took my hands and placed them over the makeshift bandage. "Keep holding it," he ordered.

He brushed the hair away from my face, his touch lingering on my skin a moment longer. Then I watched as the cold mask of the Prince fell over his features. His focus shifted to the Ignios guards and his fist tightened, his mouth forming a harsh line.

He reached for his weapon and stood.

The powerful presence engulfing my body pulled away—just slightly. "Luther," I breathed. "*Your magic.*"

A deep rumble of thunder rolled over the sea.

Slowly, so slowly, his face turned back to me. Our eyes locked, his widening slightly in understanding. His scimitar tumbled to the ground at his side. His nostrils flared, and his chest expanded in a long, shuddering inhale.

And then Luther Corbois *unleashed.*

Light and shadow ignited across the beach in a dazzling explosion of fury and magic. I rolled my head away at the blinding force of it, only to see glowing whips snake over the sand and impale the Ignios guards. Pale blue fissures webbed across their skin, seeming to tear them apart from within, and the air grew thick with the smell of burnt flesh.

Dark vines laced with thorns curled up their legs and tightened until bone crunched and blood oozed from a hundred punctures. Their agonized screams turned garbled as shadowy tendrils punched through their guts and emerged writhing from their mouths.

I looked away, unable to watch the slaughter continue. I didn't judge Luther for what he'd done, but I could take no pleasure in it, either.

On the other side of the beach, the King stared in blank horror as my Prince massacred his guards with vicious, bloody ease.

His gryvern, however, was watching *me*. Still staring in that penetrating way, its reptilian eyes still pulsing with some profound feeling I couldn't yet place.

There was so much anger trapped within the beast. A vast, lava-filled cavern of rage bubbled under its ancient skin like a volcano churning against a ceiling of rock. As the Ignios guards' shrieks fell silent, I wondered with a tremble what might happen if the Ignios *gryvern* ever unleashed.

The King dismounted and summoned two gauntlets of fire that engulfed his lower arms. "Kill me, and my gryvern kills you."

"As long as I die knowing my Queen is safe, that's good enough for me," Luther snapped.

The King sneered. "I'll remember that when I'm carving her up over your corpse."

I'd always known Luther was powerful.

I'd heard the whispered gossip. I'd felt it in his aura, seen it churning behind his gaze. I'd sensed it in the way even the most confident of the Lumnos Descended avoided his notice.

Though I'd only seen him use it in small amounts, I never had to witness the full extent of his power to know it was something extraordinary.

But as I watched him reduce a Crown of Emarion to a sniveling heap in a matter of seconds, *extraordinary* seemed far too inadequate a description.

It was unthinkable I beat him out for the throne at all.

A faraway song played in my ears as Luther's magic consumed the beach. Unlike before, when I'd seen him shape it into objects or weapons, this was an eruption of pure, glittering day and violent, vengeful night. It came in a deluge from every angle, swirling around the King and his gryvern and trapping them within an enormous whorl of liquid dark.

Even the earth couldn't escape his wrath. The falling rain sizzled to steam as it collided with a crackling swarm of white-hot sparks that flowed from his palms. Granules of sand flew into the air, tossed by the rumbling tremors that rippled with each deadly blast of shadow. I could almost hear the roar of Luther's godhood in the deafening thunderclaps that trembled in the clouds.

The King's once-mighty flames looked pathetic in comparison. They glanced off Luther's magic and vanished, as effective as embers in a snowstorm. The whites of his eyes grew large as he abandoned his attacks and shifted all his effort to his shield, but that, too, was no match for my Prince. A seemingly infinite swarm of obsidian hands clawed razor-sharp nails along the shimmering barrier, and though the battle had barely begun, it fractured and gave way.

The King scrambled to hide beneath his gryvern, whimpering a plea for help, and Luther paused his assault. "Any final words you'd like me to pass on to your successor?"

The gryvern snorted angrily and snapped its wings. It hissed, eyes narrowing on me, and I finally understood what I'd missed before.

"Stop," I cried out.

Luther's head whipped to me. His eyes were wild, ablaze with pale blue light. For a moment, I saw nothing of the Prince I knew, his mind lost to the frenzy of his rage.

"Don't."

The vortex of crackling starlight spinning around him stilled in mid-air. His expression turned incredulous. "You want to *spare him?*"

With my heart slowing and my lungs full of blood, it was far too much to explain that it wasn't the King's life I was saving, but his. That the Ignios gryvern, obliged to avenge its King, was offering me a trade—the life of the man it despised for the life of the one I adored.

My head collapsed back onto the sand. "*Mercy,*" I gasped.

Luther's shoulders sank. He gave the King one final look that quaked with an enduring promise: someday, somewhere, retribution would come. He turned away and came to kneel at my side.

My gaze met the gryvern's. *Take him,* I said in silent request, knowing somehow the beast would understand. *I wish I could have saved you instead.*

The gryvern loosed a frustrated howl into the sky. It snatched the cowering King into its talons and took flight, disappearing over the dunes.

Luther's magic dissolved, and the beach turned eerily quiet, save for the soft patter of falling rain. His hands returned to my wound, his fingers threading into mine as he pressed hard on the makeshift bandage. The rage that had overtaken him in battle melted away, replaced with a frantic concern.

"You're going to heal," he swore, his voice rough. "You have to."

My chest burned as I choked for air. I needed some way to make him understand. Suddenly, so many pieces were falling into place—but getting him to agree would be damn near impossible.

"Magic," I mouthed.

His eyes scoured my face. "*My* magic?"

I nodded weakly.

A twinkling blanket of woven light spread from his hands and covered my body, draping me in his warm, protective energy. A feeling of peace settled in my spirit and silenced the excruciating ache scoring through my chest. The pain, the discomfort, the fear—in the caress of his magic, it all faded away.

I felt calm. I felt safe.

And I fought against it with everything I had left.

"Attack," I managed to rasp. My lungs wheezed with an alarming rattle. I pulled my hand from beneath his and pointed to myself. "*Attack.*"

Luther's horrified expression was exactly what I'd feared. I wasn't sure he was even capable of what I was asking him. It was carved into his marrow to protect me, not hurt me.

He wrapped an arm beneath me and held me against his body. His other hand, slick with my blood, curved around my neck.

He shook his head. "I can't. I won't."

The world began to blur, the sounds of the sea becoming muffled and distant. When I opened my mouth to speak, the only thing that came out was a rivulet of blood at the corner of my lips.

Agony wracked Luther's features, his heart crumbling in his eyes. The indecision tearing through his chest was as visible as the scar that marked his skin.

With considerable effort, I managed to lift my palm to his heart. "Trust," I mouthed.

He let out a sigh and nodded slowly.

Lowered his forehead to mine.

Laid a tender kiss on my lips.

And *attacked*.

Tentative at first—prickles on my arms, light jabs at my feet. He watched me from beneath lowered lashes, probing my reaction, before increasing his power.

The tingling sensation returned. Hot and cold, fire and ice, roaring through my veins. My heart stuttered, then picked up its pace.

Whatever Luther read in my expression, it bolstered his faith. He abandoned his hesitation and slammed his magic into me full-force with a blast of searing light. Glowing cords braided around my chest and squeezed with the brunt of his might.

My vision spotted, but the tingling endured. It was exploding, shattering, overwhelming. My wound began to itch. The blood cleared from my throat, leaving me gulping for breath.

My godhood stretched its hands toward the light. It sang a quiet entreaty, hopeful and serene. I knew I should wait, take more, but I couldn't hold back any longer.

I surrendered to its call.

A soft, harmonic melody filled my soul. Luther's aura no longer felt stunted, but gloriously, ethereally fulfilled. My magic burst beyond my skin to meet it, tumbling happily over his *attacks* like playful lovers having a romp.

Luther sucked in a sharp breath, and I knew he felt it, too. Our gazes met and shone in wonderous fascination. For a moment, one fleeting moment, our hearts beat together as one.

"Fuck, is she alive?"

Taran's voice shocked us both from our daze. He ran up the beach and threw himself onto the sand beside us, glaring at our many bleeding wounds.

"Their '*plan*' was for us to leave her behind," he said to Luther with a growl. "I didn't realize until we crossed the border. I came back as soon as—"

"I know," Luther said. "They tricked us both."

Alixe jogged up behind him and stared at me with apology and alarm. "Is she...?"

They all looked at me. All I could manage was a deep draw of breath and an exhausted nod.

Taran looked around at the graveyard of Ignios corpses. "Where's the King?"

"Alive," Luther answered with a glance at me. "He left with his gryvern."

"Then we should get as far away as we can before he comes back," Alixe said.

Luther cradled me and fought to stand. His knees shook under the effort as fresh blood spilled from the myriad gashes and burns marking his flesh.

"Let me take her, cousin," Taran said gently.

Luther tensed and gripped me closer. My heart squeezed—I understood all too well. When he finally relented and placed me into Taran's arms, I whimpered out a quiet protest of my own.

Alixe coaxed Luther into letting her take his arm over her shoulder, and together, the four of us hobbled through the rain until a painful surge snapped across our skin to mark the border. As the flames on my body slowly faded, Taran scowled down at me, a harbinger of the fight I knew was coming the moment I wasn't knocking on death's door.

"Thank you," I whispered, smiling.

He rolled his eyes, though he held me a little closer.

"*Fucking Ignios,*" he muttered.

PART TWO

CHAPTER
TWENTY-TWO

U mbros, Realm of Mind and Secret, was everything and nothing I imagined.

Rain-soaked and exhausted, we shuffled through the long tunnel that descended into the beating heart of Umbros City and took our first look at the famed city of shadows.

The entire capital had been built underground, carved into the realm's sky-high canyons of matte black rock. Cast into perpetual evening, its residents could thrive on the sins of the night no matter the hour.

Growing up, mortal gossip had painted it as a den of depravity, a place where nothing was sacred and everything was for sale. You could buy drugs, sex, weapons, poisons, a murder, a spouse—or a murderous spouse. If you had the money, it was yours for the taking.

The main square was a cavernous hall extending a mile in every direction—including up. Several levels of carved archways were stacked along the walls, and with tunnels splintering off as far as the eye could see, I suspected this was only the beginning of what hid in Umbros's shadows.

Although there was darkness, it was also a place of *life*. The mammoth, bustling central market was packed with merchants selling every creation I'd ever imagined and even more I hadn't. The air was rich with a medley of smells—roasted meats, heady incense, fragrant spices, intoxicating perfumes—and fluttering with textiles that painted the room in vibrant colors. A steady buzz in the air hummed with voices, punctuated by the pluck of stringed instruments and warbling singers. Crowds of raucous spectators ringed sandy fighting pits, and caged beasts chirped, snarled, and hissed at passersby.

Most shockingly for me, eyes of every color were woven seamlessly throughout the throng. There was no segregation, no poor village where mortals were shoved to be subjugated and unseen. Vendors and consumers alike were a melange of mortal and Descended, man and woman, local and foreign, and everything in between.

"Is that Lumnos light?" Taran asked, gaping up with jaw slung low. A web of spotlights springing from the ceiling littered the hall in tiny blue speckles.

Alixe nodded. "Descended who pay tithes to the Queen are permitted to use their magic. Looks like she put some of them to work."

"Keep your heads down," Luther warned. "We can't afford to attract any attention."

"Where are we going?" I gritted out. Though my wounds had healed enough for me to walk without coughing up blood, I was still badly injured.

"I have a contact here who can arrange passage," he said. "I'll need time to find them."

"I'm coming with you," I insisted. Alixe and Taran exchanged a tense glance, and I hurried on. "I know it's a risk, but I—"

Luther took my hand. "Agreed."

I couldn't tell which of the three of us looked more shocked.

"Alixe, Taran, we'll meet you by the fighting pits when we're finished." His features hardened. "If you're caught, you know what to do. Remember the oath of the Royal Guard."

They both nodded solemnly. I frowned.

Luther's eyes narrowed on Alixe. "You do still remember that oath, I hope."

She bristled. "I do."

"Good." He pulled me away, tucking me under his arm as we were swallowed up into the market.

"What's the oath of the Royal Guard?" I asked.

"Protect the Crown at any cost."

My frown deepened. "Shouldn't it be to protect the realm or protect its people?"

"That's your job. Ours is to protect you."

"I'm adding *that* to the list of things I need to change," I muttered.

His jaw tensed, but he said nothing.

As we pushed into the horde streaming between the stalls, I couldn't tear my eyes from the sharp lines of his face, silhouetted by pinpricks of light. To the rest of the world, he looked blank and impassive, but I recognized the temper within.

"Luther, if you're angry with Alixe for leaving us back in Ignios—"

"Angry doesn't begin to describe it. She'd be out as Vice General, if I had anyone I trusted enough to replace her."

I stopped and turned to him. "She followed my orders. You can't hold that against her."

"I can and I will," he said tightly. "I have to know there are people who —" His mouth snapped closed, and his expression shuttered. "We'll discuss it later."

He glanced down at the wound on my chest, which I'd haphazardly bandaged. He'd insisted on it—while refusing to let me tend to his own wounds, of course.

His eyes bounced back up to me and narrowed. "She's not the only one I intend to have words with about what happened today."

I swallowed. "I did what I had to do."

"We'll talk about *that* later, too."

"Luther, this is—" A passerby bumped against my side and sent me stumbling into Luther's chest. We both winced as the movement jostled our injuries, but despite his obvious pain, his arm curved around my back, drawing me closer.

"*Later*," he said again, gentler this time. He pulled my hood lower. "Right now, let's just get out of Umbros unseen and go home."

FOR ALL ITS SECRECY, Umbros was anything but *quiet*. From the moment we'd arrived in the city, my head had been filled with the buzz of voices. Here in the heart of the central hall, they pressed in on me like a tangible force.

The deeper we pushed, the louder they grew—whispering and shouting, cooing and sneering. It was deafening, infiltrating my thoughts in a muddled jumble of words. I cringed at the throbbing headache already beginning to form.

Though I wanted to seal myself off in a silent room and lose myself in a warm bath, a warm meal, and a warm bed, a part of me thrilled at the exotic newness of it all. I couldn't resist stealing curious glances at each stall we passed.

More than a few drew me in with the urge to see more, like one offering the rarest medicinal herbs and another packed with messy stacks of dusty, leather-bound tomes. Others had me burrowing into Luther's side, like the woman with turmeric eyes who tended a pit of live snakes beneath rows of bottled venom and, for thrice the price, antivenom.

In another, dirt-smudged children no older than ten stood in a long line, hands clasped, their eyes cast low. When a portly, gap-toothed man stepped forward and beckoned a finger to two young girls, I froze in place, seconds away from turning the market into a warzone.

The girls reached into their tattered, dirt-soiled garments and whipped out narrow blades. They launched into a display of whirling footwork and jabs that would have put even Alixe's prowess to shame.

"Assassins," Luther explained. "They pose as beggars, so their targets ignore them until it's too late."

"They're only children," I breathed, though in truth, I'd witnessed far darker fates for the orphans back in Lumnos. At least these girls had the means to protect themselves.

The man turned to a dark-haired woman, who dropped a pouch in his hand with a metallic clink. The girls looked at each other and beamed.

"I can't wait," the woman's voice carried to me as she turned. Something about it sounded strange—hushed, like a whisper, even though she was yards away. "They'll do to him what I should have when I was their age. I just wish I could see the bastard's face when it happens."

Her words faded as she disappeared into the crowd, the girls giggling and scurrying like ducklings behind her.

Luther's voice caught my ear as he muttered to himself in that same odd, hushed tone. "Need to get out of this market. Too many people here need saving, and her heart's too big to leave any of them behind."

I sighed and fell in step beside him. He wasn't wrong. It was easy to romanticize a place like Umbros, but it was another thing to see the reality of what it took to fulfill all those dark desires. Turning a blind eye had never been my strength. It was only a matter of time before I set this whole place ablaze.

"Give it time," he said, his voice returning to normal. "You will remake this world. You will be the voice they never had and the sword they were never allowed to wield."

"In Lumnos, maybe, but what about everywhere else?" I argued. "What power will I have in a place like this?"

My gaze dropped to my feet, and his hand stilled on my back. Again his voice took on that odd, whispered timbre. "Does she really not see it?"

I glanced back up. "See what?"

His brows jumped. "Did you—"

"Quit blocking my booth, will ya?" an irritated voice snapped.

An exceptionally short woman wedged herself between us, placing her hands on our thighs and shoving us apart. She grabbed a rag hanging from her shoulder and whipped it at Luther's groin. "If yer wantin' to feel her up, inns are over that way." She gestured to a far corner, then paused. "Now if yer lookin' to put on a public show..." She tugged on my cloak. "Lemme see your face girl, I may know a buyer."

Luther growled and snatched me away, leaving the woman cackling behind us.

At the edge of the market, a row of lopsided signs pointed to different areas of the city, labeled by the items sold within: *Gems, Weapons, Skin, Rooms, Boats—*

"Luther, look—I think the docks are this way."

"We're not going to the docks yet. We need someone who doesn't know who you are to book our passage in case they're stopped by the Centenaries."

The Centenaries.

A shiver rippled through me.

Umbros was a wild, lawless place, but one fundamental principle underpinned each and every clandestine arrangement: no matter who you were or what you sold, the Queen of Umbros *always* got her cut.

And she did it with the help of the Centenaries.

After the Descended's near-loss in the Blood War centuries ago, many realms set limits on Descended breeding in order to prevent their magic from becoming diluted and weak.

But none had gone as far as the Umbros Queen. She selected the one hundred most powerful of her Descended—the rest, she put to death. Over the years, she'd kept the number consistent, a small but formidable personal army known as the Centenaries.

According to rumor, if you were unlucky enough to cross them, your heart became ice and your skull became glass. Their staggering thought magic could read your mind like a book and bend you to their will.

It made them the perfect enforcers in a realm populated with liars and thieves. There was no secret the Centenaries couldn't uncover, no deception they couldn't detect. They collected their Queen's share of the profits with perfect efficiency, and because she could read *their* minds, even they didn't dare cross her.

Luther's plan was clever. If the Centenaries found us, they would know instantly the Queen of Lumnos was here, but if the person who booked our passage did not know of my presence, even the Centenaries would not be able to pry it out from them.

Although...

A small, pestering urge told me the Umbros Queen might have the answers I sought. She had already taken a special interest in me, ambushing me with strange riddles in the alley the day my mother had gone missing. At my Rite of Coronation, she'd been the only one unsurprised by the destructive effect of my blood on the heartstone. In fact, it had almost seemed like she was *expecting* it.

Seeking her out would be an enormous gamble, but if she knew something that could help me in the coming war...

"This way," Luther said. I kept close to his side as he led me out of the main hall and through the labyrinthine pathways. The buzz in my head began to die down, allowing my crowded thoughts some room to breathe.

"How do you know where to go?" I asked, rubbing my throbbing temples.

"I don't. I'm following those." He pointed to a spot high on the wall, where a sleek feline was carved into the rock, its long tail curled to the right. A fork appeared a few steps later, and Luther swiftly turned down the rightmost path.

"My contact here is known as the Jaguar," he explained. "I don't know much about him. We've only communicated through messenger hawks. We kept our identities secret in case either of us was caught. He said if I ever needed to find him in Umbros, his symbols would guide me there."

Another etching came into view, its tail in a sharp line to the left. Again, we shifted our route.

"How did you meet him?"

"Your mother, actually. He worked with her to—look, I think that's it."

Straight ahead sat a cozy-looking inn lit by a curtain of floating blue orbs and a sign that read "The Second Chance." Just above the entrance, a sleeping cat was engraved into the rock, its tail hanging lazily over the door.

I kept my head down as we passed through the sparkling drapes. The quiet dining room contained a handful of lone travelers hunched under heavy cloaks. A gaggle of children in white aprons scurried from table to table, refilling drinks and delivering plates of steaming food.

"Welcome to The Second Chance," a woman chirped brightly from behind the counter. "Are you in need of a room or just a meal?"

"Neither." Luther edged closer to her and lowered his voice. "I'm here to see the Jaguar."

She blinked, her smile unmoving. "There's no one here by that name."

"I know he's here." He pulled a handful of gold coins from his pouch, then set them on the wood beneath his cupped hand and slid them toward her. "Perhaps this will help lure him out?"

She slid them back. "Sorry. You have the wrong inn."

I risked a quick glance up. The woman was striking, with full, plum-colored lips and dark curls, but it was her brilliant cobalt blue eyes that sent my heart staggering.

A Lumnos Descended.

I had no right to claim her. She was clearly of age, old enough to decide for herself where she wished to make her life. The shadows twisting like jewelry around her arm suggested she'd paid her tithes and was a citizen in good standing with the Umbros Queen.

But she was one of *mine*. My godhood strained against the walls of my chest, begging to push out and enfold her within its protection.

She shivered, goosebumps rising on her arms. Her eyes moved to me. I swiftly lowered my chin until my hood dropped forward to conceal me.

Luther tapped a gold coin against the counter. "If there is anyone here by that name, he should know the Phoenix has come to see him."

She blinked again. "As I said, there's no one here by that—"

A door opened behind her, and a man emerged.

If this was the Jaguar, his name was well-earned. He moved with a cat-like grace, fluid and effortless, seeming to glide rather than walk. Though he was slender, cords of muscles swelled along his elegant frame, which was draped in swaths of black silk. A gilded metal collar rose high on his neck, while bands of gold wire encircled his thighs and biceps. His dark skin looked freshly oiled, shimmering under the dim light and setting off eyes of the palest ice blue—another Lumnos Descended.

But it wasn't just his beauty that overwhelmed me. The second he stepped forward, a wave of power brushed against my skin, similar to how I felt around Luther. Whoever this man was, his magic was strong—immensely so.

The man glanced my way, catching me mid-stare. A bolt of panic sliced through me as our eyes locked, but he gave me only a bored skim before settling his attention on my Prince.

With Luther, the man's gaze dragged slowly, deliberately, appraisingly. Luther's chin lifted, though he made no move in response.

It was a bizarre thing to watch Luther get sized up as a threat. In Lumnos, the strength of his magic made him infamous. Even those willing to provoke him, like Aemonn and his father, knew when to back down to avoid a battle they were certain to lose.

He was practically untouchable, and after he'd trounced the Ignios King, I'd begun to wonder if it was not just the Descended of Lumnos who should fear him.

But Luther's magic had disappeared again after crossing the Umbros border, leaving him vulnerable for now. If this *Jaguar* was weighing his strength against another Descended aura, it wasn't Luther's he felt—it was mine.

I let my godhood slip its leash for just a moment, sending a pulse of my magic rippling across the room. The man's eyes went round.

"You've been misinformed," he said, swallowing. "There's no Jaguar here."

Liar, I thought irritably.

Both Luther and the man shot me looks.

The man shifted his weight. "Perhaps you'd like to stay the night in our inn instead?"

"I don't need a room," Luther said. "Just a conversation."

"Our rooms are quite private. Ideal for conversations of all kinds." The man's slow cadence sounded curiously deliberate. "One might even say they're fit for a *prince*."

I tensed. So he did know who we were—or at least who Luther was.

Luther nodded once. The man looked at the woman at the counter. "Would you please show our guests to Suite 10?"

"Of course, Zal." She plucked a key from beneath the table and gestured for us to follow. "Right this way."

The man gave a tight smile and turned back to the door from which he'd entered.

Luther hesitated. "Aren't you coming with us?"

"My staff will take care of anything you need," he called out over his shoulder. "Have a lovely stay."

The door slammed shut.

CHAPTER
TWENTY-THREE

A s we walked through the long hallways of the inn, a number of workers scurried past, most of them young, all bearing eyes in shades of Lumnos blue. There were so many of them—far more than an inn of this size warranted.

Luther watched them with rapt interest. He seemed to be studying each of their faces in search of something. He was so distracted, he nearly collided into the woman when she stopped.

"Suite 10," she announced, unlocking a door and pushing it open. "You're very lucky. It's our nicest room."

I frowned. The other rooms we'd passed were clearly numbered, with brightly lit orbs floating over the entry. This door was blank, nondescript, and cloaked in darkness. Though I tried to peer inside, there was nothing illuminating the ominous space.

"The room is rather... dark," I said carefully. "Perhaps another room would be more—"

Before I could finish, the woman snapped her fingers at two older children nearby, a boy and a girl. As they dashed past me to enter, the feeling of another strong aura breezed over my skin. I could feel that it was young, but deep in its potential.

I raised an eyebrow at Luther in silent inquiry: *Did you feel that?* His lips pressed tight as he gave a subtle nod.

Within seconds, the children had adorned the suite with bouquets of luminescent flowers that bathed each room in a soft glow. Once lit, the space looked normal enough—a large sitting area, lined with bookshelves and packed with cozy settees, flanked on each side by twin bedrooms.

Luther nudged past me and stepped inside. His eyes swept over the room as he paced in an arc along the walls. He paused at the dining table and ran his fingers over a few of the light-made flowers, causing flecks of light and shadow to bob along the ceiling.

"These are lovely." He turned to the two children, his demeanor warming. "The details are impressive. I hardly know any Descended your age in Lumnos who could craft something so intricate."

The children looked at each other, proud grins bursting across their faces.

He walked over and kneeled to bring himself to their eye level, then pulled several gold coins from his pouch. "May I buy two more of them from you?"

Their blue eyes bulged at the extravagant sum. They nodded excitedly and set to work fashioning a pair of long-stemmed dahlias. Rather than each making one, their magic wove in harmony to craft the blooms together. Each row of tiny petals was edged with glimmering blue light and faded to a shadowy center.

When they were done, they handed the flowers to Luther with bashful smiles. He hummed his approval. "Using your magic in tandem like that is a very rare skill. Are you family?"

The girl wrinkled her nose, and the boy smirked. "Nah, just friends. I've only got light, but she can do both, so she helps me sometimes. She can mix her magic with anyone."

"Interesting." Luther studied the girl more carefully. "You must have a very good tutor."

She perked up. "We do. The best in Umbros. We practice every day."

The boy nodded. "Zalaric says we have to keep our magic strong just in case we—"

"That's enough," the woman at my side blurted out. She beckoned for them to join her. "Come along, let's leave our guests to their room."

Luther frowned at her, though he didn't argue. He placed a gold coin in each of the children's hands, then leaned forward to whisper in the girl's ear. Her mouth sprung open, her eyebrows shooting up.

She pulled back and gaped at him. "Really? The *Queen of Lumnos?*"

"Of course. I know Her Majesty very well." He tucked one of the flowers behind the girl's ear, then waved the other one. "I'll take this back to

Lumnos to show her. Bring one just like it to the palace, and my Queen will know I sent you."

"Could I..." She bit her lip and glanced at the boy at her side. "Could I bring a friend with me?"

He smiled, a rare sight in the presence of strangers. "Bring as many as you'd like. The Queen will welcome you all."

The girl squealed and threw her arms around Luther's neck. As he returned her embrace, his eyes met mine with a knowing gleam, and my heart somersaulted in my chest.

The woman stiffened beside me. "He should not give them such hopes," she said quietly. "They cannot ever go back to Lumnos."

"Why not?" I asked.

"They would be executed if they returned."

My breath caught as understanding crested over me. Luther's secret contact, my mother's involvement, all the blue-eyed Descended...

These were not just any children.

These were the half-mortals Luther and my mother had smuggled out of Lumnos. And with what he'd just done, he had given them a path to come *home*—and the promise that their Queen would accept them with open arms.

Warmth surged through me, my chest squeezing tight. As I watched Luther talk with the two children and surreptitiously shove a few more coins into their pockets, the depths of my feelings for him overcame me.

Suddenly, the kind of commitment I'd always feared no longer felt so alarming. A life with this man—this kind, selfless, fiercely loving man, who had been fighting for the vulnerable with zero fanfare and at great personal risk long before I ever met him, who believed in me and my dream and was willing to sacrifice everything for it, who would walk to the ends of the continent and back just to put the briefest smile on my face—I didn't just envision a future with him. I *wanted* it.

"He's right," I said, a little hoarsely. "The new Queen will welcome them. She'd never allow them to be executed—nor any other half-mortal."

"That's a big gamble." The woman faced me directly, her tone turning nosey. "How do you two know so much about what the Queen would do?"

"I don't," I rushed out. "But he does. The two of them are..." I forced down a lump in my throat. "...*close*. If he says she'll do something, she'll do it."

The children finally ran past us into the hallway, giggling. Luther's face had a contentment to it I hadn't seen on him in days. I crossed the room, lured in like a fish on a line, unable to stop my fingers from stretching out to brush his as I returned to his side.

"Take some time to settle in," the woman called out. "I'll send up ale and hot food."

"That's generous, but we don't intend to st—"

Before Luther could finish, the door shut, followed by a loud *click* and fading footsteps.

His eyes narrowed.

But my gaze was fixed only on him, my heart still reeling. "These children—they're the ones you've saved, aren't they?"

He stared at the flower in his hand. "That little girl looked so familiar... it took me a moment to realize why." A muscle feathered on his cheek. "I got her out, but her mortal mother decided to stay behind."

I recoiled. "She gave her daughter up?"

"The girl was the product of an affair. The mother had three mortal children already, and she was afraid that if her husband found out, he would take the others and leave." He gave me a hard look. "It wasn't a choice she made lightly."

I bit back my judgment. I knew well the ugly choices the mortal women of Lumnos were forced into making. "That little girl's aura..."

"I know. If it's that strong already, by the time she matures, she'll be quite formidable. She could be a valuable ally to you when she's older."

I laid a hand on his arm. "But that's not why you invited her to return to Lumnos, is it?"

He stared at it, something indecipherable passing across his eyes. "No, it isn't." He pulled down my hood and gently brushed back a wavy lock of hair hanging over my eyes, still damp from the rainstorm we'd escaped in Ignios. He tucked the flower the girl had created behind my ear. "They should all come home. I'll make sure the Jaguar knows they can, if they wish."

My heart felt near to bursting. I lifted to my toes and pressed a kiss to his stubble-lined cheek. He closed his eyes and leaned into my touch, his hand slipping beneath my cloak and curving around my ribs.

We stayed there for a moment, temple to temple, the press of his fingertips ever so gently pulling me closer. An undeniable sense of longing burned off him—the waning patience of his desire, the desperate need to claim me as his and never let go. My own restraint was wearing thin. In the quiet solitude of the room, with no one to disturb us, I found my lips grazing his jaw, my fingers roaming over his waist.

Abruptly, he pulled away and gave me his back, walking to the table and offloading his satchel.

I flinched at the sudden emptiness against my skin. "Luther, is everything—"

"The man at the front—did you feel his magic?" His voice was strained, unsteady.

"Yes, I did." I started toward him. "Luther..."

"He's powerful, too. Perhaps the strongest Lumnos Descended I've ever felt, other than King Ulther."

"Stronger than me?"

"No. You..." His hands stilled. "You're in a class of your own. In *every* way."

It sounded more like a warning than a compliment.

I shrugged off my pack and set it on the table. "Are you going to tell Alixe or Taran?"

"Not unless there's a reason they need to know." He shot me a loaded look. "There's an unspoken rule that those of us who can sense power levels keep that knowledge to ourselves."

"Why?"

"Because information can be as dangerous as magic. That's precisely what makes the Umbros Queen such a threat." He lifted an eyebrow. "Why? Do you wish to tell them?"

I hesitated, then let out a heavy sigh. "Back in Lumnos, you and I agreed to give each other honesty. I confess, I haven't entirely been upholding that."

Luther looked away.

"It's not because I don't trust you," I rushed out, guilt knotting in my stomach. "My entire life has been about secrets. Some I've kept, some kept from me. I went along with it because I thought I had to in order to stay alive—and because, until you, I had no one I felt safe enough to share them all with. Keeping things to myself has become second nature. I know you of all people understand that."

I reached for him, and he tensed.

The knot inside me jerked tighter. "These past few days, I've seen how much these secrets are driving us all apart. Not just us, but Alixe and Taran, Teller, everyone we care about. Our pact for brutal honesty has to include them, too. The truth about my mother, the Guardians, the half-mortals... it will all come out eventually, and when it does, it's going to hurt ten times more because we lied to them."

"Withholding information is not lying," he said, sounding almost defensive. "Taran and Alixe understand that I have to keep things from them. They trust me to tell them when the time is right. I feel the same way toward you."

I gave a small, sardonic smile. "Because you were so *understanding* when I didn't tell you my plan to sneak back into Arboros?"

He bristled. "That was different."

"Was it?"

"Yes. I—I wasn't—it wasn't about..." He raked a hand down his face, his shoulders falling. "It doesn't matter. You're right. You need a group of allies you can be honest with. Once we're in Lumnos, we'll gather everyone together and..."

I frowned as his voice trailed off and his eyes turned distant.

This wasn't Luther. He wasn't a man who stumbled over his words and lost himself in thought. He'd always been confident, impeccably controlled. Even the rare few times he'd come unbound, each glimpse behind his walls had been focused, precise, a sunbeam through a magnifying glass. In those moments, his feelings—good or bad—had been knee-wobblingly clear.

But the man in front of me now... his mind was in turmoil, that much was evident, but the *what* and *why* were a mystery.

"Luther, what's going on? Is this about Taran? I'm not pretending anymore—I really do think he's going to heal." I teasingly rolled my eyes. "I had a moment of weakness and asked Lumnos to save him. I suppose I'll finally have to make peace with her after all."

I'd expected him to look pleased, or at least relieved, but the misery hiding beneath his features only burrowed deeper.

He darted around me, heading for the door. "I'm going to find the Jaguar and ask him to book our passage. You stay here, get some r—"

He slammed against an invisible wall and staggered backward. He frowned and extended his hand. Though he was several feet from the door, his palm seemed to hit something, and a faint ripple wavered through the air.

"A shield," he growled. "They've locked us in."

CHAPTER

TWENTY-FOUR

I walked to his side and pressed forward until I felt my palms hit a solid wall. Rings of pale blue light radiated out from my palm.

"It *is* a shield," I said, recognizing the telltale shimmer. "I think there's an illusion over it to hide it, like one of Alixe's."

"Clever. They didn't want us knowing they'd trapped us inside." He looked at me. "Can you get through it?"

"My magic is still weak. I'm not sure I have enough to destroy a shield."

"Not destroy it—push through it. Every time a Descended has used their magic against you, it hasn't hurt you. In fact, I think it made you *stronger*. That's why you had me attack you in Ignios, isn't it—to give you more strength to heal your wound?"

I nodded. "Is that normal?"

He cocked his head. "*Nothing* about your magic is normal."

I frowned at the invisible wall. I pressed down as hard as I could, feeling only a slight give beneath my hand. I reared back and pushed off my heels, launching my shoulder forward, then bounced off with a cry as pain shot from the half-healed wound on my chest.

Luther caught me as I stumbled back. "You're trying too hard. Those other times, you weren't fighting the magic, you just absorbed it. Almost like it was a reflex."

I rubbed at my sore arm and stared forward for a moment, then closed my eyes. I lured my magic out until I felt my aura brush against the shield.

It was as strong as iron and delicately woven to blend seamlessly into the room. It thrummed with a slightly older energy than what I'd felt from the little girl, but not the kind of ancient power I'd felt in older Descended, either. Whoever built this had been strong, well-trained, and likely in their prime—the Jaguar himself, if I had to guess.

I gave myself over to my godhood. My magic sprang to life, curling over my skin and coating it in that tingling, contradictory frozen heat. I took one step, then another. The sensation increased, coursing through my veins and injecting me with a boost of raw energy.

A gasp broke from my lips.

"Diem? Are you alright?"

I couldn't answer. My magic had control now, and it was too busy savoring the power, gulping it down like a fine wine. My wound itched as the healing quickened and mended my skin. As my magic surged, voices rose to a murmur in my head—not the *voice* of my godhood but a melee of words, thoughts, and feelings I couldn't parse, all of them unfamiliar except one.

"Diem, talk to me."

My limbs were frozen, my body captive to my godhood and its ravenous demands to soak up every last drop of the shield's magic, then follow its trail back to the owner and bleed them dry, too.

Panic warred against curiosity. Could I do that? Could I steal magic right from within its bearer—and what would happen to them if I did?

"Diem, *please*—come back to me."

I latched on to the sound of Luther's voice. I let it anchor me, guide me, remind me who I was and what I could do. I thrashed against my own magic, and it exploded in a sudden burst, shattering the shield into a fine, iridescent dust.

Instantly, Luther's arms were on me, turning me, searching me, holding me close. He clutched my face and tilted it up, and my eyes fluttered open. The room was awash in a silvery glow. It took a moment to realize the light was coming from me—from my illuminated, moonlike skin.

"Are you hurt?" he demanded.

I shook my head, a bit dazed. The magic I'd absorbed left me feeling intoxicated with power—part euphoric, part spinning wildly out of control.

"That shield," I breathed. "He's even stronger than I thought."

"You think it was the Jaguar?"

"It wasn't the little girl. How many powerful Lumnos Descended can there be in one inn?"

Luther kept me nestled against him as he reached for the door, but the latch wouldn't give. He swore. "I'll have to break it open."

I laid a hand on his arm. "Wait—what if there's a good reason he put us here? Maybe he plans to come to us."

His dark eyebrows knit inward. "Or maybe he plans to turn us in to the Umbros Queen."

"You worked with him before. You trusted him then. Why would he turn on you now?"

"The Jaguar didn't help me out of kindness. There was always a fee—a large one. If he believes he can sell us out to the Queen for a reward, I wouldn't put it past him."

"Maybe that wouldn't be such a terrible outcome." Luther balked, and I chewed on my lip, avoiding his eyes. "I think the Umbros Queen knows something about me. When I met her in Lumnos, she knew about the flameroot."

"Your mother visited Umbros many times. One of the Centenaries must have read her mind and reported back to the Queen."

"But she knew things even my mother couldn't know. She called me *'Daughter of the Forgotten.'* And at my coronation, before the Guardians attacked, something went wrong with the ritual. My blood... there was a stone, and it broke, and she... she *knew*, somehow, she..." I saw his confused stare and huffed, scrubbing my face. "I don't understand it, either. But you told me to trust my instincts, and they're telling me to talk to her. Maybe we should delay going back to Lumnos and—"

"No."

"I know you want to get back home, but if what she knows could help us, wouldn't it be worth—"

"*No.*" The word came out of him like a snarl, so forceful it pushed me back a step. "The Crowns want you arrested. Even if the Queen doesn't execute you for coming to her realm uninvited, she could turn you over to them. It's too dangerous."

"I'm not afraid of her—or the Crowns," I insisted, not entirely honestly. "In a few days, my magic will be back to full strength. We can wait here until then."

"You need to return to Lumnos."

"I've been gone for weeks. What difference does it make to stay a few more days?"

"It makes *all the difference!*" he shouted, his voice echoing through the dark corners of the room. He seemed to grow in size as his muscles coiled with furious restraint, his features as sharp as the blade at his waist. "Your brother is worried sick—do you not care to see him? Do you not care what could be happening to the mortals under my father's rule? Or the half-mortal children Aemonn could be slaughtering every day you're gone?"

I flinched, my shoulders curling inward. Hurt pressed down on my chest and forced the air from my lungs. "Of course I do," I whispered. "How can you ask me that?"

He lumbered over to a nearby armchair and hunched over it, knuckles white where he gripped its high back. His dark hair fell around his face, concealing his expression.

"I don't—" He stopped himself to take a labored breath. "We don't have enough time."

"Until what?"

He didn't answer.

"Enough time until *what*, Luther?"

He raised his chin to look at me, his expression stricken. Everything about him—his slumped stance, his weary voice, his dull, lightless eyes—seemed utterly defeated.

"There's something I need to tell you."

A frosty sense of dread skittered up my spine.

On the other side of the room, a muffled scratching interrupted the silence. A cloud of dust took flight as one of the bookshelves rattled, then swung out with a wobbly creak.

"What in Kindred's name did you just do?" an angry voice called out.

The man from the front desk emerged into the room, glaring, arms crossed. His draped silks floated ethereally, unmoored by gravity, and I realized they weren't fabric at all, but a gown of living shadow.

Luther's demeanor changed instantly. He straightened and steeled his shoulders into a defensive stance, hands gripped on his weapons. The stony mask of the Prince fell into place and erased all trace of the agony pouring out of him moments ago. He stalked to position himself in front of me, looking fearsome and unstoppable.

"You trapped us in," he barked.

"You destroyed my shield," the man snapped back. "And you stole my magic."

"Stole your magic?" I asked.

The man's eyes moved to me and narrowed. Luther shifted to block me from his sight. "So you're the Jaguar."

"And you're the Phoenix. Or should I call you the Prince?"

"The point of the codenames was to keep our identities concealed."

The man gave him a strange look. "Did you think I would forget you?" Luther tensed, and the man's eyebrows lifted. "I see. It's you who forgot me."

My curiosity lured me out from behind Luther as the man pushed the bookshelf until it clicked back into place, its grooves disappearing behind strategically placed moulding.

"Forgive my delay." The man stopped to fluff the bouquet of flowers on the table before perching on the side of a settee, arm draped across its back. "After you so *loudly* demanded to see the Jaguar, I couldn't risk anyone seeing me come to you."

Luther didn't move. "Have we met?"

"A long time ago. I can't blame you for forgetting. We were both much younger then." He pulled off the gold collar from his neck, revealing a cruel scar encircling his throat. "Perhaps you'll remember this."

"Blessed Kindred..." Luther dropped his grip on his blades. "You survived."

The man nodded. "Thanks to you."

"I asked what became of you, but I never got a straight answer. I thought you'd died and Margie was keeping it from me to spare me the guilt."

"You should have known better. Miss Margie was never one to spare anyone's feelings." The man's smile was fond, yet tinged with sadness. "She found homes for the others, but I was too old and too wounded, so she raised me herself."

"So that's why you took over after she died," Luther mused. "I'm sorry for your loss. Margie was an incredible woman."

The man's lips tightened. A buried hurt surfaced for the briefest moment before he shrugged and gave a graceful flick of his hand. "As she always said, no sense weeping over the past. She's gone, and I'm in charge now."

He rose and strode lithely toward us, one hand extended. "Zalaric Hanoverre. Pleasure to meet you again."

Luther gripped his hand, brows rising. "You use your sire's name?"

His eyes gleamed with defiance. "Is that not my birthright?"

"If House Hanoverre discovers that you survived and are living in Umbros—"

"Then it could put you in danger?"

"It could put *you* in danger. The Hanoverres are ruthless when it comes to their bloodline."

"I'm aware," Zalaric said dryly, tapping his scar. "Don't worry, I'm careful about revealing my name to protect us both. But if my darling family does find me..." He gave a bitter smile and conjured a ring of sizzling sparks. "I've got my own score to settle with House Hanoverre."

That makes two of us, I thought to myself with a smirk. *I like him already.*

His face whipped to me. "And you are...?"

"None of your concern," Luther clipped, stepping back in front of me. "And she was just about to retire for a rest." He turned to face me with a pointed, urgent look. "Weren't you, *cousin?*"

I shot him a glare, my temper prickling at being shoved to the side.

Luther's nostrils flared. He leaned in, whispering, "We can't risk him getting a good look at you—at least not until after he's booked our passage home."

Though I wasn't ready to let go of my unexplainable urge to seek out the Umbros Queen, even I was not reckless enough to have that argument here and now. I scowled, pulled my hood back up, and skulked off to one of the side chambers, feeling both their gazes burn into my back as I left.

Once inside, I pulled the door until it was barely ajar. I curled up on the floor, then pressed my face into the narrow opening to watch.

"You don't trust me," Zalaric observed, sounding amused.

"You locked me in, then trapped me with your shield. Are those the acts of a trustworthy man?"

"Letting you wander all over Umbros asking for the Jaguar would only bring trouble on us both. Besides, I felt your aura. I knew you could defeat my shield, if you truly needed to leave." He gave Luther a slow once-over. "How did you do it, anyway?"

"Pierce your shield? Surely you know how that's done."

"It was more than that. You were draining my magic right out of me. Here in Umbros, we've got every type of magic that exists in Emarion—but I've never seen anything like that."

Luther played the lie well, crossing his arms and feigning a smug pride.

"Could you teach me?" Zalaric asked.

"No."

"I would pay you. Handsomely."

"No."

"Name your price."

214

"I have plenty of money. I don't need yours."

"How fortunate," Zalaric drawled. His tone dripped with a specific flavor of anger I knew intimately: the bitter injustice of a person who'd grown up scrabbling for every last coin, faced with the casual indifference of someone who couldn't fathom having a *last coin* at all.

As a mortal, everything had its price. Love and life, freedom and family. It could all be bought, for those who could pay, or withheld, for those who couldn't. No mortal was so rich that they weren't for sale. We'd sell our own souls for the right price—and many did.

I wondered vaguely if Zalaric's life here in Umbros had not been so different from the mortals in Lumnos, eking out a meager living as second-class citizens under the thumb of the Queen and her Centenaries.

He settled onto the settee, his demeanor markedly cooler. "So what brings the Prince of Lumnos from his shiny castle all the way to the dark markets? And does it have anything to do with this mysterious new Queen everyone's abuzz about?"

Luther stiffened. "What have you heard about her?"

"Mostly rumors too outlandish to believe. '*She's a mortal, she's a long-lost royal, she has no magic, she's more powerful than a god, she's in hiding, she's starting a war.*' Every day it's something different." He arched a single brow. "Care to confirm or deny?"

Luther sank into an armchair. His cloak fell open, revealing a sweater scattered with puncture wounds and bloodstains. He covered it quickly, but Zalaric's shrewd eyes took silent note.

"I can tell you this—she is a friend to the half-mortals," Luther said. "She would welcome you home, if you wished to return."

"I have a life here. A successful business, plenty of friends. I pay my taxes, and the Umbros Queen lets me do as I please. Why would I ever go back to Lumnos?"

A lie lurked beneath his haughty tone. I felt it more than I heard it—the quiet, buried longing to return to his *terremère*, to build the life he was so cruelly denied.

Perhaps Luther sensed it as well, because his voice softened as he leaned forward. "The offer remains open, should you ever change your mind."

"I couldn't leave the children. They need me."

"Bring them. You're all welcome to return."

Hope sparked in Zalaric's eyes, though he quickly shut it down. "We have nowhere to live. Without my business, I'd have no way to provide for them."

"There's plenty of room at the palace. And Lumnos has need of inns and taverns, if you prefer your independence."

Zalaric fell quiet. I laid my head back against the wall and closed my eyes as my heart soared at Luther's dogged persistence. He wasn't just opening the door to the banished half-mortals—he was actively calling them home.

Because he knew it's what I would want.

Because he knew *me*.

"And what would this generosity cost me?"

"From Her Majesty? Nothing. She only wishes to right the wrongs of the past."

I nodded my agreement from my unseen nook.

"And *your* price?" Zalaric prodded.

"Your loyalty to my Queen." Luther paused. "Her Majesty needs allies. Strong ones. Allies who are not afraid of the Twenty Houses."

Zalaric chuckled. "I see. She wishes *us* to do her dirty work."

Luther and I bristled in unison.

"No," he said firmly. "If there is one thing I know of my Queen, it's that she will never let anyone fight her battles on her behalf."

There was a ferocious pride in his words, but something else, too. Something bleak and unsettled.

"But," he continued, "I do not want her to fight them alone. All I ask is that you stand with her, if she needs you."

Zalaric stroked his chin. "She means a great deal to you."

"She is my Queen. She is a gift from the Blessed Mother herself. She is..." Luther swallowed and dipped his chin, and he was no longer talking to Zalaric. "I gave myself to her the moment I met her, and I have not regretted it for a second. I have laid my life at her feet, and I would do it again and again, a thousand times over. She has my faith, my loyalty, my vow... I believe in her with everything that I am. There is nothing I would not do to see her fulfill her destiny. No matter the cost."

My chest burned with a fiery emotion I dared not name.

"If she has such devotion from you, I can't imagine she'll ever be fighting alone," Zalaric said.

Luther was quiet for a long moment. "I would fight for her until the world was ash, if the Kindred allowed it."

Zalaric studied him, squinting, then finally sighed. "I'll consider the offer. I'm happy here, but... I'll think on it."

"And you'll tell the others, as well?"

"I will." He cocked his head. "I presume you didn't come all this way to deliver a message you could have sent by hawk. Tell me, Prince, what's the real reason you're here?"

"I need your help securing passage to Lumnos. Tonight, if possible. But it can't be just any ship. I need to keep it away from the Centenaries' notice. I'm traveling with... sensitive cargo."

"All ships in this port have *sensitive cargo*. As long as your tariffs are paid, the Centenaries don't care."

"They'll care about this."

Zalaric sat up, his interest clearly piqued. "And I suppose you don't wish to share it with me, either?"

"Believe me, it's better for us both if I don't."

"Is this going to get me killed if you're discovered?"

Again, Luther said nothing.

Zalaric lounged back against his chair and considered. "What you ask is impossible. The Umbros Queen prides herself on knowing everything that happens in her city, and in all the years I've lived here, I've never seen anything slip her notice."

"Are you saying you cannot help me?"

"No." His lips curved into a smile. "It's Umbros. Even the impossible is for sale somewhere."

They began to discuss the more trivial details of our escape, and I let their voices fade to a hum as I slumped against the wall, my posture sagging.

Luther had made the decision over my head. We would be leaving immediately—without any conversation with the Umbros Queen.

My heart was painfully torn. I wasn't happy that he'd overruled me with barely a discussion, and the accusations he'd made earlier had cut me deep. If I hadn't just heard him profess his devotion, I might have begun to suspect his affection for me had changed.

But I had heard it. And more than that—I'd *felt* it. Luther's feelings for me were profound, so strong they were nearly tangible. I saw them in every look, felt them in every touch, their presence filling each room we shared.

I tried to push aside the hurt lodged in my chest and remind myself that he was just worried. He was so used to playing the avenging angel for everyone he loved, guarding their safety in his hands. His self-worth was inextricably tangled in the safety of others, and now, we were all more in danger than we'd ever been.

Once we're home, he'll be himself. I repeated it like a mantra, my eyes drooping closed. *Once we're in Lumnos, everything will be okay.*

217

CHAPTER

TWENTY-FIVE

I woke up some time later in bed, head resting on a pillow and a pile of blankets tucked around the outline of my body. On the bedside table, the flower had been plucked from my hair and laid atop a note:

Gone to find the others. Please don't leave.

The *please* was underlined. Twice.

I sat up and yawned, then realized my arms were free of the crusted sand and dried blood from the fight in Ignios. Luther must have wiped it off before moving me to bed. He'd even set out a clean change of clothes beside a pitcher of ale and a silver dinner cloche emanating a delicious smell. I leapt up and wasted no time ravaging the food in rather embarrassing fashion. When I finished, I padded to the washroom to find a hot bath already drawn.

My stomach fluttered as I peeled off my bloody, ruined clothes and sank into the steaming water. Even in the midst of his own inner unrest, he was always protecting me, always thinking of me, even in the smallest of ways.

The woman he loves.

Taran's words echoed in my thoughts as the heady buzz from the ale sent me in and out of sleep. I might have stayed there all night—I might have stayed there all *year*—until I heard voices drift in from the other room.

I finished washing up and reluctantly abandoned the water's comforting warmth.

For the first time in weeks, I was clean and rested, my mind finally clear enough to take stock of the mess I was now at the center of.

I was not ready to be a Queen—my catastrophic Period of Challenging had proven that much. I didn't have the right temperament or the right upbringing, and I'd been pushing away the few people willing to serve me. I was better equipped to start a war than to end one.

But the Crown sat atop my head nevertheless. Ready or not, my reign had begun, and so had the war.

It was time to start building my army.

I nodded firmly to myself and wrapped a towel beneath my arms, then marched out of the washroom—and straight into Luther's chest.

His broad hands caught my hips to keep me from stumbling backward. He'd cleaned himself up as well, his fresh clothes and clean hair smelling strongly of his woodsy musk.

"You're back," I said.

"You're awake." His gaze wandered over my bare skin, sending a rush of heat everywhere it roamed. "It's healing well."

I blinked, distracted by his murky expression. "What?"

"This." His right hand slid up my side and grazed the swell of my breast. My breath hitched.

It was an effort to tear my eyes away from him. When I did, I saw that the wound I'd taken in Ignios was gone, with a patch of new, pink skin in its place.

"Oh. Right. Yes." I scoured his body for injuries, but nearly every inch of skin was covered in thick fabric. Even his throat was wrapped in a heavy scarf. "And yours?"

His face darkened. "Fine."

I frowned. "If they're still bothering you, I can make a salve—"

"They're fine. Taran's back, if you want to check his wounds."

"Any news from Zalaric?"

"Not yet."

We stood in silence, eyes locked. Though I made no move to leave, his grip tightened on my hip, as if I was being dragged away and he was fighting to hold on.

I drew in a breath, and his focus dropped to my mouth. His fingers grazed over my collarbone, lingering for a moment over my crescent-shaped scar, then traced the column of my throat, curving around my nape. He pulled me in like he might kiss me, then paused, forehead creasing as his lips hovered a breath from mine. His mind seemed far away, waging some internal battle he refused to let me join.

As the carousel of emotion spun across his face and I waited to see where it would stop, for a moment, his mind appeared to me like a cloud of smoke, as if the simplest wave of my hand might lay open his soul.

The urge to do it was thrilling—to finally know all his secrets and unearth the truth of why he'd been pulling away. It would be treachery of the darkest kind, a violation for which I might never atone—but if it was just the tiniest glimpse...

A shudder passed over me. *What in the Flames was I thinking?* Even if I were willing to betray Luther in such a horrific way, I couldn't *read minds.*

"You're shivering." He pulled back and ran his palms over my arms in long strokes. "You should get dressed."

"I should," I agreed.

Neither of us moved.

A crackling energy buzzed in the air between us, my heart thundering against my chest.

"Looks like we're finally alone," I said, barely above a whisper. I leaned closer until my chest brushed against his. The movement jostled my towel, causing it to slip an inch. Luther's hands stilled.

"Diem," he breathed.

A desperate urgency took over. I closed the distance between us and poured my need for him into a feverish kiss, fingers knotting in his hair and clutching at his sweater.

Whatever had been holding him back vanished as our lips collided in a fury of taste and tongue. He hauled me into his arms, then staggered forward until he had me pinned hard against the wall. My back arched in teasing defiance, crushing my body to his.

Large, commanding hands worked their way up my thighs and slipped beneath the edge of my towel, kneading my flesh and easing my legs apart. Every touch sent me spiraling, writhing, pleading. My hips rolled against him and drew a groan from us both.

"The nights I have spent dreaming of you," he murmured against my throat. "Of *this.*"

Eager sounds whimpered out of me as he tasted his way across my skin like he might devour me, consume me. My mind had gone hazy, unable to think past the throb of hunger that grew with every rough sweep of his hands and insatiable press of his hips.

The grinding of our bodies loosened my towel, and it fell to the floor, leaving me naked in his arms. Luther let out a low, animalistic sound. He pulled me away from the wall and set me on the washroom's marble countertop, then leaned back for a better view.

I flushed and wrapped my arms over my waist. I'd never been ashamed of my body, but the partners I'd been with before were all mortals who shared the same scars and curves. The partners Luther was surely used to—well, I couldn't bear to think about that.

"I lied," he said, his voice stilted. "Before."

My shoulders hunched. "About?"

"I said *looking* would be the least of what I would do once we were alone." He gently peeled my arms away until I was bare once more, his eyes full of wonder as they drank me in. "But this... *you*..." Muscles leapt on his throat. "I could look at you forever, and it wouldn't be nearly long enough."

My skin felt too tight, ready to burst, my body incapable of containing the firestorm of emotion sparking inside.

The newness of it left me unsteady. Lust, I understood. Lust, I could control, I could wield like a sword and shield. But these feelings I had for Luther... this was no mere lust. This, I had no idea what to do with.

My godhood, on the other hand, knew exactly what it wanted. The *voice* purred and paced, hissing at me to stop being a coward and take what I desired. The corner of Luther's mouth quirked up in a knowing smile, and sparks of light danced at my fingertips as my magic swirled in blissful response.

I summoned my courage and looped a finger into his belt. "What if I want you to do more than just *look?*"

He fixed me in a predatory stare. This Prince was a hunter, and I felt every bit his prey—trembling, waiting, wondering if I'd make it out of this alive.

His hand brushed against my knee, then began a slow trek up my leg. His thumb trailed with exhilarating pressure along my inner thigh. As he neared my hips, his touch dangerously close to my core, my lashes fluttered and my gaze dropped down.

His hand stilled. "Look at me."

I did.

He nudged my knees. "Open."

I did.

"Wider."

221

I did, and my mouth went dry. There was nowhere to hide. Everything was bared to him—*everything*.

His other hand rose to my chin and tilted it up. "That's my girl."

A confusing excitement seared through my blood. It would surprise precisely no one to learn that, with my previous lovers, I'd craved control. Henri once teased that I treated sex the way I treated a fight—never retreat, never surrender. I made up for it with enthusiasm, and my partners had always been more than happy to submit.

With Luther, I had expected the same. He was so committed to serving me, I'd imagined that when we finally crossed this line we'd been dancing, our dynamic would stay the same: a headstrong Queen and her obedient Prince.

But this was something else. Something I'd never truly had before—a worthy opponent. The man staring at me now, lips parted and pupils black as night, had no intention to *submit*.

And I liked it.

A lot.

"Eyes on me, Bellator," he ordered as his palm slid between my legs. We both sucked in a breath at the revealing wetness he found. The hard calluses on his palm from years of wielding blades created excruciatingly sweet friction against my slick skin. His fingers circled in a way that had my body arching and my hands clawing at the marble.

A satisfied rumble built in his throat. His touch turned deeper, harder, more demanding. One finger pushed inside me, then another.

I writhed against him, and his watchful eyes caught every tiny reaction. His movements adjusted—faster or slower, harder or lighter—as he shrewdly studied the nuance of my pleasure. In minutes, he had worked me into a panting, trembling frenzy.

My body was alive in a way I'd never known. Each breath hung on the stroke of his fingers, my heart seeming to pound in time with his movements.

I couldn't tear my eyes from him. I felt entranced, entirely at his command—yet somehow free. Unchained. Invincible.

I thrust my hips against his hand, and he grunted his approval. His other hand mapped my body, touching every line and curve in a slow, methodical path, as if committing each one to memory. Each time he passed over one of my many scars, his nostrils flared wide.

The mounting pressure threatened to crack me open. Pleasure merged with my magic and infused my aura, igniting the air around us with a silvery shimmer. His eyes widened in surprise, and it gave me a small thrill and more than a little comfort to know some part of this was new and unexplored for him, too.

I reached for the button on his trousers, and he grabbed my wrist.

"Let me touch you," I pleaded.

"No."

His voice was soft, but firm. Unyielding.

"Luther—"

His fingers plunged deeper, and my protests garbled into moans. My control slipped, my head falling back as my eyes squeezed shut.

He buried his face against the curve of my throat. "There's so much more I want to give you," he breathed into my skin, sounding nearly as shaken as I was. "So much more you deserve. At least I can give you this."

I had the vague sense there was something wrong with his words, but I was drowning in need, and the thought floated away before I could catch it.

The pressure built and built and built, excruciating and elating. I was a bomb, a volcano, a match in a powder keg, fire eternal and passion aflame. My fingernails dug into his arms as I trembled on the precipice of release.

"Please," I begged.

"Tell me what you want," he growled in my ear.

It took every last shred of willpower to force my eyes open and lean back until our gazes locked.

"You," I whispered. "All of you."

Something heart-wrenching filled his expression. His fingers curved into that perfect place inside me, and all semblance of control imploded. Release shuddered through me as I cried his name and collapsed, trembling, into his arms.

More magic poured from my hands unbidden, glowing cords that twined around him and drew him closer. A fond smile touched his lips as he happily obliged, nestling my pleasure-wracked body to his chest. He worked me through each cresting wave with slow, tender strokes, and I clung to him as if his touch were the only thing keeping me whole.

He brushed my hair back from my face, his touch warm and achingly gentle. "Perfect," he said so quietly I thought he might be talking to himself. "You are so perfect." His eyes shone with affection, though a discomforting darkness lurked at the edge.

"I am very naked, and you are *very* dressed," I joked, trying to laugh off my unease. "Why is it you and I never seem to be unclothed at the same time?"

My hands moved down his chest, and his back stiffened. He gave me a chaste kiss, then began to back away. "Get dressed. Come join us in the parlor."

I pouted and tugged him back. "The others can wait a little longer."

I toyed with the hem of his sweater and began to lift it away. He jerked back violently, nearly crashing into the wall behind him. He tried to recover quickly, smoothing his hands over the fabric and bending to grab the towel I'd dropped, but the muscles in his shoulders were still tight as a spring.

He offered the towel out to me. I ignored it, frowning. "Luther, what's wrong?"

"We should get back to the others."

"Why won't you let me touch you?"

"We just did quite a lot of touching." He gave me a look that was surely meant to be teasing, but it came across strained.

"*You* did a lot of touching. Do you..." I slid off the counter, wrapping my hands around myself as my insecurities resurfaced. "Do you not want me to touch you?"

His hesitation said too much.

"Of course I do, but we've been in here long enough. Alixe and Taran are waiting."

He held out the towel again, and again I ignored it. He sighed and set it beside me, then turned to leave.

"Wait," I called out.

"I'll meet you in the parlor."

"Luther, stop."

He continued across the room, heading for the bedchamber door.

"Your Queen *commanded* you to stop," I snapped.

He halted immediately, frozen mid-step.

I blinked a few times, shocked at my own words. Shocked that it had gone that far.

I took a deep breath and forced my voice to soften. "Look at me, Luther. Please."

Slowly, with palpable reluctance, he spun on his heel. His face was fixed in a hard stare, jaw set and eyes cold.

I took a step toward him. "Earlier, you said there was something you wanted to tell me."

"It was nothing. I misspoke."

I balked. "Now you're *lying?*"

"I'm not—" He scrubbed a hand down his face. "Can you please put on the towel?"

"Forget the gods-damned towel!"

His teeth ground together. "I cannot think straight with you standing in front of me naked."

I rolled my eyes and walked to the washroom, snatching the towel and knotting it around me. "Better?"

His eyes fixated on the bare hip still peeking out between the folds. His hands flexed at his sides. "Not really."

I studied his frosty expression, all its harsh angles and severe lines. All trace of the sweet contentment from moments ago was long gone.

Hurt crept its spindly fingers into my heart. How could his emotions change so quickly? Had what we just shared meant so little that he could turn away from it on the flip of a coin?

And then it hit me.

"Luther, if you... if you think... that is, if you're not interested in..." Nausea rose in my throat. "What we just did... I don't need to be *served* that way just because I'm Queen. You are under no oblig—"

"*What did you just say?*"

His dark timbre had my blood chilling in my veins. Never had a simple question seemed so much like a drawn blade.

His eyes met mine, pitch black and pulsing with ire. "You think what just happened was me... *serving* you? Because you're Queen? That I made you come because—what, Diem, I'm just your fucking advisor?"

A blush of shame burst across my cheeks at the disgust snarling his features. But *I* was the one with the right to be angry, not him.

I forced my back straighter. "What else am I supposed to think? You seem to have no interest in me reciprocating."

He glared at me for a long moment. Veins popped beneath his skin, his body seeming to vibrate with the effort of holding back.

I shrugged, trying my best to look unbothered, even as my heart collapsed. "If you don't desire me, just be honest. I'm a grown woman. I can take it."

"Desire?"

His voice was whisper-soft, dangerous, rumbling with the ominous promise of a blow about to be unleashed.

"You think I do not *desire* you?"

My cheeks felt hot. "In Arboros, I thought... what we said to each other..." I swallowed thickly. "But now you're pushing me away, so I—"

He crossed the room in a split second, a snarl ripping out of him. In a blur of motion he had me pinned against the wall, one hand clenched around my neck, trapping me at his mercy. The other hooked behind my knee to open my thighs as he ground his hips forward with near-bruising force. The hard ridge of his arousal was undeniable where it strained against his trousers and dug into the still-tender flesh between my legs.

"Does *this* feel like I do not *desire* you?" he hissed.

Something between a gasp and a moan slipped out as a darker, more primal kind of pleasure split through me. The ferocious bite in his voice, his dominating grip on my body, the ruthless savagery in his eyes. This was no measured, guarded Prince. This was Luther at his core, raw and out of control.

He forced my chin up and tipped his mouth to mine. "I did not know what it was to *need* until I met you. One look from you—just the fucking sound of your voice—and my cock gets hard. One touch of your skin, and I can barely think beyond dragging you into the nearest bed. Every second I'm not *inside* you is another wasted moment of my miserable life."

His fingers tightened on my throat—not enough to hurt, just to send my pulse hammering. If I had any sense at all, I might have been scared, but the energy tingling at the peak of my thighs was giving a very different response.

"There is no place in all of existence I would rather be than between your legs, and there's no part of you I do not long to consume. With my eyes." His gaze dropped brazenly to my chest. "With my hands." He squeezed my breast in his palm, kneading the sensitive point until I gasped. "With my mouth." He kissed me, harsh and insatiable, his tongue sweeping greedily over mine.

When he had reduced me to a mewling, quivering puddle, he released me and took a step back. The loss of his touch was an agony, but his lethal focus still had me entirely in his hold.

"It is not just my body that craves you, Diem. It is my heart." He clutched at his chest. "My scarred, ruined scrap of a soul. Your smiles, your affection, the way you look at me, the way you *see* me... that is my lifeblood. I would sooner wither without food or water, sink into the sea until my lungs burst, abandon my magic and let my godhood burn me alive from within than endure one more day of life without you in it."

Suddenly, his magic sparked back to life, and its potent presence flooded the room. It swirled in the air and encircled my skin, and my godhood crooned in eager response, undaunted by the wrath thrumming in its ferocious energy. I fumbled for breath, suffocated by the mix of his aura and his powerful words.

"Desire?" He gave a dark, throaty laugh. "Desire is a pathetic word for what I feel for you. I require you. I am sustained by you. You are the flame that fuels my fire. Don't you dare question that—not for a second."

"Then why are you pushing me away?" I whispered.

He went preternaturally still. Slowly, almost too subtly to notice, the fury faded from his features, replaced by an emotion I couldn't interpret. Wisps of light and shadow cracked in the icy blue pools of his eyes. I couldn't tell whether he wanted to take me to bed or take off running.

I wasn't sure *he* knew, either.

I pushed off the wall, hating the way his muscles bunched as if preparing for an attack. I stood in front of him, close enough to touch but not doing so. Not yet.

I started with his hands—innocent, simple. A slight brush of our knuckles. My finger, hooked around his. A reassuring squeeze.

Patiently, I waited for him to react. He stared at our joined hands, but he didn't move.

My hands lifted to his face. I swept my fingers across his sharp cheekbones, his full lips, his broad, angular jaw. I traced the lines of his scar, smiling when he closed his eyes so I could follow its trail across his eyelids.

I raked my nails through the coarse stubble that darkened his jawline, winning a grunt of pleasure from him that emboldened me to keep going.

When my touch moved to his neck, shadows seeped from his palms. They pooled at our feet, then began climbing up the walls. They snuffed out the scattered candles and smothered the light-crafted flowers. Even the faint glow from his eyes disappeared as he closed them, turning the room to moonless night.

Darkness for my touch—these were his terms of engagement. This moment seemed too fragile, too important, to question it aloud.

I blindly tugged at his scarf, loosening it enough to stroke the column of his neck. I looped a hand behind his nape and pulled him down so I could lay a kiss in the hollow of his throat. I felt him swallow, felt his pulse pound beneath my fingers, and still, he made no effort to resist. Encouraged, I pushed myself further.

My hands strayed beneath his collar, following his warm skin over the muscular planes of his shoulders. I gently rolled my thumbs into the hard knots I found until his tension eased and his posture loosened.

As surprisingly good as it had felt to surrender and let him take control of my body, I longed to return the favor. I wanted to cover him in loving hands and tender kisses, then ignite in him the same kind of cataclysmic bliss he'd just given me.

The thought of it made me brave and a little more reckless. I nibbled at his jaw as I dragged my hands over the front of his sweater.

Luther stiffened.

I kept going as if I hadn't noticed, but his tension remained. We both held our breath as I grabbed the edge of his sweater.

"Arms up," I said with a teasing lilt, "unless you prefer me to burn your clothes off you again."

He didn't move. I waited, still and silent. He didn't so much as twitch.

My lips grazed his skin in blind search of his mouth. When I found it, I kissed him—light at first, delicate pecks that lengthened into slow, adoring caresses, then heated with an insistence that forced him to respond with his own urgent strokes. A hand tangled in my hair and tugged, angling me to deepen the kiss.

I began to lift his sweater. Slowly, agonizingly slowly, it rose, my knuckles brushing against the rippled steel of his torso, and then—

His hands clamped around my wrists and pushed them away. I heard the rustle of movement, then a cluster of orbs appeared across the ceiling to light the room. Luther stood a few feet away, tightening the scarf around his neck.

"Get dressed," he said flatly.

My throat burned. "Why are you doing this? If you desire me, why are you pulling away?"

His expression stopped my heart still. There was no warmth, no fondness, no emotion at all. He was an empty husk—the cold, vicious Prince.

"Because life is cruel," he snapped. "And we don't always get what we desire."

He turned to leave.

"Luther, wait."

He kept walking.

"Don't you dare turn your back on me."

He reached the door and threw it open.

"As your Queen, I *order* you to st—"

The door slammed, and I was alone.

CHAPTER
TWENTY-SIX

He disobeyed me.
Luther Corbois.

Disobeyed *me.*

His *Queen.*

It wasn't even that I minded the disobedience. Though my stubborn temper didn't always show it, Luther's willingness to tell me no was something I both needed and cherished.

But this felt different. This wasn't a simple disagreement, a debate that could be won or lost, shouted over or talked through.

This felt like a decision made. Like Luther was closing a door. On us. On *me.*

The thought sat heavy on my heart as I towel-dried my hair and slipped into the clean clothes he'd set out. The lingering burn of his rejection was tempered by the powerful confessions he'd just made.

There is no place in all of existence I would rather be than between your legs, and there's no part of you I do not long to consume. With my eyes. With my hands. With my mouth.

I pressed a finger to my lips, still swollen from his kiss. How could he feel so strongly and still turn me away? Did he somehow believe he wasn't worthy? Because if so, I would happily persuade him otherwise. Preferably with my own eyes, hands, and mouth.

But what if *I* was the one unworthy of *him?* What if my mistakes as

Queen had left him regretting his decision to support me, but he cared for me too much to admit it to my face?

Stop, I scolded myself. *You doubted him before, and you swore never to do it again.*

Every time Luther had done something I didn't understand, it had always come down to him protecting me in some way. If he was holding back, there had to be some threat he didn't want to reveal, and though it pricked my temper to know he was keeping secrets to protect me again, I had no right to be upset when I still harbored secrets of my own.

If I wanted to be a good Queen, I needed to lead by example. I would have to come clean to him, to *all* of them, and pray I could earn back their trust.

I took a deep breath and stalked out of the bedchamber, into the center of the main parlor, facing the three Corbois cousins with arms crossed.

"We need to talk."

Alixe and Taran looked up at me in surprise. They were both lounging on a couch, Alixe nibbling on a bowl of dried fruits while Taran twirled a thin, dark blade between his fingers.

Luther stood by the fireplace, a tumbler of amber liquid in his hand, staring into the flames with that same hollow, uncaring expression.

"Look, Queenie," Taran said, grinning. "My magic's back again."

I looked closer at the weapon in his hand. The edges swirled with the telltale sign of a shadow-crafted blade. He twitched a finger and it grew in size to a small axe, which he precariously balanced upright in the palm of his hand.

"Luther's is, too," I said.

Taran and I both looked his way. Luther swirled his glass silently. Taran glanced back at me, raising an eyebrow.

"Mine returned for a moment while we were in the markets," Alixe added.

"It seems to be happening more frequently," I said.

She nodded. "And it's not just happening to us. We overheard a couple from Meros say it's going on there, too, and a Descended from Sophos bragged that he was using magic without paying his tithe to the Umbros Queen."

"Have you ever heard of this happening before?"

"Never," Luther mumbled.

"Care to elaborate?" I asked, a bit testily.

The silence stretched on. He took a long sip from his glass, and Alixe and Taran shared a look.

I glowered and poured myself a glass of whiskey, then slammed it back in a single gulp. Taran whistled low.

"Did something happen while we were gone?" Alixe asked carefully.

"Yes," I said, just as Luther answered, "No."

Taran leaned over to Alixe. "Mom and Dad are fighting," he whispered loudly.

"This—" I gestured to the four of us. "—isn't working. We're all arguing, keeping secrets, not trusting each other. We can't keep going like this."

"Don't look at me," Taran said. "I'm not keeping any secrets. I trusted all of you, and look where it got me."

A stab of guilt needled at me. "You're right."

He blinked. "Wait—I am?"

"Yes." I sighed and sat down beside him. "If I had been more honest with all of you from the beginning, maybe I could have stopped what happened on Coeurîle. You all wouldn't have had to rescue me, and you would never have been hit by that godstone blade." I took his hand. "I am so sorry, Taran. I will never forgive myself for that."

Luther whipped around so quickly his drink sloshed over the side of his glass. "That was not your fault."

My back straightened in surprise. *Now* he had something to say?

"Looking back," I went on, "I saw enough that I should have been able to put together what they were up to. If I had, we would never have had that fight with Vance, and—"

"*You will not blame yourself for that,*" Luther thundered, his mask slipping to reveal a flash of bitter anger before he managed to lock it down again.

It was such a volatile, disproportionate response that I was left momentarily speechless.

Taran squeezed my hand, his voice softening. "I was just teasing. I don't blame you for that, and Luther's right—you shouldn't, either."

"Regardless, I owe you an apology. There's so much I've been keeping from all of you—so much that I don't even know where to start filling you in, to be honest—but I want to. You all have become my family. You stood by me through the worst weeks of my life, and you trusted me when you had no reason to. You deserve better than what I've given you, and I'm truly sorry."

231

I looked between the three of them, trying to convey my sincerity with my expression. Luther took another drink and turned away.

"What exactly have you been keeping from us?" Taran asked. Though Alixe said nothing, I saw the same question in her eyes.

I winced, wishing I'd poured myself a second glass. I rose to my feet and drew in a long breath.

"My mother is the leader of the Guardians of the Everflame," I began. "I think she met my birth father while on a mission for the Emarion Army, but I won't know for sure until I get her out of prison—which I plan to do once we get back to Lumnos. I don't know who he was, but I know he's alive, and he knows I exist. The Umbros Queen told me so last Forging Day, when she showed up in Lumnos and told me to stop taking the flame-root that was suppressing my magic. Also, when her Centenaries came to the Ascension Ball, I released their magic to get their help stopping a Guardian attack, so the Centenaries have probably read all my thoughts and memories—and all of yours, too."

I paused, bracing for what I knew would be the hardest pill.

"I'm *still* working with the Guardians. I want to help them wage war against the Crowns to restore what was taken from the mortals. But only some of the Guardians—the ones that aren't trying to kill us. But I also want to help the good Descended in the war, too. And bring all the half-mortals home. So I guess I'm not really picking a side..." I frowned and shook my head. "I haven't really figured out the *war* part yet, this is all kind of a work in progress."

All three of them blinked at me.

"Oh, and Luther and I have been having visions. About each other. And the war. And some glowing man who called me Daughter of the Forgotten. Also, there's a prophecy, I think. The Umbros Queen told me some of it, and then King Ulther said more, and—I'm not sure, I'm still figuring this part out, too—then everything went sideways at my corona-tion, and Sophos called me an imposter. Which, actually, they might not be wrong about, because there's something bizarre about my magic, and—"

"Blessed Kindred..."

"Your birth father is alive?"

"What kind of visions?"

"You never mentioned a prophecy."

"What do you mean, '*imposter*'?"

"And what do you mean, '*bizarre*'?"

"We're going to need a bigger Royal Guard."

232

I cringed. "I know it's a lot. And there's probably more." I shot Luther a pointed look. He would have to have his own *come clean* moment soon enough. "I don't want to keep any of it from you all. Not anymore."

"What prophecy?" Luther demanded. "What did it say?"

"It was all gibberish. It can't possibly be true. Something about chains, and a debt, and blood falling on a heartst—oh." My lips parted. "*Oh.*"

"What?"

"It might be true after all."

Luther slammed down his glass and came to stand in front of me. "Tell me. Every word."

I dove into my memories and pulled out the cryptic lines the Umbros Queen had spoken that day in Paradise Row. "*When forgotten blood on heartstone falls, then shall the chains be broke. Life for life, old debt requires, or eternal be his yoke.*"

"Creepy," Taran said, helpfully.

Luther's eyes wandered as he mouthed the words over and over.

"Why do you think it's true?" Alixe asked.

"At my coronation, there was a stone at the center of the Kindred's Temple. The other Crowns called it the heartstone. They use it for the rituals. It seemed... important."

As in, the source-of-all-Descended-magic, the-world-will-crumble-if-it's-destroyed kind of important, I thought to myself.

"As part of the ritual, we each spilled drops of our blood on the heartstone, but when my turn came and my blood touched it, it cracked down the middle."

"If you're the 'forgotten blood,' what are the chains?" Taran asked.

"I'm not sure." I glanced at Luther. "I was *hoping* to ask the Umbros Queen if she knows..."

"You can write her a letter from Lumnos," he clipped. "What about Ulther—you said he told you something?"

"That part was even less clear. He called me all of these titles... '*Devourer of Crowns. Ravager of Realms. Herald of Vengeance.*' Then he said '*They told me your blood would shatter our—*'" I paused, sucking in a sharp breath in realization. "'*—shatter our stone and lay waste to our borders.*' I guess that part is coming true, too."

"The borders must be breaking down," Alixe said. "That explains why our magic keeps returning."

"Is that all the King said?" Luther asked.

"Not exactly. After that, his voice changed. It sounded... old. Not elderly, more like—"

"Ancient," Luther answered for me, and I nodded. His expression lay somewhere between awe and concern. "What did they say?"

"*Give him our gift, Daughter of the Forgotten. When the end has come, and the blood has spilled, give our gift to my faithful heir, and tell him this is my command.*"

His eyes went wide.

"The voice you heard," he said, sounding suddenly urgent, "did it sound like a woman?"

I balked. "Yes—how did you know?"

"Has anyone given you anything?" he pushed. "Has anything appeared to you?" I shook my head, and his expression darkened. "Think hard, Diem. There must be something."

"There's nothing. I never even met Ulther before that day."

"Not Ulther—*Lumnos.*"

My brows flew up. Was he right? The goddess was certainly ancient, and if she were going to speak through an earthly body, it would make sense she would choose the bearer of her Crown.

But that would mean she could now speak through *me*. The thought made me feel like there was poison slithering under my skin.

"If it was Blessed Lumnos, maybe her Crown is the gift," Taran said.

"More like a curse," I muttered. "And if she wants me to give it away, I apparently have to die first. Whoever her *faithful heir* is, he can wait his turn. I didn't survive the Challenging just to give my life up for some prophecy."

Luther's hands fell away from my arms. His face looked pale. "No. You won't."

I took a deep breath. "I know you don't like this, but I really think we should speak to the Umbros Queen while we're here."

That seemed to shake him out of his trance and shove him right back into *irritable* territory.

"She could have you executed, Diem."

"If she wanted me dead, she could have killed me in Mortal City. I think she wants me to seek her out."

"And if you're wrong, you die. It's not worth the risk. We're going to Lumnos, end of discussion."

I ground my teeth, my temper beginning to boil. "It's not up to you."

His eyes narrowed. "I will carry you out of this realm myself, if I must."

"*Luther*," Alixe warned. "She is the Queen."

His cutting glare shot to her. "You dare tell me that, after you left her behind in Ignios? I brought you along to protect her, not abandon her."

"She was following my orders," I cut in.

"*Fuck* your orders."

Taran leapt up and crossed in front of Luther, placing a firm hand on his shoulder. "Cousin, let's step out and take a walk."

I let out a wry laugh. "No, if Luther suddenly has so much to say, let's hear it. It's about time some *brutal honesty* comes out, isn't it?"

Our eyes locked in a battle of scowls.

Luther lowered his chin. "You want brutal honesty? What happened in Ignios was a disaster. We barely survived."

I shrugged. "It turned out fine in the end."

"Fine? *Fine?*" His voice grew louder, angrier. "Do you not remember how close you came to dying in my arms on that beach? If my magic hadn't come back—" He stopped himself, closing his eyes as a tremor rocked through him. "I'm the one who takes a blade to the heart for you, Diem. Not the other way around."

"No one is taking any blades to the heart," I muttered. "The wound wasn't as bad as it looked."

A lie. A shameful, extravagant lie. Had his magic not made a miraculous appearance at the last possible second, we'd both be corpses.

But if Taran and Alixe had stayed behind, so would they. Sending them away had saved their lives—that I was sure of, and that certainty was fuel on the fire of my indignant pride.

"Why do you refuse to accept that our job is to protect you?" he demanded.

"Because your job isn't to protect me, it's to serve me. Are you still willing to do that, or have I lost your faith already?"

His jaw tightened. "You know I have faith in you. You, above all else. You are *everything*."

My heart stumbled, but my anger marched on. "Ignios was messy, but it was the right call. It was the only way for all four of us to make it out alive. The real *disaster* is that I couldn't trust you to retreat when I ordered it. Either of you," I added with a sharp glance at Taran. He rubbed the back of his neck, looking abashed.

Luther was unmoved. "The High General of the Royal Guard is entitled to overrule the Crown if necessary to save their life."

"Then you can't be my High General."

The room went deathly silent.

"I've been thinking about it for a while, and..." I looked down, unable to bear his reaction. "I'm making Alixe my High General."

No one spoke. No one moved. Even the air seemed to still.

When Luther finally broke the silence, his voice was quiet. "Is this about what happened in the bedchamber?"

My cheeks warmed. "No. This is about what happened in Ignios, and in Arboros, and at the Challenging. I need a High General who can accept my choices to put myself at risk. I trust you with my life, Luther, but I can't trust you with my orders."

He opened his mouth to argue—then stopped, shook his head, and turned away. "Fine. Good. It was inevitable."

"I still want you by my side," I said, my tone softening. "Just... in a different way."

Taran let out a nervous chuckle. "You hated all that administrative work anyway, cousin. Now you can focus on trying to keep Diem alive, despite all her best efforts." He winked at me. "That's an all day, every day job."

Alixe, wisely, said nothing, though when I glanced her direction, she placed a fist over her chest with a slight nod, and I knew it was her way of showing her grateful acceptance.

I placed a hand on Luther's back. "This changes nothing between us. Whatever battles I face, I want you there to fight them with me. I can't do this without you."

"You can. And you will." He pulled out of my reach and grabbed his glass, draining it dry. "We're still going back to Lumnos. High General or not, I'm getting you home safely. I'll take on all three of you, if that's what it takes."

Tired of arguing and feeling guilty over my decision, I let out a heavy sigh and nodded. "Alright. We'll go home."

"No tricks, Diem. Promise me."

I shouldn't have been hurt by his distrust—I'd earned it.

But I was.

"I promise," I said quietly.

CHAPTER
TWENTY-SEVEN

After my fight with Luther, the communal discomfort was so thick I could taste it—bitter and slimy, like cream gone bad.

I grabbed Taran's hand and dragged him to the table. "Let me check your wounds."

I gestured for him to remove his tunic, then opened my satchel to dig out the bundle of herbs I'd collected in Arboros.

"Shit," I said, frowning. "I'm running lower than I thought."

Luther looked over.

"Do you not have enough?" Taran asked.

"Depends on how fast you heal."

"Can you get more in Lumnos?"

"Nothing this strong." I saw his face go pale, and I quickly forced a smile. "I'm sure I won't need them. You're going to be fine."

He sulked. "This must be bad. She's lying again."

I set to work removing Taran's bandages. Though the poultice was still white—usually a sign it had not worked—I was relieved to see that the cut on his side showed no sign of the godstone's dark poison, and the wound at his shoulder had only a fading trace.

Even the wounds had mended better than expected. Godstone typically slowed a Descended's natural healing to that of a mortal's, but Taran's injuries looked like they'd been healing for weeks.

I set about preparing a new batch. "Lumnos must really like you. These are almost healed. And *that's* not a lie."

His worry seemed to ease, and he cracked a smile. "You never should have doubted me."

"I recall it being *you* who doubted *me.*"

He had the gall to look offended. "I would never, Queenie."

"No? You didn't doubt my plan in Ignios and come running back to save me?"

"Well, see, about that—"

"You didn't doubt my ability to survive the Challenging?"

"To be fair, we *all* doubted—"

"You didn't doubt that I would choose Luther when you gave me hell about it that day in Lumnos?"

"Fine, that one I should have seen coming."

"What did you say to her in Lumnos?" Luther asked.

"Nothing," Taran and I answered.

Luther's eyes narrowed.

"If I'm on the Blessed Mother's good side, I've got to milk it while it lasts," Taran blurted, hurriedly changing the subject. "Maybe I should ask for a mate, now that you've overruled my father's ban on mating cere-monies without his permission."

My brows rose. "I didn't realize you were such a romantic."

"I'm not."

Alixe snorted, and Taran shot her a scowl.

"I'm *not.*"

"You swoon at every mating mark you see." She gestured to me and Luther. "And you get bouncy every time these two touch each other."

"Maybe *some of us* are just happy to see our friends find the person they're meant to spend forever with."

A flush of emotion glowed inside me. I couldn't stop my eyes from lifting to Luther, but his were on my hands, watching me work.

I gave Taran's arm a squeeze. "You'll find your mate, I'm sure of it. And when you do, she's going to be a very lucky woman."

He smirked. "Actually—"

A section of the bookcase shook loose and swung open with a loud creak. Taran shot to his feet and shoved me behind him, using his magic to conjure a dark axe in one hand and a spear of shadow in the other.

Zalaric prowled inside in his elegant, cat-like way. His magical aura unfurled like a rich perfume, crowding the room alongside mine and Luther's.

He paused in front of Taran and gave him a withering appraisal. With the flick of a single finger, a twinkling mist surrounded Taran's hands and dissolved his weapons into smoke.

"What—I—how?" Taran sputtered. He reached for his real blade, but Zalaric was faster.

A cord of sizzling blue light snaked around the sword's hilt as Taran's fist closed on it. He yelped and snatched his hand away, shaking it like he'd been burned.

The corner of Zalaric's lip curled up. Taran growled and lunged forward, promptly slamming face-first into a glimmering shield.

I had to practically scrape my jaw off the rug. I knew from our training sessions that Taran was a skilled fighter, quick and adaptable, but Zalaric had reduced him to a fumbling novice.

"Are you done embarrassing yourself?" he asked blandly, arching a slender eyebrow pierced with golden hoops.

I grabbed Taran's arm. "It's alright—he's a friend." I eyed Zalaric. "I think."

Zalaric's focus sharpened on my face, no longer covered by my cloak. He cocked his head, curiously looking me over.

Luther and Taran edged forward to block me from view. "What news do you bring?" Luther asked.

"I can get you out of Umbros without a Centenary checkpoint, but my contact can't leave until tomorrow night."

Luther shook his head. "We need to leave tonight."

Zalaric shrugged. "Then I cannot help you."

"What price will it take to change your contact's mind?"

"It's not possible. Either wait or find your own way back."

"Surely we can wait one day," I offered.

Luther glared in silence, frustration wafting off him like steam. A long moment passed, and he said nothing.

I leaned out from behind him and tried again. "Crossing the sea in winter will be cold and rainy. We could all use a warm bed and another hot meal before we go."

I glanced at Luther. His jaw tensed and adjusted, but he offered no response.

Finally, I turned to Zalaric. "Thank you. We'll leave with your contact tomorrow night."

His eyes darted from me to Luther, gleaming with unasked questions. He held out a hand. "I don't think we've been properly introduced."

I stepped past a bristling Luther to clasp Zalaric's wrist. "Please, call me D. I'm Luther's, um, cousin." I gestured to the others. "This is Alixe—" She gave a shallow bow. "—and Taran." He crossed his arms with a scowl.

Zalaric gave Alixe a fleeting wisp of a smile. His focus lingered on Taran's chest, still bare from where my ministrations had been interrupted by his arrival. "Godstone?"

I nodded. "How did you know?"

He strolled to Taran, who stiffened bodily, and hovered a hand just above the wound at his shoulder. "May I, Terry?"

"It's Taran," he grumbled.

Zalaric shrugged. "Whatever."

Taran's mouth popped open. I bit my lip to hide my smile. A speechless Taran was something I never thought I'd see.

Zalaric waited patiently until Taran managed a nod, then brushed his fingers delicately over the planes of Taran's golden-tan skin. "I've learned a bit about healing so I can tend to my customers' needs. Over the years, I've seen quite a few godstone cuts."

He traced the dark veins that still webbed from the wound while Taran gawked. Without even looking away from the injury, Zalaric crooked a finger under Taran's slackened jaw and pushed it closed.

"Do you know much about treating them?" I asked.

"As I understand it, they can't be treated. It's simply up to luck whether the person survives." He clicked his tongue. "Brutal death. Terribly painful. But this..." He swiped a thumb over the ridge of Taran's collarbone and hummed. I began to genuinely worry Taran might pass away from shock. "This looks almost healed." His gaze dragged up to Taran's face. "I've never seen anyone survive godstone. You're very lucky."

Taran swallowed. "Well you're very... very..." He swallowed again. "Very..."

"Rich," Zalaric answered for him. He spun on his heel and strode toward the bookshelves. "And unlike you royals, I earned my fortune. Something I must now get back to doing."

I followed behind him. "Thank you again, Zalaric. Your generosity is much appreciated."

"I'm many things, D, but *generous* isn't one of them. The bill for all of this will be outrageous. I hope you're prepared to pay."

"We are," I insisted, having no idea whether we were or not, but Alixe was busy smirking at Taran while Luther had resumed his staring match with the fireplace.

As I watched Zalaric go to leave, my heart twisted with the urge to shower him in questions—about his upbringing in Umbros, about the half-mortal children, about his relationship with my mother. This was a man with endless stories to tell, and I yearned to hear them all.

Maybe he yearned to tell them, too, because he hesitated at the last moment. "If you wish, I could take you on a tour of the city tomorrow morning. I'd be happy to show you the lesser-known markets and all the best food vendors." He gave a feline smile. "For a fee, of course."

A disapproving growl rolled out from behind me, no doubt from Luther's throat.

I sighed. "It's a lovely offer, but we can't risk being stopped."

"Oh, the Centenaries won't bother you if you're with me. I bribe them *extremely* well to leave me and my people alone. And I can disguise your faces with my magic, in case there's anyone who might recognize you. I'm quite good at being invisible if I don't want to be seen." His eyes cut briefly to Taran. "And being noticed if I do."

I didn't have to see Luther to know he was mentally snarling at me to say no. But deep within, something was daring me to say *yes*. Though I knew the others would see it as rebellion or reckless curiosity, it was beyond that. My soul felt certain we'd been brought here for a reason—and that Zalaric's path and mine were paved with the same stones.

Trust your instincts, Luther had said.

He was definitely going to regret saying that.

"We would love a tour," I said with a warm smile. "Add it to our bill."

"Cousin," Luther said darkly. "We should discuss this. In *private*."

"No need. I'm sure Zalaric will take good care of us."

"Even so, it would be best to stay here until—"

"Then stay here," I said, my tone sharpening. I threw him a hard glance. "But I intend to go. A few hours in the city, then we return to Lumnos."

A compromise for a compromise, I thought tartly. Luther's eyes widened for a split second, then narrowed, a faint crease on his brow.

I spun back around. "We'll meet you after breakfast, Zalaric."

He eyed us both with a fascinated glint, then moved to leave, waving a dismissive hand in Taran's direction. "Try to find a shirt to wear tomorrow, Thomas."

"It's Tar—"

The bookshelf snapped into place, and Zalaric was gone.

Taran scowled. "I *really* don't like him."

I grinned. "I *really* do."

"Traitor."

I laughed and nudged him back into a chair to finish changing out his bandages. "You don't have to come. It's a risk I'm willing to take, but I won't ask the same from any of you."

"Like I'm going to trust you with *him*," he shot back. "Besides, watching you get yourself into trouble is my new favorite hobby."

"There's not going to be any trouble." I smiled sweetly. "I'm going to be on my very best behavior, just like I promised Luther. In and out of the city, no complications."

Taran snorted, and I poked him in the ribs.

"What about you, Alixe?" I asked.

"Well, actually..." Her eyes flitted apprehensively to Luther. "I would like to come. There's something I'm working on in Lumnos, and this is the only place I can find what I need."

"Perfect." I beamed at Luther. "And you, my Prince? Will you be joining us?"

"No."

My smile fell. Taran and Alixe stared at each other in shock.

"What I said," I stammered, "I—I didn't mean... it wasn't that I don't want you to come, I—"

"You three can handle it." He grabbed his cloak and threw it over his shoulders. "It's safer for one of us to stay back, in case the others are captured."

"Luther—"

He started for the door. "There's something I need to take care of while I still have my magic. I'll be back in a few hours."

I ran to follow him. "Come with us. I want you there."

"It's time to get used to having them at your side, not me." He gave me a fleeting stare. "A compromise for a compromise, Your Majesty."

He pulled away and disappeared down the hall.

AN INTENSE COCOON of heat coiled around me, stirring me from what was already a restless sleep. Two strong arms looped around my body and pulled me into the air. A flash of panic gave way to relief as a familiar musk filled my nose.

"Luther," I murmured drowsily.

"Go back to sleep."

My bone-tired body whimpered to do exactly that, though I fought the pull.

After Luther left, Alixe and Taran had distracted me with lessons on how to use my magic, until eventually they surrendered to exhaustion and retired to bed. Unable to get Luther's last words out of my head, I had curled up into an armchair by the fire to nurse an overfull glass of whiskey and stare at the door, awaiting his return. At some point, I must have drifted off.

"You finally get a bed and you choose to sleep on floors and chairs," he said softly.

His teasing tone soothed my nerves. I nuzzled into his chest and the blissful warmth soaking through his sweater. "You were gone so long."

"I'm sorry I worried you. I lost track of time."

"Where did you go?"

He rested his chin atop my head. "To pray. I saw a shrine to Blessed Mother Lumnos on our way in, and I wanted to make an offering."

"What were you praying for?"

He didn't answer for a long moment. I shifted my hand until it sat above his heart.

"*Peace*," he whispered with a shaky exhale.

He laid me on the bed and covered me in downy blankets, then fussed over a hearth in the corner until the room warmed.

He moved to the edge of the bed beside me and placed his hand next to mine. I was instantly taken back to the morning after the armory fire, when I'd woken up in a palace bed with him at my side. It was the first day he'd let me see his smile—that true, brilliant, world-illuminating smile I hadn't yet realized was only for me.

What I wouldn't give to see that smile on his face again.

He let out a sigh. "I owe you an apology for how I acted earlier. I was out of line." He hooked a finger around mine. "I've never cared for anyone the way I care for you. Knowing you're in danger brings out a darkness in me I'm not proud of."

"Are you angry at me?"

"I am angry. But not at you." He tucked my hair behind my ear. "Never at you, my Queen."

"At Alixe? Luther, she didn't—"

"Not at her, either. She did exactly what I would have done, if the Crown were anyone but you."

I looped another finger through his. "Then who are you angry at?"

He stared at our joined hands, the muscles along his throat flexing as if struggling to pull the words forward—or fighting to keep them down.

He leaned down and set a kiss on my temple. "Sleep, my Queen."

"Wait—don't go. I promise I won't touch you."

He flinched, like my words had struck a blow.

"Stay," I pleaded.

An unreadable emotion swam across his face, while my heart held its breath in hope. His eyes glowed faintly with the final embers of his magic before it flickered and disappeared, silent once more.

With a deep breath, he rounded the bed and climbed in beside me. Even the two feet of empty space between us and his awkward position— flat on his back and fully clothed, his guarded expression fixed on the ceiling —couldn't dampen my relief.

I turned on my side and laid my hand out, palm up. Not pushing him —I was determined to respect his boundaries, even if I didn't understand them. Even if they were breaking my heart.

But offering.

Hoping.

The dim wash of the firelight painted his skin in soft amber and sienna. I watched the dance of colors over his handsome features until my eyelids grew heavy. Though I couldn't be sure whether it was real or a dream, I swore I felt rough, warm skin close around my hand as my mind slipped away.

CHAPTER
TWENTY-EIGHT

"The market in the main hall is mostly overpriced junk to make an easy coin off casual travelers," Zalaric explained as we walked. "The real show is hidden in the lower levels like these."

We were on hour three of Zalaric's grand tour of Umbros City, having already spent the morning wandering through the luxurious gowns of the cloth market, the fragrant aromas of the spice market, and, to my delight, the book market. They nearly had to physically restrain me from buying every book on mortal history—which, I was relieved to discover, were plentiful. I'd reluctantly sulked away with a silent vow to establish a mortal library back home and enlist Zalaric's help to fill it.

Though all the markets had been filled with treasures of the most unexpected sort, strolling into the gem market was like stepping into a different world.

My eyes bulged at the opulence on display—rubies as large as my fist, platinum filigree resembling shimmering lace, and brightly colored stones emanating with their own internal light. I thought I'd seen the ultimate extravagance on the Descended at my Ascension Ball, but the baubles here put even the Twenty Houses to shame.

"Who can afford this?" I asked breathlessly.

"Royals, mostly," Zalaric answered. "Many of the dealers here work directly with the Crowns."

Alixe nodded. "King Ulther sent guards to pick up shipments here often. I heard he practically emptied the market out in preparation for his mating ceremony."

Zalaric gave me a probing glance. "I'm sure your new Queen has her fair share of shiny objects."

I absently touched my throat, thinking of the only jewelry I owned—the pendant Luther had given me at my Challenging. I'd opted not to wear it to my Rite of Coronation, aiming to look humble for my first meeting with the other Crowns. Though that had been a fortuitous choice—it surely would have been stolen or destroyed by the Guardians—I longed to return home and secure it back on my neck.

"She has what she needs," I answered.

Alixe nudged my arm. "We could take a gift back to her, if you see anything she would like."

I tried to wrap my head around any of the pieces belonging to me. Growing up, even if I could have afforded jewelry, wearing it would have only made me a target in the alleys of Mortal City.

But now I was Queen of a realm. And not just any realm—Lumnos, where beauty and extravagance were currency. Soaking myself in rare stones and precious metals was practically in the job description.

My eyes hooked on a stunning collar of black pearls studded with pale sapphires. I reached for it, then hesitated, flushing and feeling oddly unworthy.

"Try it on," Zalaric urged. "I know the vendor, she won't mind." He lifted it from its black velvet pillow. "Come, there's a mirror over here."

The breath tore from my lungs as I spied my reflection. Staring back at me was a wholly unfamiliar face, courtesy of Zalaric's illusions. The woman in the mirror was much older, refined, with a voluptuous figure and a stick-straight emerald bob. A smoke-hued gown that matched my eyes—my *real* eyes, not the navy ones he'd given her—draped over her curves and pooled at the floor.

I had to glance down at my body and my plain, rumpled clothes just to confirm I hadn't actually transformed. Zalaric secured the collar at my neck, then took me by the waist and spun me around.

I looked over my shoulder and gasped. The rear of the necklace cascaded into a low point that dripped down my back. In the dim light of the caves, the pearls nearly disappeared against my gown's dark fabric, making the scattered blue gemstones look like a cape of falling rain.

"It's breathtaking," I gushed. I moved and the strands swayed, setting off the fiery sparkle of the sapphires. "I've never seen anything like it."

"It was made for you," Zalaric said. "Would you like me to negotiate the price on your behalf?"

His face lit up with the prospect of whatever enormous commission I was sure he would tack on—but that wasn't what held me back.

"I—I can't. I'm not..." I shook my head. "Whatever it costs, I'm sure I don't have enough."

"Oh, I'm sure you do," Taran deadpanned over his shoulder from a nearby booth, where he was admiring golden arm cuffs that looked suspiciously similar to the ones Zalaric had worn yesterday.

"You can always charge it to House Corbois's account," Alixe offered.

Zalaric's smile pulled tighter. "Indeed. The Lumnos royals keep an open tab in the markets at all times."

A part of me deeply, *deeply* wanted to say yes. I'd never known the thrill of buying something impractical just because it was pretty. Perhaps it made me frivolous to want that, but why shouldn't I? Didn't everyone deserve to feel beautiful?

"No. I can't." I pulled the collar off before my resolve buckled. "I need to save my money for other things."

Like a war.

Zalaric's brows lifted. "Interesting. I've never heard a royal talk about *saving money* before."

I tensed, remembering the part I was supposed to be playing. A real Corbois would have bought it without a second thought, wouldn't they?

"She's very frugal," Alixe jumped in. "Always has been, ever since she was a little girl."

I nodded vigorously.

Zalaric pursed his lips. He took the collar and stared at it, running a thumb over the sapphires, then looked up at me. "I don't think I noticed until now, but your eyes are not quite blue, are they?"

"They were," I rushed out. "Born brown—I mean blue. Lost the color in a childhood illness."

He angled his head. "Interesting."

I cringed at my mistake. I'd repeated the same excuse so many times, the words had become a reflex.

Alixe glanced in the mirror and let out a surprised laugh at her reflection. She wore the disguise of a large, burly man, shirtless and coated head to toe in intricate tattoos.

"How are you able to make us appear normal to each other, but different to everyone else?" she asked. "I've never seen that done before."

"I bend the light around a shield so the illusion is only visible from the outside."

"But it's so crowded—how do you keep other people from walking into the sides of the shield?"

He waved a hand and, for a split second, the shield shimmered into view. It wrapped like a second skin around each of our bodies and skimmed the floor, so that anyone passing between us would walk over it like a carpet, rather than bumping into it.

Alixe looked impressed. "That's very clever. Where did you train?"

"I didn't. I'm self-taught."

Taran dropped what he was holding with a loud *clang*. "*What?* You have no training? At all?"

Zalaric bristled. "We half-mortals don't get the luxury of attending your elite Descended academies. I was raised by a mortal, so I had to learn how to use my magic on my own."

Raised by a mortal? My heart tripled in size as my fondness for him grew.

Taran blinked repeatedly. "But... your magic... yesterday, you... you were so..."

"So much better than you? I guess your academies aren't that elite after all." Taran growled, and Zalaric's amused expression took on a mischievous twinkle. "Don't worry, I saved my best disguise for you."

"Oh, no," Alixe mumbled.

Taran stomped over to the mirror and let out a strangled, horrified noise.

"You made me *a little girl!?*"

Standing across from Taran, his infuriated expression mirrored on her cherubic face, was an adorable child of about eight with golden ringlets and a petal pink dress, carrying a basket of daisies.

My hands clamped over my mouth, but not before a loud cackle burst out. I shot him an apologetic look, my shoulders shaking uncontrollably.

"Change it," he hissed at Zalaric.

"I don't think so. It fits you quite well. Although I might consider it—for a price."

"Change it, or I swear to the Kindred, I'll—"

"You should thank me. It's a boon for haggling. The sellers will be much more likely to give a discount to a little girl."

"Look at me," Taran shouted. "I'm four feet tall! My head barely reaches above the tables!"

"At least that explains why the vendors have been smiling down at your crotch all day," I teased.

He glared at me. "You're supposed to be on *my* side, Queenie. This is how you repay me for rescuing you from the Guar—"

Alixe elbowed him hard in the ribs and gave him a wide-eyed look.

"What?" he snapped. His face blanched. "Oh."

If Zalaric noticed Taran's slip-up, he showed no sign. "I can't change it here or someone might notice. You'll have to live with it for now, Tristan."

Taran's jaw clenched. "That's not my name."

Zalaric frowned. "Tybold?"

"That's a gods-damned *gryvern* name."

"My apologies. I remember now. It's Tulip."

"That's a *fucking flower!*"

Alixe and I looked at each other, both of us pressing our lips tight to hold back laughter.

"One of us should probably break this up before there's bloodshed," I whispered to her. "But I'm enjoying it too much to intervene."

"So am I. Even Aemonn doesn't get him this worked up."

"*Taran! T-A-R-A-N! It's not that difficult!*"

Alixe jogged forward to grab his arm. "Cousin, look, I see some booths with armor. Maybe we can find something useful."

As they walked away, I noticed Zalaric's haughty veneer crack as a genuine smile warmed his features.

"Did I go too far?" he asked.

"Not at all. He's usually the one teasing me, so you have my full support."

"Perfect. Feel free to hire me any time you need revenge."

"For a fee?" I joked, and he grinned.

"Of course. Though I might consider a discount if he always looks that handsome when he's mad."

My mouth hung open. Was Zalaric...*flirting* with Taran?

"Oh, actually, um, I'm not sure he's interested in—" I stopped myself. I didn't really know what Taran was interested in. I had made assumptions, but I'd never bothered to ask. That realization left me a little ashamed.

Zalaric held his elbow out. "Walk with me?"

I slipped my arm through his, and we began to stroll. "Thank you again for offering to do this."

"Anything for my guests."

"In that case... I have a request. I was hoping you might be willing to tell me about yourself."

"Don't you already know how Luther and I are acquainted?"

"I do. I'm not asking about him—I want to know about you. *Your* story. I so rarely get to meet people like you back in Lumnos. I'd love to know what your life has been like here—if you're comfortable sharing."

He eyed me with a hint of skepticism, then turned me toward a staircase that led to a walkway around the perimeter of the market where the crowds were thinner.

"I was born in Lumnos," he began, "in Mortal City, in a neighborhood called Paradise Row. You've probably never even heard of it."

I bit down hard and didn't respond.

"For seven years, I lived in hiding while my mother worked in a tavern. It wasn't the safest place, but she did the best she could, and we were happy enough—until one day, she didn't come home. I never discovered why."

I squeezed his arm. "I'm so sorry for your loss, Zalaric."

His jaw flexed. "It was long ago. I barely remember her now."

"You were so young. What did you do?"

"At first, I was too scared to leave. I'd never left our home before that day. Eventually I got hungry and left to wander the streets and beg. It didn't take long for someone to see my eyes and hand me off to the Royal Guard to get the very large reward for turning in half-breeds."

I scowled. "That's awful. Those bounties are a vicious practice."

"Don't tell Luther that. They were his idea."

I couldn't hide my shock. "They were?"

Zalaric nodded. "Once he put the bounty in place, people stopped executing the half-mortals themselves and started delivering the children to him alive to collect it. That's how he was able to save so many."

I stared forward as my world reoriented. I'd long despised the Crown's system of trading rewards for information, believing it immeasurably cruel for turning neighbor against neighbor. What if it had all been Luther's way of ensuring he could intervene for those who deserved saving?

"Oh, Luther," I murmured, my heart skipping several beats.

"If only I'd known then that I could trust him. When they took me to him, I thought I was going to be killed, so I tried to escape. One of the guards caught me and slashed my throat." He lowered the high neck of his robes to reveal the scar across his neck. "Luther managed to stop the bleeding enough to get me here to Umbros. To Miss Margie."

His eyes took on a faraway look as he smiled fondly. "She was a hell of a woman. Smart and resourceful. Fiery, too. She could reduce you to ash with just a few words, but only if you deserved it. And she was loving. Generous to a fault. She helped Luther find homes for the orphans she could, and the rest, she kept herself. She treated me like a son, and I loved her like a mother."

"She sounds like a wonderful person."

"She was. She was beautiful, too." He gazed out over the market, his expression hardening. "She made a good living selling her body in the skin market, but she was a mortal. Her body aged, the money dried up, and we fell into poverty." He sighed. "She never stopped taking in the orphans. Even when she had nothing to give them, she found a way."

Zalaric and I walked in silence for a while, his sadness palpable in the air. I slipped my hand in his. He gave me a tight smile, his throat working.

"One day Margie got sick, and she couldn't afford a healer. I begged her to ask for money from Luther or the families she'd placed children with. She refused, of course. She didn't want to scare them off from working with her." His voice turned pithy. "She told me '*Zal, money should never get in the way of doing the right thing.*'"

"I get the sense you disagree," I said gently.

"You can't do the right thing if you're dead."

I couldn't argue that.

His shoulders rolled back. "After she died, I decided I would never be poor again. I started as a pickpocket, keeping the gold and reselling whatever else I stole. Then I moved to the blood market—that's what they call the fighting rings. I couldn't afford to pay my tithe to the Queen, but fighters get their magic back while in the ring. It was the first time in my life I'd ever used it—that's when I realized I was stronger than most."

I laughed. "That's putting it mildly. Other than Luther, no one I've met in Lumnos even comes close."

"Except the Queen, of course."

"Oh, um... right, yes. Except her, of course."

His lips curved up. "And you."

"I, uh... yes, I suppose." I cleared my throat. "Is that where you taught yourself how to use magic—in those fights?"

"It is. You learn fast, when your survival depends on it. I started winning frequently there, then did some time of my own in the skin markets. By then I'd won the attention of the more powerful people in Umbros. They hired me for odd jobs, and over time, I earned a reputation for handling difficult tasks discreetly, for those willing to pay the right price. That's what I still do today."

"And the inn?" I asked.

"I own it, but the other Lumnos half-mortals run it and split the profits among themselves. It gives the younger ones a place to call home and the older ones a place to earn a living safely. I make sure none of them ever have to make the choices Margie and I were forced to make."

I nudged his side. "I thought you said you weren't generous."

He shot me a good-natured glare. "Don't tell anyone. You'll ruin my reputation."

"Don't worry—I'm good at keeping secrets." We shared a smile and continued walking. His remarkable openness was making me braver. "I noticed the children at the inn are very skilled for their age."

"I make sure they all get the best education money can buy." He beamed proudly. "Some of mine have even been invited to study in Sophos."

My stomach turned. I knew the dark fate that awaited mortals invited to study there—would it be the same for the Lumnos half-mortals?

"That's... nice, but I didn't mean their education. I was referring to their magic. Luther said they're better trained than the Descended children in Lumnos."

He hummed indifferently. "Is that so?"

"I suspect they have a very good teacher. A very powerful one. One who could, let's say, make quite an embarrassment of a certain '*handsome*' Corbois cousin."

Zalaric's smirk gave him away.

I stopped and turned to face him. "Come to Lumnos and teach me. Name your fee, and I'll pay it."

"You're a member of the royal family. Surely you have access to the best training in the realm."

I didn't answer at first, weighing my words. That same unexplainable instinct was cajoling me again, that prodding urge to push forward despite all good sense and reason.

"I did not have the typical Corbois upbringing." I glanced around and dropped my voice low. "I, too, know what it's like to have to work to survive."

To my surprise, he didn't react at all. His expression remained flat as he studied my face. "You're a half-mortal, aren't you?"

Alarm bells blared in my head. I couldn't admit that—I *couldn't*. The only way a half-mortal could so freely interact with the royal family was if they were immune from the laws, and the only person with immunity was the Crown. A man as smart as Zalaric would make the connection in a second.

But before I could deny it, a grin spread across his face. "I knew it! I knew as soon as I saw you. You have that same look that all the rest of us have."

I glanced around nervously. "What look?"

"The look of someone trying to find a place in the world where they belong."

I huffed and pulled him back into a slow stroll. "I refuse to confirm or deny."

"You don't have to, I know I'm right. I can *always* spot another one." His lip hooked into a wicked smirk. "Which reminds me—where is the Prince today?"

It took every atom, every hair, every drop of blood, every last spark of resolve in my body to suppress my reaction.

My heart hammered furiously, a frightened bird in a tiny cage. This was Luther's darkest, most closely guarded secret. Did Zalaric know? Had my mother told him? Had he told anyone else?

"He's resting," I said stiffly. "We had a long journey."

My mind flashed back to this morning. Though we'd fallen asleep on separate sides, I'd woken up tangled in his embrace, his lips against my temple. He'd been drenched in sweat, skin flushed. The temptation to peel away his scarf and heavy clothes to cool him off was nearly insurmountable.

He'd been sleeping so soundly he didn't even stir when I pried myself free. I sat at his side for longer than I wanted to admit, staring at him and wondering what he was so adamant to hide.

Alixe and Taran waved, so I led us back down the stairs and into the market. "You'll come to Lumnos, then? Nothing would make me happier than emptying a Corbois coffer or two for you."

"I think I need to know more about this mysterious new Queen first. Do you know her well?"

"No," I blurted, a little too fast. "I've only met her once or twice."

"Luther seems *very* fond of her." Zalaric was watching me intently. "And he's convinced she's a friend to the half-mortals."

"Then it must be true. He knows her best." I glanced at him. "Can I ask you a personal question?"

"Sure, but I may charge you for it."

"The scar on your neck—why did you keep it? Surely there are Fortos healers here who could have removed it."

"I considered it, but I always remembered the Prince who saved my life. I told myself if he wasn't ashamed of his, I shouldn't be ashamed of mine. And besides..." He tipped his face to me with a knowing look. "I find scars quite sexy, don't you?"

My cheeks heated. "Yes, I do."

CHAPTER
TWENTY-NINE

We caught up to Alixe and Taran, the latter of whom was hurling obscenities at a merchant who had declared him too much of a *cute little doll* to buy any of the weapons at their booth.

Zalaric sighed dramatically. "I suppose this is my fault, so I have to fix it, as well."

"Must you? I want to see everyone's faces when a little girl chokes a grown man half to death."

Zalaric chuckled as he strode on ahead. "There you are, Theresa. Why are you arguing with that nice man, my pretty poppet?"

"I hope Taran remembers he can't actually kill Zalaric or we'll never get home," Alixe said.

I'd like to see him try, I thought.

She laughed. "Me, too. It would be a hell of a match."

I frowned. That was... odd.

She gestured for me to follow, then led me to a secluded corner. "I never got a chance to thank you properly for making me your High General."

"No thanks needed—you earned it. You're the best person for the job."

She nodded low. "Your trust honors me greatly."

"I'm sorry for putting you in a difficult spot with Luther—with both this and what happened in Ignios. I hate that I've come between you two."

"He'll get over it." My brows rose in surprise, and she gave a wry smile.

255

"I love Luther like a brother. He's taught me so much, and I can only hope to be half the leader he's been."

"But?" I prodded.

"But... what you said to him was right, and I respect you all the more for seeing it. Under Ulther, the realm and its people were always Luther's priority. That's what made him such an admirable High General. Under your reign, though, he is..."

"Distracted?"

"Not at all. With you, his focus is *crystal* clear."

I frowned. "It's just in the wrong place."

Her expression turned pensive. "When you first took the Crown, Luther told me a war was coming and you were the only one who could lead us through. He claimed you were hand-picked for that purpose by the Blessed Mother herself."

The same words Luther had said to me at the Ascension Ball—a declaration of faith, his wholehearted certainty that I was fated to bring the people of Emarion together.

"He doesn't just see you as our leader, Diem. He sees you as our salvation. *Everyone's* salvation."

I stared at my wringing hands. "That's a heavy mantle to carry. I'm not sure I'm worthy of it."

"Tell me about it," she teased. "I'm now supposed to lead our salvation's personal guard into war. No pressure at all."

My laugh was tempered by the worry sinking in my chest. "Alixe, have you noticed a difference in him these past few days? Has he seemed... perhaps... a bit sad?"

She gave me a strange look. "Do *you* think he's sad?"

I blushed, suddenly feeling silly for asking. "Forget I said anything. You and Taran have known him so much longer. If something were wrong, I'm sure you'd know."

"It's true we've known each other a long time, but we don't know him the way you do. I'm not sure anyone does—or ever has."

My heart perked its ears. "What do you mean?"

"Tell me—do you know how Luther knows Zalaric?" I nodded, and she shot me a pointed look. "I don't."

"That's only one story."

"Do you know how Luther got his scar?"

"Well, yes, but—"

"I don't. I didn't know about the visions he was having, either. I defi-

256

nitely didn't know he's been helping the Guardians. Neither did Taran, and they're even closer. And I'm willing to bet there are several more of his secrets you know that we don't."

I stared blankly, unsure how to respond.

"Luther has always made time to listen to whoever needs him, no matter how trivial the issue, but he never shares his own burdens." Her expression turned solemn. "Except with you."

My insides squirmed. I wrestled a burning urge to sprint back to the inn and curl up in his arms.

"Let's head to the food market," Zalaric called out to us, waving us over. "Tabitha here is getting peckish."

An exasperated moan rang out behind him, and Alixe and I shared a smile as we set off to join them.

"What is this special project you're working on?" I asked.

"Actually, I've been wanting to discuss it with you. It's a tool of sorts. Something that could protect us against any enemy. But the details are... sensitive." She glanced around. "Too sensitive to discuss so publicly."

I nodded. "Keep working on it. We need every advantage we can get. Let's talk more when we're alone."

As Zalaric led us across Umbros City toward the food markets, we approached the cavernous central hall. It was louder now than the day we'd arrived. Voices, so many voices—a deafening roar that left my thoughts grappling for space.

It made my magic restless, too. My godhood paced, awake and alert. Analyzing. *Listening.*

I winced and rubbed my temples. "In a hall this large, you'd think the sound wouldn't be so intense."

Taran grinned and threw an arm over my shoulder. "I don't think that's the sound, *cousin.* I think that's the half-bottle of whiskey you polished off last night. You're lucky this city has no sunlight."

The pressure mounted with every step, a crushing weight against my skull. "It isn't loud to you?"

"Not really. No more than any ball usually is."

"I don't exactly have much experience with balls," I grumbled. Only my Ascension Ball, which hadn't felt anything like this.

"I do. Do you need some advice? See, men *really* love it when you put them in your—"

I punched him hard in the side, drawing raucous laughter from Taran

257

and stern looks of disapproval from onlookers who believed me to be attacking a defenseless little girl.

"You two do remember you're supposed to be avoiding attention?" Zalaric scolded.

We were almost past the main hall when a flash of light flared up just as I passed. I stumbled, nearly knocking over a table of large glass jars. Inside each one, tiny fires danced in a spectrum of colors. They seemed to glow brighter the closer I came.

My focus caught on one containing a sapphire glow. As I reached for it, my fingertips brushed the smooth glass, and the flame arched to meet my touch. A calming burst of warmth shot through my arm.

I pulled back just as the proprietor turned to face us. "Hail, madam. You'll not find anything like this in all the nine realms."

"What is it?" I asked.

"Bottled dragonfyre, pulled from the throats of the gryverns themselves. Got almost all nine of 'em. Even..." His voice hushed. "Her Majesty's own."

He lifted the fabric draped over his table. Hidden beneath, barely visible, a line of jars contained whirling black flames.

"Used to have the full set," he said proudly. "Sold the last of my Fortos stock a few years back. There'll be no more where that came from, but I still have one left from the dead Montios beast." He jerked his chin toward a sole jar in the center of his stash, where a pale lavender flame burned low and slow, little more than an inch in height.

My fingers twitched closer, pulled by some innate urge. I hesitated, hand hovering in midair.

"What do you use them for?"

"Whatever you like, madam. That's none of my business."

"How did you get them?"

He smirked. "That's none of *yours*."

"It's a ruse to scam the tourists," Zalaric whispered in my ear. "A bit of oil set alight."

I wasn't so convinced. Something about them called to me, and I was finding it harder and harder to ignore the lonely violet flame burning quietly at the center.

Like the Fortos gryvern, the Montios gryvern had been killed centuries ago during the Blood War. If this truly was its dragonfyre, it might be the last existing remnant of the creature that once guarded the desolate mountain realm.

"You must be new to Umbros," the man mused, a gleam in his eye. "You should know better than to ask about the provenance of items sold in the dark markets. That kind of mistake can get you killed." He rocked on his heels. "Lucky you only slipped up with me. I can be very forgetful—for my customers, of course."

My magic stirred at the threat underlying his tone. Zalaric must have felt it in my aura, as he subtly edged away.

I pointed to the lilac flame. "How much for this one?"

"Ah, exquisite taste. For you, a special price." He paused, sizing me up. "A thousand gold marks."

I nearly choked. I'd never owned that much money in all my days *combined*.

I shook my head. "I don't have—"

"Fifty," Zalaric countered.

My face snapped to him in surprise.

The man scoffed. "Don't insult me. It's worth a hundred times that."

"It's only worth what someone's willing to pay," Zalaric shot back. "That gryvern's been dead for centuries. If you haven't sold it by now, it's time for a discount."

The man's eyes narrowed. "Nine hundred, not a mark lower. This here's the rarest item in the market. There won't be another for sale ever again."

"Until next month, when your stock has mysteriously replenished," Zalaric muttered.

"You *dare* call me a liar?"

"We both know these don't come from any gryverns. Give us a fair price."

The merchant spat at his feet. "I should open one and make you stick your hand in. Then we'll see if you doubt the power of my dragonfyre."

"One hundred."

The man waved him off. "Get out of my sight. I wouldn't sell to you for any price."

Zalaric rolled his eyes and tried to nudge me away, but I resisted, my gaze fixed on the lone jar at the center. My godhood hummed, equally intrigued.

"The Montios gryvern—what was its name?" I asked.

"Rymari," the man answered gruffly. "She was the oldest of the gryverns, even though Montios was youngest of the Kindred. She was the most beautiful, too. Pure white from tongue to tail, with scales like opals. They say it never stops snowing in the place where she died."

Zalaric leaned in to my ear. "You truly want it?"

I didn't know how to answer.

My throat tightened watching the pale flame sway in its vessel. The other jars seemed to blaze with defiance, but this one was so small and weak, so dreadfully *alone*.

Rise, the *voice* inside me hissed.

"Rise," I echoed without thinking.

The flame fluttered, then sparked as if lit anew. It flourished to twice its size, then doubled again, then once more, leaving the jar blazing with a blinding violet light.

"Another trick," Zalaric said under his breath, though he sounded significantly less certain.

The merchant reached for the jar. As his fingers skimmed the glass, a sizzling sound rose from his hand, and he jerked back with a swear.

"Looks like this one found the owner it wants," he said, laughing nervously. He rubbed at his hand, his skin now blooming bright red. I realized with a start that his eyes were brown—a mortal.

I turned to Alixe. "How much gold can we spare?" I was surprised as anyone to hear the words come out of my mouth.

She handed over her pouch. "The three of us brought ten thousand marks each. We can pull more from House Corbois's account, if needed."

I closed my eyes briefly. The ease with which she talked about such staggering, life-altering wealth, the kind no mortal in Lumnos would ever know...

I forced my resentment away and dug into the pouch, grabbing well over a thousand marks and shoving it toward the man. "Here."

Zalaric stepped in front of my hand. "At least let me negotiate a better price."

"Why bother?" I asked. "I did nothing to earn this gold. I'd rather a mortal have it than House Corbois."

Amazement darted over his face, then softened into something deeper, a complex understanding. He gave me a slow once-over as if meeting me anew.

I turned back to the merchant and handed him the coins, then reached for the jar. The man lunged to stop me.

"Madam, wait, you'll burn yourse—"

He fell silent as I cradled the jar in my hands. Though the glass was cool to my touch, once again a warm, soothing tingle spread up my arms.

"It's not too hot for you?" he asked. The beginnings of suspicion threaded through his voice. "Where did you say you're from?"

"She didn't," Zalaric said firmly. He plucked another gold coin from the pouch in my hand and held it up. "We're not from anywhere. And you never saw us, isn't that right?"

The merchant smiled. "Of course. I forget all my best customers. It's the Umbros way." He took Zalaric's coin and scurried around the table. "At least let me wrap it up for you."

I clutched the jar to my chest, feeling strangely protective of it. "No, thank you. I'll be fine."

"It's unwise to carry your purchases so openly. It will attract attention to us both." He began to walk toward me. "Here, let me take—"

His hand closed around my wrist, and I froze.

And so did the flames.

All of them.

Every row, every jar, every hue of blazing fire—completely, *impossibly* still.

"Don't touch her," Taran growled, his hand moving to the hilt of his blade as he stepped forward.

The man's jaw hung agape. "How... how did you...?"

The flames abruptly grew, both in brightness and heat. Within seconds, our entire half of the market was illuminated with their rainbow glow.

"Make it stop," the man hissed, releasing my arm. "*Now*, before the Centenaries come investigating."

I backed away, shaking my head. "I didn't... I don't even know how—"

The jars began to vibrate. Glass clinked as they rattled against their shelves. In my arms, the purple flames thrashed against the walls of the vessel, almost as if it was trying to get to me—to *protect* me.

"*Stop*," I pleaded under my breath.

The rattling immediately fell silent.

"Calm down," I whispered. "I'm safe."

Slowly, the flames faded back to their original state, and the brilliant light receded to a muted, flickering burn.

"How did you do that?" the man demanded.

Zalaric didn't wait for me to answer—not that I would have had any answer to give. He threw an uneasy glance at a pair of red-caped men in

261

thick body armor sauntering toward us, then pushed me in front of him. "Let's go."

I tucked the jar under my arm as we hurried away. Zalaric gave a languid roll of his wrist, and shadows crept in thick at our backs to shield us from sight.

"I—I think I've seen enough of Umbros," I stammered, my mind reeling.

Alixe nodded. "Let's go back to the inn."

Zalaric looked disappointed. "Are you sure? I thought you might like to see the iron markets." He glanced at Alixe. "There's a vendor there who can help with the project you asked me about earlier."

"You should go," I told her. "That's important. You too, Taran—I don't need a chaperone. And Luther's at the inn, so..." Taran grinned as I trailed off, his eyebrows wiggling, and my cheeks turned hot.

"We'll at least walk you back," Alixe said. The hard edge in her tone said it was a declaration, not an offer.

I relented, and we walked together through the maze of tunnels leading to the inn. The deafening buzz in my head eased, though it didn't go silent until I waved goodbye and slipped into our suite.

I slumped against the door and leaned my head back, forcing my still-racing heart to calm. The room was dark and silent except for the crackle of the fireplace. I walked over to stoke it and noticed Luther stretched out on a divan, propped at an awkward angle with a newspaper open in his lap. His head had lolled to the side, his eyes closed.

Even in sleep, his face looked troubled. His skin was unusually pale, making his scar less prominent but his dark features even harsher.

On the table in front of him sat a stack of fresh gauze and a large bundle of herbs. They were the same kind I'd used to make my poultice, but these had been harvested differently and tied with twine.

I set down the jar of flame, then eased beside him, gingerly lifting his head and laying it in my lap.

For a long time, I sat in silence and watched him sleep, wrestling with my need to know whatever secret he was still hiding. It had become more than simple curiosity. It had taken on a sense of urgency, a foreboding warning not to let it go. It was the same feeling that had pushed me to buy the lavender fire—and the same feeling still nagging me to speak to the Umbros Queen.

But being Queen meant making compromises. I'd pushed Luther far enough. I would respect his wishes—even though I feared what might come of it.

I laid one hand on his chest and ran the other over his hair, my nails gently scratching his scalp. He made a satisfied noise low in his throat and stirred slightly. His eyes opened on me and lit with recognition.

He stiffened.

I stilled. "Is this alright?"

Stormy emotions rolled through his eyes, though eventually he nodded, and I continued my slow strokes. He set a small gold object down on the table and laid his hand on mine on his chest.

"Was that the compass?" I asked.

"I like to keep it nearby," he said, his voice rough from sleep. "Where are the others?"

"Still out with Zalaric." I glanced at the herbs on the table. "I see you went shopping. Without me." My eyes narrowed in jest. "How dare you."

He gave a small smile, and my heart smiled back. "You said you were running low. I bought more, in case..." His muscles bunched under my hand as he swallowed. "...in case Taran needs them."

I brushed my thumb along his sweat-beaded forehead, trying to smooth the deep creases of worry carved between his eyes. Though I felt confident Taran was healing, Luther's distress hadn't eased—it almost seemed to be *worsening*.

He glanced at the jar of purple flames. "What is that?"

"According to the seller, it's bottled dragonfyre from the Montios gryvern. According to Zalaric, it's a scam for gullible suckers. I'm choosing to believe the former."

I smirked down at him, but he didn't react, still watching the flame intensely.

"Why did you buy it?" he asked.

"I'm not sure. I had a feeling I should. A hunch, I suppose."

He nodded slowly, like he'd already known that would be my answer.

"Have you ever been to Montios?" he asked.

"Not really. Henri and I went once, but we didn't stay long."

His chest rumbled at the mention of Henri. "Who did you visit there?"

"No one. We just wanted to step over the border and defy their ban on mortals. We thought it would be fun to see if we would get caught."

"Fun? You could have been killed."

I grinned. "That's what made it fun."

He closed his eyes and sighed. "It's a miracle you made it to adulthood."

"Father used to tell me that almost daily." I tried to sound lighthearted, but my throat went tight at the memory of my father, my voice wobbling. Luther kissed my palm in silent support.

"What other realms have you been to?" he asked.

"All of them except Sophos now. This is my first time in Umbros. I'd never been to Ignios before, either. Hopefully I'll never have to go back."

His hand tightened on mine. "You should go to Sophos. Find an excuse to request a visit. It doesn't have to be long—a day trip to the libraries, perhaps."

"I doubt the Sophos Crown would welcome me. They already think I'm an imposter."

"Then do what you did in Montios. Sneak to the border and step over it. Just for a moment."

I frowned down at him. "What good would that do?"

"Call it a hunch." He sat upright and closed the newspaper that had been sitting in his lap, then handed it to me. "I found this on a table in the tavern. There's something in it you should see."

I scanned the pages with genuine interest. We had nothing like this in Lumnos—at least not in Mortal City. The only news we got came from tavern gossip or mortal travelers passing through on the Ring Road.

Most of the newspaper highlighted local news—marriages, babies, and the like. It was unexpectedly quaint, given Umbros's depraved reputation. Among all the sin and excess, thousands of refugees who had fled their own realms had built a thriving community here all their own.

What really caught my eye, though, were the images scattered among the printed stories. They were lifelike and vivid, seeming almost lit from within. They shimmered with hints of movement—hair blowing in the wind, eyes crinkling with a smile. It was a novel trick of magic, perhaps from a Lumnos illusion or one of Sophos's innovations.

There were stories from elsewhere in the realm, including one on my coronation-gone-wrong. I was shocked to see an acknowledgment that the rebels had taken Coeurîle, especially since the Crowns had formally denied it.

"Do you think the Umbros Queen has seen this?" I asked incredulously.

"I'm not sure—but there's something more important." He pointed to a story on rebel attacks in the northern realms. Apparently, the Emarion

Army had deployed a battalion of eighty Descended soldiers to Montios—and every last one had disappeared without a trace.

"Gods, an entire battalion? I didn't realize the Guardians were that strong."

"They're not. But someone helping them is." He reached over to turn the page for me, and my heart jumped into my throat.

Staring back was a face I'd never forget. Striking features, colorless and pale. Silvery, glittering skin. A brilliant glow radiating around him, illuminating a horde of armed mortals at his back.

"It's the man from our vision," I breathed. "The one who called me—"

"Daughter of the Forgotten," he finished. "The same one who asked you to help him kill all the Descended."

I stared into the man's eyes. A shiver rippled along my spine and seemed to burrow straight down into my bones. It was like he was watching me somehow, seeing me from a continent away.

Like he knew me.

Like he was waiting for me.

The vision I'd had the day of the Challenging flashed through my mind. The battlefield. The dead bodies. The sword in my hand, and Luther at my side.

The man offering me his hand as I was torn apart by a desperate need to *fight* and a senseless urge to *surrender*.

I slammed the paper closed and shoved it to the side. My heart was thundering, my godhood reeling. "He's real. And he's here in Emarion."

"And helping the Guardians," Luther said.

"I should be happy to see Descended and mortals working together... but this doesn't feel like a good thing, does it?"

When I met Luther's gaze, his eyes were dark with shadows.

"No. It doesn't."

CHAPTER

THIRTY

As a continent surrounded by water both inside and out, Emarion's ports were crucial to its existence. Though each realm had its own, there were only three of significance.

The port in Fortos, while large, was controlled by the Emarion Army. Its tightly regulated activity dealt mainly in weapons and soldiers.

The port in Meros, Realm of Sea and Sky, was the primary port for all nine realms. Ships carrying passengers and cargo alike moved in and out around the clock, a highly organized dance carried out under the always-shining Meros sun, thanks to its Descended's ability to manipulate the weather through their wind and water magic.

The port of Umbros, however, was its close rival. Though located nearby, Umbros offered something Meros would not: a blind eye for all those willing to share their profits—and their secrets—with its Queen.

No one really knew what passed through its dark docks, because unlike in Meros and Fortos, every ship in Umbros was off the books. Boats wove their way through a tangle of underground passages, stopping in solitary caves to be loaded and unloaded under the cloak of darkness, often with a cadre of paid mercenaries to keep prying eyes and ears at bay.

Only the Centenaries knew the true scale of their port, and they weren't talking—at least not to anyone but their Queen.

"There are Centenaries stationed at all the places where the canals open up to the Sacred Sea," Zalaric explained as he led us through the tunnels, draped in an illusion to hide us from sight. "They scan the minds of everyone on board to ensure all tariffs have been paid. Many have tried to outwit them, but no one's ever succeeded."

"Ever?" Taran asked uneasily. "You're telling us this *now?*"

"You're not going to outwit them. You're going to avoid them entirely." I expected a smirk or some teasing banter, but Zalaric's expression was somber. "My contact knows a hidden way out. I don't know any more than that—I can't, or else it would be compromised the next time I report to the Centenaries to pay my tariffs."

"Does that mean the Queen will eventually know we were here?" Luther asked. He walked close at my side, one hand on my back and the other on his weapon.

Zalaric's eyes darted to me before he answered. "She will. I cannot hide it forever."

There was a deliberate tone in his voice that set the hair on my nape prickling.

"Will you be in trouble when they discover you helped us?" I asked.

He looked away. "Don't worry about me. A jaguar always lands on its feet."

Although the hallways were pitch-black save for a handful of glowing orbs at our feet, the shining prospect of home was drawing me forward.

Until now, I hadn't allowed myself to dwell on what awaited me back in Lumnos. It was too easy to succumb to the anxiety of what horrible things might have happened in the weeks I'd been gone.

My brother. My mother. Henri. Eleanor. Vance and the Guardians. Maura and the mortals.

But soon, so soon, I could finally take my throne and oust Remis as Regent. The flameroot was nearly gone from my system, and by the time our boat arrived, my magic would be restored in full. I would have the authority—and the might—to put my plans in action.

Luther was right. Wasting any more time here would have been a folly. The Queen of Umbros, and whatever answers she held, would have to wait.

Luther slowed our pace until we were out of earshot of the others, then leaned in close. "Are you having any more hunches?"

"No, why?"

He didn't answer. His pale eyes were on high alert, jumping warily around the shadows.

"Are *you* having any?" I asked.

He shook his head, but it was far from convincing.

"We'll be home soon. That will put us all in higher spirits." I tugged on his cloak until his gaze dropped to mine, then offered a hopeful smile. "Then we can get to work saving the realm. Together."

His features turned stony. "*You* will save our people. You don't need me or anyone else."

"Of course I need you. I can't do this without every one of my advisors, but you most of all."

He stopped walking and set a hand on my shoulder. "This is war, Diem. People are going to die—people you care about—and when they do, you must keep going. You cannot lose yourself to grief like..." He hesitated.

"Like I did with my father?" I said, my voice cutting like a blade. Hurt bloomed as Luther stared at me without answering. "Is that why you're pushing me away, because you think I'll let my heart get in the way of my duty?"

"The world needs you. That is more important than anything else."

My tone turned to ice. "Who are you really trying to convince, Luther? Me—or yourself?" I pushed his hand off my shoulder and briskly stalked forward to join the others.

"Everything alright?" Taran asked.

"Fine," I snapped.

He looked back at Luther, then at me. "You two really need to just fuck this out of your system already."

I scowled at him. He raised his hands in surrender, though his grin was poorly hidden.

We walked in silence the rest of the way. The air turned humid and musty, and the walls glistened with a buildup of moisture. Scattered archways, locked with gates and marked with lit torches, led to stairs that descended into darkness as the faint sounds of sloshing water echoed down the corridor.

After a time, the archways ended, and the caves took on a rougher, unfinished appearance. We squeezed around large boulders and carefully maneuvered slippery, uneven terrain. I studied the jagged ceiling with apprehension. If we were discovered and I was forced to use my magic, I wasn't confident its precarious structure would hold.

Seemingly out of nowhere, the tunnel ended. A sheer rock face stretched over our heads, thick and impenetrable, no openings in sight.

Zalaric clasped his hands and turned to face us. "I'll go with you as far as I can, but beyond this point, you'll be in the hands of my contact. I will not be able to help you if anything goes wrong."

"Beyond what point?" Taran asked, scratching his head and staring at the wall of stone.

Zalaric ignored him. "There's no turning back. Are you sure you want to do this?"

Though he'd spoken the words to Luther, his eyes shifted to me.

"Do we have reason to fear?" Luther asked. "Do you not trust your contact?"

"It's *Umbros*. I trust no one here—and neither should you."

"Wonderful," Taran grumbled.

Still, Zalaric's eyes weighed on me. "I would not deliver you to them if I believed they intended to do you harm, but if they do, I cannot prevent it." His shoulders lifted in a slow shrug, but there was none of the haughtiness in it he normally displayed. Instead, he looked... resigned. Sad, almost. "I have only the power I can afford to buy. Such is the way of life in Umbros."

"We have no other choice," Luther said. "We'll have to trust your contact. Even if you do not."

Zalaric didn't move.

Just as I'd experienced once before with Luther, Zalaric's mind appeared to me as a thin wall of mist.

Look, the *voice* urged.

I jerked back a step, startled at my godhood's sudden appearance and its novel demand.

Look, it urged again.

I squinted my eyes, and the haze parted like a curtain drawn back from a window, revealing what felt like an infinite library of images that felt at once wholly foreign and yet intimately familiar. A wave of thoughts and emotions overwhelmed me, but among them, one stood out—a secret buried under a deep layer of sorrow and regret.

And suddenly, I understood.

I glanced over my shoulder at the dark tunnel at our backs, second-guessing my choices and wondering if I was leading us all to ruin.

I reeled my godhood back in and looked back at Zalaric, then subtly dipped my chin.

Understanding. Accepting.

He seemed to understand, too. His shoulders sank. His head hung as he swept one hand in a graceful arc at his side, and the stone along the wall began to shimmer in place.

A bird-like chirp rang out, sounding muffled and far away. Zalaric balled his fist, and the shimmering disappeared, revealing a narrow crawl-space carved into the rock.

"Go ahead," he said, gesturing toward it.

Taran crossed his arms. "You first."

"I have to go last, so I can conceal the opening once we're all through." Zalaric raked his eyes over Taran, one eyebrow raised. "But if *you* can do that, just say the word, Terrance."

Taran growled.

"At least he's getting closer to your name," Alixe whispered to him with a sly smile.

"I'll go," Luther said. "Don't follow until you hear from me."

He crouched low and wobbled. His eyes squeezed shut as he grabbed a nearby rock to steady himself. A moment later, he dropped to his knees, and slowly, stiffly, he disappeared through the crawlspace.

We waited in tense silence for a minute, then another, then finally, Luther's voice came echoing back: "All clear."

Taran followed next, then me, then Alixe. I wasn't sure Zalaric would— if for no other reason than to avoid soiling his silk robes—but he came as promised, sealing off the small opening behind us and casting us into total darkness.

"You're late," a woman's voice called from the shadows.

My heart leapt into my throat.

"Apologies," Zalaric said. "I took a longer route to avoid being followed."

Sparks rose from his palms and formed a fluffy, twinkling cloud above our heads that illuminated the woman standing before us. She was short and stout, clad in full-body leathers and laden with blades. Her cropped cherry-red hair, styled into rows of spikes, matched her crimson eyes—a Fortos Descended.

"This is the Cardinal," Zalaric said. "She'll be getting you home. Cardinal, this is—"

"Don't wanna know," she said brusquely. "Don't wanna hear your names, why you're here, or what you're up to. I know where you're going. Keep the rest to yourself." She harrumphed and spun on her heel. "Follow me."

Questions spun in my mind as we descended a set of rough-hewn stairs. How long had she been in Umbros? Had she been in the army when my mother was there? Had they known each other? Is that how she and Zalaric met? I cursed myself for being too afraid of blowing our cover to ask Zalaric about my mother when I had the chance.

The bottom of the stairs opened up to an enormous flooded cave. A stone landing ran along its edge, while a pontoon boat carrying a large wooden crate rocked gently in the water. Zalaric snuffed out his magic, leaving us in the sole light of a torch affixed to the ship's bow.

The Cardinal climbed onto the boat and opened the end of the crate. Inside, I spied a handful of bedrolls and a bucket. "Get comfortable," she said as we all shared uneasy glances. "It's a long trip."

Alixe gave Zalaric a shallow bow, and Luther stepped forward to clasp his wrist. "I believe our work together has come to an end. Her Majesty is repealing the progeny laws, so there will be no need for you to take in any more half-mortals."

"I'm grateful for what you've done all these years." Zalaric cleared his throat, his gaze skimming the ground. "So many of us owe you our lives."

"You owe me nothing," Luther said. "Those lives never should have been at risk to begin with."

"Indeed," Zalaric murmured.

"But should you wish to repay me..." Luther paused until Zalaric met his stare. "If Her Majesty needs you, answer her call. She is a Queen worth fighting for. Give her a chance, and she will earn your loyalty as surely as she has earned ours."

A more rational, more adult part of me melted at his sweet show of devotion. But the rest of me belonged to my temper, and it—and I—were still simmering in hurt from his earlier words.

If I'm worth fighting for, then why aren't you fighting for me? I wondered.

Luther's gaze snapped to me. I let out a quiet huff and looked away.

Zalaric stepped back and fidgeted with the fabric along his collar. "Be well, Phoenix."

Luther nodded stiffly. He gave me a long, lingering look, then he and Alixe set off for the boat.

Taran rubbed the back of his neck as he walked past Zalaric. "Thanks," he mumbled. "It was, uh... interesting."

Zalaric finally cracked a smile. "You were quite an unexpected surprise."

Taran grunted and started to shuffle away, then stopped and looked back. "You know, if you ever come to Lumnos... and if you ever learn to say my name correctly... maybe you could teach me some of your tricks." Zalaric's grin widened, and Taran's cheeks turned pink. "With your *magic*."

271

"I'd love to, but I'm afraid I can't visit a realm with no hairstylists."

Taran frowned at Zalaric's short, tight curls. "Lumnos has hairstylists."

"Really?" Zalaric took a strand of Taran's messy dark blonde waves and twirled it in his fingers. "Are they just too expensive for you, then? I can loan you some gold if—"

Taran scowled and snatched his hair away. "Nevermind. Forget I offered." He stormed off toward the boat.

"Goodbye, Taran Corbois," Zalaric called out. Taran looked back in surprise. "Whatever else fate has in store for us... I'm glad I met you."

Taran shook his head and continued on, muttering under his breath, "*What's wrong with my hair?*"

Zalaric watched him go with a wistful smile. He turned to face me, his back to the others.

"I will be praying for your return to Lumnos," he said. "I hope you make it there safely."

Words unspoken hung in the air.

His mantle of calm, self-assured strength faltered, and for a moment I saw a flash of the little boy who crossed a sea, wounded and alone, exiled for the crime of being born.

"I only wish you and I could have met under better circumstances," he added softly.

I laid a hand on his cheek. "I'm glad I met you too, Zalaric Hanoverre. Whatever else fate has in store."

He closed his eyes and lowered his chin. I leaned in to kiss his cheek, then paused, my mouth hovering near his ear.

"If the others leave without me, will they be safe?" I whispered.

Zalaric stilled. Slowly, he shook his head. "I'm sorry. It's too late."

I pulled back with a sigh. At my sides, two balls of whirling magic—one of light, the other of shadow—formed at my palms.

"Is there a problem?" Luther called out.

"Hurry up, lady," the Cardinal barked. "The longer we stay here, the riskier it gets."

I didn't move. "Zalaric, if any of them are killed, I swear on the gods—"

"Well, well, well," a new voice purred from the back of the cave. "I knew we would see each other again, Your Majesty. I just didn't think it would happen so soon."

CHAPTER
THIRTY-ONE

The metallic scrape of unsheathing blades hissed from the boat behind me as a fair-skinned man sauntered from the shadows—a face that had haunted my nightmares since the night we'd met at my Ascension Ball.

Symond.

The Umbros Queen's Chief Centenary.

"You're looking as beautiful as ever, Diem Corbois," he crooned, striding toward me, stroking his dark goatee. "Or should I call you by your real name... Diem Bellator?"

"Bellator?" Zalaric said, his eyes going round. "You're Auralie's daughter?" At my nod, his expression turned to horror.

"Hello, Symond," I said wryly. "I'd say it's a pleasure to see you again, but why bother lying to someone who can read minds?"

He stopped a few feet away and chuckled. "You're a long way from Lumnos, Your Majesty."

"You hired me to smuggle *a fucking Crown?*" the Cardinal snapped at Zalaric.

Symond cocked his head at me. "Do you know what happens to foreign Crowns who make visits without permission?"

"Your Queen has experience with that," I answered. "Perhaps she can tell me."

I threw on a cocky smirk to conceal my own fear while I calculated my odds. Though my magic was recovering from the flameroot, I was still a Crown. Even weakened, *one* Descended should be no problem.

Then, from the shadows, another emerged. Then another. Five, then ten, then fifteen. All clad in black leathered armor and fluttering crimson capes.

"Cooperate," Zalaric warned quietly. "Fighting back will only make it worse."

Symond gave a cruel smile. "Her Majesty the Queen would like a word with you."

The claws of Umbros magic scraped at the edges of my mind. Like a swarm of tiny insects, the Centenaries scratched and burrowed their way into my thoughts.

"Ignios?" one cooed. "How fascinating."

"A Guardian-loving Crown," another laughed. "Now I've really seen it all."

Another clicked her tongue. "Naked and begging, and he still didn't want you."

"Get out of my head," I gritted out, my cheeks burning.

Symond surveyed my body, dragging his teeth over his bottom lip. "He's a fool. I would never turn you away. But you already knew that."

Just as he had at the Ascension Ball, he forced a wave of dirty, sinful, scandalous images of the two of us into my mind. My skin tingled with the sensation of a hand drifting down my stomach and along the ridge of my hips. I sucked in a breath as I realized it was my *own* hand, moving of its own will—or rather, Symond's will.

Fight, my godhood hissed.

I didn't hesitate. The floodgates opened and a cascade of icy flame swirled around the corners of my mind, purging the intruding magic until I was alone in my own head. A silvery light haloed my skin and pulsed in the cave around me.

Several Centenaries staggered back in alarm, though Symond's ominous smile curved higher. "Clever. Who taught you that trick?"

"You've learned enough from me already. But I do have more where that came from." With a twitch of my wrist, a tangle of sizzling, white-hot whips unfurled around me, the crack of their snapping ends reverberating off the stone walls.

"Stop," Zalaric pleaded from behind me.

"I wouldn't do that if I were you," Symond said in a knowing, sing-song voice. "Those blades look terribly sharp."

I narrowed my eyes. "What blades?"

"*Diem.*"

My head turned at Luther's hard tone, my breath choking in my throat at the sight of Luther, Alixe, Taran, and the Cardinal holding their own knives against their necks.

Symond chuckled. "For their sake, I hope your magic is fast. Take care not to miss—a single thought from just one of us, and they all slit their throats."

"Do it, Diem," Luther gritted out. "Don't worry about us. Kill them and run before more come." He grimaced as his blade cut deeper, slicing through the fabric of his scarf. Trickles of red dripped down the front of his sweater.

"You hurt him, and I will slaughter every last Centenary," I snarled at Symond. "And I don't mean just the ones in this cave."

My glowing whips lashed at the stone walls in warning. Rocks carved loose and clattered loudly across the cave floor.

Symond's cold smile wavered, then tightened. "Come peacefully, and your friends will be spared."

I glared. "You'll let them go if I come with you?"

"Oh, no. They're coming with us. Her Majesty wants to meet you all." Symond shrugged lightly. "But I give my vow your friends will not be hurt, so long as they behave."

I glanced at Zalaric, who was in the same psychic stranglehold as the others. He watched me with a clouded expression as the edge of his blade pushed against the pale scar along his throat.

"Can I trust them to keep their word?" I asked.

"It's *Umbros*," he said.

"Right—trust no one," I muttered.

"Diem," Luther warned, "don't do th—" His words cut off in a strangled grunt, and panic seized me by the chest.

"Fine," I blurted out. I waved a hand, and the whips dissolved into mist. "I'll come. Just don't hurt them."

The others marched stiffly back to land and lined up at my side, their unnatural gait suggesting they still weren't moving of their own accord. The Centenaries approached and felt them up with lascivious smiles as they snatched weapons from sheaths and baldrics.

Symond reached for the stolen Ignios dagger strapped across my breasts.

"Are you *trying* to lose a hand?" I snapped, and he paused. "I'm coming willingly. You have no need to take my weapons."

"No blades in the Queen's presence. You've got your magic, that's weapon enough."

"You touch her, and if she doesn't kill you, I will," Luther growled. "And I don't give a damn whose throat you cut for it."

Symond shot him a venomous smile. "Curious that a man who rejects her touch thinks he gets a say in what other men do with her."

"You can stop airing our private matters now," I grumbled, handing over my weapons—though I didn't *entirely* disagree with him.

"What a shame." Symond winked at Luther. "I was just about to get to the juicy part."

I jerked my chin at Zalaric and the Cardinal. "Let them go. They shouldn't be punished. They didn't even know I was Queen."

Zalaric stared at me in surprise.

"Aye," the Cardinal said. "I was just hired to drive a boat. I didn't know nothin' about this."

Symond pointed at me. "You don't know this woman?"

The Cardinal shook her head emphatically. "Just met her."

"Hmm." He took the Cardinal's blade from the Centenary who had confiscated it and strolled toward her. "So you wouldn't say you're her *friend?*" He drew out the word slowly, methodically.

"Nope. She's nothin' to me."

"Well, then." He held her knife out to her, handle first. "If you're not her *friend.*"

Suddenly, I realized what he was implying. My blood froze to ice. "No, Symond, don't—"

So quick I almost missed it, the Cardinal snatched her knife from his hand and plunged it deep into her own throat.

Luther and I lunged forward to grab her as she collapsed. Blood bubbled up into her mouth, her chest shuddering with a wet sucking sound. He laid her on the ground as I pulled the knife free, then tore off my cloak and pressed it firmly against the wound.

"You said you wouldn't hurt anyone," Taran shouted.

"I said I wouldn't hurt her friends." Symond gave a bored look at the woman dying in my arms. "They weren't friends. I kept my word."

"Jemmina," Zalaric cried out, looking genuinely heartbroken. "Oh gods, I'm so sorry."

Symond's vicious stare shifted to Zalaric. "And *you*. You've become quite wealthy thanks to the Queen's favor. Now you repay her with treachery?"

Taran pushed Zalaric back and stood in front of him, fists clenched and growling. "You can't hurt him. He *is* our friend. And a subject of Lumnos, which means he's under our Queen's protection." His eyes cut nervously to me. "Right?"

It was hard to say whose jaw was lower, mine or Zalaric's.

"R-right," I stammered. "He's with us."

"You can save your lies. He already made his bargain." Symond picked up the Cardinal's fallen knife and tossed it into the water before turning back to Zalaric. "Her Majesty may be letting you live for turning them in, but don't think I've forgotten your original plan. I'll ensure you pay for it eventually."

"Zal... you betrayed us?" Taran asked softly.

"What happened to '*I owe you my life*'?" Luther snarled.

Symond chuckled. "So much for being friends."

Zalaric scowled at him. "You were supposed to keep my role a secret. That was the agreement."

"It's *Umbros*," Symond said mockingly. "Trust no one, remember?"

"How much did they pay you?" Taran demanded, disgust dripping in his tone. "How many gold marks were our lives worth?"

Zalaric pursed his lips, his expression shuttering to an icy indifference.

Taran pushed in closer. "Really? Nothing to say for yourself?"

Hands curled into fists, Luther began to rise.

"Leave him alone," I said. "I'm the one to blame."

Every head in the cave swiveled to me.

Symond crossed his arms and grinned, apparently content to watch our drama play out.

I looked down at the Cardinal. Her eyes had closed to thin slivers, her lips now a dull grey, and her pulse was slowing at an alarming rate.

"You knew?" Luther asked.

His delicate, lethal tone should have warned me, but I was too distracted to realize how thick the air had turned.

I swore to myself, racking my brain for a solution. The herbs in my bag were useless for this kind of injury. I could pack the wound with gauze, but she would still suffocate on her own blood before her Descended healing could repair the wound.

I hunched over the Cardinal's body, my thoughts circling around what happened with Zalaric in the tunnels. If I could do *that*, then maybe, just maybe...

"*You knew?*" Luther demanded again.

"Yes," I mumbled absently as my eyes closed. I laid my hands over her throat, her blood-soaked skin slippery under my touch. My magic was thrumming in a way that felt excited, unchained.

Voices volleyed above me as the men began to argue—Luther's rumble, Taran's growl, Zalaric's aloofness, Symond's snark. They were all shouting, accusing, trading barbs and threats.

Alixe kneeled at my side. "How can I help?" she asked quietly.

"I... I can't let anyone see," I murmured.

She nodded and turned her back to me, then subtly spread her coat wider to block me from view.

I released my hold on my godhood, trusting in its magic to do the impossible. A cold-hot sensation rippled over my body and concentrated at my palms with a sharp prick of pain. A soft glow pooled beneath my touch, flared to a blinding pulse, then faded away.

The Cardinal's eyes flew open. She gasped for breath, and I clamped a hand over her mouth.

"Close your eyes," I hissed. "Don't move."

A single nod was her only response.

With my hands still quivering at the shock of what I'd just done, I took my cloak and laid it out over her body and covered her face. I drew in a steadying breath to calm the thundering in my chest, then stood and faced the others.

Taran and Zalaric were nose to nose, looking ready to come to blows at any second. Luther was on his knees, face twisted in pain as he rammed his fist into his own side, while Symond stood above him with palms extended, chuckling darkly. The other Centenaries had circled Alixe, some with hands extended, others hovering near their blades.

This was a *disaster*. I needed to get us out of this cave before anyone saw what I'd done and keep Symond's attention on me and off my friends.

And I knew exactly how to do it... I just hoped Luther would forgive me.

"She's gone," I said loudly.

The fighting stopped.

Again, a sea of faces turned to me.

"I'm sorry, Zalaric. The Cardinal didn't make it."

His poised features melted into a slump, guilt swirling in his eyes.

My gaze cut to Symond. I cocked a hip and crossed my arms. "Are you done murdering innocent people, or do you intend to make your Queen wait even longer before you obey her orders?"

Symond bristled. "That woman wasn't innocent. Bypassing the checkpoints is treason."

"What's treason," I purred, sauntering toward him, "is how badly you're drooling over me. I can see the bulge in your pants from across the cave. I doubt your Queen would appreciate that."

His eyes flared with heat. My stomach turned.

"Her Majesty encourages her Centenaries to indulge in all of life's pleasures with whomever we please." He ran a finger up my arm. It was all I could do not to shudder. "If she doesn't kill you, she might even join us."

I forced a coy smile. "Then what are we waiting for?"

He gave a low laugh and extended his arm.

I glanced back at the others and immediately wished I hadn't. The confusion, the anger, the disgust, the *betrayal*...

Only Zalaric seemed unaffected. He watched me with dead eyes, his expression revealing nothing.

I swallowed tightly and turned away. My hand slid through Symond's arm as I gazed up at him and smiled.

"Lead the way. I'm ready to meet the Queen of Umbros."

CHAPTER
THIRTY-TWO

The palace of Umbros had also been carved into the canyons, high above the city. A system of pulley-drawn lifts carried the Queen and her Centenaries up and down at their leisure, but Symond had gleefully informed us those were off-limits to foreigners.

Instead, we were forced to trudge up a seemingly endless set of narrow spiral stairs. By the time we reached the top, we were all panting for breath, our heads spinning and calves burning.

Unlike the perpetual night of the underground city, daylight spilled in through tall, narrow slits carved into the black rock walls. It was currently sunset, and thin streaks of orange-red sliced like bloody knives through the halls.

The floor was inlaid with gold-veined marble, and towering columns carved into the shape of dragons guarded each corridor. Elaborate, flame-lit lanterns hung from frescoed ceilings depicting scenes of debauchery. Pools of velvet cushions and golden carts bearing liquors and spirits seemed scattered at random, as if the palace's residents might find themselves in need of a bed or a drink on a moment's notice. The air was heavy with rich incense, languid music—and moans.

Carnal, orgasmic moans.

If I'd thought Umbros City was a den of indulgence, it was *nothing* compared to this. As Symond led me through the palace, the others following at our backs, each room we passed was filled with naked, writhing bodies engaged in pleasure in all its forms. The kind you smoke, the kind you drink, the kind you f—

Well, you get the idea.

"Do you like what you see?" Symond crooned in my ear.

"It's really... something." I cleared my throat. "Are they all Centenaries?"

"Not at all. Her Majesty is the skin market's best patron." He brushed his knuckles against my wrist and pinned me with his depthless black eyes. "She ensures her loyal guards can have everything—and everyone—they desire."

"Not *everyone* they desire," I said with a smirk.

He gave a throaty laugh. "Well, I do love the thrill of a chase. It's such a rarity for me."

"Given our history, I can't help but wonder how *willing* your partners have truly been."

He stopped short. "Such a vile thing is strictly forbidden. I would *never* —and if I had, the Queen would have made me rip out my own heart and hand it to her."

"And yet you had no hesitation forcing yourself into my mind."

He shrugged. "A simple prank. Thoughts are harmless."

"They're anything but harmless," I shot back. "Our thoughts make us who we are. Violating someone's mind is no better than violating their body."

He sneered in a way that made me think I'd struck a nerve. "So what would you have us do, never use our magic?"

"Not without consent."

He leaned closer. Luther rumbled a low warning behind us.

"Tell me," Symond said smoothly, "did you ask that woman's consent for what you did back there in the cave?" My eyes grew, and so did his smile. "You may have forced me out of your mind, but I could still read hers." He looked me over. "So many unusual tricks you have up your sleeves."

I swallowed. "Are you going to kill her?"

"That depends." His hand slid to the curve of my waist as he brought his lips a breath from mine, and Luther's rumble turned into a snarl. "What will you give me if I don't?"

I trembled in place, wondering just how far I was willing to go to save the life of a stranger.

Symond threw his head back in loud, body-shaking laughter. "Blessed Kindred, you should see your face. You might have a point about not using our magic. Taunting you is much more fun when I have to guess what offensive name you're calling me in your head."

"Here's a preview: You're a prick."

I punched his side, and he took the blow with a grin, then snatched my hand and threaded it back around his arm. "Her Majesty is going to *love* you."

I scowled as we continued walking. "So you'll let the Cardinal live?"

"I will. She received her punishment. What happened after is none of my concern."

"What about Zalaric?"

"Why do you care? He betrayed you, even knowing it might cost you your life."

I couldn't answer. I *shouldn't* care. Zalaric's deceit could have cost us our lives—it still might. And yet, when I thought about what I'd seen beyond that strange misty curtain, it wasn't outrage I felt, but pity.

"Will it cost me my life?" I asked instead.

The gleam in his eyes raised the hair on my neck. "That's for Her Majesty to decide."

We climbed another set of stairs leading to a circular throne room lined with ten arches that opened up to the sky on all sides. At the center, on a raised platform, sat a throne carved from dark jade that resembled a swarm of battling dragons. Concentric rings of black velvet cushions fanned out across the floor.

Symond released my arm. "Her Majesty will join you shortly. In the meantime, I'm afraid I have to take your bags."

I clutched mine closer, remembering the jar of lavender flame. "Why? You have our weapons."

"Do I?" He cocked his head. "Before you somehow pushed me out of your head, I saw you frolicking with the Guardians. How do I know you haven't stashed one of their pesky bombs?"

Luther moved to intervene. Symond's eyes shot to him and narrowed as he lifted his palm.

I rushed forward and toyed with the collar of Symond's leather armor, feverishly fluttering my lashes. "Come now, Symond. We both know I don't need a bomb to take you down."

His gaze slid back to me. "You have a point. I'll go down on you any time you like."

I let out a vapid, girlish giggle that would have had Taran snorting loud enough to be heard in Lumnos, if only he weren't glaring at me like I'd poured out his favorite whiskey.

Symond took my hand and pressed a kiss to my wrist. "My, you are *delicious*." I tensed as his mouth worked its way up my arm—my elbow, my shoulder, my neck. Luther's growls grew thunderous in the background. I held my breath as Symond stopped just below my ear. "I'm still going to take your bags."

I huffed and pulled back, then shoved my satchel into his waiting hands. "I'm calling you a prick in my thoughts again, in case you couldn't tell."

"I could." He chuckled and strolled to Luther, whose jaw was clenched hard enough to form diamonds, though not a muscle moved across his entire body as Symond threw an arm across his shoulders. "She is especially beautiful when she's angry, isn't she, Prince? I bet she's a firecracker in bed. Not that you would know, of course."

Luther didn't answer—couldn't, probably—but the rage boiling in his eyes said enough.

Symond laughed again and pulled Luther's bag off his shoulders. "Don't worry. I'll take good care of her when you're not around." He clapped a palm hard against Luther's hip. "*Very* good care."

Luther's eyes closed. His face went bloodless, his body shuddering as if it might collapse.

Hard as it was, I held my tongue. If Symond thought he could drive a wedge between me and my Prince, perhaps I could use that to convince him to let Luther go.

The remaining Centenaries took the bags off Taran and Alixe, who were similarly frozen in place, and descended the staircase with Symond following behind.

"You're just going to leave us here alone?" I called out.

Symond paused and glanced at Luther. "Hear that, Prince? She misses me already." His laughter echoed as he walked out.

The moment the door shut, the Centenaries' hold on the others dissolved. Alixe wasted no time checking whether the door had been locked —it had—then scouring the room for makeshift weapons or an exit.

Luther staggered forward and leaned his hands on the throne's dais, his head hanging low.

I started toward him, then froze as Taran stormed past me—with Zalaric in his warpath.

283

Zalaric summoned shadows at his palms, but he didn't attack. Even when Taran shoved him, sending him stumbling backward, and grabbed him by his robes to pin him against a column, still, Zalaric's magic held back.

"You *traitor*," Taran shouted in his face.

"I owed you nothing. I'm a subject of Umbros."

"Look in a mirror, Zal. Your eyes are blue, not black."

My eyebrows flew. ...*Zal?*

"Taran, stop," I said.

"You're a *Lumnos* Descended," he spat. "Your loyalty is to your terremère."

"My loyalty is to myself," Zalaric shot back.

Taran made a disgusted noise. "That's all you care about, isn't it? Yourself and your money."

"Taran," I warned. "Leave it be."

"Tell me, how much did you sell Diem's life for? What about mine? Did you haggle for a better price, or were we not even worth that effort?"

Zalaric's hand fell limp at his side, his magic vanishing into wisps.

I looked to the others for help. Alixe was on the balcony staring over the side, and Luther was still doubled over near the throne.

"You don't get to judge me." Zalaric's voice was soft but harsh. "You, who have never thought twice about where your next meal will come from."

"At least I'd never sell a person's life for a little gold. Especially someone I had just..." Taran's throat bobbed, his anger faltering.

I rushed over and grabbed his arm. "I said *leave it*. Zalaric's right. He owed us nothing."

His glare shot to me. "How can you defend him?"

"I'm not. Or... I guess maybe I am, but—"

"And why are you flirting with that asshole Centenary?" He jerked his chin toward Luther. "Where's your loyalty to *him?*"

My cheeks burned hot.

Zalaric let out a short, surprised laugh. "Do you not see what she's doing?"

Taran scowled at him, then at me.

Zalaric's eyes rolled. "It's a good thing that empty head of yours is so pretty, Tammy, because you—"

"*My name is Taran*," he bellowed, throwing his fist forward into Zalaric's face.

Only it didn't hit his face.

At the last moment, Zalaric ducked out of reach, sending Taran's fist colliding into a thick stone column with a fleshy, stomach-turning crunch.

"By the Flames," I breathed. I reached for his hand. "Are you alr—"

"Is that the best you've got?" Zalaric taunted. "I've seen better punches from an armless newt."

"Zalaric, *stop*," I hissed. "This isn't—"

Taran launched himself forward, and the two of them tumbled to the ground in a flurry of fists. I debated intervening, but despite being half Taran's size, Zalaric was more than holding his own. And he was *smiling*.

"Let them fight it out," Alixe called out. "They'll be fine."

I pinched the bridge of my nose and shook my head as I walked back to Luther. He was finally upright, now staring grimly at the Umbros throne.

"I think those two might kill each other before the Queen gets her chance," I said, only half joking.

Luther's chest rose in a long, slow breath as his hands squeezed into white-knuckled fists. "You gave me your word."

Shit. He must have believed my ruse with Symond. "Luther, what you think you saw..."

"Was this always your plan?" His livid stare shifted to me. "Did you lie to my face, knowing you would do what you want anyway?"

I recoiled at the visceral hurt in his voice.

"Luther, Symond is not—"

"I don't give a damn about Symond," he snapped, "except that I'm going to rip his fucking hands off if he keeps touching you when you clearly don't want it."

I frowned. "Wait. You *know* that I don't...?"

"You promised me, Diem. No tricks. No Umbros Queen. But you knew Zalaric had betrayed us, and you did nothing?"

Understanding washed over me, quickly shifting to panic. Then horror.

His eyes narrowed. "Or was it a betrayal at all? Did you two plan this together?"

"No," I gasped. "I didn't... it wasn't—"

"Incoming," Alixe shouted from the balcony.

A slow, repetitive thumping grew louder as a dark silhouette formed in the setting sun.

Alixe backed toward me. "*Gryvern.*"

Luther's posture switched dramatically. All hint of emotion cooled away. His spine snapped rod straight as he pushed me behind him and set his focus on the sky.

Taran looked over from where he was pinned to the ground with Zalaric straddling him. He set his jaw and shoved Zalaric off, jumping to his feet and striding toward us. At the last moment he paused, let out a quiet grunt, and doubled back. He grabbed Zalaric's wrist and dragged him along.

"Stay behind us," he muttered. He pushed Zalaric into my side and joined Alixe and Luther's protective arc.

"You three do realize Zalaric and I are the ones with magic, right?" I asked. "It should be us protecting you."

Alixe cracked her knuckles as Taran tied back his hair and glared, all three of them ignoring me.

Zalaric shot me a stunned look, and I shrugged.

As the gryvern approached, a door opened, and a flood of Centenaries marched in. Some were still in their caped armor, but others were in flowing, sheer robes that put their bodies on display. Several carried trays of fruits, nuts, and cheeses, while others carried goblets and jugs of wine.

Perhaps the Umbros Queen was planning to have a feast over our executions.

"Don't fight back," Zalaric warned. "She's ruthless about protecting her reputation. Don't insult or threaten her, Diem. Be quiet and polite and—"

Taran groaned. "We're all gonna die."

The Umbros gryvern landed on the balcony with a floor-rattling thud. It was larger than Sorae, with sleek, feminine lines and a graceful gait. Its wings and fur were a dark caramel hue, while its scales glittered like godstone. Its eyes fixed on me, two slitted pupils shrinking and growing as it studied me with wary curiosity.

I didn't see the Umbros Queen at first, her body blocked by the gryvern's wing.

But I felt her.

Her power was incredible. The intensity of her aura rivaled even Luther's. It exploded through the room with a force that could only have been intentional and coated the air so thickly I seemed to inhale it with every breath, pulling it—pulling *her*—into my lungs, into my blood.

Two Centenaries ran forward. One dropped to all fours at the gryvern's side. The other extended their arm, and a delicate hand with nails sharpened to points settled into their outstretched palm. A slender leg swung into view and set a high-heeled foot onto the other Centenary's back, using him as a stepstool. She glided smoothly to the ground and sauntered, hips swaying, into the room.

Her beauty overwhelmed me as much as her power. She was sex in human form, a buffet of curves to satisfy the most insatiable lust. Long lashes brushed against high, rosy cheekbones, her pillowy lips swollen with a just-kissed flush. Ebony hair flowed unbound over her shoulders, curling at the dip of her ample hips. Despite her advanced age, her skin was flawless —and her tiny dress left a great deal of it to see.

Zalaric dropped to his knees and turned his gaze to the floor. The Centenaries did the same, but my three companions—bless their loyal, courageous hearts—remained standing.

"Well, that isn't very polite," she chided.

Behind her, the gryvern snapped its jaws.

"*Kneel*," Zalaric whispered frantically.

"Listen to your friend," Symond warned. "Kneel, or I'll do it for you."

"He's not our friend," Taran grumbled.

Luther rolled back his shoulders. "Force us if you must, but I only bend my knee willingly to Blessed Mother Lumnos and my Queen. And you, madam, are neither."

Her scarlet lips curved into a smile.

The Queen strode toward me. The Corbois closed their ranks, shifting until their shoulders touched in an imposing wall of muscle. She paced slowly in front of them, back and forth, trailing a finger in a line across their chests.

"And if I told you that if you did not kneel, I would make you toss yourselves over the balcony and bash your lovely heads open on the canyon floor? What then?"

My stomach dropped.

"Then we will die with honor," Alixe said.

Taran smirked. "I've always wondered what it felt like to fly."

The room fell silent and lethally still.

Then, abruptly, the Queen began to laugh. She placed a hand on her chest. "Blessed Kindred, how faithful you all are. Lucky for you, I have a great deal of respect for loyalty to one's Crown."

Still chuckling, she turned and strolled toward her throne. "Fair enough," she called out over her shoulder. "Unwilling it is."

She snapped her fingers and the three Corbois slammed to the marble floor in forced supplication, knees bent and foreheads scraping the ground.

I sucked in a breath and shifted to face her. It was now just the two of us standing—two Queens, towering over their subjects. Would she try to make me kneel, too? *Could* she?

She sank into her throne and lounged against an armrest. The final rays of sunset gilded her in a wash of honeyed tones. Her legs crossed, exposing a smooth expanse of bare flesh that ran to her hip.

Her gaze settled on me. "Hello, Daughter of the Forgotten."

I gave a subtle, but respectful, nod. "Hello, Umbros."

"We're not on Coeurîle, dear. You can call me Yrselle." Her eyes flashed across the room. "But if I hear that name on anyone else's tongue, I'll feed it to my gryvern. Am I understood?"

Murmurs of "*Yes, Your Majesty*" rippled across the crowd.

I shifted my weight. "I apologize for my unannounced visit to your realm. After the attack—"

She waved her hand. "Yes, yes, I already know. Don't bore me with details I've already plucked from your companions' heads."

"Then you know I did not come by choice. I'm only trying to get home."

"Doesn't matter." She clicked her nails against the arm of her throne. "You're in my realm. Your life is mine to take."

My heart picked up speed. I flexed my fingers at my sides, conjuring gauntlets of shadow. "*If* you can take it."

Though already night-black, her eyes seemed to darken. The golds of sunset vanished as the sun dipped beneath the horizon, shifting the room to a palette of frosty twilight blues.

Careful, a feminine voice hummed in my mind. *I cannot let a challenge go unanswered in front of my Centenaries.*

My godhood snarled, begging to force her out, but I held myself back. For whatever reason, she was warning me. Guiding me.

"Or," I said slowly, "perhaps I could offer you a... favor. In exchange for your mercy."

Her smile stretched higher. "I might be open to that—if the *favor* is sufficiently interesting."

I studied her for a beat. This felt like a game of words, a delicate dance whose steps were ever-changing. "Is there something you had in mind?"

"In fact, there is. That discussion is best had over wine, don't you think?"

She waved a hand, and everyone kneeling slumped as if they'd been hanging from a rope that finally snapped. I realized with a start that she'd been forcing them *all* to kneel, even her Centenaries—an unnecessary show of power, just to prove she could.

The Centenaries rose as one and began lighting candles and taking up posts around the room, save for Symond, who stood by the throne with arms crossed. Those carrying refreshments crowded around the dais, contorting in odd positions to ensure every delicacy was within arm's reach of their Queen.

The most scantily dressed among them flocked to her side. Two sprawled at her feet, stroking the lines of her legs. Another perched on the throne's arm and combed her fingers through Yrselle's hair. One particularly beefy man even wedged himself beneath her so she was sitting on his lap—a visibly aroused, very well-endowed lap.

Zalaric and the Corbois rose as well, the latter joining my side. Though Zalaric held his head high with his usual composure, I felt a pang of sympathy. He was alone in enemy territory, no ally in sight—just as he had been as a boy all those years ago.

A Centenary approached with a tray of wine. Taran, Zalaric and I accepted, while Luther and Alixe declined.

I studied the goblet, noting the way a pewter dragon twined its way up the stem. "Is a dragon your sigil? I've noticed them throughout your palace."

"Very perceptive," she said. "Did you know dragons feel every piece of gold in their hoard? If even a single one is taken, they know—and they take their repayment in blood." She held my gaze as she sipped her wine. "I find that *inspiring*."

"They are fearsome creatures, though I confess, I don't understand them. With as much power as they wield, what use does any dragon have for gold?" I swirled my goblet. "Or any Crown, for that matter?"

"Power takes many forms. Even among the Descended, strong magic will only get you so far. Isn't that right, Zalaric?"

He dipped his chin. "Of course, Your Majesty."

She smiled warmly at him. "Zalaric has always been one of my favorites. He understands the importance of collecting every last coin."

Taran snorted softly, and the Queen's smile fell. I shot him a look, eyes wide in warning.

"I've watched him grow up here, you know." She leaned forward, her tone markedly colder. "After your people scarred him and threw him away, I welcomed him. I gave him a home."

Zalaric's throat bobbed, his eyes dropping.

"You gave many a home," I said. "Mortals, half-mortals, even Descended. An honorable thing, to open your arms when no one else will." I lowered my chin deeply, hoping she saw the honesty in the gesture. "You have my gratitude—and my admiration."

Mollified, she lounged back and shrugged. "Perhaps I should be thanking you. I could fill this room with the gold I've made off your exiles." Her gaze drifted to Luther. "Or perhaps I should thank your handsome Prince."

"I'll thank him for you," one of her attendants cooed, looking Luther over with a hungry gaze.

My eyes narrowed.

Yrselle smiled. "I don't think the Lumnos Queen likes that suggestion. Best keep your distance, dear, or I'll be down a Centenary."

The attendant pouted. "But he doesn't even want her."

Heat rushed to my face, and hurt rushed to my heart. Luther glanced at me, and shame won out over pride as my eyes lowered to the ground.

Yrselle tutted. "*Want* isn't the problem, is it, Prince?"

Their stares met, and charged energy buzzed in the air between them. As the silence drew on and his nostrils flared, I wondered if she was speaking into his mind, as she had with me. The thought made me feel like a dragon watching someone touch their gold.

I cleared my throat loudly. "You spoke of a favor, Yrselle?"

"Ah, yes. The favor."

She took a long drink, and her attendants' hands began to roam. They wet their lips as their palms grazed hungrily over her bronzed skin, at times disappearing beneath the hem of her dress.

"You and I have a great deal to talk about," she said, her voice taking on a husky lilt. "About you. About Emarion. About your parents."

"My parents?" I straightened, stepping toward her. "What about them? What do you know?"

She arched her neck as the man beneath her ran his tongue along her throat. "I know more about them than they know about themselves."

"How is that possible?" I took another step forward. Symond tensed.

The man beneath Yrselle shifted his hips. She closed her eyes and leaned back with a breathy sigh.

This was all getting *very* distracting.

"My mother—you know where she is?" I asked.

"Of course I do."

"Is she...?" The words stuck in my throat, burning with the question I both did and didn't want to ask. "Have the Crowns...?"

"Executed her?"

My hands trembled, and my wine goblet slipped and clattered to the floor.

If my mother was gone...

If I'd lost them both...

"She lives." The Queen's tone had softened. "As a prisoner of the Crowns, her execution requires a vote of six. Without mine, they have only five."

I grabbed the edge of the dais and nearly collapsed with relief. Rustling, footsteps, and grunts rose around me.

"Take care, dear. If you come any closer, you'll either have to die or join in on my fun."

I looked up to see Centenaries surrounding me with weapons drawn. Symond was staring down from the dais, the point of his sword an inch from my nose. Behind me, the Corbois had been forced back down to their knees.

One of the attendants at her feet crawled forward and twirled a lock of my hair in her fingers. "I'd rather see her come than bleed."

"So would I," Symond said with a sly smile.

I raised my hands in surrender and took several steps back. The Queen nodded, and the Centenaries sheathed their swords.

"You said they need six votes to execute her—who else voted against it?"

"I am the only vote against it. Montios and Arboros have yet to respond, and your Regent has declined to vote until you return."

I'd never been more grateful for Remis's cowardice, though the news of the Arboros Queen's silence left me uneasy. I had hoped she'd found a way to escape the Guardians. If they still had her...

Then again, if she did escape, her vote alone—or the Montios King's—would be enough to sentence my mother to death.

I had to get my mother out of Fortos. Quickly.

"What is the favor you wish?" I asked.

Yrselle snapped, and the attendants around her pouted and moved away. She set down her goblet. "I want you to stay here as a guest in my palace. Only a few days—three at most."

"*No*," Luther gritted out.

The Queen looked at him, her expression flickering with something I

291

didn't understand. "I understand your objection, Prince, but it will have to wait. This is more important."

"Why?" I asked, feeling like I was missing something vital.

"We have much to discuss, and I haven't had a formal Crown visit in centuries." She clasped her hands together on her knee. "We'll make your visit official. I'll even host a dinner tomorrow with all my Centenaries. You can return home on my personal boat the following day."

"You're not going to turn me over to the other Crowns? The Ignios King said I've been summoned—"

She made a disgusted sneer. "That *edict* isn't worth the paper it's written on. A Crown holds no authority over other Crowns. I don't answer to them." Her chin tipped down. "And neither do you. Until you return home, you and your people will have my full protection."

I frowned. It was a generous offer. *Too* generous. "Why? What do you gain from all this?"

She smiled slowly. "You'll see."

I made the mistake of looking at Luther. He was staring at me, brows pinched, eyes pulsing with a near-rabid insistence. The betrayal he'd accused me of earlier was written all over his face.

You promised.

"And if I decline," I asked her, "will you execute me?"

"No. But I may reconsider my vote on your mother's fate."

Defeat flooded Luther's expression. He knew that was one risk I would never take.

I sighed heavily. "Alright. We'll stay."

CHAPTER
THIRTY-THREE

True to her word, the Queen retroactively sanctioned my visit. We were now being treated as honored guests, though we were still very much unwilling captives.

We, it turned out, included Zalaric. She had insisted on including him in my delegation as an ambassador between our two realms. For the time being, he was as stuck here as we were.

She returned our weapons and bags and granted us a private wing of the palace for our own use. She had even unlocked the three Corbois' magic —after warning that any attack on her or her Centenaries would mean a death sentence for us all.

She also gave her word that her Centenaries would not intrude on our thoughts any further. Notably, she made no such promise for herself.

I now found myself alone in my suite, nervously pacing the floor. I'd requested a private dinner, claiming we were weary from the day's drama and in dire need of rest. It wasn't entirely a lie, but I was anxious to speak with the others—especially Luther.

A knock on the door brought the arrival of Alixe and Taran, followed by a host of Centenaries who laid out a buffet of food and wine, the latter of which barely hit the table before Taran grabbed a jug.

"We're still on duty," Alixe chided, snatching it from his hands.

"Queenie doesn't mind." He grabbed another one from the table and looked at me. "Do you?"

"Don't ask me. She's your High General."

Alixe smirked triumphantly and held out her hand. Taran passed the jug over, scowling.

I looked around the spacious parlor of my suite. Although it was a lavish space, laden with luxurious comforts, the room was entirely enclosed within the canyon walls without even a glimpse of sky. I felt like a pretty bird in a gilded cage.

"I wish I had a balcony. I'd feel better if I could call Sorae and keep her close in case things go wrong."

"I don't think it's a coincidence that none of our rooms have openings to the outside," Alixe said.

"Neither do I." I frowned. "Do you think she'll keep her word and let us return home safely?"

"If she wanted to harm us, they could have simply killed us at the boat."

"Maybe she likes toying with her food before she eats it," I muttered.

A series of soft thunks caught my attention. I looked over to see Taran inspecting the jar of purple flame I'd purchased. He was holding it upside down, tapping loudly on the glass and squinting.

Though I couldn't possibly explain it, the fire almost seemed to be staring back. And, oddly, looking miffed.

Another knock rapped on the door. When I opened it, Zalaric was standing in the hall, hands clasped behind his back.

"I wasn't sure if your private dinner included me," he said hesitantly.

"It doesn't," Taran yelled out.

Zalaric cleared his throat. "I'm not even hungry, really. I can return to my—"

"Of course it does." I moved aside and gestured for him to enter. "Ignore Taran. He's sulking because the Montios fire doesn't like him."

Taran frowned at the jar. "She likes me." He gave it a violent shake, and the flame snapped angrily against the glass.

"Have you ever been to the palace before?" I asked Zalaric.

"Only during my time in the skin markets, when the Queen would hire me. Never as a guest." He gazed around my opulent room. "Never like this."

"I'm sorry you got caught up in all this. I know it might complicate things for your life here."

Taran scoffed. "Don't apologize to *him*. Not after what he did."

I rolled my eyes. "It's time to move on, Taran. We're all trapped here together. We have to figure out the Queen's intentions, and Zalaric knows more about her than any of us."

"I'll help however I can," Zalaric said, "but I must warn you to guard your words in my presence. Anything you tell me, the Centenaries will learn eventually. Whether I want them to or not." He cut a glance at Taran, who sniffed and looked away.

"I'm not sure it matters now. I doubt we have anything left to hide they haven't already seen." My stomach churned, thinking of how they'd taunted me over Luther's rejection.

The need to clear the air with him was eating away at me. There was *so much* we needed to discuss.

"I'll go check on Luther," I announced, bounding for the door.

"Oh, uh, about that..." Taran set down the jar. "Lu's not coming."

I blinked. "He's not?"

He raked a hand through his hair, his eyes darting everywhere but at me. "He said he was going to bed. Asked me to, um, fill him in tomorrow."

I stared at him, mouth ajar, as the air thickened with awkward tension.

"I'm sure he's just resting," Alixe said gently. "He was fighting hard to break the Centenaries' control and get to you. It looked like it took a lot out of him."

I wasn't so convinced it was a lack of energy keeping him away.

I manufactured a painfully bright smile. "Right. It's just us for dinner, then. Let's eat." I took a seat and the others followed, all of us stretching to load our plates with the generous spread.

I glanced at Zalaric as I filled my glass. "Tell me, what is the Queen like?"

"Unpredictable. I've seen her kill entire families for a small discrepancy, and I've seen her let severe crimes go because she was having a good hair day. With her, you never know what to expect, but it's best never to find out."

"Is that why you told her about us, because you feared her?"

Though Taran dug into his food like it was his only interest, I spied him watching Zalaric intently from the corner of his eyes.

"After you all returned to the inn this afternoon, a Centenary stopped me to chat. I pay a lot of money to avoid their attention, so I knew something wasn't right. I suspected the Queen already knew you were in Umbros, and she was testing me to see where my loyalties would lie."

"And now we know," Taran grumbled.

"If I hadn't told her, she would have taken it from my head anyway,"

Zalaric snapped. "Then I'd be dead like my friend, instead of here helping you."

"The Cardinal isn't dead," I said.

His eyes shot to me. "She isn't?"

I smoothed the napkin in my lap to avoid their stares. "She wasn't hurt as badly as it seemed. I told her to play dead, then I distracted Symond to get us out before they noticed."

Alixe tilted her head. "Are you sure? When I saw you helping her, she looked nearly gone."

"I'm sure."

I pushed some food around on my plate, feeling guilty for lying after promising them honesty, but the truth... the truth was more than even I could handle. I needed time to think through what this new revelation meant for me before I could share it with anyone else.

"Thank you," Zalaric said quietly. "I knew what you did with Symond was an act, but I didn't realize why. Jemmina is a good person. I... *we* owe you a debt."

"No, you don't. My presence put her life at risk, so it was mine to protect. Besides... at least *you* knew I wasn't really flirting." I shot Taran a pointed look. He glowered and flicked a roasted beet at me.

"Do you have any idea why the Queen asked us to stay?" Alixe asked Zalaric.

He gazed off thoughtfully. "I have wondered if, perhaps, she is scared of Diem."

I laughed, though no one joined me. "Scared of me? Why?"

"Because of the strength of your magic."

"*My* magic? Did you feel hers?" I shook my head incredulously. "Surely not. At best, we're equally matched."

Zalaric's eyebrows leapt. Alixe coughed on a sip of her drink. Taran rolled his eyes.

"Do you not remember the Challenging?" he asked. "You put thousands of people in a chokehold, Queenie. At the same time. You *turned day into night.*"

"Those were tricks of light," I argued.

"You shattered the arena barrier," Alixe said. "That's Forging magic—it's supposed to be unbreakable, even by the Crowns."

Zalaric leaned forward, steepling his hands. "Normally, if someone's magic is strong enough to sense, I can feel them when they enter the room. I could feel your magic when you entered the *city*." He rubbed his chin. "I wasn't sure what it was until I met you at the inn. I guarantee you the Queen felt it, too. She is very strong, but you..." He shook his head. "You're something else."

I slouched back in my chair as I fought an urgent reflex to insist they were wrong.

My upbringing had made me an expert at living in denial. In order to pose as a mortal without getting caught, I'd had to genuinely believe I was one. Every sign was ignored, every inconsistency dutifully explained away. I mastered the art of looking the other way and putting all my doubts in a dark, locked room.

I'd done the same with so many other aspects of my life: My career as a healer. My relationship with Henri. My feelings for Luther.

How many more hard, scary truths were staring me right in the face that I was still too in denial to acknowledge?

I didn't want to live that way anymore. I wanted to be brave enough, strong enough, to face the path ahead.

But what if I wasn't?

"If she's scared of me, why not let me leave?" I asked.

"She may want an alliance," Zalaric offered. "The other Crowns don't trust her. She may see you as a chance to build a strong faction against them."

Alixe nodded. "Voting to save your mother could be her way of showing you she's willing to take them on, if you are."

I drummed my fingers on the table. I didn't trust the Umbros Queen any more than the other Crowns did. But I didn't trust *them*, either. And Yrselle alone seemed interested in helping me.

And, even if it had been motivated by money, she had opened her realm to refugees of all kinds. Perhaps I could win, or at least buy, her assistance in the coming war.

I thumped my head back against my chair. "I'll keep working on Symond. If I get him comfortable, maybe he'll slip up and let me know Yrselle's plans."

"Luther's going to *love* that," Taran said.

I briefly closed my eyes, but Luther's face followed me into the darkness, his hurt, betrayed expression stamped on my thoughts. "He's already angry with me. Might as well make it immeasurably worse."

"Diem, whatever happened between you two..." Alixe hesitated and shared a look with Taran. "Not that it's any of our business, but..."

I wasn't sure my face could get any redder. They'd surely heard the Centenaries' comments. Gods only knew what they thought of it.

"It doesn't matter," I rushed out. "Right now, I need all three of you to focus on getting friendly with the Centenaries."

Taran's lips curved up. "*How* friendly?"

Zalaric frowned.

"Whatever it takes," I said. "Get them to let their guard down, and find out everything you can. If they're going to lock the wolves in the henhouse, then we're going to have a feast."

"Are you sure you don't want me to wake him up?" Zalaric asked.

I gently wedged a pillow beneath Taran's snoring head and covered him in a blanket. "He must have had two barrels' worth of wine. I'm not sure *anything* is waking him up."

After a long dinner discussing theories and strategy, I'd wheedled Alixe into another magic training session. To my surprise—and Taran's irritation —Zalaric had offered to stay and help. For the next few hours, I watched in rapture as Zalaric put on a display of innovative magic that even Alixe could not reproduce, while Taran brooded in a corner, stealing gulps of wine every time Alixe looked away.

When the candles burned to their bases, Alixe excused herself to sleep, but Taran was passed out cold on a settee in my parlor.

Zalaric peered beneath a corner of the blanket. "I could brand a 'Z' on his ass. I bet that would do the trick."

I laughed, though my heart squeezed at the subtle sadness that had persisted on Zalaric's face all night. "I'm sorry he's giving you such a hard time. Taran is incredibly loyal. It makes him the best friend you could ever hope to have, but I know how bad it feels to be on the wrong side of it."

Zalaric shrugged, trying valiantly to look unmoved. "I cannot blame him. I only wish I had friends so loyal at my back. In Umbros, friendships and fortunes tend to go hand in hand. When one disappears, so does the other." He smiled tightly. "Good thing I am very rich."

"I heard Symond threaten you earlier. Will you be safe here once we leave?"

"I'll be fine. As long as I still have the Queen's favor, Symond won't risk angering her." He hooked his arm in mine as we walked toward the door.

"You know, your mother was a dear friend of Miss Margie. She came to treat Margie when she fell ill, but by the time she could get here, it was already too late." A deep crease dug into his forehead. "Auralie was the only person who was really there for me after Margie died. If I had known you were her daughter..."

"You would have done the exact same thing." His head dipped guiltily, and I squeezed his arm. "When my realm exiled you, you were forced to look out for yourself—I cannot judge you for doing so now. Sometimes there are no good choices. We do the best we can, and we hope we find forgiveness along the way." I stopped and pulled him in for a tight embrace. "For what it's worth, you have mine."

His muscles softened beneath my hands, and when we broke apart, his deep blue eyes were gleaming and wet. The tendons on his throat tightened, drawing my focus to his scar.

"Being stuck between two worlds is not easy, is it?" I asked softly.

He sighed. "No. Especially when neither of those worlds really wants you."

I laid my palm on his cheek. "I suspect there are a great many people who want you in their world, Zalaric Hanoverre. And you can count me as one of them."

He flashed a smile, though there was no joy in it—only a wistful resignation. "Luther was right. You are a Queen worth fighting for. In another life, I wish we could have been allies."

"Perhaps we still can."

We shared a long look, a quiet understanding seeming to pass between us.

Zalaric turned to leave. He reached for the door handle, then paused.

"Diem," he said carefully, "how did you know I'd betrayed you?"

I stiffened. "I... I didn't—"

"I know what it feels like to have an Umbros Descended reach into my mind. Earlier, in the tunnels, it almost seemed like..." He trailed off, his clever eyes darted over me and noting the signs of my panic—my drawn-up shoulders, my wringing hands.

I staggered back a step. "Zalaric, I—"

He pressed a palm to his chest. "Blessed Kindred, where are my manners? Any citizen of Umbros knows not to ask questions unless they're willing to pay for the answer. It appears I'm all out of gold tonight. Another time, perhaps?"

"I, uh—yes," I stammered. "Another time."

He winked and threw open the door. "Good night, Your Majesty."

I stood speechless as I watched him saunter down the hall and disappear into his quarters, though as my eyes came to rest on the door opposite mine, Zalaric's alarming question gave way to a larger concern.

The knowledge that Luther was so nearby was as much a torment as a relief. My heart pleaded to burst into his room and swear that I hadn't broken my promise—but how could I?

How could I explain that Zalaric had never told me his plan, and yet I knew? That I had looked at him in those tunnels and *seen* his secret—that he'd been so desperate to warn us, his mind had been screaming it? How could Luther believe what made no sense, even to me?

But if anyone deserved for me to at least try, didn't *he?*

I went back into my chambers and loaded up a plate with the leftovers of our buffet, topping it with a silver cloche and wedging a carafe of fresh water in the crook of my arm. I returned to the corridor and pulled my shoulders back.

"Be brave, Diem," I scolded myself. I knocked on the door, held my breath, and waited.

And waited.

And waited.

I knocked again—no answer. I banged my fist so loudly I half expected the others to come investigate. Still no answer.

I frowned deeply at his door. I knew he was inside—I could feel his aura, though something about it was *odd*, like a song sung slightly off key. Perhaps he was asleep.

My stomach tangled in a monstrous knot as I reached down to the door handle and pushed.

But the door didn't budge.

He'd locked me out.

He'd *locked me out.*

I set the plate and the carafe down in the corridor, then leaned my forehead against his door.

"Please, Luther," I whispered, eyes burning. "Don't give up on me yet."

CHAPTER

THIRTY-FOUR

"I don't want to be Tiffany anymore."

I stared down at Taran, hands propped on my hips. Morning had come and he was still dozing in my suite, clutching the bundled-up blanket in his arms and murmuring gibberish.

"Taran," I sang brightly. "Good morning."

"You want me to put that *where?*" he mumbled.

I crouched at his side and gently pushed his arm. "Time to wake up."

"Zal, that tickles!" His eyes shot open, his pupils dilating before fixing on me. "Oh—uh, Queenie. Hi."

"Hi. You fell asleep in my room. I think it was all that wine you swore to Alixe you didn't drink."

He smiled sheepishly. "I don't know what you're talking about."

"Uh huh." I grinned. "You were talking in your sleep." My grin spread further. "About Zalaric."

His smile twisted into a scowl. "Must have been a nightmare."

"Mmhmm." He sat up, and I perched beside him. "Taran, did something happen between you two yesterday?"

He sighed heavily and scraped a hand down his face. "After you went to the inn, he introduced Alixe to a weaponsmaster he knew. She wanted to learn some technique from the guy, so Zal and I wandered off for a while, and we, uh... talked. Once he stopped making fun of me, he turned out to be a pretty good guy." He grunted. "Or so I thought."

301

"He is a good guy. Zalaric didn't want to betray us, Taran. He didn't really have a choice."

"There's always a choice," he snapped. "You sound just like Aemonn."

I flinched. Coming from Taran, that was a deep blow. I wasn't sure there was anyone he hated more.

"I'm sorry," he said quickly. "I didn't mean that." He hunched forward, forearms on his knees. "I guess you've heard the rumors about our father."

I nodded. Eleanor once told me Taran's father had been suspected of violently abusing his sons, but after their healing abilities manifested, no one knew for sure.

Taran's voice got quiet. "I used to beg Aemonn to protect me. He was older, he could heal. And he had his magic." Taran's knuckles blanched. "But he never would. He said we had to be tough, show Father we could take it. He said we didn't have a choice. That's bullshit—he had a choice. He just chose Father."

I leaned my head on his shoulder. "I'm so sorry, Taran. You should have had someone to look out for you."

He shrugged, though he laid his head against mine. "Luther did. He's my real brother, in all the ways that matter."

My chest warmed with a swell of emotion. Of course Luther had protected Taran. He protected everyone—that was who he was.

"Can I say something you don't want to hear?" I asked gently.

"Let me guess—you're going to say '*Zalaric isn't Aemonn, and you shouldn't hold your issues with your brother against him*'?"

"Well, I wasn't, but now that you mention it..." He groaned, and I nudged him until he looked at me. "Aemonn was a victim, too. And he was a child, just like you."

"But he grew up," Taran shot back. "After everything we went through, he became Father's pet, like it never happened."

"I worked with patients in similar situations. Children hurt by parents, wives hurt by husbands. Sometimes their reactions didn't make sense to me. Sometimes it even made me angry. Wounds take many forms, and not all of them are physical. Healing from a trauma like that can be..." I sighed sadly. "...complicated."

I squeezed his arm. "You have every right to feel the way you feel. No one is owed your forgiveness, not even Aemonn. But you have so much love and kindness in that big heart of yours... maybe Aemonn needs you to be the kind of brother to him that he wasn't strong enough to be for you."

He wrinkled his nose. "Yeah. Maybe."

"And also—Zalaric isn't Aemonn, and you shouldn't hold your issues with your brother against him."

He let out another loud groan and stood up, grabbing me off the couch and throwing me over his shoulder. "That's it, I'm finding a balcony to toss you over."

I squealed with laughter and beat my palms against his back in protest as he marched me to the door of my suite and pulled it open.

"Morning."

I stilled at the sound of Luther's voice.

"You look like shit," Taran said. I wriggled to get free, but he held me in place. "Did you get drunk without me?"

"Hardly. I'm still recovering from the last time I joined you for a night out."

Taran barked a laugh.

"Hello?" I called out, squirming in his grasp.

"Cousin, do you mind putting Her Majesty down?" Luther asked. "As much as I'm enjoying this view, I'm rather partial to her face."

Taran slid me off his shoulder and deposited me on the ground. I whacked my palm against his arm and glared at his smirk, then turned—and froze.

Luther looked *terrible*.

He was slumped against his doorframe, his head drooping with the effort of staying up. Stringy, rumpled hair had matted to his forehead. The dark circles beneath his eyes were stark against his sallow skin, which sagged from his bones like melting wax.

Even at his lowest, Luther had always burned with a spark from within. The man staring back at me now looked hollow. A candle blown out.

"Good morning, my Queen." He smiled, but it was all wrong.

I must have looked like a trout, staring with large eyes and an open mouth, no words coming out.

His focus shifted to Taran. "Could I have a word with Her Majesty alone?"

Taran threw an arm around my neck, planting an obnoxiously wet kiss on my temple. "Thanks for the sleepover, Queenie. It was a night I'll *never* forget." He winked at Luther and clapped a hand on his shoulder before strolling away with a laugh.

Luther grimaced and braced himself against the wall.

"Are you hurt?" I asked.

He straightened with some effort. "I haven't been sleeping well."

I frowned. He'd slept most of yesterday, and a full night of rest both days prior. After our time on the road, the last few nights had been a luxury.

"I left some food for you," I said.

"I saw." He shifted his weight. "Thank you."

"We missed you last night." I took a step closer. "*I* missed you."

He hung his head and closed his eyes, allowing the silence to hang for a painfully long moment. "Diem, we need to talk."

"I know," I blurted out, all my feelings suddenly bubbling up in my chest. "I agree."

"I wanted to wait until we were back in Lumnos—"

"What happened yesterday—I didn't plan it, I swear. In the tunnels, I saw—"

"It doesn't matter. There's something more important."

"It does matter. I don't want to keep things from you. We promised each other brutal honesty."

Luther grimaced. "*Fuck.*"

I straightened. "What is it? What's wrong?"

He finally looked up at me, his face the portrait of agony. He took a stiff step forward and raised a hand, the tips of his fingers just barely grazing my face, as if he feared my touch—or his own.

I placed my hand over his and pressed it to my cheek, surprised—and a little alarmed—at the fiery heat of his skin. I slowly closed the distance between us. "Whatever it is, we'll get through it."

He shook his head, his forehead falling to mine. "Diem," he breathed. "Will you ever forgive me?"

Before I could answer, a cheerful whistling cut through the air.

We both went still.

"Well look at that, if it isn't just who I was coming to see."

Luther deflated against me.

With reluctance bordering on despair, I pulled out of his arms, then glowered down the hall. "I thought this wing was for our *private* use."

Symond strolled out of the shadows with his hands in his pockets. His dark trousers were skintight against his slender legs, his silk shirt unbuttoned to his waist. "I come bearing a message from Her Majesty. Nothing in this realm is private from her."

"What do you want?" Luther snapped.

"From you? Nothing. From her?" He ran his hand along his bare chest.

"I have a few ideas. Would you like me to show you again, Prince, or did you get enough of that yesterday?"

Luther lunged unsteadily toward him. I threw myself in the way, gently nudging him back.

"You're an ass, Symond," I muttered.

A sinfully arrogant smile hooked his lips. "Her Majesty wishes you to join her for an early lunch."

"Fine. I'll collect the others and we'll be down in an hour."

"The invitation is for one, and I've been sent to retrieve you immediately."

I threw him an annoyed glare. "Can't it wait?"

"Her Majesty waits for no one. Even Queens."

I glanced back at Luther, who looked one snide comment away from turning Symond into a rug. I lightly touched his chin to pull his attention back to me. "Can we discuss this after lunch?"

He nodded stiffly, though his expression was screaming *no*.

I hesitated. "If it's really important..."

"Just go." His glare sharpened on Symond. "Touch her again without her consent, and mark my words, I'll take you down with me."

Symond chuckled and extended his arm. "Your Majesty?"

I gave Luther an apologetic glance before laying as little of my hand as I could on Symond's forearm and following him down the hall.

As we turned out of the corridor, I cast one last look over my shoulder. Luther was still waiting, still watching. The darkness in his eyes lingered in my thoughts even after he fell out of view.

"He's a real ray of sunshine," Symond quipped. "I can see why you're so in love."

My heart tripped and tumbled across the floor. "Love? I... I haven't—"

He grinned. "No? Hmm. My mistake."

I swallowed down the massive lump that had formed in my throat. "Leave him alone. We've been through a lot the past few days—which you very well know."

"But I'm having so much fun."

I shot him a scowl. "How did you get so..."

He glanced back to confirm Luther was out of sight, then pulled me closer. "So charming? So handsome?"

"So gleeful at other people's misery."

His smile tightened. "I'm a Centenary. We can read each other's minds, and we're allowed to be as wicked as we want. In a world like that, you strike first or you get struck."

"You can *all* read each other's minds?"

"The strongest can shield their thoughts from the weakest, but most of us are equally matched."

"What about the Queen?"

"No one can breach her shield. Not that anyone would dare try."

I hummed thoughtfully. "It must be difficult never having any privacy, even in your own mind."

"On the contrary. It's quite nice never having to lie." He leaned his face to mine. "Unlike your Prince, *brutal honesty* is all I know."

I gave him a withering glance, though I couldn't deny there was something liberating about the idea of living without secrets and never having to hide any part of who you were.

Symond turned me down another hallway, this one notably more extravagant. "We have to make one small stop."

"I thought the Queen waited for no one?"

"She doesn't." He eyed me head-to-toe. "But she also insists on proper dress."

"What's wrong with my—"

I paused and looked down. My stolen linen clothing was wrinkled and stained with flecks of blood, the hems dusted with dried mud. Holes dotted my scarf from where I'd partially burned through it in Ignios.

"You're a Queen," Symond chided. "Best to look like one."

My cheeks flushed. In so many ways, I was still a poor-born mortal at heart. I had not yet grown used to the idea that anyone cared how I looked.

Symond led me through a series of corridors to a lamp-lit room lined with gowns and glittering baubles.

"What is this?" I asked, gazing around in awe.

"Her Majesty's wardrobe."

I nearly choked. "Are you mad? I can't take her clothing."

"It's better than insulting her by showing up in rags."

"You're trying to get me killed, aren't you?"

He laughed and leaned against the wall, crossing his arms over his chest. "Believe me, you don't get to my position without learning what the Queen will and won't tolerate."

I turned and let my eyes wander. There were enough gowns here to clothe every person in Lumnos, with accessories to match. I wondered if

Yrselle even bought them, or if the cloth market vendors simply showered her with gifts to stay in her good graces.

"Does that mean you also know what the Queen wants from me?" I asked, running my hand along the shimmering fabrics.

"I don't. Honestly, I've been wondering the same thing myself."

"Are you telling the truth, or are you taking advantage of someone you can finally lie to?"

"I don't know. Am I?"

I peered over my shoulder and studied his smug expression, looking for the lie. Oddly, my godhood stirred, and I felt a sudden certainty he was telling me the truth.

I turned back to the gowns, grabbing a white gossamer frock that I hoped was too plain for the Queen to remember owning. I gestured for Symond to turn his back, and though he rolled his eyes in dramatic fashion, he obliged.

"Do you at least have any theories on what she wants?" I asked as I disrobed.

"Now *you're* trying to get *me* killed." He was silent for a moment. "I know she thinks you're valuable somehow. But don't get any ideas—your *friends* are not, and you're not so important that she'll spare them if they step out of line."

I walked to a mirror and stepped into the gown. "Valuable how?"

"Whatever that riddle she told you means, she spends a great deal of time thinking on it." He paused again. "Her Majesty has been Queen for many years. She survived the Blood War. I don't think she desires to see Emarion have a second one."

A knot of worry formed. If Yrselle was determined to avoid war, she might not be the ally I'd hoped for.

My gaze caught on a pair of eyes in the mirror—gleaming, lust-filled black eyes devouring the sight of my exposed back.

He grinned. "Couldn't resist." He kicked off the wall and strode toward me, then took the back of my dress in his hands. His knuckles brushed my skin as he drew up the fastening.

Symond leaned in, his breath hot against my neck. "I would say the Prince is a lucky man, but..."

Our eyes met in the mirror.

Abruptly, he turned for the door. "We're late. Leave your clothes here, I'll have them sent to your room. Or maybe burned."

I grabbed a pair of silk slippers and clumsily slid them on as I scrambled to catch up.

"That dress is a lovely choice," he said. "You look ravishing."

"You'd say that to anything that breathes, Symond. I'm not sure the bar is even *that* high."

He gasped in mock offense. "I'm hurt, Your Majesty. I have quite exacting standards for my partners."

I arched an eyebrow. "Then what *exactly* is it you're attracted to?"

"Power."

He stopped in front of a grand set of dark-stained oak doors carved with the Queen's signature dragons, then pushed them open and swept inside. "May I present Her Majesty, the Queen of Lumnos."

I took in a deep breath and walked inside. Yrselle was seated at the head of a long table laden with platters of food. A host of fawning Centenaries crouched around her, feeding her berries and pawing at her skin.

"Diem, darling, come join me," she called out, gesturing to a chair beside her.

I took my seat while side-eyeing her entourage. They seemed oblivious to my arrival, entirely fixated on her pleasure. "Are they always like this?"

She cast them a surprised glance, as if she hadn't noticed them until I brought it up. "Only when they're not on duty. We take our work and our play very seriously here." She leaned forward and smirked. "Most of them are as high as the clouds."

I looked closer—though it was hard to see with their black irises, several indeed had blown pupils and glassy eyes. "And this is... by choice?"

"If I wish to bend someone to my will—" She tapped her temple. "—I don't need *drugs* to do it."

Yesterday had been reminder enough of that.

She flicked a wrist, and the Centenaries scattered to the exits, taking Symond with them. Her eyes raked over me. "There's something about your appearance today. Something that disturbs me."

My blood froze. I wrapped my hands over my chest in a pathetic attempt to cover up the borrowed gown.

"Ah. Now I see."

I braced for impending death.

"Your Crown is missing." Her head tilted. "That will not do. We are Queens, dear. We must look the part."

I absently touched my forehead. I hadn't worn my Crown since escaping in Arboros. It had been nice to walk the markets unnoticed and feel somewhat normal, even though my life was anything but.

I reached in and immediately sensed the spark of divine magic I'd tucked away. It was easier than expected—my body seemed to recognize it as something foreign, something not entirely *mine*.

I pulled it up through my chest and throat, up to the top of my head, until a warm heaviness settled on top of me—a glowing reminder of the burden that lay on my shoulders.

Yrselle's eyes fixed on the space above my head and grew in size.

"*Incredible*," she breathed.

I frowned. Surely she'd seen the Crown of Lumnos before. "Is something wrong?"

Her gaze snapped to mine. "Not at all. You wear it so well." She lounged back in her chair. "My dress looks lovely on you, too."

"Oh, uh, I'm sorry. Symond said—"

"I'll have a few more sent to your room. Or do you prefer to select them yourself?"

"No! No... I trust your expertise."

She nodded approvingly and gestured for me to eat.

"How did you find me?" I asked, loading a plate with fluffy whipped eggs and a ham gleaming with glaze. "I'm guessing Zalaric's confession wasn't really news to you."

"No, it wasn't. I told him nothing happens here without my knowledge. I tell everyone, and still, the fools think they can deceive me. He'll have to learn the hard way." She stabbed her fork into a roasted tomato. "Shame. I quite enjoyed him."

My stomach dropped. Maybe Zalaric wasn't as safe here as he thought.

"How is it that you're able to know so much with only one hundred guards? Can you read everyone's minds from here?"

She laughed. "Well I can't go revealing *all* my secrets, can I?" She grabbed her butter knife, then reached for the bread. "For you, I suppose I can share one tiny piece. You've felt the Forging magic, yes? When you released my representatives at your ball?" She paused, and I nodded. "That magic runs through everything in the realm. Every plant, every creature. Even the stone. When you've been Queen as long as I have, you learn how to use it to your advantage." She shook the knife in my direction. "Though your spectacle at the coronation has made that more difficult than it used to be."

"You knew what was going to happen with the heartstone, didn't you? I remember—you were the only one who wasn't surprised."

"Do you know what I remember? You pointing and blaming me when everything went wrong."

I cringed.

Yes. I *had* done that.

She popped a piece of bread into her mouth. "You're lucky I don't care what the rest of those nitwits think of me."

"Why did you vote against them to save my mother?"

She chuckled. "It made them furious. That would have been reason enough for me."

I arched a brow. "Is that the *only* reason?"

"No. Your mother has a role to play in what's to come."

"And what is that? What's to come?"

Yrselle didn't answer. She leaned forward and lifted up a porcelain kettle. "Tea, dear?" She filled my cup before I could answer.

"Did you know my mother? When she came here to Umbros, did you read her mind? Or was it when you came..." I paused, my head tilting. "Wait... *did* you come to Lumnos? The woman I saw looked—" I glanced at her regal gown and curvy body. "—not like this."

The corners of her eyes creased slightly. I felt a tingling buzz between my temples and the scratch of sharp nails on my mind.

Are you sure? her voice crooned in my head.

I blinked, and suddenly her skin was wrinkled and spotted with age, her shoulders hunched and draped in tattered fabric—the old crone I'd seen in Paradise Row on Forging Day.

"Appearances can be deceiving, child," she croaked, her voice sounding much older and weaker.

I blinked again, but the illusion persisted. My godhood jerked unhappily at the mental invasion.

Fight.

I yielded to the *voice*'s demand. A burst of cool warmth cascaded over my head. My skin sparked with light, and her presence in my head was gone.

"Marvelous," she gasped, her appearance back to normal. "Just *marvelous*. I've never felt anything like it."

I sat up straighter, feeling slightly energized—though more than a little unnerved.

"I did read your mother's mind, both here and in Lumnos," Yrselle admitted. "She didn't know that, of course. Auralie thought she was very sneaky." Her dark eyes rolled. "They always do."

"If you knew about the attack, why didn't you stop it?"

"Stop it? I was grateful for it. If it gets me out of those awful rituals, the mortals can keep that damn island forever. Do you know how many of those ceremonies I've had to attend? How many hundreds of Forging Days I've had to trek out there just to shed a drop of blood?"

I gaped, unable to believe I'd heard her correctly. "You're not opposed to the Guardians' occupation? Won't that disrupt the Forging magic?"

"The Forging magic is already disrupted."

"Because of me? Because..." I held my breath. "'*When forgotten blood on heartstone falls*'?"

Her smile was wide and proud. "Clever girl."

"Does that mean my birth father is the '*forgotten*'?"

She shrugged lightly. "Words in prophecies can have many meanings. Some quite obvious, some less so."

"What about the rest? What chains? And the debt—whose yoke?"

"If I give it all away this early, you won't stay for the whole trip. We can discuss the rest tomorrow, before you leave."

I sank in my chair, frustrated. "You said my birth father was alive—where is he?"

"That, I do not know. You'll have to find him on your own." A spark of something glimmered in her midnight eyes. "Perhaps your mother will know."

"But she's in prison."

"Yes. As a prisoner of the Crowns. And what are you?"

"A Crown." My pulse picked up speed. "So I can get her out?"

"For that, you need a vote of six Crowns—unless you intend to start a war. But you are entitled to question her. And if Fortos says otherwise, you remember what I told you."

"'*A Crown holds no authority over other Crowns*,'" I repeated. My mind reeled at this new possibility. I could go see my mother, speak to her, hold her in my arms—but I still had no idea how to get her free.

Yrselle sneered. "I never approved of this 'vote of six' rubbish. That's a new creation, you know. Put into place years after the war, over my protests."

Her fist slammed onto the table with a violent *crack*, rattling me and half the dishes.

"There's a reason it takes all nine Crowns to renew the Forging magic," she hissed. "We act as one. That's what the Kindred intended. Even a single dissent should stay our hands. These fools and their egos thought they knew better than the Kindred, and look where it got us. Look what's happened! Look how much we'll have to sacrifice now that—"

She stopped short, huffing angry breaths. She'd talked herself into a furor, the wildness of her gaze betraying the unpredictability Zalaric had warned of. Her mighty aura had a disturbingly unhinged energy, a bomb that might erupt in dragonfyre or daffodils.

She brushed her hair back with a shaky hand. "Well. We've lost sight of *many* things the Kindred intended, haven't we?"

I nodded to placate her, keeping as still as I could muster.

Her breathing steadied, and she picked up her teacup. "Lumnos is not the only one who speaks to her disciples, you know." She raised the cup to her lips, watching me from beneath her dark lashes. "Blessed Father Umbros has *much* to say about you."

My fingers tightened around the arm of my chair. Whatever I'd been expecting, it wasn't that.

Umbros... a *Kindred*... a dead, super-powerful divine spirit... had spoken to *Yrselle*... about *me?*

I sat up straighter. "The prophecy... is that how you—"

"I've answered enough questions. Now I have a few for you." She shoved her chair back with a noisy screech, extending her hand. "Shall we discuss them on the balcony?"

It didn't feel like a request, so I stiffly rose and took her hand. Her nails scraped lightly against my wrist as she led me to an outdoor terrace. Her gryvern was there, curled up and dozing, though it cracked one amber eye as we approached.

The balcony was lined with the flimsiest railing imaginable—swaths of ribbon draped between potted olive trees. I peered over the edge, spotting white, skull-shaped objects in a heap on the canyon floor, and I began to understand why.

"You and that Prince," she began, stealing my attention back. She took my hands in hers. "You have plans for a new Emarion, don't you?"

Oh, no.

My mouth went dry. "What? No, I—"

"Don't bother lying, dear. Everything your Luther knows, I've already seen."

Oh, no no no.

This was bad. This was *so* bad. Was this why she'd brought me here—to expose me and kill me?

Suddenly, the edge of the balcony was uncomfortably close. I looked around for an exit or a weapon. Could I resist, if she pushed me? Could I push her first?

A growl rolled from her gryvern's throat.

"Careful, dear. Gryverns can sense intentions. And unlike that miserable Ignios beast, mine actually likes me." She squeezed my hands. "You want to change the order of things in Emarion, yes?"

Slowly, I nodded.

"And these plans of yours... how dedicated are you to seeing them through?"

My lips pressed tight.

She stepped closer. "How far are you willing to go for them? How much will you sacrifice?"

"Whatever it takes," I said. "I'll die for them, if I must."

She rolled her eyes. "That part's easy. Anyone can die." Her head shifted with a predatory tilt. "Can you *kill?*"

That question had been haunting me for weeks. Could I? I'd taken a life, but it had been accidental, a reflex of self-defense. Could I kill with purpose? Could I *slaughter?*

"I... I think so."

"Can you watch the people you love die?"

My chest tightened. "I already have."

"Can you watch them *all* die?"

"Surely that won't—"

"Can you keep going when everyone you care for is lying in a grave?" Her gaze sharpened. "Can you be the one who puts them there?"

She crooked a finger under my chin, the sharp point of her nail digging into my flesh. "How far will you go? This world of peace and unity you think you can build—how much are you willing to give to see it come to life?"

"Everything."

The word came out instantly, dragged up by some innate certainty, out of my mouth before I'd consciously thought it through.

"Are you sure?" she snapped. "Be *certain*, child. Everything has a price, and the more precious the item, the more devastating the cost." Her hand gripped painfully around my jaw and jerked me forward. Her mental claws scraped against the walls of my mind, and for reasons I couldn't explain, this time I let her stay there.

"I'll ask you one last time," she snarled. "How much of your soul are you willing to set ablaze?"

"All of it," I whispered.

Silence hovered, thick and deadly.

"Good." She let go of my chin and gave me a light pat on my cheek. She turned and walked away, and her presence slithered out of my head. "I have something to show you."

I swayed on my feet, unable to move. Her gryvern watched me with a probing gaze.

"Come along, dear. It's rude to dawdle."

I followed her out of the room and down the hall, my heart still hammering in my chest.

A few moments later she stopped in front of a stained-glass door depicting what looked to be a history of Emarion. On one panel, bloody bodies were scattered over a red-drenched battlefield. On another, nine Crown-wearing figures stood on a circular black platform.

But what rendered me speechless was the panel on top. A tree, its branches engulfed in flames, a red-haired man leaning against its base.

The Everflame.

"What is this place?" I asked breathlessly.

She swung the door open, revealing an enormous room. Each side was lined with fully stocked bookshelves, while tables with soft-hued lanterns dotted the center path.

"This is my library," she explained. "I saw in Zalaric's memories you have an affinity for books."

I nodded, too overcome to speak.

She gestured to one side. "The mortal section is there. Peruse it to your heart's content. The Descended books are on the other side." She pointed to a small alcove walled off by an iron gate. "That's the Kindred section. It has some of the rarest books in Emarion. Only the Sophos Crown's library could hope to compete."

My jaw dropped further. She pulled back her shoulders, smirking with no small amount of pride.

She slipped a key out of her corset and dangled it just above my hand. "I don't even give my Centenaries this access. But you are not a Centenary." The key fell into my palm. "And I think you will need this in the weeks to come."

She promptly whirled around and began walking away. "I'll see you tonight at dinner."

I cringed. This was a gift, a once-in-a-lifetime opportunity. Any other day, I would have walled myself into a fort of books and refused to ever come out.

But today, Luther needed me.

"Wait," I called out.

She paused and looked back, eyebrows high.

"Thank you for this offer. I would love nothing more, really, but..." I sighed. "I need to get back to my friends."

"Oh, they aren't here." She made a face. "They were disgustingly unkempt. I sent them to a bathhouse in the city to be cleaned up and fitted for appropriate clothing. They'll be back for dinner."

My shoulders sank.

"Happy reading, dear," she chirped, strolling away. "And don't forget why they banned these books for mortals in the first place."

"Why is that?"

"Because an education is the most powerful weapon of them all."

THIRTY-FIVE

The next few hours were some of the most enjoyable I'd ever had. I lost all sense of time as I dove head-first into the depthless well of knowledge the Queen's library contained.

I rifled through the books at lightning speed, my eyes furiously skimming the pages of the ancient tomes. There were books I thought had been lost forever—histories of mortalkind that stretched back long before the Kindred's arrival—and references to Emarion's original cities, names we'd been banned from knowing, let alone writing or speaking aloud.

There were treatises on systems of government the mortals had experimented with. Monarchies, councils, parliaments, even self-rule. Though none was without its flaws, the mortals of old had at least been learning from their mistakes. Each successive attempt had been getting more open and more fair—until the Kindred stopped that progress in its tracks by removing mortals from the process entirely.

Perhaps the most interesting find were the scriptures of the ancient religions. Sadly, these were not intact—the true names of the Old Gods had been meticulously burned away, page by page, leaving only vague, ambiguous descriptions.

The Kindred must have believed there was power in names. Why else go to such great lengths to strip them from our collective memory? One could not hold on to what one could not define. In erasing a name, they erased everything that name once stood for. The results had been ruthlessly effective.

The Everflame was the one name that had persisted, and as a result, it had become the rallying cry of the rebellion. If the Everflame's name had been stolen from us as the Old Gods had, would the Guardians of the Ever-flame be so united? Would they even exist at all?

The Crowns must have had the same questions, because they'd finally banned any mention of the Everflame after the Blood War. Though mortals still revered it in private, each new generation of mortals knew less and less of its lore. If my plans failed, someday its memory might be lost forever.

For now, at least, it endured—in the pages of these books, if nowhere else.

Stories of the Everflame were plentiful. Apparently, the Old Gods once plucked flames from its branches and gave them as blessings, flames that burned forever and kept their bearers warm even in the coldest of nights. Pregnant mothers would risk their lives to travel the sea once labor began, believing a child born on the Everflame's blessed soil would be imbued with its sacred power of life. And the glacial pits of hell beneath its roots were not eternal, as I'd been told. Unworthy souls condemned to its ice could petition for a second chance to earn their way into the warm haven of the Undying Fire.

When the clock's chimes jolted me out of my reverie, I realized the entire afternoon had come and gone. Surely Luther had returned by now.

I stowed the books back on the shelf, wishing I had a lifetime to consume them. Perhaps I'd have another chance once this war was over.

If I survived that long.

As I grudgingly dragged myself to the exit, my focus snagged on the locked cage containing the books on the Kindred. I'd never been particularly interested in their stories, but something Yrselle said had stuck with me.

Umbros had talked to her about me.

And so had Lumnos to Luther.

If two of the Kindred had seen fit to discuss me with their most loyal adherents, perhaps there was something I should know about *them*.

I walked to the cage and unlocked it with Yrselle's key. The space was small and well-maintained, with glass cases for each of its books to preserve their delicate condition.

A large, pencil-drawn sketch of Emarion hung on the back wall. A golden plaque described it as the original map used by the Kindred.

I stepped closer and squinted. Faint lines were still visible where old borders had been erased and modified several times over, likely as the Kindred had apportioned out each realm. Only one seemed not to have been redrawn: a barely there scratch through the middle of Montios.

At the center, more erased lines peeked out from where the Everflame had once been labeled, obscured by a rough sketch of what would become the Kindred's Temple.

My temper prickled. These Kindred, with their divine egos, had defaced our home and rebuilt it in homage to themselves. My interest in anything they had to say was rapidly dying.

I gave a cursory, half-hearted skim of the books in the cases, mostly fawning biographies of the Kindred written by the earliest Descended. Only one item piqued my attention—a small, well-worn notebook on a lavender pillow. Unlike the others, there was no label for its contents.

I lifted the lid and gingerly picked it up. The inside was all handwritten in a fluid, elegant scrawl without dates or sections. I flipped to an early page at random and began reading:

> The locals, too, are at war. The hate reminds us of home and all we have lost. It grieves me. I do not wish these people to know the despair we have seen.
>
> We try to help them with our gifts. We end their diseases and feed their hungry. They call us their saviors and bow to us as gods. My siblings welcome it. I do not.
>
> They even gave us names in their language. They call me Montios, for my love of their beautiful mountains.

I gasped.

This was the diary of a *Kindred*.

I'd always known they existed—the Descended were proof of that—but it was oddly disconcerting to imagine them not as gods but as people, each with thoughts and feelings of their own.

I flipped to another page:

> When Lumnos fell, it was expected. Her heart is a soft place where love thrives. Nor were Meros or Umbros any

surprise. *They are drawn to pleasure, and we have all been lonely for so long.*

My siblings and I warned them against their unions. Then our eldest fell. Sophos, our guiding light! I could not believe it.

Though it may have been I who sealed our fate. I have always preferred solitude over the company of others. Once I found my love, that changed. When he and I steal away on Rymari to the mountains, I feel the peace I have always longed for.

Every day, our beloveds age. The thought haunts us all. Sophos believes there may be a way to bind their short lives to ours.

Whatever the cost is, I will pay it. An eternity with him is worth the highest price.

A chill skittered over my skin. Montios had hoped to give her lover eternal life—instead, she'd sacrificed her own immortality to age and die at his side. She had indeed paid the ultimate price, but in a twisted way she hadn't expected.

I'd made a similar vow earlier to the Queen—to sacrifice everything for my goal. Was I destined for the same fate?

I flipped to the end and frowned. The final section had been ripped out, leaving shredded edges along the center as evidence. I thumbed back a few pages and began reading:

The locals are grateful, though some resent our presence. They fear Lumnos's unborn child, as well as the life growing in Fortos's mate. What role will our descendants play in this new world?

There is a plan, but our youngest will not agree. Our lives are shorter now. We must persuade him before our time expires.

I confess, some days I fear him. What happened in our

319

homeland did not scare him, as it should have. Instead, he speaks of it with reverence. Even our Mo—

"Your Majesty?"

My head snapped up. Symond leaned against the doorway, head cocked and smiling. His shirt from earlier was missing, and his skin was coated in dried blood.

"What happened?" I asked. "Are you hurt?"

His smile pulled wider. "It's not my blood. But your concern is noted."

I rolled my eyes. "Whose blood is it?"

"Someone who should have known better than to cross the Queen of Umbros." He stood upright and jerked his chin. "Come. There are Centenaries waiting in your quarters to help you dress for dinner."

"Have you seen this?" I breathed, holding up the diary. "This was written by a *Kindred*."

"I have not. I'm not allowed to step within this room." His smile tightened. "I didn't think anyone was, save for Her Majesty."

I reluctantly set the book down in its case and closed the glass lid, then left the room, locking the door behind me with Yrselle's key.

"She must think highly of you, to have given you such access," he said smoothly as we walked. "I take it your lunch went well?"

"I'm not laying at the base of a canyon or digesting in a gryvern's belly. I'll call that a success."

In truth, I wasn't sure if it had gone well or not. I felt a little like I'd pledged my soul to something I hadn't fully understood.

I was grateful for his silence the rest of the way. My mind was still spinning from what I'd seen and trying to piece together what significance, if any, it had. Something about what I'd read was gnawing at me, but I couldn't quite place what it was.

When we reached the corridor leading to my suite, Luther returned to the forefront of my mind. I should have come back earlier—now I would have to rush our conversation.

I gave Symond an awkward wave. "I can find my way back from here."

"I should hope so," he drawled. "I need to pick up two of my own. They've been here all afternoon."

"Here? Why were two Centenaries in our private wing?"

His lips twitched with a secretive smirk. "They were requested by one of your guests."

My frown slowly deepened as Symond accompanied me the entire way down the hall. When we reached the end, he gave me his back, facing Luther's door and knocking loudly.

Muffled voices came from the other side.

Feminine voices.

The door swung open, and two pretty Centenaries appeared.

"Come, ladies," Symond ordered. "You've had enough fun for today."

"Hope you feel better now, Princey," one called out loudly, waving. "Let us know if you want us to come back later tonight."

"It was a real *pleasure*," the other said, drawing out the final word with a seductive purr.

They walked out arm in arm, whispering in each other's ears.

"Did you see that scar? It's *huge*."

"That wasn't the only thing that was huge."

They collapsed in a fit of laughter as they walked away.

Symond pulled the door closed, but not before I caught a glimpse of Luther—laying naked in bed among rumpled sheets, his back to the door and his clothes scattered along the floor.

"Oh, dear," Symond said. "I forgot—he requested that you not be told. Be a sweetheart and pretend you didn't see that."

I could hardly think over the sound of blood rushing in my ears. Surely that wasn't what it seemed. Luther cared for me, he would never...

Or would he? He'd been with Iléana, and he never cared for her. Maybe that's how he preferred it—no strings, no emotions. Maybe that's why he'd been avoiding my touch, why he'd been afraid I wouldn't forgive him.

In the moment we had in the inn, he'd said I deserved *more*. More that he couldn't give me...

Oh, *gods*.

"Diem?" Symond tipped a finger under my chin, snapping me back to the present. "You should get ready. Her Majesty doesn't tolerate lateness."

I nodded numbly and turned to my room.

"Try not to fret," he called out from behind me. "I'm sure it's nothing to worry about at all."

I BARELY HEARD a thing as the Centenaries bathed and dressed me. They painted my nails, curled my hair, even oiled my skin with a sweet-smelling perfume. I stared mutely at the wall the entire time, replaying every word Luther had ever spoken. First I convinced myself that what I saw meant nothing; then I convinced myself it meant *everything*.

If I found any clarity at all, it disappeared the second I stepped into the corridor and met his gaze with mine.

His hair had been trimmed and pulled back, his sharp jaw cleanly shaven. His suit was pressed and perfectly tailored to show off his broad, high shoulders. Though I could still sense a heaviness wearing on him, regaining some control over his appearance had restored a glimmer of the light missing from his eyes when I'd seen him last.

An excruciating tightness wound around on my chest. I couldn't deny the appeal of the rugged side of him I'd seen while traveling, but this stately, well-groomed royal was the Luther I'd first met. The Luther I knew on a soul-deep level. The Luther I'd fallen for. And I wasn't sure why, but that *hurt*.

"My Queen. You look..." He stepped toward me, the breath rushing out of him all at once. He admired me like the finest work of art, the wonder in his expression bringing a flush to my cheeks.

Taran gave a low whistle as he looked me over. Alixe nodded, smiling wide.

"Finally, a dress befitting your status," Zalaric said.

I broke my daze long enough to look down at myself. The Centenaries had dressed me in sheer black gossamer, draped to cover as little as possible, with a plunging neckline that dropped to my navel and a slit at the thigh that ran nearly to my ribs. An array of tiny, glittering rubies resembled splattered blood after a gruesome kill.

It was violent and sexual, perfectly suited to the court of Umbros. Though I would never have chosen it for myself, I had to admit, the look injected me with a boldness I hadn't felt since emerging victorious in my Challenging.

It was an intriguing contrast to my companions, who had been dressed in Lumnos's traditional blue and silver. Luther was characteristically formal in a high-necked brocade jacket, while Alixe stunned in a flesh-colored bodysuit with strategically placed diamond clusters and a navy overcoat that trailed in a pool behind her. Taran wore breeches of blue-black leather and a harness of straps and chains that left his tanned muscles on display, his godstone injuries now nearly gone.

Even Zalaric's Lumnosian heritage was evident in his clothing—if it could even be called clothing, considering his open vest and billowing pants were fabricated entirely from shadow magic, with glowing light-made cuffs snaking up his forearms. The Lumnos Queen in me was proud to see him embrace his homeland so openly—but as I remembered Yrselle's cryptic comment about his fate, worry grew in the back of my mind.

Indeed, I was the only one who looked as if I belonged in the Umbros court. This felt strongly like Yrselle's way of stamping me with her claim, but to what end, I still wasn't sure.

"You are stunning no matter what you wear," Luther said. "But I agree with Zalaric. It is good to see you adorned as the Queen you are."

Despite his adoring tone, his words were swallowed up by the thoughts plaguing me over what I'd seen.

"Especially with your Crown," Zalaric added. "I've never seen it in person before."

Alixe's smile fell. She frowned, then exchanged a look with Taran, whose head had gone nearly sideways, his brows similarly furrowed.

"The Crown," she started, "does it look...?"

"Different," Luther answered. His eyes locked on the space above my head.

I smoothed a hand over my milk-white curls, swept back on one side with a garnet comb. I'd been too distracted to look in the mirror before leaving. "Perhaps it changed form due to the coronation."

"Perhaps," Alixe murmured, "though it's always looked the same in old paintings."

The clock chimed to signal the dinner hour. I shrugged off their scrutiny and gathered my skirts. "Let's get on with it," I said dully.

Luther stepped to my side and offered his hand—gloved, I noticed. An odd choice. Overly formal, even for him.

"May I escort you?" he asked.

"I think I'll walk alone tonight." I tried not to notice the slight drop of his shoulders as I breezed past him down the corridor, where a Centenary was waiting to lead us to dinner.

The others followed, Alixe and Taran bantering about their day at the bathhouses with the occasional quip from Zalaric. I picked up that Luther had gone with them, but returned early—"to rest," he claimed.

I steeled my jaw and focused on our march through the palace. With the exception of our guide, there wasn't a soul in sight, not even a Centenary on guard. The unexpected emptiness set my hackles rising, especially when we turned into a very extravagant—and entirely vacant—banquet hall.

"Where is everyone?" I asked our chaperone.

"They'll be along shortly," he answered, his onyx eyes gleaming with hidden knowledge. He bowed and excused himself, leaving the five of us standing awkwardly by a fireplace.

Alixe flipped back the train of her coat, revealing a glimpse of the many blades she'd tucked into its inner pockets. "Did you learn anything at your lunch with the Queen?"

"She knows more than I thought, and she seems inclined to help me— or at least to not join the Crowns against me. I'm still not sure why. Or what she expects in return."

Taran rocked on his heels, a smile creeping in at the corners of his mouth. "Does that mean our plan for tonight is still the same?"

"There's a plan?" Luther asked.

"Oh yes. Queenie's plan. A *great* plan. We discussed it last night."

Alixe sighed. "He means the plan where he gets to drink all night and sleep with the Centenaries to coax information out of them." Her eyes rolled skyward. "He's been reminding me all day that it's Her Majesty's plan, so I can't overrule it."

Taran nodded excitedly. Zalaric glared.

"Yes, Taran, you can enjoy yourself tonight," I said. He fist-pumped the air, and my smile finally broke free. "You too, Alixe."

She looked uneasy. "Are you certain? We're going to be heavily outnumbered."

I shrugged. "The Queen had a clear chance to kill me at lunch. If she didn't strike then, I doubt she'll try now. As long as we keep playing her game, I don't think we're in danger."

Taran pounced and threw his arms around my ribs, crushing me against him. "Of all the Queens I know, you're my favorite."

I clutched at my dress to keep from spilling out. "Thanks, Taran. That's a high honor."

He gripped me tighter until I squeaked for air.

Luther cleared his throat. "Cousin, please stop grabbing Her Majesty's chest in public. It's bad enough you're sleeping in her bedroom."

I stiffened and pushed Taran off. "He fell asleep. Nothing happened between us."

Luther's frown deepened.

Taran barked a laugh and prodded me with his elbow. "Don't worry, Lu's not really jealous. He knows you're not my type."

I pretended to look offended. "What *is* your type? Wait, let me guess—a tall, blonde goddess with giant breasts and a tiny waist?"

Alixe started coughing.

Zalaric blinked.

Taran grinned. "Not exactly."

His eyes shifted to something over my shoulder and grew two times in size. "Wine," he breathed reverently, lurching toward the bar like a doomed sailor caught in a siren song.

Alixe and Zalaric shared a look and followed behind him, leaving Luther and I alone. I stared at my hands, my feet, my dress, everywhere but at his eyes. All the while, his heavy gaze stayed on me, watching in his all-seeing way.

The silence became unbearable, and the words tumbled out of me. "I came by your room earlier."

"I'm sorry I missed you. I must have been at the bathhouses."

"You weren't. But you were... occupied." My stomach reeled. "With two Centenary women."

I finally, reluctantly, agonizingly dragged my eyes up to his.

His expression was dark and carved in stone. A muscle twitched on his sunken cheek. "It's not—"

He stopped. Looked away.

His silence stung, but I forced myself to wait. Any second now he would explain, and then we'd make a joke of it, him teasing me about Taran while I ribbed him over... whatever it was, and then I would scold myself for ever having worried.

He retreated a step.

"I'm sorry I missed you," he repeated.

The words came out like an empty clang, painfully curt yet reverberating without end.

"That's it?" I asked, choking on the words.

"You should focus on the dinner," he said gruffly. Tightly. As if every word hurt to force out.

I stared at him, shaking my head.

"What happened to you?" I whispered.

His eyes shot to me. Beneath the churning shadows, there was hardly anything left of the glowing blue-grey.

"What happened to *us?*" I asked, my voice breaking. The emotions were rising too violently to stop. The hurt and the anger, the rejection and the confusion. It was a swirling cyclone, a tempest of feeling I couldn't contain.

Luther's throat worked as he watched me collapsing. His mask began to fracture.

"You'll understand soon," he said, sounding anguished.

It was his pity, of all things, that finally broke me. A hot, angry tear escaped from the corner of my eye. I stormed away before he could spot it and marched to Taran's side.

"I need a drink. Fast."

Taran smirked and bumped me with his hip. "Your wish is my command, Your Maj—" He stopped, his smile vanishing as he watched me wipe my glistening cheek. "Is everything—"

"A strong one," I interrupted. "A large one. And is there something to drink while I'm waiting?"

He wordlessly handed me his own half-finished glass, and I threw my head back and swallowed its contents in a single gulp. Heat flooded my chest as the alcohol burned through my bloodstream.

His eyebrows rose. "Should I be worried or impressed?"

"What in the Flames was in that?" I gasped between coughs. My mouth tasted like I'd swallowed a gaslamp whole—metal, glass, and all. "That was vile."

He shrugged. "I grabbed a bottle at random."

"I'm not sure that was for *drinking*, Taran. You might have just found the secret ingredient in the Guardians' bombs."

He snorted and rifled through the bottles, sniffing and tasting and crafting a new concoction.

As I waited for him to finish, my focus lifted to the mirrored panel behind the shelves, and I got my first glimpse of myself in all my regal glory —but it was the glowing Crown that stole my focus.

It *was* different.

The dark, thorny circlet had shifted slightly in shape, the peak in front now mirrored on the opposite end. Nestled between the glimmering points of light, shards of broken crystals seemed to form and dissolve at random.

My gaze dropped to my face—that, too, looked different. Smoky kohl had been smudged around my eyes, while a deep, sanguine red stained my lips. With the dress and the Crown, the effect was striking.

I was fearsome, deliciously decadent, a predator on the hunt, fierce and unflappable.

The opposite of how I really felt: wrecked, vulnerable, and painfully raw.

Perhaps the alcohol had already gone to my head, but the hurt in my heart began to harden into an indignant, almost defiant confidence.

Why shouldn't I be that woman in the mirror? I was a Queen of Emarion, for gods' sakes. I would not let this, or anything, break me.

And if Luther was determined to push me away, then I would show him what he was missing.

"Where's that drink?" I asked.

Taran popped upright and offered me a glass brimming with fizzing blue liquid. Without looking, he pulled an unmarked bottle from a shelf and ripped the cork out with his teeth.

"To the Blessed Kindred," he crooned. "May they find us more useful alive than dead."

"I'll drink to that."

I clinked my glass to his and downed a large sip. Taran, refusing to be outdone, chugged half the bottle in one go.

"Has anyone ever told you that you might have a drinking problem?" I asked, only half joking.

"Alixe and Luther, sometimes." He scowled. "My brother, daily."

"Do you ever think they might be right?"

He shot me a look. "Do you want to talk about why you were crying?"

I glared. He smirked. We both threw back another guzzle.

The sound of creaking doors floated through the room. We turned as a group to see Yrselle striding in. Her body was nearly bare, save for an embroidered dragon with emerald eyes that wrapped around her intimate areas, its gold-tipped wings splaying into a gauzy train that floated in her wake.

Behind her, the female Centenaries followed in two lines, each wearing matching skimpy crimson slips that draped low on their chests and even lower on their backs. Another small group followed, its members androgynous in appearance. Their outfits were crafted from the same fabric, the designs more varied but equally revealing.

"They know how to make an entrance," Alixe said.

"I think I'm overdressed," Luther muttered.

"I think *I'm* overdressed," I agreed.

Finally, Symond led in two lines of swaggering men. They ranged from svelte to muscular, but all wore scarlet satin pants slung outrageously low on their hips, their oiled bodies gleaming beneath sheer mesh tops.

Taran leaned into my side and grinned. "*That's* my type."

CHAPTER
THIRTY-SIX

W e sat at a long, narrow table that stretched the length of the room, the center piled high with arrangements of food, flowers, and candles. Yrselle and I shared the place of honor at the center on opposite sides. On her right, Symond had the perfect position to throw smug glances at Luther, seated to my left. Taran sat beside Luther, while Alixe and Zalaric sat to my right.

Courses came and went as conversation probed the details of my life as a mortal, something Yrselle and her ilk found fascinating. Though I tried to sate their curiosity, it was hard to say which was more distracting: the Queen's sharp-edged questions, Symond's relentless flirting, or the way Luther leaned in his chair so his arm brushed mine with every gesture. I felt a bit like a favorite doll being fought over by siblings.

It didn't help that the noise in the hall echoed deafeningly off the marble walls. Ever since arriving in Umbros, I'd found it difficult to think around more than a handful of people. Even the hushed whispers penetrated my thoughts and competed for my focus.

As wine flowed, I began to wear thin, and my answers grew shorter and snippier. Alixe smoothly interceded, maneuvering the topic to safer waters.

"When you said your Centenaries would attend this dinner, I didn't think you truly meant *all*," she said. "Is no one guarding the city?"

"We have our ways of guarding it from afar," Symond answered with a cryptic smile.

"What about new boats arriving at the docks? Have you closed the port for the night?"

A Centenary down the table scoffed. "The Umbros port *never* closes."

"Even the Blood War never shut us down," Symond agreed. "Your presence certainly won't."

"Does that mean the ships passing through tonight will go untaxed?" Alixe asked.

"Never," another Centenary hissed. "Her Majesty always gets her share."

"*Drink!*" Taran cheered, raising his glass.

I winced. Over the course of the night, Taran had turned the discussion into a one-man drinking game: Symond pokes at Luther? A small sip. Someone gloats about the Queen's absolute control of her city? Take a drink. A Centenary propositions one of us for sex? Finish his glass.

"But how can you collect payments?" I asked.

"You can hardly expect us to reveal our tricks to *you*," a Centenary said snidely. I recognized her as one of the women I'd seen leaving Luther's room. We shot each other mirrored glares.

"The Lumnos Queen is our new friend," Yrselle said. "Surely we can trust her to keep our secrets." Her piercing gaze challenged me to deny it.

I shrugged. "If you doubt my motives, you can always look in my head and see them for yourself."

Yrselle's mouth tightened.

I sat straighter in my chair.

She recovered quickly with an unbothered smile. "We hire Lumnos Descended to craft the illusion of Centenaries throughout the city." She tipped her glass to Zalaric. "Usually you're the one who collects my tariffs at the port."

He stilled, his fork frozen in midair. "I am?"

Laughter rippled among the Centenaries.

Symond smiled nastily. "You don't remember because we erased it from your memory."

Blood drained from Zalaric's face. He looked like he was wondering what *else* he might have done on Yrselle's command he now had no knowledge of.

"You can do that?" I asked. "Erase pieces of someone's memory?"

More laughter rose around the room.

"Oh, we can do *anything*," the Luther-admiring female Centenary said with an arrogant sniff.

Hagface. I decided to name her Hagface.

"We can erase memories. Create them. Replace your emotions with pain." Hagface smiled at Luther and bit her lip. "Or replace them with pleasure."

Yrselle sipped her wine. "When you control someone's mind, you control everything about them. You can make them say or do anything. Believe they're someone else. Turn them against the people they love." She ran a finger along the stem of her glass, her gaze hard on mine. "I could make your Luther put a sword through your heart, if I desired."

Luther's hand fisted on the table. "I would *never*," he growled.

"Would you like me to prove it?" she snapped, slamming her glass down.

The room went silent.

"No need," I said quietly. "I believe you."

Her glare cut to me. "Good. Because that's not even the worst of what our magic can do." She rose, planting her palms on the table and leaning forward. "I could remove every thought from your head and turn you into a walking corpse. Everything you love, everything you are, gone *forever*."

Goosebumps prickled my skin. I offered a small smile. "Then let us all be glad we are allies."

Nervous chuckles rose from both our groups, but they were quickly silenced by the clattering of plates and glasses falling to the floor as Yrselle swiped her arm across the table and cleared the space between us.

I jumped to my feet in surprise. She crawled across the table and snatched my wrist, yanking me closer until we were nose to nose.

"Are you listening?" she hissed. "Once a mind is crushed, there is no saving it. Memories cannot be rewritten. Even Blessed Father Umbros cannot restore what no longer exists."

To anyone else, it surely looked like a threat. The Corbois had drawn their magic in my defense, though the Centenaries had frozen them still.

But there was something else in the crazed darkness of Yrselle's eyes. A message. A warning of a different kind.

"Do you understand?" she demanded. Her nails dug into my flesh. "The soul is gone. *Gone*. Death is the only salvation you can give them."

I nodded. "I understand."

"You don't." Her eyes narrowed. "But you will."

She released me and flopped backward into her chair. "Someone clean this mess up." She lazily flicked her wrist. "And bring us *gaudenscium*, too."

I stumbled back a step, my companions jolting free of their mental binds. Centenaries leapt up and surrounded us to clear the fallen items.

Luther placed a hand on my waist to steady me. "Are you alright?"

I nodded dumbly and leaned into him, still stunned from the Queen's outburst. His grip on me curved tighter.

"I hate this place," he mumbled. "The sooner we leave here, the better."

I'd briefly forgotten my irritation with him amid the commotion, but now it was slamming right back in place. "You seemed to enjoy yourself today."

His wounded look took me by surprise, and my righteous ire deflated. I avoided his eyes as I pulled free and slid back into my chair.

Once the table was clear, a Centenary appeared with a silver tray and set goblets containing a reddish liquid in front of us.

The Queen lifted her glass. "A toast... to our very *special* guests."

A cheer went up around the room. I flashed her a strained smile as I raised the drink to my lips.

The smell hit me first. A smell I knew—and despised: smoke and citrus.

Stop!

The word exploded in my head, an urgent thought borne of panic and fury.

Instantly, every hand in the room stilled.

Including the Queen's.

"This is flameroot," I snarled, shoving my goblet away and yanking Luther's from his grasp.

Yrselle beamed, looking oddly proud. "Bravo, dear. You're even more clever than I thought."

"You call us allies, then try to drug us and steal our magic?" I snapped.

Zalaric and Alixe quickly pushed theirs away. Taran grimaced, staring into his already empty glass.

"This is an attack, Yrselle," I warned.

"I would have told you after the first sip." She motioned for her Centenaries to replace our drinks. "Can you blame me? The last time I saw you under its effects, you and I had such great fun."

She flashed a savage grin. An image of our first meeting blinked into my mind: me, whimpering under her control in a darkened alley.

When we meet again, remember this moment, she'd told me that day. *How I could have made you kneel. How I could have made you beg.*

The image vanished, along with the faint drag of her mental claws retreating.

I gritted my teeth. The Umbros power was dangerous, indeed. If you weren't looking for it, and if the wielder was skilled, you could fall captive without even knowing you'd been caught. I wondered if I could craft a mental shield to keep them out of my head once and for all.

My godhood swelled, knowing instinctively what to do. It bloomed and coated my scalp, pulsing ice and fire against the inside of my temples.

The room went quiet.

I looked around. Centenaries were still laughing, talking, flirting, yet the maddening roar of voices plaguing me all night was inexplicably... gone.

And then it hit me—it was never voices I'd been hearing, here or in the markets.

It was *thoughts*.

The realization left me deeply unsettled—and a little intrigued.

Five fluted glasses were placed in front of me. Yrselle took a bottle and filled them with a pale green liquid, then topped up her own glass and took a sip. "There. If this one is poisoned, we're both doomed."

I reached forward, and Luther seized my hand.

"Wait," he insisted. He grabbed a glass, then downed its entire contents.

Symond rolled his eyes. "What does that prove? If he falls over dead, it's hardly *our* fault."

The Queen tutted at Symond with a disapproving look. After a tense moment where no one spoke—and, more importantly, no one died—I pulled my hand free and distributed the glasses to the others.

The liquid was pleasantly sweet and went down smooth, leaving a warm buzz on my lips. "What is this?" I asked, taking another sip.

"*Gaudenscium*," Zalaric answered. "A local favorite. You can buy it down in the markets."

"Though none compares to Her Majesty's blend," Symond said with a simpering smile at Yrselle. "We go through it so quickly, we can barely keep it in stock."

I could see why. After only a sip, the tingling had spread to all my most *intimate* areas. My cheeks flushed, my body throbbing, my nipples peaked. I became acutely aware of the friction as they brushed the fabric of my dress with each breath.

"It's quite strong," I said breathily.

Symond gazed at me and stroked a thumb across his lower lip. "It's an aphrodisiac. It opens your mind and your legs."

"*Drink!*" Taran shouted and emptied his glass.

"We should play the mirror game," Hagface suggested, wearing a devious smirk I didn't like one bit.

The Queen clapped. "A brilliant idea!"

"What's the mirror game?" Alixe asked.

"It's simple," Hagface said. "We ask you a question, and you have to answer it truthfully. We'll use our magic to make sure you're not lying."

"Sounds more like an interrogation," Luther said. His voice sounded different—like warm honey and rough gravel. Like lips on my skin and a hand on my throat. I wasn't entirely proud of how my thighs squeezed in response.

Hagface giggled a little too hard. "The game is in the questions. Each one forces you to look at yourself and admit who you truly are."

"Like a mirror," the Queen added. "It's always great fun."

I nervously tapped my glass. "Surely there's nothing you can ask us you don't already know."

Her shadowy eyes gleamed with a whirlwind of plans. "How about another trade? Play our game tonight, and tomorrow, I'll answer whatever questions you wish."

My heart skipped a beat. "You'll answer them all? And you'll answer truthfully?"

"You have my word." She propped a hand under her chin and smiled. "May Blessed Umbros strike me dead if I lie."

I took a deep breath. "I'll play. But only me—not the others."

Hagface pouted, and Yrselle clicked her tongue. "It's not a game if you're not all playing."

"I'll play," Taran slurred. "I *love* mirrors."

"I'll play, too," Alixe said.

"You don't have to do this," I said to her.

She smiled. "I know. But you need those questions answered, and I swore to serve my Queen."

"My, what loyalty you inspire," Yrselle said.

Hagface grinned. "We'll see how long that lasts once the game starts."

Yrselle's focus slid to Luther. "Well, Prince? Are you willing to sacrifice your secrets for your Queen?"

He didn't answer. Though I couldn't begrudge him his hesitation, the knife in my heart twisted a little deeper.

He looked at me, conflict thrashing in his eyes.

"You can say no," I said quietly. "I understand."

"What's wrong, Luther?" Symond jeered. "Can't handle a little '*brutal honesty*'?"

"*Drink*," Taran mumbled sadly, staring at his empty glass.

Luther's jaw twitched. "Fine. I'll play, too."

Yrselle slapped her palm on the table. "Wonderful! And you, Zalaric? Will you play with all your new friends?"

I tried to shoot him a warning look—this game was most dangerous for him of us all—but his attention was fixed on Yrselle.

"Does Your Majesty wish for me to play?"

Her cruel smile stretched wide. "I do."

Don't do it, I pleaded silently. *Find a way out.*

He looked at me, and from the helplessness in his expression, I knew he'd heard me.

He swallowed. "Then I'll play, as well."

The Centenaries chattered eagerly and moved their chairs nearer, and our glasses were refilled, much to Taran's delight. Others crowded around the Queen and resumed their ritual of groping her body while she ignored their presence.

All eyes locked on us as a hush fell.

"I'll start off easy," Yrselle said. "If Blessed Lumnos gave you the power to decide which of you wore the Crown, who would you choose?"

"Diem," Luther answered immediately.

Yrselle nodded. "Truth."

"Myself," Zalaric said, smirking.

"Also truth," she said, followed by a chorus of laughter around the room.

"Luther," I answered.

He stared at me again. Though I avoided his eyes, I could sense the shock in his reaction.

"Is that true?" Yrselle pushed. "You would give up your Crown to him?"

I took a long drink, the *gaudenscium* fueling my bravery. "Why don't you tell me?"

Her gaze narrowed. I felt a scrape at my mental walls, but it felt distant this time, muffled and frail.

Her hands tightened on the arms of her chair. My shield had worked— she couldn't get in.

The thought sent adrenaline pulsing in my veins. How many years, how many *centuries*, had it been since she'd been locked out of anyone's head?

And what would her Centenaries do if they found out?

"Knock, knock," she cooed, her tone light but laced with menace.

After her stunt with the flameroot, the temptation to expose her weakness was strong. Reluctantly, I withdrew my godhood. It lingered at the edges, still poised to strike, not trusting her any more than I did.

Her posture eased. "You speak the truth," she said matter-of-factly. "You would make Luther the King." Her lips pressed to a thin line. "An interesting choice."

"I would choose Diem," Alixe said. "The Blessed Mother chose her. Who am I to decide differently?"

Luther grunted in agreement.

Yrselle gave a low, husky laugh and lifted her glass high. "We have our first liar of the night."

The Centenaries roared their satisfaction and applauded, tipping their heads back to drink.

Alixe blanched. "It's not a lie."

"It isn't? You don't think Luther is more well-known, more respected? More levelheaded and capable of leading an army in wartime?" Yrselle cocked her head. "You don't think *you* are, too?"

"I... Luther would be a fine King, and I would try my best, but Diem, she... she's proven that—"

"It's not whether you think she can do the job," Symond interrupted. "It's whether you think she can do it better than the rest of you." He swirled his glass. "And you, High General, clearly do not."

Alixe shrank into her chair.

"It's fine," I told her. "I understand." I smiled, trying to be reassuring, though I couldn't deny her answer had stung. Not because she was wrong —because she was right, and I knew it.

"I choose Queenie," Taran drawled. "Lu never wanted the Crown anyway, and she makes my father miserable."

"Truth," Yrselle declared.

"Thanks," I said dryly.

"Plus Queenie's a better nickname than Kingy." His nose scrunched. "Kingy Kingy Kingy. See? It's all wrong."

"I have a question," Hagface chimed in. "Who in this room do you most wish to have in your bed?"

A Centenary beside her rolled their eyes. "That's a terrible question. Their answers are obvious." They nodded to Luther. "Especially for him."

Yrselle lifted an eyebrow at Luther. "Well?"

"There's only one person I desire in my bed." He glanced at me. "And she should know who she is."

"I think we all know who she is," someone quipped, followed by a wave of snickers.

My cheeks turned pink. The heat of it mixed with the liquor in my blood, prodding mischievously at my temper. How should I know anything, when he continued to push me away?

I rolled back my shoulders. "The only man I'll welcome in bed is a man who desires me—*and* who wants me there. As I've come to learn, those can be two different things."

"I volunteer," Symond drawled.

Shrugging, I raised my glass to him. "I suppose we'll see where the night takes us."

A pulse of energy exploded through the room with menacing force. Some jolted back in their chairs, others shuddering as the ferocious presence rumbled over their skin.

Though my hand wobbled at its impact, I didn't have to guess who caused it. I knew that aura more intimately than any other.

"I don't think the Prince liked Her Majesty's answer," Symond teased with delight.

"But it's an honest answer." Yrselle gave me a knowing wink. "Technically."

I carefully avoided all the eyes locked on me as I sipped my drink. "What about you, Alixe?"

She gazed out at the clustered Centenaries. "I'd be happy to have any of you in my bed tonight. Or all of you. The more the merrier."

"That's truth," Yrselle said.

"Same answer for me," Taran said.

"*That's* a lie."

The Centenaries cheered and drank another round. Taran huffed. "Fine. Half of you. No offense, ladies."

"Another lie."

The celebrations grew louder, and Taran paled. He looked around the room. "Look, you're all very handsome, I can't possibly pick just one—"

"*Still* lying," Yrselle sang in a teasing pitch.

"It's not a Centenary he's interested in," Hagface sneered.

My nose wrinkled. "Gross, Taran. Luther's your *cousin*."

Luther shook his head. "Not me. Try again."

Taran scowled at him. "Traitor."

"You've exposed my feelings for Diem several times. You've earned a little payback."

Luther and I shared a glance. I forced myself to look at him, really truly look at him, for the first time tonight. Even in his finery, polished and trussed up with all the trappings of the mighty Prince, something wasn't quite right.

His expression was weary, and his eyes looked inexplicably sad, but as he stared at me like I was the only creature in all the world, his lip still curved up with a tentative smile.

The woman he loves, Taran had said.

I closed my eyes, my throat squeezing tight.

Alixe, our eternal and long-suffering peacemaker, turned to her right. "What about you, Zalaric? Does anyone here strike your fancy?"

He swirled his wine slowly. "With all due respect to our two beautiful Queens, I think I'd be better off alone than with anyone here."

"Another lie," Yrselle said. The Centenaries whooped and clinked their glasses.

Taran's bloodshot eyes rolled to the ceiling, though not quite at the same time. "What Zal, none of us are good enough for you?"

"As a matter of fact, no."

Taran snorted, and Zalaric glared.

"So many lies," Yrselle taunted. "At this rate, you two are going to get my Centenaries drunk within the hour."

Zalaric looked so alarmed, I had to take pity on him and clear my throat. "I don't think Zalaric is lying. No one would rather be alone than with the person they desire. But if that someone doesn't want you back..." I swallowed thickly. "Maybe he's just waiting for a person who cares enough to fight for him."

Luther's hand flexed at his side.

"That's a beautiful sentiment," Yrselle said. "But it's still a lie. At least for dear Zalaric."

Taran barked a laugh as Zalaric sulked low into his seat.

"New question," Yrselle declared. "My palace is burning, and you can only save one other person." She crossed her legs and lounged casually against the arm of her chair. "Who do you choose, Zalaric: Diem or me?"

The energy in the room shifted. The Centenaries hushed, their eyes volleying between Zalaric and their Queen. Even Symond had paused his vigilant taunting of Luther to watch.

This was exactly what I'd feared. I wiggled in my chair and quietly coughed, trying to catch Zalaric's eye and cursing myself for not warning him sooner.

He reached for the bottle of *gaudenscium*, then refilled his glass. "I have an answer, though it might get me killed to admit it."

"Zalaric," I started, "you really don't—"

"Hush," Yrselle snapped. "Let him answer."

I winced. Still, Zalaric would not look my way. He took a long drink, then raised his chin. "I'm only saving myself. The rest of you are on your own."

A tense silence hung in the air as we all awaited Yrselle's response. Her expression stayed fixed in stone, unimpressed and unmoving.

Then, without warning—a cackle burst out of her. "Oh Zalaric, this is why I've always respected you. A man who knows his priorities."

My shoulders relaxed as the other Centenaries joined her laughter. Zalaric finally looked at me, his expression mildly apologetic.

I grinned. "I respect it, too. I'd rather have your honesty than your loyalty."

Luther visibly stiffened. I hadn't intended it as a dig at him, but I sipped my drink with a small kick of satisfaction.

"Alixe," Yrselle started, "who would you save, your Queen or—"

"My Queen," she answered immediately.

"I didn't finish the question."

"It doesn't matter what name you choose. My oath is to my Queen. I serve her above all others."

I braced for Yrselle to declare it a lie. Alixe tensed, and I wondered if she feared the same.

Yrselle nodded. "She speaks the truth."

Alixe let out a quiet exhale.

"Taran," Yrselle said. "Your turn. Would you save your Queen or Luther, your closest friend?"

He groaned. "Too easy. I'd save Diem."

I tossed him a teasing grin. "You're only saying that so Alixe's answer doesn't make you look bad."

"And he knows I'd kill him myself if he chose me," Luther rumbled.

"No." Taran thumped his glass down on the table, glowering through his drunken haze. "I swore an oath too, you know." He gestured wobbily at us. "Just because I don't argue about it all the time like the three of you doesn't mean I don't take it—" He hiccupped. "—seriously."

"Truth," Yrselle said, looking amused.

His face turned somber as he pointed at random to several Centenaries. "I mean it. If you try to hurt her, you'll have to—" He hiccupped again. "—come through me first."

"We're positively terrified," Symond droned, drawing a round of laughter.

"You should be," I said coolly.

He bristled as I gave him an unimpressed once-over. Like most Centenaries, he was lean and soft-edged—a body accustomed to comfort, not combat.

"You all have been coddled in Umbros," I went on. "No one dares challenge you for fear of angering your Queen. But war is coming, and your enemies are not all so afraid. When the fighting starts, you better pray to the Kindred you've got someone like Taran on the battlefield to save your pampered asses."

Taran crossed his arms and smirked.

Symond's stare hardened. So much for flirting to get information—by the look on his face, I'd just made my first enemy in Umbros.

Well... second, if you counted Hagface.

Right on cue, she scoffed. "We're not fighting in any war. We let the mortals do as they please. The Guardians aren't coming for *us*, and our Queen doesn't bow to other Crowns' demands."

My stomach dropped. I'd hoped to rely on Yrselle's help, maybe even recruit her to my cause, but if she believed doing so would make her look weak...

I turned to her. She was already watching me, her expression murky and deep in thought.

"You reigned through the last Blood War," I said. "Do you really think it's possible to escape this one?"

She leaned her arms on the table, trapping me in the mesmerizing lure of her midnight gaze. "I think..." Her sharp nails drummed against the table. "I think we haven't finished the game."

"The game isn't important."

"I beg to differ."

"Yrselle, you and I have already been caught in the midst of one battle, we can't—"

"What was the question?" she cut in. "Oh yes—who would you save? Well, I doubt we need to bother asking who the Prince would save."

"No," Luther said darkly. "You don't."

Yrselle hummed, then rolled her head back to me. "That just leaves you."

Taran snorted a laugh. "You don't have to ask her, either."

Yrselle was undeterred. She held my stare with a piercing look. "Tell me, Diem, who would you choose? Who will live, and who will *burn?*"

My pulse picked up speed. The time might come, sooner than I was ready for, where I would be forced to make this very choice. And not just these four, but others. Teller, Maura, Henri, Lily. How could I choose which of the people I loved to save and which to sacrifice?

"I can't answer."

"You have to, that's the game," Hagface said.

"I can't."

"You can choose him, Your Majesty," Alixe urged. "Taran and I wouldn't expect anything else."

"Nor would I," Zalaric agreed.

I frowned. "But that would be a lie."

Yrselle smiled and nodded slowly. "Go on."

"I wouldn't let any of them die."

"But that's not *the game*," Hagface whined. "We know you don't want any of them to die. That's what makes the question hard to answer. *Obviously.*"

Gods, I was going to enjoy dreaming tonight about wiping that sniveling look off her face.

"It has nothing to do with what I want. The game requires an honest answer, and if I gave you a name, it would be a lie."

"You're just like Zalaric," she said, looking smug. "You'd only save yourself."

"No, Hagface. That's not it."

"What did you just call m—"

"Because I'd never leave any of them behind. I'd find a way to save them all, or I would die trying."

"But—"

Yrselle raised a palm to stop her. "It may not fit the game, but it's indeed the truth. Any other answer from Diem would be a lie."

"And that's why we swore her our oath," Alixe said, tapping a fist to her chest in salute.

Taran echoed the gesture. "Agreed."

"Agreed," Luther said softly, setting his palm flat over his heart.

Emotion burned at the back of my throat.

My eyes caught with Zalaric's. He looked confused—almost conflicted. Like he couldn't imagine why I would do that for him. Like he wasn't sure he even wanted it.

That, I could understand. To have someone willing to die for you—it was a gift, but it was also a burden. A *liability*, Alixe had called it. For someone like Zalaric, so adept at navigating a dangerous world all on his own, that burden might not be so welcome.

He shook it off with a nervous laugh. "I think Her Majesty just won the game." He grinned down the table at Taran. "Now whose answer is making you look bad?"

Zalaric's tone was playful, empty of spite, but Taran's face soured. "At least we're willing to fight for someone other than ourselves."

Zalaric flinched, his smile falling.

"I agree with Zalaric," Yrselle declared. "Diem's answer wins the game. No mirror could look deeper than that. And as your prize for winning, I'll answer your question about the war."

She drank until the final drop of emerald liquid disappeared between her lips. Her hand cupped the bowl of her wine glass, then she held it out in front of her and *squeezed*. It shattered in her palm with an explosion of glittering shards.

I gasped and jerked forward to help her on instinct. As a mortal, broken glass had been a harmful, wounding thing—but Yrselle was no mortal. Instead of trails of blood spilling on the table, the jagged pieces harmlessly dimpled her skin, then tumbled like sparkling pebbles from her fist.

"Look at that." She wiggled her fingers. "Not even a scratch. All because the blood of Blessed Father Umbros runs in my veins. You know, even the most distant relation to a Kindred will bestow such gifts. The Sophos Crowns have been researching it for centuries—breeding Descended with mortals, then breeding that child with a mortal, then breeding *that* child with a mortal, on and on for generations. The Kindred blood never fades. No amount of mortal blood can destroy it. Only the blood of another Kindred can do that."

I frowned. "I don't understand."

"One of my girls, Drusila—" She pointed to a woman nearby with blush-colored curls and a shy smile. "—is mated with a Meros man."

Drusila waved, revealing a shimmering tattoo on her wrist.

"I've granted them leave to bear a child. Because her magic is stronger than her mate's, the babe will be one of ours, with black eyes and thought magic—our next Centenary. It may take its father's nose or laugh or personality, but his Meros blood will simply *disappear*, defeated by her Umbros blood." Yrselle's lip curled back. "Sophos has been studying that too, trying to recruit my Centenaries for their tests. The Crowns would love nothing more than to breed our line out of existence."

"That's terrible," I said. "No group should be forced to die off—mortal or Descended. But I still don't understand what this has to do with the war."

"Tell me, do you know why we named it the Blood War?"

"Because of the blood sun on the morning the war began," I said, parroting what I'd been taught in school. "And because of how many people died."

She laughed. "That's the safe answer we give the mortals." She pointed to my Crown. "It was the old Lumnos King who coined it. He said the war was about blood—whose would triumph, whose would survive. We Crowns were certain we would prevail, because we believed the blood of the nine Kindred would always win out—in war, as in life."

"And you were right," Symond said snidely, joined by a wave of nods and snickers.

Yrselle's nostrils flared. Silence abruptly choked their responses as they all froze mid-movement.

"We were fools," she hissed. "Our hubris cost us dearly. We lost two gryverns, thousands of lives, and we almost lost the war. These new Crowns have learned nothing from that lesson."

She held out her palm to me, beckoning with an expectant look. I hesitantly set my hand in hers. She grabbed it by the wrist and flipped it over, then dragged a fingernail down my palm. I felt a bite of pain, then watched in surprise as a line of blood sprang to the surface. Only then did I see the glint of a dark blade fastened to the edge of her nail.

Luther tensed at the sight of my blood and reached for my arm, sparks of light and shadow swirling at his palm. My other hand shot out to his leg and pressed gently in a wordless order to stand down. He stilled, the softest rumble rolling low in his throat, then slowly eased back into his chair.

His hand slid over mine, holding it in place on his thigh. Despite the emotions churning between us, the simple gesture filled me with an unexpected calm. His magic caressed my skin as it dissipated, and my godhood swirled happily in response.

"This." Yrselle tapped her finger at the blood pooling in my palm. "The war will be fought over *this*. But this war will be unlike any we've ever seen. Those who are most certain they will win will find themselves among the first to die."

I studied her carefully. "Does that mean you intend to fight?"

She smiled, and for the first time, there was no taunting in it, no malice, no amusement, no joy—just the bittersweet tightness of acceptance.

"My fate on that is sealed. The war has begun, and there's not a soul on the continent who can escape it now."

CHAPTER

THIRTY-SEVEN

After dinner, we were ushered into a small room awash in the trembling glow of firelight. Hundreds of candles were nestled into nooks along the walls, trails of dripping wax cascading over every ledge. Smoky trails of sweet incense marbled the air, mixing with the twang of a stringed instrument from a musician that was nowhere to be found.

The Centenaries sprawled across plush chaises and nests of cushions scattered around the room. Silver platters of powders and pills were offered up alongside various liqueurs, and eyes glassy as sobriety slipped off to bed.

After I'd assured her—repeatedly, vehemently—that she was off-duty for the night, Alixe became a popular attraction. She was currently holding court in the center of the room, surrounded by a gaggle of lust-addled Centenaries scooting closer with every word she spoke.

Luther, on the other hand, had isolated himself the instant we walked in. He'd tucked into a corner, enrobed in shadows that seemed to fit his mood. Hagface briefly joined his side, where her overloud giggling turned my dial from annoyed to murderous, but whatever he said sent her sulking away moments later.

While the Queen had vanished to places unknown, Taran, Zalaric, and I had acquired our own pack of curious Centenaries.

"Is this what you do every night?" I asked them, and they nodded as one. "You don't ever spend your evenings in the city?"

"Why would we do that?" one asked. "Everything we need is brought to the palace for us."

"Unless we're working, we have no reason to go into the city," another added.

"But it's so remarkable! The food stalls, the markets, all the things to see and do. There's nothing like it on the continent. If I lived here, I'd be in the fighting pits every night." My mischievous grin was met with a sea of blank stares.

One of them angled their head. "Why would we do that when we could be here?"

I looked at Zalaric. He raised his eyebrows with an amused smile and silently sipped on his drink.

For someone as sheltered as me, Umbros was mesmerizing. The diverse mix of cultures was exotic and fascinating, teeming with life. I could explore its secrets for decades and barely scratch the surface of what this realm had to offer. I couldn't understand how these apex predators could have such power and access, yet isolate themselves so completely.

"This never gets boring?" I prodded. "Spending every night locked away up here, drinking and..." My eyes grew larger as I spied a trio of Centenaries across the room, naked and fucking on a daybed. "...everything else?"

"Boring?" another asked incredulously. "Her Majesty ensures our every desire is fulfilled. How could that be boring?"

"Sounds like a great deal to me," Taran said brightly. I shot him a frown, and his grin vanished. "Er, not a great deal. A... terrible deal? Awful!"

"Your upbringing is showing, Your Majesty," Zalaric teased. "It takes being denied what you want to understand the power of wanting more. Satisfaction is the death of curiosity. And this group has been satisfied in abundance."

"I don't get everything I want," Taran grumbled.

"No? Name one thing you've ever really, truly yearned for that the Corbois name couldn't buy."

Taran glared down into his glass. Zalaric laughed triumphantly, taking his silence as an admission of defeat, but I saw the shadow that passed over Taran's face. The strife in his family was a painful rift no amount of money or power could resolve. I tucked my hand in his and gave it a squeeze.

"I understand," a voice called out.

The group shifted to reveal Drusila, the mated Centenary. Now that she was standing, I could see the prominent swell of her growing belly beneath her dress—likely well into her third trimester, I'd guess.

"Her Majesty lets my mate live in the palace. He enjoyed all the luxuries at first, but lately..." She sighed, rubbing the mark on her wrist. "He's from Meros. He's a sailor at heart. He longs to explore the world, but as a Centenary, my place is here."

"We warned you this would happen," another said. "You should have mated with your own kind."

Drusila stroked a thumb across her tattoo, and its glimmering ink brightened. "The heart doesn't care who it *should* love. Only who makes it sing."

"Indeed," I murmured. I thought of my father, who walked away from his career for my mother. Teller and Lily, and their ill-fated love. And Luther...

My eyes found him instantly. Yrselle had returned, and they were talking alone in his corner. He didn't look happy about it, his scowl carving progressively deeper.

His gaze snapped to mine. I started to turn away, but something roiling in his stormy expression made me linger. Something that sent icy fingers raking down my back.

"Can I see it?"

Taran's voice dragged my focus back to the group. He was looking at Drusila's wrist, his eyes round and aglow. She held it out to him, but as he reached for it, she jerked back.

"You may look, but I don't let anyone touch it," she said firmly. "Only my mate."

He let out a dreamy sigh, seeming almost enchanted by her scolding. He nodded eagerly and clasped his hands behind his back.

She held it out again, and Taran and I both leaned in. It wasn't a tattoo at all, I realized, at least not one I'd ever seen before. The symbol—an intricate knot of swirling lines that resembled two hearts forging into a dagger—seemed alive beneath her skin. It had a dull, silvery shimmer, but when her finger ran across it, it pulsed with a soft, warm glow.

"It's so beautiful," Taran breathed. "No matter how many I see, I never get sick of them."

She beamed. "I know all marks look similar, but I really think ours is the prettiest."

"It's lovely," I agreed. "But, um... you'll have to forgive me, but... what is it?"

346

The entire group gawked at me, save for Taran, who looked lost in a daydream. I flushed, embarrassed by my ignorance.

"My mating mark," Drusila said. "The ritual requires you to shed a drop of blood and commit your heart for all eternity. If the magic determines your love to be true and unconditional, then the bond is formed, and this mark appears where you bled. It connects you, in a way. He can feel when I touch mine, and—" She looked down as her mark flared brighter, then smiled fondly. "I can feel him, too."

Taran clutched my hand to his chest and whimpered, resting his head against mine. "I want that."

"You're a hopeless romantic after all," I teased. I glanced at Zalaric with a scheming grin. "What about you—would you like a mate?"

He kept his expression guarded. "Perhaps. If I ever meet someone worth mating."

Taran tensed against me. He abruptly pulled away and stalked off across the room.

Zalaric's eyes lowered, his mouth pulling tight.

"What about you, Your Majesty?" Drusila asked. "When you take a consort, do you plan to make them your mate, as well?"

"Oh. I, um ..."

Don't look. Don't look. *Don't look.*

Like a moth to a crackling flame, a bee to a thorny rose, my gaze was lured against its will to Luther's corner.

A corner that now stood empty.

I glanced around the room in search of him, but he was nowhere to be found. Gone—without even a goodnight.

"I'm not sure," I murmured. "Excuse me."

I turned away from the group and sulked over to Taran, who was rifling through a coffer of small glass carafes. "Whatever you get, pour me one, too."

He grunted in response.

I watched with increasing worry as he prepared the drinks in hard, angry movements, splashing liquids haphazardly into glasses and slamming bottles down like they'd done him a grievous wrong. By the time he handed me my drink, more liquid had made it onto the table than into the glass.

He threw his drink back in a single gulp, then grumbled and started on another.

"We're leaving tomorrow, you know," I said gently.

"The sooner the better," he growled.

347

"Once we're gone, you might never see him again."

He stilled for a long moment, then resumed his violent bartending. "Fine. Good. *Great.*"

"He was only teasing you at dinner." I arched my neck to catch his eye. "I think what you said really hurt him."

"I doubt anything I said mattered to him. He only cares about himself."

I laid a hand on his arm. "You know he helps Luther get the half-mortal children out of Lumnos?"

His movements slowed. "I know."

"The Lumnos Descended at the inn—he saved them all. He provides shelter and training, and he gives them all the money from the inn. Does that seem like someone who only cares about himself?"

Conflict flickered over his features. He glanced over his shoulder just in time to see Zalaric burst into a fit of laughter with the Centenaries, two of whom had moved in close, their hands stroking his arm and back.

Taran scowled. "He doesn't care what I think." He waved a bottle at me. "Anyway, you're one to talk. Were you *trying* to hurt Luther with your answers?"

I recoiled back. "No. I—" I stopped, frowned, then sighed heavily. "Maybe."

"Thought so."

I took a drink and grimaced at the bitter aftertaste that chased the fiery alcohol down my throat. Somehow, it felt fitting. "It's complicated, Taran."

"Everything's complicated with Lu. He never gets the luxury of a simple choice. Lives are always hanging on his shoulders. I thought you of all people would understand that."

"I do." Guilt gnawed at the last remnant of my anger. "I do," I said again, quieter.

"Judging from how mad you are and how miserable he looks, I can guess whatever happened must be his fault, and I'll give him hell for it if you want. But I'm certain of one thing." Taran clamped a hand on my shoulder. "He would never hurt you on purpose. Never. *Never.*"

I took a shaky breath. "Taran, what if..." My voice dropped to a raw, vulnerable whisper. "What if he changed his mind? I know he cares for me, but what if it's not... what if he doesn't want—"

Taran straightened abruptly. "What are you, drunk?" He snatched the glass from my hand. "You've had too much. If *I'm* saying that, you know it's bad."

"I'm serious, Taran. What if—"

"Did you huff one of those glittery powders they were handing out? Did the Queen do that mind-wipey thing where she turns your brain into mush?" He squinted at me. "She did, didn't she?"

"Taran."

"Have you already forgotten the Challenging? The compass? The way he looked when you almost died back in Ignios? 'Cause I'll *never* forget that. He held you like you were his own heart, ripped out of his damn chest and beating in his arms." My eyes burned, and his fists clenched. "It was that shithead Symond, wasn't it? He put this in your head. Where is he, I'm gonna—" He turned to the room with a growl.

"No!" I clutched his arm. "No fighting while drunk. That's an order."

He groaned. "Now you sound like Luther."

"That probably means I'm right."

"Come on, I've been wanting to kick that scrawny creep's ass for days. It'll be fun. Quick, you distract the Queen, then I'll—"

"Looking for me?" Yrselle said smoothly.

Both our heads snapped to the side as she approached.

"Oh, no," I rushed out. "We were only—"

"As a matter of fact, we were. I have a bone to pick with y—"

I slapped my hand over Taran's mouth. "He's drunk. *So* drunk. Talking gibberish, really."

"Nrrr, *yrrr* drnnnk," his muffled voice shot back.

The dark arches of her eyebrows lifted slowly. "If there's a problem, please, allow me to address it."

"No problem here." I speared Taran with the fiercest glare I could manage. "Right?"

He glared back silently.

"In fact, I think Taran was just about to go talk to Zalaric. *Right?*"

His glare turned lethal.

I not-so-gently pushed him toward the group, and he reluctantly began to skulk away, glowering and mouthing: *This isn't over.*

"Oh—Taran, was it?" the Queen called out. She smiled frostily. "Kill one of mine, and I kill one of yours. Understood?"

He glanced at Zalaric, then back at her. "Can I pick which one?"

"*Taran,*" I hissed.

"Fine," he moaned, shoving his hands into his pockets and stomping away.

I half-smiled, half-cringed at Yrselle. "Don't worry, he's harmless. I think."

349

"Oh, my warning was for his benefit, not mine. He may be a skilled fighter, but against our magic, even the finest warriors are brought to their knees."

"So I've noticed," I murmured, remembering how a single Centenary turned away a mortal army two hundred strong at my Ascension Ball. "I understand why the other Crowns fear you. Your Centenaries alone could turn the tide in a war."

"I'm glad you recognize that." She looked out, surveying the room. "You know, the others were quick to condemn me for culling my people down to one hundred. They called me barbaric and heartless." She smiled bitterly to herself. "But they were secretly grateful. They wanted my people dead even more than the mortals did."

I bit my tongue to hold back my opinion—that they were right, it *was* barbaric and heartless.

"It must have been difficult," I said instead, "choosing which of your people to live or die."

"Most were volunteers, actually."

I balked. "They willingly chose to die?"

"It's a long tradition in Umbros for our people to choose their own deaths. It's a great honor, especially when done in service to the realm. Our elders and those whose magic was weak—they were happy to have a choice for a death that was meaningful. We have a Hall of Remembrance here with their portraits so their sacrifice will never be forgotten."

"And those who didn't volunteer?"

"As Crowns, we're called to do whatever is required to protect our people. Even when it pains us."

Again, I held my tongue.

"Did you enjoy my library today?" she asked.

"Indeed. I could have stayed there all day. Oh—I still have your key in my room."

She waved me off. "Keep it. Consider it an open invitation to visit whenever you like." Her eyes gleamed. "There is much here you may find useful."

"I was surprised to see so many books on the mortal histories. There were several in the markets, too. I thought they'd all been destroyed."

"I never agreed with those policies. And I never implemented them in my realm." She sneered and shook her finger at me. "I've been a good friend to the mortals, you know. Never treated them badly. The Blessed Father knows. That's why he told me everything. That's why he showed me your—"

She stopped herself, pursing her lips.

"Showed you my what?" I stepped closer. "What did Umbros tell you?"

"We'll discuss that tomorrow."

"Please, I need to kn—"

"*Tomorrow*," she repeated curtly. "You've waited twenty years to know your fate, Diem Bellator. You can handle a few hours more."

I huffed an irritable sigh. Yes, it was only a few hours, but I was sick of my future always feeling just out of reach. Close enough to fascinate me, terrify me, taunt me, inspire me, but never enough to take a firm hold.

"Mortals do have much freedom here," I forced out, frustrated but resigned. "I hope future Umbros Crowns follow your example."

She let out a short, loud laugh. "Oh, the next Crown isn't going to do *any* of this."

"How do you know?"

"I know my successor, and I know their plans. Crowns can always sense their own heirs—though most are wise enough to keep it to themselves, lest they find their death arriving sooner than expected."

My eyebrows danced, leaping and dipping, as surprise mixed with dismay. "But the late Lumnos King was certain Luther would be his heir."

"The knowledge only comes near the end of a Crown's life. Your predecessor was unconscious in his final months. Had he awoken and met you, he might have recognized you as his heir."

The King did have a brief moment of lucidity the morning of his death —he'd seemed to know me, even recognize me. I'd believed he was crazy, lost to the delusions of his illness.

You, he'd gasped. *You've finally come.*

I straightened suddenly. "Wait—you said you know your heir now. That means..."

"My reign is coming to an end."

"Yrselle... Gods, I'm so sorry."

She gave a wry smile. "You're more sorry than you know. We could have been quite the allies, you and I."

My heart sank. "How much time do you have?"

"Impossible to say. The awareness of one's heir can come months before death for some Crowns, mere minutes for others."

"Is there anything I can do? Any way to stop it from happening?"

"Don't be silly, dear. Fate cannot be changed. That's why it's called *fate*."

A heavy unease settled in my chest, though I wasn't sure why. "Perhaps you might tell me your heir, so I may begin building an alliance with them now?"

She looked down, smiling to herself, then shook her head. "I don't think that would be wise."

"I'll keep it to myself, I swear it."

"That's not what worries me."

"Then what is?"

"You," she said simply. "My successor will be your most difficult adversary. They will stand in the way of what you need to do. They will drive a wedge between you and those you love, they will cost you a terrible price, and there's a strong chance they'll put you in a premature grave. I fear telling you now will only make it worse."

I blinked. "Can you ask them to... *not* do any of that?"

"Wouldn't matter if I did." Her lips curled up. "Unchangeable fate, remember?"

My hopes at an alliance crumbled to dust. Her words at dinner had lit an ember of hope in my soul that I might not lead this war alone—but now that ember had faded to dark, cold ash.

"Well, I don't believe in fate." I gritted my teeth. "Whatever you've seen —I can change it. Just tell me, give me a chance, and I'll show you."

She swished a hand. "You young new Crowns are always the same. So temperamental. Insist on making all your own mistakes."

"Then why tell me anything at all? If the future's set in stone, what good will it do?"

"Not everything is fated. You were destined to wear a Crown, and you're destined to fight a war. Whether you win or lose remains to be seen."

I scowled. As a mortal, my life had followed the narrowest of roads bordered by towering walls that left only the illusion of choice. When I became Queen, I'd naively believed those barriers had come tumbling down —that I might step off the paved path and forge a trail all my own.

But lately I felt like I'd only traded stone walls for gilded, bejeweled ones.

"For a bunch of dead people, the Kindred love meddling in our affairs," I said under my breath, then immediately regretted it as she fixed me with a reproachful look.

"The Kindred are not dead, child."

"I thought they died with their mortal lovers?"

"They bound their physical bodies so they could age and pass from this world together. But they did not die as you and I understand it. The afterlife is only for those with mortal blood in their veins—the mortals, the half-mortals, the Descended. The Kindred have no mortal blood. Their bodies perish, but they endure."

"So they can't ever die? They just... *'endure'*? Forever?"

"Oh, their kind *can* die."

"Then how?"

"Shockingly, the Blessed Father kept that detail all to himself," she said wryly. "But it is an interesting question, isn't it?"

She sipped her drink, then set her glass down and looked at me. "We have much to discuss tomorrow. It's time you finally learn who you are and what you're meant to do. But for now..." She reached across me to grab a trio of bottles by their necks, then tapped me on the nose. "I'm going to enjoy this evening like it's my last."

She winked one onyx eye at me, then turned and strode toward the fleshy pile of moaning, undulating Centenaries in the back of the room.

The sounds of their pleasure ignited my own smoldering desire. The *gaudenscium* had worked as advertised, leaving my blood heated and my core aching. But unlike Yrselle, the object of my longing could not be so easily fulfilled.

The reminder of it was more than I could take. I set off for the door. As I was exiting, I heard my name.

"Are you leaving?" Alixe asked, jogging toward me. "Perhaps I should escort you, just to be safe."

"I'd prefer some time alone. I'll be fine." I glanced at the quickly growing orgy behind us. "I think the Centenaries have other things on their minds tonight."

She rocked on her feet, seeming to hesitate. "I spoke with Luther today. He apologized. He told me he was proud of you for making me High General, and proud of me for earning the job, and..." Her cheeks flushed pink. "...well, he said many kind things. All is well between us now. I thought you'd want to know."

My muscles eased from a tension I hadn't even realized I'd been carrying. "That is a relief, Alixe. I'm happy to hear it."

"There is something else, though..." She tucked her hair behind her ear, her forehead wrinkling. "I've been thinking on what you asked me—about Luther acting strange. Today at the bathhouse, it was as if he wasn't really there. Not distracted, but as if a piece of him was somehow... *gone.*" She worried her lip. "I thought I'd seen him at his lowest when he failed to rescue you from the Guardians. Now, though..."

The somber gravity on her face rattled my nerves. "And you don't know why?"

"He claimed he was only tired." She gave me a hard look. "Luther Corbois does not get *tired.* And if he does, he certainly doesn't let anyone see it. You were right—something is very, very wrong."

CHAPTER
THIRTY-EIGHT

By the time I reached my suite, I'd talked myself into barging into Luther's room and insisting we talk—though whether I wanted to yell at him or beg his forgiveness, I still wasn't sure.

But when I pressed my ear to his door and heard only silence, I forced myself to return to my quarters instead.

It was only one day.

Tomorrow, we would go home, and then everything would be better.

I tried to focus on my meeting with Yrselle. I scrounged up some ink and paper and scribbled the questions I wanted to ask: Who was my birth father, and what did he know? What had Umbros told her? What did the prophecy mean? And what did any of this have to do with the war?

But even that couldn't keep my mind off the man across the hall. I shoved the papers aside, then ambled around the room, collecting my things in my satchel for the journey home.

Still, my eyes drifted again and again to my door.

At the sound of footsteps, I almost burst outside to greet them—but I was stopped by Taran and Zalaric shouting and a slamming door. I groaned and threw myself onto my bed, fully clothed and not at all tired.

For the next hour, I laid there, my mind spinning, then slowing, then settling. Much as I'd tried to ignore it, I was coming to a realization wholly against my will. Something I'd known for a while, if I was truly being honest, though I'd been too stubborn, too scared to admit it.

355

Even thinking on it now triggered every awful, self-doubting thought: *Don't do it. Stop. You're being reckless again. Give it more time. You don't want this. You're going to regret it.*

But deep down, I knew.

And running wasn't going to make it go away.

I dragged myself out of bed and smoothed my wrinkled dress, then closed my eyes and tucked the Crown out of sight. This was about *us*. Diem and Luther, not a Queen and a Prince. I'd already let those lines blur too far.

Those titles might create other relationships between us—relationships that might look very different after tonight—but for now, it was long past time to put the private *us* in its proper place.

I opened my door.

Crossed the hall.

Took a deep breath.

And knocked.

This time, I wasn't giving up. It was the middle of the night, and most of the palace was likely slipping into a booze-induced slumber, but I would knock as loud and as often as it took. I might never find the courage again if I didn't.

After two knocks, I heard his voice, indistinct and muffled. After a third knock, I heard him again—louder, but strained.

"Just a moment."

"I'm sorry it's so late," I called out. "I only need a minute."

Sounds of rustling and thumping rang out, followed by a silence so long I thought he'd fallen back asleep.

I knocked again. "Luther? I really think we need to t—"

The door opened, and my breath choked.

He was dressed the same as at dinner, but everything about him was wrong. His clothes were rumpled, jacket misbuttoned and boots unlaced. His gloves sat awkwardly over his cuffs, and his dark hair was sweat-soaked against his sallow skin.

"What happened?" he asked. His eyes quickly scanned me, his innate urge to protect sparking to life. "Is something wrong?"

I opened my mouth to respond, but all my carefully planned words vanished on my tongue.

"Can I come in?" I asked instead.

He started to move aside, then paused and glanced over his shoulder. "One moment."

356

He pushed the door almost closed, then disappeared from sight. The shuffling and quiet grunts that followed needled my curiosity, and I peered around the door's edge.

His room was in total disarray. Clothes strewn about, a chair knocked on its side, bedsheets crumpled in a pile on the floor. Luther stood at a table, hurriedly shoving items into a bag. I almost thought I caught sight of a strip of gauze...

Again, a dark foreboding shivered over my skin. This was alarmingly unlike him. Luther was always organized, controlled to a fault. There wasn't a single thing about him anyone could ever call *messy*. Everything he did had purpose. But this—it wasn't even a mess.

It was more like he'd... given up.

He reached down to grab a bowl that had fallen, but halfway to the ground he stopped, swaying on his feet. He gripped the edge of the table.

I hurried over and picked it up. "There's no need to tidy on my behalf."

He pushed himself to his feet with noticeable effort, turning quickly to face me. "I'm not normally so..."

"I know," I rushed out, hating the shame on his face. "I think this journey has pushed us all to our limits."

He nodded and said no more, and for a long moment, we bathed in the quiet calm of the midnight silence. Our eyes locked, saying so much without uttering a word.

"We need to talk," I murmured.

He sighed slowly, then nodded. "Yes, Diem. We do."

"And I know there's a better time and place for it than right here and right now, but I can't wait. This... whatever this is, it's killing me."

He flinched, then nodded again.

"You've been different this past week." I stepped closer. "In Arboros, despite everything going on, you and I—it felt... good. Right. But after you told me about the compass, everything changed. You started pulling away."

His back straightened. "Is that what you think this is about?"

"I thought you were worried about Taran, and then I thought you were angry with me, then I thought maybe your feelings had changed, and you were just too kind to say so."

"Diem..."

"You said you wanted me, but every time I got close, it was like you were afraid of me. And then today—"

"What you saw," he growled, "it wasn't what it looked like."

"Are you sure? Because what it looked like is you keeping a secret from

357

me, either because you're trying to protect me or you're afraid of my reaction. Is that true?"

He looked down, the muscles on his throat straining as he struggled for words. "Yes," he said finally, and I winced. "But not for the reason you think."

"You know how I feel about secrets, Luther. We promised each other honesty. I know I haven't been perfect, but I've at least been *trying*."

"I know." His arm shook, and I realized he was leaning his entire weight against the table. "I never intended to keep it from you. I only wanted to wait until we were back in Lumnos. But it can't wait—not anymore."

"Yes, it can."

He looked up, frowning.

"It *can* wait. In fact, you don't have to tell me at all. Because it doesn't matter. I've thought through every possible explanation you could have, the most innocent and the most unforgivable, and none of it changes the decision I've made." I steeled my shoulders. "No explanation you give me will change how I feel."

He looked stricken. Devastated. "I understand," he said quietly. "Whatever you've decided, I accept it, but before you say anything, there's something you should know."

"No. I need to get this out first."

"Please, Diem, let me explain—"

"I have trusted you from the very beginning, Luther. For reasons I can't begin to understand. Even when I despised you for what I thought you did to my mother, something inside me still wanted to believe in you. I think because..." I sighed. "You made me feel safe. You protected me in every way you could. Not just my body, but my heart, my happiness—you were always guarding them, right from the start. Even when we were fighting, I always felt *seen* by you. Heard by you. Understood, in a way no one else ever has, even the people who have known me all my life. You're the first person that made me think about the future in a way that excited me. You gave me *hope*."

His features warped in agony, every word a harsher blow. The cracks in my broken heart fissured deeper, threatening to shatter me completely.

"But lately," I said, "it feels like that hope is gone. Like you've left it behind. Left *me* behind." I took a deep breath and looked down as my nerves began to rattle. "Maybe that's my fault. I know I've made mistakes. In Ignios, I never should have—"

"No," he said harshly. "This has *nothing* to do with that. This is not your fault. None of it is."

"Then why are you—" I stopped and squeezed my eyes shut for a moment. "It doesn't matter. I told you, I've made up my mind."

"Diem—"

I placed a finger over his lips, and he fell silent. My shoulders rose and fell, my pulse hammering in my ears. "At the Challenging, when I realized the truth of why you'd Challenged me, I swore to myself I would never doubt you again. And that's a promise I'm trying to keep."

My palm slid to his cheek. His skin was on fire beneath my touch, triggering a wave of alarm bells somewhere deep in my brain, but the words were coming faster than I could stop them.

"My father told me that loving someone doesn't always mean brutal honesty. He said you don't have to *see* all of someone to *love* all of someone. I didn't believe him then, but now... I think I understand." I smiled softly. "Love isn't contingent on never keeping a secret. It's about trust. It's about standing together, even when you don't understand, and never giving up, even when things get hard."

His eyes grew wide. I stepped closer until our chests pressed together. Like clockwork, his hands curved around my waist and folded me in, our bodies becoming a single, pulsing thing.

"You said I was a Queen worth fighting for. Luther Corbois, you're worth fighting for, too."

My forehead leaned to his. "If you don't want to be with me, tell me, and I'll let you go." I raised on my toes and pressed a soft, tender kiss to his lips. "But I don't think that's what you want at all, is it?"

His arms wrapped tighter around me in wordless response.

"So keep your secrets. Push me away, if that's what you need. When you're ready, I'll still be here." I kissed him again, deeper this time, leaning into him as my hand trailed down his torso. "For you, I will always be h—"

As my hand crossed his hips, his body shuddered and hunched inward, a pained groan bursting from his lips.

I recoiled as he collapsed against the table and sank to the floor. I reached for him, then froze, horrified at the sight of a blackish-red liquid coating my hand.

"Luther, you're *bleeding*."

His head hung low as he clutched at his waist. "I know."

"You're wounded." I knelt in front of him and began yanking at the buttons of his jacket. He made a halfhearted attempt to stop me, but after I

359

shoved his hand away, his head thumped back against a chair, his eyes dull and pleading. "I'm sorry. I'm so very sorry. I've failed you again."

"You've never failed me," I scolded. "How did you get hurt? What happened at the bathhouse?"

I grunted in frustration at my hands, which were trembling too hard to manage the intricate fastenings. I spied a small dagger on the table and snatched it, then ripped its blade along the fabric.

"Not the bathhouses," he panted. "Arboros."

I stilled. "Arboros?"

The dread that had been quietly pacing in the depths of my chest reared its ugly head and roared with all its might. I dropped the blade and clawed frantically at the fabric, yanking it free of his chest.

And I screamed.

Only it wasn't a scream—no sound came out at all. Because it wasn't my voice. It was my hopes, my joys, my every happiness fleeing my soul at once.

Low on his hips, a wrap of gauze was soaked through with dark blood, the surrounding skin swollen with infection. Spreading in every direction, stretching up his scarred chest and circling his neck, was a thick, tangled web of blackened veins.

Poisoned veins.

Godstone.

CHAPTER
THIRTY-NINE

I t all made sense.

Awful, horrible, dreadful sense.

Why he had been so fixated on getting back to Lumnos. Why he wouldn't let me touch him or see him unclothed. Why he got so furious every time I risked my life for him or anyone else.

It should have been me, he'd yelled.

Will you ever forgive me? he'd asked.

We don't have enough time, he'd pleaded.

Everything slotted into its proper place, a cruel puzzle whose image was forming before my eyes.

There were so many signs. *So many.* His moodiness, his fatigue. His pale, hot skin. His inability to sleep. I was supposed to be a healer—how could I miss what was right under my nose?

"*How?*" I choked, the only word I could get out.

"In Arboros, when Vance found us. After you and—" He stopped. "Just after Taran was hurt."

After I fled.

Alixe and I had left them behind to run to safety. If I had stayed, if I had fought with them...

"Stop," he snapped. "You're blaming yourself. I can see it on your face."

"But... in Ignios, I asked if you were hurt, and you said—"

Is it right to lie to someone you love when you know death is coming? To let

361

them believe the future might stretch on forever, when you know your time left together is far shorter? Or is that adding cruelty to tragedy?

A visceral sorrow tore through my soul. It wasn't Taran's heart he had been trying to protect—it was *mine*.

I gingerly pulled away his bandages and let out a broken cry at what I saw. The wound was rank and festering, the flesh grey at its center, and it reeked with a putrid smell. A slurry of crimson blood and dark poison oozed down his side.

I forced off the rest of his jacket and yanked his gloves away, and another sob slipped out. The black tangle of veins had spread down his arms and wrapped around his fingers. The only skin untouched by the poison's reach was the spot above his heart—the same patch his scar had mysteriously missed.

I placed my palm over it as my tears turned the world watery and bleak. "Why didn't you tell me?"

He laid his hand over mine and closed his eyes. Calm settled over him for the first time in days, and I realized how much keeping this secret had taken out of him.

"I almost did, so many times. But then you would smile at me or laugh at Taran, and I knew once I told you, I would never see you happy again." His voice turned rough. "That was more than I could take."

I crumpled over him beneath the crushing weight of my anguish. He was right—smiling, laughing, it all now felt foreign. Something I'd done once upon a time, but not now. Not ever again.

No, I yelled at myself. *You can't let this happen. You're a healer—so heal him.*

I sat up and angrily swiped my tears away. "We'll figure this out. I fixed Taran. I'll fix you, too."

"My wounds were deeper than his," he said gently. "Before we made it to Mortal City in Ignios, the toxin already covered my chest."

"My poultice can still draw out the poison. It might take longer, but—"

"I've been using your poultice. I took what was leftover each time you made it for Taran."

"Maybe it wasn't enough—I can make more."

"I did make more. I watched you to learn how, then I stole your ingredients and made a larger batch. It didn't work."

"*Then you did it wrong!*" I shouted.

He didn't flinch or react. He watched me, ever patient, ever calm.

I shook my head, desperate to deny the truth written in his grief-dulled eyes. "I'll go down to the market. Maybe they'll have something stronger. Or... or I'll get a healer. There must be—"

"I've already seen one." He let out a long sigh. "I collapsed at the bathhouse. The Centenaries you saw earlier brought me back, then the Umbros Queen sent for a healer. They brought two, a mortal and a Fortos Descended. Both agreed nothing could be done. Once the poison reaches the heart, godstone is always leth—"

"Don't you dare finish that sentence," I hissed. "You and I—we don't give up. Whatever happens, we keep fighting. Until the absolute last breath, do you hear me? We *fight*, Luther. To the very end."

Defeat hung over him like a storm cloud. For him, this was the end. He had been fighting this war all alone for days in every way he knew how, and now he was kneeling on the battlefield, the enemy's sword at his neck, ready to face the inevitable with honor.

Whether for my benefit or for his own last tiny scrap of hope, he bit back his protests and nodded.

"Promise me," I pushed. It was a ruthless card to play, and a cruelly selfish one. But for him, for *this*, I'd sink to any low. "If you truly love me, you'll give me your word that you'll keep fighting."

His hand rose to my cheek. "Then I have no choice. You have my word."

My heart shattered, then healed, then shattered anew.

I nodded. "We have to get you home. Maura will know what to do." I took a deep breath and let the reality settle over me of what I had to do— and what it might cost me.

I closed my eyes, spearing my mind and heart out into the ether.

"*Come,*" I whispered. "*Hurry.*"

Across the sea, a pulse of acceptance thrummed in response.

Luther's eyes narrowed. "Diem, what did you just do?"

I pressed lightly on his heart, then pulled my hand away and stood. "Don't move. I'll be back."

"Diem, this is too big a risk, the Queen won't—"

His protests faded behind me as I fled from the room and ran down the corridor. I stopped in front of Taran's door and pounded my fist against it.

"Taran," I shouted. Waited. Pounded again. "Taran, open up!"

Silence.

He was gone—off in the palace, gods knew where with gods knew who, unaware that his best friend, his dearest confidant, lay dying a few hallways away.

I sank to my knees and wept, reality smothering the breath from my lungs. My shoulders shuddered with uncontrollable sobs as I thought of the agonizing pain Luther must have been hiding, the grief, the fear, the devastating knowledge that he might never see Lily again...

And he'd borne it all alone, suffering in silence.

All for me.

He'd done everything for *me*.

A light appeared beneath the door. The latch clicked open and Taran's bleary-eyed face peered through the crack. "Queenie?"

"Taran," I said weakly.

He took in my tear-stained face and pulled the door all the way open. "What's wrong?"

"It's Luther... he's..." My voice broke on the words, my heart refusing to speak them aloud. "We're returning to Lumnos. *Tonight.* Sorae is on her way. The Queen's not going to let me leave willingly, so we're going to have to run."

The bloodshot fog of his drunkenness instantly cleared. He grabbed my arms and helped me to my feet. "What do you need me to do?"

"Get your things, then come to Luther's room. Do you know where Alixe is?"

He frowned. "I don't."

"I do."

I looked over to see Zalaric sit up on Taran's bed, his chest bare and his legs tangled in the sheets. Only then did I realize Taran was fully naked, save for a pillow he was clutching to his groin.

"When I left, she was with a group of Centenaries," Zalaric said. "Things were getting very... well, let's just say she wasn't leaving any time soon. I'll go get her."

I hesitated. "Perhaps it's best if you stay here."

"I'm not going to betray you," he swore. "Not again." He looked at Taran, then back at me. "Let me make up for what I've done. I can be subtle—they won't know anything's amiss."

I didn't have much choice. If I went out there, they would see the despair on my face and know—

Gods, they already knew, didn't they? They had seen it all in Luther's mind. Symond's taunting, his cruelty—he'd been toying with a dying man.

And the Queen... she knew he needed help, yet she'd forced me to stay here, forced him to play the part of pampered guest. She told Luther her concerns were '*more important.*'

The fury that swelled inside me was volcanic.

No, I couldn't fetch Alixe myself. I'd end up leaving a bloodbath in my wake.

"Go," I ordered. "Be careful, but hurry."

He nodded, and I turned for the hall.

"Diem, what's going on?" Taran called out. "Is Luther alright?"

My lips trembled. I shook my head as fresh tears welled, and Taran's face went ashen. His jaw set in silent acknowledgement.

I ran back to Luther's room. He had slumped all the way to the stone floor, his head turned at an awkward angle.

Eyes closed. Chest still.

I staggered toward him, hands clamped over my mouth.

No. Please, no, anything but this.

I buckled beside him, teardrops splashing over his chest. Losing my mother had set me adrift. Losing my father had drowned me alive. Losing Luther... that would drag me so deep, I might never find the surface again.

He stirred, one hand reaching to stroke my arm. A half-destroyed, half-relieved sob cracked out of me. "I thought... I thought you'd..."

"Not yet," he murmured.

Not yet.

I eased him back up to sitting and fussed over him, propping up his back with cushions and covering him with a quilt I snatched from his bed.

"You're going to be fine," I repeated over and over, a mantra to ward off the hovering fate. "Wounds can look worse than they are. Maura will know what to do. And if she doesn't, my mother will. I'll go get her from Fortos."

"I know you won't listen, but you should stay," he gritted out.

"You're right—I'm not listening to that."

"Get the answers you need from Yrselle, Diem. If you anger her, you may not get a second chance."

"*Fuck* her answers." I cupped my hands around his jaw. "You're my answer. The only one I need."

The bittersweet flicker of happiness in his eyes broke me in an unfixable way. I kissed him, slow and deep, tasting the warm salt of my sorrow on his lips. On my end, it was a plea—a desperate, frantic prayer for him to stay. On his, it was all sweetness, all affection—one last chance to bask in the glow of the woman he adored.

It felt too much like a goodbye.

I badly wanted to break it off, but his hand grazed so tenderly around

365

my neck, his touch featherlight and loving. I couldn't bear to do it, knowing I might never feel that again.

"There's so much I need to tell you," he whispered against my lips. "I thought we'd have more time."

"We *will* have more time. You remember that vision of us on the battle-field? That's our destiny." I forced a smile. "Fate cannot be changed. That's why it's called fate."

His thumb swept along my cheekbones to brush away my tears. "That doesn't sound like my Diem. She doesn't believe in fate."

"I will. For you, I will."

He returned my grim smile. "Then I'm afraid we've each convinced the other. I see now that even the most certain of fates can be changed. The Kindred's promises are too easily broken."

I might have laughed, had any spark of light been left inside me. "That's blasphemy. My Luther would never say such a thing."

"'*Your Luther*' is exactly what I am. Now and always."

My heart collapsed, my voice disappearing beneath an aria of hopeless cries. I curled into his side with my head on his shoulder and wept, each of us holding the other, no more words left to say.

After a few minutes, footsteps came down the hall, and the door swung open.

Taran's bag slid off his shoulder and crashed to the ground. His face went slack, his wide blue eyes filling with shadows. "Cousin," he whispered. "No."

He looked at me, his heartbroken gaze pleading for some happier expla-nation, but I had none to give. It was as bad as it looked. Worse.

He took a stiff, lumbering step toward Luther, then another, then skidded to his knees at his side. "*Cousin.*"

Luther said nothing, though I could tell he was fighting his own emotion by the feathering of the muscles along his jaw. He gripped Taran by the arm, his knuckles blanching as he squeezed him tight.

"It was Arboros, wasn't it? You just *had* to rescue me." Taran swung his fist into a nearby chair, sending it shattering into splinters against the wall. "You asshole. You should have left me behind. *I told you* to leave me behind."

"I would never," Luther gritted out. "And neither would you. That's what we do for each other. And now it's what you have to do for her."

I shook my head, but Taran and Luther were lost in the ferocity of their shared glare.

"Swear it, cousin," Luther demanded. "You'll take care of her for me. Keep her safe. Whatever it takes."

"Stop," I begged.

"I will," Taran vowed. "Always."

"*Stop it.*" I shoved Taran's shoulder, his watery eyes snapping to mine. "Take it back. If he wants me protected so badly, he can live and do it himself."

Taran glanced between us, looking torn.

"He's not going to die," I hissed.

"You're going to heal him?" Taran asked slowly. "Like you healed me?"

I nodded feverishly.

"Taran," Luther warned. "I've already tried the poultice. It didn't work."

Emotions cycled across Taran's face—grief, fear, uncertainty, hope—before landing solidly on rage. He turned his glare on Luther. "I do take it back. Fuck my oath. My loyalty to her dies with you. You want her safe? Then *live.*"

I nodded once in firm approval.

Luther's eyes narrowed at him. "Liar."

"You know I've always hated Lumnos. I only stayed for you. If you die, why shouldn't I leave? There's no one left for me there. There or anywhere."

I didn't think my heart could shatter any further, but the raw bitterness in Taran's voice cut deep. This was no longer about goading Luther into living. There was a festering pain hidden in those words, and it devastated me to know that some part of Taran believed them to be true.

More footsteps came pounding toward us. I braced for Centenaries, but to my short-lived relief, two familiar faces appeared.

Alixe turned sheet-white as she sucked in a breath. Zalaric's shoulders sank.

Alixe came and kneeled beside me. Her eyes darted over Luther's chest—analyzing, assessing, putting the clues together and searching for a solution in her clever, strategic brain. We watched in silence, perhaps sharing some collective hope that she, of us all, could find a way out.

But when she turned to me, her expression despondent, it became real in a way it hadn't been before. Real in a way that clung to my bones and soaked into my marrow, infected my blood and wormed into my brain.

"I called Sorae," I told her. "How fast can she get here?"

"Three hours, maybe four. It will take at least twice that to get home." She eyed Luther. "And the journey won't be easy."

"Can she carry all of us?"

"I think so. She's carried four before."

My focus darted to Zalaric, then back to Alixe. "What about five? Can she handle that?"

Zalaric visibly reacted, taking a step back.

Alixe frowned. "It'll be tight. And it will slow her down."

I drew in a shaky breath. Could I abandon Zalaric to Yrselle's wrath in the hopes that an extra hour might make a difference to Luther's fate? Would I ever forgive myself, if I did?

I looked at Zalaric. "Yrselle has not forgiven you for helping us. I had hoped to barter with her for your protection, but now... Zalaric, you should come with us to Lumnos."

His expression hardened. "This is my home. There are people here who rely on me."

"They can come, too—I'll charter a boat to bring them all. Or I'll send money, if they decide to stay. Whatever you need."

"I'm sorry," Luther said quietly. "This is my fault. I shouldn't have brought you into this."

Zalaric shook his head. "I could have turned you away. I knew the risks, and I made my choice. I live and die by my own terms, no one else's."

"Come with us," Taran begged. "I don't want to wonder if you're going to die, too."

Zalaric's expression softened, but still he hesitated. "Let me think it over. In the meantime, I'll help you prepare."

While Alixe left to gather her things, Taran and Zalaric helped Luther dress then moved him to the bed. Over his protests, I made a new batch of poultice to dress his wound.

It was an excruciating process for us both. Even the lightest touch sent him writhing, and the closer I got to his injury, the harder it became for me to deny his grim prognosis. If I was just a healer, and he was just my patient, our conversation would look very different.

When I finished, I stroked his hair until he drifted into a restless sleep, then I grudgingly forced myself to return to my quarters and grab my bag.

Every second away was torture. Was I missing his final moments? His last words, his last breath? Would I return to find him gone forever?

Would I burn the world to the ground if I did?

I rushed back to his room and stared at his chest, holding my breath, until I saw its shallow rise.

Taran and Zalaric waved off my attempts to help them gather Luther's things, insisting I stay at his side. I obeyed, quietly grateful for that small kindness, and folded myself against him, one hand at his heart, its slow rhythm like a flickering match held just beside a fuse.

Near Luther's desk, Taran's expression darkened as he gazed at a pile of papers. "He wrote each of us goodbye letters," he said quietly. "Lily and Eleanor, too."

"Burn mine, I don't want to see it. This isn't goodbye." My stomach twisted so hard I flinched. "But... save the others."

He ignored the first part of my order and threw the entire stack into his bag. He started to toss the compass in as well, then paused. He flipped it open, and I heard the soft whirr of the spinning arrow as it sought out the object of his heart's desire.

The compass clicked to a stop.

Taran frowned. Deeply.

I studied his face for some sign of what he saw, but he gave none. His throat bobbed, and he slammed it closed in his fist, then tossed it to me. "Put that in his hand. It calms him to know he can always find you."

I pressed the golden disc into Luther's palm. Sure enough, as if on reflex, the tension eased from his muscles. Even now, even in sleep, he kept his vigil.

Alixe burst through the door, panting for breath. Like me, her focus cut straight to his chest.

"He's fine," I assured her. "Just sleeping."

She looked at me, and I caught the hint of pink in her eyes, the skin around them swollen. She locked his door, then perched on the side of his bed. Taran sat near his feet, Zalaric standing behind him, one hand on Taran's shoulder.

"How close is Sorae?" Alixe asked.

I closed my eyes and reached across our bond. Sorae sent me a glimpse of the sea through the clouds, Coeurîle to her left, followed by a tremble of concern. I looked down on Luther and let Sorae see his condition through my eyes. I could almost hear her roar of sorrow ripple across the water's surface. Like a second heartbeat, I felt the thump of her wings quicken as she strained to get to us faster.

"She's almost halfway," I answered.

"Good. It will still be dark. If we're clever and a little lucky, we might be able to slip away unseen."

I stared at the snarling knot of veins on Luther's chest, feeling far from clever and the opposite of lucky. "Even if the Centenaries don't see us, Yrselle's gryvern will."

"Then we'll be prepared to fight," Alixe said. "We have our magic. We're not as vulnerable as we were when they captured us."

Taran cringed. "About that... the flameroot I drank at dinner is still wearing off."

"It doesn't matter," I said. "Yrselle could take all your magic back at any time. Or worse. You heard what she said at dinner—what she's capable of."

A silence fell in the room. I could lose more than Luther tonight. One stray thought from Yrselle, and all of them would be as good as dead.

What good was being immune to her magic if I couldn't protect the people I loved?

"Maybe..." My voice quivered at the words rattling in my thoughts. "Maybe I should stay."

"You think we should leave tomorrow?" Alixe asked.

"No. I mean... maybe *I* should stay. Just me."

"Diem," Taran warned.

"Their magic can't hurt me. I can fight them off while you all get away."

Alixe frowned. "Your Majesty..."

"I'm the one Yrselle wants. If I stay—"

"Don't even think about it," Luther grumbled.

His eyes slowly cracked open. Despite myself, I smiled at his menacing glare.

"You told me once there was nothing you would not do to save me, Luther. You think I don't feel the same way about you?"

"I'm going to die, Diem. Having you at my side until it happens is my only mercy." His voice fell quiet. "Don't take that away from me, too."

My throat tightened to a close.

I could have argued with any other plea.

Anything.

But not that.

"We need a balcony where Sorae can land," Alixe said, wisely steering the subject to safer ground. "The throne room, perhaps."

"I wouldn't recommend that," Zalaric cut in. "The Centenaries sometimes sneak up there and use the throne for their, um... activities."

"Yrselle's private dining room," I said. "There's a large terrace, and no one will be using that room this late."

Zalaric nodded. "We should go now. If she's still in the lounge, the path may be clear of guards."

"*We?*" I asked, eyebrows rising.

Taran sat straighter. "You'll come with us?"

Zalaric quietly stared at his hands for a moment. "If I do, I will not hide who I am, where I've been, or what I've done. I am a half-mortal and a Hanoverre. And I refuse to be anyone's dirty little secret."

He glanced at Taran, who gave a subtle nod.

"Good," I said firmly. "I can't promise you'll be safe—I can't even promise *I* will be safe. But I can promise you'll have a Queen as your ally."

He took a deep breath. "Then let's go home."

CHAPTER

FORTY

O ur plan was simple.

Alixe and Zalaric would use magic to cloak the group from sight. I would remain visible—if the Centenaries sensed someone nearby, they would see me and think nothing of it. If anyone stopped me, I'd claim I couldn't sleep and I was visiting Yrselle's library to pass the time, flashing her key as evidence of her consent.

But as I strode brazenly down the palace pathways, spinning Yrselle's key in my hand, something she'd said didn't sit quite right.

An *"open invitation to visit,"* she'd called the key. Yet, moments later, she'd admitted her death was arriving soon—and that her successor would make themselves my enemy.

Why, then, would she encourage me to return? Did she *want* me to challenge her heir—here, in their own realm? What would that accomplish, other than putting my mother's life at risk and—

I froze mid-step.

My mother.

Yrselle's vote was the only thing preventing her execution. Leaving now, like this—how far would Yrselle go to get her revenge?

"Is something wrong?" Alixe's voice whispered from what looked like an empty corner.

I didn't answer, my mind lost in my grim choices. This was Yrselle's dinner game made real. The palace was burning, and it fell to me to choose whom to save and whom to abandon to a fiery fate.

Who will live, and who will burn?

"Diem," Luther's voice called out.

I closed my eyes, letting the steadiness of it, of him, calm me.

If this was the game, my answer had not changed. I would save them all —or I'd die trying.

"I'm fine," I answered. "Let's keep going."

Though laughter and sex-addled moans rang out unnervingly nearby, we somehow managed to reach the dining room unnoticed. To my relief, the room was dark and uninhabited, and the terrace was empty, no gryvern to be found. We crafted a paltry barricade of chairs in front of the door and settled in for an anxious wait.

While Taran tended to Luther, I tucked Yrselle's key into my dress and slipped off to the balcony. The moon was no more than a fuzzy glow behind a canopy of winter clouds. She'd watched and laughed at my disastrous sail from Arboros. She was nowhere to be found during our escape in Ignios that set this awful path in motion. Tonight, it seemed she was hiding her eyes, unable to bear watching what was about to unfold.

Perhaps she was still mad at me for showing her up at my Ascension Ball.

Scattered stars peeked through the haze, twinkling enthusiastically as if cheering—or perhaps goading—me on.

"You lot have always been there," I murmured to them. "You've seen it all, the good and the bad. And I've always given you a show, have I not?"

They sparkled in wordless response.

"If you have any wishes to grant, I could really use five or six of them." My eyes burned with fresh tears, my voice falling to a whisper. "Though I'd be grateful for just the one."

I laid my palm over my heart and thought of Drusila and her mate. Their mating bond ensured they'd be together in the afterlife. If I lost Luther, would he be waiting for me on the other side? Or would this be the end of us, our affection a forgotten blip on the eternal timeline of the ageless gods?

A wild, reckless instinct flared up in my heart. It hissed at me to run inside and beg him to be my mate—*now*, while we still had time. I gritted my teeth and forced it back with all the reasons it couldn't happen. It was too soon—he'd think me a lovesick schoolgirl. Or maybe he would refuse, his ridiculously noble heart wanting me to move on and love again after his death. Or worse, he'd accept out of pity. Then the ritual would fail, and we'd both die of embarrassment before the godstone did its work.

Besides, I wasn't the mating type, right? I was too selfish, too headstrong, too independent. I didn't believe in fates and forevers.

But I did believe in love.

"Is this the part where you tell me to run off and leave you behind?" Alixe said as she strolled out on the balcony. "Because I'm not sure Luther or Taran will fall for that plan again."

She stopped at my side, and I gave her a glum smile. "Not this time. I'm staying with Luther, for better or worse."

She nodded. "I know that's not an easy choice for you."

"Do you think it's the right one?"

"I'm not sure there is a right choice this time." She stared up at the stars. "Ask me again in a few hours."

I shut my eyes and reached out to Sorae. The Umbros coast was now clear in her horizon. She'd be here within the hour. I sent her our location and the plan for our escape—and a warning of what she might face when she arrived.

"Have you ever seen two gryverns battle?" I asked.

"No, but I've heard stories. The Ignios gryvern took on three at once during the Blood War when the other Crowns were trying to force Ignios into joining. It gravely wounded the Montios gryvern—they say that's why she was weak enough for the Guardians to kill." Her brows knit together. "I wonder if they dislike it, fighting each other. Especially being the only ones left of their kind."

I looked over the edge at the pile of bones on the canyon floor. "I think they regret a great many things they've been ordered to do."

"Sorae told you that?"

"No. Tybold did, in his own way."

"The Ignios gryvern?" She turned fully to me. "He protected us that day in the desert, didn't he? He led his King away so we could escape." She shook her head, looking stunned. "I thought gryverns couldn't disobey their Crowns."

"They can't." I smirked. "His King is just shit at giving clear commands."

"But why protect *us?* We're not even from Ignios. And that gryvern is infamous for being a vicious monster."

I fixed her with a hard look. "Spend a few millennia murdering innocent people against your will. You might turn into a monster, too."

She fell silent after that, and we stood shoulder to shoulder in the evening darkness, the winter chill whipping through our hair.

"If I lose him," I whispered, "I fear what I'm capable of, Alixe. What I'll do if left alone to my rage."

I wasn't even sure she heard me amid the roar of the wind through the rocky gorges, but after a moment, her hand slipped into mine.

"You won't be alone. We'll all grieve together. We'll be furious together. And then we'll fight together. For him."

I pressed hard on my trembling lips. "Yes. For him."

Alixe's fingers stiffened in mine. Her eyes narrowed on a clump of clouds to the north. "Do you hear that?"

I squinted and strained my ears, but I heard nothing over the whistling wind.

"Is it possible Sorae is here?" she asked.

"Doubtful. Why?"

She slowly stepped backward, dragging me along with her. "Any chance the Umbros gryvern wants to protect us, too?"

Then I heard it—*thump, thump, thump.*

"*Run.*"

We sprinted inside to find the men seated at a table passing around a leftover flagon of ale.

"Gryvern," I shouted. "Hide!"

They jumped to their feet. Taran slung Luther's arm over his shoulder, and they hobbled to the shadow of an oversized wooden buffet. Zalaric slid behind a hanging tapestry, a shimmer of his light magic helping his outline disappear.

"Do illusions work on gryverns?" I asked Alixe.

"Perhaps. But it won't stop the gryvern from hearing us. Or smelling us."

The thumping grew louder, and I shoved her away. "Go. Hide."

She hesitated. "What about you?"

"*Go!*"

Her jaw tensed, but she obeyed. She fled to a far corner and crouched low, giving me a final nod before vanishing into thin air.

I grabbed the flagon of ale, then ran to the terrace and splashed it over the entry. It wasn't terribly pungent, but its odor might mask us long enough for the gryvern to lose interest and fly away.

A winged silhouette emerged from the clouds. My head whipped around in search of a hiding place, but in my panic, the best I could find was a gauzy, fluttering curtain. I swore softly and tucked myself into its pleats.

Seconds later, the floor rattled from an impact, followed by clawed talons clicking against stone. Through the filmy fabric, I spied the yellow eyes of the Umbros gryvern shining in the darkness.

Help, I said silently to my godhood. *Do something. Hide us.*

My magic turned its curious gaze my way. If it answered, I couldn't tell. It seemed to be waiting. Watching.

The gryvern paced along the terrace edge, its long tail slapping loudly against the stone. My stomach churned—if it decided to rest here for the night, a violent confrontation would be unavoidable.

The beast dropped its nose to the floor and snuffled loudly in wide, sweeping arcs. I held my breath as it prowled past the area where Alixe and I had been standing.

Suddenly, it stilled. Turned around. Sniffed again. Tilted its head. Took another long, deliberate smell. Then snapped its attention to the dining room.

My sharp inhale was muffled behind my hand. The creature stomped toward me, then paused at the puddle of spilled ale. It sniffed and licked at the liquid, its head angling right, then left.

Broad feathered wings tucked in tight against its body as it splashed through the ale and stepped to the massive archway leading inside. With lethal focus, it surveyed the room, its scrutiny catching on the overturned chairs at the table, then again at the barricade we'd pushed against the door.

A skittering trill rumbled from the creature's throat. It sank into a predatory crouch as it scanned the room again and settled its piercing gaze on the buffet near the wall.

Right where Taran and Luther were hiding.

My heart hurled itself against my ribs, desperate to get to him, as the gryvern moved closer. It jabbed its snout against the buffet, and the hefty wooden chest jostled as if it were no more than a pile of sticks.

I jolted in fear, causing the curtain to sway. The gryvern glared in my direction.

Time stretched on for an eternity as I cringed and waited to be discovered, but after an excruciating moment, the creature turned back to the buffet.

I craned my head to see more clearly and let out the tiniest sigh. Luther and Taran were invisible, cloaked behind what I guessed was Alixe's illusion.

But my relief was cruelly cut short.

Trickles of crimson blood dripped seemingly from mid-air and pooled on the floor. Luther's wound must have already seeped through the new dressings—a fact that terrified me almost as much as realizing I wasn't the only one who'd noticed.

The gryvern gazed at the ruby splatters, tendrils of smoke curling around the end of its snout. With each new drip, it followed the trail upward, stopping eye-level with where I knew Luther's wound must be. The creature's lips curled back, its fangs bared. A harrowing growl reverberated through the silence.

Its jaw cracked open, and a dark glow began to swirl in its throat.

Dragonfyre.

I shoved the curtain aside.

"Looking for me?" I yelled across the room.

The gryvern's head twisted back to face me, its slitted pupils growing wide.

Luther's voice called my name, then cut off with a strangled sound—Taran's intervention, no doubt.

"I'm the one you want," I shouted. "Come over here and face me."

The creature leapt toward me and crossed the expansive room in a handful of strides. I straightened my shoulders, refusing to cower, even as my hands trembled at my sides.

The gryvern stretched its head high and its wings wide to show off its impressive size. Fire-warmed breath brushed across my skin.

"I have no desire to hurt you. Or her."

The gryvern watched me, giving no reaction.

"You can let us go. Fly away, pretend you've seen nothing. Your Queen will never know."

Hot smoke hissed in my face in unhappy response.

"Fine. Tell her, then. But I beg of you, give me a head start—enough to avoid a battle so your Queen does not get hurt."

The beast crouched back onto its haunches, seeming to weigh my pleas against its orders.

I took a risk and stepped forward. "You know she's going to die soon, don't you?"

Its golden eyes dimmed as its wings lowered almost imperceptibly.

"You gryverns can sense it, can't you? The coming of a new Crown." I edged forward another step. "I don't want her to die, either. I want us to be allies. Look at my intentions—do you see it in me? Do you see that I only desire peace?"

Its gaze lowered to my chest as if it was reading my heart right through my skin. Its wings folded back against its body. Slowly, carefully, I raised my palm to its snout, letting my hand hover for a knee-shaking moment before I set it on the gryvern's rough scales.

"Help me," I pleaded. "Let me escape, and I will protect her as best I can."

A tense, quiet moment passed between us. A ripple passed across its muscular body, and I felt the faintest press of its snout against my hand.

I let out a heavy breath. "Thank you. You w—"

Thump, thump, thump.

The gryvern and I looked toward the terrace in unison, then back at each other, two sets of wide eyes.

"It's only my gryvern," I rushed out. "She means no harm, I swear, she—"

A pulse of terror shot through the bond from Sorae as she swooped low in the sky and caught sight of me standing beneath the Umbros gryvern's bared fangs. She speared for the balcony with a piercing war cry that promised death and destruction on my behalf.

The Umbros gryvern snapped at me, betrayal in its eyes.

"No, wait—it's a mistake. She doesn't know!"

Too late.

I winced at the deafening boom of the beast's enraged roar. There wouldn't be a soul in the palace who hadn't heard it—and who wouldn't come running, weapons drawn, in response.

"There," I snapped, "you did your job. Now go find your Queen."

The gryvern returned my angry scowl, then launched for the balcony.

"If you truly care about Yrselle," I shouted after it, "keep her the hell away from me."

My threat was met with another thunderous roar as it jumped and disappeared into the sky.

The others emerged from their hiding places and rushed to my side.

"What was that about?" Alixe asked. "The Umbros Queen is dying?"

I nodded and grabbed Luther's other arm, then pulled it over my shoulder. I jerked my head at Taran and we started toward the terrace, Luther limping between us.

"How soon?" Luther gritted out between pained grunts.

"Doesn't matter."

"Diem." His tone was sharp. "You need to get your answers from her *now*, don't you?"

"I need you," I shot back. "*Alive.*"

Rattling sounded from the corridor, followed by a cacophony of voices. A wood-cracking smack hit the door, and our makeshift barricade of chairs swayed precariously.

I swore under my breath. "Alixe, you take Luther. Get to the balcony and mount Sorae the second she arrives. Zalaric, you're with me."

They launched into action. I fortified my mental shield as Zalaric joined me, swirls of light and shadow already conjured in his palm.

"You plan to fight them?" he asked.

"Not exactly. Send your magic beneath the door. Try to keep them away from it, if you can. But if they get through, you run—fast. Get to the balcony. Don't wait for me."

He splayed his palms wide in front of him. Waterfalls of sizzling light unfurled in a pool at his feet and flowed toward the doorway, then disappeared beneath the gap at its base. Almost immediately, the angry shouts turned into yelps and cries of protest, and the forceful pounding came to a sudden stop.

I left him there and ran outside just in time to see Sorae skid onto the terrace, her claws screeching as they gouged a trail in the stone behind her. I didn't know whether I ran to her or her to me, but we collided into each other, my arms clamped around her neck, her snout nuzzling protectively over my shoulder.

She trilled softly.

"I missed you, too," I murmured. "This won't be easy."

She huffed and stomped a talon.

"I know you can do it. I trust you."

I pressed a kiss between her eyes, a wordless burst of fondness passing between us.

"Take care of him," I said sternly. "Whatever happens to me, get him home safe, understood? He is your priority. That's an order."

I didn't wait for her acknowledgement. She couldn't withhold it even if she wanted to.

"Is this necessary?" Luther grumbled as Taran used two belts to strap Luther to his chest.

"You nearly passed out in there," Taran said. "If you go unconscious, we can't have you falling, or Diem might swan dive off Sorae's back to get you."

"He's right," I said. "I would."

His eyes narrowed at me, but there was no malice in it. Only a silent, simmering affection.

The sound of splintering wood shot from the dining room as chunks of broken chains flew out onto the balcony. I ran back inside to see Zalaric frozen in place, palms out, eyes glassy and dark.

He was still. Too still. Unnaturally still.

Torchlight leaked into the room from the corridor as the barricade crumbled and the door pushed inward, inch by inch. I grabbed Zalaric by the waist and dragged him outside.

"The Centenaries got to him," I warned. "We have to get out of reach of their magic."

Sorae crouched low so Taran could haul himself and Luther onto her back. Alixe swung her leg over and helped me wedge a stiffened Zalaric between her and Taran. Sorae's legs quivered under the strain of their combined weight as she pushed to her feet.

Another boom echoed from inside. A door crashed open, and a flood of silhouettes appeared in the glow of the hallway.

"Get on," Luther demanded. "Hurry."

I avoided his stare and ran to Sorae's front. "You remember the plan?"

Her golden eyes gleamed bright. A wave of worry shot through our bond.

"I know." I lowered my voice so only she could hear. "I hate it, too. It's the only way this works."

The sound of running boots came rushing toward the balcony.

"Go, Sorae. Remember my order."

"Diem, *no*," Luther snarled. He reached for me, and I lunged back, barely missing his grasp.

"Go!" I yelled.

With a final, helpless trill of protest, Sorae pushed off her back legs and launched into the sky. Luther's furious shouts faded beneath the sound of beating wings.

Her figure grew smaller, and my heart wrenched in two. Even the patter of the Centenaries' footsteps crowding behind me couldn't pull my eyes away.

"That was a mistake," a voice purred at my back, newly laced with poison rather than desire. "Her Majesty will not be disobeyed."

"Her Majesty can get over it," I sniped. "And if I were you, Symond, I'd tread *very* carefully. I'm feeling like a woman without much to lose."

I turned on my heel and glared, orbs of blazing light hissing to life at my palms.

"Don't be a fool," he warned. "You might have pushed me out of your head, but you can't take on all one hundred of us at once."

"Why not? I've always loved a challenge." An explosion of crackling sparks shot out in an arc at my feet, and the Centenaries stumbled over each other to back away.

Only Symond held his ground. The muscles under his goateed jaw pulled taut. "She's going to kill you for this. He can't be worth it."

"He's a better man than you'll ever be." My hands curled into claws, rage bubbling to the surface. "You knew he was dying, and you mocked him. You *tortured* him."

"And you were happy to let me do it. I enjoyed his pain, and you enjoyed his jealousy." He smirked icily. "He might be a better man than me. But if he is, do *you* really deserve him?"

Something cracked deep within me. I hurled my magic at Symond's chest and growled as it snaked around his ribs and squeezed. He gasped for air, bones creaking, then snapping, but all the while, that taunting superiority stayed plastered on his face.

"Let him go, dear."

The Centenaries parted, and Yrselle sauntered forward into the moonlight. As she did, her gryvern dove from the sky and slammed onto the terrace at my side. I eyed them both, backing a step toward the balcony's edge.

"Let him go," she said again, harsher.

Our gazes met, horns locked. I loosened my magic from Symond's chest, though I let it hover an inch away.

"I warned you an attack on my people would not go unanswered," she said.

"This is your fault. You knew Luther was hurt, and you kept it from me."

"It wasn't my truth to tell. Here in Umbros, we know how to keep a secret."

My scowl darkened. "If he dies, I'll hold you responsible."

"He was doomed long before he crossed my border." She frowned. "I admit, I did believe he had a larger role to play. The visions I saw..." Some inscrutable emotion fluttered over her features, then she shrugged. "There's no coming back from injuries like that. His fate is sealed. It's time you accept it."

"No fate is ever sealed."

"Oh, how I wish that were true." She looked equal parts sympathetic and annoyed. "You accomplished what you wanted. Your friends are free. Now come inside."

She swept an arm toward the dining room. I looked at it, then looked at her, taking the smallest step backward.

"I'll come back," I offered. "Once Luther is healed and my mother is safe, I'll come back to Umbros, and we can talk for as long as you want."

Her lips pressed tight. "I can't let you leave, Diem. My people's lives are on the line."

"Lives are at risk in Lumnos, too. Give me a few days, that's all I ask."

"We do not have the luxury of time. Every day, he grows stronger. Soon, even you will not be able to stop him—and if that happens, this entire world will fall, and so will everyone in it."

"Who, Yrselle? Who is '*he*'?"

"Come inside, and I'll tell you."

Doubt swirled in my chest. I didn't much trust Yrselle—she seemed to have a fondness for answering disobedience with death—yet there was a grave sincerity in her voice that gave me pause. If there was any chance she was telling the truth...

But Luther.

Luther...

Across the bond, Sorae felt my indecision. Even from this far distance, I could hear the soft rumble of her answering roar.

Soon, I soothed her. *It's only for a little while.*

The Queen huffed. "This is boring me." She looked at her Centenaries and flicked a hand in my direction. "Bring her inside. By force, if necessary."

Immediately, a swarm of sharp-clawed fingers slammed against my mental shield. The impact punched the breath from my lungs. I staggered back and collided into one of the potted olive trees lining the balcony's edge. It wobbled, then toppled to the side and disappeared over the rocky cliff. The ribbons tied to it pulled taut, and one by one, each of the other plants along the edge fell in a cascading wave, until there was nothing between me and the open canyon but a gust of winter wind.

A few Centenaries began to approach. I threw up my shield to keep them at bay, smirking as they smacked face-first into the shimmering dome. I was gloating so confidently I almost missed the rustling feathers of the Queen's gryvern rearing on its hind legs. Rows of jagged fangs cracked wide with a bursting dam of black flames that surged in waves toward my feet.

Fight, my godhood snarled.

Panic shot through me, and instinct took over.

Magic spilled from my hands. Its angry energy seeped from my skin into the night air—air that suddenly felt unseasonably cold for a realm this far south, even in winter.

When I looked, I understood why. The half of my shield facing the gryvern was now coated in a blanket of glittering ice. Droplets of water slid in an arc to the ground as the dragonfyre heated the frozen barrier, but the shield held, each melted drop replaced by more ice, more frost, more snow.

I sucked in a gasp at the crust of shimmering ice crystals that tipped my fingers. My skin pebbled and my breath clouded in the impossibly frigid air.

Unable to get to me on foot, the Centenaries doubled their mental attacks. My own thoughts were crushed by the relentless hammering of voices in my head—*Stop. Give in. Obey.* I ground my teeth as I fought them off, my muscles twitching against the urge to do as they commanded. Though my vision spotted and my knees wobbled, I managed to hold them off.

"Impossible," Symond breathed.

"You can't begin to fathom what is possible," the Queen crooned, her eyes on me. "End this, Diem. Let me show who you are and what you're meant to do. It's time to claim your inheritance in full."

Something deep in me purred at her words, almost as if my godhood was... *agreeing* with her.

"We can't get through, Your Majesty," Symond admitted. "We need your help."

"Careful, dear," I said, taunting her with her own words. "This could be very revealing."

She hesitated. Lines creased at the corners of her eyes and mouth as she weighed my challenge. If she backed down now, she'd look like a coward. But if she took me on and lost, she'd be blood in the water—surrounded by one hundred hungry sharks.

Apparently, the sharks won.

Her thought magic sliced into my head like a flaming arrow. My mental shield was weakened by the Centenaries' barrage, and I felt her honeyed voice pierce through.

Give in now, she warned. *I know your weaknesses. Do not force me to use them.*

383

I shouted in protest as one leg involuntarily buckled. "It doesn't have to be like this, Yrselle. Let us be allies, not enemies."

Give in, she snarled in my head. *You will dearly regret it if you don't.*

Her hold on me sank its claws deeper and forced me down to my knees.

"You see?" she said haughtily, flashing a triumphant smile to her Centenaries. "Even the mightiest of Crowns must kneel to me."

I fell still.

Above my head, a circle of shadow took form. The dark matter swirled, thickening into ropey vines tangled in sharp thorns. Pinpricks of light winked into existence, along with hunks of jagged crystals.

"I am Diem Bellator." I stared up through my lashes, the glow of the Crown casting ominous shadows down my face. "And I kneel for no one."

Fight.

My godhood roared, its wrath mirroring my own. I gave myself over to its smoldering rage.

My mental shield dropped, and her thought magic crashed in from every angle. But instead of controlling me—it *ignited* me.

A silvery moon-bright glow shone from my skin, a wave of fire and frost coating me like armor. My blood boiled away to a rush of newfound energy searing through my veins.

I was invigorated. Indestructible. Invincible.

Immortal.

"You and I stood right here on this balcony at lunch," I said, my voice sounding unearthly and foreign to my own ears. "Do you remember what you asked me?"

I pushed back up to my feet, heels at the edge of the cliff. My shoulders rolled back.

"You asked how much of my soul I was willing to set ablaze to see my plans through." My chin rose. "And do you remember my answer?"

Yrselle's eyes grew. "Diem—"

I spread my arms wide.

"All of it."

I tilted my head back, and I fell.

CHAPTER

FORTY-ONE

F*alling in love* is an interesting metaphor.

I was never Emarion's foremost expert on love. With Henri, it felt a lot more like running. Running to him, then from him, then beside him, though on different paths.

But recently—*very* recently—I had become pretty acquainted with falling.

Most people would say to fall is to give up. To accept total helplessness to one's predicament. For those fleeting, frightening moments in the air, both time and your heart stand still, and you're at the mercy of gravity's pull—and whatever awaits you on the ground.

But that's only what happens when you're pushed.

When you jump—when you stand on the ledge, look down, and embrace what you see with arms wide open—there's nothing helpless about it at all. Instead of terrifying, it's liberating. You're not in freefall... you're in *flight*.

And when I stepped off Yrselle's balcony and began my rapid descent to the canyon floor, the beautiful, scarred man I loved was exactly who I had in my mind.

My body twisted in the air to face the ground, my snow-white waves whipping in a trail behind me.

I held my breath.

Closed my eyes.

And when three clawed talons closed around my ribs and snatched me into their grasp... I smiled.

"*Are you out of your fucking mind?*" Luther shouted from Sorae's back. "Two more seconds and you would have been dead."

I looked up and guiltily bit back my grin at the worry etched so deeply in his features it might now be permanent. "I knew Sorae would catch me. She's the best gryvern there is."

She purred proudly, but even her reptilian face looked as ashen as my companions.

"You could have warned us," Taran grumbled, grabbing my hand to haul me upward.

I threw a leg over Sorae's back and settled into place just behind her wings. "I couldn't risk one of them reading your minds and seeing my plan."

Luther's arms locked around me with bruising force, the thump of his heartbeat vibrating into my back. He lowered his lips to the curve of my neck and lingered there, breathing in deep, as if needing the smell and taste of me to assure himself I was safe.

"I'm sorry I worried you," I said softly, curling a hand over his. "I'm not going anywhere. Not until you're healed."

He tensed, and my grip on him tightened.

"Why didn't you come with us?" he asked.

"I had to at least try convincing Yrselle to let me go without a fight, for my mother's sake."

A silent moment passed. I felt the guilt roll off him. "Did it work?"

I glanced over my shoulder at a dark spot in the distance. "No. Everyone —hold on tight."

I shot an order out to Sorae. She immediately pulled up, and we disappeared into a blinding mass of clouds.

For a single, peaceful minute, total silence ruled the sky. Sorae angled her outstretched wings, allowing us to glide on the wind as both the sea and the sky disappeared from sight. Other than the breeze through our hair, I might have thought we were hovering, suspended in time and space, a serene harbor where trouble could not find us.

But find us, she did.

A piercing shriek rang out from below as Yrselle and her gryvern appeared at our flank. Sorae felt the fear stab through me and slammed her wings downward, shooting us above the cloud layer and pitching Yrselle in our turbulent wake.

The dense muscles beneath Sorae's skin bunched and pulled. On a normal day, she could outrun any gryvern with little effort, but this was no normal day. She was overloaded with too much weight and already worn down from her urgent sprint across the sea. Just getting home without resting would be an effort—if we couldn't shake Yrselle, we'd be ground-bound in no time.

"Use your illusions," I yelled back at Alixe and Zalaric, who I was relieved to find back in control of his mind. They each threw out a palm, and we melted into the star-flecked night just as Yrselle and her gryvern smashed through the clouds.

Her dark gaze swept over the seemingly empty sky. "I know you're up here," she shouted. "Return to Umbros, and no one will get hurt."

Sorae slipped back into a glide to hide the sound of her wings, though the air current had shifted, now pressing us lower.

A ball of churning dragonfyre hurtled past and missed us by inches.

"You're not the only Queen who will do whatever it takes to save her people," Yrselle called out. "Do not make me force your hand."

I conjured a flock of shadow-crafted beasts and threw them out in a swarm behind us. With my still-untrained magic, their forms were wispy and grotesque, but they did the job. Yrselle shrieked as they tangled in her hair and the fabric of her dress, and her gryvern bobbled with each smack against its wings.

"Now you're just pissing me off," she snarled.

Sorae's body shuddered beneath me. We exchanged a mutual jolt of panic at the cloud line quickly edging nearer.

I sent another volley, but Yrselle's gryvern was savvy, and this time it dodged them with ease. Its golden eyes sharpened on the sky just above us as it pinpointed the origin of the attack.

Its jaw yawed open with a plume of onyx fire. We flattened against Sorae's back to duck the lick of the flames, their blistering heat searing our skin.

And they didn't stop coming. Again and again, Yrselle's gryvern renewed its attacks. Sorae zig-zagged in evasive maneuvers, leaving us digging our nails into her skin—and each other's—in a desperate fight to stay mounted.

"There!" Yrselle shouted, pointing.

I looked down. We'd dropped too low, and Sorae's talons had carved a revealing groove in the clouds. With a triumphant howl, the Umbros gryvern unleashed its dark inferno.

Fight, my godhood growled.

I spun in place, Luther holding me steady, and thrust my palms forward. A glittering crystal wall slammed into the fire, then vaporized into steam.

Alixe gaped at me. "Was that *ice?*"

Luther squeezed my hip to snag my attention. "Diem—you've been to Meros?"

I frowned briefly at him, then looked back at Yrselle. Her lips had curled upward, like my defense had not bothered but *pleased* her.

"Not just the port," he prodded. "You've touched Meros soil? You're sure?"

I barely had time to nod before twin streams of flame shot for Sorae's wings, which I hurriedly met with glistening frost.

"The wind," Luther shouted. "Use the *wind*."

I frowned at him, not understanding.

He pulled me closer, his glacial eyes boring into mine. "The day we first met, you healed Lily. That's Fortos magic. Just now, the ice—Montios magic. The flames in Ignios, and in Umbros—you heard Zalaric's thoughts, didn't you? That's how you knew he betrayed us?"

Old instincts rose in me to deny it, to hide from the hard truths that scared me, even as I stared them right in the face.

"All of it," Luther murmured. "I knew it. You can wield all the Kindred's magic."

"This isn't possible," I said, sounding like I was pleading. *Feeling* like I was pleading. Because if this was true, then everything I thought I knew about myself was even more uncertain than I thought. Who even was I? *What* was I?

Sorae's wings slumped. She flapped wildly to recover, stirring the clouds and revealing our position. Yrselle's gryvern yipped and dove to intercept us.

"You can do this, Diem," Luther yelled over the melee. "Have faith in yourself. This is what you were born to do."

My body betrayed me, my hands rising even though my head shook in pointless denial. My hair danced over my shoulders in a gust of warm, whirling wind as shimmering magic flowed from my palms. The dark panels of my dress billowed slowly like ribbons in the sea. Air filled Sorae's wings, relieving the strain on her overtaxed muscles and lifting us forward.

Though the others gawked in confusion and more than a little alarm, Luther beamed, his eyes bright with fiery affection.

He loved me.

He *loved* me.

How could I ever have questioned it? It was as sure as the sunset, as steady as the dawn. Even now, even hurt, even dying, the strength of his heart was a force to behold. He believed in me, right down to his marrow, in a way I'd never believed in myself.

He was my rock. My cove.

My sword and my shield.

My guiding light and my calming dark.

My Prince. My *love*.

He was my everything.

And he was dying.

A sharp, desperate anger took hold of me, borne of the loss I refused to accept. I offered up my rage to my magic, and my godhood accepted with violent glee. A cry ripped from my throat, broken and vicious, as the wind bowed to my will.

Air slammed into Yrselle's gryvern with the force of a marble wall. The beast toppled sideways, sending Yrselle airborne and screeching. Both figures disappeared in a freefall through the clouds.

The others gaped, muttered, frowned, twisted to watch for Yrselle's return—save for Luther, whose gaze never left my face.

His fingers swept tenderly over my cheekbone. As his hand fell, I spied the glisten of my tears on his skin. My anger crumbled, and so did I.

He cradled me into his chest, and the others fell quiet as I wept in his arms.

"You are the greatest gift," he murmured in my ear. "To everyone you meet, and to this continent and all its people." He placed a kiss on my shoulder. "But especially to me. I only wish..."

His voice fractured, and I pulled back to look at him. He cupped my face between his rough, protective palms, his eyes gleaming. "I only wish I could be there to see all that you will become."

He let out a long exhale, and with it seemed to go his turmoil. A calm acceptance settled over his weary features. His muscles softened, his jaw relaxed.

A better woman might have been glad to see him finally find the peace he so deserved.

I was *not* a better woman.

"Stop looking at me like that," I hissed. "I am not doing this without you. It's us, or it's nothing."

His lips parted, his desire to convince me dancing on his tongue.

So I gave them something better to do. I grabbed his lapels and smothered his protests with a kiss—not a desperate prayer, but a declaration of war. An echo of his vow to the gods at my Challenging: *Take him from me, and I will come for you, too.*

"You should know better than to argue with a Bellator," I panted against his lips.

His expression heated, revealing a spark of the warrior still fighting inside him. "I can't help myself. You Bellators are stunning when you're angry."

"I'll pass that along to Teller on your behalf."

He laughed, and the sound filled my heart with the most exquisite joy. Sorrow and rage were pacing monsters at the gates, but at least for now, we held them both at bay.

I pulled more wind into Sorae's wings to propel us forward, anxious to put distance between us and Umbros.

"Do you think she's coming back?" Taran asked.

"I think she's learned her lesson." I gestured for Alixe and Zalaric to drop their illusions, then reluctantly spun in Luther's grasp to face forward. "But if she does come back, this time I'll be read—"

One second, I was talking.

The next, I was flying.

Through the bond, Sorae's pain and panic commingled with my own. The world was spinning, bodies soaring, voices shouting. Something firm hit my palm. I grabbed it, clutching with all my might, barely keeping hold as my body crashed against a wall of muscle and bone. The flash of a dark-scaled gryvern whizzed past my face, along with the sound of Yrselle's cackles. Somewhere, someone was screaming, the sound getting further and further away.

"Diem!"

Luther's voice sliced through the chaos. My head jerked around until I spotted him—dangling below me, along with Taran, the belt connecting them hooked on Sorae's claw. My body swayed erratically as I clung to the thick cartilage edging her wing. She listed to one side, fighting to stay airborne under the lopsided pull of my weight.

A hand closed around my wrist.

"Yrselle hit us," Zalaric shouted as he dragged me onto Sorae's back. "Alixe fell off."

My gaze snapped downward—to the flailing figure growing smaller by the second.

"Hold on," I yelled to Luther and Taran. "Sorae—*go!*"

She arched her head, and we dropped like a stone through the sky. Sorae flew at impossible speed, but Alixe was already so far away, her body falling so fast. Even my magic couldn't reach her as I tried and failed to coax the wind into slowing her descent.

"*Faster*, Sorae," I pleaded.

Her frantic heartbeat drummed beneath my hands—not for her own life, or even Alixe's, but for me. For my happiness. A fraught desire to please me at any cost.

Before these past few weeks, I might have thought that a sad thing—something superficial, manufactured by the spell that bound her life in service. But I'd now seen the heart of a gryvern whose obedience was built on enslavement alone. Unlike Tybold, Sorae's affection for me was as real as mine for her.

Faster we dove as Alixe grew nearer. She threw out a tendril of her magic, but it was still well short of our reach.

Yrselle circled above us in leisurely pursuit. "I tried to warn you," she chided. "Come back with me now, or you'll lose them all."

I ignored her and stroked Sorae's neck. "Almost there, girl—go, *go!*"

The sea's surface grew alarmingly close. My gaze locked with Alixe's, and in it, I saw the same sad defeat I'd seen in Luther's eyes.

She was making peace. Accepting her fate.

"No," I screamed at the gods. "I will not let you have them! Not any of them, do you hear me?"

I hurled my magic out. Alixe jerked sharply, and I *felt* the wind curl beneath her like an extension of my palms.

"Got her!" Taran cried, his hand wrapped around her wrist. Her boot skimmed the water's surface as Sorae banked hard and shot us back into the sky.

With help from Zalaric, Alixe grappled her way onto Sorae's back. Her face was chalk white and her hands were trembling, but true to her nature, she jumped right back into battle.

"Luther and Taran are stuck," she warned. "Their strap is tangled. We'll have to cut them fr—*watch out!*"

Yrselle's gryvern rammed into our side. I smashed forward into Sorae's neck, my vision going woozy. Alixe grabbed me with one hand and Zalaric with the other, miraculously managing to keep us both astride.

My satchel jostled loose at the impact and spilled its contents into the air. I watched helplessly as my jar of lavender flame plummeted toward the Sacred Sea, then shattered against its ink-dark surface.

My heart stung with unexpected sadness. I forced myself to look away with a reminder that gryvern was long dead and beyond saving—unlike the one who needed me now.

"I'll give you one last chance," Yrselle called out. Her gryvern fell into pace beside us. "Turn back now if you want your friends to live."

Fight, the *voice* of the godhood seethed, its timbre lower, angrier, more savage.

This time, it wasn't a mystery what it planned. The wolf in the forest, the man at my Challenging, the godstone bolt in the Arboros clearing—I'd wiped from existence with a single silvery flash.

I could do it again now. A Queen and her gryvern, dead without a trace.

I shivered at the thought.

"Give it up, Yrselle," I shouted back. "I'm going home."

She sighed. "Very well. If it's Luther you insist on returning for, it's Luther I'll get out of the way."

Her fingers twitched, and my stomach filled with dread.

"Taran, *no!*" Alixe screamed.

I followed her horrified stare down to Sorae's talons. Both men had gone slack-jawed and stiff, arms limp at their sides—except for Taran, whose right arm had crooked around Luther's throat. Though their expressions were vacant, both sets of eyes blazed with terror as Taran's hold involuntarily tightened.

Alixe threw a tendril of light around Taran's arm and yanked. It sizzled and blistered welts against his skin, but his chokehold was unrelenting.

Luther gasped for air. His face turned pink, then red.

"Let them go or I swear on all the gods, Yrselle, your reign will end *tonight*." I raised a palm in her direction, and she wagged a single finger.

"Might want to rethink that, dear. You've got your hands full." She winked and jerked her chin to the space behind me.

I looked back to find Alixe and Zalaric wearing the same glassy-eyed expression. They began to lean, then slide, then *fall*.

I grabbed Alixe's arm with one hand and called a gust of wind to push Zalaric upright with the other, but one look down had my heart in my throat. Luther's eyes were rolling back, his lips turning blue.

A chill of terror paralyzed me. Sorae felt it, letting out an anguished trill. Her talons tightened around Taran, one claw dimpling into his chest, just above his heart. An offer from my devoted gryvern—Taran's death for Luther's life.

"*No*," I yelled, but her grip did not loosen.

Taran's eyes locked with mine. In them, I saw his plea to let her do it. He would rather die than live with the knowledge he had murdered his best friend.

Fight, my godhood demanded again.

"I'm not a murderer," I cried. "Don't make me do this."

Zalaric jerked sharply and tilted backward. I lunged and managed to snag the edge of his robe, but just as I did, Alixe nearly took me with her as she pitched herself over the edge.

Help, I begged to anyone and no one as I fought to hold them both, though I knew my prayers was futile. There was no way out without destroying some vital part of me in the process.

How much of your soul are you willing to set ablaze?

I gave one final look at Luther as the last embers of my ruined heart curled to ash.

Suddenly, a blinding flash of light filled the sky, followed by a wave of sweltering heat. The smell of burnt skin singed my nose.

I blinked. Unlike before, I hadn't *felt* the magic work. Had I used it without realizing what I'd done?

But Yrselle and her gryvern were still there. They dropped into freefall and hurtled toward the sea. They were screaming, wailing, tumbling... *burning*. Bright, roaring flames coated them both.

Lavender flames.

Alixe and Zalaric blinked rapidly and shook their heads, now free of the Queen's control. Zalaric helped me pull her up, then I slumped forward in relief as Luther gulped in air and Sorae's claw eased from Taran's chest. With a bit of wrangling, we cut them free and managed to haul them up to safety.

Once everyone was secure, the five of us collapsed in an exhausted, breathless heap.

Alixe pulled an illusion around Sorae to conceal us, and I called forth a swift westbound wind. Luther's arms slid around my waist as my head thumped back against his chest.

"Home," I sighed heavily. "Let's go home."

CHAPTER
FORTY-TWO

Hours later, after the sun had crested in the sky, the coastline of Lumnos emerged on the horizon. Winter had turned its emerald forests into a gloomy cluster of lifeless branches that reminded me far too much of the poison spreading beneath Luther's skin.

"Thank the Blessed Kindred," Alixe said.

"Thank Diem and Sorae," Taran muttered.

The others had taken turns catching what little sleep they could, though I'd declined. I sensed Sorae's exhaustion and knew she needed the help of my wind, and with the Umbros Queen's fate unknown and Luther's feverish body burning hot at my back, there was no hope of me getting any rest.

"We're home," I murmured against his temple, where his head lay asleep on my shoulder. He didn't move, so I squeezed his hand, which had fallen limp on my thigh. "Luther, look—I can see the palace."

Still, he did not stir.

"Luther?" I said again, louder.

He didn't answer. Taran and I shared an anxious look.

Taran gripped him by the shoulders and pulled him upright. Luther's head lolled forward, chin to his chest, unmoving.

Taran gave him a hard jerk. "Cousin, wake up."

"What's wrong?" Alixe asked, her voice strained. "Is... is he...?"

I spun around and cupped his jaw. I heaved out a relieved breath at the feel of his pulse beneath my hand, but it was too slow, too weak.

"He's unconscious." My eyes darted around his face, taking in his grey pallor and the pale color of his lips. I looked down to see a steady flow of red streaming along his leg. "He's bleeding too heavily. He needs fresh gauze and medicine and..."

A miracle.

He needed a miracle.

I turned forward, pressing a hand to Sorae's neck. "I know you're tired girl, but—"

She trilled her agreement before I could finish and furiously beat her wings to push us forward. Breath after shuddering breath, I fought to slow my panicked heart to match her cadence.

As we passed over Mortal City, people scurried outside to marvel at the return of their missing Queen. And they weren't alone—soldiers in Emarion Army uniforms dotted the main streets, and a barricade ten heads deep blocked the road to Lumnos City. Even in the back alleys of Paradise Row, I spied glimpses of their ominous presence.

I looked back at Alixe. "Were there this many soldiers when you left?"

She shook her head, her expression as flinty as mine.

Near the palace, an unbroken ring of them circled the royal grounds, and large groups were stacked at each palace entrance. Every last one turned to watch as we approached.

Finally, *finally*, Sorae glided to a halt on her perch outside my suite. I pushed off her side and slammed to the ground. "Get Luther to my bed and get his clothing off. Alixe, come with me."

Inside, my desk was still cluttered with the baubles and cosmetics Eleanor had set out the morning of my Coronation. I shoved them haphazardly to the floor and grabbed some ink and paper.

My hands trembled as I tried to scribble a list of medicines, but all that arose were illegible words, half-formed thoughts, and impossible-to-fulfill requests. What should have been second nature felt like dreaming in a foreign language.

I swore and folded it up, then shoved it into Alixe's hands. "Go into Mortal City and find Maura. Tell her what happened, and tell her to bring what's on this list. No, wait—tell her to bring *everything*. My mother's notes, too. And—"

She nodded sharply. "I understand."

We ran back to Sorae. I closed my eyes and pressed my forehead to her muzzle, sending her my orders—and a plea to do it all as quickly as her worn-out wings could bear.

"She knows where to go," I shouted at Alixe. "If the soldiers try to stop you—" Our eyes locked. "—do whatever you have to do."

She thumped a fist to her chest in salute. A moment later, they were gone.

I shot back into the room and peered over Taran's shoulder as he sliced the clothes from Luther's body. The web of veins had grown thicker and darker, now stretching to his feet and past the bend of his jaw. The skin around his wound looked as if it were coated in tar.

Only the space over his heart remained untouched. I clung to the foolish hope that that meant something, *anything*, that might spare him from what now seemed inescapable.

"Diem?"

My head snapped around at the sound of my brother's voice. He stood at the door to my bedchamber, bright-eyed and grinning.

"You're home," he cried out.

We ran to each other and collided in a bone-crushing hug, a balm I'd badly needed. The fragile pillars of glass I'd been erecting to stop my plummet into the dark, depthless pit of fear that yawed open beneath me— they fortified to steel the second we touched. My brother's steady strength flowed into me and restored me at a more profound level than any magic ever had.

He pulled back and gripped me by the shoulders. "Thank the gods you're alright. He told me you were, but I was too scared to believe it."

"Who told you?"

"Luther. He sent a messenger hawk from Umbros to let me know you were safe."

My heart squeezed. *Of course* he had.

Teller's eyes roamed over me, taking in the ruby-encrusted gown I was still wearing from dinner, the tear-streaked kohl that stained my cheeks, and the crusted blood all over my skin from Luther's wounds.

"By the Flames, D. What *happened?*"

My body drooped at the weight of that story—a story that was still unfolding behind me.

"I'll tell you everything soon. Right now I need to focus on—"

A scream ripped through the room. A heart-wrenched, soul-shattering cry, a hot knife that seared straight through my chest.

"*Luther?*" Lily choked out. She stared, horrified, at the bed, her round eyes already full with burgeoning tears.

Teller looked at me in alarm. The sight of my anguish answered the question he didn't ask.

Taran stepped forward to block her view. "You shouldn't see this, Lil. Let us clean him up first."

Her hands flew to her mouth as a sob cracked out. "Is—is he...? Did he...?"

I ran to grab her arm and spun her to face me. "He's alive, just ill. I know it looks bad, but he's going to be fine. I'm going to heal him."

"Diem," Taran rumbled in warning.

She looked between me and her brother, bottom lip quivering. "You can do that? You can save him?"

I knew the right thing to do was to be honest. This would be hard enough on Lily as it was. But admitting the truth to her meant admitting it to myself, and that was something I couldn't yet bring myself to do.

Though I also couldn't bring myself to meet her eyes as I answered, "Yes, I can."

"*Diem*," Taran said again.

"What?" I snapped at him. "I never gave up on saving you, did I?"

Muscles twitched on his forearms as his fists clenched at his side. He ground his teeth. "Fine. What can we do to help?"

I immediately put them to work—Zalaric filling a basin of warm water, Taran gathering soap and clean gauze, and Teller and Lily collecting the medicinal herbs I'd planted in the palace garden. Though their doubts were unmissable, I could also tell they were grateful for the distraction of being useful.

They set off to complete their tasks, and for a brief moment, Luther and I were alone. I gingerly slid onto the bed beside him and brushed back the hair from his face.

He still looked so formidable. His sharp jaw was a weapon, his scar a banner of war. He was a warrior. *My* warrior. Ever ready to face my enemies in battle—and now, that enemy was death.

I set a kiss on his lips, hating the stillness I felt in response. Would I ever again feel the dominant crush of his mouth on mine, the possessive tug of his fingers in my hair, that fiery passion that was a twin flame to my own? Would I get to see the sliver of sunlight that was his true smile, the hard-won joy he so rarely let shine?

"Come back to me," I begged. My hand shifted to the unblemished patch of skin above his heart.

I knew it, he'd said. *You can wield all the Kindred's magic.*

He'd seen it in me before I'd seen it in myself. All the way back to Ignios, when he'd braved the flames engulfing me to get to my side, knowing they were mine—and knowing they would not hurt the man I loved.

And if he was right about me healing Lily, there was a chance I could heal him, too.

I poured my magic into him, hoping my godhood understood what I could not. It tingled through my palm and into his chest, cascading around him in an anxious search.

It *wanted* to help him, in its own way and for its own reasons. Though it was weakened from how much I'd used during our long flight home, it pulsed with a shared urgency, as if it knew some essential part of us burned in him, and if it extinguished, so too might we.

As my magic pushed deeper, Luther's godhood rose gratefully to meet it. Side-by-side, they hummed a cryptic harmony, locked in that same strange ethereal dance that had always drawn us closer for reasons unknown.

I felt the godstone in him, too. It was death given physical form, a ruinous substance that leeched the life from all it touched. It wove through bone, flesh, and tendon, and where it stretched, tissue withered and decayed. Luther's blood seemed to flee from it, rushing to his wound and oozing out in a last, desperate attempt to escape the coffin his body had become.

My magic shuddered as I urged it closer. I briefly leapt with joy as I sensed his organs mending, but the damage returned as quickly as it healed. When I tried to fight the poison directly, my godhood hissed and recoiled as if burnt, and no amount of pleading could persuade it to hold on.

The true devastation came when I finally reached his heart. Tendrils of blackened death enclosed it in a shrinking cage. Miraculously, it was still strong, its flesh healthy and alive despite being surrounded by death. It thumped valiantly in defiance, determined to keep his promise to me to *fight,* but it was suffocating under the godstone's unrelenting might, and my magic seemed powerless to help.

My hope guttered. If I didn't find some way to relieve the pressure soon, even Luther's warrior heart would fall.

I reluctantly withdrew my magic. I flinched as I felt Luther's godhood cling to mine, begging us to stay. To save them both.

"Diem? I just heard the good news that you're ba—oh. Is that...? Oh... Oh, no..."

Near the door, Eleanor's hands were at her chest, her lovely face twisted in sorrow.

"It can't be," she whispered. "Not *him*."

"He's going to be fine," I rasped. My throat constricted as grief crowded every hollow place inside me. "A healer's on the way. She'll mend him."

She eyed Luther's poisoned body, her sapphire gaze heavy with disagreement. She walked over and sat down at my side, then folded my hand in hers.

"I'll stay with you," she said. "Until he's... better."

We said no more. Taran and Zalaric returned, then Zalaric helped me wash the blood from Luther's skin while Taran and Eleanor embraced and murmured quietly in a corner.

I knew what they were discussing—the truths they were admitting. But I forced my eyes to divert, and I hummed to fill my ears. For now, I needed the lie.

After a while, they returned, and Eleanor nestled beside me while Taran sat at Luther's side, hand resting on his friend's arm. I continued my ministrations as the silence thickened.

At the sound of approaching wings, the four of us jumped to our feet.

"Diem!" Maura cried, sounding as relieved as she was panicked. She was flat on her stomach behind Alixe, where she clung to Sorae's back with a green face and bone-white knuckles.

I eased her to the ground. She wobbled in my arms, gawking up at Sorae.

"I just flew," she gasped. "To the palace. On a *gryvern*. It didn't even try to eat me! And you, you're..." She seemed to catch her composure and straightened, her eyes scouring me tip to toe. "She said you were bleeding badly. Where is the wound?"

I frowned and glanced at Alixe, who cringed. "I told her you were the one injured. I thought it might give her more motivation to bring every treatment she could."

Perhaps it was a terribly cruel lie, but I couldn't have been more grateful to Alixe for it if I tried.

Maura scowled. "You're *not* injured?"

"No. It's Luther, he's..." My voice broke, and Maura's anger softened.

"Show me," she insisted.

Our years as healers had desensitized us both to all manner of gruesome injuries. We had become skilled at controlling our reactions, knowing patients and their families would watch with eagle eyes, judging their loved one's fate from our expressions alone. On a normal day, even the most brutal of wounds could barely earn a raised eyebrow.

Though Maura hesitated for only the briefest moment as she took him in, that split second—a tic downward of her lips, a blink-and-you'll-miss-it bulge of her eyes—sent my heart spiraling.

I rattled off every detail I knew of his injury and treatment, then I found his satchel and dumped its contents across the floor. I snatched up the herbs he'd bought in Umbros and painstakingly recreated the poultice I'd used successfully on Taran.

Maura listened, asking the occasional question but otherwise saying nothing. She examined Luther's wound, his pulse, his eyes, his breathing. Through it all, I hovered an inch away, flinching each time she touched him.

Her eyes darted to me. "You said he's seen a Fortos healer already?"

"Yes. Yesterday, in Umbros. And..." I paused. "Here. Just a moment ago."

The others exchanged confused looks, though Taran, who'd been close enough to hear Luther's revelation about my magic, met my eyes with a glint of understanding.

"And they weren't able to help?" Maura asked.

"The toxin doesn't respond to magical healing. It needs to be drawn out some other way."

She examined the herbs I'd used, still offering only vague hums and thoughtful, drawn-out stares.

"The poultice that worked—I used water from a spring in Ignios. Perhaps the spring had some healing quality. I can go back and get more—"

"No," Taran and Alixe said in unison.

I glanced to Sorae, wrestling over whether she could make another long journey—and who we might encounter on the way.

"Your Majesty," Alixe said gently, "Luther wouldn't want you to do that."

"We barely made it out of there alive the first time," Taran said.

"I don't care," I muttered.

He stepped toward me and growled. "*Luther* would care. If something happened to you... you know he'd rather die than live with that."

I echoed his movement, meeting his challenge with a glare. "When he wakes up and tells me that himself, I'll take it into consideration. Until then, it's *my* life to risk."

"I don't think that's necessary," Maura rushed out. She placed a hand on my back and nudged me toward the door. "You must be tired from your journey. Why don't you rest while I tend to the Prince?"

My bones went rod-straight. "I'm not tired."

"Then why don't you tidy yourself up? Perhaps a nice warm bath?"

"Maura, I'm not leaving."

"*Diem.*"

For a moment, it was my mother standing in front of me. Not in the kind, parental manner Maura had taken to treating me with since my mother's disappearance, but in a real, all-too-visceral way.

My mother's unyielding tone, leaving no room for argument. Her age-worn face, her stern yet patient stare. Those golden-brown eyes that felt like the warmest hug when they crinkled.

And I missed her. *Gods*, did I miss her.

"Please," I whispered. "I can't lose him, too."

Deep lines carved across her forehead as understanding dawned. Long ago, she'd teased me over the apparent interest of a brooding Prince. My despair was proof there was a great deal more between us now than *interest*.

Eleanor took my arm. "Why don't you sit with me? We'll pull up some chairs in here by the fire."

I took up her offer before Maura could object. Eleanor carefully eased me into a chair—facing away from Luther. Zalaric and Alixe joined us while Taran stayed back to help Maura maneuver Luther's unconscious body.

Eleanor peppered me with questions about our journey to keep me distracted. I couldn't muster more than a handful of words to each, and the others eventually chimed in to fill in the details.

As they talked, I gazed blankly into the hearth and lost myself in the dance of the fire. Perhaps subconsciously, I threw my magic into it, and it swelled to engulf the fireplace, hot flames licking at the stone mantle's edge. The others jumped, startled, and eyed me with uncertainty.

In the orange-red glow of the blaze, Luther's face kept staring back at me. The inferno during the armory attack. The dragonfyre in the Arboros clearing. The explosions in the Guardians' camp. The wall of flames on the beach in Ignios.

In some ways, it was fire that had brought us together. Fire that had forged us—melted us down, welded us together, and hardened us into a single, indomitable force.

Fire that would receive him, if I failed—the Undying Fire of the sacred Everflame, the final resting place for worthy souls.

If only fire could also save him.

My hand absently rose to my throat as I thought of the phoenix medallion he had gifted me. I stood to retrieve it when shouting voices came from the main salon.

"You can't go in there!"

"This is my palace, I can go wherever I want."

"Those are Her Majesty's personal quarters."

"Father, please, wait—"

The door to my bedchamber slammed open and bounced off the stone wall. Luther's father, Remis, stepped inside, followed by Remis's wife, Avana, then Lily, Teller, and Perthe, the Descended who had devoted himself to my service after I'd saved his life by dragging him from the burning armory.

"Your Majesty, you're back," Perthe gasped, dropping to a knee in salute.

"Indeed, you are," Remis murmured. He offered only a curt nod as his eyes trailed me in scrutiny before sweeping across the rest of the room.

Teller grabbed Lily's wrist and tugged her over to me. "Sorry," he muttered. "He saw us coming back from the gardens and followed us."

I gestured to Perthe to stand, and he rose, rushing to my side.

"I stayed with your brother the whole time you were gone, Your Majesty," he vowed. "I never left him, not even for a second."

"He sure didn't," Teller said with a scowl.

"Thank you, Perthe," I said, squeezing his hand. "Your loyalty is greatly appreciated."

Lily handed over a basket of garden cuttings. I traded it for a grateful, albeit strained, smile and hurried to set it at Maura's side.

"I thought we could try adding the star nettle and blushroom to a drawing salve," I rushed out. "I don't think it's been done before, but—"

"Is that... *godstone?*" Avana shrieked. She and Remis stood at the foot of the bed, looking equally pale. "Blessed Kindred, he's going to die."

Lily walked to Luther and took his hand. "No, Mother. Diem and Maura are going to save him."

Maura looked at her, then at me, frowning.

Remis stared down at his son with a haunted look. His head shook slowly. "Sweetheart, I'm sorry. It's too late. No one can save him now."

"That's what you thought when he got his scar too, wasn't it?" I said coldly. "Yet here he is."

He stiffened. "Luther told you?"

"Oh, he told me everything." My wrath-darkened gaze flitted briefly to Avana. "*Everything*. And you better hope that when he's healed, he's willing to ask for my mercy on your behalf."

Several eyebrows raised as Remis glanced uneasily at the now-crowded room. His eyes paused and sharpened on Zalaric. "Who are you?"

He raised his angled jaw. "My name is Zalaric Hanoverre. I'm an old friend of Luther's."

Remis's brows carved inward. "I know every member of House Hanoverre. Why have I never heard of you?"

My hackles raised, but Zalaric was unruffled.

"I'm a half-mortal," he said matter-of-factly. "I escaped to Umbros as a child. I've been living there until now."

"And he's here at my invitation," I added.

"You brought a Hanoverre bastard to Lumnos?" Remis hissed. "Do you have any idea what they'll do if they find him?"

"I know all about their pureblood pride," I said, rolling my eyes at the memory. Even House Hanoverre's sigil, a white rose with a single red drop, symbolized their obsession with keeping mortals out of their bloodline. Zalaric's mere existence would be scandal enough—his invitation to the palace would be a drama for the ages. "He's under the protection of the Crown, so they better not *do* anything, unless they wish to declare war on me and on House Corbois."

"Everyone has already declared war on us—or have you already forgotten what happened at your Challenging?"

"Oh, I haven't forgotten at all." I smiled sweetly. "House Hanoverre best not forget, either."

"And they don't need to find me," Zalaric piped up. "I intend to find them myself."

Remis pinched the bridge of his nose and heaved out an irritated sigh, then looked again at his son. To my surprise, some of the heat cooled from his expression. "Why is she here?" he asked, pointing to Maura. "We should send for a Fortos healer."

"Godstone doesn't respond to magic," I said. "Only a mortal remedy can stop it."

"And she has one that will work?"

Maura and I exchanged a silent look.

I came around and inserted myself between Remis and the bed. "We're giving her space to work—which means *you* can leave."

"I'm staying here."

"No, you're not."

Remis didn't budge. "It wasn't a request. I'm staying with him."

"The hell you are. He wouldn't want you here." Gloves of sizzling light coated my hands and forearms. "But you're welcome to fight me for it, if you'd like."

I flashed a cold smile to remind him of our shared secret—that ever since he'd lost his magic from our broken bargain at the Challenging, he was powerless against me. Against *anyone*.

He flexed his jaw. "Luther and I have our differences, but he's still my son. Whatever you think of me and my methods, I do care for my family. Everything I've done is to protect them. Even Luther would tell you the same."

I glared at him, and he glared back, the room silent except for the magic crackling at my palms.

My resolve wavered. Family was my weakness—a weakness Remis surely knew and was exploiting at my expense.

But Luther despised his father. Remis had insulted him, threatened him, *scarred* him. He'd murdered Luther's mortal mother and nearly killed him in the process. If this truly was Luther's end, he deserved to be surrounded by those he loved, not the man who'd caused him so much pain.

"Your Majesty?"

Lily's soft voice called out to me as she walked to join her parents. Her eyes were red-rimmed and swollen. "Let them stay. Please? For me?"

Avana put an arm around Lily's shoulders, and Remis clasped his daughter's hand.

Thoughts of my own mother and father bombarded my wounded heart. I swallowed hard. "Of course, Lily. Anything for you."

She threw me a grateful smile and, cleverly, led them away to a seating area far across the room.

I flicked away my magic and turned back to the bed. As I stared at Luther's tainted skin, the darkness that covered it seemed to leech inside my own soul.

Teller and Taran appeared on either side of me. Teller put a hand on my shoulder, a gesture so much like our father. The gruff familiarity of it almost did me in.

Taran crossed his arms. "Lu's going to be pissed he missed that show-down between you and Remis."

"I'll be happy to put on another one any time he wants."

He huffed a laugh, then looked down. "I'll go to Ignios and get more water from that spring, if you think it will help. You should stay here. He'll want to see you if—" He paused, clearing his throat. "—when he wakes up."

I leaned my head against Taran's shoulder. "Let me think about it," I murmured. Risking my life for a wild guess was one thing; risking Taran's was another. "Maybe there's a better way."

Burns still coated his arms from our battle over the sea. I placed a palm against his skin and let my magic soak into him. He shivered as the welts flattened, then faded, then disappeared, taking with them the last hint of his godstone wounds from Arboros, as well. We exchanged a silent, loaded look, but said nothing more of it, and after a long moment, his head arched over to rest against mine.

Zalaric came to stand at his other side and subtly hooked a finger around Taran's, and Eleanor and Alixe gathered close to Teller. The six of us stood in wordless vigil, each of us lost in our own murky shades of grief and fear and the unknown.

"I never told him I love him," I whispered. "What if I never get the chance?"

"He knows," Taran said firmly.

Alixe and Eleanor nodded, and Teller's hand tightened on my shoulder.

Much time passed as Maura slipped countless mixtures into Luther's mouth and onto his wound. She sat at his side and joined our watch, waiting to see if any of them might have an effect.

Eventually, she began repacking her bags and giving me furtive glances that said we needed to talk. Bile rose in my throat at what that conversation would bring.

I extricated myself from my friends and walked with her out to the balcony. Sorae was flopped on her side, resting but not sleeping, her golden gaze flitting between her Queen and her Prince.

Maura turned to me and took both my hands in hers. "I've done all I can, my dear. I've used all my strongest remedies. His body simply isn't responding." Her eyes began to water. "If there was anything I could do, anything at all, you know I would do it for you. You've already lost too much."

I blinked at her, feeling suddenly numb.

She placed a hand on my cheek. "I'm so sorry, Diem. It's time to say your goodbyes."

I blinked again. "Did you bring my mother's notes?"

"I did. I left them on the table by the bed. I've already been through them, though. There's nothing—"

"Thank you." I stared at her blankly. "What do I owe you for the visit?"

She gave me an anguished look. "Nothing, dear."

I didn't have the energy to argue. I made a mental note to send a pouch of gold later and shot a silent request to Sorae, who dragged herself tiredly to her feet.

"Are you alright returning by gryvern?" I looked out over the balcony. "I could arrange a horse, but with all the soldiers on the streets..."

"Gryvern is fine," she rushed out, though she jumped as Sorae shook out her matted fur.

I helped her load onto Sorae's back and murmured a request in my gryvern's ear to fly gently. As I stepped back, Maura reached forward and grabbed my wrist. She slipped something cold and glassy in my palm, then curled my fingers around it and patted the back of my hand.

"If his condition declines," was all she said.

I backed away as Sorae took flight and the two of them shrank on the horizon. The sun hung low in the sky, but there was no sign of the usual jewel tones of sunset. Only an infinite expanse of dreary grey.

I walked to the edge of the balcony and unfurled my palm on the stone balustrade. Inside was a small jar with a blue-green liquid I recognized. A sleeping draught—our most powerful one. It would cut through pain, no matter how excruciating, and offer the patient blissful relief from their misery.

It would also slow their heart and lungs. Only a little, if given no more than a drop. But if given more, it was a painless way to ease a terminal patient into the release of death.

A final mercy for a soul already lost.

CHAPTER

FORTY-THREE

L ate afternoon gloomed into evening, and evening sulked into night.
Luther's condition remained unchanged.

After I promised to send for them if there was any news, Alixe, Taran, and Zalaric left to have a bath and a hot meal. When I refused to do the same, Eleanor scurried off to have food sent up, while Perthe resumed his post at my door. Remis insisted on staying, though he kept his distance, only occasionally walking to Luther's side and watching him in silence.

To keep myself busy, I alternated between tending Luther's wound, which was now bleeding through his gauze at an hourly rate, and curling up on the bed beside him to scour my mother's notes. It took only ten minutes to read all she'd written on godstone, and even less to realize it was nothing I didn't already know.

Still I persisted, flipping page after page, in obstinate search of some key to his salvation.

There was one note that nibbled at my heel and refused to let go. An offhand comment scrawled and circled in the margins:

Diem—Coeurile
godstone=death
life=?

It was strange enough seeing my name in the notes I'd been forbidden from reading, but the placement was especially intriguing—just beside her section on possible remedies.

My leg jiggled restlessly as I chewed on my lip. Could I break her out of prison in Fortos? Could I do it before Luther's time ran out?

"I'd know that look anywhere," Teller said, sitting beside me. "You're planning something. Something bad."

I didn't bother to deny it.

"Look." I handed him the journal and pointed to the curious note. "Any idea what it means?"

He frowned and looked closer. I tried to stop myself from hoping, but when he finally shook his head, my stomach sank even lower.

"Maybe she thinks there's a cure on the island," he suggested. "If she knew you were Descended, she could have been worried you would need it one day."

"The flameroot?" I asked. "It only grows on Coeurîle."

He shrugged. "Do you think it might help?"

I sighed and rubbed my face. I was willing to try anything, but some gut instinct told me this was a dead end. It was the same reason I hadn't yet sent Taran to Ignios, the same reason I was here rather than on gryvernback heading to Fortos.

Luther had urged me to trust my hunches. So far, that advice had served me well. But sitting here doing nothing as he lay dying was tearing me apart.

I glanced down at his wound, fresh blood already staining the new gauze. I could *feel* there was something I was missing, some clue glaring at me right in plain sight.

I closed the notebook and set it aside. "I guess you've heard the news about Mother."

"I have." He leaned his forearms on his knees and stared down at his hands. "They said she was arrested on Coeurîle. Did you see her there?"

"Only for a second, before the attack." I nudged him with my arm. "She looked healthy. Unhurt."

His head hung lower. "They're going to execute her, D. I didn't think anything could be worse than not knowing what happened to her, but now..." He rubbed his eyes. "Is it horrible that I wish she'd just stayed gone?"

"I'm not going to let them kill her," I vowed. "I'm going to get her out of that prison."

He looked up. "You're going to prove to the Crowns she's innocent?" He jumped to his feet, suddenly excited, and grabbed my hands, pulling me up to join him. "I don't believe what they're saying—that she was the leader of the Guardians. The kids at school say she was using me to get information on the Descended for the rebels. But she would never do that, right?" His eyes filled with hope. "We can do this, we can prove the accusations are wron—"

He froze at the look on my face.

"What?" he asked quietly.

"The accusations aren't wrong, Tel. She was—*is*—their leader."

His expression fell. "You knew?"

"No—I had no idea, I swear. I found out from the Guardians who captured me after the attack. I thought it was some man named Vance."

A selfish part of me wanted to leave it at that, but he deserved the full truth, and I'd been withholding it for too long.

I shot a quick glance at Remis, Avana, and Lily and lowered my voice to keep them out of earshot.

"But I did know Mother was alive," I admitted, grimacing. "I didn't know where she was, only that she was likely safe."

He blinked, then drew back. "And you didn't tell me?"

"I was worried she'd never come home. I didn't want to give you false hope."

"False hope?" he shot back, yanking his hands from mine. "Like the kind you're giving everyone here about Luther?"

I flinched.

His voice began to rise. "Did you know the whole time? Was all that searching we did for her just pretend?"

"No! Gods, no. I didn't know for months. Luther only told me after I became Queen."

"Luther?" he shouted. The others started looking our way. "How in the Flames did *he* know?"

"He's the one who took her to the island. They were... working together, in a way."

"*Working together?* Was he a Guardian, too? Wait..." He staggered back a step. "You said you thought their leader was named Vance. How could you possibly know that, unless you...?"

I didn't dare admit it aloud, but the answer was plain on my face. My silent plea for forgiveness was met with a glare of betrayal.

"I stood by you the entire time, Diem. I did whatever you asked of me. I was grieving Mother and Father, my life was falling apart, but I put it aside —to help *you*. And the one thing you could have done to help me, you didn't."

His words hit like a punch to the gut. I reached for him, and he jerked back.

"You're just like her," he snapped. "Keeping secrets. Lying. Using me. You've been so angry at Mother all this time, but you're just as bad as she is."

"Tel, I'm so sorry. I know I was wrong. I should have told you. I was only trying to—"

He stormed for the door. Lily popped to her feet, her gaze darting between us. He breezed past her into the parlor and she ran after him, calling his name. Moments later, I flinched as a door slammed on the other side of the suite.

Shame and guilt towered high over my head. So many mistakes, so many rash choices, and the people who had paid the price were the ones I loved most. I buried my face in my hands as dark, vicious thoughts hissed in my ear.

Blood on your hands, corpses at your feet.

You're going to get everyone killed.

You're a selfish, reckless fool.

You don't deserve to be Queen.

No one believes in you. The only one who did is about to die—all because of you.

A pair of arms timidly wrapped around my waist. I stiffened and dropped my hands to see Lily embracing me, her head resting on my arm.

"He'll forgive you," she said, her voice soft but confident. "Whatever happened, Teller loves you, and he thinks the world of you. You're his hero."

"I'm not sure that's true anymore," I whispered.

"Is there anything Teller could ever do to make *you* stop loving *him*, or make you think less of him?"

"No," I conceded. "But I kept secrets from him. Big, important ones. Ones he deserved to know."

She shrugged. "Luther does that to me all the time. He thinks I don't know, but I pay attention. I know what he's up to."

My eyebrows slowly rose. "You do?"

"I'm his little sister, it's my job to spy on him and find all the things he doesn't want me to know. At first it hurt my feelings because I thought he didn't trust me. Then I realized it makes him think he's protecting me, so now I play dumb to make him feel better." She gave me a coy smile and lowered her voice. "He told you, though, didn't he? About his real mother? The mortal one? I bet he told you about the half-mortals he saves, too."

My mouth dropped open.

"Don't worry about Teller. I'll talk to him for you. It's the least I can do." She looked over at Luther, her smile holding strong, though it was painted with hues of grief. "Luther's always doing things for me and for all the cousins. For Father and Uncle Garath, too. Even for strangers. Oh, and Blessed Mother Lumnos, of course. But I've never seen him want anything for himself. Not until you. And *Blessed Kindred*, did he want you." She laughed between sniffles. "Ever since I was little, he has snuck into my room to hide from all the people who want something from him. Usually he just sits on my bed and listens while I ramble, but after he met you, *he* was the one rambling. My brother! Luther! Can you imagine?"

I shook my head, unable to speak. Words seemed like a complex, foreign concept that only Lily had mastered.

"I used to play a game where I would change the subject and see how long it took him to bring you up. It never took more than three sentences. He had it *bad*." She sighed. "And then you got mad at him, and he was so sad. The kind of sad you can only get from being in love, you know? The kind where you think you'll never feel happy again? But then you kissed him at the Challenging, and that whole night, he couldn't stop smiling. For the first time in my entire life, I saw my brother really, truly happy. Not just for you, but for himself, too."

She threw her arms around me again and crushed me against her. "I will love you forever for that. And even if—" Her voice wobbled. "—even if he doesn't make it, he'll die knowing what it means to be happy. That's what he deserves."

The earth began to give way beneath me.

"I... I'm going to... get some things from his room," I stammered, gently prying Lily off. "Will you stay with him... until I come back?"

She swiped at her tears and nodded. "Of course."

"I just need to get some, um..." I wandered away midsentence. Perthe moved to follow me, and I waved him off with an order to stay with Luther.

I barely made it to the parlor before my knees gave in. My hands clamped across my mouth to muffle the sound as sorrow tore out of me in great, heaving sobs. Not for me, but for the man in my bed, from whom so much had been taken and so little given in return. A man for whom something as simple as *happiness* had been a rare, fleeting gift.

A gift the gods hadn't even let him keep for more than a day.

I screamed internally at the Kindred and their fickle favor. My godhood thrashed, my vision went red, and my self-control frayed to a tenuous string. I started to feel the way I had after my father's death—unhinged and unsteady, an emotional bomb rolling toward an open flame.

Sorae felt it, too. She paced outside on the balcony, whipping her tail and arching her neck to the sky in piercing wails that rattled the furniture.

My skin began to illuminate with a silvery light. I needed to get out of here before I self-destructed and took half the palace with me.

I clambered to my feet and lurched across the parlor. When I placed my hand on the door, the wood charred black beneath my fingers. I swore and jerked away, the smell of burning wood filling the room.

Sorae howled again, and the door to my chambers creaked open. "Your Majesty?" Perthe called out. "Is everything—"

"Fine," I yelled. I called on the Montios magic and summoned a layer of frost to cool my skin. It bubbled and dissipated almost instantly into steam.

I threw the door open and flew out, rushing past the guards in the hallway before they could get too close a look. "Stay there," I barked as two of them moved to follow me. "That's an order."

Their footsteps stalled, and I broke into a run, my eyes locked on Luther's door at the end of the hall. I forced air into my lungs, forced my heart to steady, forced the magic churning in me to—

"Diem?"

Fuck.

"Aemonn," I gritted out, turning slowly.

He strolled down the corridor, hands in his pockets. He looked prim and polished as usual, his blonde hair swept perfectly over his brow and his handsome face set in a charming smirk. He wore a colorful, gold-trimmed abomination that, as he came closer, I recognized as an extravagantly customized version of the Royal Guard armor.

"I just heard that you returned," he said. "I'm glad to see that you're unharmed."

"Are you?" I clipped.

He studied me warily, his eyes lingering on my faintly glowing skin. "I heard what happened to Luther. I'm sorry. I know you two were close."

"Are close. *Are*, not were. Save your celebrations, he isn't dead yet."

Aemonn frowned. He pulled his hands from his pockets and straightened his back. "You and I have some things to discuss."

I crossed my arms. "Are you going to threaten me like you did the last time we spoke? If I remember correctly, that didn't end too well for you."

His fingers flexed at the reminder of how I'd nearly taken his arm off when he demanded to speak with me and refused to take *no* for an answer. "I was only trying to help you. If you had talked to me then instead of attacking me, I could have warned you—"

"If you truly wanted to help me, you never would have taken Luther's titles and threatened to send all my allies to the other side of the realm."

"I admit, sending Alixe away would have been a mistake. The guards respect her, as do I. But my brother... you'd be better off without him here. He will only let you down." He pressed a hand to his chest. "*I* can be your ally, Diem. Tell me your plans. Let me show you I can help."

"My plans?" I huffed out a harsh laugh, my temper still roaring. "My *plan* is to save Luther, break my mother out of prison, take on the Crowns and probably the entire Emarion Army while I'm at it, and fight a war all by myself. Still want to be my ally?"

He balked. "Your mother—the rebel leader? You're going to free her after all the violence the Guardians are responsible for?"

"And how much violence is *your* father responsible for?" I snapped.

Aemonn's confidence wavered, a flicker of the scared little boy he once must have been, the defenseless victim of his father's vicious rage. My anger slipped at the sight, losing its jagged edge.

"You of all people should understand, Aemonn." I turned to walk away, muttering under my breath. "The great man you could be, if only your loyalty wasn't so one-sided."

"What is that supposed to mean?" he called out.

I almost kept going. Almost abandoned Aemonn there, standing alone in the corridor. I was on the sheerest of emotional cliffs, my most malicious vices jeering in my ear. My temper had always been my downfall, and at the moment, I was more than ready to give myself over and embrace its destruction.

But I thought of my brother and how deeply I'd hurt him. I thought of what might become of us, if we left that wound untended. How it might fester with bitterness, infect with resentment, how it might spread and deepen and scar. How it might eat away at us, bit by tiny bit, and leave us permanently ravaged, unable to heal.

Perhaps I might never save Luther from the godstone. But this was a poison I could fight.

"It could have been Taran in there dying, you know." I managed to reel my temper back, and my magic with it, then turned around to face him. "When the Guardians attacked us, Taran was stabbed with godstone, too—twice. He should have died. I still don't know how he didn't." I cocked my head. "What if your brother had never come home—is that really what you want, for him to be out of your way forever?"

Aemonn's throat bobbed, his expression indecipherable.

"All this hate the two of you are holding—you're directing it at the wrong person. I'm sure Taran has made his share of mistakes, but I don't think he's the one you're really angry with, is he?" I glanced at my chambers, my heart and mind still trapped in that room at Luther's side. "Life is too short to hold these grudges, Aemonn. Even for the Descended."

He stared at the stone wall, saying nothing, his features uncharacteristically dull. All his suave charm had fallen away, leaving a bitter, rotting core.

Again I walked away, ignoring the sound of footsteps following close behind. When I reached Luther's chambers, I paused in front of it and frowned. Since I'd been gone, he'd added a bloodlock. I could take a few drops from his wound, but bloodlocks required willingly given blood.

Aemonn leaned a shoulder against the wall at my side. "I haven't been enforcing the progeny laws, you know. It hasn't been popular, but I insisted on delaying executions until you returned."

"Really?" I threw him a brief, surprised glance before returning my focus to the door.

"I'm not a man who murders innocent children, Diem. Despite what your *allies* tell you, I'm not a monster."

"Tell that to the mortal boy you killed in Lumnos City," I said bitterly. I ran a finger over the bloodlock as a question sprouted in my mind.

A crease formed on his brow. "What mortal boy?"

"The one you trampled with your horse and left to die on the street." I turned to face him. "Do you have any blades on you?"

Aemonn pushed off the wall, his face going pale. "That was an accident. How did you—"

"Henri saw it happen. He was going to kill you for it before I stopped him."

My eyes grazed over him and paused on a hilt at his hip. I grabbed the handle and plucked it free over his scoff of protest, then nearly groaned.

The entire weapon was cast from pure gold—too soft a metal to cut through Descended skin.

A shiny, useless distraction. Just like Aemonn's reign as High General.

"That boy—h-he was running in the street. I didn't see him. I... I didn't mean for him to get hurt."

As I looked closer, I spied a thin line of dark grey metal embedded into the blade's gilded edge. I pressed the tip of my thumb to its point and smirked as a single bead of scarlet appeared.

A hidden edge sharp enough to draw blood—also like Aemonn.

"You didn't try to save the child though, did you? You didn't call for a healer?" I spun the blade in my hand, offering it back to him handle-first. "Did you even dismount from your horse?"

His nostrils flared. "You have no idea what it's like. The pressure my father puts on me to be perfect, to never show weakness." His head shook rapidly. "I'm not a bad person."

"Then prove it." I gave up waiting on him and tucked the blade into the sash of my dress. "When I first met you, I saw good in you. I believed there was more to you than this shallow, callous person you pretend to be."

I swiped my bloody thumb across the black metal disc of the bloodlock, sucking in a breath at the soft click that followed.

Me.

Luther had keyed his locks to *me*.

The reason hit me like a stab to the heart—I was the only other one who knew about his journal recording the exiled children he'd smuggled out. In the wrong hands, that list could be deadly. Some of the Twenty Houses would go to the ends of Emarion to rid half-mortals from their lineage.

Luther had known he might not come home—and he'd trusted me to protect them in his stead.

I stepped in the room and turned to face Aemonn. "Taran got a second chance. I'm giving you one, too. Show me I was right to believe in you. You don't have to be perfect, Aemonn. Just honorable."

I began to close the door, then paused, popping my head out into the hall.

"Oh, and if you really want to make amends with your brother, tell your best friend Iléana Hanoverre to keep her House away from Zalaric."

He frowned. "Who is Zalar—"

I slammed the door shut in his face.

CHAPTER

FORTY-FOUR

I leaned back against the door as a wave of *him* hit me. His smell, his presence. It lingered, even after weeks of his absence.

I hated thinking of him as he was now—bed-bound and weakened. The Luther I knew was larger than life, a man from whom even Crowns trembled and shrank. Though he was quiet, an ocean of intensity surged beneath his skin. It seemed unthinkable that this modest room could have ever contained him.

He'd clearly left in a hurry. Pieces of him were scattered across the main parlor. Drawers hung ajar with clothes flung haphazardly to the floor, and weapons and empty sheaths cluttered a table.

The mess was so unlike him, and yet so perfectly apropos. I smiled, imagining the moment when he realized the compass would lead him to me —the ferocious resolve it would have provoked, the struggle poor Taran and Alixe must have had to force him to wait long enough just to pack a bag.

I walked into his bedchamber and sat on the edge of his perfectly made bed, running a hand along the cool fabric of his pillow where I'd woken up the morning after the armory attack.

He finally let his guard down with me that day. He showed me his smile, his laugh, his doubts, his trust. I hadn't realized it then—and I would have fervently denied it for weeks that followed—but that was the moment the spark between us became a flame, the beginnings of our inevitable blaze.

I'd left here that day questioning everything. Despite all the time that had passed and all that had changed, I wasn't any closer to knowing who I was.

But I finally knew what I wanted—with all of my heart.

I sighed and wandered back into the main parlor, my attention falling on the place where Luther had shown me his journal, entrusting me with the most vulnerable part of him. I'd hated him then, or at least I'd been *trying* to hate him, making him the scapegoat for everything I despised about the Descended.

But he never gave up on me. Never stopped fighting—for my vision of Emarion or for my heart.

I glanced at the bust of the goddess Lumnos that sat in a niche along one wall. Gathered at its base was a pile of dried flowers, glossy stones, and blown-out candles. I glared at her for a long moment, hating the calm serenity sculpted on her face as the world she left behind suffered for her mistakes. I rolled my eyes and stalked over, then conjured a single flame of Ignios fire at my finger to light each of the candles. Whatever my own feelings, Luther would want that.

"Why *him?*" I shouted at the bust. "He's done everything you've asked of him, and this is how you repay him?"

The bust of Lumnos stared back at me silently, her glossy marble eyes half-lidded and still.

"Choose someone else." I flung a hand toward the window, the snow-brushed rooftops of Lumnos City just barely visible in the distance. "If our misery is what makes you happy, there's a whole city of pricks out there in their mansions planning how to crush the mortals under their expensive heels. Pick one of them to torture for your amusement. Pick someone who deserves this." Hot, angry tears sprung to my eyes. "Pick *me*. Let *me* suffer. I'll take it all. Please, just... not him." I sank to my knees, my voice turning hoarse. "Not my Luther."

I wrapped my arms around myself, hunching forward under the unbearable drag of my sorrow. "Is this because of me? Because I haven't bowed and worshiped your name like everyone else? Is this some depraved attempt to force me in line?"

My palms fell open in front of me, and I let my magic tumble from them unrestrained. Light and shadow swirled in a twinkling fog and spread across the floor, then crept up the walls. Dark clouds coated the ceiling, sparks glittering in the air, until the bust and I were floating alone in an infinite expanse.

"Here," I pleaded. "My offering of magic. Take it—take every drop I have. Take the Crown, too. If that's what you want from me, you can have it all."

More magic began to pour out—a circle of crackling fire, chunky white snowflakes fluttering in a gust of wind that whirled through my hair, flowering vines that pushed through cracks in the stone walls, a cacophony of chirps from nocturnal creatures in the woods outside. I gritted my teeth and forced the magic out of me, screaming internally at my godhood to lay itself bare.

The bust's silhouette wavered in my watery vision as my sobs grew more desperate.

"If you're trying to break me, you've won. I'll submit. I'll be loyal. I'll do whatever you ask. *Anything*. Just please... don't take him from me."

The tears fell hard and fast, splashing against the cold stone beneath me. My soul felt as if it were rending in two, and I collapsed forward as I surrendered, with my words and my heart.

"Is my magic not enough? Do you need my blood, too?" I pulled Aemonn's blade from the sash at my waist and slashed it across my hand, the blade cutting deep enough to scratch against bone. Blood gushed out in a heavy stream, though I felt no pain, my body already overwhelmed with a greater agony.

I threw the knife against the wall and offered up my bleeding palm. "Here. A bonded bargain—his life in exchange for whatever you want. My life, my soul. I'll fight this war in your name. I'll die for it, if you wish. I'll pay any price you ask. You hear me? *Any price*." My head sank low, too heavy to lift, my voice choking beneath my sobs. "Take it. Please. *Please*. I'm begging you..."

Words gave way to a long, sorrowful wail as I collapsed forward and succumbed to my despair. I knew my prayers would go unheard.

She wasn't listening. The gods never listened.

But as my tearstained cheek pressed to the rough, cold stone, an unexplainable instinct lured my gaze back up.

And my breath caught in my throat.

Streaming down the smooth marble of the bust, beginning at the eyes and rolling over the apples of its cheeks, were tears. Dark, crimson-black tears.

Blood tears.

My heart seemed to still, watching, as I climbed to my feet and slowly walked closer. I reached out and brushed a finger across them, my eyes growing large as the blood trickled down my palm and mixed with my own.

"*Diem! Diem, are you in there?*"

Lily's voice rang out from the corridor, shrill and panicked, followed by a string of rapid knocks.

I dissolved my magic, then sprinted to the door and threw it open. "What happened?"

Her face was ghastly white. "Come quick—it's Luther."

A delicate hope sprouted inside me. Had it worked? Had Lumnos answered my pleas?

I ran beside her down the hallway, through the parlor, and into my bedchamber. Remis and Avana were standing in front of the bed, clutching each other and blocking my view.

I darted around them—and froze.

Luther was convulsing, his body stiff and jerking in sharp, erratic jolts. Choked sounds rasped from his throat as he struggled to breathe, and lines of blood streamed from his nose.

"No," I breathed, shaking my head.

I ran to the bed and grabbed his shoulder, grunting as I fought to turn him, but his body was too heavy, and my quivering hands were too weak.

"Help me," I screamed at Remis.

He startled, his face as pale as Lily's. He stepped forward and slid his hands beneath his son's back, then pushed him onto his side.

The web of poisoned veins had grown significantly in my brief absence. Their spindly lines now stretched across Luther's face and swirled around his temples.

I threw my magic into him and let out a sob when his godhood did not stir in response. I couldn't even feel it now, the blanket of poison too thick, too smothering. His heart was almost invisible beneath the blackened cage of the godstone's grip. When I listened for its beat, the thumps were soft and defeated and so, so few.

Luther was dying.

Not eventually.

Not soon.

Now.

I bowed my head. "Go get the others, Perthe. Tell them to hurry."

His face twisted with sympathy. "At once, Your Majesty."

Lily sat at Luther's back and laid her arms around him, weeping quietly against his skin. She knew what my order implied.

I stroked my fingers through his hair. "My Prince. My brave, kind, handsome Prince. Please don't go."

His breathing cleared, though it was shallow and labored. His features pinched as guttural groans of discomfort rolled from his throat. He was clearly in pain, and from what I knew of a godstone death, it would be excruciating.

I looked at the small jar on my nightstand—the one Maura had given me before she left.

I can't do this without you, I'd told him back in Umbros.

You can, he'd answered. *And you will.*

There had been so many times he had tried to warn me. To prepare me.

I will always be with you.

You have a world to lead.

I believe in you, Diem. Don't ever forget that.

Go, my Queen. Live.

My trembling hand closed around the blue-green vial. "Is this what you want—for us to let you go?"

Lily raised her head, her stricken expression shattering what little was left of my heart. "What is that?"

"It will take away his pain. It will give him..." I let out a shaky breath. "*...peace.*"

I held her eyes until I saw that she understood what I wasn't saying. She sobbed and pulled him tighter to her, but after a long moment, she looked back up and nodded through her tears.

When his convulsions faded, I propped pillows behind him and carefully eased him onto his back. My palm curved around his cheek, and I placed my final kiss on his lips, lingering as my tears fell and streaked over his skin.

"You thought you failed me. You never did. *Never.* I'm so very sorry, my love. I was the one who failed you." I pulled the cork from the vial and raised it to his mouth. "Please forgive me."

The glass rim pressed into his lip, and the last rays of light in my soul went dark as I began to tilt it forward.

The sound of metal jingled behind me—from where I knew no one stood.

I stopped and glanced over my shoulder. As I thought, the room was empty at my back. Then a glint of metal caught my eye near Luther's palm.

I sat up straighter and pulled the vial away. A glimmer of *something* sparked deep in my gut.

An instinct. A hunch.

I pried his fingers open. Tucked inside was a small golden disc—the Meros compass. Taran must have grabbed it when I'd dumped out Luther's bag earlier.

Put that in his hand, he'd said. *It calms him to know he can always find you.*

I grabbed the compass and flipped it open in a frantic prayer that its magic might lead me to a last-minute solution, but its quivering red dial only pointed to Luther, just as it had every time I'd looked at it since the night of the Challenging.

"What is it?" Lily asked, looking hopeful.

My shoulders sagged as my hand flopped to my side. "Nothing. It's noth—"

The compass shuddered with a strange whirring sound. I looked at it again and squinted, then glanced up, my eyes following the line of its arrow to Luther—then further, to an area of the room just beyond him.

"What's going on?" Remis asked.

"I'm not sure," I mumbled. I stood up and walked around the bed. Remis and Avana began pelting me with questions and demands, but I didn't listen, my brows dipping as I strode toward my desk.

I'd thrown everything off it when I arrived, but one object had escaped my sweep. Another vial—this one a dark emerald green, a gift from the Arboros Queen at my Ascension Ball.

I turned to Remis, interrupting him mid-sentence. "Arboros—do they have a cure for godstone toxin?"

"You're asking this *now?*"

"Answer the question," I shot back.

He looked at his son and sighed. "No, they do not. Arboros and Sophos have been researching it for centuries."

"Is it possible they lied? Maybe they found one but kept it secret for only their use?"

"Unlikely. A cure would give them all the leverage they could ever want over the other Crowns. They could trade it for any demand they pleased."

I looked back at the vial on my desk, my frown curving deeper. The Arboros Descended had claimed the potion could cure any disease—except for ailments sent directly from the gods.

"What are you looking at?" Remis asked.

I didn't respond.

"*Answer me*," he snapped.

My fists clenched at his entitled tone, aggravating the gash I'd cut in my palm and sending a fresh torrent of blood dripping from my hand. I snatched the vial from my desk and whipped back around to hiss some furious reply—then stopped stone-still at the sound of a *click*.

A burst of heat shot up my arm. I slowly raised my palms and unfurled my fingers. In one hand, the vial from Arboros. In the other, the compass—its arrow now missing, the blood-smeared dial aglow with a brilliant light.

The compass's sign that I'd just found what my heart most desired.

Numb and stunned, I shuffled back to Luther. My body moved on its own, my mind trapped outside myself, watching each step with bated breath. My hands uncorked the Arboros vial and raised it to Luther's mouth, letting the tonic trickle down his throat.

When only a handful of drops remained, I swore and jerked it back. I'd assumed it was meant to be swallowed—but I didn't know for sure.

I peeled the soiled gauze from his wound and grimaced at the grey, decaying flesh. I turned the vial over and shook it hard as blood splattered from my hand across his skin. I scraped my fingers inside the glass to collect every last drop, then pressed them directly into his wound, the healer inside me cringing at the crude yet effective method.

"What was that?" Lily asked. "Will it help him? Or..." She swallowed. "Is it like the other vial?"

I had neither honesty nor false hope to offer. I gave a vacant blink and shook my head. "I truly don't know."

We shared a long look, neither of us saying any more.

I crawled into the bed beside him and laid my cheek over his chest to listen for his heartbeat. It was unchanged—still weak, still struggling.

Lily followed suit and nestled into his other side. She tucked under his arm and set her head on his shoulder. She reached out for me, and I took her hand, our fingers entwining as they lay joined on his chest.

I closed my eyes and focused on the rhythm of his heart—the one I cherished more deeply than any other.

Listening.

Praying.

Hoping.

CHAPTER

FORTY-FIVE

"Let her sleep."

A voice stirred me from my dreams. Dreams of battlefields and swords and trees of fire. Dreams of blue-grey eyes and glowing gold hearts.

"We should wake her up."

A different voice. Lily's voice.

She was sniffling.

No—*sobbing*.

"She's going to be furious we didn't wake her when it happened."

Eleanor's voice this time. She was huddled behind me, her hand draped over my hip.

But there was a second hand, broad and strong, burrowed beneath my hair and resting flush at the back of my neck.

I felt Luther's chest beneath me, his skin markedly cooler than I remembered. I listened for a heartbeat, but all I could hear was Lily's weeping, all I could feel was her shuddering body.

"She hasn't slept in two days." Alixe's voice. "She'll find out eventually. Let her rest while she still can."

Dread sank like a stone in my chest. I cracked my eyes open a sliver to see Taran curled up at the foot of the bed, sleeping. Alixe stood just beyond, rubbing her face, while Zalaric and Teller dozed in chairs behind her.

My focus slowly rose to Lily. She was sitting up, staring at Luther, an ocean of tears flowing down her reddened cheeks.

I slammed my lids closed. I couldn't bear to see the truth yet. I needed a little longer here, safe in the darkness of my denial.

"She needs to know," Lily said. "We have to wake her."

"She's already awake."

That voice...

That voice.

I knew that voice. I *felt* that voice. It rumbled beneath my cheek, its timbre coating my skin like a warm, heavy blanket.

I sucked in sharply. The hand on me twitched, then its thumb stroked a slow line down my neck.

My eyes shot open—and I saw skin. A broad expanse of it, bronzed and olive-hued and marked with the ridges of a long-healed scar.

A scar... and nothing else.

My gaze locked with Lily's—and through her tears, she *smiled*.

Slowly, so excruciatingly slowly, I lifted my head and turned it upward. A pair of bright, pale eyes were waiting for me, their corners crinkled with joy.

"Hello, beautiful."

I bolted upright, nearly knocking Eleanor off the bed in the process. The poisoned veins had receded from his head and limbs entirely. Their reach now barely touched the base of his ribs—and perhaps I was delusional in my shock, but I swore I could see them *shrinking*.

Even his wound was in far better shape. There was no more blood or poisonous ooze. The skin around it was a light, healing pink, and the beginnings of a scab had already begun to form.

I pressed my palms to his chest and let my magic rush into him. His godhood leapt to meet me immediately, its song trilling with elation. The cage around his heart had vanished, and the traces of toxin still inside him now seemed to cower from my reach. His ravaged organs mended where my magic soothed over them—but this time, the damage didn't return.

Luther let out a quiet, contented grunt, then gave me a knowing look. "Fortos magic?"

All I could do was nod.

Pride gleamed in his eyes. "Careful with my scars. I've grown fond of them, thanks to you."

I pulled back my magic before it reached his skin and leaned in close as I studied him. Color had returned to his cheeks, and the sunken hollows had faded from beneath his eyes. He looked healthy, happy, *alive*.

"Impossible," I breathed.

His smile could have lit the realm. "Around you, 'impossible' seems merely a suggestion."

"Luther," I choked out, my voice hushed for fear that a joy too loud might shatter this precious illusion. My arms trembled, and I collapsed against him, sobbing uncontrollably into his shoulder.

He pulled me in and kissed my temple. "I couldn't leave my Queen when she needed me."

Lily clutched my hand, and we both dissolved into weepy, wailing messes. Luther's chest bounced beneath us as he chuckled at our pitiful states, the sound of it filling me with a bliss I never thought I'd feel again.

"Holy sh—Lu? Are you...?" Taran sat up, gawking at Luther's chest. "Lumnos's tits, you're alive."

"*Taran*," Luther scolded, though it lost its punch as his laughter grew louder.

Taran dove forward and tumbled on top of us. His arms spread wide around Lily and Eleanor and squeezed the four of us into a crushing embrace. Though Luther stifled a grunt from the pressure on his wound, he was beaming from ear to ear.

Around us, the others began to wake. Alixe grinned, tears shining on her cheeks. Zalaric rolled his eyes dramatically at Taran's antics, though relief was evident on his delicate features. Teller sat forward, flashing me a tight half-smile before turning his focus to Lily, where his face warmed considerably.

Even Remis and Avana came to join us, their arms hooked on each other's waists. Avana looked tired—simply ready for the ordeal to be over, I suspected—while Remis watched his son with a guarded expression.

Excited chatter continued around us, and I didn't hear a word of it. I kept my face buried in his neck and let the world around us fall away. I needed to feel his skin, hear his heartbeat, smell the cedar musk of his scent. I needed to be convinced this was real and not a cruel hallucination that might end at any moment.

While Luther did his best to join in the conversation, I could tell he needed the same. I felt it in the way his face stayed turned to mine, his soft sigh each time he breathed me in. The way his hand roamed over my back, always gripping, always pressing harder, my body never close enough.

"I'm here," he murmured in my ear. "I'm alive."

It felt as much like a question as a declaration, so I laid my palm over his heart and nodded.

He threw his head back and gazed at the ceiling. "Thank you, Blessed Mother. You have given me yet another gift. I will not waste it."

I tensed at his reverence, remembering what happened in his chambers. He noticed and gave me a questioning glance that I pretended not to see.

I forced myself to sit up and gently pushed at Taran's shoulder. "You're crushing my patient."

With obvious reluctance, Taran shifted to the end of the bed. He brushed the back of his hand over his cheeks and cleared his throat, trying —*badly*—to pretend he hadn't been messily weeping.

"What happened?" he asked me. "When we came back, we thought it was the end."

"So did I," I admitted.

"The vial you gave him," Remis said, "I remember now—it was the Arboros gift from your ball?" I nodded, and his eyes darkened. "You were right. Their Queen has been keeping a cure to herself."

"That's what healed me?" Luther asked.

I stared down at my hand, still crusted with a glove of dried blood. The gash I'd cut on my palm was nearly healed, only visible by a shiny pink line. A faint pressure seemed to tingle around my wrist, though I was so overwhelmed, I might only have imagined it.

"I think so," I said quietly. Luther took my hand, his curious expression seeming to sense there was more I wasn't ready to say.

"You cured three godstone wounds," Taran said. "You're going to go down as the best healer in Emarion. Take that, Fortos."

The others burst into laughter and discussion of the happy ending we'd somehow scraped out, but my gaze returned to my crimson-stained hand.

To heal godstone once was a rare stroke of fortune. To heal it twice was a blessing from the divine. To do it three times...

That felt like an imbalance I would be called to repay.

I raised Luther's hand to my lips and kissed his knuckles. It didn't matter now. I'd offered up my soul for his, and I had no regrets.

If the gods came calling, I'd be ready to answer.

THE REST of the day passed in a blur. My fussing reached never-before-seen levels as I forced Luther to eat and drink until he begged me to relent.

He and his father had a stilted conversation that the rest of us tried our best to pretend we weren't eavesdropping on. They clasped wrists and exchanged amicable nods, which was more than Avana offered before they both said their goodbyes and left.

We all crowded into my bed around Luther, laughing and talking and retelling stories of the past few weeks. After sending Perthe away for some well-deserved rest, I revealed the same truths I'd admitted in Umbros—about my time in the Guardians, the so-called prophecy, and what I'd learned about my mother and birth father. Eleanor and Lily took it surprisingly well, but Teller's mood soured with every new revelation. Soon I could barely get him to look me in the eyes.

Here in Lumnos, Remis had never officially announced I was missing, though the truth had quickly leaked. After news broke of my mother's capture and her role in the island attack, speculation had exploded about where I was and why.

My brother had taken the brunt of the gossip, to the point his school was now pressuring him to end his final year early. I swore to him I wouldn't let that happen, but he merely shrugged and mumbled something about making the decision himself.

The others took right to Zalaric, as I knew they would. Eleanor squealed with delight when I proposed she take him shopping for whatever he needed, and Teller and Lily promised to find him a palace room of his own, an offer Taran quietly pouted over.

Though Zalaric's confident facade was composed as always, I sensed he was relieved to be so welcomed, while also worried for the half-mortals he'd left behind in Umbros—a concern I shared.

Under my protests and heavy teasing from Taran, I grudgingly agreed to leave Luther's side for a quick bath and fresh clothes. Just as reluctantly, Luther agreed to the same, though with his body still weak, Taran insisted on "helping." The rest of us crowded with our ears to the washroom door and laughed until we cried at the shouted obscenities and promises of payback that followed.

When the sun's light disappeared from the sky, Eleanor proposed we arrange an extravagant dinner feast. Luther instantly made a show of yawning.

"I think my patient needs rest," I said quickly, catching his grateful wink. "Why don't we save the rest of the celebrations until he's fully healed?"

"Oh, yes, of course," she said. "I'll go to the kitchens and have some platters brought up for us instead."

Luther slumped his head back on the freshly changed linens and let his eyes droop. "That's kind, cousin, but I'm not all that hungry."

Eleanor frowned. "Then I could fetch some—"

He interrupted her with another loud yawn.

"I think the Prince is politely suggesting we all go elsewhere," Zalaric said, looking amused. "Well... almost all of us."

"Oh." Eleanor looked between Luther and me, her eyebrows slowly rising. "*Oh.*" She jumped to her feet. "I'm exhausted. Aren't you all exhausted? Some sleep would do us all good, don't you think?"

"I agree," Luther rumbled.

She eagerly herded everyone toward the door. Lily squirmed free to steal a hug from her brother. Luther clutched her tight, kissing her forehead before whispering something in her ear that made her glance at Teller and flush bright red. She scurried off and slipped her hand into Teller's as they left.

Taran jogged over and wrapped me in his strong arms. "Take care of him, Queenie."

"I will," I promised.

"And tell him how you feel," he whispered with a pointed look.

I poked him in the ribs, nodding toward Zalaric. "Just as soon as you tell *him* how you feel."

He blinked innocently. "I don't have a clue what you mean."

I rolled my eyes, then a wicked smirk grew on my lips. "You know, being *thrust* into a new world like this, Zalaric is bound to find everything *hard.*"

Taran's eyes narrowed.

"All this tension could make him really *stiff* and *worked up.*"

He groaned and turned away. "I'm leaving."

"Make sure you help him find a way to *relea—*"

"Goodnight," he yelled. "Take care, Lu. If anything swells up, just ask Diem to give it a nice long rub."

"*Taran,*" Luther growled.

The sound of laughter rang out as the door snapped shut.

Luther threw the quilts off his body and swung his legs over the side of the bed, grunting with discomfort.

"Wait—no," I protested, running to stop him. I grabbed his shoulders and tried to ease him back, but he pushed forward, wobbling as he rose to his feet. "What are you doing? Luther, stop—you need to rest."

"I've been waiting a long time for this, and I'm not going to be lying on my back when I do it." He held on to me as his legs steadied, then lifted his eyes to mine.

A tender, perfect silence passed between us. He brushed my hair over my shoulder and cupped a hand behind my neck. The other slid low on my back, drawing our bodies together until the calming cadence of his heart purred against my chest.

He leaned in, and my eyelids fluttered closed at the graze of his lips. I arched my neck up to meet him, but he hesitated just beyond my reach.

"Look at me," he said.

When I did, my breath caught. The crystal blue of his irises was more vibrant than ever. It was as if the godstone's defeat had also destroyed some deep-rooted veil that had kept him muted and withdrawn all his life. Now, the light in him blazed with wild abandon, not a wisp of shadow in sight.

"I love you, Diem Bellator."

His smile stayed on his lips as his mouth fell to mine. Even as the kiss deepened with passion, I failed spectacularly at withholding a grin of my own.

Happiness consumed me, overwhelmed me, restored me. It flourished and bloomed, filling the dark fractures in my broken soul and welding them back together with gold. The joy filled me near to bursting, and a blissful laugh bubbled out by surprise.

"That is my favorite sound," he said with a reverent sigh. "I didn't think I'd ever hear it again."

"If you had died, I'm not sure *anyone* would have ever heard it again."

He kissed me once more, sweetly, tenderly.

"I heard you. I couldn't move or respond, but I heard everything you said."

I cringed. "Everything?"

He smiled. "Everything. And Taran was right—I did know how you felt." He kissed the corner of my mouth, then brushed his lips along my jaw to my ear. "Though I wouldn't mind hearing it again."

Another laugh broke free. I looped my arms around his neck and beamed. "I love you too, Luther Corbois. But I'll only *keep* loving you if you swear never to almost die on me again."

He hauled me up against him and into the air, trying his best to steal kisses between our unstoppable grins and laughter. Every bit of me felt illuminated with the brightest, most exquisite delight.

The path ahead for us would be anything but easy, and I'd be lying if I said all my misgivings about commitment were gone. But if this was a cliff, we were jumping off together, hand-in-hand, ready to face our fates as one.

Though he tried to stifle it, I spied flickers of pain behind his smile. "Back in bed," I scolded and tried to push him off. He resisted, his hold on me a vice. "*Luther.*"

"You first." He spun us around together and tossed me on my back onto the mattress, then wedged himself between my legs. He stared down at me, desire flooding his hungry gaze. "I could get used to this view."

My mouth went dry. I reached up and tugged at the waist of his loose linen trousers until he leaned over me, his elbows propped beside my head. I dragged my teeth slowly over my lower lip, and his nostrils flared. He leaned down, eyes closing.

I clamped a hand to his chest. "Not unless you let that wound heal, you won't."

He glared, and I smirked. I pushed him off, and he rolled onto his back with a scowl, then hooked an arm beneath me and tugged me into his side. I beamed at my victory and pressed a grateful kiss to his cheek.

"Say it again," he rumbled.

"I love you."

His eyes closed, his mouth twitching in a losing fight not to smile.

"I didn't say it just because you were dying, you know. I was trying to tell you that night in Umbros."

"I know. What you said to me that night..." He looked at me, his expression solemn. "I have much to apologize for, Diem. I lost my temper. I said callous, careless things. I made you doubt how I feel about you. The fact you were still willing to fight for me through it all..." He traced the curve of my jaw. "It means more to me than you could ever know."

I leaned up and stole another kiss. "Well I do love a good fight."

His lips quirked up again. "For what it's worth, I think I've been in love with you since I tried to stop you from running into a burning building and you threatened to cut off my '*precious royal balls.*'"

I grinned proudly. "One of these days you'll stop trying to keep me out of danger."

"Unlikely," he muttered. "I've never cared for anyone the way I care for you. When I think of something happening to you, I can barely breathe. It's a constant war against my instincts to lock you up somewhere safe, where no one can ever hurt you. But a phoenix isn't meant to be caged— it's meant to fly." He let out a long sigh. "I will never stop trying to protect you, but I know I can't keep you from danger, either. All I ask is that you don't do it alone. From now on, we face it together."

"Agreed."

"You promise?"

I smiled. "I promise." My eyebrows raised. "So if you heard everything while you were unconscious... you must have heard what I said to your father."

"I did." He chuckled darkly. "And I intend to take you up on your offer for a round two."

"Much as I despise Remis, I have to admit, he never left your side. He was worried about you."

Luther was quiet for a long time. Theirs was no simple family feud. His mother's murder was a chasm they might never cross. "My father knows what you mean to me. If he wants my forgiveness, he can start to earn it by supporting you."

"He did withhold his vote to condemn my mother. I owe him a debt for that, even if it was for his own self-preservation."

"Your mother..." Luther frowned. "If Yrselle changes her vote..."

"I know. And even if she doesn't, Montios and Arboros still could. I have to go get her, Luther. Tomorrow."

He shifted his body toward me. "Let me go alone instead."

"Luther, we *just* agreed—"

"This isn't about protecting you, this is about strategy. If the Crowns see you breaking her out, they'll declare war on Lumnos. If it's only me, you can tell them I acted on my own. Declare me a traitor to save face."

I shook my head hard. "You're still wounded."

"You can heal me."

"I'm not closing your wound until every drop of toxin is gone. I won't risk trapping it inside you. Besides, in Fortos, you won't have your magic."

"You saw how our magic was returning in Ignios and Umbros. I'll make sure your mother is safe, then I'll wait until my magic returns to strike."

"And if it disappears in the middle of the attack? I just got you back from certain death, I'm not sending you right back into it with an injured body and no magic."

Muscles twitched along his jaw, sending my heart fluttering. His exasperation was so familiar, so strangely comforting. We might never stop arguing over which of our lives to put in danger, but at least we still had lives to risk.

I sighed heavily. "I can't stay behind. I need to make sure she's even still alive before I risk taking on Fortos, and only a Crown has access to see her. If—*if*—the godstone toxin is gone by tomorrow afternoon—"

"It will be."

"—and *if* your body isn't still weak—"

"It won't be." I scowled, and he smiled, taking my face in his hands and pulling me closer. "I'll be ready, my Queen."

He kissed me before I could respond, his lips and tongue moving with greedy resolve, and my protests turned fuzzy as the taste of him clouded my focus. Large, firm hands slid down the column of my throat and roamed my chest, kneading my breasts through the thin silk dress I'd thrown on after my bath. Between Luther's warmth and the heat each touch sent blazing through me, my body felt on fire, the flimsy fabric begging to be peeled away—and Luther's hands seemed more than happy to oblige.

His mouth dropped to the curve of my neck, and I lost myself in the feel of his skin against mine. Hands found their way beneath clothing—his, mine—and bodies writhed, limbs tangling impatiently.

When my own heady whimper pulled me out of my daze, my legs were wrapped around him, his powerful form blanketing me from above.

"Luther," I gasped out. "You need rest."

"I need *you*."

"You need—*ah*." My back arched as his mouth moved lower. *Much* lower.

"Months," he murmured, his voice vibrating against my skin. "Months, I have waited. Imagining what you would feel like. What you would *taste* like." He nipped at me until I sucked in a breath, then licked the sting away.

My treacherous hands abandoned me to play his game, clawing at his shoulders and weaving into his hair.

"We should stop," I insisted, unconvincing even to my own ears. "This is bad for your wounds."

"I beg to differ. The best healer in Emarion once told me skin contact with a loved one has powerful healing effects." He laid his cheek against my inner thigh and glanced up with a sinful smile. "I'm just getting the most from my medicine."

I laughed breathily and pulled at the bedsheets, trying feebly to drag myself away. "I have to get out of here," I teased. "You're sleeping alone tonight."

He growled and pinned me with his forearm. "You would abandon your patient in his time of need?"

"Fine," I said, sighing, and his eyes shone with triumph. "But if you won't rest tonight, you're resting tomorrow—"

"Deal."

"—which means I'm going to Fortos alone."

He froze. Looked up. Narrowed his eyes. "That's not happening."

He crawled forward and propped himself up above me. I held his stare, jaw set, letting him see just how serious I was. As badly as I wanted him, as deeply as I, too, craved that intimacy we'd been chasing for so long, there were things I couldn't ignore.

A slight paleness in his lips. The faintest shake in his arm when he held up his weight. The flinches he tried to hide when his hips scraped against the sheets.

He was healing—but he was not healed. And until he was, a part of me would remain that scared, devastated woman who had believed she was kissing him goodbye for the final time.

I reached up to brush his cheek, my voice turning small as my throat pulled tight. "I almost lost you. If your body relapses..."

He kissed the inside of my wrist and sank to the bed at my side. "It won't. I'll rest." He took my hand and placed it against his heart, somehow knowing its strong beat would soothe me. "But only if you stay. I'll get no sleep without you at my side."

I gave him a skeptical look. "And you'll behave?"

He smiled. "I'll behave. If you can't enjoy yourself freely tonight, neither can I."

"Soon." I leaned up to kiss his cheek, then nipped softly at his ear. "Very, *very* soon."

He let out a throaty rumble.

Begrudgingly, I pulled myself out of his arms and dragged myself to my feet. "Get comfortable while I change for bed."

I padded across the room and stoked the fire, adding a touch of Ignios flame to keep it burning throughout the night, then snuck out to the balcony. Sorae sleepily raised her head in greeting.

I knelt at her side and leaned up against her. She curled a wing around me to protect me from the brisk night air.

I took her muzzle and pressed a kiss to the top. "You saved him. You saved us all, really."

She gave a high-pitched whirr, and a wave of affection flowed across the bond.

"You were incredible up there. The Umbros gryvern had nothing on

433

you. It's too bad you weren't there when I met the Ignios gryvern. I bet you could take him, too."

Her golden eyes dimmed as she laid her head in my lap.

I frowned, feeling a flicker of her sadness. "You don't like the idea of fighting him, do you?" Smoke floated from her nostrils in a soft whimper. "Did you know him once? Are you siblings, like the Kindred were?"

Her wing shuddered against me.

"Not siblings, then. Friends?" I cocked my head. "*More* than friends?"

She arched her head to the sky and let loose a low, mournful howl so thick with emotion it brought tears to my eyes.

"Oh, Sorae," I whispered. "The Kindred separated you thousands of years ago, and you still care for him, even after all this time?"

Sorrow soaked the bond in answer. She slumped her head on the ground, her wings falling limp at her sides. I squeezed my arms around her and stroked a hand down her back.

"No wonder Tybold's so cranky. He must miss you, too." I sat up and looked at her. "He saved me in Ignios, you know. He worked around his King's orders to protect me and Luther."

Sorae's head swung out toward the balcony's edge. Her ochre gaze stared into the distance—over the trees and beyond the sea, toward a land of desert and fire.

I glared at the golden chain at her neck, the symbol of her forced servitude to my Crown. I wished there was some way I could see them reunited, but I was hardly a welcome guest in Ignios now. Even if I sent Sorae alone, the King might order his gryvern to kill her on sight.

"I'll find a way," I vowed. "You and Tybold saved me and the man I love. I don't know how, but we'll find some way to repay the favor."

She nuzzled me lightly, though it was half-hearted and full of defeat. She knew I had no power to terminate the gryvern bonds, even our own. Perhaps past Crowns had made her similar promises, and she'd learned to stop hoping for a change of fate.

Lucky for her, I was a Bellator, and a stubborn one at that. Her doubt did not dissuade me. It *fueled* me.

I dropped a kiss on her forehead and gave her a sympathetic hug, then returned to the bedchamber and walked to my wardrobe. I swung its door open, blocking myself from Luther's view.

"Sorae says you're welcome for saving your life," I called out. "But next time she would prefer you not bleed all over her pretty wings."

"Tell her I'll make it up to her with all the apples she can eat."

A trill rang out from the terrace.

"Be careful," I said dryly. "I'm not sure there are enough apples in Emarion to fulfill that promise."

I began to strip off my clothes. The key to the Umbros Queen's library fell from where I'd tucked it in my bandeau and hit the ground with a clink. *Doubt I'll ever be using that again*, I thought tartly as I snatched it up and tossed it to the back of my wardrobe.

"Also," I added, smirking to myself, "I made Sorae a promise on our behalf. She's in love with Tybold, the Ignios gryvern. We're going to reunite them."

"She... Tybold... *What?*"

I peeked around the door. "They love each other, just like us. We're going to free them so they can be together."

He threw back his head and laughed loudly. "Why am I not surprised? You've never met a person or creature you didn't want to help."

My nose wrinkled. "That's not true. There's lots of people I have no desire to help."

"No? You didn't save Vance's life from Sorae's fire back in Arboros?"

I scowled. "It doesn't count if I regret it now."

"You didn't ask us to spare all the mortals who were trying to kill you at the Guardian camp?"

"They were *mortals*."

"You didn't convince me to show mercy to the Ignios King?"

"His gryvern—"

"You saved Zalaric after he betrayed us. You're nudging me to make peace with my father. You've been *far* kinder to Aemonn than he deserves. Face it, Your Majesty. You're a good person."

"Lies," I hissed. "Take it back."

"Never." He lounged against the pillows and crossed his arms behind his head with a smug grin.

A horribly wonderful idea took root. I tucked back out of sight and peeled off the last of my lacy undergarments, then flung them over the wardrobe toward the bed. Seconds later, I grinned wide at Luther's groan.

"Problem, Prince?" I asked sweetly, leaning back just enough to reveal the outer curves of my naked body.

"This is cruel. This is *torture*."

You have no idea, Corbois, I thought wickedly.

I hid once more and dug around in the drawers until I found a garment I'd spotted weeks ago. I quickly put it on, then shook out my hair until it spilled over my shoulders. As I started to close the door, I paused, eying the medallion he'd gifted me shining from its velvet box. I clasped it around my neck and adjusted it until it hung low on my chest, resting between the curve of my breasts.

The wardrobe door closed with a loud slam.

"I'm ready to sleep," I announced.

I second guessed my evil plan as Luther's expression went blank. His soul seemed to leave his body, then return, then leave again.

"I take it back," he rasped. "You're a ruthless Queen. Savage. Merciless in all things."

I strode toward him, hips swaying and a hand raking through my hair. "Much better."

He sat up straight as I approached the bed. "You're sleeping in *that?*"

I shrugged and looked down at myself. I'd chosen the tiniest wisp of fabric in my possession. It was little more than scraps held together by strings, carefully arranged to hide as little as possible.

I toyed with the end of a strategically tied bow. "If it's a problem, I'm happy to change."

"Don't you dare," he growled.

I bit hard on my lip to hold back my grin. "You were right, skin contact can have a healing effect. And I do want you to heal..." I kneeled on the end of the bed and crawled toward him. "So I'm giving you all the *medicine* you can safely take."

He held out an arm, and I happily slipped into it, wedging myself close against his side.

"I feel better already," he murmured.

His hands began to roam. His rough touch slid eagerly over my back, my thigh, my shoulders, my ass. He hooked my thigh over his leg, sliding me over until I lay nearly on top of him.

"You swore to behave," I scolded, adjusting to avoid his wound.

"That promise was made under duress." He glowered, but there was no real protest in it. His hands were hungry yet careful, boldly pushing the bounds but always stopping short of *too far*. If Luther was anything, he was a man of his word.

"I suppose I deserve this for what I did in the Umbros inn," he said.

"I quite liked what you did in the Umbros inn." I arched my back at the memory, rolling my hips against his thigh. He closed his eyes and groaned. "And this isn't punishment. It's making sure we can do more than just *touch* for many nights to come."

His wandering hands slowed, then stopped, then curved around me and held me tight. "Many nights," he agreed. "All the nights I ever have—they all belong to you."

Our eyes met and we shared a smile, and my love for him felt as wide and deep as the Sacred Sea.

"Do you see how loved you are?" I asked. "Look at everyone who gathered at your side today. All those people who would have been crushed by your loss. You mean so much to so many people."

He tucked my hair back as his expression turned thoughtful. "It was you who brought us all together. With your support, Eleanor has become a true leader. She kept me sane while you were gone. She always stayed positive and reminded us you were too much of a fighter not to survive. She's more confident than I've ever seen her. Alixe, too—you saw in her immediately what I should have seen years ago. And my sister, standing up to Father about her betrothal and showing interest in becoming a healer. She would never have done that without your encouragement. Even Taran... if you can believe it, he's drinking less than he ever has."

I blinked. "He used to drink *more?*"

Luther smiled ruefully. "He used to say his only days well-spent were the days he was too drunk to remember. Serving you is the first time I've ever seen him take his role seriously."

His eyes dropped to the pendant at my neck. He took it in his hand, flipping it back and forth between the side marked by a phoenix, the House Corbois sigil, and the side with the Bellator initial he'd added just for me.

"You gave us something to believe in, a reason to feel like we're not in this alone," he said, "We were always related—but you made us family."

Tears filled my eyes. He wrapped me in his arms, and we kissed until our lips were swollen and our hearts were full. We confessed our fears for what was to come, murmured between words of endearment and vows of loyalty. We reveled in our tiny pocket of peace, all the while knowing how brief it might be.

After hours of kissing and laughter and apologies, our eyes and words grew too heavy to hold. With my head on his chest and my hand on his heart, we fell together into sleep.

Until now, the war had been chasing us, pulling us into its battles unwilling. Tomorrow, we would finally fight back.

Tomorrow, *our* war would begin.

PART THREE

CHAPTER

FORTY-SIX

"It's good to have you home again," Eleanor said as we walked through the palace.

"It's good to be home."

My own words took me by surprise. Did I just call the royal palace—the epicenter of the oppressive regime I'd hated all my life—my *home?*

I couldn't deny it now felt familiar. My brother was here, my friends, Luther. It would never mean to me what my family's cottage had, but life here had become comfortable. Safe.

Safer than anywhere else, at least.

But a crucial element was missing: mortals. Except for my brother, there wasn't a brown eye in sight. They were a mile away in Mortal City. Though I'd done what I could to improve conditions there, they were still suffering, still scraping to get by.

And as I strolled past opulent tapestries and art, clad in fine garments, belly full from the morning feast, I couldn't help feeling like I was letting them all down.

"I'm surprised Luther let you out of his sight," Eleanor teased. "Actually, I'm surprised you let him out of yours."

"I have a secret weapon." I grinned. "I left Lily in charge of tending his wounds. He tried to get up, and she started sobbing that she was going to fail her first task as healer. When he got back in bed to calm her down, she looked at me and *winked.*"

Eleanor burst into laughter. "I'm not surprised. Our sweet Princess has a secret wicked streak. Iléana used to lunch at the palace so she could hound Luther for attention, and Lily convinced the cooks to add their hottest peppers to all of Iléana's meals. Every afternoon, she'd start sweating and turn bright red. I don't know who was more pleased when she stopped coming—Lily or Luther." We both laughed, and Eleanor's expression turned thoughtful. "I'm glad she's following in your steps as a healer. There's so much more to Lily than anyone sees. She just needed someone to believe in her."

I nudged her. "Sounds like someone else I know." Her cheeks flushed. "How are things at court?"

"I'm finding allies for you, slowly but surely. Many of the younger Descended agree our system is unjust. Believe it or not, many respect what you did at the Challenging, trying to spare that man's life."

That was a surprise. At the time, my attempt at mercy had been met with bloodthirsty jeers—but when it came to the Descended, I was learning first impressions could be deceiving.

"Can I count on any of the Houses to support me?" I asked.

"Unfortunately, the older Descended hold the power, and they are stuck in their ways. Although..." She paused. "House Ghislaine has been quite sympathetic."

"Even after I killed Rhon Ghislaine at the Challenging?"

"They blame House Hanoverre. In fact, many of the Houses do. They never wanted to Challenge you, but Marthe Hanoverre forced their hand with threats. Now they're worried they'll pay the price for her plan going wrong."

I smirked. "Did you let them know I can be *very* forgiving to my allies?"

She grinned back. "As a matter of fact, I did." After a moment, her smile faltered. "Diem, if I may speak honestly, I have won a good deal of ground for you. But I fear if you go to Fortos—"

"—they'll no longer support a Queen who frees a rebel leader?" She cringed through her nod, and I sighed. "She's my mother, Eleanor. I can't abandon her."

"I know," she said, her voice softening. "But you should know what it might cost you."

My stomach twisted. I'd been agonizing over what it would take to get my mother out—how many lives I might have to trade for hers.

Now it seemed that was just the beginning of the price I would pay.

"Is there any chance the younger Descended will break from their

Houses to support me?"

"Normally, I would say no, but there's never been a Crown like you. Descended are drawn to power, and you've got no shortage of that."

We turned a corner and nearly collided with Alixe. She cut an imposing figure in her Royal Guard uniform, adorned with the insignia of her new status as High General. Even her myriad silver piercings had been replaced with styles in a more intimidating black.

She bowed. "Your Majesty, I was just looking for you. I hoped we could discuss the project I mentioned back in Umbros."

I nodded and embraced Eleanor. "Thank you for everything. You've planted the seed that things need changing. That's work worth doing, whatever the result."

As she left, I fell in step beside Alixe. "I'm dying to know, what is this mysterious advantage you think might help us win the war?"

She tensed, seeming hesitant to start. "The day of your father's funeral, I noticed unusual black rocks covering the ground where you... *exploded*."

Pain flashed through me at the memory of the cottage I'd unintentionally destroyed after my father's death. Another thing I'd taken from Teller. Another loss I'd have to break to my mother.

"I had a suspicion about what they were," she went on. "I gathered them all and brought them to the palace, just in case."

I stiffened. "You collected the remains of my father without telling me?"

"I apologize, Your Majesty, but it was too dangerous to leave, and at the time..." She grimaced. "You weren't much interested in speaking to me."

I couldn't deny it. In my grief, I'd unfairly accused her and Luther of scheming to get on my Crown Council. Now, such an accusation seemed inconceivable.

"What do you mean, 'too dangerous to leave'?"

"It's not just rock. It's godstone."

I stopped. "*Godstone?* At my family's home?"

She nodded. "In its raw, unmolded form. I've only read about it in books. We were told only the Kindred could make it, and the supply they left was all used up. No one thought we'd ever see any more."

"Then where did this come from?"

"From you. The rocks were only present in the places your magic touched."

I started to deny it, to claim it was impossible—but these days, that word had lost its meaning.

"In Umbros, Zalaric introduced me to a woman whose ancestors had worked with raw godstone and recorded the process. For a small fortune, she taught me the technique." Her eyes lit up. "If it works..."

I held up my palms. "Alixe, I'm not sure I'm comfortable bringing new godstone weapons into the world. Perhaps I'm a fool for it, but after what almost happened to Taran and Luther..."

She gave a wry smile. "I thought you might say that. But we could use it for shields. Nothing can pierce godstone once it's forged, so even if our enemies have godstone weapons—"

"—we could protect our own from getting hurt," I finished excitedly. "Alixe, that's brilliant."

Her chest rose proudly. "I've put the godstone in the palace armory. Would you like to come with me to test the process for the first time?"

"I'd love to. I was on my way there already to gather weapons for my trip to Fortos."

Alixe smiled as we resumed walking. "Godstone also repels magic. If this works, it will make your army difficult to beat against mortals or Descended."

Complex feelings washed through me. Though I hated the thought of using my father's ashes for tools of war, it felt fitting to know he would be with me in battle. If his sacrifice kept my loved ones protected, at least some good would come from the pain of his loss.

"There's not much of it," she said. "Do you think you can make more?"

I frowned. I didn't even know how I'd made *that*. "When I return from Fortos, I'll see what I can do," I offered.

We stepped into the corridor leading to the armory, and we both came to a halt. In the past, I'd seen one guard at the door, two at most. Now, the hallway was lined with them—including several in Emarion Army uniforms.

Alixe and I exchanged a wary look.

The Lumnos Royal Guards snapped to attention in salute. The army soldiers straightened, though it seemed more an acknowledgement of a threat than of a Queen.

As we came to the door, a guard stepped in our path. "Your Majesty. Vice General."

"Alixe is High General now," I corrected him.

His blue eyes flicked to Alixe, then back to me.

"Step aside," she said. "Her Majesty is here to visit the armory."

"I've been ordered not to let you in." He swallowed. "Either of you."

"The Challenging is over," I said. "I am the Queen. Whoever gave those orders, I overrule them."

Again his throat bobbed. "The Regent says you are not yet coronated, and until you are, he still holds the authority of the Crown."

"The Regent is mistaken," Alixe cut in. "Her Majesty has been coronated."

"His Majesty the King of Fortos says otherwise," an army soldier interrupted. "He says the coronation ritual was never completed."

I thought back on that disastrous day. We'd gone around the Kindred's Temple, each of the Crowns shedding a drop of their blood to affirm my reign—until mine had split the heartstone in half.

Wait. I stiffened. The elderly Montios King, to my left, was last in the order. He never got his chance before the Guardians unleashed their bombs.

The Fortos King was right.

I *wasn't* coronated.

Alixe stood boot-to-boot with the guard. "We don't answer to the Fortos King. This is Lumnos, and you will obey the command of your Queen."

He trembled as he raised his chin. "The Regent has ordered us to use force, if necessary."

His hand moved to the hilt of his blade. A flurry of clinking signaled the others doing the same. Shimmers of light danced across the walls as shields rose into place. Alixe's fingers curled around the handles of her shortswords.

I stepped closer to the guard. "I don't believe we've met. What's your name?"

"Werrol Corbois, Your Majesty."

"Ah. A fellow Corbois. Tell me, *cousin*, did you attend the Challenging?"

"Yes, Your Majesty, I did."

"Then you saw what I am capable of." I gave him a smile thick with false friendliness. "If I want to come in, Werrol, do you really think you can stop me?"

His face went pale. Impressively, he held his ground. "No, Your Majesty, I don't. But if I let you in, the Regent will execute me. At least here, I'll die in battle with honor, not with my head on a traitor's pike."

My mind cycled through all the ways I could do it. Tie them up with

Arboros vines. Push them back with Meros wind. Trap them behind a line of Ignios fire.

I could let loose to make a point. Leave them humiliated—or worse.

But as fierce as my temper was, it had nothing on the ruthlessness of Remis and the Fortos King. If I embarrassed them, they'd take out their wounded pride on these guards.

And as much as I shouldn't care one bit whether these Descended lived or died... *godsdamnit*, I did.

My jaw clenched hard enough to snap.

"Where is the Regent?" I demanded.

The guard slumped with palpable relief. "A meeting in the reception rooms, Your Majesty."

I spun on my heel, storming back down the hall with Alixe close behind. As we passed a clump of Emarion Army soldiers, they snickered at each other and grinned.

I flicked my wrist.

Light exploded around me. Glowing tendrils speared through the soldiers' shields as easily as paper, looping around their ankles and tossing them on their backs. The cords pulled taut as I walked away, tugging them behind me in a shouting, struggling heap.

"Take this as a warning," I shouted over my shoulder. "My mercy has its limits."

I let them drag a little longer before a twitch of my fingers dissolved my magic to mist.

I raised an eyebrow at Alixe. "Too much?"

"Arguably, not enough," she said. "Mercy isn't a familiar concept here. They're going to think Remis has something over you."

I sighed. "He does. He's right about the coronation. The Guardians attacked before it was complete."

She glowered. "If you were any other Crown, it wouldn't matter. The other realms have no Challenging, so the new Crown reigns from the moment they're selected. The coronation is just a formality to renew the Forging sp—" Her eyes went wide. "*That's* why our magic kept coming back. The Forging spell enforces the borders. If the rituals aren't done promptly, it begins to break down."

"That would explain why it's getting worse over time," I agreed.

"At least this means they'll have to complete your coronation soon."

I smiled grimly. "Unless they plan to kill me and coronate my successor instead."

CHAPTER
FORTY-SEVEN

I t was easy enough to spot the room where Remis was meeting—a pack of twenty Royal Guards lined the corridor on both sides.

And the white rose insignia on half their uniforms told me exactly who he was meeting with.

One stepped forward with a hand raised to stop me. This time, I had no interest in wasting my breath. I flung out a web of shadows that tangled around the guards and trapped them in place.

My magic pulsed outward with enough force to slam open the heavy wooden door. Inside, Remis was seated with Aemonn and Aemonn's father, Garath. Across from them, Marthe, the elderly matriarch of House Hanoverre, sat with her grandchildren, Jean and Iléana.

"Look at this," I crooned. "A meeting of my most loyal subjects."

"Just when I didn't think this day could get any worse," Garath muttered.

Aemonn—and Aemonn alone—stood. "Your Majesty," he said, nodding.

Iléana snorted, glancing smugly at her brother Jean. "She's not *really* Queen, Aemonn. You can stop kissing her ass."

My focus locked on Remis. "I'd like a word."

"I'm afraid it will have to wait. This meeting is very important." His eyes flared, his expression trying to convey a silent plea to *behave*.

I flopped into a chair and crossed my legs. "Well, then. If it's such an important meeting, surely the Queen should attend."

"The *Crown* should attend," Marthe said smoothly. "And Remis is already here."

"I think my gryvern would beg to differ." I shot her a cloying smile. "Would you like to meet her?"

Her face soured and turned to Remis. "First you accuse my grandson of a revolting falsehood, now you bring her here to threaten us? If this is how you intend to make amends, Remis—"

"You should be making amends," I snapped. "What you did at the Challenging was a shot at me and at House Corbois. A shot you *missed*."

"A mistake we won't make twice," Jean said under his breath.

Marthe hunched forward on her cane, her forehead creasing as her peppery eyebrows rose. "We're not the only ones who took a shot, were we? Even House Corbois didn't deem you worthy." She clicked her tongue. "Challenged by your own House. A first in Lumnos history."

"I knew Luther would eventually see what you were," Iléana said. She leapt to her feet. "I heard he's back. Where is he? I want to see him."

I rolled my eyes. "I assure you, the feeling *isn't* mutual."

She stalked toward me with a poisonous glare. Alixe moved to block her, but I waved her off, giving Iléana a tired, unbothered stare.

"You think because you forced him to kiss you at the Challenging that you've won him?" she said archly. "He and I have something deeper than you could ever understand."

"Don't let me stand in the way of true love." I swept my arm toward the door. "You'll find him in my bed. I should warn you though, he's exhausted." I bit my lip. "He and I had a long, *busy* night."

I could almost see the steam shooting from her ears.

"How dare you?" she shrieked. "Does he know you're secretly engaged to a mortal?"

I shot a glare at Aemonn. His guilty look confirmed he'd been the one to leak my secret.

"I've been loyal to him for years," Iléana moaned. "You half-breeds know nothing of loyalty. You're just like the mortal whores, spreading your legs for any Descended man you see."

My fists clenched.

Alixe jumped forward to nudge her friend away.

"Marthe," Remis said with a sigh, "I can only control her so much. Step in, or this is not going to end well for your granddaughter."

"He only wants you for the Crown," Iléana shouted over Alixe's shoulder. "Once you're gone, he'll lose interest and come right back to me."

I cocked my head. "It must be difficult to watch him choose someone else. I might pity you, if I didn't know how you treated him all those years. How you told him his scars made him unworthy to be King." I thumbed a dagger I'd strapped to my hip. "Perhaps I should give you some scars of your own. Then you can see firsthand just how powerful they can be."

"*Marthe*," Remis warned.

Marthe pushed to her feet, bones creaking, then shuffled forward to take Iléana's hand. "Come, child. Let's not waste our time on a half-breed who consorts with rebel scum."

The breath punched from my lungs as a gruesome memory flashed into my head of my father's blood scrawled across the walls of our home.

Mortal lover.

Half-breed.

Rebel scum.

The grief of his loss came tumbling down on my head. Suddenly I was right back in that kitchen, kneeling at his body, his warm blood soaking into my clothes. I smelled the death in the air, felt his too-stiff body beneath my hands.

It had been so long since I'd had one of these days, where the sorrow felt so fresh and so inescapably permanent. Days where I couldn't stand to do much more than lay down and cry. It had been so long, I'd begun to convince myself that I had healed.

But this kind of grief didn't heal.

It *waited*.

The world spun around me as I gripped the seat of my chair. I fought to catch my breath amid the pounding in my ears.

As the Hanoverres filed out, Jean stopped in front of me and leaned down until his face was near my ear. "Can't wait to meet my long-lost son," he whispered. "Tell little Zalaric I'm looking forward to our reunion."

Everything stilled.

"You?" I rasped. "You're...?"

He winked, laughing darkly, and followed his family out the door.

My eyes squeezed shut, though it did nothing to stop the visions of my father's corpse. My godhood slammed against my ribs, roaring to *unleash* the way it had that day, and my skin began to glow with a silvery light.

Guilt. Rage. Fear. Hate.

Cycling in a vicious, relentless loop.

"Diem," Alixe said quietly, "are you alright?"

My heart was racing, my magic snarling. I focused on breathing—focused on keeping control. Focused on not reducing this entire palace to rubble.

"Do you know how hard we've been working to repair things with House Hanoverre?" Garath yelled. "You just arrived, and you've already managed to ruin it all."

My nails dug into the wood of my chair as I fought to keep control. "You told them about Zalaric?" I snapped at Remis.

He eyed me, subtly backing away. "It's better they hear it from us directly. If they found out through court gossip, there would be no hope for a truce."

"That's a decision I should have been included in. I'm the Queen."

"Not yet," Garath sniped. "Right now, you're just a stupid girl with a Crown."

My temper exploded—and so did my magic.

A crisp bite chilled the air as dark magic surged and coated every surface. Shadowy tendrils scaled up legs and twined around waists, their thorny vines encircling each man's throat. The unfurling darkness choked out the sun trickling in through the window, and the room turned an inky black. Only the light from my glowing skin remained.

A vengeful moon and her violent night.

"There's a bit more to me than just a Crown," I growled, rising to my feet.

Garath's lip curled back in a jeer, but before he could speak, the dark fronds stretched over his mouth and nose.

"Watch yourself, Garath," I warned. "Unlike your usual victims, I fight back."

I spared a brief glance at Aemonn, who was gaping at his father with a dumbstruck expression—though the corner of his mouth was the tiniest hint upturned.

Garath's face reddened amid his fight for air. His hand jerked against my hold, and because I'd used up all my good judgment and restraint last night with Luther, I smirked and let his arm go.

His palm thrust toward me in a burst of bubbling, white-hot light. I quickly flicked a shield around Alixe, but I held Garath's stare as I left myself exposed. His magic sizzled across my skin—then absorbed and disappeared.

His eyes bulged wide.

My smile spread wider. "Come on, Garath. You can do better than that."

"Perhaps we should speak in private," Remis rushed out. He tugged loose from my shadows—only because I allowed it—and positioned himself in front of his brother with hands raised. "This has escalated far enough."

"What do you think?" I called out to Garath over Remis's shoulder. "Have you had enough?"

Sadly, I didn't think he could hear me, as his eyes were rolling back, his lips a sickly blue. I grudgingly swished a hand, and my magic receded. Garath fell to the floor with a thud.

Remis shot a look at Aemonn, who jumped forward to drag his father toward the door. I turned to Alixe and lowered my voice. "Warn Zalaric and the others. I'll find you when we're done."

She nodded to me, then to Remis, then left and closed the door at her back.

Remis sighed wearily. "You should not provoke my brother. Garath is a dangerous man."

"And I am a dangerous woman."

"I'm not sure you realize just how dangerous you are. Is this your plan as Queen, use your magic to threaten everyone you dislike?"

"I'll do more than threaten," I shot back, though Remis's criticism had struck deeper than I wanted to admit.

My father's final words to me had been a similar condemnation of my temper and a lack of faith in how I chose to reign. His disappointed tone rang in my ears with each and every failure, an immortal reminder that I was still letting him down.

And if he could see me now, he would be anything but proud.

The painful thought was water on the fire of my anger. I sank back into my chair with a slump.

Remis sat and studied me carefully. "I want to thank you for saving my son. For that, I am in your debt."

"And this is how you repay me? By usurping my throne?"

"The Fortos King claims the ritual was not completed." His eyebrows rose. "Do you deny it?"

I worked my jaw, not answering.

"He also said the Crowns had some... *concerns* about your legitimacy."

I pulled the Crown into view atop my head. "Is this not legitimate?"

Remis's head angled as he frowned at it.

I speared a thought over the bond, and seconds later, Sorae's piercing howl floated through the window. "What about that—is Sorae legitimate enough?"

His attention returned to me. "There is also the question of your involvement with the Guardians. The Crowns believe you planned the attack."

"I knew nothing before it happened. I was as surprised as anyone else."

"And yet the Guardians rescued you."

"The Guardians *kidnapped* me. They chained me up as a prisoner."

"You returned in a ballgown and lipstick," he drawled. "A strange kidnapping, indeed."

"That was from Umbros."

"You were in Umbros?"

"Yes. The Guardians chased us into Ignios, and then—"

"You were in *Ignios?*" He sat forward. "Do those Crowns know you were in their realms?"

"Yes. Both."

"And they didn't kill you for it?"

"They certainly tried their best."

He pinched the bridge of his nose. "Must you make enemies everywhere you go?"

I crossed my arms. "And what have you done while I was gone, Remis? Have you found my father's killer?"

"I've had my hands full with other things."

"So you've found homes for all of Lumnos's orphans? Made sure no one goes hungry in Mortal City? Repealed all the laws treating mortals differently than Descended?"

He glowered. "No, I have not."

"Then tell me, other than conspire with Fortos to flood the realm with army soldiers, what exactly have you done?"

"I've been trying to prevent a war," he shouted, his composure finally fracturing. "Can you imagine what the Twenty Houses demanded after the attack? The Hanoverres wanted to burn Mortal City with everyone in it." He slammed a fist on the arm of his chair. "And I'm the one who stopped it."

We glared at each other in silence, each of us simmering in righteous indignation.

His anger broke first with a long sigh. "Those soldiers are here to keep peace, Diem. Believe it or not, I do not wish to see any mortals slaughtered."

I balked. "You don't?"

"The other Houses wouldn't either, if they weren't so blinded by their prejudice." His voice turned irritable. "Please, you think any *Hanoverre* is going to cook their own food, clean their own clothes, and wash their own floors? Our realm needs those mortals to function."

My surprise turned to scorn. "They're human beings, Remis, not cheap labor."

"Regardless, I'm trying to keep them alive. My orders have not been popular. If the Twenty Houses discover I have no magic to enforce the laws, those soldiers will be the only thing stopping House Hanoverre from taking this realm by force."

"Why should I believe you? Don't think I've forgotten the threats you made before the Challenging."

He rubbed a hand over his jaw. "I confess, I said some... regrettable things. At the time, you couldn't use your magic, and a Challenge seemed inevitable. I did not expect you to survive it."

It was hard to fault him for that—even I hadn't expected to survive it.

"Until things calm down, this is for the best," he went on. "If you are not in power, the Crowns and the Twenty Houses may stay their hand. And with war looming, the realm needs a strong leader."

I arched a brow. "And I am not?"

A withering stare was his only response.

The reproach in his eyes was too much like my own father's, and my gaze dropped to my lap.

"I could force you," I said quietly, my words proclaiming a confidence I no longer felt. "I could make you step down. Or kill you, if you refuse."

"You could," he agreed. "The army would invade, the Houses would revolt. You could start a civil war. Are you willing to get that much blood on your hands to seize power?"

A lump stuck in my throat. Remis knew *all* my weaknesses, apparently. And now he was expertly wielding them against me.

"It's only temporary," he soothed, eyes crinkling with barely suppressed triumph. "Just until the Crowns agree to complete the coronation ritual. If you stay out of trouble, they may withdraw their objections when the war is over."

I almost laughed. If he thought I was causing trouble *now*, he would be apoplectic at what else I had planned.

But I did have one thing working in my favor. If Alixe's theory was right, delaying my coronation much longer would break down the realm borders and wreak havoc across the continent.

I rose and paced the room. "I'll go along with this charade and let you play King, but only on two conditions."

"I'm listening."

"Make Alixe your High General. She's more qualified than Aemonn, and her loyalty is to the realm, not either of us. I've told her you're right about the coronation. She'll respect your authority until it's complete."

His eyes narrowed. "I thought Luther was your High General."

"He was. He's not anymore."

His chin lifted, his interest clearly piqued. "And your other condition?"

"Suspend the progeny laws and make no move against the mortals."

"The Twenty Houses will put up a fight."

"Then *fight back*." I fixed him with a hard glare. "This is non-negotiable, Remis. If anyone hurts the mortals or the half-mortals, you *will* have a civil war on your hands, and I promise you, that's blood I have no problem spilling."

He stood as well, pacing as he quietly pondered. It felt largely for show —he wanted power too much to turn me down.

"I accept," he said finally, "but without my magic, I cannot make another bonded bargain."

"Oh, I don't need a magical bond to hold you to your word." I smiled. "I can do that all on my own."

I strode to the door to leave. As my hand closed around the latch, I paused.

"I hope you realize I'm doing this for Luther," I called out over my shoulder. "Because I love him. And no matter how awful you've been to him, I don't want to be the reason he goes to war with his father."

A shadow passed over Remis's face. When he spoke, his voice sounded sad, almost regretful.

"I am not your enemy, Diem," he said quietly. "Nor my son's. If only you both could overlook your tempers long enough to see it."

I fought off a pang of sympathy with all the reasons I had to despise Remis: The scar on Luther's body. The mother he never got to know. The emotions he was forced to hide.

"Enjoy the throne while you can, Remis." I tapped my temple. "Just don't forget who wears the Crown."

CHAPTER

FORTY-EIGHT

M y feet felt leaden as I trudged through the palace back to my chambers. On the road, I'd been so eager to get home and start my reign, help the mortals, and protect the people I loved.

Well, I'd been here barely more than a day, and somehow I'd lost my throne, the mortals were under siege, and the people close to me were more at risk than ever.

I had one more task to complete before leaving for Fortos, and it was the one I'd been dreading most.

My ears perked at the sound of shouting coming from my suite.

"I'm going to kill him."

"You should be in bed!"

"Cousin, stop—"

"Get your hands off me."

"Your wounds—"

"You promised Diem!"

"*Where is she?*"

I broke into a sprint, flying past the guards posted at my door—but not before noting that a pack of army soldiers had newly joined them.

In the parlor, Luther was red-faced and glaring. Taran and Alixe were planted in front of him, Taran's hands on his chest, while Lily and Eleanor tugged frantically at his arms and Teller and Zalaric watched with amusement.

"What's going on?" I asked.

Luther's eyes snapped to me. A chorus of groans and cries of *thank the Kindred* rose from the others as they all sagged with relief.

He scoured my body. "Did my father attack you like Garath? Did Aemonn?" Swirls of hissing shadows coated his clenched fists. "Where are they? I'll put an end to all three of them right now."

"I told them what happened," Alixe explained. She shot Luther a stern look. "I also told them you had it under control."

"He's trying to steal your Crown," Luther snarled. "It's traitorous. It's *blasphemous*. Blessed Mother Lumnos chose you, not him."

I walked over and set a hand on his arm, but even that didn't calm him. His glare lingered on the door, violence smoldering in his eyes.

"You're supposed to be resting."

"I've rested enough. I should have been there. Garath is a dead man when I find him."

"To be fair, I attacked him first."

"I can't believe I missed it," Taran groaned. "Tell me everything. Every tiny detail. Did you hurt him? Was he embarrassed? Did he piss his pants? Ohmygods, did he *cry?*"

I grinned, an idea striking. My godhood stirred to life as I wooed it into doing something I'd never tried before.

I speared a thought into Taran's mind: *Do you want to see it?*

His eyes went wide as he realized what I'd done. He nodded excitedly.

My mind swirled around the memory of what had just occurred. I opened my thoughts and let Taran take my place as the images played out in my head.

He let out a dramatic, breathy moan. The others stared at the two of us in confusion. "This is the greatest gift you could ever give me. This is better than drinking. This is better than *sex.*"

"I'm taking that personally," Zalaric muttered.

I was so enjoying Taran's bliss, I let the memory expand, showing him how I'd taunted the Hanoverres.

He barked a laugh, then stilled. His joy abruptly dropped away. "Oh, Queenie," he said softly. "Your father..." He looked at Zalaric and blinked. "And *your* father. Fortos's balls."

I yanked back my magic in a panic. I hadn't intended to let him see *that* deep.

"What about our father?" Teller demanded.

"Nothing," I rushed out.

His eyes narrowed. "More secrets?"

"No! It's not... Tel, I just—"

He shook his head and turned away.

"Show me," Luther insisted, shrewdly picking up on what I'd done with Taran. "I want to see exactly what my father needs to answer for."

He reached for me, and I jerked back. Guilt gnawed at me for the surprise that flashed across his face, but my slip to Taran had left me feeling defensive and overexposed. The shame over my father's disappointment was a part of me I wasn't ready to share—not even with Luther.

I routed around the group and grabbed a cloak from my wardrobe as I strode toward the balcony. I tucked the Crown out of sight. "I'll be back in an hour. No one die while I'm gone."

Luther followed. "I'm coming with you."

"No, you're not."

"I'm rested. The toxin's gone."

"Not here, Luther. Not to this."

"We agreed to do these things togeth—"

I whipped around. "I'm going to see Henri."

A cloud of turbulent emotions briefly darkened his face before he shut it away behind a cold, indifferent veneer.

"Once we break my mother out, things could get worse for the Guardians," I said. "I have to warn him. I owe him that much."

He watched me in silence, his jaw flexing.

"And... he and I need closure. I owe him that, too."

In Luther's eyes, I saw all the protests he held back, all the arguments he wouldn't let himself make. Much as it bothered him, this was one area he knew to stay out of, and I loved him all the more for it.

I kissed his cheek and slipped my hand beneath his tunic to lay flat against his hip. My magic surged through his skin and scoured his wound, probing for any trace of the godstone's presence. When it came up empty, an unexpected sob caught in my throat.

Luther sighed, his hand pressing to the hollow of my back to draw me closer. He gave a soft grunt of pleasure as the wound mended and finally closed. His godhood happily entwined with mine, their combined joy so pure that I couldn't resist lingering a moment in his arms.

"Gather what we need," I said. "When I return, we'll leave for Fortos."

"Be careful. And don't..." His hand flexed. "Just be careful."

Grudgingly, I pulled away and headed for the balcony, where Alixe was waiting for me at Sorae's side.

"Let me come," she said. "Or Zalaric. Someone who can hide you, if things go wrong."

"I'm not hiding. I want the mortals to see me. The army, too. I want them both to know I'm not afraid." Sorae snorted a puff of smoke in agreement and lowered to let me mount. "Besides, it's better if we keep our distance now. You're Remis's new High General."

She balked. "I am?"

I smiled. "Even Remis knows you're the woman for the job."

"Is this a good idea? If he orders me to betray you..."

"Then do it. Stay in his favor, and use that to keep everyone safe. When this is over, I won't hold any of it against you." I paused for a moment. "He swore to me he won't harm the mortals, but if he goes back on his word..."

"I won't let that happen," she vowed.

"Good." I thumped a fist to my chest in salute, and so did she. "I trust you, Alixe. Do what you believe is best for the realm, whatever that may be."

I threw a final look to Luther, who watched in solemn silence as he leaned against an arch. Sorae launched into the air, and we left the palace behind.

FROM THE MOMENT Sorae soared above my run-down village, every eye was on us—including every soldier's. They followed my path, gaining in number until an unnervingly large group gathered to await my arrival.

I wanted to be *seen*, but this was looking more like a confrontation.

Sorae banked toward the forest, and I led her to the ground in a clearing near my old home.

"Keep them distracted," I told her as I slid off. "I'll call you when I'm ready."

She nuzzled my hand and huffed.

"Yes, I promise I'll also call if anyone needs a good roasting. Go, before they see I'm not with you."

She trilled softly, then leapt toward the sky at breathtaking speed. Her wings flattened out, angling to conceal the spot where a rider would sit.

I grinned up at her silhouette. "Clever girl."

Her answering howl rumbled across the forest.

The sound of approaching bootsteps sent me scurrying up the nearest tree just as soldiers flooded the clearing. I carefully searched their eyes, spying various colors, none of them brown.

Descended, all.

Even their search tactics reeked of their privileged upbringing. With the trees bare for the winter, I was plainly visible among the branches. Any mortal would have looked there first, but these soldiers barely lifted their eyes above the ground.

They'd been raised in mansions, their childhoods filled with tutors and toys. As adults, hunts were structured affairs for social leisure, their prey hobbled in advance to make for an easy kill on the ground. Even as soldiers, they traveled on roads and slept in inns, not in the rough of the Emarion wilds. Climbing a tree to stalk prey or gather fruit—or, Kindred forbid, just to play—was a concept their pampered minds simply couldn't fathom.

A wise man would have sent *some* mortal soldiers to guard a mortal town, and I'd heard enough from my father to know the Fortos King was a bastard, but he was no fool.

So why hadn't he?

"This must be where the gryvern landed."

"I hear it—it's back up there in the clouds."

"Is the Queen still on its back?"

"I'm not sure. Wait... yes, I think I see her."

"Follow it. Don't let the Queen out of your sight."

The soldiers sprinted off in pursuit, and I barely held in my laugh until they were gone. I shimmied down the tree, tugged my hood low, and set off into town.

The streets of Mortal City were packed, many with faces upturned to watch my gryvern doing circuits in the sky. As I ducked my head and wove through the throng, morsels of various conversations floated to my ears.

"Her fault these soldiers are here. Maybe if they catch her, they'll leave."

"I thought they put her in prison with her mother."

"That's why she never had friends. We always knew she wasn't really one of us."

"She hasn't been here once since the Challenging. She's already forgotten us."

"Is it true her whole family are Guardians?"

"*Hush.* Don't mention the rebels out loud. My neighbor did it once, and he hasn't been seen since."

I gritted my teeth. So many lies and misconceptions. So many faces I'd once treated as patients, now all too happy to treat me like a villain.

The belief that I'd abandoned them was most troubling of all. Before I left, I'd make my presence—and my intentions—known to them all.

But first, I had business to finish.

I veered into a quiet alley, following a series of turns my feet knew by heart. When I made the final left, the street lit with the amber glow of firelight through a white-paned window.

A raucous laugh echoed from inside and squeezed around my heart. Even if I hadn't been standing outside the post office he ran, I'd know it instantly as Henri's father.

This place had been like a second home. Henri and I had chased each other around its bins of boxes and letters before we were even old enough to read the writing on their labels. His family home was in the back, and we'd spent countless nights on its creaky wooden porch trading fantastical stories of the adventures we'd have together one day.

Not once had we ever imagined *this*.

I walked toward the post office door when murmurs caught my ear. A low, honeyed voice, then a giggle.

I craned my neck, and my heart leapt into my throat. Barely visible around the corner, a mop of ash-brown hair fluttered in the winter wind.

Henri.

I felt more on edge, more desperate to run, than in any combat I'd ever faced. Sword-wielding enemies, I could handle. Battle and blood were where I thrived most. But love and heartbreak? That's what I truly feared.

My breath came shallow as I crept along the building's side. Henri's hair wavered again—and I froze.

It wasn't the wind that had jostled it. It was a hand—a distinctly feminine hand, tangled in his unkempt curls.

Then came the unmissable sound of *kissing*. Deep, impassioned kissing, with its smacks and muffled moans. Another hand appeared on his back, clutching at the fabric of his shirt.

My feet moved forward, drawn more by habit than conscious thought. The wooden overhang came into view—and with it, two intertwined bodies. I knew Henri's instantly, but the other...

Petite and slender. Skin so porcelain it might never have seen the sun. Gold curls stretching down her back, neatly tied with a mint green ribbon.

Their kiss broke apart. Henri gazed down at her with his impish, lopsided grin, the one I'd looked at nearly every day I could remember.

She looked down, whispering something followed by a pretty tinkling bell of a laugh. He poked her in the side—

Then I saw the apron.

An apron I'd clung to, as a toddler. An apron I'd longed for, as a young girl. An apron I'd earned, as a grown woman.

A healer's apron.

I laughed.

I laughed.

It burst out without warning—abrupt, but loud.

Too loud.

Loud enough that two heads swung my way, two pairs of brown eyes flaring in matching shock.

I couldn't help it—I laughed again. I wasn't angry or jealous. I was *relieved*.

"Diem," Lana gasped, yanking violently out of Henri's grasp. "I mean, um, Your Majesty." She curtsied, her gaze falling to the floor.

"Hello, Lana," I said. "I told you before, you can call me Diem. After all, we've worked together for *so many* years at the healer's center."

Fine, perhaps I was a little bit angry.

Lana's face flushed fiery red.

Henri's surprise twisted into a scornful glare. "You've got some nerve giving her a hard time, after what you did."

"I guess that means Vance is back in town," I drawled. "How's his arm?"

"Gone," Henri snapped. "How's your new lover's godstone wound?"

"Healed." I smiled tightly. "A miracle from the gods."

Henri spat at his feet.

"Diem, I'm so sorry," Lana pleaded. "We wanted to tell you, but you were out of town."

"*Out of town?* I was drugged and chained up as a prisoner. Tell me, Lana, did you know about that plan too, or was it only my betrothed who kept it from me?"

Her eyes widened. Henri's narrowed.

"Don't apologize to her, Lana. We didn't do anything wrong."

"*Henri,*" she hissed. "You know that isn't true. We agreed to be honest when she came back."

He clenched his jaw and looked away.

Lana stepped off the porch, tentatively approaching me as she chewed on her lip so hard I thought it might bleed.

"I'm glad you're safe," she said. "And I'm sorry you had to find out about us this way. Things weren't handled as they should have been." Her eyebrows slowly rose. "Perhaps that's true on *both* sides. Still, I'm sorry for my part in it. I never wanted to hurt you." She took a deep breath, her shoulders straightening. "But Henri is mine. I may not be a Queen like you, but I care about him, and... and..." She swallowed. "And you can't have him."

I fought to school my stunned reaction. My eyes darted to Henri, who was looking at her warmly, clearly proud of her courage. It reminded me so much of how Luther looked at me.

"I, um... I appreciate your honesty, Lana," I said. "I wish you both the best. I won't get in your way."

She whooshed out an enormous breath.

"I would appreciate a chance to talk to Henri alone, though. One last time."

Lana looked back at Henri. He sighed and nodded, raking a hand through his hair. He reached out for her, and as she joined him, he tugged her hard and wrapped her in a showy, passionate kiss.

I averted my eyes, a strange discomfort in my chest. Even though I was genuinely grateful to see Henri find someone who truly cared for him, a part of me would always think of him as *my* Henri, the boy that young Diem thought she'd have forever at her side.

But he wasn't that boy anymore, and I wasn't that girl.

"She's a good fit for you," I said after Lana left. "She's the kind of woman I always thought you'd choose. Sweet. Sensible. Easy to get along with." I smiled grimly. "All the things I'm not."

He leaned a shoulder against the post of his porch, staring off into the distance with a glare.

"When did it start?" I asked.

"When did you and that Descended Prince start?" he shot back.

"The day of the Challenging. I came here to end our engagement the night before." Henri snorted, and my temper spiked. "I felt so guilty that night. Little did I know you were in Arboros, planning to blow me up with bombs."

He crossed his arms, saying nothing.

"I could have died, Henri."

"We were careful. We made sure you weren't hurt."

"I meant the Challenging. Do you understand how close I came to not surviving it? And you, my best friend, the man who was supposed to love me—you couldn't even be bothered to stay in the realm."

His jaw worked. "You're the best fighter I know. I knew you'd be fine."

"*Well I didn't!*" I shouted. "When I came to see you that night, I thought it was goodbye, Henri. Not just for our relationship. Forever."

His anger faltered for a moment, but when his eyes dropped to the pendant at my neck, his glare returned.

"I was fighting for the mortals. That requires sacrifice—not that you would know anything about that while you sit in your palace with your shiny gold jewelry."

My hand closed around it defensively.

"We used to make fun of the Descended, and now look at you," he said. "Wearing their clothes, living in their city. You've barely stepped foot in Mortal City since it happened. Admit it Diem, you *love* being one of them." He made a guttural, disgusted noise. "I don't even recognize you anymore."

Every word felt like a stab, every angry curl of his lip a new gaping wound.

There was too much truth mixed in his words. Part of me *did* thrill at being Queen. At being powerful and having control, at wearing pretty things and making strong men kneel. Perhaps it was because I'd grown up with none of it, or perhaps I'd been told one too many times I was special, and like a spoiled child, I'd begun to believe it.

And to have that worst, most pitiful part of me pointed out so plainly by the man who had known me best...

I looked down, fighting the burning in my throat. "You didn't answer my question. When did you and Lana start? After the Challenging or before?"

He was silent for a very long time.

"You were never around," he said finally, his voice quiet. "You were pushing me away. I thought you were avoiding me because you were too scared to tell me you didn't really want to marry me. And you were—"

"—a Descended?" I finished for him. "Look me in the eye and tell me your feelings for me didn't change the second you found out what I was."

He shuffled his feet, looking down. "Yeah. Maybe. But I did love you, Diem. I really, truly did." He glanced up. "Did you *ever* love me?"

I stiffened. "I... I care deeply for you, Henri. I always will. And... yes—yes, of course I loved you, but..."

"As a friend," he said. "Only ever as a friend."

I winced, unable to deny it.

His face turned terribly, heartbreakingly sad. "I wanted to marry you. I wanted to start a family with you."

"I tried to want that, too. I just don't think I'm that kind of person."

"Are you going to be that kind of person with *him?*"

I couldn't answer. That same question haunted my own thoughts.

Henri laughed harshly. "Well, make sure you warn him so he doesn't waste his life pining for a woman who will never fully give herself away. Give him the courtesy you never gave me, and let him leave before you break his heart, too."

My hand squeezed around the necklace Luther had given me. A burst of heat spread where my skin brushed the glowing ruby he'd imbued with a spark of his magic. My godhood stirred in recognition, as if sensing his presence nearby.

It should have calmed me. Instead, it planted a seed of fear.

"I hate them," Henri murmured. His hands were white-knuckled and fisted, his body quaking. "First the Descended took my mother, now they're taking you."

"We can still be friends, Henri. I'm not dead."

"You might as well be dead to me."

It was more painful a blow than the knife I'd taken in Ignios. I flinched and wrapped my arms around myself as tears slid down my cheeks.

"How can you so easily throw me away?" I whispered.

"You already threw me away." There was hurt in his voice too, buried deep beneath the anger. "You went off to Lumnos City with all your new Descended friends, and you forgot that I existed."

"You know that's not true. I *begged* you not to give up on me. I risked my life to convince you I was loyal. And then my father died, and you were nowhere. My world was collapsing, and I was alone." My words choked between my sobs. "I was so fucking lost, Henri. I needed you. You can't imagine how badly I needed you."

His anger seemed to deflate at the sight of my tears. He took a step, his hand twitching in my direction, then stopped himself. "I know. I should have been there." He took a slow breath and scraped his hand down his face. "But I did try to come see you. You threw me in the dungeon, remember?"

"You came there to kill Descended. Not for me."

His face hardened. "And if you had let me, maybe Mortal City wouldn't be overrun with soldiers. Do you know how many mortals have gone missing since they arrived? It's not even Guardians—they're choosing people at random to keep everyone on edge."

I swore and wiped at my cheeks, desperately scrabbling to pull some strength back into my bones. "I didn't know. They found a way to keep me off the throne, but I'll do what I can to stop them."

"Isn't the Crown supposed to be the strongest Descended? Why not just kill anyone who tries to stop you?"

"I'm not Vance. I don't solve every problem with murder."

He scoffed. "You had no problem murdering mortals in Arboros. Vance told me everything before he left here for Montios."

"Everything?" I snapped. "Like how he held me down and sliced my wrists open? How I saved his life by sending my gryvern away? How I tried to escape to save my mother, but he and his men chased me down and nearly killed me?"

Uncertainty surfaced on his features. The small part of him that still trusted me was wrestling with whatever lies Vance had fed him.

"Vance is not a good man, Henri. All he cares about is hate and violence. I know you—you're a better man than that."

His eyes shadowed. "Maybe I'm not anymore. Maybe hate and violence are all I have left."

I walked toward him, my heart aching at the way he bristled. Slowly, tentatively, I reached for his hand. He went rigid at my touch, but as I laid my other hand on his, tension loosened from his shoulders.

"I would never ask you to leave the Guardians," I said. "I know how much you want justice for the mortals, and so do I. But I am begging you, Henri—don't follow Vance. His brand of hate will destroy you, and I care about you too much to see that happen."

He stared at our joined hands with a deep frown. "Vance is our leader."

"My mother is your leader."

"Your mother's in prison. She can't lead us from there."

"That's why I'm breaking her out."

His head snapped up. "You are?"

I nodded. "Today. But when I do, things could get worse here. The Regent's new High General is a friend—she promised to help the mortals, but the army doesn't answer to her, and there's no telling what they'll do."

He perked up with sudden excitement. "I'll warn the others. We'll be ready. Whatever happens, it's worth it—the Guardians need Auralie back. Without her, everything has fallen apart. The cells are fractured, no one can agree on what we should do. She kept us united. Under her, we were strong."

His face glowed as he gushed over my mother's leadership. The way he spoke about her with such admiration sparked a light in him I thought had died forever.

"With Auralie, we really might win this war. When Vance told me she had gone to the island, I—"

He froze. Stiffened.

It took me a moment to realize why.

"You knew," I breathed, understanding dawning. "This whole time, you knew where she was."

He pulled his hand free and edged away. "You weren't a Guardian then. You know the rules. I couldn't say anything."

My godhood raised its mighty head, sensing a brewing storm.

"I cried in your arms for *months*."

"I told you the Old Gods had showed me she was alive. I thought it would give you hope."

"Hope?" I shouted. "*Hope?*"

My temper flared sun-bright. I wanted to rage at his deceit—but the memory of Teller's voice, thick with scorn over my similar betrayal, still played in my ears.

My skin lit with a glittering radiance, light and shadow rising to my palms. In the sky, Sorae let out a piercing snarl.

Henri's face went pale.

"Tell the Guardians the blood Vance stole from me won't work," I growled. "And if they attack the palace again, I'll kill them myself."

"Diem—"

"I wish you and Lana happiness. I hope she gives you everything I couldn't."

His expression shuttered. He shoved his hands in his pockets and tightened his jaw. "I hope he does for you, too."

"I'll see you on the battlefield, Henri. I pray we'll still be fighting on the same side."

I turned and walked away, feeling like a cave was collapsing at my back. Every step was a falling boulder, cutting off that path forever and obliterating the treasured moments we'd never share again.

My best friend, my lover, my betrothed.

And soon, perhaps, if the gods were cruel—my enemy.

Heartbreak and anger mixed with bittersweet relief, turning me into a volatile emotional cauldron. I poured it all into my godhood, who ate it up like wind to a wildfire.

Magic leaked into the air around me. Streams of light formed a whirling arc that sizzled and cracked. Wind whipped at my hair as pebbles trembled under every step. Trees in the forest creaked as their branches stretched toward me.

"Lumnos magic only," I murmured. "We'll keep the rest our little secret for now."

As if in answer, the magic pulsed across my skin. Shadows coated my cloak and cascaded to the ground in a train of smoky curls. Glowing swords formed in my hands as I restored the Crown to its place atop my head.

At the midday hour, the town square buzzed with a swarm of bodies. Within seconds of my arrival, a hundred heads had turned my way.

A circle formed as they edged away. I let my gaze drag lazily over the throng, noting so many familiar faces. Some screamed and cowered, others ran. Several reached for their blades.

A few began to kneel, faces ashen with fear. I held their eyes and shook my head.

"Don't kneel to me yet."

They shared confused glances, some moving closer as they arched their necks to see.

I raised my chin and threw my voice to the edges of the market. "I was raised in this village. I know the struggles you face because I faced them, too. I went to school with your children. I healed your loved ones. I feared the Descended, just as you do. I *hated* them, just as you do. I watched as they treated us lower than rats, and I, too, dreamed of a day when their reign would end."

Scattered heads nodded, eyes narrowed. A few spit and muttered low epithets.

"All that time, I believed I was a mortal. Though I now wear a Descended Crown, do not think for one second that I have forgotten where I'm from. Mortal blood runs in my veins." I raised a sword. "And that's blood I'm not afraid to spill on your behalf."

The hum of murmurs grew louder.

"These past weeks, I've lived among the Descended, learning their ways. I did so expecting to loathe them all. Indeed, many are as wicked and soulless as we all believed." I took a deep breath. "But there are others. Good people. Some I now call friends. Some... even more than friends."

The chatter rose to a roar, a resentful tide turning back with ire. Shouts of *traitor* and *Descended scum* rang out, a few beginning to walk away.

My heart picked up speed.

"One of them believes I was chosen by the gods to unite our people and bring peace to Emarion." I laughed. "If you don't believe that, you're in good company. I'm not certain I believe it myself. But I'm willing to try—for all of you, and for all the mortals who died fighting for us over the years. And everyone who will keep dying if I fail."

The din fell to a silent, expectant hush.

"My mother, Auralie... she taught me to *heal*—to save lives every chance I get. My father, Andrei, taught me to *fight*—to end lives, but only when I must. And my brother, Teller, taught me to *think*—to lead with reason, not prejudice. That is the Queen I strive to be. I will not demand that you bend your knee. Past Crowns have done enough of that. I will only vow, on my blood and my soul, on all that I am, and all that I hold dear, if you give me your faith, I will do my best to earn it—" I crossed my swords at my chest. "—and I won't stop until my dying breath."

Conversation stalled, no one quite sure what to do with me and my grand declaration. Mortals whispered in huddled groups, looking between me and each other with doubt in their eyes.

"She's here! Commander—in the square."

Shouting arose from a back corner as Emarion Army soldiers violently shoved a path through the crowd.

"Took you long enough," I called out. "The army's gone downhill since my father retired."

As his soldiers fanned out in a circle around me, a man with heavy regalia and red eyes—Fortos eyes—stepped forward and assessed me with contempt. "You're not supposed to be here."

"This is my realm. I can come and go as I please. You, on the other hand..."

"An edict has been issued," he barked. "You've been summoned for questioning by the Crowns."

"How about I issue my own edict instead?" I spread my arms wide. "I formally declare to the good citizens of Lumnos that the Crowns of Emarion are summoned to kiss my half-mortal ass."

Laughter rolled through the crowd. The soldiers looked around and rocked uneasily on their feet.

"If you will not go willingly, I'm authorized to bring you in," the man warned.

My smile stayed, but all the humor in it vanished. "Go ahead, then. Bring me in."

His sword hissed as it slid from its scabbard. His other hand curved into a claw at his side. Though I couldn't see it as easily as Lumnos light, I knew how lethal the death magic of Fortos could be.

"Come peacefully, without a fight," he urged.

"All these people came to see a show." I shrugged. "Can't let them go home empty-handed."

The crowd cheered their agreement. The man's eyes darted around at his soldiers, but he made no move to attack.

"What are you waiting for?" I teased. I let my swords dissolve into mist and wiggled my fingers. "I'll make it easy. No weapons."

His hand tightened on his hilt. Still, he held his ground.

I grinned. "You can't, can you? You have no authority to attack a Crown."

"You haven't been coronated. You're not yet considered a Crown."

Sorae swooped from the sky and soared across the open square. Her wings snapped in a thunderous beat, the powerful downdraft sending the soldiers stumbling backward.

"I think she disagrees," I said.

His glare hardened. "Soldiers, take her in."

I tutted in disapproval. Tendrils of light sprouted from my palms and slithered across the ground. The soldiers hacked in vain as the glowing vines wrapped around their hands and hilts, then swore as the metal in their hands turned a molten red. Melting blades dripped to the dusty stone in puddles of steaming orange-yellow sludge.

"You'll have to do better than that," I taunted.

"Fine," the man ground out. "No weapons. We'll do this the Descended way."

The soldiers hesitated. Descended were reluctant to use magic in front of mortals for fear it might reveal their weakness, and in this crowded square, there was no shortage of riveted mortal eyes.

But the Fortos commander's pride was on the line, and there was no greater enemy to good sense than a wounded ego. His eyes glowed scarlet as his palm rose and his fingers curled.

Unlike the female Fortos Descended, who all had healing magic like the kind I'd used on Luther, the Fortos men wielded a rotting, deadly force that decayed their victims' bodies from within.

It left me wondering—if I had *all* the Kindred's magic... did that include the Fortos power to kill?

His magic hit me like a foul odor, a rank wave of rot and mold. My skin briefly tingled, then flared with light as it harmlessly absorbed.

I cocked my head. "Is that it?"

His nostrils flared wide. "Soldiers, attack!"

This time, there was no hesitation. The crowd gasped as magic erupted from every angle and pummeled me in waves of sparks and fire and wind and snow. I held my ground, and my chest rose in a slow, calm cadence as my energy built.

Alixe once told me that godhoods fed on our emotions—perhaps that's why mine was so strong and so frequently out of control—and with each brush of magic, I caught glimpses of its wielder. Some hateful, some angry. Some terrified of my reaction. Some wishing they could just go home.

My skin grew brighter, and so did my smile. "Are you done, or shall we keep going?"

The soldiers gawked at their commander, awaiting an order I knew would never come. The thinly veiled panic in his eyes told me I'd finally made my point.

I jerked my chin to the left. "I'd move, if I were you."

He frowned. "Why would I—"

A massive shadow fell over his body, and his words cut off in a yelp. He dove out of the way with not a second to spare as Sorae slammed to the ground where he'd just stood. She growled, low and vicious, and snapped her jaws at the circle of soldiers to push them back.

I mounted her back and turned my glare on the Fortos commander. "Know this—I am not afraid of the Emarion Army, and I am not afraid of the Crowns. If I hear of one more mortal going *missing* from my realm, every last one of you will repay their loss in blood. I am the gods-damned Queen of Lumnos. If my people suffer, so will you."

Sorae arched her neck and snarled out a sapphire fireball that swirled into curling smoke.

I let my gaze linger on the soldiers' faces until both they and I were certain I'd committed each one to memory. With a thunderous howl, Sorae stretched her wings and sent us airborne.

As we soared for the clouds, a ripple of movement drew my focus back to the ground. In the dirty, downtrodden square of my beloved Mortal City, one by one, the mortals lowered to their knees.

CHAPTER
FORTY-NINE

I half expected Luther to be waiting in the same spot I'd left him, keeping watch from afar, but when Sorae touched down on the palace terrace, there was no sign of him.

There was no sign of anyone.

My bedchamber was empty, door ajar, parlor silent. I tried to remind myself the others had their own matters to address. No reason for them to be lingering at my beck and call.

No reason for me to worry.

I quickly changed into the fighting leathers I'd worn during the Challenging. They'd brought me victory when I needed it most, and today, I'd take all the help I could get.

Though my plan to raid the armory had gone awry, the supply of blades Luther brought me on my first night as Queen was still stashed in hidden nooks throughout my room. Gathering them brought a faint, much needed smile. I'd hated him more than ever that night—and he knew it—but he'd still been protecting me, trying to keep me alive against all the odds.

That task was about to get much harder.

I strapped on as many blades as I could fit, then pulled my hair into a tight braid that circled my head just below the floating Crown. I tucked my pendant safely under my neckline and strolled into the parlor.

"Your Majesty," Perthe said in greeting from where he stood at attention by the suite door.

"Where is everyone?" I asked.

"The Regent came by. He was quite angry about something. He left with the High General, and the others followed."

I frowned. Had Remis found out about my spectacle in Mortal City already?

"I thought you'd prefer that I stay with your brother," Perthe added, inclining his head toward the closed door leading to Teller's room.

"Yes, of course. I owe you a debt for taking care of him in my absence."

"You saved my life. The debt is mine to repay."

I winced. "Perthe, there's something you should know. The night of the armory attack..." My eyes lowered. "I saved you out of guilt, not bravery. Weeks before, I made a stupid, reckless decision that made the Guardians' attack possible. I didn't know what would happen, but I cannot deny my share of the blame. You owe me nothing, and if that changes your desire to serve me—"

"It doesn't change a thing, Your Majesty."

I looked up. "It doesn't?"

His sky-blue eyes crinkled with a kind smile. "I've been a member of the Royal Guard for many years. Risked my life for the late King many times. He was a good man, but he would never have run into a fire to save me, even if he was the one who lit the match."

My chest warmed at his words. "Still... I don't want you putting yourself in danger out of some sense of obligation for what I did."

"Then let me do it to honor my oath as a Royal Guard. An oath I'd happily take again knowing the kind of Queen I'd be vowing to serve."

I smiled and raised a fist to my chest. "You're a noble man, Perthe. An honor to your family, and a credit to my guard."

He inflated with pride and returned my salute, bowing dramatically low.

I took a hesitant step toward Teller's room, then paused. "Is anyone... *else* with my brother?"

Perthe's lips twitched up. "No, Your Majesty. Princess Lilian left. Prince Teller said he wishes to be alone."

I blinked. "*Prince* Teller?"

"Siblings of the Crown and their children are entitled to a royal designation, if they wish to use one."

"And Teller does?"

"Oh, no, Your Majesty. Not at all. But I thought perhaps *you* might wish him to."

"I do, indeed." A mischievous smirk slowly grew. I strode toward Teller's room and rapped my fist on his door.

He didn't answer.

"It's your sister. Let me in."

I knocked again.

He still didn't answer.

"Fine. It's your Queen, and I command you to open. You can't ignore *that*."

"Yes, I can," a muffled voice shouted back.

"I'm leaving town. Aren't you going to say goodbye?"

The door cracked open. A sliver of Teller's face appeared. "You're leaving already?"

I grinned. "Hello, *Prince* Teller."

His eyes narrowed. "Goodbye."

I wedged the toe of my boot to stop the door mid-slam. "I think you should use the title. It suits you. You're very princely."

"I don't want it."

"Why not?"

"Because I don't want *any* of this," he snapped. "I don't want to be royal, I don't want to live in this palace, and I don't want guards following me everywhere I go. I never get to see my mortal friends anymore, and the Descended think I'm a Guardian now. I want my home back. I want my *life* back."

My smile vanished. "Tel... I didn't—"

"Nevermind." He scratched the back of his neck, looking down. Like me, my brother was horrid at hiding his true feelings. Dejection was screaming from every pore. "I'm fine. Forget I said anything."

I sighed. "Can I please come in?"

He let go of the door and turned away.

"I guess it went badly with Henri," he muttered as I walked in.

"Why do you say that?"

"Your eyes are still puffy from crying."

I stared at my feet, my cheeks turning warm.

He looked me over. "You're going to get Mother, aren't you? That's why you're dressed like you're going into battle?" I nodded, and he let out a harsh breath. "Maybe... maybe you shouldn't. Maybe you should just leave her there."

I frowned. This wasn't like him. Even when Teller was angry, he was never cruel. "You want me to abandon Mother?"

"This is *Fortos*, Diem. You'll be surrounded by soldiers. If they catch you, they'll kill you, and even if you don't, you'll be an enemy of the Crowns. Then they'll arrest you and execute you both, and then I'll be..." His shoulders crumpled. He sank onto the edge of his bed, dropping his head in his hands. "After your coronation, we didn't know if you or Mother made it out alive. For days, I thought..." His hands clenched in his hair. "I thought I was the only Bellator left."

My heart broke at the thick despair roughening his voice. He'd had so little choice in all that had happened. Even before I became Queen, he'd been a pawn in my mother's plan. He'd put on a strong face through it all, but everyone had their breaking point, and I feared I had finally pushed him to his.

I sat beside him, my arm brushing his. "They won't catch me. And if they do, they can't kill me."

"Come on, D. I know you're strong, but—"

"Luther and I discovered something about my magic. I haven't told everyone yet."

His eyes darkened. "More secrets?"

"Yes," I said, sighing. "But when you see, you'll understand why."

I took his hand and flattened it out, my brow furrowing as I focused on his palm. At the center, a single flame began to grow.

Teller jerked upright. "Is that...?"

"Watch," I urged.

The flame twirled, then extinguished into smoke with the force of a tiny windstorm. A droplet of water wobbled in midair, then crystallized into an icy, frost-coated orb.

"That's Ignios magic," he breathed. "And... and Meros. And Montios."

And Umbros, I spoke into his mind.

He jerked away and leapt to his feet.

"And Arboros and Fortos and all the others," I went on. "The only one I can't use is Sophos. Luther thinks it's because I've never been there."

His forehead wrinkled in that earnest way it did when his clever brain was puzzling out a problem. "Descended magic is tied to the soil of their terremère. They can't use it if they've never set foot in the realm." He looked me over slowly, like he was studying some new, fascinating creature. "But no Descended has even had *two*, let alone all of them."

"It gets stranger. When Descended attack me with their magic, it doesn't hurt me. It *helps* me. It's like I'm stealing their magic right out of them. It even helps me heal faster, if I'm wounded."

His eyes grew wide. "Mother said your birth father had a rare condition. Maybe that wasn't a lie. If he could do this, too, that would explain why she tried so hard to hide you."

"I'm going to get her and ask her that myself today."

His look of wonder fell away, hardening back into his scolding frown. "This doesn't mean you can't be killed. Fortos has weapons. And *godstone*."

"I'll be careful."

"You're never careful," he shot back. "We always joked you were lucky to be alive after all the things that should have killed you. It was never luck. It was all of *this*." He gestured angrily at my body. "You're not fighting weak mortal men anymore. These are real threats."

"I will be careful this time," I said again. "I'm coming back, and I'm bringing Mother with me."

He stilled. "You're going to bring her back here—to the palace?"

I nodded emphatically. My better judgment shouted at me with reservations, but I shoved them away, frantic to win back my brother's trust. "We'll have to hide her somehow. I'll find a way. We'll be together as a family again by day's end. I promise."

He eyed me with blatant doubt. "Are there any other big revelations I should know?"

"No. I've learned my lesson—no more lying to protect you."

"Swear it, D," he insisted. "Promise me there are no more secrets."

I pressed my hand to my heart. "I swear on my life."

He blew out a long breath through his nose, his face still etched with lingering hurt. We'd never had a rift like this, nothing more serious than fleeting sibling spats, and I was desperate to mend it. Teller was my one constant, the one person who had been there through it all and had never let me down. Losing his trust would destroy me.

His eyes shifted up above my head, his cross expression giving way to curiosity. "Your Crown..."

"It's different, I know. It changed after the Rite of Coronation. I'm not sure why."

"The new part of it..." His head angled to the side. "This is going to sound crazy, but it almost looks like..."

I let out a sudden groan as a wave of foreign pain and confusing shock knocked me to my knees.

"Diem!" Teller lunged to grab me.

I gritted my teeth against the visceral sensation seeming to come from everywhere and nowhere at all. My skin glowed silver-bright as my godhood thrashed in search of some wound to heal, some enemy to vanquish.

"Are you hurt?" Teller asked.

"Not me," I rasped. "*Sorae.*"

The bond between us was engulfed with her panic. Somewhere, she was under attack.

Her physical agony mixed with her fury. And terror—not for herself, but for me, for fear that her attackers would come for me next.

"I have to get to her," I choked out. Teller helped me to my feet, and we ran together through the parlor. An excruciating pain splintered through my chest. I stumbled to the ground just as Sorae's enraged howl carried through the terrace archways.

"Your Majesty," Perthe cried, rushing forward.

I clutched my throbbing side. "I think we're under attack."

Perthe pulled his sword and coated it with a corona of shadow. "I'll come with you."

"No—stay with Teller. If something happens to me, get him to Mortal City. Maura will take him in."

Teller's face blanched. "Diem..."

I didn't wait to argue. I pushed to my feet and ran to the balcony. Sorae was missing, but I sensed her presence nearby. My eyes slammed shut as I slipped into her head like it was my own.

The world was vivid and shimmering through her golden eyes. I was momentarily lost in an ocean of colors I'd never seen, shades of light too delicate for my human eyes to detect. I felt the thump of every heartbeat in the palace and caught the pungent scent of every man and creature wafting on the winter wind.

And intentions. They blazed in the air around each person's form, a halo of their heart's darkest hates or brightest loves.

And everywhere I looked, I saw a hunger to *kill*.

She was writhing on the ground outside the palace entrance, struggling to get free, though something held her still. Her wings were bent at an awkward angle that sent bolts of agony down both our spines.

In front of her, a barrel of apples lay overturned, some half-eaten. I could taste their cloying aftertaste coating my mouth. A circle of both Lumnos guards and army soldiers surrounded her with long, metal-tipped spears, some of which were lodged in bloody gashes across her hide. A few guards clutched chains as thick as my thigh, and when they pulled taut, Sorae's throat—and mine—squeezed closed and gasped for air.

I yanked out of the bond, sending her a wave of calm and a promise to get her free, and bolted for the corridor.

"Move," I shouted at the horde of waiting guards. "Get out of my way!"

They closed their ranks. "I'm sorry, Your Majesty," a woman said, stepping forward. "We've been ordered by the High General to keep you in your chambers."

"Those orders are empty. Aemonn's not High General anymore." I tried to shove past her, but the guards tightened around me.

"The orders weren't given by Aemonn."

I went stiff. "Alixe did this? She's the one hurting Sorae?"

"The gryvern is only being subdued, not harmed."

"I can *feel* her pain," I hissed. "And if you don't get out of my way, I'll make sure you feel it, too."

The woman's eyes glowed bright blue as her chin lifted. "Return to your chambers, Your Majesty. Don't force us to harm our own Queen."

"Don't worry, there's no danger of that." I stalked forward and clipped her with my shoulder to force her aside.

Her arm swung out across my chest. She gripped me by the elbow, yanking me toward her.

I stilled. My gaze slowly lowered to my arm as my voice went soft. "Remove your hand."

"Simply return to your chambers, and no harm will come to you or your gryv—"

Her words cut off as every guard in the hall was flung backward by the explosive force of my magical pulse. I'd only put a fraction of my power into it, but it was enough to crunch bone as soft bodies met stone walls.

I set off in a sprint. More guards spotted me, calling out demands to stop—only to find themselves pinned against the nearest wall with a searing rope of light or a razor wire of darkness.

When I reached the stairs to the foyer, thirty army soldiers were ready and waiting. They raised their weapons, and I raised my palm to condemn them to the same fate as the others.

Then I stopped. A few held weapons made not of dull grey Fortosian steel, but a telltale glittering black.

"You threaten me with godstone in my own home?" I snarled.

"And we're not afraid to use it," their commander barked. "Go back to your chambers."

I slowly walked down the staircase, my rage boiling to a dangerous heat.

I had to be careful—one reckless blast of my magic and godstone blades would go flying. If they did, there was no telling how many lives it could cost. Even a minor nick could be a death warrant.

I could use my Umbros magic to persuade them all to turn away, but then my secret would be out. If the Crowns wanted to question me before, that would make me enemy number one—if I wasn't already.

My fists clenched at my sides. Until now, I'd been blunt-forcing my way through every battle, making up for lack of skill with sheer power and dumb luck. I was the magical equivalent of a toddler with a hammer—able to do enormous damage, but only if I was willing to smash everything in sight.

This required a delicate touch. Sophisticated precision, the kind of magic one only gained after years of training. And I'd been deprived of that chance by the progeny laws and my mother's lies.

"Step aside," I said. "I don't want to hurt you."

"You're delusional," their commander sneered back. "Even the King of Fortos couldn't take us all."

I arched an eyebrow. "I didn't realize the King of Fortos was so weak."

The commander narrowed his eyes—red, like his counterpart in Mortal City.

"Sheath your blades and fight me like a Descended," I taunted. "I'll level the odds for you—I won't even raise my shield."

He pointed his sword toward me, and I stared at the blade as it hovered inches from my face. The sunlight streaming through the palace windows cast twinkling specks on the onyx stone, like moonlight glinting off the choppy waves of a midnight sea. It was paradoxically beautiful for something so vile.

"I hear you're a Guardian sympathizer," he jeered. "I wouldn't mind putting this right through your neck. Give me a reason, and I'll do it."

I held his stare and sent a wave of my magic rippling through the air. Not an attack, but a warning.

A warning their stillness suggested they were not inclined to heed.

"Diem?" Luther's voice called from outside.

The door to the palace flew open, revealing my furious-looking Prince. His chest and thighs bore glowing armor of pale blue light, while barbed shadows coiled up and down his sinewed arms.

His eyes thinned to slits as they stopped on the sword now pointed at my throat. He raised his fists, forearms dark with swirls of roiling night.

"Touch her," he snarled, throaty and vicious, "and I'll peel every last vein from under your flesh and strangle you with them."

Though I shivered at his words, my godhood was exhilarated at the sight of him. It pried at my ribs, yearning to be let loose and join him in battle.

Fight, its *voice* demanded.

Some of the soldiers whipped toward him, their dark blades swinging his direction. A panicked cry stuck in my throat.

"Luther, please," I begged. "Go back outside."

The commander looked between us, his mouth curving. "Ah. I see."

I didn't need Umbros magic to understand the plan forming in his head.

I shook my head in warning. "Don't do it."

He smirked. "You wanted us to fight like Descended. That means using every weapon we can get. Soldiers, *take him down!*"

My protests drowned in the roar of the surge. Luther moved with the grace of a leopard, prowling expertly through gaps in their swings, but the godstone sliced through his shield like it was nothing. If he made one wrong move...

Fight.

I hurled a globe of blazing light at the commander. It burned straight through his armor and left a circle of charred flesh across his chest. His screams rang in my ears as I leapt past him and waded through a swarm of sparkling black blurs, a few missing me by inches.

"Diem, *no*," Luther shouted. He launched toward me, each of us turning reckless in our race to rescue the other.

The soldiers took quick advantage. They hacked at us as we passed, a deadly gauntlet we couldn't survive for long.

I'm going to lose him, I thought, my heart breaking. *The gods won't let me save him again.*

A soldier appeared at Luther's flank, two black daggers in his fists. One blade punched forward.

Fight.

Destroy.

I screamed.

And I surrendered.

The room flooded with silvery light. Its blinding brilliance forced my eyes shut as a wave of frost and fire tingled down my spine.

Then... silence.

"No," I whimpered. I clamped my hands over my face. I couldn't bear to face the horror of what I'd done. All those soldiers, all those lives...

"What in Kindred's name did she just do?"

My eyes popped open at the Fortos commander's voice.

Luther sank to his knees before me. His lips parted, his eyes aglow with reverence. The air rushed out of him as he laid a palm on his chest.

"My Queen," he breathed.

"How did she do that?"

I tore my eyes away to see the commander staring at his open palms—his *empty* palms.

Across the foyer, every soldier was gaping at their hands, looking lost, and every palm was empty, not a weapon in sight.

"How?" the commander demanded again. "Godstone can't be destroyed."

"Yes it can," I protested. "After the war, the Crowns confiscated all the godstone weapons and—"

"—and stored them," Luther finished. "The weapons were locked in a vault in Fortos, because even the Crowns couldn't destroy them. No one could... until now."

We gazed at each other, his face dazzling with wonder, mine fraught with shock.

"She's too dangerous," the commander said. "Capture her and bring her in. Use your magic—whatever it takes."

I moved to raise my shield, but Luther beat me to it. With a twitch of his wrist, he surrounded us in a shimmering blue dome.

The foyer erupted. Outside our bubble, lethal magic clouded the air. Attacks teemed in a dizzying melee of chaos and violence. The soldiers screamed until their faces were red and beat their fists against the shield's glowing wall.

Inside, our world was calm. Nothing could reach us. It was all so far, far away.

All the while, my Prince's eyes stayed on me. Deflecting the full force of an entire army battalion didn't even warrant a glance. He rose to his feet and curled a hand beneath my jaw, gazing at me like I was the brightest star in the sky.

"Some days, I pray for these surprises to end. I beg for time to stop and the world to still so I know that, at least for a moment, you are safe. Then you do something like this..." He laughed softly. "And I thank the Blessed Kindred I'm lucky enough to see it."

I could have stayed there for an eternity, basking in the warmth of his love. He had a way of making me *feel* it—see it and touch it, nest it in my hands like a tangible thing.

Most days, my self-doubt felt as powerful a beast as my magic, but in the light of his gaze, all my uncertainty fell away.

But, desperately as I wanted to, I could not linger.

"Sorae's under attack. We have to help her."

His expression darkened. "I know. I was loading her with our bags when they lured her away. My father knows our plan to get your mother. He thinks he can stop us by capturing Sorae."

"Oh gods, Alixe must have—"

"She didn't tell him. It was Aemonn."

I swore under my breath.

"You told him?" Luther asked, noticeably struggling to keep the disappointment from his tone.

"You were dying. I wasn't thinking clearly." I sighed. "I wanted to give him a second chance."

"Like I said last night, your compassion knows no bounds," he muttered flatly.

I scowled and took his hand. "Let's go."

Luther's shield burst outward in an explosive arc, sending soldiers skidding across the marble floor.

Outside, a pack of Royal Guards crowded Sorae's panting body. Her snout was locked in an iron muzzle while a contraption pinned her wings at her back. Heavy chains encircled her throat and trailed from shackles clamped around her limbs.

Eleanor and Lily clutched each other nearby, watching with sorrow. Taran was screaming at Aemonn and Garath, both of whom were eying Zalaric as he tried in vain to hold Taran back. At Sorae's side, Alixe and Remis were huddled in discussion.

My gryvern's eyes slid to me, and a mournful wail trilled from her throat. She dug her talons into the ground in a frenzied attempt to crawl to me. The guard holding her chains scrambled to pull her back, the metal links rubbing her scales raw where they squeezed her neck.

"Let her go," I shouted at Remis. "You have no right."

"I have every right." He stormed toward me, his careful composure long since shattered. "The Lumnos gryvern serves the Crown, and right now, that Crown is me."

"She'll never serve you. She doesn't even *like* you."

481

Sorae swung her head with a wild snarl of agreement. She shoved to her feet and strained at her chains. A few of the spear-carrying soldiers closed in and jabbed their blades into her soft underbelly.

I let out a cry and hunched forward, feeling the blades as viscerally as if they were in my own side. Luther's arms wrapped around me to hold me steady against his chest.

"That's enough," Alixe barked at the soldiers. "Your orders were to hold her down, not hurt her."

My eyes locked with Alixe. Her expression was brutally severe, so unlike the warm friend that I knew. The message was clear: she would obey her orders, even if she hated it. I'd made her my High General for that very reason.

"Sorae *will* serve me," Remis argued, "because you are going to order her to do it. If you don't, she'll be spending her future in chains."

"No. She's coming with me."

"I heard about your plan," he hissed. He stormed closer, lowering his voice. "Fortos? Are you *insane?*"

I dragged my glare to Aemonn. "I gave you a chance, and this is the man you chose to be?"

A brief flash of shame surfaced before it twisted into something bitter and cruel, so much like his father. "You had me replaced as High General. Why should I be loyal to you now?"

"You'll never be more to our fathers than a pawn," Luther snapped at him. "Diem was the only person who ever saw good in you. You're a fool to throw that away."

Taran spat at Aemonn's feet. "Coward. Always have been, always will be."

Aemon jumped away and glowered at the three of us. He swallowed and straightened his jacket, then stomped off toward the palace, his chin hanging low.

I glanced at Luther. *Can you get Sorae's muzzle off?* I asked into his thoughts.

His nostrils flared in surprise. He quickly gave a subtle nod.

Go, I told him. *I'll distract your father.*

"Why do you care what I do in Fortos?" I asked Remis haughtily. I crossed my arms as Luther slipped away. "You'd be thrilled to see me finally meet my end."

Remis scoffed. "You'll be lucky if it's only death. There'll be no coming back from this."

I shrugged. "I guess I'll find out when I return."

My eyes darted over his shoulder. Alixe had pulled her shortswords, and she and Luther were circling each other in a battle stance.

My muscles went stiff—surely she wouldn't *really* hurt him... would she?

"Don't even think about bringing your mother here," Remis warned. "The Crowns will make a bloodbath of the realm, and they won't stop until you're on the gallows."

I rolled my eyes. "The other Crowns can't hurt me."

"You better hope they can, because if they can't, they'll hurt everyone you love in your place. Your brother. My son." He jabbed a finger in my face. "If you do this, at least do *them* a favor and don't ever show your face in this realm again."

I held strong to my facade of arrogant indifference, but his words had a stone sinking in my gut. A quick glance confirmed Luther and Alixe were still locked in combat, their spinning bodies a blur of blades and magic.

"Is that a threat?" I shot at Remis. "Do you know what I do to those who threaten my family?"

"I am not the threat to your family, Diem. It's *you*. It has always been you."

I flinched. "If anything happens to my brother, Remis, you cannot fathom the hellstorm I will bring down on your head. There will be no place to hide from my wrath." My eyes narrowed. "I don't care whose fault it is. It will be *your* head that rolls. Understood?"

"Diem," Luther shouted. "Now!"

I held Remis's stare a beat longer, letting him see the depth of my vow, before breaking away and striding toward Luther. He sliced the straps from Sorae's muzzle in between thrusting out volleys of glowing arrows that sizzled into the flesh of the surrounding guards.

I caught sight of Alixe and halted. She was lying on the ground, a pool of blood spreading around her at a terrifying rate. In a panic, I ran toward her. Luther lunged to snatch my arm.

"We need to leave now."

"She's hurt—I have to heal her."

"If you do, Remis will think she was in on our plan."

I hesitated, staring at Alixe. The healer in me rose to the surface, analyzing her injury, her blood loss, her chances.

"She'll be fine," Luther said, quieter. "I know how to wound without killing."

Shadows crept into his eyes. His careful mask slipped, giving a glimpse of a tortured darkness that lurked deep inside.

A group of army soldiers came riding on horseback through the palace gates. Atop the lead horse sat the red-eyed commander I'd battled in Mortal City.

"Stop her," he yelled, pointing toward me. "She attacked my battalion!"

Luther raised an eyebrow, and I swore under my breath. "Fine. Let's go."

He nodded. "What about Sorae's chains?"

"Oh, she'll take care of those all on her own." I untied the bags Luther had secured to her side as he sliced away the last of the muzzle's leather straps. The second the iron cage slid from her snout, her thunderous roar exploded over the palace grounds.

"Go," I shouted at the soldiers holding her chains. "If you want to live, *run now!*"

A low rumble built in Sorae's throat, and the air turned blisteringly hot. Remis staggered backward, his face turning a sickly pale.

"Run," he hoarsely echoed my order. "*Run!*"

As one, their eyes grew wide. The soldiers dropped the chains and scrambled to get away. I grabbed Luther's arm and threw my body on top of him, ignoring his grunts of protest as I built the thickest blanket of ice I could craft and stretched it to cover both us and Alixe.

A sapphire inferno erupted from Sorae's fanged jaws, a cataclysmic deluge of flame that charred every surface within reach. The world disappeared within its violent, blinding glow, though I felt only a calming warmth—as her Crown, her dragonfyre could do me no harm.

Everyone else was not so lucky.

My ears rang with horrified screams, bubbling ice evaporating to steam, and, to my relief, the hiss of melting iron. When the flames receded, I didn't dare look at the damage Sorae had wrought—only a brief glance at Alixe to confirm that her clothes were singed, but her skin was unburnt.

Luther wasted no time. He hauled me to my feet and dragged me at his side in a sprint for Sorae, snatching our bags along the way. We carefully avoided the molten red ooze puddled beneath her as we vaulted on her back.

"Go, Sorae!" Luther shouted.

She held still, awaiting my command.

I spied Taran huddling by the palace walls. Zalaric crouched behind him, peering out from Taran's protective grip.

"Jean will come for him," I called out to Taran.

He growled, fists clenching. "If he does, Hanoverre blood will run in the streets."

I smiled. "Take care of him for me?"

Zalaric rolled his eyes. "I'm more powerful than him, you know. I'm perfectly capable of taking care of mys—"

"I will, Your Majesty," Taran shouted back. "I'll protect him with my life."

We exchanged salutes, and I sent a silent command to Sorae. Her wings shuddered as they flared out, the lingering pain from her capture echoing in my body through the bond. But my fearless gryvern pushed through her pain and leaned back on her haunches.

"I pray you remember my warning, Remis," I yelled to him as we leapt for the sky.

His response barely reached me over the whistle of the wind.

"I pray you remember mine, as well."

CHAPTER
FIFTY

"I can't believe you stabbed Alixe."

It was the first time either of us had spoken in the hour since leaving the palace. After I'd healed Sorae's wounds, Luther had silently pulled me against him and held me close, somehow sensing I needed his touch and time to sort through my turbulent thoughts.

"If it makes you feel better, she got me first," he grumbled.

I looked back to see his shirt torn at the shoulder and soaked in dark red. "You should have told me," I scolded, pushing my healing magic into his skin.

His eyes closed briefly with a contented hum. "Alixe won't have access to a healer. It seemed only fair I suffer, too."

I sighed heavily and leaned against his chest. Much as I wanted to, I had no ground to lecture him on guilt and self-punishment. Those flaws, we shared in equal excess.

"So you attacked the soldiers in Mortal City, did you?" he teased, his tone lightening.

"It was reckless and wildly dangerous. And it felt amazing." I grinned. "You would have hated it."

He huffed a laugh. "I really shouldn't tell you this..." His mouth grazed a line up the bend of my neck, then nipped at my ear. "I actually enjoy your rampages. A little *too* much."

My grin spread wider. I opened up my thoughts to him and pulled the

486

memory to the forefront, letting him hear my impassioned speech and feel the fire of my devotion to the mortals, then letting him bask in my vengeance as I provoked the soldiers into their embarrassing defeat.

A dark laugh rumbled from his throat. His hand slid low on my hips as his fingers circled in teasing strokes. "About that night alone I was promised," he murmured.

I hummed my agreement and arched my back against him, my hand gripping tight on his thigh. Our mouths met in a kiss smoldering with long-suppressed desire.

He rolled his hips forward, letting me feel every rock-hard inch of the effect my vision had aroused. His touch was deliciously rough as his hand dragged up my body and gripped possessively at my nape.

Our kiss broke, and I leaned in for another. Luther hesitated, pulling back. When I looked up, his eyes were sharp with hunger, but a spark of something more troubled waited, too.

"Do you want to talk about what happened with Henri?" he asked carefully.

My lust cooled to ice.

My back went rod-straight, my muscles rigid. I twisted to face the sky ahead, leaving Luther staring at my back.

"I didn't mean to pry."

"It's fine. He hates me. It's... it's fine."

"I know you better than that. If he does hate you, you're anything but fine."

No, I wasn't fine at all. Ending our betrothal was always going to strain things between me and Henri, but I'd naively hoped our friendship might endure. Instead, it lay buried ten feet deep beneath more prejudice, hurt, and resentment than we might ever be able to overcome.

Another painful wound, another permanent scar on my heart.

But as awful as that conversation had been, it wasn't just Henri's hatred that haunted me.

Well, make sure you warn him so he doesn't waste his life pining for a woman who will never fully give herself away. Give him the courtesy you never gave me, and let him leave before you break his heart, too.

I forced down the lump in my throat. "There's something you should know about me before things between us go any further."

Luther sat up straighter. His head craned to the side, trying to catch my eye. I kept my gaze locked on the horizon ahead.

"I care about you. I *love* you. But... I may never want anything more than this."

"Good," he said slowly. "I pray I never leave you wanting more."

I shifted my weight. "*You* might want more. More than I'm able to give."

A beat passed. Luther's silence was excruciating.

I cringed and forced myself on. "I've never been the kind of person who dreams of weddings and babies and mates. The idea of being tied to *anything* forever makes me feel like it's hard to breathe. I couldn't be that person for Henri. I'm not sure I can be that for anyone." My words picked up speed as my nerves grew. "Maybe I'll change. Sometimes, with you, I want to change. But maybe I won't. And the last thing I want is to hurt you if you want a piece of me I can never give."

"You think I don't already know this?"

I spun around in surprise. "You do?"

"Diem, you're the most independent person I've ever met. You treat your life like it's disposable. You insist on doing every hard thing alone. When I told that guard in Ignios you were my mate, I genuinely thought you were going to be sick." I winced, and he squeezed my hip with a smile. "I know what I'm getting with you. And it is more than enough for me."

My heart stumbled. "But... at the ball, you said you wanted *all* of me. What if I can't give you that?"

"You already have."

I gave him a confused frown, and his arms tightened, tugging me closer.

"'All of you' means I want Diem the Queen *and* Diem the woman. The Diem that's courageous and bold and inspiring. The Diem that taunts Crowns and armies into battle, then leaves them wondering what the hell they just faced." We both laughed, and his fingers brushed across my cheek. "But I also want the Diem that worries and cries. The Diem that's scared. The Diem with a temper hot enough to melt Fortosian steel." He shot me a pointed look. "The Diem who doubts herself too damn much."

I blushed, dipping my chin. He crooked a finger under my jaw and nudged it up.

"I want there to be no part of you that you hide from me because you fear it's a part I will not love. I treasure your darkness as much as your light." He dropped his mouth a breath away from mine, his words a whisper on my lips. "Show me your worst, my darling, and I'll show you how far my love can go."

The caress of his lips was a song on my heart. I arched my neck up to meet him, and my worries carried away in the fluttering wind.

Each kiss from Luther carried its own promise. Some were offers of love, others oaths of devotion. Some were vows of the flesh, a hint of steamy nights to come.

But this was a promise that I was *enough*, and that was the promise I'd needed most of all.

"I didn't dream of those things either, you know," he said. "I thought I would spend my life in a loveless arranged marriage to Iléana."

I scowled, scrunching my nose.

He rewarded me with a rare unrestrained grin. "Being with someone I chose for myself already exceeds any hope I ever dared have. Of course I would be honored to share those things with you someday—but only if you decide you want them. And if you never do, I'll be grateful still." He teased me with an almost-kiss that hovered just beyond my reach. "Will you put this doubt out of your head now?"

"I will," I said, and for once, it was true. "There are plenty others to take its place."

He groaned. I stole a kiss while he was distracted, but not to be beat, he cradled my head and held my mouth to his, turning my sweet peck into a fiery embrace. I happily surrendered and lost myself in the bliss of his hungry, roaming hands.

As usual, the gods were cruel, and our joy was short-lived.

A snap of burning pain shot through me. Luther and I both jolted, his hands gripping hard on my shoulders.

"It's the border," he said. "We must have crossed into Fortos."

Sorae dipped below the cloudline, and the ground came into view. Sure enough, the shift from forest to rock that marked the Lumnos-Fortos border was fading fast in our wake.

When I'd crossed this border months ago on a trip with Henri, the change had been stark—not a tree out of line, not a stone out of place. Now, bushes and young saplings had sprouted in the rocky Fortos flatlands, and the usually lush soil of the Lumnos forest was littered with scattered grey stone.

"The borders are getting less defined," I said. "Alixe thinks they're breaking down because my coronation ritual isn't complete."

"That would explain why I still have my magic," he said, pulling a spark to his palm in proof.

"Thank the gods," I breathed.

"Thank the *Kindred*," he gently corrected. "It's their magic."

"The Kindred wanted these borders. I'll thank whatever god of chaos is helping me work against them instead."

He sighed and raised his eyes to the sky. He murmured a quiet prayer, then sent an offering of his shadows into the ether.

I watched his reverence with conflicting emotions. I'd never believed in anything the way he believed in Lumnos. He never wavered in his confidence that she was watching him, his guide and his guardian, sending him blessings in good times and comfort in bad. Much as I enjoyed taunting him with my heresy, in truth, some part of me longed for the solace his faith seemed to bring.

"What would you say to her if you met her?" I asked.

"The same thing I say when I pray. I'd thank her for bringing you into my life."

My heart fluttered and twirled.

"But what if she could answer, what would you ask her then?"

"She answers me already, in her own way." He gave me a strange look. "What would *you* ask her?"

I turned my focus to the town approaching in the distance. "I'd ask her what it's going to cost for us to win this war."

His fingers wove into mine as the imposing grey heart of Fortos grew larger and nearer.

"I wish I'd spent more time learning illusions and less time learning a thousand ways to kill," he muttered. "This would be far easier if we could slip in and out unseen."

"The killing part might come in handy, too."

He grunted in agreement. "I'm afraid to ask... do we have a plan?"

"The Umbros Queen said I have a right to see my mother. Once I know she's alive, we'll pretend to leave for Lumnos, then sneak back in late tonight."

It wasn't much of a *plan*. Kindly, he didn't say so, though his frown said enough. "Perhaps we should go back and get Alixe and Zalaric."

I shook my head vehemently. "I won't let them ruin their reputations to save my mother. It's bad enough that you're here."

"Diem." He paused until I looked at him. "Once she's out... where will we take her?"

I didn't answer, and he didn't push.

As we approached Fortos City, I gave a silent order to Sorae to save

Luther and my mother if the worst came to pass. Her snort of objection stirred a troubling question in my mind.

The spell that bound Sorae to the Crown required that she protect me from harm and obey my every command. If my life was at risk, but I insisted she save Luther... which order would triumph?

The question seemed to bother her, too. A heavy pulse of disquiet rumbled through the bond. Her head turned, her golden eyes sliding back toward me.

He's the next Crown, isn't he? I asked her. *If I die, you'll be bound to protect him next?*

If she knew the answer, she kept it to herself.

Her wings shifted, and we began our descent.

"I'M HERE to see the King."

I slapped on my widest, friendliest smile, then cocked my hips, one hand propped at my waist.

"Could we not have chosen something a little more subdued?" Luther mumbled. Standing at my side, he was my opposite—arms crossed, face scowling, ever my cruel, unapproachable Prince.

"What better way to show him I'm not afraid than by landing in the center of his training field?"

My eyes swept over the stunned faces. There were at least a hundred of them, perhaps more.

All in uniform. All armed.

"Maybe he'll be less inclined to kill me with all these witnesses," I added.

He shot me a look. "Don't count on it."

Scattered blue-eyed soldiers dropped to their knees, fists rising to their chests. I beamed warmly and returned their salute.

"If he does attack, will the Lumnos soldiers come to my defense?" I asked Luther quietly.

"No. For Descended soldiers, allegiance to their terremère is second to their army oath. For the mortals, it's even worse. They're deemed subjects of whatever realm they're currently in. Even your own brother couldn't show fealty to you outside of Lumnos."

My smile vanished. "So we're on our own?"

He answered with a somber stare.

I drew in a deep breath and stepped forward, raising my voice. "*I said* I'm here to see the Fortos King. Which of you can bring me to h—"

"They heard you. They just don't obey you."

The crowd parted.

The Fortos King was a boulder of a man. His massive frame made even Taran look small in comparison, his body so over-swollen with muscle his shoulders bunched at his ears. As he strode toward me, I swore the ground rumbled with each flat-footed stomp.

He wore only leather breeches and his Crown, which appeared as a throbbing ring of veins. His bare chest gleamed with sweat and speckled blood, and thick trails of red dripped from the ivory-handled broadsword dangling in his hand.

"You dare come to my realm without an invitation?" he growled.

"The soldiers you sent to my realm said you wanted to chat." I spread my arms and smiled. "Here I am. I do so *love* to talk."

He glowered at Sorae, an old bitterness in the sneer of his lip. Though the Fortos gryvern's death during the Blood War was a true tragedy, after my time in Umbros and Ignios, I was grateful for an advantage he couldn't match.

His focus stopped on the Lumnos Descended still on their knees. "Don't kneel to her," he barked at them. "She's not Queen yet."

I shrugged. "I've got a Crown and a gryvern. The Kindred seem to think I am." I let my voice carry further. "Surely you would *never* blaspheme the Kindred by questioning their decision."

"What happened at the ritual suggests the Blessed Kindred are questioning it themselves." His crimson eyes narrowed on me. "I should arrest you right now."

I held his glare. "You're free to try."

I didn't bother showing off my magic. The King's formidable aura had hit me the second we landed, which meant he felt mine, too—and Luther's.

There were other auras powerful enough to sense scattered among the soldiers. I couldn't place exactly who they came from, but too many carried a taste of the malice that burned within their hosts.

None—including the King—carried a candle to Luther's power, but they were many, and we were two. Even my shield couldn't hold forever.

You could kill them all, my darker instincts purred. *One flash of your silver light is all it would take. A show of power like that, and every mortal would follow you into war.*

A shudder rattled my body.

"Let's speak elsewhere," I called out. "Somewhere more private."

The King's lip curled higher. "I think I've got you right where I want you out here."

"If you insist. I'm sure they'll all love to hear about what happened on Coeurîle. Especially about the heartst—"

"*Enough,*" he growled loudly. His muscles twitched.

I grinned at my victory as he turned and jerked his chin for me to follow. I gave Sorae a light tap on her haunches, and she reared back and leapt upward into flight. After what happened in Lumnos, I didn't trust her in their hands on the ground.

"There are fewer soldiers here than I expected," I mentioned as we fell in step behind the King.

"There's more than enough to handle you," he snapped.

I raised my hands in mock surrender. "I've no doubt of that. I'm just wondering. I've been to Fortos many times, and these yards had ten times the soldiers."

His square-cut jaw ground tight. "In case you haven't noticed, we're at *war.* Between the rebels on the island, the attacks in every realm, and having to babysit your Regent, my men are in high demand."

"If you're only using the men, I'll be happy to take the rest," I joked, earning his withering glare.

My hackles rose as we moved indoors. The King's complex was a concrete fortress of labyrinthine hallways and foot-thick metal doors, with scowling soldiers on guard at every corner. I kept my chin high, refusing to acknowledge their scrutiny, though Luther let out quiet growls as he brazenly stared down each one we passed.

"We were never formally introduced," I said. "This is my Prince, Luther Corbois. You can call me Diem."

The King grunted. "You can call me Your Majesty."

"Well I won't be doing *that,*" I mumbled, half under my breath. "Don't you have a name?"

"No one here has names, only ranks. And mine is King. If you must, you may refer to me by my realm, as we do on the island."

"Surely there's something I can call you other than *Fortos.* What did people call you before you had a rank?"

"Child 1593-30."

I slowly blinked. "Fortos it is."

We turned into a long hall that ended in a set of vault-like doors. Even from a distance, I recognized the unmissable sparkling black stone.

"You come alone." He pointed at Luther. "He stays here."

Luther edged forward. "Crowns are entitled to a guard."

"Only when invited for a formal visit."

I rolled my eyes. "Your little edict *formally invited* me to come in for questioning."

"Are you always this difficult?" the King asked irritably.

"It's part of her charm," Luther drawled.

I shot him a scowl, though it faded at the hidden smile gleaming in his eyes.

"If you wish to discuss the coronation ritual, we do so in private," the King said.

I let out a dramatic sigh. "Well, if you're *that* scared of my Prince…"

He glared and turned on his heel. I gave Luther an apologetic look, his nostrils flaring unhappily, and scurried down the corridor.

We passed through the godstone doors, and the King slammed them shut with an ominous bang. He secured a convoluted series of bolts and locks, then nudged a chair with his boot. "Sit there."

He grabbed a tunic from a small armoire, then began cleaning the blood off his chest at a water basin.

"Nice doors," I said as I sat. "Is that what the army did with all the godstone they were supposed to destroy—turn it into royal decor?"

"It's a saferoom to protect the Crowns in case of attack."

"And yet *you* are the only Crown with access. How very convenient."

His eyes slid to me, his expression unamused.

"The soldiers you sent to my realm had godstone weapons," I went on. "I thought those had been banned by the Crowns."

"The army is permitted to use them when necessary."

"And what in my realm makes it necessary?"

He toweled himself off and threw on his tunic, then sank into a leather chair behind his hammered steel desk.

"There's a rumor the Guardians have allies among the Descended. Very *highly placed* Descended." He leaned his forearms on the desk. "I don't suppose you know anything about that."

I bit back all the snarky responses that rose to my lips. "I know you think I planned the Guardians' attack on Coeurîle. I assure you, I did not."

He snorted. My hands tightened on the arms of my chair.

494

"I was kidnapped by the rebels. They held me as their prisoner until I escaped."

"All the Crowns were attacked, yet you were the only one spirited away." He flashed a mocking smile. "How *very convenient*."

"They took Arboros prisoner, too."

"The Arboros Queen?" He swore, his hands curling into fists. "Well that explains why she hasn't responded to give her vote."

"Is there some way to tell if she's... that is, if something..."

"...if she's dead?"

I winced, nodding.

"If she is, the Arboros fire at the Kindred's Temple would extinguish. But now—" He shot me an accusatory stare. "—between the rebels and the winter fog, we can't get close enough to see it."

Worry tangled in my ribs. It had been weeks since I'd seen her dragged away. Cordellia hadn't seemed the murderous type. But Vance...

"Isn't there an Umbros soldier here who can read my mind and confirm I'm telling the truth?"

"The Umbros Queen forbids her subjects from serving in the army," he said bitterly.

I sat straighter. "We can do that?"

His glare sharpened to a vicious point.

I cleared my throat. "Regardless—I speak the truth. The Crowns can issue all the edicts they want. My answer won't change."

He stared at me for a long minute. "You came all this way just to tell me that?"

"No. I did not." I drew in a deep breath. "I've come to see a prisoner. Auralie Bellator."

He sneered. "You've made a long trip for nothing. You can't see her."

"She's a subject of my realm."

"Not anymore. And we both know that isn't why you want to see her."

I gritted my teeth. "Fine. *Yes*, she is my mother. All the more reason I should be allowed."

"All the more reason my answer is no."

"She's a prisoner of the Crowns, and I am a Crown. I have the right to question her."

He slammed his fists on the desk with a loud metallic *clang*. "You are implicated in her crimes. I don't believe your claim of innocence for one second. You think I'm going to let you conspire with a Guardian on my own soil?"

"You can't stop me." I crossed my arms. "A Crown holds no authority over other Crowns."

He stilled. His chin dipped with predatory focus. "So you're colluding with Umbros, too."

I held my tongue. The Crowns already considered me a threat. Perhaps it was to my advantage if they believed I didn't stand alone.

"I will see my mother today, one way or another," I said instead. "It's up to you how much blood is spilled in the process."

He laughed harshly and shook his head. "You threaten me in my own realm, in my own fortress, surrounded by my own army. You're either the biggest fool I've ever met, or..." He trailed off, eyes sweeping over me.

I leaned back and smiled. "Or *what?*"

His aura crept toward me. He was careful at first—not tentative, but targeted, pushing hard at the center of my chest. The air grew thick with his magic, choking me in his ego and his toxic, violent pride.

My stillness made him angrier. His lip curled, and his godhood began to prod. Poking me, goading me, like two hands shoving my shoulders to provoke a punch. I held his gaze, unmoving, fighting the urge to respond in kind.

Finally, his magic took its shot. My nose filled with the smell of death, followed by the familiar tingle of frozen heat. My skin began to glow.

And my smile grew wider.

His eyes bulged for a fleeting moment before he hurriedly reeled his magic back. He stood, striding for the door. "Wait there. I'll bring her in."

I popped to my feet. "No need. I'll question her in her cell."

"The only visitors allowed inside the prison are the prisoners' mates."

I craned my neck, studying his hands as he unfastened the plethora of locks along the door. He eyed me and shifted his body to block my view.

"I'm not a visitor, I'm a Crown. If you can trust their mates, surely you can trust me."

"Lady, I trust the *prisoners* more than I trust you."

"Funny, I was just thinking the same thing."

He speared me with a glare, and I beamed cheerily in response. He threw the door open and stalked off down the hall.

Luther straightened on our approach. He raised an eyebrow, and my shoulders twitched in a subtle shrug.

"You're not going in," the King said again as we trailed behind him. "You can return to my office and wait, or you can go home to Lumn—"

Without warning, I thrust my aura out. Soldiers flew off their feet, their bodies flung like discarded dolls, while the King slammed face-first into a concrete wall. Debris crumbled to the ground as a fissure webbed across the ceiling, and a metal door to my right now bore a fancy new inward dent.

My Prince was another unfortunate casualty. I hadn't yet learned to direct my aura the way the Fortos King had, so poor Luther had gone skidding across the floor. I flashed a smirk as I helped him to his feet.

"Still enjoy my rampages?" I whispered.

The heat in his eyes rivaled the summer sun. He yanked me up against him, his arousal digging into my hip. "Do that again," he murmured in my ear, "and we're going to need to find a room."

We walked back to rejoin the King, who was peeling himself out of the crackled, impacted wall.

"Sorry about that," I chirped. "Happens every time I sneeze."

Luther nodded solemnly. "If she ever catches a cold, we're going to need a whole new palace."

I bit my cheek to hold back my grin. "You were saying something?"

The King brushed bits of concrete from his shoulders, looking dazed. His crimson eyes swept over me in renewed assessment—once an annoyance, now a threat.

My brows arched in silent challenge.

He cleared his throat. "Hurry up, then. Follow me."

CHAPTER
FIFTY-ONE

After being forced to turn over our weapons, we marched outside through a maze of boxy, soulless buildings. As we walked, he threw out gruff orders to soldiers he passed, all of whom had red eyes—and all of whom were male.

"Where are the female commanders?" I asked.

The King flicked me a sour look. "Blessed Father Fortos saw fit to make our men fighters and our women healers. *Healers* don't make *commanders*."

There was oh so much I wanted to say.

About the fact that his most prized Descended were the select few who were neither male nor female, and thus carried both sides of the Fortos gifts.

About the fact that my mother—a healer—was the leader of his greatest enemy, the same group that had bested him on the island.

About the fact that *this* woman, *this* healer, had just made a King-shaped dent in his fortress walls.

But I knew men like him. I'd outsmarted and outmatched them all my life. They didn't trifle with silly things like *logic* or *reason*.

They were bullies.

And bullies only responded to fear.

I let out a soft, thoughtful hum. "Do you think the Kindred decide together who gets their strongest magic?"

"Doubtful. The other Kindred choose Queens. Blessed Father Fortos has never made that mistake." He threw me a smirk, goading me to argue. I brushed it off with an agreeable smile.

We stepped into a small, nondescript building, notable only for the heavy presence of soldiers. Inside, a single hallway led to another godstone vault and another pack of beefy guards. They saluted their King and began unlocking the doors.

I edged closer to Luther and hid my hand behind his thigh. "Do you think he might ever change his mind? Maybe realize he was wrong to determine a person's worth by what lay between their legs?"

The King scoffed. "The Blessed Father is no fool. He knows men are more capable of handling leadership. Only men are strong enough to wield—"

He paused.

Swallowed.

Wriggled his shoulders. Wrinkled his brow.

His face turned pale, then a little green.

"Something wrong?" I asked.

A pungent odor of decay rose in the air. The King tensed, his bulbous muscles straining.

"Is there a problem, Your Majesty?" a soldier asked hesitantly.

"No. No, everything's fine." The King tugged at his collar and coughed. A shimmering veil draped around him as his shield dropped into place.

"You're not looking so good," I tutted. "Perhaps you need to lie down? Have a little nap?"

I twitched my fingers. The King groaned and clutched at his gurgling stomach, his throat seeming to work at keeping its contents down.

"Which of you is doing this?" he hissed at his men. "This is treason. I'm your *King*."

The soldiers exchanged baffled looks.

"Your Majesty," one said, pointing. "Your *nose*."

The King's hand touched his nostrils, then pulled away smeared with glossy red.

"Oh, dear," I cooed. "That's not good at all."

I walked forward, smoothly breaching the wall of his shield, and brushed away the blood from his chin.

His men fell silent. The King's eyes grew.

"Careful, Fortos," I said. "Wouldn't want you to catch something your *weak, incapable* healers can't fix."

Accusation raged behind his eyes—followed quickly by doubt, then utter confusion. I said nothing, enjoying the visual tour of what his walnut-sized brain was attempting to parse.

I touched his arm and released my healing magic. "Feeling better now?" I asked. "If so, I'd like to get on with it. I intend to be back in Lumnos by sunset."

He jerked away and gripped the hilt of his sword. Luther responded in kind, shoving himself in front of me and conjuring gauntlets of sizzling light. Metallic clinking and the stink of rot filled the air as the soldiers followed suit.

I clasped my hands behind my back. "Goodness. You men are so emotional." I glanced at Luther. "Put that away, my Prince. We didn't come to do anyone harm."

He instantly withdrew his magic. "As you wish, my Queen."

I stared expectantly at the Fortos King. Though I hid it well, his dumbfounded look matched my own thoughts. When I'd called on my godhood to use the King's own deadly magic against him, I hadn't actually believed it would work.

He glanced around at his frowning, bewildered men, then eyed me, far less cocky than before.

A soldier nudged forward. "Your Majesty, are you hurt? Should I call for a heal—"

The King stiffened. "Don't just stand there," he shouted at his men. "Open the door, you idiots."

They scrambled to obey, blades returning to their sheaths. The godstone doors swung open to a stone staircase leading down further than I could see.

The King gestured for me to go ahead. I really, *really* didn't like the knowing gleam in his eyes.

"It's your realm," I demurred. "I wouldn't dream of taking the lead."

He flashed a murderous smile. "I insist."

Neither of us moved.

"Afraid to turn your back on a Queen, Fortos?" Luther taunted.

Eyebrows flew up on the soldiers' faces.

"There's nothing on this earth I fear," the King snarled. "Least of all a *woman*." He scowled and shoved past us, trudging down the narrow steps.

Luther held me back until the King had gained some distance, then tugged me close as we descended together.

"Did you just do what I think you did?" he asked under his breath.

I shrugged coyly. "Did you enjoy it?"

His hand flexed on my hip. "I am going to do such *filthy* things to you tonight."

An eager warmth pooled low in my belly. My toes curled as we exchanged a look simmering with mutual promise.

After a seemingly eternal descent, the stairs smoothed into a long, vaulted hallway, though it was blocked by a gate of glittering black stone bars.

The King unsheathed his blade and drew its point across his thumb, then swiped the finger on a small metal disc on the gate.

Shit.

Bloodlocks.

Only willingly given blood would unlock them. Even if I took the King himself hostage, no amount of threats or mind control would bypass *this*.

We followed the King through, his stare holding steady on me as he slammed the gate closed. "Like what you see? It might be your home too, someday. Someday *soon*."

I gazed up and tapped my chin. "I wonder if a pissed off gryvern could make it all the way down here." I frowned. "Oh, I forgot, you don't have one. I guess you wouldn't know."

His face filled with so much rage, Luther stiffened and nudged me behind him.

Sensitive subject? I asked into Luther's mind.

He shot me a half-amused, half-wary look.

We continued on, following more long halls, passing through more bloodlocked gates. Oddly, there wasn't a single soldier in sight.

"Where are all the guards?" I asked.

"We don't need guards," the King answered. "No one can get past these gates. Even if they did, there's only one exit, and it's nothing but flatlands for miles. They'd be spotted in minutes. There's never been a successful escape in Emarion history."

My stomach lurched.

The corridors thinned, and iron doors began to appear along the stone walls. Behind grates in their panels, the interiors were shrouded in darkness.

I paused in front of a door and raised a hand to the opening. Pale blue light spiraled out from my palm, illuminating the bleak cell. There was very little inside—a flattened mat of moldy hay, a dingy bucket, and a tray of food that looked like it had been rotting for weeks.

And curled up in a back corner, shielding his face from the glow, sat a green-eyed man.

He looked shockingly fragile for a Descended. Soiled muslin rags drooped from his bones, which had become nearly visible through his sallow, paper-thin skin. His face had lost all its color, and his eyes had lost all their light.

I sucked in a breath. Instinctively, I reached toward him and pushed healing magic into the air.

"What are you doing?" the King snapped, lunging to grab me. "Get away from there."

Luther blocked his path with a threatening snarl. "Lay a hand on her, and this realm will have a new Crown by day's end."

I had to admit, *his* rampages had quite the stimulating effect of their own.

"You two can't just come to my realm and threaten me," the King roared.

"These conditions are inhumane," I shouted back. "This man is barely alive."

"He's lucky. If I had my way, there'd be nothing left of him but ash. My only mandate is to keep the prisoners breathing. Beyond that, I run things how I please. If you don't like it, take it up with the Crowns." He began to walk away. "Something tells me they won't be receptive to complaints from *you*."

I gazed back at the cell. Luther took my hands and gently tried to pry me away.

"You will remake this world," he said, echoing his words in the Umbros markets. "Right now, your mother needs you."

I reluctantly let him lead me away. My eyes fell in shame with every new cell we passed, knowing now of the horrors that lay inside.

"Why are they so quiet?" I murmured. There were at least forty cells in this hall alone, yet not even a whisper emerged from a single one.

"They're drugged," the King answered. "It suppresses their magic and keeps them docile."

Flameroot, I realized. Though the small amount I'd taken daily had dulled my emotions, for the most part, I'd still been myself. These prisoners must have been given an enormous dose to have this strong an effect.

A sudden crush of emptiness hit me. It was visceral, more physical than sadness, like a piece of my soul had been sucked out from within. I clutched at my chest and looked up at Luther in alarm—only to see his face had gone pale.

His expression turned grim as his gaze locked with mine. The storm of light and shadow that usually churned in his eyes had vanished.

My heart sank.

His magic was gone.

The King stopped mid-step and glanced over his shoulder, a cruel smile hooking at the corner of his lips. It seemed he had noticed, too.

Luther's knuckles blanched where they fisted at his side. "Don't get any ideas," he rumbled. "All I need is my bare hands and a good reason."

The King's ominous chuckle echoed down the hall.

After a shorter set of stairs, the corridor opened up to a wide central room partitioned by walls of iron bars enclosing several large, hay-covered pens. Like the other cells, they were brutally sparse. The air reeked of a putrid scent, the scattered buckets overflowing with waste.

The room was freezing, raising bumps along my arms, yet no prisoner had more than a thin, threadbare tunic and no blankets were anywhere in sight. Thick metal chains draped from the walls and tangled on the ground where shivering bodies huddled in groups, emaciated arms draped over bony shoulders.

"You're a monster," I breathed. "These are human beings, Fortos."

He grunted. "I thought you'd be happy. At least we let the families stay together."

"Families?" I choked.

As I dared to peer closer, I spotted smaller, younger bodies hidden amid the horde. Their brown eyes peered at my Crown with a deeply understandable fusion of terror and hate.

My temper exploded. I whirled on the King and stormed toward him as magic sprang to life at my palms. "You put fucking *children* in here?"

He threw up his shield, momentarily bouncing me backward. I slashed a hand across the filmy grey dome and it shattered to dust.

The King stumbled back a step. "They were captured in a rebel camp. The laws apply to everyone equally. Even children."

"Equally?" My enraged shout reverberated off the stone walls. "*Equally?*"

Fight, the *voice* purred.

My godhood blazed alongside my fury, swirling in tandem to a blistering heat.

"My Queen," Luther said. "There's something you should see."

I barely heard him over the roar of my temper. My self-control was unraveling and taking my magic with it, sparks flurrying in the air and shadows dripping from my palms.

Fight.

The mortals began to rise and press curious faces to the bars of their cells.

The King edged further back. "Put your magic away, Lumnos. I can have a hundred guards here in a second."

"How *dare* you claim the laws apply equally?" I snarled. "This continent hasn't seen equality since the day your cursed, gods-damned Kindr—"

"Your Majesty," Luther cut in sharply. "*Look.*"

His hand pressed between my shoulders. The tender touch blunted the edge of my ire, but I was too far gone in my rage to tear my glare from the King.

Fight.

Destroy.

My skin ignited with glittering light. "One day soon, you will answer for your crimes, Fortos. And when you do—"

"Diem?"

My voice hitched.

My heart paused.

My magic stuttered and died.

Time slowed to a crawl as my head turned toward the weak, familiar voice that had called out my name.

From deep within the shadows of the cage, the brown eyes of Auralie Bellator stared back.

CHAPTER
FIFTY-TWO

"Mother?"

It was a whisper. A prayer. A plea.

"Diem? Is that you?"

I lurched forward a few steps, then froze. It seemed too much to hope that this was real.

For months, I'd lived in the limbo of her absence. If she was dead, I'd have to mourn her. If she was alive, I'd have to confront her. I feared both with equal dread, so I'd never allowed myself to plant my feet in either camp.

Even after learning she was alive—even after seeing it with my own eyes on Coeurîle—I'd barricaded myself in the 'we can't be sure' of it all. With no guarantee I'd ever see her again, I'd pushed away the hope just as fiercely as the grief.

And now my purgatory was over.

"*Diem!*"

My mother's voice shattered as she hoarsely called my name. Her copper-red hair was dark with filth, but even in the shadows, it shone like a ruby in the moonlight.

I threw myself against the bars and reached an arm through, desperate for the feel of her beneath my palm. Her hand stretched shakily toward me.

"Mother," I gasped. "Come here—let me see you."

Her hand trembled, then fell limply to the floor. She struggled to get up amid stifled whimpers.

I stilled. "Mother? Are you alright?"

Two mortals rushed to her side. Gingerly, they hooked her arms around their necks. A soft cry of pain escaped her at the sudden movement.

"What's wrong with her?" I hissed at the King.

His mouth set in a firm line. "She was given a chance to cooperate with our interrogations. She chose not to do so."

"Diem," she croaked.

I strained toward her again and let out a sob as my fingertips grazed her shoulders. "Mother, please, look at me."

The mortals carried her closer. Her drooping head lolled to the side, then tilted up to the light.

Red clouded my vision.

The red of her vibrant hair, hacked in choppy pieces above her too-thin shoulders.

The red of the blood on her hollowed face, coating her swollen-shut eye and half-bent nose.

The red of my rage, reawakened and screaming for retribution.

"You *tortured* her," I shouted.

"What do you expect?" the King said testily. "She has information that could stop the war and save thousands of lives. We have a moral obligation to get it by any means necessary."

I might have murdered him right then and there had Luther not intervened in my place.

"There's nothing moral about beating a defenseless person," he thundered. He flew into the King's face, sending him staggering until his back collided with a wall. "These people are in your care. It's your duty to keep them *safe*."

The King flicked up his shield and sneered. "I'm keeping the people who matter safe."

Luther slammed his fist against the shimmering dome. The King flinched, then growled and raised his palm.

I threw my shield around Luther and turned back to my mother.

"Diem," she whispered. "I missed you, my little warrior."

Fire burned through my throat. "I missed you, too. Oh gods, Mother... I missed you so much."

Her head bobbled in a fight to stay up. I cupped my hands beneath her jaw, my heart aching at her grimace of pain. I darted a glance at the shouting match behind me, then unleashed my healing magic into her skin.

I flowed alongside my godhood as it surveyed her many wounds. Broken bones galore, a punctured lung, a shattered knee. Her back was slashed to ribbons. One tooth was missing, another loose.

My wrath nearly escaped in a feral scream. I poured it into my magic and growled at my godhood to make my mother whole.

A bright light flashed beneath my hands, and she slumped forward with a breathy groan. Slowly her legs trembled, steadied, then straightened. She stared at me, mouth agape. "Did you...?"

I hushed her, nervously glancing at the King.

Her eyes rose to my Crown. "But... I thought..."

"I'll explain later," I whispered. "Don't let him know what I've done."

She gave a shallow nod. The mortals hovered close, watching me with blatant doubt. She patted their shoulders. "Thank you, Brothers. Would you give me a moment with my little girl?"

I bristled, then nearly laughed. I was a grown woman, a Queen, a conquering hero come to break her free—but in her eyes, I was still *her little girl*.

She pressed her palm to my cheek. "It's only been a few months, but you look so different. Older. So much stronger, too."

"It's been almost a year. Much has happened."

Her gaze flicked again to my Crown. "It seems it has."

All my thoughts warred in a race to my lips. A thousand burning questions demanded to be asked, each one more urgent than the next. But it wasn't the questions that choked me silent.

"Teller is well," I managed to croak out.

Her eyes squeezed closed. "Thank the gods. I heard news of you, but nothing of him."

"He's fine. Sad, but fine. Healthy. Living in the palace. I get to call him a Prince now." I laughed between sniffles. "He *hates* it."

Her smile wobbled with the tremble of her lower lip, eyes gleaming with unshed tears. "When they were torturing me, they told me things. About you... and about Andrei."

My father's name on her lips was more than I could take. The dread of this revelation had been haunting me for weeks.

"What did they say about Father?" I forced out.

"Vile things. Cruel things, to hurt me." Her voice began to shake. "They said he's..."

She didn't finish.

And I didn't answer.

The despair on my face, and the horror on hers, spoke the words neither of us could bear to say aloud.

She collapsed against the bars, her broken-hearted sob filling every corner and every shadow. My arms pulled her closer, but my own knees felt unstable as sorrow lacerated through my soul. The wound of my father's death ripped open anew, and we clung to each other, bleeding out our agony.

The shouting behind me stopped. The mortals fell quiet in their cells. An awful silence settled around us, broken only by my mother's weeping.

We stayed like that for a long while, my tears tumbling silently as hers fell in loud, heaving gasps. I held her as close as the bars would allow, tugging her so hard I feared we'd both be left bruised.

"They mentioned a fire," she whispered.

I winced. "That's just the story we told."

"Story?"

"He was stabbed." My throat worked. "Murdered."

Her body deflated. She clutched the bars, her forehead sinking against them.

"After the attack on the island?" Her voice was barely audible. "Because of me?"

"No. Before. Because of me." I couldn't look at her. "Whoever killed him left messages for me."

"What kind of messages?"

Memories of the blood-smeared walls of my family home flashed through my head.

"Mortal lover. Half-breed."

Rebel scum, I thought, though I held that detail back. This was my guilt to bear, not hers.

The anguish on my mother's face slowly sagged away, replaced by a hardened wrath. She seemed to have aged ten years in that one moment, the slaughter of her beloved stealing the final traces of hopeful youth. "Do you know who it was?"

"I have suspicions, but no proof. There were plenty of Descended with a motive. I had few allies then." I shifted uneasily. "I have few allies *now*."

"You must go to the Guardians. They'll help you find the killer."

A bitter laugh escaped before I could stop it. "The Guardians have no interest in helping me. Especially not now."

She frowned. "They will not let an attack on my family go unanswered. I am their leader."

"And I am a *Descended*."

My tone cut too sharp, and my mother balked. "You have mortal parents. A mortal brother. You were raised in Mortal City, at mortal schools. Your friends, your career... Diem, you are—"

"—a Descended," I finished. "That's all I am to them now."

She dropped her hands and stepped away. Her gaze roved over me, eyebrows tugging low, expression awash with inexplicable denial. If I didn't know better, I might have thought it hadn't occurred to her until this very moment what she'd raised.

"How could you keep this from me?" I asked.

Her expression looked pained. "The man who sired you was... different. Not like any mortal or Descended I'd ever met. When you were born with brown eyes, I thought the gods had blessed us, and you had escaped it. Then your magic came in..." Her shoulders fell. "You were only ten. I wanted to give you a normal life for as long as I could."

"My life *wasn't* normal." My voice grew louder. "You drugged me. You told me I was having visions—you made me think I was crazy. You hid me away."

"They would have killed you, Diem. Every day, I lived in fear they would discover the truth."

"And what is the truth? Who is my birth father? *Where* is he? I know you lied about him dying, too."

She recoiled a step. "That wasn't a lie. He died the day you were born."

I searched her face for some hint of dishonesty, but she was either Emarion's greatest liar or she truly believed it. I didn't know which conclusion was more likely.

"He isn't dead," I said. "He's alive. And he knows about me."

The color drained from her face. "No. *No.* That can't—"

She stopped, her attention cutting over my shoulder. I looked back to see the King notably closer than where he'd stood before. He was staring at his feet, hands clasped at his back, his ear ever so subtly leaning in.

My mother's lips pursed closed. She gave me a glare that told me she'd say no more in his presence.

I spun around to face him. "I want to question her in private."

His back snapped straight. "Prisoners don't ever leave their cells. You can question her here."

"Ever?" I cocked my head. "So when you beat her and whipped her, you did it right here?"

"Sometimes," one of the mortals muttered. "But when he questioned her, he took her away."

"He told us she betrayed the Guardians," another added. "He thought we'd turn on her and kill her, since the Crowns won't let him do it. But we didn't believe him. We know her better than that."

Nods rippled through the cages. The mortals looked at my mother with admiration in their eyes.

The King glowered. "You'll all pay for this later."

Dread crept up my spine at the promise in his tone. "Why don't we take her back to your office?" I offered. "It's safe there, isn't it?"

"You think I'll let her walk outside this prison with *you?* Do I look like an idiot?"

I gave him a look that said *do you really want me to answer that?*

He scowled and marched to the cage, pricking his finger on his blade to swipe across the lock. "I'll take you to an empty cell, but she's not leaving this prison unless it's in a coffin."

He held up a fist, and the stench of rot filled the room. A shared groan of pain rose as the mortals clutched their stomachs and fell to their knees. The shield I'd placed around Luther rippled like it had been struck, and my skin blinked with light and a sudden burst of energy.

"Was that necessary?" I asked archly.

"Yes. And if any of them move, I'll give them far worse than a stomach ache."

He threw open the cage door and stalked to my mother, then gripped her arm and dragged her back to her feet. He paused, looking at her knee. "How'd you heal so fast?"

Panic flared. "Get off her," I shouted, running toward her. "She's clearly still wounded. I'll help her walk."

The King threw a blast of his magic out to stop me. I glowed bright as it absorbed without effect.

I snatched my mother's arm out of his grasp and threw it over my shoulder. Without missing a beat, she collapsed against me and let out a convincing whine.

"Why is your shield different?" The King jerked his chin toward Luther. "I can see it cover him, but not you."

"Because I'm stronger than he is," I lied. Luther smirked in confirmation. "And he's stronger than *you*."

The King eyed Luther, whose expression shifted from proud to ferocious.

With my pretense of help, my mother faux-hobbled out of the cage. Luther moved forward to take her other arm, and my mother jerked away, shooting him a warning glare. I glanced between them with a frown, looking to Luther for explanation. He disappeared behind his mask of indifference and turned away.

As the door to the iron gate swung closed, a mortal woman lunged forward to grab it. She slipped through the closing gap with a cry that rang of vengeance as she dove for the King's neck.

I tried to untangle my hands from my mother to raise a shield, but I moved too slow. The King's palm curled in, and the woman decayed before my eyes. Her flesh turned grey, then ashen, then crumbled away in rotting hunks. When nothing remained but hair and bones, her form collapsed amid a puddle of putrid mess.

My mother screamed. She lurched at the King, and I jerked her back with barely enough time to stretch my shield around her before he launched another wave of deadly magic through the room.

As promised, this blow delivered much more than discomfort. Blood leaked from mouths and noses amid excruciated shrieks. A few collapsed, and I watched in horror as not all got back up.

"*Stop*," I shouted at the King in between grunts as I wrestled to hold my mother back. "You killed the one who ran. Isn't that enough?"

"You killed them," he shot back, slamming the cage door in an echoing clang. "You rile up my prisoners, these are the consequences. That woman would be alive if you'd never come."

I stiffened.

"I have given you more latitude than you deserve, Lumnos. You should be locked up with them. One more outburst—" He jabbed a finger at my mother. "—from *either* of you, and my patience ends. The law may not let me kill you, but I can kill them. And now you see I have no problem doing it."

My mother clamped her mouth shut. I felt her emaciated muscles shudder beneath my hands.

I spoke a thought into her mind: *He will pay, Mother. I promise.*

The fight in her faltered as she looked at me in surprise, and I confirmed with a subtle nod.

The King started up the stairs, and we followed, Luther marching protectively in front of me. I tried not to think about the mortal stretching her arms toward the dead woman's remains, but her sorrowful wail rang in my ears long after we'd walked away.

I noticed my mother marking each turn we took with rapt attention. She whispered to herself: "*right, ten paces, left, twenty-four paces, left.*"

Don't try anything, I warned in her head. *No running. No fighting him. Let me handle this.*

She stared at me and furrowed her brow, her face expectant, like she was awaiting a response.

"Can you hear mine, too?" she mouthed after a moment.

I pushed my magic out and let it swirl around her temples. A sound hit me—through my *head*, not my ears—resembling the strange, hushed whispers I'd heard in Umbros.

Can you hear me? my mother asked again.

This time, her lips didn't move.

I nodded, my eyes going wide. Would this magic ever stop feeling so uncanny and new?

The Umbros magic in particular felt *wrong* to wield. My mind spun with all the ways it could be useful in our war—persuading the staunchest haters into unity, forcing surrenders before any lives could be lost—but if it wasn't willingly chosen, could there ever be true peace?

I have to escape, my mother said. *I may never get another chance.*

I know, I answered back. *I'm not leaving this realm without you.*

Her eyes lit up. *Did you bring the Guardians?*

I shook my head. *Only Luther. And my gryvern.*

I tried not to flinch at her crestfallen expression. She sighed heavily. *Diem, if I don't make it out—*

You will, I insisted.

She grabbed my hand and squeezed. *If I don't... tell Teller how much I love him. And how sorry I am for not being there.*

Her eyes glistened, my father's loss casting a bleak shadow over our reunion.

"Here." The King stopped and swung open the door to a dark, empty cell. "We reserve these for our most dangerous prisoners." He smirked. "Perfect for the likes of you two."

I studied it apprehensively. Unlike the cells I'd seen earlier, this door had no grates, no openings—just a solid slab of glittering black.

"The door stays op—"

"*No*," he cut me off. "No more concessions."

I shared a glance with Luther. The godhood door would trap my magic inside the cell, leaving him at the King's mercy without my shield.

"What's wrong?" the King taunted. "Don't trust me with your Prince?"

I forced my chin high. "Nah. You're not really his type."

Luther's lip hooked up for a second before settling back on the King with a menacing scowl.

Behave, I said in Luther's head as I led my mother inside. *No rampaging without me.*

I caught a sliver of his wink before the door slammed shut and cast me into darkness. I crafted a globe of light and tugged my mother to the furthest corner of the cell.

"Do you have a plan to get out?" she asked quietly.

I nodded confidently—a lie. A big, ugly, glaring, outrageous lie.

"How are we getting out?" she pushed.

"Let me worry about that."

"Diem—"

"Tell me what you know about the prison. The bloodlocks—who do they open for?"

Her reddish brows furrowed into a skeptical crease. I'd forgotten how well my mother knew me—how clearly she'd always seen through my false confidence. "Diem, I know Luther is very powerful, and..." She looked me over, plainly unconvinced. "I'm sure you are, too. But there are thousands of soldiers here. You need weapons, you need an army—"

I bristled. "You have *no idea* what I am capable of."

She stroked my hair, one hand cupping around my cheek. It was such a familiar gesture, rich with well-worn love and easy memories. Memories that now felt like they belonged to another person.

I flinched away. That life was gone. The touch that had once brought me such comfort had become a painful reminder of all that I'd lost.

"Why don't you distract the King?" she suggested. "I'll run for it. I can find a place to hide, perhaps slip out when no one's looking."

"Are you mad? You won't make it five feet."

"I'll be fine. I have some... experience with these kinds of things."

"You're just a *healer*, Mother."

She smiled a pitiful smile, one of secrets and regret. "Diem, I have never been just a healer."

My attention was stolen by muffled voices in the hall. I put a finger to my lips, then crept on quiet feet to the door. I crouched low and pressed my ear to a thin flap at the base I suspected they used to deliver meals.

"—with instructions they were to be delivered to you directly."

"Who sent them?"

"The first hawk was sent by Her Majesty the Queen of Arboros."

"So she's alive, after all." The King chuckled darkly. "And she's finally sent her vote on Auralie Bellator's execution. Tell me, Prince, if your Queen spoke true and Arboros was the Guardians' prisoner, what do you think her vote will be?"

My heart sputtered and stalled, then dropped into a gut-clenching freefall.

"Who sent the other hawk, Lieutenant?"

"The Regent of Lumnos, Your Majesty. It arrived minutes ago. It was marked as *extremely urgent*."

My falling heart plummeted straight into hell.

Remis hadn't just betrayed me. He'd signed my death warrant—and his son's, too.

Waiting until nightfall was no longer an option. We had to leave this prison.

And we had to do it now.

CHAPTER
FIFTY-THREE

The King laughed loudly. "Have the messages brought to me here, Lieutenant. I want Lumnos to see me when I read them out loud."

Luther's growl rolled through the air.

"And bring a battalion when you come," the King added. "In case our *guests* get any ideas."

I threw my thoughts out in a desperate bid to reach Luther, but the godstone's effect was brutal. Like it had in his toxin-ravaged body, every time my magic brushed against it, my godhood shrieked and retreated in fear.

It felt unthinkable that I'd destroyed it in my earlier battles. The glimmering ebony rock seemed hopelessly impenetrable now.

"Change of plans," I hissed at my mother as I stood. "The King needs six votes to execute you, and I think the last one just arrived. We have to do this now."

She blanched, then a calm focus settled over her face. "Tell the *Prince* to distract the King while I run. Let him take the fall."

She said Luther's title like a swear. I frowned. "I'm not putting Luther at any more risk than he is already." My mother balked. I grabbed her arm with a warning scowl, then rapped my other hand against the door. "And *you* aren't running."

"Yes?" the King's voice called out.

"We're finished," I yelled.

515

"So soon? It's only been a few minutes."

"I work fast."

"Don't you want to make the most of your mother-daughter time?" His tone turned cruel. "Might be the last chance you ever get."

I clenched my teeth and pounded the door. "Let us out, Fortos."

Even without magic, the godstone's repellant nature had an uncanny effect. The longer it touched my skin, the more my bleakest emotions bubbled to the surface—hatred and anger, sorrow and gloom. The material was smooth beneath my palm, but it somehow *felt* like the worst thing I'd ever touched, like death and wrongness given tangible form.

I fought the urge to recoil as I knocked again. "*Now*, Fortos."

"I'm not quite ready. I'm enjoying my time alone with your Prince."

My blood went cold. I heard Luther's voice, too low to decipher. I pressed closer to the door, straining my ears to hear, and the godstone's wicked influence deepened its claws.

"Touch him and you're a dead man," I shouted.

"Don't worry. I don't have to *touch* him at all."

A foul smell wafted beneath the door, followed by pained grunts.

"Luther?" I called out, my panic rising.

"I'm fine," he answered in a stilted rasp. "Fortos is just... trying to make up... for his... tiny di—"

His words cut off, followed by the thump of a body hitting the floor.

My banging turned frantic. "Luther? *Luther!*"

Fight, the *voice* demanded.

I hurled a blast of light at the door. The rays shattered into splinters on impact, ricocheting in white-hot sparks throughout the cell.

"The Prince might need a healer," the King taunted. "Your mother was one, wasn't she?" He snorted, as if that were some clever joke.

I glanced at her. Her eyes quickly darted away.

"I'll make a deal," he said. "Tell me everything you know about the attack on Coeurîle, and I'll leave him alone."

"I already told you, I didn't know anything."

"How unfortunate for your Prince."

Fight.

My irritation enflamed to wrath, my worry spiraled to terror. My godhood was feeding off the turmoil, and with nowhere to go, it built inside me to an unbearable pitch. I clawed at the door, my nails screeching against the impenetrable rock.

"I can't tell you what I don't know," I pleaded.

"You claim you were kidnapped and held for weeks. You have to know something. Give me names. Locations."

I grimaced, torn by conflict. Even after all the Guardians had done, I didn't want to be the reason more mortals died in cages. "I didn't know where I was. They drugged me with flameroot."

"They have *flameroot?*" the King roared.

"Diem, no," my mother hissed, yanking me away from the door.

"I have to give him something. Luther—"

"Forget about the Prince. He's just a Descended." She saw my incredulous stare and seemed to realize what she'd said a moment too late. "I didn't mean—"

"That's a lot of blood," the King crooned. "I better get more details quickly."

Fight.

My skin glimmered and glowed, my magic whipping into a frenzy beyond my control. "Get out of my way," I warned my mother.

She spread her hands across the door. "No, Diem. I won't let you betray the Guardians for him."

Fight.

"Move," I growled. Pebbles rattled against the floor, the air crackling with the buzz of a brewing storm. I ground my teeth near to dust in a fight to keep it contained.

She held fast to her place. "I'm so sorry, my little warrior. This is one battle you won't win."

"Luther, are you alright?" I called out.

An awful silence answered back.

"*Luther?*" I pleaded.

"I think he might be sleeping," the King crooned. "Permanently."

Fight.

I stormed into my mother's face, her frightened features awash with the light from my blazing eyes. She shrank back, and something inside me broke at the knowledge I'd become a monster my own mother feared.

"Get out of my way," I snarled.

She steeled her shoulders. "I will not."

Fight.

"Mother, *move!*"

Her brown eyes turned glassy, her expression going blank. With limp arms and a sagging head, she stiffly shuffled into the far corner of the cell.

Destroy.

I didn't even surrender to the magic—my heart did it all on her own. She was still healing from the near loss of him to the godstone, and she'd be damned if we let the gods take him now.

The odd, destructive silvery light burst from my skin. I'd once believed it a reflex, some uncontrollable force that worked in ways I couldn't predict let alone control, but every time I used it, I came a little closer to bringing it to heel.

I honed in on its essence—where it came from, what it did. My usual magic flowed from my godhood, but this power seemed imbued in my blood itself. And when it brushed against the toxic bleakness of the godstone's touch, it did not cower.

It merged. It *fulfilled.*

I thought I'd been destroying the godstone. But it was never destruction—it was balance.

Hot and cold, light and shadow, life and death.

In the center of that all-consuming glow, a preternatural wisdom bathed me in its eerie, quiet calm. A knowledge of all that was and ever will be, a glimpse from the gods themselves at a truth too pure for human minds to comprehend.

And yet, for that moment—one perfect, ephemeral moment—I understood.

But it was an answer I wasn't yet meant to know.

Not until my worth was proven.

Not until my soul had been judged.

I cried out as it slipped away, evaporating like a wet stone baking beneath the sun. It tingled at my fingertips and whispered in my ear of choices and prophecies and fate, but when the light ebbed, so too did it fade.

"How did you do that?"

The King stood in the corridor, jaw agape.

"That... that was *godstone*," he stammered. "How...?"

I raised my palms, and a burst of shadow slammed into the center of his chest. He grunted and hit the floor, wrestling with the writhing darkness that pinned him down.

Luther lay nearby, eyes closed. My heart plunged as I ran and collapsed on top of him, healing magic pouring out before my hands even found his flesh.

His insides were in ruins—organs failing, tissue rotting to an ashy grey

—and yet his heart had once again been miraculously spared. It was defiant, that warrior heart of his. Just like the woman it loved.

Its fierce, persistent beat grew louder as my magic did its work. His hand twitched, then closed over mine, and when his blue-grey eyes opened and met my gaze, all the air in my lungs rushed out.

"I leave you alone for *five* minutes," I joked, though my voice was a hoarse, shaken mess.

"Whatever it takes to get your hands on me." We shared a relieved smile as the last of the damage mended, then his face turned grim. "The messenger hawks."

"I heard. We can't wait anymore."

As I helped him stand, I spied my mother lurking in the doorway of the cell, watching me with a clouded expression. I felt a stab of guilt—I hadn't *intended* to use the Umbros magic on her, but given her willingness to let Luther die, I didn't exactly regret it, either.

"How did you do that?" the King bellowed, wriggling free of my shadowy web. "What kind of weapon do you have? Where did you get it?"

I schooled my face to confusion. "I don't know what you mean."

"That door was solid godstone. Nothing can destroy it."

My head cocked. "That door was made of iron. I melted it away with Lumnos light."

He scowled. "Don't play games with me. That godstone dates back to the Blessed Father himself."

My mother slowly began to creep away.

Don't, I warned into her thoughts.

"You don't know your own prison, Fortos," Luther said, chuckling. "That door was clearly iron."

The King scoffed and glanced at the cell, where my mother froze and nodded quickly in agreement.

He stiffened. "That door... it wasn't—I'm sure of it..." He gazed down the hallway. "All these cells are fortified with godstone."

"You said it was being repaired." I flashed a helpful smile. "Squeaky hinges."

The King looked down, scratching his head. "*Squeaky hinges?*"

My mother started moving again, creeping slowly as she moved beyond the King, then scurrying faster. Luther's arm brushed mine—he'd spotted it, too.

Mother, I warned her. *The King will kill you.*

I heard her answer back: *Then tell the Prince to stop him. He should want his revenge.*

I glared at her. *I'm not letting you run a—*

She turned and bolted. The King's head snapped toward her, and to my surprise—and my horror—he began to laugh.

"Finally," he breathed, grinning. "I've been waiting for her to give me a reason. Now I don't need a sixth vote." His gaze slid back to me and sparkled with malice. "Escapees can be slaughtered on sight."

My eyes narrowed.

"Go get her," I murmured to Luther. "Be careful." He nodded and took off after my mother.

The King lunged to grab him and collided into my shield. He stumbled back, grabbing his nose with a snarl. "Helping a prisoner escape is treason. You're just as dead as she is."

My head spun as my plans unraveled. Getting my mother out quietly, leaving no proof, convincing the Crowns to coronate me—those hopes had gone up in a bigger blaze than the Everflame itself.

I squared my shoulders and crouched into a battle stance. "I'm not dying in this prison, Fortos. Do what I say, and you won't, either."

His lips slid sideways. "I can't *wait* to hear this."

I pointed to an empty cell. "Open the door and get inside. Your soldiers can let you out once we're gone. I don't want to have to kill you."

He threw his head back and laughed. "You're very cocky for a woman. What is it you think you have that I don't?"

"Knuckles that don't drag when I walk. The ability to breathe through my nose. A neck."

His mirth vanished. "If you're so certain you can kill me, why not do it now?"

"I'm not here to take lives. You and the other Crowns have put too many bodies in graves already."

"This is your problem, Lumnos. You've got all the confidence of a man, but none of the balls." He pulled his broadsword from its scabbard and pointed it at me. "If you want me in that cell, you'll have to chop me into pieces and sweep me under the door."

My insides tangled in knots. I was being forced into a crossroads I'd tried desperately to avoid.

Shadows hissed at my palm, and a long, dark sword took form in my hand. "Don't make me do this, Fortos. Let me take my mother and go."

He grinned and lifted his blade. "Maybe I'll get lucky, and she'll come back just in time to see her '*little girl*' die."

He lunged forward and struck. I'd never used a magic-made sword for anything but show—when I raised mine above my head to block his attack, I wasn't entirely certain the shadows would hold.

My eyes screwed shut, and I braced for death.

A violent ripple rocked through my arms as his blade clashed against mine and bounced away. Though my magic had held, the brutal force of his swing sent me stumbling back.

He was strong. Very strong.

Dangerously strong.

He was also dangerously skilled. It seemed all five of his brain cells had been devoted to the art of the fight. He wielded his strength with shrewd precision, using momentum to compensate for my greater speed. As we danced in violent tandem, trading parries and thrusts, my nerves rose higher with every blow.

But I had skills of my own. Though it pushed my training to its limits, I managed to land a few critical strikes in an aggressive flurry of attacks.

He retreated a step, looking amused. "A Queen who can wield a blade. I didn't expect that."

"You forget who my father is. Andrei Bellator taught me everything he knew."

"And who do you think taught *him?*"

I sliced a line at his throat, shifting at the last second so my blade only drew a minor nick. "Yield, Fortos."

Blood trickled down his chest. He touched his fingers to it and smirked. "Never."

In a flash, he jabbed straight for my heart. I spun away and crashed into the corridor wall, wincing at both the King's smug laughter and my now-tender arm.

"Andrei must not have taught you everything. You're making a mistake my men never would." He rolled his sword in a lazy arc. "You're holding back."

I feinted left and sent him lunging for open air, a distraction to mask my unease at being so easily read.

I didn't want to end him. But I needed to convince him I *could*—then perhaps I might rattle him enough to comply.

My godhood howled to be let loose. I firmly clamped it down, feeling some innate push to do this on my own. Perhaps it was an homage to my father—using his training to defeat the man he'd served all those years. Or perhaps the King's comments were getting to me more than I wanted to admit.

A quick strike landed a deep gash on his arm. He hissed at the blade's sharp bite.

"My mother taught me everything she knows, too. I can have a look at all those wounds you're taking on." I smirked. "Once you yield, of course."

"Ah, yes. Your mother. The *healer*."

Again, he said the word with a curious timbre.

His blade swung up and clipped my thigh. I bit down on the pain and lurched forward on my injured leg, slicing my sword at his unguarded side. Panic flashed briefly in his eyes, but he deflected surprisingly fast, and our blades locked in an X at his neck.

"Yield."

"*Never.*"

His strength won out over mine, and I was forced to stumble back.

"Why do you speak as if she wasn't a healer?"

His head cocked. His eyes trailed curiously over my face. Finally, he barked a laugh. "I shouldn't be surprised. She was always good at keeping a secret."

Pattering footsteps echoed down the hall—far too many to be just my mother and Luther.

The King's grin stretched wide. "Time's up."

In a panic, I sent him hurtling backward with a burst of Meros wind. His head cracked against a godstone door, and his unconscious body slumped to the ground. I crouched beside him, wrapping him up in dark vines and raising a veil of shadows to cover us both.

A group of his soldiers appeared at the end of the corridor carrying two hawks with scrolls clamped to their legs.

My pulse set into a gallop. If the soldiers came any closer, my sloppy makeshift illusion would be too obvious to miss.

"I thought the King was here," one of them said.

"They must have taken the prisoner back to her cell."

"We passed the mortal cages. They weren't there."

The King stirred at my side, his groggy voice emerging from the dark. "I'm over he—"

I slapped a thick patch of shadow over his face.

"Did you hear that?" a soldier asked. He crept our way, warily craning his neck.

An idea struck.

They already left. I pushed the thought out with force. *The King must be in his office now.*

The man stopped. "They already left. The King must be in his office now."

My heart leapt.

Another soldier raised his brows. "No one saw them leave."

The man blinked, then frowned, then shook his head as if clearing a fog. "I... I'm not..."

How dare he question your command? I thought.

He spun on the other with a glare. "How dare you question my command?" He shoved him in the shoulder. "Get going. Back to His Majesty's office."

The others hustled to obey. The soldier whose mind I'd spoken into lingered and stared down the dimly lit corridor. After a moment, he was gone.

My magic dissolved. The King gasped for air, his face alarmingly blue.

I swore and reached for him. "Are you al—"

He launched at me in a rage, slashing at my head with enough force to shatter bone. I yelped and rolled across the ground as his blade carved a gouge in the floor.

He didn't spare a second before trying again. I abandoned my shadow sword and frantically crawled out of his path. A whiff of air whistled past my ear, his strike missing by a hair.

My godhood snarled to answer in kind. I snarled right back, still determined to do this my way.

"Wind," the King wheezed between pants. "You used *wind* to push me back."

I climbed to my feet. "You hit your head too hard," I said, desperately trying to keep my tone light as panic spiraled in my chest. "Wind belongs to Meros."

"Earlier, in the hall—it was *you* using my magic." His eyes blazed a bloodthirsty crimson. "Sophos was wrong. You're not just an imposter, you're an abomination."

He swung for my neck, and I struck fast. I crafted another sword, this one sizzling with white-hot light, and glanced a blow across his wrist. His blade clattered to the floor as his hand went limp, skin bubbling and raw from the magic's burn.

He screamed and clutched it to his chest. I pinned him against the corridor wall with the length of my sword, its scorching edge pressed to his throat.

"You've lost. Yield, and leave with your life."

"Fortos never surrenders. We fight until we die."

I scowled. Without him offering his blood by choice, I couldn't open the cell doors to lock him in, but the longer our eyes stayed locked in mutual rage, the clearer it became he would never give in.

He arched his neck against the blade. "Go on then. Do what you must."

I let out a loud, frustrated groan, then stepped back and dissolved my sword.

The King balked. "You're not going to do it?"

"I told you. I didn't come here to kill." I grabbed his fallen blade. It glowed red in my hand, then melted to the ground in a useless sludge.

"By the Kindred... a Queen who won't kill." He began to laugh. "How pathetic."

My eyes rolled hard.

His chuckling grew louder. "This is precisely why my realm will n—"

His words choked. His bulging eyes shot upward, then back to me as his breathing turned shallow. "You?" he rasped. "That—that's not... but you're..."

"Yes, I know. I'm *pathetic*."

Blood drained from his face. "I won't let this happen. You—you can't do this. It's not possible."

I shrugged and turned away. "Watch me. I'm taking my mother and leaving."

As if on cue, a seething Luther turned the corner, carrying my squirming mother under his arm. His clothes were disheveled, his glare hot enough to melt glass.

"Why is it the traits I find endearing in you are so *gods-damned annoying* in your mother," he snapped. He clamped an arm around her legs as she tried her best to kick him in the groin. His eyes darted to the King. "He's not dead yet?"

"Sadly, no," I answered with a sigh.

"You win," the King said suddenly. "I'll let you go without a fight."

My brows flew up. "You will?"

He nodded and extended a hand. "You bested me in battle. It's only fair."

I eyed it—and him—my skepticism plain. Warily, I extended my own.

The King held statue still until my fingers curled around his wrist, and his closed around mine. His other hand swept across his hips, and he bent into a waist-deep bow.

"There's just one thing," he said. "A lesson your father must not have taught you."

The hairs on my nape stood on end.

His eyes snapped up. "Never leave a fight unfinished."

He jerked my arm, forcing me off balance. Before I could react, he had me pinned against his chest, his hands clamped to the sides of my head.

"*Diem!*" Luther shouted.

The anguished panic in his voice seemed to slow time as each second of the tragedy played out.

The King's fingers digging into my skull. His excited heartbeat hammering at my back. The muscles of his arms pulling taut in preparation to snap my neck.

I might have died that day, in that dirty, hopeless, gods-forsaken prison.

But Fortos was wrong—Andrei Bellator *had* taught me that lesson. That one, and many others.

And though I'd forgotten it for a time, there was one lesson I now carried in my heart wherever I went.

To be disarmed is to court death. By wits or by weapon, be ready at all times.

Years of training ignited on instinct, a well-worn path I could walk even in the darkest of nights. I twisted in the King's arms, my knees going slack. In the confusion, his death strike faltered, a split second's hesitation.

Just long enough for my small, shadow-crafted blade—the one I'd hidden in my palm the second he came near—to slide deep into the apex of his thighs.

He doubled over, hands clutched at his groin. I kicked the knife, jabbing it further into his flesh. He collapsed on his back with a blood-curdling scream.

"Never underestimate a Bellator," I muttered.

Luther stared, face still ashen from the terror of nearly watching me die. He let my mother fall from his grip, and when she climbed to her feet, she took in the scene with equal surprise.

"The guards might have heard him," I said. "We need to go. I'll have to hope my magic can burn through all the bloodlocks."

"Do you have enough left?" Luther asked. "You've used so much already."

I frowned, unsure how to answer. The only time I'd ever exhausted my godhood was the day my father was killed. At the time, I hadn't exactly been noting my body's subtle magical signals.

I did feel *something*, though. A hot kind of pressure over my temples, like the beginnings of a brutal headache.

"I'm fine," I lied. "Let's go."

My mother planted her feet. "What about the mortals? I'm not leaving here without them."

I sighed heavily. "Mother, I understand, I really do, but—"

Something brushed against my ankle. I jerked back with a yelp, then looked down to see the King's hand stretching toward me. The lake of ruby red around his body confirmed my aim for his artery had hit its mark. His slow, vacant blink and his tormented stare sent a chill of dread slithering over my skin.

"You," he croaked out hoarsely. "You're..."

"Leaving," I finished. My focus returned to my mother. "I'm not even sure the three of us can—"

"*Daughter of the Forgotten.*"

My blood turned to ice.

The King's voice had... changed.

There was nothing wounded in it, no dying rattle of a final breath.

In fact, he sounded strong. Impossibly strong.

Impossibly powerful.

And impossibly *ancient*.

My godhood responded to its call like a reunion with a long-lost friend. It brushed excitedly against my skin and hummed with an eerie anticipation, as if straining for some long-sought prize it deeply craved.

The King's skin began to glow. The scarlet of his irises faded to a churning smoky grey.

"*Never before have I made this choice,*" his voice boomed throughout the hall. "*It was not an easy one for me. Nor will it be an easy one for you.*"

I sucked in a breath as the pressure on my head sharply increased. My senses felt heightened and overtaxed, every sound too loud, every smell too noxious. The stifling air became a sea of liquid fire that my gasping lungs couldn't quite draw in.

"What choice?" I gritted out.

The *voice* of my godhood answered back. It screamed and shouted, whispered and sang, all at once and in a language I wasn't sure I even knew.

The King's skin had grown almost too blinding to gaze upon. I stared down at my own hands, both alight with equal, star-bright brilliance.

"*Guard my people well,*" the King said.

"Blessed Kindred," Luther murmured. "I think that's—"

My legs trembled and gave way. I fell forward, the stone blissfully cold against my scorching skin. Luther rushed to grab me, but on some buried instinct, I raised my shield to keep him away.

The King's back arched unnaturally toward the sky. "*Remember my sister's words. Beware my brother's wrath.*"

The pressure spiked, an excruciating pain inexplicably mixed with the sweetest pleasure. Light exploded in a wave around me, and I let loose a piercing scream.

Claim me, Daughter of the Forgotten.

It was a calling my soul would not, *could not*, ignore.

I closed my eyes, and I surrendered.

The light in the corridor shifted—the blinding, ethereal silver warming to a sunny gold. The force on my head began to ease, though a heavy presence lingered as if something sat upon my brow.

"By the Flames," my mother gasped.

"My Queen," Luther breathed.

My eyes opened to see him fallen on his knees, palm pressed against his heart. He looked as if he were gazing at something profoundly sacred, something as worthy of his reverence as the Blessed Mother herself.

I dropped my shield and staggered toward him, then nearly tripped over a ring of fallen soil and stone. My face turned up with a sudden gasp. Rising in a line from where I stood, a tunnel had formed through the prison's ceiling. A perfect circle of sunlit sky beamed its spotlight into the bleak, dim center of the prison hall.

Luther pushed to his feet, and we strode toward each other, pulled together by a soul-born, irresistible draw.

"My love," he whispered, "you are so much more than we ever dreamed."

"Show me?"

Somehow, he knew what I meant. He took my trembling hand and pressed it firmly to his cheek.

An image arose in my mind—me, through Luther's eyes, courtesy of my Umbros magic. A fiery red corona ringed my body, the shimmering glow slowly receding from my skin.

Above my head, my Crown had changed. A new peak had formed, and woven among the thorny, star-dotted vines and glittering crystal was a ring of throbbing, tangled veins.

I pulled my magic back, and our gazes met.

"My Crown," I rasped.

Luther tenderly cupped my face.

"Your Majesty... you just became the Queen of Fortos."

CHAPTER
FIFTY-FOUR

"But... there's never been a Queen of Fortos."

Luther's face glowed with affection. "You never were very good at following the rules."

My confidence shuddered beneath this new burden. "I don't want this," I whispered. "I can't even be a good Queen to Lumnos, and that's my home."

"Don't mistake the pain of change for failure." His large, protective hands curled beneath my jaw, tipping my face to his. "You may not be the Queen anyone expected, but you *are* the Queen they need."

I clung to his faith like a lifeboat against the rising tide of my usual urge to deny. "Maybe this isn't what it seems. Maybe I'm not..." I trailed off, glancing back at the King. His chest did not rise, his limbs did not stir.

My attention slid to my mother, who seemed less interested in my Crown and more interested in Luther's thumbs as they grazed reassuring strokes across my skin.

Suddenly I felt like a naughty child caught doing something wrong. I forced myself to pull away.

I stared up at the new skylight I'd blasted into the prison roof. "It's too small for Sorae, but maybe I can grow roots so we can climb to the surface."

"Not without the mortals," my mother insisted. She had that jaw-set, brow-creased, feet-planted look that said she wouldn't be swayed. If I was stubborn as a mule, my mother was a mountain.

Luther looked only to me, eyebrows raised.

I sighed. "She's right. We can't leave them." I rubbed my aching temples. "If I'm the Queen, can I just order their release?"

"Unless they were captured here in Fortos, you need the other Crowns' consent to let them go."

"And if I let them go anyway?"

He gave me a dark look. "Fortos Descended live and die by their rules. The last time a Fortos King broke from the law, his own men quartered him and strung the pieces up as a warning to the next one."

"Lovely," I muttered, hiding the Crown away. "I think I'll wait a while before telling everyone the good news."

I started toward the King's body. When my toes brushed the edge of his bloody moat, my muscles unexpectedly locked up. Memories of my father's death jolted through me in a painful overlay of the grisly scene at my feet.

The pool of blood. The vacant stare. The murder weapon, still protruding from his corpse.

My palms turned sweaty as my legs refused to move. I didn't realize I was shaking until Luther's hands gripped my arms to hold me still.

He gently guided me away. "It's not him."

I nodded stiffly, grateful he understood without explanation. Luther had tried so hard to talk me out of seeing my father's corpse. Most days, I wished I'd let him.

"M-make sure he's dead," I stammered. "His—his pulse... check—"

"I will." He gave me a light nudge toward my mother.

She studied my face with concern as I joined her side. "Have you ever taken a life before?"

"Yes," I admitted, wincing. "But that's not why—" I paused. My eyes met hers. "Have *you?*"

She sighed heavily. "Yes, Diem. Many times."

Her answer rocked me. Of course I had suspicions after learning of her role in the Guardians, but hearing her confirm it...

In my head, my mother existed within tightly defined walls. She was a healer—*the* healer, the standard to which all mortal healers were held. She'd dedicated her life to saving lives wherever she could. It was everything she was, all she'd ever been.

As the pedestal I'd perched her on collapsed to rubble before my eyes, I wondered if the woman I thought I knew had ever existed at all.

"Who *are* you?" I breathed.

"I'm your mother. I'm the same woman you've always known."

"I'm not sure that's true."

Her features pinched. She reached for my hand, but I shrank away.

"He's dead," Luther said as he joined us. "We should burn the body. If the soldiers see him, getting out will be much harder."

Without looking back, I raised a hand toward the King and set him ablaze in an explosion of Ignios flame.

I waited to feel some shame or hesitation, but I felt nothing of the sort. In fact, when I thought on the life I'd just taken, I felt... nothing.

And that scared me most of all.

Movement above us caught my eye. As the smoke billowed to the hole in the ceiling, curious faces peered down from its edge.

I grabbed Luther and my mother and set a brisk pace for the mortal cages. "Getting them out of Fortos won't be easy. My gryvern can't carry them all."

"If you can cover us until the border, I can take them from there," my mother said.

"Us?" My head whipped to her. "I promised Teller I'd bring you home today."

"Well I can't just leave them. They're my people. They need me."

"*Your family* needs you," I snapped. "We've needed you for months."

"Then you can wait a few days more." She gave me an exasperated look, as if *I* was being irrational. "I'll be fine. I've handled bigger dangers than sneaking through the Lumnos forests."

I gawked at her, then looked to Luther for support. He was staring ahead, lips quirked up at the corner.

"You're enjoying this?" I hissed at him.

"I'm realizing just how much you are your mother's daughter." Laughter gleamed in his eyes, unaffected by the daggers shooting through my glare.

An idea began to form.

"I'll get them to the border," I said to my mother, "and I'll arrange a guide from there. But you're coming with us." She started to protest, and I cut her off. "I sacrificed too much to come here. I'm not leaving without you now."

The mortals perked up at our arrival, craning their heads in note of the King's absence.

"I'd like to make a deal," I announced to them.

"We don't negotiate with Descended," one said tersely. "Especially Crowns."

I tossed my mother the most obnoxious *I-told-you-so* expression I had in my arsenal.

"Good," I said, "because this isn't a negotiation. If you want to get out alive, you're all going to have to do something you hate—trust the Descended." I gestured to myself and Luther. "Us, and anyone else I tell you to trust."

Heads shook fervently, mutters of protest rising to a roar. Luther crossed his arms, glaring.

"You could try to look a little less intimidating," I said under my breath. "I'm trying to win them over."

"I see how they look at you when you're not watching. Being intimidating is the wiser choice."

"If you don't trust her, then trust me," my mother said loudly. "She is my daughter. I know her heart."

"And what about *him?*" one mortal asked.

She and Luther exchanged a stare dripping with hostile tension.

"He has helped other mortals." Her slow, jerking cadence suggested each word was being chosen with care. "I doubt he intends to do you harm."

"A ringing endorsement," Luther muttered.

"Can you blame me?" she snapped quietly.

Muscles twitched along Luther's jaw. He'd warned me their interactions were not always friendly, but I could barely fathom how they'd worked together at all.

"There will be Descended you trust far less than us," I said. "I won't let them harm you, but I can't ask them to help you if you intend to harm them, either."

A mortal man stepped forward, his brown eyes fixed on me. "You said you wanted to make a deal. What is it you want in return?"

I let out a heavy sigh. "I know your reasons for distrusting the Descended. I share them all. There are many, *so many*, wrongs to be addressed. I believe in the Guardians' mission of bringing justice for the mortals—but some Guardians won't stop until every Descended is dead."

Murmurs—too many—of agreement rumbled through the group, turning my stomach into stone.

"Do you think they'll stop there?" I pushed. "They wish death on anyone they deem *different*. What happens when they find you different because of your gender, your skin color, or your realm? Or the gods you worship or the people you love? What the Kindred did was a great injustice, but before they arrived, the mortals were at war with each other over these very things. We can't abide that, either. Isn't injustice our *real* enemy—in whatever form it takes and whoever it comes from?"

The mortals fell quiet as they looked to each other, reluctant agreement flickering in many an eye.

"I will raise an army against the Descended's unjust rule, that I vow that to you. But the world I'm fighting for is one where *all* are equal, no matter the blood in their veins. Let's not make hate our guiding light. Let's choose love. Choose fairness. Choose..." I thought of the strange peace I'd glimpsed in the silvery light. "...*balance*. Someday we'll all answer to the Everflame for our choice. This is mine."

The mortals looked unsure.

My mother looked stunned.

My Prince looked proud.

"So if we want out of here, we have to join your army?" the man asked.

"I won't force you," I said quickly. "I see the fire in your eyes. I know you want to pick up a sword and fight. All I ask is that you consider wielding it for me."

I didn't waste any more time begging for their answer. If I really wanted to win them over, I'd have to prove myself through actions, not words.

I raised ropes of blistering light that wove through the iron bars and melted them down into puddles of muck, then Luther stood guard while I made the rounds to heal any lingering wounds.

The King's neglect had left them weak and emaciated. I used Meros magic to conjure water—surprisingly easy—and Arboros magic to conjure food—surprisingly hard. When I called on the soil to sprout through the stone with fresh fruit, I ended up flooding the cages with a field of dandelions instead. It did little for sustenance but wonders for mood. The children giggled and ran through the room, grabbing fistfulls of fluffy blooms and puffing their seeds into the air.

"Thank you," a mortal woman said as she watched them beside me. Her caramel-brown eyes were bright with unshed tears. "It's been a long time since they've had a reason to laugh."

I smiled sadly. "I'm sorry for what was done to all of you. It ends here and now."

She tucked her short dark hair behind her ears and extended a hand. "I'm Runa."

I clasped it with a nod. "Call me Diem."

"You're really going to take on the other Crowns, Diem?" she asked.

"I am." I gave her a cautious look. "But I'll also take on the Guardians, if I must."

She chewed thoughtfully on her lip. "And you truly think we can all live in peace someday, after everything that's happened?"

"Honestly, I'm not sure." I shifted my gaze to the children. "But I think I owe it to them to try."

My attention drifted to Luther. His daunting glare had softened as he stole glances at the children playing, the faintest trace of a smile toying at his lips.

Still no sign of anyone? I asked into his thoughts.

His happiness vanished. He shook his head, the disquiet in his features an echo of my own.

After my blast through the ground, the soldiers had to know *something* had gone wrong. Why hadn't they come? What were they doing?

And what would we face when we emerged?

"THEY'RE GOING to be waiting for us out there," my mother said as she fell in step on my right, Luther joining on my left. The mortals followed behind us in a tightly huddled group, whispering quiet doubts I was trying not to hear.

"I know," I said.

"We're going to need weapons."

"I know."

"So where are we going?"

"To get weapons."

She looked at me expectantly. I didn't elaborate.

"Diem, we need a plan."

"I have a plan. You'll see."

The hallway where I'd fought the King was silent, save for the crackle of the dying fire and the occasional rustle of soil falling from the hole I'd left. The column of light cascading from its opening seemed almost heavenly— the gods smiling down on what I'd done, giving their blessing to the slaughter.

My muscles stiffened. I turned and kept walking.

"I thought we were going to escape through the hole?" my mother asked.

"We are."

"Then where are we going?"

"You'll see."

"Diem, this isn't like the games you and Teller played as children. This is real. Lives are at stake."

My jaws ached from the force of holding back.

Some days it felt like there wasn't a soul in all of Emarion whose life didn't hang on my success or failure. It was a constant punctuation to every thought, a weight dragging down the corners of every smile.

"Diem." She snatched my arm. "Sweetheart, this is serious."

"You think she doesn't know that?" Luther said testily. "Have some faith in the woman you raised."

I could have thrown him on the floor and taken him, right there and then.

She balked at him. "You're fine with this?"

"Of course. She is my Queen."

"You never had trouble disobeying your Crown before." A hint of accusation rang in her tone.

"Diem is not Ulther." His hand brushed mine. "For *many* reasons."

We reached the corridor I'd been searching for, and I turned to face him. "Stay here with them?"

He frowned. "I have no weapons or magic. There's not much I can do if soldiers come."

I let out a resigned sigh. "About that..."

My eyes fell closed. My godhood arched its neck curiously as I retreated within. I passed it by, to its dismay, along with the hidden Crown glowing in my soul like a candelabra in a pitch-dark room.

I wondered if I'd find it—part of me hoped I didn't—and yet it rose right to my grasp, somehow knowing my intent before I'd even asked.

The Forging magic.

That buzzing, tingling energy imbued within the soil that wove the Kindred's magic throughout the continent, enforcing the terms of their Forging spell.

I'd only used it once, just before my Ascension Ball. Its edges had been so clear that night, a current flowing to the realm's borders, both land and sea. Its magic was pure, a seemingly infinite well, flowing smooth and rich across the realm.

This time, it felt very different—like an overworn blanket, edges frayed to threads, littered with rips and unraveling seams that allowed frosty air to sneak beneath and taint its warmth. And its reach didn't stop at the Fortos borders. It stretched on, into Lumnos and beyond.

However, one thing felt very much the same: This magic was not for just anyone to see. Only its master. Only its Crown.

Only *me*.

The finality of it sank my head low. I searched and found Luther's aura, trapped within a hard cocoon, and shattered it to bits. A tidal wave of *him* flowed free, and I welcomed its caress with bittersweet relief.

He sucked in a breath, eyes glowing with the sudden return of his magic. "It's true, then. You *are* the Queen of Fortos."

I swallowed, nodding, unable to keep the conflict off my face.

He smiled faintly. "You needed an army. The Blessed Kindred have a sense of humor."

"If only the joke wasn't always on me."

He closed the distance between us and lowered his face to mine. "You are worthy of this, my Queen. The Kindred see it, and so do I."

I leaned against him, absorbing his warmth, his faith, his love, letting it forge the armor I needed to guard my soul in the battle ahead.

My mother cleared her throat.

We both went stiff. My fingers grazed the tips of his as I forced myself to peel away.

"Wait here," I said to them both.

I strode down the hall until I was well beyond earshot, then stopped in front of an iron door. "I'd like to speak," I called out.

Two dull green eyes stared blankly from the darkness, giving no indication they'd understood.

I reached through the grate and conjured a sprinkle of glittering stars that cast a dim glow over the grimy walls.

"The King isn't here," I said, softening my voice. "I've come back alone. I'd like to help you."

The man didn't move. From the state of his cell, I wasn't sure he'd moved for a very long time.

"I know why you're here," I went on. "You were helping mortals get out of Faunos. You crossed too far over the border, and the army caught you."

My words were a careful dance to conceal that I'd slipped into his mind to pry the information out. I wasn't proud of the intrusion, but I'd needed to be certain before I took this risk.

"You tried to heal me," the man croaked, voice hoarse from disuse. "I felt it."

I fought a grimace—so much for keeping my secret. I stretched my arm toward him. "I can heal you now, if you'd like."

He stared bleakly at my hand like it might as well have been a thousand miles away.

"Can you walk?" I asked.

He pulled back the tunic draped over his legs. They were turned at an unnatural angle and bent in more places than any leg should bend. "They healed me like this so I couldn't run."

I muttered a vibrant string of curses. As I pulled back and glared at the door, I spied a familiar black disc.

A shadow blade took form in my hand. I drew it across my thumb several times with no effect, internally bickering with my godhood to let down its guard. Finally, a dot of red pooled on my skin. I held my breath as I swept it over the smooth circular plaque.

The door swung open, and the man's eyes grew wide. "How?"

I opted not to answer. I crouched at his side, my hands hovering in the air above him. "May I?"

His mouth hung agape and speechless, but he managed a nod. I pressed my palms against his ice-cold skin and sent my magic through his legs.

This was unlike any healing I'd done before. Repairing wounds was easy—the body already knew what it was meant to do, my magic simply fueled its natural drive. But the brutal work of these Fortos "healers"—*they don't deserve that title*, I thought bitterly—had convinced his body that his mangled limbs were already healed. Though I could soothe the damage done from thirst and malnutrition, his legs remained unchanged.

Fight.

The *voice* sparked in concert with my temper as resentment reared its angry head. I could have had *years* to train so that advanced magic like this was not so far beyond my grasp. My mother had stunted my growth, and it wasn't just me who paid the price.

Fight.

All the patients I'd watched suffer over the years, the key to their relief sitting dormant in my blood.

All the needless losses I'd mourned, wishing there was more I could have done.

All the hands I'd held through their final moments, when a single thought from me could have stopped death in its tracks.

Fight.

Help him, I pleaded to my godhood. *I don't know how to do this, but you do.*

No answer came.

I turned my frustration into fuel and unloaded more magic into his body. A tiny, nervous bell clanged in the back of my mind at the hollow chasm forming in my chest. I pushed it away—I refused to abandon this man to the monsters of Fortos.

Think, Diem, I told myself. *You're a healer. If you could mend this with your hands, you can mend it with your magic.*

Jaw clenched, I dove in deeper. This time, I let my healer's instincts guide me, weaving my mortal upbringing with my Descended gifts. My years of studies on the human body led the way, identifying bones I knew were broken and the ways the joints were not quite right. I gave instructions to my magic—clear and specific, encouraging and firm—the same way I'd taught trainees at the center.

Fight, the *voice* demanded.

Heal, I demanded right back.

The man suddenly let out a hoarse, blood-curdling scream. I froze, panicked, certain I'd done something utterly, terribly wrong—until I felt a stirring in my chest. My godhood flowed beneath his skin and set to work obeying my commands: reforming the bones, shifting them into place, and restoring the atrophied muscles. I gave a final, unrestrained pulse of power, and a blink of light flashed across the room.

"Blessed Kindred," the man gasped. "You... you healed me. *You healed me!*"

My eyes flew open, and a triumphant laugh burst free. "Lumnos's tits," I said, grinning. "I wasn't sure that would actually work."

He lunged forward and wrapped his arms around my waist, burying his head in my side. "You are Kindred-sent. I haven't walked in decades."

"Decades?" I choked out. My heart shattered at the horrors he must have endured. "What's your name?"

"Enness, Your Maj—" His brow furrowed with a glance at the now-empty spot above my head.

I took his hand and squeezed it, ignoring the question in his expression. "I'm Diem, Enness. I'm so happy I could help you. Now, I need *your* help."

"Anything," he breathed.

"I've got a lot of mortals I need to get out of this prison. If I help you escape, will you use your magic to protect them until they get home?"

His shoulders fell. "I don't have my magic. They drugged us with—"

"Flameroot," I muttered, remembering. I chewed on my lip. "I wonder..."

I let my magic rush into him again, this time focusing on his blood. I felt the flameroot's presence flowing in his veins, but much like the godstone's toxin, my magic fizzled at its touch.

But the light... the strange, silvery light. The one that demanded *balance*. Some inscrutable hunch urged me to turn my eyes that way, but I'd only ever used it when life and death were on the line.

I focused in on that—the needless tragedies I yearned to avoid. Children trapped in joyless cells. Broken bodies scattered on the Fortos flatlands. Corpses strewn throughout my beloved Lumnos forests. I pleaded with my heart, my magic, the gods, not knowing which of them held the key—*help me do this. Help me save them all.*

A light burned frail within me, like the last smoldering ember of a long-extinguished fire. I held it close, cupped within my hands, the blow of my breath keeping its stubborn glow alive. I let my magic be its vessel and carry a spark through my palms. The moment it hit Enness's skin, he illuminated with a fleeting burst of silver light.

We stared at each other in mutual shock.

I blinked at him. "Did it work?"

He blinked back. "You don't know?"

I shrugged. "I'm a little new at using magic."

He laughed abruptly, then straightened in surprise. It had been decades since he'd walked—how long had it been since he'd *laughed?*

He held out a palm. Twisting green vines slithered through the cracks in his cell. They sprouted vibrant leaves and clusters of fat grapes. He plucked one off and popped it in his mouth. The moan that followed was borderline indecent.

"Blessed Mother, I've missed that," he sighed, his eyes brightening to a brilliant emerald green.

"Enness, I don't mean to be rude... can you use that magic to do more than grow fruit?"

"You mean, can I fight the Fortos Descended?" I nodded, and he smiled. "I can. And frankly, there's nothing I'd rather do more."

He wobbled unsteadily to his feet, and I clutched him as he got his bearings. "Are there others like you? Any Descended I can trust to help these mortals?"

His heavy look suggested I had no idea the box I'd just opened. "How many can you take?"

"As many as I can get."

He nodded firmly. With my help, he staggered out of his cell and into the corridor. His body shuddered violently, and I looked at him in alarm.

"I... I never thought I would..." He gazed down the corridor as a tear broke free and streamed over his cheek. "People don't leave this place, Diem. They bring us here to die."

I wove my fingers into his and held him close. "Not anymore."

CHAPTER

FIFTY-FIVE

E nness and I made our way through the prison, stopping cell by cell. Mostly abandoned by the guards, the prisoners had become a kind of family over the years. Enness knew every name and every crime, those I could trust and the dangerous few I was best to leave behind. Though I believed in his best intentions, I quietly used my Umbros magic to verify the honesty of each person's promise that I could trust their word.

Our numbers grew to a shocking size. Perhaps I shouldn't have been so surprised. Each realm had its own prisons and punishments—Descended who ended up here had either crossed the army or a foreign Crown. Neither outcome was common unless mortals were involved.

Their stories gave valuable insight on the Crowns. Unsurprisingly, none had been captured by the Umbros Queen or the Ignios King, both of whom would rather kill their targets than hand them over to Fortos. There were none from Lumnos either, though I suspected Luther's years of intervention were at play. Most had been captured from Sophos, Meros, Montios, and Faunos, whose Crowns seemed content to play by the rules.

As I healed away wounds and flameroot, the hollow in my chest took on a greater heft. The *voice* of my godhood was growing distant, and fatigue had turned my brain fuzzy and my movements slow. I wrestled with my better judgment to stop and conserve my power, but that would mean leaving good people behind, and after seeing the squalor they'd lived in and the torture they'd faced, I couldn't bear to walk away.

541

At the end of the corridor, the mortals watched with palpable trepidation. By the time I rejoined them with the Descended, the tension in the air had grown thick enough to choke on.

"But they're criminals," someone said. "Dangerous ones."

"So are all of you," I said dryly.

"How can we trust them when they're not even trusted by their own kind?"

"Maybe being distrusted by their kind is a good thing," Runa offered. I flashed her a grateful smile.

A host of brown eyes settled on my mother as they looked to her to take their cues.

She crossed her arms, lips pursing. My anger at her still roiled beneath my skin. I considered bursting into her mind to rant about how badly we needed them, how they were worthy of saving, how I thought better of her than petty prejudice. Just as my temper was about to win, she walked forward and extended a hand to Enness.

"Thank you," she said simply. "We appreciate your help."

He clasped it with an easy smile. Throughout the hall, muscles relaxed with fading worry, not the least of which was mine. I led the newly combined group down the corridor while I explained the details of my plan.

I felt their suspicious stares as they took in the charred bones and pool of blood in the hallway where I'd killed the King, but either for fear of me or apathy for what I'd done, no one said a thing. A few mortal children shrank away, and a Meros Descended brought a wave of water to sweep the remnants of my carnage under a door and out of sight.

I raised my palms to the opening in the ceiling and pushed out Arboros magic, conjuring ropey roots that stretched to the prison floor. Enness and another Arboros Descended joined in to thicken the cords and craft knots to make them easier to climb.

Luther's hand closed around my arm. "Your magic is running low," he said, too quietly for the others to hear. "I can feel it in your aura. Let the Descended give you some of our magic to strengthen yours."

I shook my head. "You'll need all the magic you can get to shield the mortals, and I need those Descended strong when we part ways in Lumnos."

Luther's brows carved low, his muscles twitching at the clash of his instincts to keep me safe at everyone else's expense.

I forced a smile. "I'll be fine. Their magic can't hurt me."

"But their weapons can," he said darkly.

His thumb swept across my wrist. Somehow the simple gesture felt deeply intimate, bringing a blush to my cheeks and heat pulsing over my skin. My heart broke into a sprint that had nothing to do with the battle we were about to face.

I leaned in closer, my chest brushing his. "Chin up, Prince. I'm about to put on a show just for you."

His eyes dropped to my lips and blazed. I stretched toward him, yearning to feel his mouth on mine, but from the corner of my eye, my mother's glare was a siren in the silence. I needed them to work together—setting off this particular bomb would have to wait until we escaped.

If we escaped.

I love you, I said into his mind. Just in case.

His hunger deepened to something more profound. He grudgingly let go, though his knuckles brushed my arm in silent response.

"Enjoy the view," I crooned as I grabbed the vine and started my ascent.

The air was eerily quiet when I approached the edge. No voices, no sounds of running, no clink of blade-on-blade from the training fields. Heavy clouds obscured the sunset, and the sky had darkened to a flat, portentous grey.

I cast a thought out to Sorae. Her wingbeats broke the silence as her silhouette soared above my head.

Now, I commanded.

A deafening snarl rippled through the air. I pulled my head above the ground—and the blood drained from my face.

Soldiers.

Soldiers and more soldiers.

Far more than we'd seen before.

Hundreds, maybe thousands. Mortal and Descended.

A massive circle all around the opening. Weapons drawn, shields up, magic conjured.

I frantically ducked back down before the draw of Sorae's distraction wore off, gasping against a flood of rising, burning fear. Not for my own life, but for the faces staring up at me—the people who'd put their faith in me to lead them to freedom, a vow I wasn't so sure I could keep.

I sent Luther an image of what I'd seen, and—gods bless him—he gave no reaction. He simply nodded and turned to the others to calmly convey what they needed to know.

My nails sunk deep into the fibrous roots as I swayed just beneath the surface, willing my trembling to subside. A gust of wind fluttered through the hair that had come loose from my braid, and my father's words swirled around me in the whispering breeze.

If you are outnumbered or overwhelmed, or if all seems lost, just keep moving. Onward, until the very last breath.

I drew air into my lungs, wrapping his guidance around my heart like a glittering shield, then hoisted myself up onto solid ground.

A hundred swords raised in response, a thousand eyes trapping me in place.

"You sure know how to make a girl feel special," I called out. "Do all Crowns get this treatment, or does your King have a little crush?"

"Our King is dead." A red-eyed soldier walked forward, his heavy regalia marking him as the Fortos High General. The aura of his potent magic slammed into me with a hostility that matched his acrid scowl. "And I think you killed him."

I cocked my head. "Now why would I do that?"

He held up an object in his hand.

I swore softly. A messenger hawk's scroll.

"It seems the Regent of Lumnos believes you should not be allowed inside the prison. He sent a warning that you came here with the intent to kill."

Rage smoldered through me. I wasn't the least bit surprised at the lengths Remis would go to see me off the throne, but throwing his son's life away for temporary power was low, even for him.

I feigned a casual shrug. "My Regent can't bear it when I'm away. He'll say *anything* to get me home." I gave a long, exaggerated sigh. "Perhaps he has a crush, too."

A quiet snort rose from underground.

The High General was not so amused. "I saw the column of light. I know what it signifies. Whoever our new King is, he was right there when the old King died."

"Well whenever you find him, send him my thanks for the easy exit." I took the excuse to glance down at the hole, my nostrils flaring wide at what I saw.

I quickly looked back at the High General. "The King *was* looking quite sickly earlier." I pouted. "If only he'd seen a healer in time."

He strode closer. My hands curled at my side, and a dome shimmered over me, wide enough to encircle the opening, as Sorae's growl rolled through the air.

"Turn yourself in now, and you won't be killed," he said. "We'll designate you a prisoner of the Crowns. You can beg them for your life."

I tapped my chin in mock consideration. "A generous offer. There's just one tiny problem."

He sneered. "And what's that?"

"A Crown holds no authority over other Crowns."

My hand flew out toward the north. A wave of writhing shadow sliced through the air like a blade, carving through the ranks and sending soldiers diving across the rocky soil to flee its bite.

Around the clearing, battalions advanced. With a flick of my finger, magic spread across the perimeter in a wall of dancing darkness that cracked its whip at any who came near.

"*Now!*" I shouted.

The escaping prisoners tumbled out in a mad dash, streaming from the opening like an anthill overturned. An onslaught of magic slammed against my shield, and the wall of shadows wavered as my power diverted to fortify the dome.

With a pulse of devotion and a howl of wrath, Sorae swooped low, unleashing a stream of dragonfyre that sent soldiers scrambling and a wide berth forming in their lines.

My eyes locked with Luther, who kneeled along the edge, helping mortals to the top. "Get them out of here," I ordered. "Keep the shield strong."

He thrust a spear of light whizzing over my shoulder. Splinters and shrapnel exploded behind me, remnants of a spiked bolt that had been on a collision course with my head.

"Watch your back," he snapped. "If something happens to you, I'll suffocate this entire fucking realm in darkness."

A shiver prickled my skin. His vicious tenor left no question that was a promise he would keep.

"Diem," my mother shouted. She had a mortal child cradled on her hip, another cowering at her side, their tiny hand clutched in hers. Her expression was resolute, but I saw the glint of fear in her eyes at the mass of soldiers closing in. "Be careful, my little warrior. Remember everything Andrei taught you."

My throat burned. I managed a stiff nod. "Stay close to Luther. He'll keep you safe."

Luther scooped up the child at her feet and led the others toward the break in the ranks. My shield strained to stay with them, though its glittering canopy faded with every step.

The earth shook as Sorae slammed to the ground at their backs amid a tempest of sapphire flame. My skin stung with the painful echoes of the spears that sliced across her hide.

I fled in the opposite direction, chased by a hailstorm of arrows and an encroaching ring of men. I threw out a pulse of magic with as much power as I could muster, and my heart sank—the soldiers stumbled, but held their ground.

The abyss in my chest spread at a startling rate. My godhood felt darker, heavier, its *voice* too far away.

Time for a change of course, I thought. *Flash over substance.*

With a crook of my finger, glittering sparks exploded across the field. A harmless illusion, but the soldiers scrambled to get away, buying me precious time while commanders barked orders to reform the lines.

Luther and the others hit the edge of my magic's reach. Making a careful gamble, I dissolved my shield and the barrier of shadows I'd built across the clearing.

"Oh, no!" I held up my hands, wiggling my fingers. "I'm out of magic. What *ever* will I do now?"

The High General bristled at my taunting tone. He raised a palm to attack, then paused, jaw working with indecision.

"Don't tell me Fortos men are afraid of one weak little woman," I mocked.

My arrow struck its bullseye in his pride. His magic barreled toward me, marked by its telltale stench of death. As my skin flashed with light and my energy rose, I dipped my chin to hide my triumphant smile.

He doubled his efforts, joined by his soldiers, and my body became a brilliant, shining star. I egged them on with pleas for mercy and a theatrical crumple to my knees. Scattered laughs arose from soldiers gleeful to see a Queen of Emarion beg for her life at their feet.

"The prisoners are getting away," a man yelled. "We can't get past her gryvern to follow them."

The High General whipped his head toward them, then frowned. Slowly, he slid his gaze back to me, brows dipping as he watched his solders' magic pelt my skin. "Gryverns always come when their Crowns are hurt. Why isn't hers here?"

Awareness dawned in his eyes.

"Send the mounted cavalry." He grabbed his sword and strode toward me. "I'll draw the beast back here."

Shit.

"Give me a blade and make it a fair fight," I called out, backing away. "Or do you only get off on hurting women when they're defenseless?"

The High General laughed. "You're not defenseless. You're the *distraction.*"

His blade whistled toward my head. I hurriedly cast a shadow sword to deflect the strike.

"The Crowns will have your head," he growled.

I smirked. "They'll have to catch me first."

"You think you can hide? You're not even in power in your own realm. There's no place on the continent where you'll be safe."

Dread tied a noose around my throat. His words were landing where his blows had not.

I ducked another swipe of his blade, my focus darting to the soldiers racing away on horseback. In a burst of panic, I hurled out my arm—and prayed.

A shocked but victorious cry tore out of me as the horses reared on their hind legs, courtesy of Faunos magic. Angry neighs joined bucking backs, sending their Descended riders plunging to the ground.

Searing pain lanced through my side.

The High General had taken advantage of my distraction. Hot, sticky blood oozed from a gash below my ribs.

The air rippled with Sorae's distant, enraged snarl. Across the bond, I yelled an order to hold her position, assuring her I could survive without her help, but my doubt in my own words seeped through, weakening the binding force of my command. Her winged silhouette soared back and forth across the battlefield as she wrestled with the conflict.

I pushed the High General back with a shot of light, but I could barely lift my arm, let alone a weapon. I needed to heal—and I needed *magic.*

I turned and ran at the nearest line of Descended soldiers. Just as I'd hoped, they reacted on instinct, pelting me with a violent buffet of magical attacks.

Energy surged through my blood and awakened my nerves in a deluge of fire and ice. Soldiers shielded their eyes and looked away as my skin grew blindingly bright. It was intoxicating, the highest high, a euphoric torrent of liquid *life* injected directly into my veins. My wounds stitched together as my godhood gorged with abandon.

"Stop," the High General bellowed. "*Stop attacking her!*"

Hundreds of heads—including mine—swiveled at once. His crimson eyes were as vibrant as fresh-drawn blood. "I don't know how, but you're getting stronger. You *want* us to attack."

"You do that a lot, don't you?" I asked.

His scowl wavered. "Do what?"

"Convince yourself that women *want* what you're offering."

A venomous smile that I very much disliked the look of unfurled across his face. "You know what? I think I've finally figured you out."

He sheathed his sword.

"Vice General?" he barked at a man behind him. "Pull back the Descended. Send in the mortal battalions. Let the Queen have a go at them instead."

My stomach dropped to my feet, taking my smirk with it. The High General's dark laughter reverberated in my head as a wall of brown-eyed soldiers stepped through the front lines.

I threw up a barrier of sparks, ominous but harmless. The High General either didn't believe I would hurt them or simply didn't care—either way, he bellowed an order, the mortals advanced unscathed, and my bluff was called.

My heart lurched. I was outnumbered, outsmarted, trapped between harming the very people I was fighting to save or reveal the secret I was desperate to keep.

"Fine—you want to meet your King's new heir?" I shouted, jaw tight. I summoned the Crown into view atop my head. "Here I am. Now get on the ground and fucking *kneel*."

"That's not our Crown," he stammered, though recognition blanched his face.

"It's the Crown of Lumnos *and* the Crown of Fortos." My smile was frosty. "It seems the Kindred have learned to share their toys."

His head thrashed in stunned denial. "This—this is some kind of trick."

"And what of the Descended prisoners—what *trick* restored their magic? What *trick* opened the bloodlocks on their cells?"

"You are a woman," he spat. "The Blessed Father would never choose—"

His words choked as my palm stretched toward him, fingers twisting in. He gripped at his gut, wobbled on his feet, then sank, features gnarled in a horrified stare.

Fury flickered in my eyes. "Tell me again what the Blessed Father would not do," I seethed.

The battlefield turned eerily quiet. Swords began to lower. A few knelt in wary salute. Even the mortals fell still, caught in a Descended political landmine.

My chin jutted high. "You will stand down and let me leave. I have business in Lumnos. When I am done, I will return to Fortos, and we—"

"No."

The word exploded through the field.

The High General climbed back to his feet, knuckles white along his fists.

I swallowed tightly. "I am your Queen, and you will obey my com—"

"*No,*" he said again. "I don't know what blasphemous spell you've managed to weave, but this is Fortos. We do not kneel to bitches like you." He pointed a finger. "Mortals—kill the traitor."

An awkward silence hung. Not a single mortal advanced. They shrank back, faces drawn with conflict.

"Kill her," he barked again. "And if anyone refuses, I'll use them as kindling on her pyre."

To prove his point, he raised a palm at the mortal nearest me, a ruddy-cheeked young recruit. The soldier managed only a choked-off grunt before his boyish face slackened in heartbreaking, excruciating realization, then faded to a deathly shade of grey.

"*Stop!*" I screamed.

My shield whipped forward a beat too late. By the time it glimmered into place, the only thing it guarded was a pile of bones and rotting ash.

"Every minute she's not dead, one of you meets the same fate," the High General warned.

This time, no one hesitated. They crushed in on me in a swinging, snarling fight for their own lives that I met with magic and chaos.

Everything unleashed—thrashing vines mixed with watery torrents, patches of slippery ice spun with bursts of churning air. While I fought desperately to push them back without taking their lives, my godhood hissed a plea to ignite a bonfire of sinew and blood. I yanked on its reins to hold back its most violent desires, but as mortals broke through my defenses, I feared my own panicked heart would betray me—and them.

Two dark swords took form in my hands. With bedlam all around me, I had to trust my training to guide me as the song of combat struck up its bloody tune. I parried and feinted, thrusted and lunged, leaning on my father's lessons and emulating Alixe's savage grace.

The crush pressed in and in and in. For every soldier I stopped, two more took their place. My reflexes turned sluggish, my instincts began to fail.

I was tired, frantic, overwhelmed. Wounds throbbed in every limb, and fresh blood—mine, theirs—painted a crimson carpet at my feet. Pain became such a constant I could no longer distinguish between the damage I took on and the damage I dealt.

"Kill her already," the High General roared.

He bent his fingers in a twisting knot. A trio of mortals screamed in agony as their bodies disintegrated to a stinking muck.

Something snapped inside me.

My heart went numb. Darkness clouded my vision, brought on by my fury and my weakened state. It felt as if all my goodness and love had withered alongside those mortals and left me with a core full of rot.

If this was my end, I'd go down in a blaze—and I'd be taking someone with me.

My glare narrowed on the High General.

End yourself.

His eyes turned glassy and vacant. The sword dropped from his hand.

I sent the last ounce of my magic in a harsh burst of air that sent the mortals flying. My shadow swords dissolved, and the hollow in my chest consumed me at last.

Though the High General's face was slack, doom thrashed behind his gaze. My lips curled in a cold, malicious smile.

My conscience tugged at my sleeve, its quiet voice whimpering for me to stay my hand. But even if I wanted to—and I wasn't sure I did—I had no magic left to rewrite his gruesome fate.

His quivering fingers pulled a small knife sheathed at his waist and brought its edge to his throat.

The mortals had recovered from my final blast. They angrily climbed back to their feet, no longer needing any encouragement to want me dead. They raised their swords and ran toward me.

I had no weapons, no magic.

No allies.

No hope.

Only darkness. Only *death*.

A grim acceptance settled through me.

The soldiers were shouting something—one word, over and over again —but it was lost in a cacophony of voices and wingbeats and bootfalls.

The battlefield faded away, leaving only me and a red-eyed High General whose pleading stare I held as blood splashed across his chest.

A shadow passed over me. Loose hairs tickled my cheeks with a sudden breeze blowing at my back.

The soldiers stopped advancing. And looked up.

"*Gryvern!*"

Something jerked me backward. My stomach dropped with a weightless flutter as the world became a falling, spinning blur.

I went slack, paralyzed by confusion. Where were the soldiers? Where was the *ground?*

"Diem—grab my hand."

The growling command cut through the chaos. It was a voice my heart trusted so completely, my body obeyed before my mind understood. My arm stretched up until my fingers brushed against warm, coarse skin, and I clutched it like a leash to life itself.

An arm curled around my waist and dragged me up against a wall of steel-hard flesh.

"You're safe," the voice rumbled in my ear, breathless and rough. A second arm braced across my shoulders and caged me in. "I'm here. You're safe."

The horizon finally leveled, and my eyes dropped to the ground. The field was now a hundred yards beneath me, but in the center, one man stood out.

Red eyes, unblinking. A dagger in his hand. A gash across his neck.

CHAPTER
FIFTY-SIX

W e didn't talk the entire way back to Lumnos. The danger wasn't over, and there was little I dared to say.

Though he was almost drained from shielding the others, Luther pushed his magic into me the way he had in Ignios, allowing me to absorb enough to heal my wounds. My mother sat behind him on Sorae's back, and while I longed to hold her, I was secretly grateful for the distance.

The darkness I'd succumbed to in battle refused to ebb. Its fangs had sunk deep, and now my resentment toward her festered as a quiet, spreading venom.

The escaped prisoners were, for now at least, out of harm's reach. The army horses I'd diverted earlier with Faunos magic had caught up with them and allowed them to mount. With the prisoners on horseback and Sorae roasting anyone who followed, the army eventually abandoned their pursuit.

By the time we reached the border, the dark of evening had captured the sky. I tucked away my Crown before its glowing beacon lured any more trouble.

I guided Sorae to land, and the horses slowed to a stop. I was surprised to see so many saddles with a Descended in the back and a mortal taking the reins. It was a wise arrangement—leaving the Descended's hands free to wield magic, if needed—but one that required more trust in them than most mortals, especially Guardians, were willing to give.

Luther kept watch as my mother and I dismounted along with the group.

"Beyond this point, my gryvern's escort will do you more harm than good," I said. "I wish I could do more."

"You've done enough," Runa cut in. She gave my body a pointed look.

I looked down and balked. My clothes were slashed to ribbons, my skin coated in blood. I'd taken far more blows than I thought. Once I'd given in to the dark call of my fury, I'd barely felt a thing.

Even now, the numbness lingered. The empty abyss within my ribs felt as if it had consumed far more of me than just my magic.

Enness bowed his head. "I can't thank you enough. We all owe you our lives."

"Make sure everyone gets home safely, and I'll consider the debt paid," I said.

"Don't worry about us." Runa said. "Your Prince gave us a map showing the Royal Guard patrols and how to get around them, and a list of safe places to hide." She grinned, shaking a large, jangling pouch. "And enough gold to bribe our way out of trouble, if we get caught."

I glanced at him in surprise—not that he'd helped them, but that he'd had the foresight to bring along those kinds of supplies.

"Find a man named Vance in Mortal City," my mother said. "He'll help you get home."

"Do *not* go to Vance," I hissed at Enness. "He might help the mortals, but he's just as likely to kill the rest of you on sight."

My mother frowned. "You don't know that."

"Yes, she does," Luther rumbled.

"Find Maura at the healers' center instead. She can get word to me..." I hesitated. Tensed. "...or to a royal named Taran. If we're not in Lumnos, he'll get you whatever you need."

"Where else would we be?" My mother's gaze narrowed on me, shrewdly picking up that there was something I left unsaid.

I shrugged lightly but didn't answer. Between her uncanny skill at sniffing out a lie and her ability to read me like a book, silence was my only hope.

"Take care of each other," I said instead. "I know this arrangement is unusual, but you're better off together than you would be apart."

Runa and Enness exchanged a look. I might have been hallucinating from blood loss and exhaustion, but I could have sworn the faintest blush touched their cheeks.

The group mounted and led their horses into the trees. Soft grunts arose from the Descended as the border snapped across their skin and their magic sputtered out. I reached inward and once again released them from the binds of the Forging spell.

A few glanced back at me in confusion. I let the Crown briefly flicker before hiding it back away, and their eyes went wide with understanding.

"You said you're building an army," Runa called out. "What if we decide we want to join it after all?"

A true smile brightened my face, and the void inside me eased the smallest bit.

"Go home for now," I said. "Tell your families you're safe and hold the ones you love. When you're ready to fight... come find me."

Once they were finally out of sight, we returned to Luther and Sorae. He dismounted and rifled in our bags, tossing me a small blade to replace the ones we'd left behind in Fortos and my mother a hooded cloak to stay hidden.

"Maybe we should wait here," I suggested. "Give our magic a few hours to rebuild."

"You'll need more than a few hours," he said. "And they may have seen us land. If we don't get airborne soon, they might come looking."

"And if they do, they'll find the others," my mother said. "So let's get going."

Her tone had taken on that stubborn, emphatic edge that warned against debate, so I reluctantly nodded. Luther mounted and held out an arm to help my mother.

"Move back," she said archly. "I'll be sitting behind my daughter, not you."

His jaw strained. His icy gaze slid to me for confirmation, and I gave a helpless shrug. My mother's dislike of Luther bothered me more than I'd expected, but at the moment, I was too anxious to mediate and far too tired to care.

He stiffly slid back to make space. "Diem," he began, "we should really talk ab—"

"You're very *familiar* with my daughter," she interrupted. "Shouldn't you address her as 'Your Majesty'?"

Luther and I both blinked in surprise. I could count on one hand the people brave enough to speak to him that way—and one of them was me.

His brows pulled inward. "Your daughter has permitted me t—"

"*Her Majesty,*" she corrected.

A low, unhappy noise rolled from his throat.

I managed a weak smile despite my mood. "She has a point, Prince. You are so fond of titles."

His stare dragged to me. "As you wish, Your Majesty. I certainly wouldn't want to get too *familiar* with my Queen." His eyes darkened with the same ravenous focus I'd felt when he'd stripped me bare in Umbros. I could almost feel the rough grip of his hands as he'd stroked them up my thighs, the heat of his tongue against my skin...

A breathy hum slipped past my lips. My mother shot me a sharp-eyed glare, looking almost like she somehow knew where my mind had been.

Behind her, Luther's mouth curved up. He *definitely* knew where my mind had been.

I cleared my throat. "Hurry up then, let's go."

The second my mother and I were mounted, she began prodding at the slashes in my clothes.

"What happened to your wounds?" she asked. "Even Descended don't heal this fast."

"I'm not like most Descended," I said simply, urging Sorae back into flight. "Something you've apparently known for a while."

She offered no response to that.

"There was something you wanted to discuss?" I called out to Luther, already missing the feeling of being tucked within his arms. I regretted not standing up to my mother—now that he and I were apart, my unease had worsened tenfold.

"If we cannot safely land in Lumnos—"

"We will," my mother and I said at the same time.

A long beat of silence passed.

"Of course, we'll do our best," he began again slowly, "but if we cannot do so safely—"

"We have to," I said. "I promised Teller."

"Di—*Your Majesty*." His tone was firm. "My magic is low. Yours is gone. The army soldiers already tried to kill us once, and my father seems willing to do the same. If we're not careful, your brother might never get to reunite with her at all."

My soul ached at the truth in his words.

I glanced back at him over my shoulder. "I promised him, Luther."

Pain flashed across his face. If anyone understood how deeply it would wreck me to break my word, it was him.

He reached for me, and my mother shot forward to grab my hand before he could take it. "Let's try the palace," she urged, squeezing it tightly. "It's worth an attempt."

My focus moved back to Luther. "How long can you hold a shield before your magic drains?"

His throat worked with all the warnings he was holding back. "A minute or two at most. But you—"

"That will have to be enough." I sat forward and stiffened my back. "I'm not giving up."

"As you wish, Your Majesty," he murmured.

Guilt hounded me for brushing him off, but this was something I had to do. After letting my father and brother down so completely, in so many ways, this felt like my chance to finally make it right.

Even in the brisk wind of our flight, tension hung in the air. The moon, always my mischievous nemesis, seemed to be shining brighter than ever, bathing us in a vivid glow that denied any hope of arriving unnoticed.

"Keep your hood low," I warned my mother when the palace spires came into view. "Don't let anyone see your face."

Remis had known my plan to rescue my mother, but Descended hoarded information like they hoarded wealth and power. If he'd kept it from the army soldiers, we just might make it back in one piece.

I aimed first for the coastline. I'd pinned my hopes on Luther sneaking my mother in through the royal dock while Sorae and I created a distraction, but as we passed over the inlet entrance, my heart sank. The usual post of two had increased to twenty, with more lining the canal where it disappeared beneath the ground.

My shoulders sagged. I grudgingly turned Sorae inland, skimming low over the forest canopy and avoiding any roads where sentries might be waiting.

A broken sob sounded from behind me. I looked back in panic to see my mother staring at the ground, her expression torn with sorrow.

In my attempts to stay unseen, I'd unintentionally directed Sorae right over the marshy land that once held our family home. Against the glittering winter snow, the dark circle of charred earth looked more like a sinkhole— one that had swallowed our memories and our joy right along with our home.

"It's all gone?" she choked out. "His killer destroyed *everything?*"

"No," I said quietly. "I did that."

I was too much of a coward to look back, or to explain, or do anything beyond locking my focus on the horizon.

The palace loomed larger, and the royal grounds came into view. The pale blanket of frost stopped abruptly at the garden's edge, almost as if the palace's heat had melted it away. I squinted, trying to make out more detail —and my blood froze.

The snow hadn't melted.

It was covered with *people*. Scores and scores of them, uniformed and armed.

All the soldiers from Mortal City and the entire Royal Guard, together in a legion encircling the palace in a thick, unbroken line.

Sorae let out a thunderous warning howl before I could stop her, and a hundred weapons turned our way, including several large wooden structures laden with boulders and giant metal-tipped bolts ready to shoot us right out of the sky.

I nudged Sorae into a sweeping circle just outside their reach. The dark ring of soldiers rippled as their weapons trailed our path.

"There he is," I breathed. On the balcony outside my chambers, Teller had run outside, drawn by Sorae's call. Perthe and Taran emerged not far behind.

"Now," I said to Sorae. Her wings angled down, and we shot toward him in rapid descent. His eyes grew large, his focus stuck on the woman at my back.

"*Launch!*" a voice shouted from below.

Sorae's panic burst across the bond. Her right wing dropped, and we banked hard an instant before a bolt grazed its feathered tip.

"Your father really is trying to kill us," I yelled to Luther, the three of us clutching each other in a fight to stay upright.

But as my eyes scoured the horde, there was no sign of Remis—or Alixe. Near the front, the Fortos commander I'd confronted in Mortal City sat on horseback, shouting orders to the army soldiers and Royal Guard alike.

"Archers ready," he bellowed.

"Shield up," I told Luther as I sent a wordless order to Sorae. Her jaws yawed open with a plume of blue flame to send the soldiers scattering.

"*Launch*," the commander said.

A throng of arrows emerged from the ground. Luther's hand shot toward them, his shimmering blue dome sparking into place just in time to send them bouncing back to the soil below.

She's coming, Tel, I thought to myself as the balcony came near. My brother was so close, the honey-brown of his eyes almost visible in the moonlight. *Mother is finally coming ho—*

A soft whistle flew past my head.

"Archers on the roof," Luther shouted. His shield rose back into place, but not quick enough.

Agony burst through my shoulder. Instinctively I reached for the pain —and my hand brushed against the end of an arrow's shaft.

"Diem's hit," my mother cried out.

Sorae's head reared back with a snarl as she sensed my pain. She pulled up and soared for the clouds, leaving Teller behind and the palace growing smaller at our backs.

Luther called out my name, his voice frantic. I felt his broad hand grip my arm, then the hot-cold tingle of his magic absorbing.

I shoved him away. "Save your magic. We'll need it on the next pass."

"There can't *be* a next pass," he growled. "It's time to retreat. We're too outnumbered."

"Can't we land somewhere else?" my mother asked. "I know ten different ways to sneak into the palace."

I could almost hear the crunch of Luther's teeth grinding. "You got in because I allowed it," he bit back as she scoffed. "Alixe will not be so permissive, nor will the army. And Sorae is too large to miss—they'll spot her wherever she lands."

"What do you suggest we do instead?" she snapped. "If we cannot land, where *can* we go?"

"Montios."

"*Montios?*" I whipped around. "How is that any safer?"

"It isn't. But the Montios Descended dislike weapons. They prefer to use magic. That gives you an advantage if we're attacked. If we can find a place there to hide..."

There was something in his expression as he held my gaze. Something loaded, like there was more he wanted to say, but he didn't dare bring the words to life. I wondered if it was because of my mother—if there was something he didn't trust her to know.

I glanced down at the soldiers' lines. With my magic, I could easily take them. Without it, the odds felt nearly insurmountable—unless I was willing to unleash Sorae in all her fury and paint my own realm in dragon-fyre and blood.

A chill swept through me. The darkness I'd embraced in battle still loitered, waiting just below the surface to see what I would do.

"Look," Luther said. "By the entrance."

At the grandiose doors of the palace foyer, Alixe and Remis were surrounded by a thick pack of Fortos soldiers. Remis looked uncharacteristically flustered, shouting at the soldiers, who were shoving him against the palace walls. Beside him, Alixe was oddly pale. Her eyes kept darting to an area hidden by boxy hedges.

She looked up, and our gazes met. She slowly shook her head and mouthed a single word: *Go*.

I shoved away the massive pit sinking in my stomach and snapped off the protruding tail of the arrow, tossing it aside.

"Again," I ordered. "Shield up."

Luther growled a warning that went unheard. My determination to get to my brother had risen to a shadow I was lost in, unable to see the light beyond.

Sorae swooped across the parapets where the upper row of archers were hiding. Her talons hung low, dragging a gash into the stone. The archers dove to escape her path, providing a small window of respite.

Again we shot toward my brother. His arms strained toward us as if he might pluck us down from the air himself. Arrows and spears clinked against Luther's shield with an endless, steady patter, a violent hailstorm against a windowpane growing thinner every second. He roared with the effort of maintaining it—his well of power was so near empty, I no longer felt his aura at all.

Sorae's wings began to tuck as she prepared to land, and I held my breath at our imminent victory.

"Sorae, abort," Luther shouted suddenly.

"No!" I screamed. "We're almost there!"

"Diem, they're launching god—"

His words were cut off by the unmistakable squelch of a blade ripping into flesh. Sorae shrieked, and fiery pain blasted through my side. We slammed against the edge of a palace spire, the gritty stone scraping like sandpaper against my skin. I clutched Sorae's wing in a desperate effort to keep from falling.

My vision swam with pain, chaos, confusion. Sorae jerked unsteadily through the air. I hung on for dear life with one hand and clawed at my side in search of a wound with the other.

But the pain wasn't from my body—it was from my bond.

"Sorae's hurt," I cried, spying a wooden pole hanging from her soft underbelly.

Luther swore and flattened on his stomach crossways over her back. He shot a fierce glare at my mother. "Grab my legs and hold on tight."

She nodded and gripped him with both hands. He slowly slid forward until he was draped down Sorae's side, arms dangling in the air.

Terror raced through my veins. Luther's life quite literally hung at my mother's mercy. I snaked my uninjured arm around her waist to steady her, but he was out of my reach, and with my wounded shoulder, I was barely holding on myself.

There was nothing I could do but trust her.

"I'm sorry, girl," he yelled, "this is going to hurt."

A sickening sound accompanied the excruciating feeling of flesh ripping near my hip. Sorae and I both cried out, her outstretched wings shuddering in pain.

With some effort, my mother managed to pull Luther upright. He held up a blood-soaked bolt tipped with a point of glittering black.

"Godstone," I breathed, eyes growing wide.

He nodded grimly. "Thank the Kindred, the toxin isn't as deadly for gryverns. She'll heal fine now that it's out. But if they'd struck her heart..."

Or if they'd aimed any higher, I thought as I realized how close Luther's leg had been to where Sorae was hit.

"It's the same weapon the Guardians had in Arboros," he added, darting a judgmental look at my mother, who stiffened. "Alixe was trying to warn me, but I saw it too late."

I looked out toward the palace, now a fair distance away. "I think I know where they were hiding it. Sorae can burn it with her fire, then we can try again to—"

"Diem," my mother said softly. "It's time to cut our losses."

"Not without Teller. If I can get close enough to grab his arm, he can come with us, and then—"

"And then *what?*" Luther asked. My eyes flashed angrily to him, which he met with his own harsh resolve. "Returning to the palace was risk enough, but at least the consequences were on us alone. If your brother leaves that palace at your side right now..."

My eyes fell closed, my brother's words replaying in my head. His grief, his betrayal, his raw, vulnerable pain.

I swiveled forward and finally retreated to the numb darkness I'd been flirting with all evening.

For better or worse, my decision was made.

I opened my heart to Sorae across the bond, and she let out a doleful trill at what she found. She arched back toward the palace to obey my orders, though a pulse of protest rippled back forcefully enough to send a tremor through my spine.

My mother grabbed my arm. "Diem, Luther's right. We can't go back. It's too dangerous."

I didn't answer. The palace grew nearer, and my lips flattened to a thin, angry line.

At my back, I heard Luther's quiet sigh, then felt the faint swirl of his nearly depleted godhood. "Shields ready, my Queen."

"Save your magic, Prince," I said.

Sorae's pace abruptly slowed, then stopped just outside the soldiers' reach.

I met my brother's gaze. Taran and Perthe gripped his arms as he strained against them to get to me. Even at this distance, I saw the desperation on his face—and when his expression shifted, I knew he saw the plea for forgiveness on mine.

Luther was right. He and I had chosen our fates, and so had my mother. Whatever consequences would come from this, they were ours to bear. If Teller left the palace at our side, he would become our accomplice.

On the run as a fugitive, if I could protect him.

Prison or execution, if I couldn't.

I knew how badly he wanted our family together. Perhaps he'd be willing to sacrifice the rest of his life for it—but he deserved to make that choice on his own.

"I'm so sorry," I called out.

"No!" he shouted.

He rammed an elbow into Taran's ribs, catching him by enough surprise to slip his hold, then twisted until Perthe's wrist bent unnaturally and he was forced to let go. Both men lunged to stop him, but Teller deftly sidestepped and broke away.

I would have smiled, were my heart not breaking. Teller might be an academic at heart, but he was still a Bellator, through and through.

He ran to the edge of the balcony, shaking his head. "Please don't go!"

I fought the burning in my throat as I tugged my mother's hood down to her shoulders and her identity was laid bare. It might condemn me to be a fugitive for life, but I couldn't leave without letting Teller see that she was alive and well.

Murmurs arose, growing louder and angrier. Troops advanced in our direction. Sorae's ochre gaze kept a careful watch, edging us further out of range.

I barely noticed. All I could see was my brother's face and the stream of tears falling down his cheeks. My mother stretched an arm toward him, and he leaned over the balustrade to do the same.

"I love you so much," she shouted in a wobbling voice. "Be strong, my little scholar."

"*Please*," he begged.

I dropped my chin and placed a hand on Sorae's neck. "Let's go."

CHAPTER

FIFTY-SEVEN

S torm clouds greeted us in Montios and shrouded the moon in dismal grey. The temperature had taken a dramatic plunge, turning our breath into clouds and our fingers into ice.

We touched down just inside the border in a sunken valley at the base of a towering, snow-capped peak. With little vegetation, we were dangerously exposed to both our enemies and the weather. We exchanged anxious glances and settled in for a long, restless night.

I showered Sorae in pets and scratches for her loyalty, promising to grow her a thousand apples once my magic returned. Thankfully, she seemed unbothered by the cold. She offered up the space beneath her wings for us to sleep, and I breathed a sigh of relief when I saw her wound was healing fast.

My own weren't faring quite as well. Luther had pushed the last of his magic into me knowing he'd lose it at the border anyway, but it had only been enough to stem the bleeding. My arm was useless, and the throbbing pain had set my already sharpened nerves on a razor's edge.

"How long until your magic is replenished?" my mother asked me.

I glanced at Luther, brows arched, internally irked that this was something I should already know.

"We have a saying—'the stronger, the longer,'" he said. "It's the downside to being powerful. Most Descended take a few hours. Mine takes a day, sometimes two. Yours... I'd guess three or four, at least."

"Three or four *days?*" I choked.

"Maybe more." He shot me a look. "Assuming your magic works like normal."

He didn't elaborate, but I caught his point. When it came to me, *normal* never seemed to apply.

My gaze swept across the landscape, a vast expanse of lavender peaks. In any other situation, I might have enjoyed the chance to spend a few days exploring. Something about this realm, with its breathtaking vistas and mysterious secrets, called to my soul in a primal way.

"Let's get comfortable then," I conceded. Luther nodded and stepped away to unpack our supplies.

"Diem," my mother said slowly, lowering her voice to a hush. "There is another option. A Guardian camp nearby."

"The last time I was in a Guardian camp, I was chained up and drugged, and both my Prince and my gryvern were nearly killed."

"*Your* Prince?" she asked, brows lifting.

I worked my jaw. I'd have to tell her soon enough, but I dreaded the fight the truth was sure to bring.

"We're safer on our own," I said instead.

"You and I could go. There would be food, water, and shelter from the cold. They'll have weapons and lookouts. You'd be safe from Descended attacks."

"And what about Luther?"

She pursed her lips. "He's a Descended Prince, Diem."

"And I'm a Descended *Queen*. I'm not sure you understand that, Mother. I'm not the sheltered mortal daughter you left behind. That girl is dead."

She flinched, looking for a moment not like a legendary healer or a fierce rebel leader, but a grieving, heartbroken widow whose family was irreparably changed.

I sighed. "I'm sorry. Can we discuss this tomorrow? It's been a long day."

"Of course." She tentatively stroked a hand along my arm. "Come, let's get some rest. Luther can take first watch."

My gaze shifted to find him standing on the other side of Sorae, rummaging through our bags and pretending like he hadn't overheard every word.

His eyes met mine. He nodded silently, then held out a bundle of fabric. As I walked over and reached for it, my hand brushed against his, sending a tingle coursing through my blood.

"The Montios gift from your ball," he explained. "The cloak that's spelled to always keep you warm."

I stared at it for a long moment. "You knew we would end up here, didn't you? That's why you brought this—and the map and gold you gave to the prisoners?"

"Those were meant to be for us," he muttered. "I suspected going back to Lumnos wouldn't be an option. I wanted to be prepared in case we were forced to stay away indefinitely."

"You went with me even though you knew you would be exiled from your home?"

His brows knit to a deep crease, as if my question made no sense. "Diem... *you're* my home."

A breath rushed out of me, crystallizing in the air into a glittery fog. The darkness inside me finally began to recede.

Luther took the cloak and secured it around my shoulders. Though I felt its magic seal me off from the winter chill, it was the emotion in his eyes that set me simmering from within.

"Thank you," I said. "For stopping me from making a mistake with Teller I would have regretted forever. And for standing by me when it looked like I was going to do it anyway."

"You're not angry?" he asked. I shook my head, and his muscles eased from a tension I didn't realize he'd been hiding. "I'll stand by you through anything, Diem, even when I disagree. I hope you know that. Whatever consequences may come, we face them together."

I gazed at him, unable to form the words I really wanted to say. I was overwhelmed by the stirring in my soul—not just of carnal desires, but of a future I was beginning to let myself imagine.

It wouldn't be so scary, giving myself to him forever.

The thought arose suddenly, taking me by surprise. I'd always feared commitment because I thought it meant sacrificing who I was. But being with Luther never felt like a sacrifice. He'd go to hell and back to help me achieve my dreams—and not just because he loved me, but because they were his dreams, too. Because we were the same in deeply fundamental ways that were etched in our bones and dyed in our blood.

Had I held myself back all these years because I didn't *want* to give my heart away, or had I simply never found someone worthy of giving it to?

And if so... what happened when I finally did?

Luther cut a quick glance to my mother. She must have been watching us, because all the warmth in his expression immediately shuttered. He used Sorae as a shield to hide his hand as it slipped beneath the cloak and settled on my waist.

"Are you alright?" he asked.

A loaded question.

One that, were he anyone else, I would brush off with a joke and a promise I was fine.

But he wasn't anyone else. And I wasn't fine.

My eyes fell. I focused on the feeling of his palm on my hip: Solid. Strong. Certain of its place.

"I killed a King today," I whispered.

"He deserved it."

"And I killed the High General."

"He deserved it, too."

"And I betrayed my brother."

His voice softened. "You did the right thing. You saved a lot of lives today, too. In Fortos *and* in Lumnos."

I wanted so badly to believe him, but every time I closed my eyes, I saw the High General's face. Felt the numbness in my heart as I forced him to take his own life.

I could try to convince myself it had been noble—he would have killed more mortals. Or maybe self-defense—he certainly would have killed me.

But I knew the truth. He was dead because I'd *wanted* him dead and because I'd known I was strong enough to do it. I'd killed him simply because I could. No more, no less.

It was that sense of total power, that addictive draw of wielding fate in my hands that haunted me most of all.

I shook my head sharply, needing to outrun those thoughts as fast as I could. "It looks like our night alone will have to wait a little longer."

His eyes narrowed at my change of subject. I waited to see if he would push, but whatever he saw on my face, it convinced him to let it go for now.

"Although..." I cracked a tiny smile. "We could tell my mother we need to go collect firewood."

A noise rumbled in his throat. "I didn't really want to have you for the first time against a rock with snow up to our knees." His fingers found a slice in my tattered clothes and grazed over my flesh. "But I could be persuaded."

I hooked a finger into the weapons belt slung low on his hips and tugged him closer. His eyes darkened with desire.

"Diem," my mother called out loudly. "Leave the Prince to his watch, dear. Let's get some sleep."

I bit my lip and shrugged. "Sorry, Prince. Better luck tomorrow."

I reluctantly pushed him away and turned toward my mother. He grabbed my hips and jerked me backward, grinding into me so roughly I felt his hardened cock against my back.

He leaned his mouth to my ear, his voice dominant with command. "Dream of me."

Despite the emotional turmoil of the day and the enormous trials that lay before us, I fell asleep with a smile on my face.

And dream of him, I did.

CHAPTER

FIFTY-EIGHT

S orae's feathers ruffled in the wind as I carved a line through the spun-silk clouds, soaring above endless lilac slopes that stretched to the horizon in a rugged sea of snow and stone.

Despite its beauty, the Montios terrain seemed desolate, too harsh for life to survive. After nearly an hour of flying, I hadn't laid eyes on a single soul.

But much like the black canyons of Umbros, the true story of this realm lay under the surface. Somewhere beneath, a Descended court thrived.

And though I couldn't seem to find them, I was all but certain they were watching me.

Last night, Luther had not just taken first watch—he'd kept his vigil all night, claiming I needed the sleep to refill my magic and my mother needed to rebuild her strength from her mistreatment in prison. I'd put on a good show of rolling my eyes and scolding him, but my heart couldn't stop twirling at the gesture.

If he'd been trying to win my mother over, his efforts went sorely unnoticed. She'd offered a stiff smile and a muttered thanks, then they both fell right back into their silent standoff.

The rift between them tore through the center of my heart. My mother had treated Henri like a son, caring for him as genuinely as I had, and I hadn't realized until now how much that had meant. It wounded me to watch her scowl at the man I loved and watch Luther retreat behind his walls as a result. A confrontation was inevitable, but after waking in the night more than once to find my mother softly weeping over my father's death, I begrudgingly held my tongue.

Besides, my mother and I had our own battles to fight. My questions for her loomed large, casting us in their shadow. I'd planned to wait until our reunion with Teller, knowing he deserved the same answers, but I wasn't sure how much longer I could last.

She was a fuse, and I was a bomb. It was no longer a question of whether I would explode, but where and when—and who would get hurt in the blast.

At dawn, we'd moved to a cave where Luther could sleep while my mother and I kept watch. When I felt the brush of his aura as his magic temporarily slipped through the Forging spell's grip, I gave my mother a vague excuse about *scouting for food and water* and jumped on Sorae's back, hurriedly flying away.

It hadn't entirely been a lie, but within minutes, I spotted a nearby stream with an abundance of animals we could hunt. When I bit down and urged Sorae to keep flying, I had to admit to myself I had a bigger reason to get away.

I needed air. Air, space, and solitude. Time to think, time to come to terms with what happened in Fortos and the new Crown that sat on my head. Time to wrestle the conflicting emotions that were fueling me on while simultaneously burning all the oxygen from my lungs.

Time to plan a war.

And, if I *happened* to find some Montios Descended to provoke into a fight so I could absorb their magic and go home—well, I wouldn't complain.

Barren as it was, there was a gentle beauty to the Montios terrain. The immovability of the mountains was strangely soothing, a reminder of their calm permanence through millennia of conflict. These slopes had been here long before the Kindred, and they would still be here long after the Descended died out. They'd outlasted the rise and fall of countless rulers, and they would survive the horrors of any war. Whatever became of me and my fate, these mountains would endure. Somehow, that gave me peace.

Sorae whirred excitedly, which I'd learned the hard way was a warning to tighten my grip. My stomach went weightless as she plunged into a spiraling freefall, then snapped her wings out at the last second to send us skirting along an incline of jagged rock. She banked to the left and swept past a waterfall, her wingbeats stirring the mist into tiny droplets that clung to my unbound hair.

Stuck at the Crown's side century after century, Sorae so rarely had the chance to fly for her own pleasure. When I'd commanded her to let loose and explore, the bliss that coated the bond was as heady as a drug. I whooped and hollered, egging her on with my laughter, embracing every surge of adrenaline her aerobatics sent blazing through my veins. It was a relief to feel my heart pounding from welcome excitement for a change and exactly what I'd needed to return a smile to my face.

"Come on," I mumbled as I scoured the ground. "Show yourselves. Come outside and play."

Sorae snorted in agreement, clouds of smoke puffing from her nostrils.

I grinned. "Aren't you supposed to keep me *out* of trouble?"

A proud kind of confidence flickered back. She'd seen enough of my battles to know I wouldn't be in any real danger from a minor skirmish, and after being wounded yesterday, she was champing at the bit for a brawl, too.

It struck me suddenly that Sorae must have done this same thing with the goddess Lumnos all those millennia ago, traversing the skies over the forests she would eventually claim as her own.

"Did you love Lumnos?" I asked Sorae, stroking my hand along her dark, iridescent scales. "Do you miss her?"

Jumbled emotions came answering back. An enduring love for her Kindred master, whom Sorae had followed to this world out of loyalty, not obligation. Sadness, even now, at her loss. Resentment, for the chains the Kindred had imposed on her kind, prioritizing the safety of their Descended offspring over the gryverns' freedom. Betrayal, for the separation from her beloved Tybold.

My temper rankled, wondering how the Kindred could have done such a thing to the creatures who had stood by them so faithfully. Then again, what moral superiority could I claim, when my own choices had entrapped my brother's freedom though his loyalty to me rivaled even Luther's?

"So you cared for Lumnos," I mused aloud. "What of the other Kindred, were you fond of them?"

A strange, strangled feeling came washing back. Like there was something she wished to share but could not.

My eyebrows rose slowly. "Were there some you disliked?"

When her gaze shifted back to me, her golden slitted pupils seemed to deepen to an ominous bronze. A dark rumble rolled in her throat.

I sat up straighter. "Which one? Fortos? It was Fortos, wasn't it? I knew he must have been a prick."

A ripple of amusement shot back, but beyond that, she didn't answer. "Was it Montios? Sophos?"

Again, no answer. I listed off each of the remaining Kindred, and though flickers of mild feeling accompanied some, none inspired the harsh darkness I'd felt in her a moment ago.

I frowned. "Who was it, then?"

My throat went tight in phantom pains as Sorae strained against the bounds of whatever held her back.

Her head slowly turned to the east, snarling and fangs bared. My heart skipped a beat. I searched for some sign of danger, but nothing was there.

I looked again at Sorae—her gaze wasn't on the sky, but on the ground.

In the distance, the mountains gave way to a dark forest set on a series of steep, undulating hills. Its trees were blackened and gnarled, like each one had been burned—or poisoned. At its center, set into a low valley whose base I couldn't see, several columns of smoke rose into the air.

My godhood stirred. It was still deeply weakened and lethargic, but wide awake, and sharply aware in a way I'd never felt it before. It pressed to the edges of my skin, tugging me toward the shadowy trees.

Claim me, Daughter of the Forgotten.

I jolted upright in surprise. My godhood had only spoken that phrase to me twice before—each time I'd surrendered to a Crown.

Something else tickled at my mind. A memory, perhaps, or a dream. An image of screaming and bloodshed, of explosions and a blinding light. Of my mother's arms around me and a crushing pain.

Sorae let out a low whine. I shook my head to clear the vision.

"That must be the Guardians' camp my mother mentioned," I said, squinting at the distant smoke. Sorae's muscles tensed beneath my legs. I suspected she wasn't keen for another showdown with the mortals like the one we'd had in Arboros. Neither was I.

Still... something was calling me toward that forest. A pull from deep within. A sense that the course of my fate ran through those hills.

Trust your instincts, Luther had told me.

And my instincts were telling me there was something I needed to see.

A glance at the sun warned I'd been gone longer than I'd planned. I blew out a frustrated sigh. I couldn't risk being away when Luther's magic went dark again, and I'd promised him no more running into danger alone.

Begrudgingly, I pushed my instincts aside and set Sorae into a swift pace for our return. My heart broke a little at her disappointment, and I silently renewed my vow to find some way to set her free.

"Were you friends with Rymari, the Montios gryvern?" I asked.

A heavy sadness bled across the bond, a sorrow tinted with shame that left me wondering if she'd been involved in the battle that had weakened Rymari enough for the Guardians to strike her down.

I stroked my hand gently along the fur of her leonine haunches. "Whatever happened, it wasn't your fault. That blame lies on her killer."

She sent back a pulse of gratitude, but her guilt didn't ebb, and I understood—no amount of hating my father's murderer would ease the blame I felt over his death, either.

"I think Rymari saved our lives back in Umbros," I said, thinking back on the jar of lavender flame that had put an end to the Umbros Queen's attack. "I wish I had some way to thank her."

Sorae took a sudden sharp turn off our path.

I opened my mouth to order her back on course, but Sorae snapped her jaws before I could get the words out, her clicking fangs seeming to beg me to stop before she was bound to obey.

As we drew closer to the ground, I noticed something odd. This part of the mountains had no snow, but at the center of a grassy plateau lay an impossibly perfect circle of unblemished white.

Sorae landed just beside it. The draft of her wings sent a whirl of snowflakes flying out of the circle and into the air. She bent to the ground to let me dismount, then crept forward to the circle's edge. She hung her head low, her eyes closing, her wings folding back. There was something almost reverent to her stance.

I walked to the circle and stared up, slack-jawed. Snow fell in a steady flurry—*only* above the circle. I reached out a hand into its perimeter and marveled at how countless glittering flakes settled softly onto my fingers, but not a single speck of white made it further than my wrist.

"This is where Rymari died, isn't it?" I whispered, remembering the lore I'd heard about this place from the man in the Umbros market.

Sorae let out a mournful whine. I dropped to my knees at her side and laid a hand on her muzzle. We sat together for a long while, saying nothing, my gryvern grieving her lost friend while I lamented the death of a creature I'd never known.

I held out a palm. My brows pulled together in sharp concentration as I wrangled the small bit of magic that had restored overnight, and a shape began to take form.

At first, the best I could manage was a sharp, ragged spear of crystal-clear ice. I'd never used my magic in such an intricate way, and I was surprised at how much energy and focus it required.

I'd learned from my training with Alixe that the more familiar we were with an object, the easier it was to replicate with magic. That's why crafting weapons had come naturally to me. Sharp points and blunt objects, I could handle with ease, but this... this required so much more than might alone.

Sorae watched curiously as the glassy shard thinned to a delicate strand, then sprouted with a pair of curling ovals that stretched to a point. A rough globe spun at the top, then shaved into a hundred paper-thin slices, ruffling and spreading like petals opening to the sun.

My hand sank to my side. At the circle's center, sunlight gleamed off a single rose of pure ice.

I bowed my head and murmured the sacred Rite of Endings. When I finished, Sorae's snout nuzzled against my side, and I wrapped my arms around her, holding her close.

Perhaps I should have conserved my magic in case we ran into trouble, but after Rymari saved my life from beyond the grave, I felt I owed her *something*. The last of my magic seemed a worthy trade for the last of her fire.

A cloud passed over the sun, casting us in a gloomy patch of shadow. A sudden weight pressed on my head, and light flickered across the snow.

I frowned in realization. My Crown had appeared, emerging entirely on its own. I quickly tucked it out of sight and shared a bemused glance with Sorae. "That was odd," I mumbled. "I wonder wh—"

A skittering sounded behind us. Sorae was on her feet in an instant, teeth bared and growling. Blue dragonfyre glowed from the depths of her throat.

"Easy, girl," I whispered, rising. "Let them attack. I need their magic."

I crept forward, eyes narrowing. The barren rock was static and inhospitable—no sign of life, let alone movement.

"Hello?" I called out. "Is someone there?"

A slow creaking broke the silence, like old bones moving after a long rest—this time from our flank. We whipped back around. Sorae's wing curled protectively around me, but again, we saw only infinite stone.

Sorae trilled and turned her head to the distance, where a column of dark shadow curled its way to the sky.

Luther's magic.

I swore and swung myself onto her back, and she instantly launched

573

into flight. My heart hammered—had they been found? Had they been attacked? Had my reckless choice put them in danger yet again?

But as the cave came nearer, my pulse raced for a different reason. Luther stood at its mouth, arms crossed over his chest, looking absolutely *murderous*. My mother stood beside him, hands balled at her sides, her eyes dark.

They weren't in danger.

But *I* was.

Sorae grumbled a warning at them both when we landed, her protective instincts prickling as she sensed their malice. Though neither of them would ever do me any real harm, ever since my father's murder, my sweet gryvern had guarded my happiness as fiercely as my safety.

"You're awake," I said to Luther with false brightness. "I'd hoped to be back before you woke." I lowered my lashes, offering my flirtiest smile. "Any good dreams?"

His glare was the stuff of nightmares. His normally pale eyes were now a swirling midnight, the shadow magic within him stirring thick in his gaze.

Something must have been deeply, *deeply* wrong with me, because as he stared at me looking like he wanted to uncage the fearsome monster that lived beneath his skin, warmth tingled between my legs.

I wet my lips, my eyes dropping to his mouth. His knuckles turned white where he gripped his arms.

"Where have you been?" my mother seethed.

I forced myself to tear my heady focus off Luther. "I found a stream with trees we can hide under and plenty of animals to hunt. It's only a short walk. We should be safe there until we can leave."

"You said you'd only be gone a few minutes. It's been half the afternoon."

I shrugged. "I lost track of time at the stream."

"You're lying," Luther ground out.

My mother nodded sharply. "Indeed, she is."

I had to admit, I was enjoying the sight of them working together, even if it was to lecture me. "I took a short flight to get a look at our surroundings. I didn't think you'd even notice I was gone."

"You think I wouldn't notice your aura disappearing, like you'd died at my side?" Luther snarled, his voice rising. "You think that wouldn't pull me out of the deepest sleep and reach for you in a panic to make sure you're alright?"

My pathetic heart swooned a little.

I walked forward and laid a hand on his arm. His muscles were fully taut, solid as steel beneath his skin. "I'm sorry I worried you," I said gently. "I felt your magic come back, and I knew it wouldn't stay long, so I had to act quickly."

He eased slightly at my touch, though his scowl was still fierce. "You should have told me first."

My mother looked between us, anger slowly turning into suspicion. "Why are you apologizing to *him?* You took off and ran, Diem. I was terrified."

"I wonder where she picked up her habit of disappearing on the people who love her with no explanation," Luther said flatly.

My mother whirled on him. My mouth popped open as she jabbed her finger into his chest. "You stay out of this. You have no authority over what she does. She is a *Queen.*"

He squared his shoulders to her, towering over her tiny form. "A Queen whose Crown you do not even recognize."

So much for them working together.

"She is my daughter," my mother hissed.

"*And she is my—*" He stopped himself abruptly, his roar echoing off the stone. His jaw clenched and unclenched. "At least I have sworn her my oath. You and your rebels would die before you did the same."

I cocked my head and shot her a look. He had a point.

She bristled. "What I think of her Crown is irrelevant. She and I are family. You are just her subject."

"He is *not* just my subject," I said, a bit too quickly. A bit too intensely. "He is my..." I shifted my weight, swallowing thickly. "...my closest advisor. It is his duty to speak his mind to me freely."

I stole a glance at Luther. His expression slammed down behind the icy, unbothered veneer of the Prince, but not before I caught a flicker of disappointment in his eyes.

My stomach twisted with regret. I wasn't ashamed of him, or of us, and I hated that he might think I was. Avoiding a fight with my mother wasn't worth it if it came at his expense.

Luther had told me that I was *enough.* He deserved to know that he was, too.

I drew in a long breath. "Mother, there's something I—"

Sorae's low rumble cut me off. The hair along her spine prickled. She turned to face a line of wild vegetation nearby, her wings puffing out to shield us behind them.

Luther nudged my mother into the back of the cave. He tried to do the same to me, but I resisted, craning my neck to see what had caught her notice.

Snow cascaded off the leafless branches of the shrubs as they jostled with movement. Sorae's growl deepened, vibrating through the stone at my feet. Luther and I shared a somber glance.

"Who's there?" I called out uneasily.

A group draped in dark cloaks, their hoods pulled low to conceal their faces, stepped forward into the open. Luther and I dipped beneath Sorae's wing to stand at her shoulder.

"Show yourself," I demanded.

The man at the center raised his chin. Red eyes gleamed from beneath his hood as he raised a crossbow loaded with a godstone-tipped arrow. "Hello again, Your Majesty."

The Fortos commander. The same one we'd fought at the Lumnos palace—the same man who had launched a bolt at us with the aim to kill.

The others threw back their cloaks. More soldiers. More weapons, many tipped with glittering black.

"The Regent of Lumnos ordered you to stay in Lumnos and turn over that gryvern," he called out.

I rolled my eyes dramatically to hide my relief that they hadn't heard the news of what I'd done in Fortos. "If Remis wants my gryvern, he can get her himself. I'm not stopping her." I glanced at Sorae. "Do you want to go serve Remis?"

She snarled loudly, and I looked back to the man with a smirk and a shrug.

"It doesn't matter what either of you want," he said coolly. "You defied the Lumnos Crown's orders. That makes you subject to arrest."

"*She* is the Lumnos Crown," Luther shot back. "My father is a usurper. And this is Montios, not Lumnos. The army can't enforce his orders here."

The man chuckled with disquieting triumph. "Well then, if *she* is the Crown, then she's subject to arrest for visiting a foreign realm uninvited. Either way, she's coming with me."

I stared at the wave of sharp godstone pointed at me—and more importantly, at Luther. "If my gryvern and I go with you, will you let my Prince remain here?"

Luther's head snapped to me. "Diem, no."

I didn't look at him, only the Fortos commander, whose hateful grin continued to grow. "Only if you come peacefully. If you resist, *he* pays the price."

I nodded slowly and walked toward him. Luther moved to block me, and the commander's finger tightened on the trigger of his crossbow.

"Stop," I begged. My eyes stayed on the commander, but my plea was all for my Prince.

Stay with my mother, I said into his thoughts with the last tiny shreds of my magic. *Get her to Teller.*

"Don't do this," he begged.

I cleared my throat. "Sorae, return to the Lumnos palace. Once you're there, obey Remis's commands as if they were my own."

Her steps were heavy and sluggish, as if she was fighting against the magic that bound her to my orders, even knowing her protests were in vain. With a hung head and a heartbroken whirr, she leapt into the sky, disappearing into the clouds a few moments later.

I couldn't bear to look at Luther as I strode forward and offered up my wrists. The commander grabbed them and jerked me forward, nearly sending me tumbling down a rocky slope.

"You hurt a hair on her head," Luther growled, "and I will hunt you down and remove yours from your neck."

The commander chuckled, unmoved by his threats. One of his men clamped shackles to my arms and ankles.

"Oh, and one more little thing," he said to me casually. Too casually. "We'll be executing your mother before we go."

"No," I breathed.

He raised his crossbow to my chest, the godstone tip so close it snagged the fabric. "Go into the cave and get the prisoner," he barked at his men. "Tell her if she fights back, her daughter dies. If the Prince fights back, they *all* die."

The soldiers stormed by Luther, taunting him with jeers and vulgar promises of what they might do to my mother before she died, trying to goad him into a reaction so they'd have an excuse to fulfill their leader's threat. But Luther, my valiant Prince, held silent and strong, his smoldering focus on the godstone bolt at my chest.

As the men reached the cave, a slow rumble filled the air. The ground began to tremble, and I staggered to stay upright as the quakes turned violent.

"What the hell are you doing?" the commander shouted.

The ground jerked beneath him, sending him crashing into my side and jolting the crossbow's trigger. I sucked in a breath as the bowstring twanged —then gasped in relief as the arrow hit the stone ground and snapped in half.

I tumbled forward, wincing at the crack of my knees against jagged rock. The strange creaking sound I'd heard at Rymari's gravesite cut through the chaos.

Then, the rumbling stopped. The earth stilled.

"Fortos's cock," a soldier swore. "How'd she do *that?*"

My eyes shot up. At the cave where my mother had been hiding, a smooth slab of lavender stone had appeared out of nowhere, sealing off the entrance completely.

"You broke the deal," the commander barked.

I shook my head frantically. "No—no, that wasn't me, I swear. I don't—"

"It wasn't her."

As one, our heads turned to the quiet, youthful voice.

"It was us."

A young girl of about seven stood at the edge of the clearing outside the cave. Her face was grave, her copper hair wild and windswept. A semicircle of twenty adults spread out at her back, all in matching grey robes wrapped with hides of white fur—and all with lavender eyes.

Montios Descended.

"I'm afraid you won't be taking anyone with you, Commander," the child said. "The Lumnos Queen is in our realm uninvited. That makes her and her guests our prisoners." Her stare shifted to me. "It's *our* Crown who will decide your fate."

CHAPTER
FIFTY-NINE

A tentative hope streamed through my panic. When I'd met the elderly Montios King at my coronation, he'd been... not *friendly*, but curious. I even thought I'd heard him whisper something in my ear.

Good luck, Daughter of the Forgotten.

If he'd sent his people to claim me, perhaps there was some chance I could count him as an ally.

"We have authority to arrest the Lumnos Queen in whatever realm she enters," the commander insisted. "She is a prisoner of the Crowns."

"On what grounds?" the little girl asked.

"She broke into our prison. Killed our King. Freed our prisoners. Attacked the army." His gaze narrowed. "And that's just what she did *yesterday*."

The girl shrugged her tiny shoulders. "Those are crimes against Fortos, not the Crowns."

"She is suspected of planning the attack on Coeurîle," he huffed, clearly losing his patience.

"Suspected." Her slender eyebrows rose. "But not yet charged?"

"It's only a matter of time until she—"

"Then you may retrieve her when she's charged... if she's still alive."

My sunny hope disappeared behind a cloud.

"Fine," he spat. "But we're taking her mother. She *is* a prisoner of the

Crowns, and she's subject to execution." He pointed at the cave. "Turn her over."

The little girl pursed her lips and spun to the group at her back. They circled around her and crouched, their whispers hidden by the howling wind.

Luther watched them shrewdly. His hands twitched, and his weakened magic misted around me, preparing to solidify into a shield at a moment's notice.

The girl glanced back our way. Her eyes fell on me, looking inexplicably sad. She began chewing on her lip, and despite her adult-like eloquence, suddenly she looked very much the child that she was.

"Godstone," Luther said suddenly, insistently. "They brought godstone weapons into your realm."

A few of the group raised their brows and looked to each other with loaded stares. One of them bent at the girl's side and whispered in her ear.

She lifted her chin. "The Lumnos Prince is correct. You may not bring godstone into our realm without our Crown's consent. Not even if your business here is legitimate."

"How are we supposed to get his consent when your King refuses to answer every messenger hawk we send?" the commander snapped.

"I must have missed the law allowing a low-level Fortos grunt to do whatever he wants if a Crown doesn't respond as quickly as he'd like," Luther said. "In fact, the law I remember says anyone brandishing godstone weapons without consent is subject to immediate execution." His smile was vicious. "Perhaps we should *all* go see the Montios Crown."

"Perhaps so," the little girl agreed with a grin.

The commander paled. "No need for that. It was a simple mistake." He shoved me, staggering back like I was poisonous. "We'll be on our way."

The other soldiers took the hint and edged away, hurriedly sheathing their godstone weapons or hiding them behind their backs.

I held up my shackled wrists. "Forgetting something?"

He threw me a nasty smirk. "Consider it our gift to the Montios King so you don't kill him, too."

He and his soldiers stumbled backward, refusing to turn their backs on the Montios Descended.

"This isn't over," the commander called out to me. "You and your mother can't run forever."

"Send my love to your new Crown," I yelled back. "I hear she's a real pain in the ass."

He paused, frowning. "*She?*"

A few of the Montios Descended raised their palms, and their magic swirled in the air, its frosty bite sending a shiver over my skin. My heart leapt at the prospect of absorbing it, but the magic brushed past me and continued on.

The snow beneath the soldiers' boots crackled and thinned to a flat, glossy sheet. Their legs floundered for grip against the slippery surface. One fell on his back, then another. The ground thundered beneath them and shifted into a steep incline that pitched them down the rocky slope, their shouts fading into the distance as they tumbled out of sight.

I breathed out a relieved laugh for half a second before realizing I was in no less danger. My mother was a mortal and I was a foreign Crown—both were forbidden here. If the Montios King wanted us dead, he had all the excuse he needed to do it.

The little girl walked up to me, accompanied by one of the adult Descended, an older woman who might have been her grandmother. The girl held out her hands with an expectant look. I frowned, offering mine in return. She thumbed at my shackles, examining them closely, then looked at the older woman, who shook her head.

"I'm afraid we can't open these here, Your Majesty," the girl said. "You'll have to keep wearing them for now."

I nodded silently, unsure what to think.

"Our Crown Council would like a word with you, if you don't mind," she added.

I blinked. *If I don't mind?*

"Do I... have a choice?"

Her freckle-splattered nose scrunched in a toothy smile. "Of course. But they've been waiting for your arrival."

I blinked again. *They have?*

"We'll come with you," Luther cut in. He shot me an urgent look, nostrils flaring.

The Montios Descended didn't move. Their gazes were fixed on me, awaiting my response.

"Alright," I agreed.

The girl beamed and beckoned us to follow. One of the adults waved a hand toward the cave, and after a brief moment of trembling earth, the slab of stone across the entrance crumbled to dust.

My mother ran out in a panic, face pale and weapon high. Her knuckles were bloody and scraped as if she'd been trying to claw her way out.

Her focus dropped to the shackles on my wrists, then snapped to the Montios Descended. She ran to my side and threw herself in front of me. "You stay away from my daughter," she shouted.

"Calm down, Auralie," Luther said. "We're not in danger."

I blinked a third time. *We're not?*

The Montios Descended clutched their furs tighter around their shoulders and walked away in a single file line led by the little girl, their tattered hems snagging along the rough terrain.

We followed until they paused at a cliff that disappeared into a deep ravine. Two of them raised their palms, and shards of glittering crystals solidified from the snowy air into bricks that curved into a spiral bridge winding into the darkness below. Pebbles from the mountainside rattled down its path and wedged into the ice to give the slippery floor a safer grit. The group parted, one half taking the lead and the other pinning us in from behind.

"Are you sure about this?" I whispered to Luther. "The Montios King could execute us, too."

"I don't think they want to hurt you. I've had a suspicion about something since Umbros, and if I'm right..." He didn't finish, but the look he gave me was bright with hopeful implication.

I cringed as ice creaked beneath my feet. I peered over the edge, my stomach somersaulting at the deadly drop below.

The world began spinning around me. My legs went liquid, and with the shackles still on my ankles, I lost my balance and pitched forward. My body hit the railing, and the ice snapped beneath my weight.

Luther's arms were around me in an instant. He hauled me back against his chest, his hammering heartbeat nearly drowning out his snarled shouts at the Montios Descended to reinforce the bridge walls.

"I've got you," he murmured over and over through heavy, shaking breaths.

"Are you alright, Your Majesty?" the little girl called out.

My face flushed hot with embarrassment. I forced myself to pull away from Luther, even though being held in his arms was the safest I'd felt since leaving Lumnos. "Lost my footing, that's all," I called back.

The girl smiled knowingly. "The height takes some getting used to. It helps if you don't look down."

I battled the urge to crawl into a hole and hide.

"Let me carry you the rest of the way," Luther said, reaching for me.

"Don't even think about it." I swatted at him in an effort to recover my lost dignity. "I'm not a princess who needs a shining knight to whisk her off her feet."

He persisted, his arm winding around my waist and tucking me into his hip. I glared up in protest, but he was slightly pale and his hands weren't quite steady—perhaps I'd come closer to danger than I thought.

"I'm a bit more dark prince than shining knight," he said. "But you're right, you're no princess. You're a queen." He leaned close and whispered. "*My* Queen."

His warm breath tickled the curve of my neck and sent energy pulsing through me. "Too bad," I hummed. "A queen needs a king, not a prince."

The corner of his lips hooked up at my teasing lilt. "Well, I was supposed to be a king," he said dryly, "and then some beautiful upstart showed up and stole my crown."

A loud laugh burst out of me, causing a few of the Descended to glance back with alarmed stares. I bit back my smile. "Who knows, my dark Prince, maybe you'll become a king someday yet."

The words came out before I could overthink them. What they might imply—what I might be offering. My heart squirmed under the burn of his probing eyes.

"I don't think so," he said after a long pause. "I'm not letting you die on my watch."

I started to correct him, then paused as my eyes caught on my mother. Her posture was taut, her biting glare locked on the place where Luther's hand had drifted high on my ribs.

I flushed and pushed him away, then immediately scolded myself for doing it. I had to tell my mother the truth—just as soon as we weren't in the midst of some new mortal peril.

Thankfully, Luther hadn't seemed to notice. His attention was on an archway that had appeared in the sheer rock face. Another ice bridge grew at its base, its winding path merging seamlessly into ours.

"Why is the child the only one who talks?" I whispered to Luther.

"Montios Descended are extremely reclusive. Once their magic comes in, they don't speak to outsiders. Some of them never speak again at all."

"Oh, they're going to *hate* me." I groaned, and the sound was amplified by the miles of barren stone, drawing a wave of frowns. I shot Luther a pointed look that screamed: *See?*

At the end of the walkway, we stepped into a tunnel of carved stone. My relief at being on solid ground vanished the moment I looked back to see the bridge crumble and plummet out of sight, destroying our only way out.

"Your companions may stay here," the girl said to me. She gestured to a room off the main corridor appointed with comfortable chairs and a roaring fireplace. "We'll have warm food and tea brought while they wait."

I stiffened. "I'm not leaving them behind."

"I must insist, Your Majesty. Only Montios Descended may go beyond this point."

"But I'm not a Montios Descended."

"Go on," Luther urged. "I'll stay with your mother." He flashed a teasingly suspicious stare at the little girl. "You look very dangerous. You won't hurt us, will you?"

She giggled and shook her head emphatically.

I eyed the adults who accompanied her. "You give your word they'll be safe here?"

They bowed their heads low, which I had no choice but to take as their agreement.

My mother lagged behind, studying the corridor and its entrance with rapt concentration. The thought of leaving her and Luther alone had me wondering if it was the Montios Descended I should really be worried about.

"Mother?" I called out.

Her gaze snapped to me. "Hmm? Oh, yes, of course. We'll be fine." She hurried over, pulling me into an awkward embrace, then hissing in my ear. "Pay close attention. Even the other Descended don't know what goes on here. Look for maps that show their cities or any sign of weapons stockpiles. And see if you can find any other way in or out."

I jerked back sharply. Was she trying to assign me a *Guardians* mission?

I pried her arms off before she could spot my disgust. I'd learned my lesson about turning information over to the rebels. I wouldn't be doing it again—not even for her.

I walked beside the elderly woman and the little girl while the other Descended fell into a line in our trail. We continued in silence down the corridor until it ended in a slab of solid rock.

The woman placed her palm against it. At her touch, a series of lines surfaced as if being carved from within. A doorway appeared with the Montios sigil etched into its face then slid away, opening a path for us to enter.

We continued on, and the corridor opened up to a brightly lit atrium.

The high ceiling looked to be glass, but from the brisk bite in the air, I suspected it was cast from solid ice. It was a clever, staggered design that left snow lightly gathered on its surface—to conceal it from view, I guessed— while allowing sunlight to diffuse through in a muted glow.

The atrium was scattered with towering stone columns, and firelit torches threw dancing swirls of amber across the walls. At the center of the room, a crystal-clear statue of the goddess Montios loomed tall, with candles in clear jars lining the steps leading up to its stone base.

It was a simple place, lacking the garish opulence of Lumnos, but there was a serene beauty to it all the same. I sensed innately that this was a place of reflection, a haven for tranquility and thought. Though Descended wove their way through the columns in small groups, the whispers of their robes carried further than their voices.

"It's beautiful," I breathed.

"I'm pleased you like it," the woman answered.

I startled at her voice—strong and steady, unafraid to disturb the sanctity of the quiet.

"You... talk," I said, a little stupidly.

She smiled. "Yes, I do." Her head lowered. "Welcome to Montios, Your Majesty."

Behind her, the other Descended bowed their heads again. I returned the gesture, feeling a mix of relief and disquiet at their politeness. There wasn't a single scowl, sneer, or suspicious glare among them. I didn't receive this kind of warm welcome from my own subjects, let alone those of a foreign realm I was in uninvited.

The woman turned to the child and gave her a gentle pat on her shoulder. "Thank you, Maybell. Service is a virtue, and you served your people well."

The girl beamed proudly for a moment, then quickly wiped the expression away and lowered her chin. "Let us seek virtue in all things," she said softly, the words sounding automatic.

"Will you serve us once more and fetch your father to remove Her Majesty's chains?"

"Yes, Councilor Hepta." The girl threw a shy smile at me before scurrying off down a nearby hall.

The woman—Hepta—beckoned me to follow. As a group, we strode across the heart of the soaring atrium. I cringed at the loud screech of my shackles as they dragged across the stone floor.

"Why do your people not speak to outsiders?" I asked.

"Blessed Mother Montios made these mountains her home because she believed being isolated and spending time in silence enhances the mind and opens us to higher truths. We carry on those same teachings today."

I quickly bit back my own terse thoughts. What good was a *higher truth* if you kept it secret from everyone else?

"The little girl said your King was expecting me?" I asked instead.

"Our Crown Council," Hepta corrected. She looked amused. "His Majesty said your arrival would be full of surprises. As usual, he was not wrong."

I frowned, wondering why the King's advisors wished to see me—and how the King had known I would be coming.

"He told us much about you," she added.

"That's strange. I only met him once, at my coronation, and... well, I'm guessing you know how that went."

As one, Hepta and the other Descended placed two fingers to their lips and murmured a word I couldn't make out.

"A terrible tragedy," she said sadly. "Such violence is a stain on our land."

"Land that is already too deeply stained," I mumbled.

She nodded. "Indeed. Peace is a virtue."

"Let us seek virtue in all things," the Descended chanted in unison.

Hepta led me into a large room with a long, narrow table bearing the snow-capped mountains of the Montios insignia. She gestured for me to take a chair at the far end, and she and the others took chairs along either side. Two older children walked in with trays, one setting paper and ink in front of a few seats, and the other distributing mugs of steaming tea.

"Would you like something warm to eat?" Hepta asked.

My stomach growled in hopeful answer, but I declined, too unnerved by this odd place to think of eating. I laughed nervously. "Does this mean you won't be executing me for coming unannounced?"

Several heads jerked to me in surprise.

Hepta frowned. "Of course not. You are welcome here." She relaxed back into her seat. "Perhaps an introduction is in order. My name is Hepta, and I am the Elder of the Crown Council of Montios. Seated here are my fellow Councilors, each of whom has been elected by our people."

"Elected?" My brows rose. "Your King does not select his own advisors?"

"Montios governs itself differently from the other realms. Here, it is our Council, not our Crown, that makes decisions for our realm. The Crown is a member of the Council, but the rest of us are chosen by the people of Montios. If we cannot come to an agreement, the Crown's will is decisive. Otherwise, they have only one vote, the same as each of us here."

Unexpected admiration flowed through me. In the Umbros library, I'd read about mortals using systems like these, but I never imagined them existing among the monarchistic and power-obsessed Descended.

"That's very, uh... fair," I stammered.

"Fairness is a virtue," one Councilor said.

"Let us seek virtue in all things," the others responded.

A man rushed in, nearly tripping over his feet in the process. He gave a hasty bow to the group and darted toward me, then paused. His eyebrows rose high, his expression implying a question I didn't understand.

"Um... hello," I said hesitantly.

"Nector has taken a vow of silence," Hepta explained. "But he will remove your shackles, if you'd like."

"Oh, yes!" I gave him a bright smile. "I'd like that very much."

His cheeks turned pink at the attention, and even pinker as his hand brushed mine to examine the iron cuffs latched to my wrist. He pulled out a stack of tools from his bag, carefully unwrapping each one from its cloth cocoon and setting them down gingerly to avoid the slightest sound.

"Thank you for intervening to help," I said to the Councilors as he worked. "I'm not sure we would have survived, had you not come when you did."

Hepta sighed wearily. "The army is getting overbold. The Fortos King has been pushing the boundaries, and now his soldiers do the same."

"This is not the Blessed Kindred's way," a Councilor said with an angry sniff. "Fortos was given control of the continent's army under the agreement it would act only with the consent of *all* Crowns. These new rules are a disgrace."

"New rules?" I asked.

Hepta nodded. "During the Blood War, the Crowns disagreed on how far the army should go to stop the rebellion. It was nearly impossible for them to come to any unanimous agreement, so a decision was made that the army could act on a vote of six Crowns, instead of nine."

"Some concessions were given in exchange," another said. "The use of godstone, as your Prince pointed out."

"Concessions the Fortos King apparently does not intend to honor," one man grumbled.

A soft clink drew my attention as the shackles on my wrists popped

587

open, even though I'd barely heard or felt a thing. Nector cringed, seeming embarrassed I'd noticed.

"That's very impressive," I said to him.

The flush on his cheeks spread across his face, and he seemed to be fighting the urge to smile.

"Humility is a virtue, Nector," one of the Councilors said in a scolding tone.

Nector looked ashamed and quickly lowered his eyes, turning to the shackles at my feet.

I frowned. "Surely there's nothing wrong with taking pride in a job well done."

"Pride is not a virtue," the Councilor said. "A job well done is its own reward."

Nector adeptly removed the last of the irons from my ankles, then painstakingly wrapped them in cloth to keep from making any noise—a task I promptly ruined by loudly and effusively praising his work. By the time he finally scurried out, he was beet red from head to toe, but there was a spring in his step I hadn't seen before.

"You disagree with our methods," Hepta noted. "You do not believe that we should seek to be virtuous in all that we do?"

"Who decides what it is to be virtuous? Where I come from, what's considered virtuous for a man is called scandalous for a woman. The virtues a Descended is encouraged toward are punished in a mortal. Acts that harm no one are labeled vices, while the loudest purveyors of virtue do the most harm of all. All this to keep some groups in power and others subservient. I admit, I find no honor in that."

Another Councilor bristled. "We do not do such things here. All our people are equal."

A bitter snort broke through before I could stop it. "The mortals you exiled might disagree."

"That was done to protect them. They cannot survive the climate here as we can. We were finding their corpses on the mountain, dead from hunger or the cold. We did not wish to see any more lives lost."

"So you cast them out instead of helping them."

"We did offer to help them," Hepta cut in. "Many times. They did not trust our Council."

"Were there any mortals on this Council?" She didn't answer, and I arched an eyebrow. "Were they even allowed to vote on its members?"

The male Councilor scoffed. "We hardly enforce the exile. We've always turned a blind eye to the mortals hiding in the Forgotten Lands. Including that damn rebel camp. And look what's come of it. Our King—"

"*Peace*, Councilor," Hepta interrupted. "Anger is not a virtue."

He sank back in his chair and closed his eyes as he swallowed his irritation.

My back straightened. "You know about the Guardian camp?"

"So do you, it seems," someone murmured.

I internally swore.

"The rumors are true, then?" Hepta asked. "You and your mother are Guardians?"

These were dangerous waters, but for some reason, I didn't want to lie to these people. They'd saved my life, freed me from my shackles, and welcomed me into their home. My plan to win over allies in Umbros had imploded—perhaps fate was offering me a second chance.

I drew in a deep breath. "I will not speak for my mother, but... yes, I was a Guardian once. I was raised as a mortal, and I joined because I, too, want to end the violence and prejudice that has gone on for so long." I sighed. "And I left for the same reason. There were some—not all, but some —who wished to see every Descended killed. I couldn't agree to that, so I walked away." I hesitated for a moment. "But I would be lying if I claimed to no longer believe in their cause. I only hope to achieve it with as little bloodshed as possible."

The room was quiet for a long time. The Councilors looked at each other, their expressions conveying messages I couldn't interpret. I shifted uneasily in my seat.

"You could be executed for admitting that," Hepta said quietly. "Even as the Crown."

"I could," I agreed. "But I'm taking you at your word that you believe in fairness, and what's been done to the mortals is anything but fair." I offered a wry smile. "And besides—honesty is a virtue."

"Let us seek virtue in all things," they answered as one.

A man who had not yet spoken hunched over the paper and ink set in front of him. The soft scratches of scribbling filled the room as everyone fell silent in deference. When he was done, he passed the paper to the Councilor beside him, who read it aloud. "The soldiers claimed you killed the King of Fortos. Is that true?"

They all leaned forward, their interest piqued.

"I did," I confessed. "He attacked my Prince unprovoked, and he nearly killed me. I did my best to avoid it, but it was his life or mine."

The Councilor who'd snapped at me earlier wrung his hands in his lap. "We never celebrate a life cut short, but perhaps this will solve some of our concerns. The new Fortos King may be less aggressive than his predecessor."

The eyes of the Councilor who'd written his question studied me like he knew the secret I was hiding. He reached for his paper, then paused, leaning back in his chair.

"Fortos's problems are its own," Hepta said. "We are called to look after *this* realm. The time has come to address our problem in the east."

My weight shifted nervously as I felt sorely out of place. I itched with an urge to demand their intentions with me, but I held my silence, worried I'd pushed my luck enough as it was.

Hepta's focus settled back on me. "Recently, we heard rumors of a powerful Descended working with the Guardians."

"I've heard those rumors myself."

"At first, we paid it no mind. The rebels have been in the Forgotten Lands for a long time. We've found that if we leave them be, they do the same."

"What are the Forgotten Lands?"

"An area of the realm we do not enter," one Councilor said, twisting his face in disgust. "That land is evil. *Cursed.* Few Descended are willing to go, and most who do are never seen again."

My eyebrows leapt to the sky. I'd never been taught about any place like this in school. Then again, if there was a place Descended feared to enter, they surely wouldn't want the mortals finding out.

"After the rumors began, Descended passing through on the Ring Road started turning up dead," Hepta continued. "Not just killed, but tortured and defiled. Their bodies were strung up from the trees with a symbol carved into their skin—a ten-pointed star."

"What does the symbol mean?"

"We don't know. We've asked Sophos to research it. Meanwhile, the violence is spreading to other realms. Last week, an entire fishing village in Meros was decimated. Three hundred adult Descended killed, and that symbol was carved into every corpse."

My breath caught. "And the children?"

Her face turned grave. "Vanished without a trace."

My fingernails screeched against the stone table as my hands squeezed into fists and my blood boiled. This sounded too much like the brand of slaughter Vance had espoused. I had to wonder if he was somehow involved —or, gods forbid, if there were more Guardians like him than I thought.

Without warning, one Councilor stood up and directed a fierce glare my way. "Is it you?" she hissed. "Are you the one helping them?"

"What?" I gasped. "Gods, no."

A few Councilors stood, placing their hands on her shoulders and urging her to calm. Tears welled in her eyes as she jabbed a finger at me. "Tell us the truth! Are they dead because of you?"

I shook my head frantically. "I would *never* bring harm to an innocent." Bile rose in my throat at the mere thought—until I remembered the guards who had died at the armory, and my body drooped with shame. "Not knowingly, at least."

"Peace, Councilor," Hepta chided.

Tears spilled down her cheeks. "You swear it? You have not come to do the same to us?"

My hands flew to my heart. "I swear it on my life. On everyone I love. I wish to end suffering, not encourage it."

The woman seemed to find some solace in my words. The anger flooded out of her in a shuddering breath, though it was replaced by a look of helpless fear.

"Forgive her, Your Majesty," Hepta begged. "Emotions have been high since the Umbros attack."

I stilled. "Umbros attack?"

"Three days past. It's too early to know how many were lost, but we hear the casualties were significant."

A chill slithered over me. Three days ago, I was meant to be spending my final day in Umbros as a guest of the Queen. My magic had been at its peak, and four of the strongest Descended I knew were at my side. If we had stayed...

If we had stayed, Luther would be dead. But how many more might be alive?

Hepta went on. "Like us, the Umbros Queen has looked the other way on the rebels in her realm. In return, they left her people alone, as they have here. But if they're no longer honoring that truce..."

"Then Montios could be the next target," I finished. They all nodded, sharing looks of concern.

I leaned my forearms on the table, my hair spilling around me as I dipped my head. The weight of the world seemed to hang on my shoulders.

Even if Montios wasn't next, Lumnos could be. Whoever this Descended man leading the attacks was, he needed to be stopped.

And if my visions could be trusted, then Luther and I were destined to be the ones to do it.

But how? I had no army, few allies. I was a fugitive on the run and the Queen of two realms who didn't want me. I wasn't even sure I was going to be allowed to leave this realm alive.

My gaze rose slowly to the Councilors. "I will help you however I can, but I have to ask... why are you telling me this?"

Hepta's head cocked, the creased lines of her aging face becoming more prominent with her frown. "I don't understand what you mean."

"Why save me and bring me here? What is it your Crown wants from me?"

"Your Majesty... you *are* our Crown."

CHAPTER

SIXTY

"I am *not* your Crown."

Even as I spoke the words, I doubted them. I had felt a calling to this place, an ownership of it humming in my blood. It was the same way I'd felt about Lumnos—and how I now felt about Fortos, even though I'd despised it all my life.

"We saw you at Rymari's gravesite," Hepta said. "You placed your hand inside the circle—it's spelled so only the Montios Crown may enter."

"I'm already the Queen of Lumnos. I can't also be—"

But I could. I *knew* I could.

"The late King warned us his heir would be unlike any other," another Councilor said. "He urged us to trust the Blessed Mother's choice. Even so, we weren't expecting..." His gaze surveyed me. "...*this*."

"When did he die?" I asked.

Again, they all placed two fingers on their lips and murmured as one, an awkward reminder of how little I knew of the people I was now meant to lead.

"The attack on Coeurîle," Hepta answered. "He warned us before he left that his end was near. When he didn't return..." She looked pained. "The other Crowns are not aware. We decided not to inform them until our new Crown was found."

My mind flashed back to my coronation. I had no clear memories after the initial explosion, but there were... fragments. Slivers of recollection that glittered in the fog, wobbly images and muffled sounds that had broken through as my mind flirted with consciousness.

A bright light and a heavy pain at my temples—not an injury from the bomb's blast, I realized now, but the onset of a new Crown. That's why my Crown had looked different, *felt* different. The Arboros Guardians hadn't been familiar enough with the Crown of Lumnos to know, but Luther and the others had.

The Umbros Queen—had she known? Was this one of the secrets she'd intended to reveal?

I reached inward for the Forging magic that answered only to the Crown. It rose to greet me like a housecat purring for its owner, nuzzling itself into my grasp and mewling to me to take control.

Luther's presence within it called to me, a lilting melody that my own godhood gasped to join, despite its exhausted state. Even as I shattered the binds around him and breathed a sigh of relief as his magic was freed, my heart sank. There was no denying it now.

I started to pull away, then hesitated. The Umbros Queen had mentioned using the Forging magic to spy on people within her realm. If this mysterious Descended killer was in Montios, perhaps I could do the same to find him.

I waded deeper, and my senses dulled. The chilly air, the faint rustling of the Councilors' robes—it faded away in the depthless abyss.

The sensation of life buzzed against my skin—creatures and people and plants, their existence inextricably interwoven. And, just as in Fortos, there were fraying gaps where the Forging spell was unwinding bit by bit.

I was caught between conflicting urges. One to heal, to mend the tears and make it whole. And one to destroy, to set it alight and watch it all *burn*. I couldn't tell where either instinct came from—or what the consequences of either choice might be.

But my attention was pulled by something else. Something that stood out among all the life forms the magic pulsed through. Not a foreign Descended like Luther, but something *other*. Something that did not belong.

I set my focus on the being, and an image took shape, bleary like a window in heavy rain. Darkness everywhere, but at the center, a dazzling light almost too bright to look at. As the vision sharpened, the shadows shifted into trees—twisted, blackened ones like I'd seen while flying with Sorae—lit by the golden dance of nearby bonfires.

The light at the center dimmed, then took the form of a man, his back turned to me.

He stiffened, his shoulders rolling. His head turned slightly, revealing the hint of a cold smile. Slowly, he turned, and I sucked in a gasp.

I'd only ever seen him from afar in my visions, but now, it was as if he was right before me, standing in my presence and staring directly into my eyes.

My dark grey eyes—just like *his*.

There was something unsettlingly familiar about him. Something deeply innate, a recognition that burned within my blood. Something not unlike my connection to Luther—that preternatural sense I'd had from the moment we met that our fates were aligned in an inevitable way.

But while Luther's aura sang to me and filled me with calm, this man's presence made me want to cower and *kneel*.

My instincts howled to run as far as I could get, warning of a danger I didn't understand.

He can't see you here, I reminded myself. *He can't touch you. He can't hurt you. It's just a vision.*

But as the man stepped closer, my certainty swayed at the way his silvery gaze stayed on mine.

My hand rose toward him, hesitating just beyond his jaw. There was something about his face...

In a flash of movement, a rough hand gripped tight around my wrist. A real hand—a *solid* hand. I cried out and tried to yank away, but he held me firm.

"Well if it isn't the Daughter of the Forgotten." His voice was satin set ablaze, the smoothest nectar and the deadliest poison. "So many years I waited for you, my sweet liberation." He chuckled, low and dark. "I will give you the world to show you my thanks."

"Who are you?" I whispered, heart thundering.

"Come find me, and I'll tell you." His mouth hooked up in a frosty smile that sent tremors rattling down my spine. "Better hurry. Our destiny awaits."

He dropped my hand and placed his palm on my collarbone, his fingers curling at the base of my throat. I held still, paralyzed by fear, as a painful heat seared my skin beneath his hand.

"Come find me," he said again, this time more order than request. His grip tightened suddenly, harshly, lifting me off my feet and choking off my air. "And if you spy on me like this again, I'll kill you."

He growled and shoved me backward. My vision blurred as I flailed for something solid, feeling like I was falling through infinite sky. I lost my grip on the Forging magic and the world slammed back into place around me as my head cracked against something hard.

"Your Majesty," Hepta cried out. She rushed to my side and helped me up from where I'd fallen out of my chair. "Are you alright?"

I coughed against the lingering sensation of his crushing grip on my throat. The Councilors stared, mouths ajar, their fear-filled eyes focused on my neck.

"What is it?" I asked.

Hepta rolled her wrist, and glassy ice formed over the stone table. I gazed down at my reflection to see a small ten-pointed star glowing at the base of my throat.

I quickly covered it with my hands. "I—I saw him. He's in the forest—the Forgotten Lands. He... he wants me to find him."

"Why?" one Councilor asked, eying me with distrust. "Does he think you will help him?"

I stormed for the door. "I need to go."

"Your Majesty, wait!" Hepta shuffled after me as quickly as her elderly body could move. "You just arrived. We should discuss this as a Council."

"There's no time," I yelled back.

I got to the corridor that marked the entrance, the door having dissolved back into a solid slab. I called on my magic to force it open, but my drained godhood managed only a few tiny cracks.

"Wherever you're going, at least take some guards with you."

I slammed my palm against the stone in frustration. "I don't need your guards, Hepta, I need your *magic*."

She reached for the wall. "Of course. I'll open it for you."

"You don't understand." I willed myself to calm, despite the fiery adrenaline pumping through my blood. "I need to take magic from as many of you as I can. Then I need to find this man and kill him before he hurts anyone else."

SIXTY-ONE

To my heir,

If you are reading this, you now bear my Crown. Blessed Mother Montios has spoken to me of our fates, and I am at peace with the sacrifice I must make. I pray you find the same peace with yours.

I leave you this note for two reasons. First, a plea: guard our people well—for they are now yours as surely as they have been mine. Teach them as much as you learn from them. What you give, they will return in kind.

Second, a message from the Blessed Mother. I know not what it means, only that it is essential you heed these lines:

Eleven must fall for one to rise.
Share the gift to pay the cost.
A dying star will rekindle the spark.
What is forgotten is not lost.

Remember my sister's words.
Beware my brother's wrath.

597

Good luck, Daughter of the Forgotten. May you strive to seek virtue in all things.

My jaw clenched as the words tumbled over in my mind. I crumpled the letter and handed it to Luther.

"What does it say?" my mother asked.

"More riddles I don't understand," I muttered. "Why can't anyone ever speak plainly?"

Luther's eyes narrowed as they roamed the page. "These last two lines... *'Remember my sister's words. Beware my brother's wrath.'* Fortos said the same thing. If this is from Montios, that must refer to the other Kindred."

"Just what I need—the wrath of a Kindred on my head."

"The sister must be Blessed Mother Lumnos. She's the only other Kindred who has spoken to you, isn't she?"

"As far as I know. I suppose Umbros must be the brother. He and his Queen have plenty of reason to be angry with me now."

Luther's eyes turned stormy. Ever since I'd told him about the Umbros attack, his mood had soured. I wished I could ease the blame I knew he placed on his shoulders, but how could I, when I carried it, too?

"I still don't like this plan," he said. "We should have sent to Lumnos for reinforcements before we left Montios City for the Forgotten Lands. It's not too late. Sorae can bring Taran and Alixe."

I groaned. "We went over this all day yesterday. Alixe is where she needs to be, keeping an eye on your father, and she'll need Taran's help. And I tried calling Sorae here already. Remis chained her up the second she got back to Lumnos. I had to call off my command before she choked herself half to death trying to get free."

His hands clenched angrily around his horse's reins. "We should at least wait until our magic is restored."

"We've waited too long already. I'm not going to risk another attack happening while I rest. The Montios Descended gave me as much magic as they could spare."

"And it *still* wasn't enough to replenish you," he grumbled, though a touch of awe lay in his tone.

Nearly every Descended in Montios City had exhausted their power into me in exchange for my reluctant agreement to stay for an extra day in case an attack occurred while they recovered.

Frustrated as I was, it was a lesson I'd needed to learn. Being new to magic made me inefficient and sloppy, too quickly burning through my reserves. Luther assured me that I could eventually train to pace myself and make my magic last longer. Until then, I'd have to choose my battles with more care.

"All the more reason we don't need reinforcements," I said. "If I have the power of all those people, surely we can handle one Descended man."

"I think we both know this is not as simple as *one Descended man.*"

I shifted restlessly in my saddle. We hadn't even reached the Forgotten Lands, and I could already sense the man's potent aura. If it was this strong already, he was more powerful than any Descended I'd met before.

Luther looked up from the letter. "'*What's Forgotten is not lost.*' If you're the Daughter of the Forgotten, perhaps that confirms your birth father is alive."

I glanced at my mother. "Anything to add?"

Her eyes briefly touched on Luther as her expression turned hard. "Not here."

I sighed wearily. "Mother, say what you have to say. I trust Luther to hear it."

"Well I do not," she clipped. "I have known him far longer than you, and trust me, your openness is not reciprocated. The Prince keeps many secrets."

"Not from my Queen," Luther snapped.

"Oh? So you've told her that you—"

"*Yes.* Whatever you're about to say, the answer is yes, but considering who lurks in these woods, I'd prefer you not shout it aloud. Diem knows everything you know and much more you don't." His voice dropped to an irritated murmur. "And she knows because I told her willingly, not because she betrayed my trust and spied on me."

I held my tongue, awkwardly riding between their volley of hostile glares.

My mother turned her focus to the road. "Your birth father is dead, Diem. Whoever told you otherwise was mistaken."

"What if you're wrong? If he's out there and he knows something about why all of this is happening to me—"

"I'm not wrong."

"Mother, if there's any chance—"

"There isn't."

"But the Orb said—"

"He's *dead*, Diem."

"How can you be so certain?"

"Because I killed him myself."

I pulled hard on my reins. "You... *what?*"

She stopped as well, struggling to meet my eyes. "He was unwell. Lost to mad delusions. The day you were born, he tried to stab you. There was a struggle, and..." She didn't finish, her expression grim.

I stared down at my hands as my head began to spin. Though I'd insisted I didn't need him, a tiny part of me had hoped he really was looking for me, wanting to know me.

It shouldn't have hurt so badly to lose something I'd never had.

She drew her horse close and took my hand. "I never wanted you to know this, my darling girl. I knew it would only bring you pain."

A lump built in my throat. "He was a Descended. He might have healed. Survived. The Orb of Answering said he was alive."

She shook her head with a heartbroken grimace. "It was a godstone dagger to the heart, Diem. No one survives that, mortal or Descended."

I jerked my hand back and prodded my horse into a trot, increasing my pace each time she tried to follow, until finally she relented and fell back with Luther, leaving me alone with my turbulent thoughts.

I blinked back tears, hating myself for their existence. I already had a father in Andrei—wasn't it a betrayal of him to mourn a sire I didn't even know?

But if my sire was unwell, what might he have become if he'd gotten help instead of death? What might we have become to each other?

A dark cloud settled over me like a cloak. As we passed into the Forgotten Lands, the landscape seemed to shift to meet my mood. The warped, knobby trees arched above us, hovering with clawed tendrils like predators poised to strike. Their barren branches knotted together in such a thick canopy, we might as well have been riding at dusk rather than noon. The soil turned black and spongy, and though I was grateful for the way it silenced our movement, it would do the same for anyone hunting us.

My heart felt buried under a painful weight, compounded by the three Crowns on my head and the oppressive pressure of the man's aura growing thicker in the air. I was being crushed from within and without by the force of everything hanging over me. Lives and fates, secrets and questions.

My eyes rose to the sky. Why had the Kindred chosen *me?* Was Luther right—had they seen something in me to make me worthy? Or was I just the reckless idiot they could count on to run into battle when every sane mind would walk away?

I despised being a pawn in their game. It made everything bad in my life feel inescapable and everything good feel unearned. I itched with a desperate need to make a choice that was mine, wholly *mine*—even if it led me to ruin.

I tensed at movement from the corner of my vision, then eased at the familiar scent of cedar and musk. I waited for Luther to speak as his horse fell in line beside mine, but he said nothing, merely lending me strength through his quiet presence the way he so often did.

"Let's run away," I said softly, my eyes still fixed on the clouds. "Let's get on a ship and sail as far as the wind takes us. Forget the war, forget the Crowns. Let's have our own adventure, just the two of us."

"Alright."

My gaze cut to him. "Alright?"

He was looking up too, a thoughtful expression on his face. "Where should we go?"

"*Anywhere* else," I breathed.

He nodded solemnly. "Keeping it to ourselves will be difficult. Taran's been wanting to do this for years. He'll find our ship and hide as a stowaway."

"If we bring him, we'll have to bring Zalaric."

A smile twitched. "I think you might be right."

"I suppose Teller and Lily will want to join us. And Eleanor. And if my brother comes, my mother will, too."

"We're going to need a larger boat," he said flatly. I laughed, surprising us both. "We could find a boring little village somewhere. Build a cottage on the sea with an apple tree for Sorae. And a goat."

"*A goat?*"

"I've always liked goats."

I groaned. "My father had one once. It was very cute—and an absolute menace."

"That's what I like about them." He shot me a sidelong look. "I seem to have a weakness for very cute troublemakers."

A grin cracked through. "Imagine that. The terrifying Prince of Lumnos and his fugitive Queen, tending goats and apples by the sea."

"Ah, but we wouldn't be the Prince and the Queen anymore. We would just be Luther and Diem."

My smile faded at the deep ache in my heart to make those words come true. "Would you really do that for me? Leave everything behind?"

"I would do anything for you. As long as I can do it *with* you."

A silent, abiding love glowed in his eyes. My mother's presence a few yards back was the only thing keeping me from launching myself at him and showing my appreciation in every way I knew how.

I had considered leaving her behind in Montios. I yearned for time alone with him, but Hepta and the others knew well who and what she was. Merely having her with me was a crack in their fragile trust. Frankly, I couldn't blame them.

There was also the issue of the mortals. I had come to kill this Descended man, but I prayed the Guardians who joined him could be persuaded to change their course. If I had any hope of that, I'd need their leader at my side.

I frowned at a speckle of movement in the clouds, barely visible through the web of blackened limbs. "Is that a bird?"

He squinted. "If so, it's the biggest bird I've ever seen." He pulled our horses to a stop. "Are you sure Sorae is still in Lumnos?"

I reached out across the bond and winced at the frantic helplessness that pulsed back in return. I could *feel* the chains around Sorae's body, leashing her to the ground, and the muzzle clamped down on her jaws to keep her dragonfyre contained. I was as furious at Remis as I was at myself for not calling her back the second the army soldiers had left.

"I'm sure," I sighed.

My mother's horse joined ours. "What's going on?"

"It's a gryvern," Luther said. "It isn't going anywhere. It's just flying in a circle."

"Maybe the Crowns realized the man leading the attacks is here," I said. "They could be looking for him like we are."

He frowned deeply. "Or they're looking for you. Either way, let's stay out of sight. We don't need the Crowns thinking you're connected to him."

My hand rose to my throat, where the ten-pointed star still glowed beneath my skin. I'd tried healing it away, but the more I pushed my magic toward it, the brighter it grew.

I caught my mother staring at it, her features pinched. "I've seen that symbol before, but I can't remember where."

"Were the Guardians working with him before you went to Coeurîle?" I asked.

She shook her head firmly. "No. I would never have allowed the kind of attacks you described."

"You had no problem planning the attack that killed the Montios King," Luther mumbled.

"That death was never supposed to happen," she snapped at him. "The bombs were only meant to make the Crowns flee so the Guardians could take the Temple."

She looked so genuinely regretful, I was tempted to believe her, but every time I looked at her, I pictured her driving a blade into my sire's heart. When it came to what she was capable of, I didn't know what to think.

"Intentional or not, that death did happen," Luther said. "Many died, and Diem was hurt. And you made me an accomplice for helping you."

Her remorse twisted into a scowl. "You had no problem being an accomplice all the times King Ulther shed a mortal's blood."

His jaw ticked. "I saved as many as I could. Which you well know—you helped me do it."

"Please stop," I murmured.

She jabbed a finger at him. "You still stood at Ulther's side knowing what he'd done."

His eyes flashed with his unraveling temper. "I was the only voice in his ear holding him back. Would you rather I had walked away?"

"You could have stopped him permanently and taken his Crown."

"*Diem* would have taken the Crown, and if she'd done so while you were still poisoning her with flameroot, she might not have survived the Ch—"

"*Stop!*" I shouted.

They both stiffened.

"I have enough to deal with without you two at each other's throats. Whatever issues you have with each other, it's time to let them go. We're on the same side now, remember?"

My mother huffed. Luther shut down, retreating behind his blank facade.

"Seeing the two most important people in my life hate each other hurts me more than you can imagine." I shot them both hard looks as I grabbed my reins. "If that's not enough to make you work things out, then go back to Montios. I've got a war to fight, and I'd rather do it alone than like this."

I prodded my horse forward before they could respond. I was one snide comment away from breaking, and galloping into a battlefield of murderous rebels and a crazed Descended was looking more appealing than one more minute here.

I set a direct course for the tendrils of smoke rising into the air. Even without that beacon to guide me, I'd know where to find him—his powerful aura was a shiny, dangerous lure.

"We're going the wrong way," my mother called out. "The camp is near the border to the east. We're headed north."

"Then he's not at the Guardian camp," Luther answered. "Diem's going the right way."

I didn't look back, but I heard the apprehension in his tone. He could feel it, too—how the man's energy crackled through the air. It wasn't protective, like Luther's, or refined and guarded, like Zalaric's. This man's aura was violence incarnate, pure apex predator, the kind accustomed to never losing a fight.

Distant voices rang out through the trees. I froze and darted a glance at Luther, his grave nod confirming he'd heard the same. My mother jerked her head toward a steep hill not far away, and we made our way to its base and dismounted our horses.

The second my feet hit the ground, a rush of energy surged into my body. My godhood went wild with an eager fervor. For some reason, it *liked* this bleak, gloomy place.

Claim me, Daughter of the Forgotten, its *voice* demanded.

Luther knelt beside his horse, clutching his chest and looking pained. "What is that? It feels like it's sucking out my magic right into the soil."

I frowned. My godhood was *growing*, getting stronger and bolder, seeming to feed off the land itself.

Luther's aura sputtered as if the Forging spell was fighting to bring it back within its grasp. I reached inward toward it, and my breath hitched.

Every time I'd dipped into the Forging magic, its energy had been abuzz with life. But this place... it felt abandoned, decayed, like unpicked fruit rotting on its vine. Though it was within Montios borders, it seemed angrily disconnected, as if rejecting the realm's embrace and aching to rip itself free.

I could see why the Montios Descended had avoided it. If this land could speak, it would snarl of long-held grudges and festering, bleeding wounds. Something bad had happened here once, and, despite its name, the land had not forgotten. It remembered—and it was waiting to claim its due.

The healer in me prickled. A visceral urge rose to cure the damage and find a way to make the realm whole. But when I tugged at the fabric of the Forging spell, it didn't gather in my hand as it had before. It snagged, caught on some force I couldn't see.

It didn't like Luther—that was *very* clear. It was attacking him like a virus, leeching his energy in a bid to force him out or strike him dead. I yanked again, harder, demanding the Forging magic bend to my will.

The symbol at my throat burned hot. The land resisted, but after a moment, it finally ebbed and released Luther from its grasp. A low, distant chuckle echoed faintly in my ear.

I rushed to Luther's side. "Are you hurt?"

"No, but whatever that was, it drained a good deal of my magic. And I wasn't full to begin with."

His glum expression said everything he wasn't saying aloud. We were woefully unprepared and almost certainly outmatched. The battle we'd come to fight had gone from a risk to a folly.

But I couldn't walk away now. We'd come too far, and the stakes were too great.

I crept to the top of the hill to survey from a higher vantage, Luther and my mother following behind. In a large clearing within the trees lay a small village, though it wasn't like any I'd ever seen. There were no roads leading in or out, and though it was populated by simplistic stone buildings, it was set up more like a camp, with a bonfire at its heart, a single pen for livestock, and a shared line of cooking pits.

"Look," Luther said, pointing at a cramped patch of crops. "Potatoes, wheat, lemons. How is that possible in the dead of winter?"

"It's not. This far north, those plants should be dormant."

"Maybe he's an Arboros Descended," my mother said. "Their kind have been friendly to the Guardians in the past."

"Those days are over now," I mumbled, absently itching the star at my throat. "The Guardians captured their Queen. I saw her chained up at the camp where they took me."

She didn't respond, but her face took on an expression I knew too well. Lips pursed, brows arched, eyes anywhere but on me.

I glared. "Mother, what do you know?"

"Nothing to concern yourself with."

Her answer was a knife screeching against porcelain. I'd heard those words a hundred times growing up, and not once had she ever given in.

"The time for secrets is over," I growled. "If you know something about the Arboros Queen—"

"I recognize some of those mortals. They're Guardians, but not particularly high-ranking ones."

"Don't change the subject."

"Leave it be, Diem." Her features were carved in a gentle scold, her tone maternal but firm.

"I could take the answer from your mind myself."

She had the nerve to shrug. "You won't. I know you better than that."

I ground my teeth, knowing and hating that she was right.

"If he is from Arboros, his magic shouldn't work here," Luther cut in. "And those buildings look made from Montios magic."

"He's not a Montios Descended." The words fell from my lips without thinking, like that was some fact I'd innately known.

"Maybe he's not the only Descended here," my mother said.

Luther and I exchanged a look. In our current state, fighting one powerful Descended would be hard enough. If there were more...

"Is that *Vance?*" she gasped. My focus snapped to see my old foe gathering the mortals into a crowd. "What happened to his arm?"

"I did," I said, ignoring her appalled stare. "I should have known he'd be here."

"He's got my sword," Luther grumbled. Sure enough, a familiar jeweled hilt glittered on a scabbard at Vance's hip.

"That thieving ass." I launched forward. "I'm stealing it back."

"*No,*" Luther and my mother said in unison, both of them reaching for my arms.

"Let him have it," Luther said. "That sword means nothing to me now. Besides, you teased me ruthlessly for it. What did you call it? A *'garish piece of tin'*?"

A sudden laugh burst from my mother, and I smirked. Luther shot us both an unamused look.

"It must have meant something if my teasing bothered you so much," I said.

"What *bothered* me was you thinking I was a spoiled royal who didn't know how to fight." He leaned in closer, his voice going dark and rough. "Hopefully I've proven by now that whatever sword I'm working with, I can get the job done."

My eyes briefly dropped below his waist. "Not yet, you haven't."

His nostrils flared.

"Besides, I'm Diem Corbois now." I shrugged. "That's my family heirloom, and I want it back."

My mother's back snapped so straight I worried she might have cracked a bone. "What do you mean you're Diem *Corbois?*"

"I made a deal to claim House Corbois. In exchange, Remis promised no Corbois would rise against me at the Challenging." I snorted. "So much for that."

"Remis Challenged you?"

"No, Luther did."

She whipped to him. "You tried to kill my daughter for the Crown?"

"It's not what it sounds like," I interrupted. I winced and rubbed my throat, which had begun to ache. "It's a long story—one we don't have time for."

Vance's voice carried to us as he addressed the crowd of mortals with an impassioned monologue. I caught enough to recognize it as his standard drivel—*all Descended are bad, all Descended must die, Guardians must be willing to die for the cause, blah blah blah.*

I threw my mother a sour look. "Is this what you believe? Is this what the Guardians stand for?"

Her lips pressed, though she gave no response.

"He wants me dead, Mother," I pushed. "He wants Luther dead. Those half-mortal children you got out of Lumnos? He wants them all dead, too."

Her caramel eyes narrowed as she watched Vance whip the mortals into a cheering frenzy with his calls for vengeance and bloodshed. "He and I have not always seen eye to eye. I try to avoid violence when I can. Vance prefers a more... aggressive approach."

"And yet you left him in charge when you went to the island."

"He's been a Guardian as long as I have, and his loyalty to the mortals is absolute. I needed someone I could trust."

"You gave me your word there would be no attacks," Luther said. "The man you *trusted* did not keep that bargain. Innocent people paid the price."

Her frown cut deeper. "I'm sorry. That should not have happened."

"Don't apologize to me. Your daughter is the one who put herself at risk to stop him—even before she became Queen."

Her heavy stare turned to me, painted with admiration mixed with hues of regret. I looked away.

"You said you recognize those mortals?" I asked.

She nodded. "They're Guardians, but they're from different realms. The only common factor I can think of is that many have been critical of me over the years for being too weak."

"So it's a mutiny," Luther said.

"Henri mentioned the cells have fractured since you've been gone," I said. "You need to unite them again and put a stop to all this."

She lit up. "You discussed this with Henri?"

Luther pretended not to notice, though he went marble still.

A raucous cheer split through the air, drawing our focus and sparing me from the wide, hopeful look in her eyes—and the curiosity in his.

I nearly gasped aloud at the brightly glowing figure emerging in the clearing. If his ethereal appearance hadn't given him away, the sudden spike in his aura would have. Merely breathing was a struggle with his magic saturating the air.

My hand shot out and clamped on Luther's arm. "It's really him."

He nodded grimly. "He's not shielding. My magic can't reach that far, but yours can. You have a clean shot from here, if you want to take it."

A strange kind of coldness took me over as I crafted a bow and arrow of shadow magic. It wasn't the callous numb I'd felt in Fortos, but something perhaps even more bizarre. If I wasn't certain this path was the right one, I might have thought it was anticipatory regret—like some part of me was already grieving this choice and its consequences.

But I *was* certain. This man had killed hundreds with no regard for guilt or innocence. Gods only knew what he'd done with those missing children. He was a risk not only to my realms, but to the peace I was fighting so hard to achieve.

I nocked my arrow, raising the bow to my eyeline and aligning its lethal path. The man's back was to me as he spoke to the mortals in a voice too quiet for me to hear.

My hands trembled.

One good shot, I thought. *One shot, and I save countless lives.*

"Aim for the heart or the spine at his nape," Luther urged. "It's the only way to ensure he dies instantly." I swallowed, and he set a hand on my shoulder. "I'll have a shield ready. Just in case."

I nodded stiffly. My fingers tightened on the arrow as I drew it back.

My godhood stirred unexpectedly, and I nearly let the arrow slip. It thumped alongside my heart and swirled in my arms, keenly interested in what I was about to do. Not supportive, nor judgmental—more like a held breath, waiting to see if I would prove my mettle once and for all.

The man turned his head, the line of his profile just barely visible.

"Now," Luther said. "Before he sees us."

My hands were frozen, too terrified to fire, too defiant to give up.

My mother's face had gone moon-white, her lips popped ajar. She was staring at the camp, murmuring something I couldn't make out.

I clenched my jaw and drew the arrow back as far as the bowstring would stretch. This was my moment. My chance to end more slaughter before it started.

But it would make me a murderer in an inescapable, inexcusable way. There was no chaos of battle this time, no self-defense, no imminent harm to force my hand. This was a calculated killing. No good intention could ever change that.

War is death and misery and sacrifice. War is making choices that will haunt you for the rest of your days.

"Now, Diem," Luther urged.

I took a deep breath, and offered up a silent prayer for forgiveness.

"No," my mother whispered.

Too late.

My fingers relaxed, and the arrow flew.

It sliced through the air with a whistle, carried by my will and a fierce burst of my power. My heart and my godhood squeezed each other close as we awaited my victim's demise.

The magic struck true. Its shadowy point speared into the soft, vulnerable flesh at the base of his neck.

Then... it disappeared.

It didn't cut clean through or fly off course. It didn't fall to the ground or bounce off a last-minute shield. It simply *disappeared*.

Absorbed right into his skin.

The man's supernatural glow flared bright, his aura pulsing with new strength. Goosebumps prickled across my skin.

Luther swore and threw up his shield, then grabbed my arm. "We can't fight him. We need to run."

But I couldn't move. My mind fumbled for some explanation other than what my heart already knew to be true.

"Impossible," my mother breathed. "It's *impossible*. He can't be..."

The man slowly turned on his heel. His smokey eyes—so like my own —found me in an instant.

"He's seen us," Luther hissed. "We have to run."

A panicked cry cracked out of my mother. "Diem... that man... he's—"

"Hello, Auralie," the man crooned.

His voice carried as if he were standing right at our side, his tone smooth and rich with power. His silvery skin glittered as his lips curled into a malicious smile.

His eyes slid back to me. "Hello, daughter. At last, we finally meet."

CHAPTER

SIXTY-TWO

I *tried to kill my father.*

Hours had passed, and the same six words ricocheted inside my skull, drowning out the sounds around me—the crackling fire, the quiet whispers between Luther and my mother, the chirps and howls of the forest creatures lurking in the night. All of it dimmed in the echoes of that one horrifying thought.

I tried to kill my father.

No—Andrei was my father. This man was something else. Something powerful and unnatural. Something terrifying.

Something just like me.

I wrapped my arms tighter around myself as a shudder rolled down my spine. Luther jumped up and grabbed the spelled Montios cloak, draping it over my shoulders, then stoked the fire until its heat seared against my skin.

But it wasn't the cold making my hands tremble.

He crouched at my side. "How can I help?" he said softly.

"You've done enough," I rasped.

After being spotted by the man—by my *sire*—my mother and I had gone into matching states of shock. We'd both stared dumbly as Luther hauled us back down the hill. He'd thrown my mother onto her saddle and pulled me into his, leaving my horse behind as he took both reins and launched into an urgent retreat.

The Guardians must have seen us coming from the mountains, because a group of them were waiting for us at the pass. Rather than fight, Luther changed course for Sophos, pushing our horses to a punishing pace until the day faded to black. Just shy of the border, he'd found an overhang tucked into a hill where the three of us waited in tense silence, jumping at every rustle and snapped twig. When the moon rose high with no sign of pursuit, he'd set up our camp for the night.

He had singlehandedly saved our lives. Meanwhile, I couldn't string together more than that one singular thought.

I tried to kill my father.

I gazed into the flames. "He wanted me to find him," I mumbled. "So why hasn't he followed us?"

It was our only reassurance of safety. Though I still felt a faint trace of his power, it was clear he was nowhere nearby. The Guardians might still be on the hunt, but for whatever reason, *he* was not.

"It's for the best. At least until we know what he wants."

"I tried to kill him, Luther. He's my father, and I almost..." My voice dropped away as another tremor rattled through me.

"You didn't know."

"But I do know now. And it doesn't change what I have to do."

Concern carved deep on his brow. He squeezed my hand, his desperate urge to ease my pain evident in his grip. "Tell me what you need."

My gaze lifted to my mother, pale and shivering, on the other side of the fire.

"The truth," I breathed.

Her watery eyes rose to mine. She'd barely spoken since we'd fled, the weight of this revelation hitting her just as hard.

Luther stood. "It's going to be a cold night. I'll go gather some more firewood."

I threw him a grateful look for what he was really offering—the privacy he knew my mother would require before she would give me any answers. His focus dwelled on me for a moment, an invisible caress against my cheek, then he left.

I shrugged off the cloak, preferring the way the sharp frost nipped at my skin and cut through my daze. I walked to my mother's side, setting it on her instead, then took a seat beside her on a fallen log.

"I need to know everything, Mother." I'd been aiming for stubborn resolve, but it came out like a pathetic plea instead. "I know you were only trying to protect me, but these secrets are more dangerous than the truth."

She nodded stiffly but didn't speak.

My voice softened. "I won't tell anyone else, if that's what worries you. Not even Luther."

A frown flickered over her face. "How did you two become so close?"

"He and I..." I winced. "This isn't about Luther. It's about *us*. And it's time you told me the truth about who I am."

"Your heart is what makes you who you are, Diem. Not Ophiucae. All he did is give you his blood."

Ophiucae.

For so long, my birth father had been no more than a missing word in my story. Like the names of the Old Gods in the mortal books, his name had been burned off the pages of my life in the hopes that I might forget he was ever there.

But now he had a name. He had a *face*.

And our story was still being written.

"Please, Mother," I begged. "Aren't you tired of carrying this alone?"

My words struck a chord, and a deep, soul-weary sigh rushed out of her lips. "Yes, I am."

She shifted on the log until our shoulders were square, then took my hands. Her chin lifted as she summoned strength to her voice. "You know I served many years in the army before you were born."

I nodded. "That's where you trained as a healer."

"Yes... and no." Her brows pinched. "I wasn't just a healer, Diem. I was a spy."

My back straightened. "What do you mean, a *spy?*"

"They recruited me very young. I wanted to do something important with my life, and they convinced me I could do that by serving the Crowns. For a poor mortal girl, it felt like the chance of a lifetime."

I hadn't thought it was possible to have even *more* questions. "Who did you spy on?"

"The Guardians, mostly. Occasionally they would send me to a powerful Descended with a fetish for mortal women, or a well-connected family who needed a mortal healer for their children, but even when I was spying on Descended, it always seemed to lead back to the rebels in the end."

"You broke the healer's vow?" I asked, unable to hide my scorn. Perhaps I had no right to judge her after what I'd done at House Benette, but so much of my shame from that day had come from a fear that, when I broke my vow, I'd really betrayed *her*. "You taught me that nothing is more sacred than that oath."

"It *is* sacred," she insisted.

"But you still broke it. When you were the palace healer, you spied on Luther and his family, didn't you?"

She stiffened. "I never spied on a patient. And healers also vow to save as many lives as we can. What I did at the palace was in service of that."

"So we pick and choose which vows to keep?" I knew I was being unfair, but it was a bitter wound to see her lack of remorse for her choices after months of agonizing over mine.

"I may have made mistakes, Diem, but I've always done what I believed was right at the time. In this world, right and wrong are not always so easily distinguished."

I swung away from her and rubbed at my face. When I offered nothing else, she sighed and tentatively went on.

"I was good at being a spy, and I earned the notice of the Fortos King. But I was also building relationships in the Guardians, and I began to agree with their ideals. One day, I broke down and told the Guardians the truth. The leader at the time asked me to use my position in the army to spy for them instead—and I accepted. I kept them ahead of the army's movements and passed along false information to waste the King's time."

"He would have killed you if he'd caught you."

She huffed a laugh. "Hardly a day has gone by where I have not done something to risk my own life. I tried to discourage you from turning out the same." She gave me a sad smile. "I fear you may have inherited that quality nevertheless, my brave little warrior."

I pushed the heels of my palms against my brow. So much of this made perfect sense in hindsight. She and I had similar natures, with our stubborn, fiery spirits and our passion for doing good. But it also made no sense at all. Auralie Bellator wasn't a *spy*. She was a wife and mother—and when she'd become those things, she'd left excitement behind. She lived a quiet, simple life.

And yet she hadn't. And as much as I wanted to blame her lies for concealing it, a nagging thought wondered if my own prejudices weren't partly at fault. Perhaps I'd seen in her what I'd expected to see—what society had told me to see—instead of the complex, nuanced woman she truly was.

"One day," she continued, "the Fortos King approached me for a mission of the highest secrecy. He'd heard rumors that rebels had found a way onto Coeurîle. He wanted me to hide alone there for one year to find out what they were doing. I knew from my Guardian connections the rumors were false, but I couldn't turn it down without raising suspicion. And it was a priceless opportunity—no mortal had been allowed on the island in centuries."

"Why a year? And why send a mortal?"

"At first, I thought it was a loophole in his authority—perhaps he could deploy mortal soldiers more freely than Descended. But he smuggled me to the island on Forging Day when he was coming for the annual ritual, and he retrieved me a year later the same way. He also ordered me to stay hidden from the army ships patrolling from the sea. He didn't want anyone knowing I was there, even the other Crowns." Her expression turned grave. "Then he gave me a godstone knife to take with me, and I realized he suspected a Crown was helping the rebels. He hoped I'd catch them in the act and kill them."

I frowned. "I don't understand. What does any of this have to do with my birth father?"

"When I got to the island, I began exploring, and I stumbled on a hidden door near the Temple. It was nearly invisible, grown over with weeds." Her eyes wandered. "To this day, I'm not sure why I did what I did next. So much might have been different..."

"What did you do?"

"I called out and asked if anyone was inside. It was completely foolish. This was the most secure place in Emarion, and the door looked like it hadn't been opened in generations. Even if someone had once been there, surely they wouldn't still be alive." Her gaze snapped to mine. "But then a voice *answered back*."

"Someone else was on the island?"

"I couldn't believe it, either. He sounded so scared. When I told him I was mortal, he began weeping. He claimed he'd been imprisoned for helping the rebels and left there to die, but he'd managed to survive on rodents and rainwater. He begged me to help him escape."

"And you did?" I asked incredulously.

"What else could I do? I couldn't just walk away. The door was made of godstone, but the hinges were rusted iron, and I was able to break them open." Her stare went glassy as she lost herself in the memory. "The man I found barely looked human. He was frail and thin, and his skin was grey. Not pale, but *grey*—like his body had been drained of its color. He claimed it was from going so long without seeing the sun. I should have known then there was more to the story.

"He was locked with a godstone chain. Nothing I did could break it open, but I had a year ahead of me to keep trying. In the meantime, I brought him fresh food and water and kept him company. Ophiucae was unlike anyone I'd ever met. The simplest stories would fascinate him, and he spoke of his dreams to change our world for the better. He was charming, and I was... lonely."

"You developed feelings for him," I guessed.

Her cheeks flushed a guilty pink. "I fell fast and hard. With no way to make the contraceptive tonic, I tried to resist, but he was so eager..." Her eyes closed. "Within a few weeks, we were making love. Soon after that, I became pregnant."

I stood and walked to the fire, gazing into the flames. So *this* was how I came into the world. Not as a summer romance or a drunken fling, but a tryst in an underground prison between an army spy and a man so dangerous the Crowns had locked him up where they thought he'd never be found.

"Did... did he..." I swallowed hard. "Was he happy about the pregnancy?"

"You cannot imagine how happy. It was all Ophiucae seemed to think about. He would lay for hours with his head against my belly, listening for your heartbeat or feeling for your kicks. He said he'd been dreaming of you for years."

My heart swelled, and for once, I ignored my guilt and embraced it. He had wanted me. He had *loved* me. What person didn't want to know that their birth was a precious, desired thing?

I turned back to her, frowning at her somber tone. "Why do you sound like that was a problem?"

She was silent for a moment. "His personality changed. He became obsessed with revenge. He spoke of killing off the Descended and installing himself as king. And he became very possessive. When I left the cell, he would make me vow on your life that I would come back. He was paranoid that I might leave, no matter how much I reassured him. Near the end of the pregnancy..." She flinched and looked at me, the pain of the memories stark on her face. "Are you sure you want to know this, Diem?"

"I need to know, Mother. Even if it hurts."

Her head hung low. "One day, I tried to go outside, and Ophiucae became violent. He threw me against a wall and said I wasn't to leave his sight until you were born, but I was able to get away. For weeks, I slept out in the cold, listening to him plead for me to come back. He apologized and said his captivity had made him unwell. He swore that he loved me and would never do it again... I was pregnant and alone. I didn't know what to do.

"The stress of it sent me into early labor. I was afraid of him, but I was more scared of what might happen if I tried giving birth on my own. When a blood sun rose at dawn, it felt like a sign that if I made the wrong choice, I might lose you forever. I prayed to the Old Gods to protect us both, then I went back down to his cell and told him you were coming. Ophiucae became just like his old self again. He made no demands, and he did everything I asked. When you finally made your appearance, he was overjoyed. I believed he'd really changed."

My throat strained with the burn of emotion, a stray tear breaking free. I wanted to stop the story here and let that be my only truth—a man who was flawed, but willing to grow. A man who had loved us.

"But he hadn't changed, had he?" I whispered.

She looked anguished. "When I'd healed enough to walk again, he insisted I leave to get some fresh air. I thought he was trying to earn back my trust. I left you asleep and went outside, but as soon as I walked away, a feeling in my gut told me something was wrong. I crept back down to the cell, and I saw Ophiucae standing over you with my godstone knife." She shuddered, squeezing her eyes closed. "I'll never forget seeing the tip of that blade over your tiny heart. If I'd been one minute later..."

Her voice choked up. I returned to her side, pulling her close, and she swiped at her tears.

"The rest is a blur. He gave me some absurd story about needing your blood to unlock his chains. I refused, and we fought, and I managed to steal back the blade. He tried to grab you, and I panicked, and I—I stabbed him in the heart." Her head sank. "I took you and ran, and I never went back. When the time came to leave, I lied to the King and claimed I hadn't known I was pregnant when the mission began."

I barely heard her, my thoughts caught on one detail. "Ophiucae wanted my blood?"

"He said he wanted me to pour it on a rock and break some curse. All of it was nonsense, utter madness."

"It wasn't," I breathed. "I think he was right." We both pulled back, and my wide, stunned eyes mirrored hers. "There's a stone in the Kindred's Temple where the Crowns shed their blood for every ritual. When my blood touched it at my coronation, something went wrong. The stone broke, and—"

"The tremor just before the bombs went off," she said, her face lighting up with realization—then darkening with horror. "All those months I thought I was alone... by the Flames, Ophiucae was there the whole time."

"He must have escaped during the attack." I blew out a long breath. "No wonder he hates the Descended."

I didn't say it aloud, but a part of me was darkly sympathetic. If someone had buried me alive, I might come out on the other side with a thirst for vengeance, too.

"Who else knew what happened?" I asked.

"No one. Not even Andrei."

"Did he know you were a spy?"

"If so, he never acknowledged it. We'd both done things in the army we couldn't discuss. We had an understanding to leave it behind in Fortos." A heavy sorrow dragged on her features. "We were focused on our future together, not our past apart."

I bristled. "I met Cordellia in Arboros. She said you never told him about the Guardians, either."

"I'm sure he had his suspicions," she said slowly. "But we never—"

"He was your husband, Mother. How could you lie to him about something so important?"

My tone was harsh, and she flinched at its bite. "You see it as a lie, I see it as unconditional trust. Andrei knew there were things I couldn't tell him, and he chose to love me anyway. I pray you find that in your own partner someday."

Luther's face surfaced in my thoughts. My heart ached to let him wrap me in his arms and shoulder this burden at my side. But I couldn't —I'd have to keep all of this from him to honor my promise of secrecy to her.

And I knew he would accept it. No questions, no argument. He would simply trust me. *Love* me.

"What about me and Teller?" I shot back. "You put us both at risk. Didn't we deserve to know?"

"Diem, dear, you didn't *want* to know. There were times I slipped up, and I was sure you'd figure it out. I was prepared to tell you everything, if you asked, but you never did."

"That's not true. I always asked where you were going, what you were doing—"

"—and when I gave you an easy answer, you took it, even when it made no sense. You were happy with your life, and you didn't want it to change, so you looked away. As for your brother... he's always idolized you. He knew if there was something to worry about, you'd tell him. And since you never pushed, neither did he."

I scoffed. "So this is my fault?"

She reached for me and flinched when I jerked back. "I take responsibility for the choices I made. You have to do the same for yours. If you look back at our lives, if you truly look, I think you'll see my secrets weren't as *secret* from you as you wish to believe."

I shoved to my feet, my temper boiling beyond its limit. "Maybe you're right, maybe I did see it and look the other way. But it was only because I trusted you. I believed my own mother loved me too much for my worst fears to be true. *That* was my real mistake."

"Diem," she begged, "please—"

I walked away before she could finish, winding into the forest and leaving her staring at my back.

CHAPTER

SIXTY-THREE

I stumbled on Luther by accident, leaning against a nearby tree. Perhaps I was lucky, or perhaps his heart had drawn me toward him, knowing my injured soul needed the balm of his touch.

He straightened as I approached, his brow creasing with worry. "What happened?"

I grabbed his hand and kept walking without a word, tugging him further into the darkness until I was certain we were out of earshot and out of sight.

"I can't tell you what she said," I gritted out. "I promised her I'd keep it to myself."

"I understand."

"That's it?" I snapped. "You're not mad?"

He frowned. "Should I be mad?"

"We're supposed to be honest. Tell each other everything." I scowled. "Isn't that what real love is all about?"

"No couple tells each other everything. I know you wouldn't keep something from me if it wasn't important." He brushed my hair away from my face, then dragged me closer. "My love for you *is* real love, Diem. No secret you keep is going to change that."

I huffed, equal parts cranky and swooning. "Stop being sweet. I'm trying to be angry over here."

His lips twitched as he fought his smile. "Very well. What would you like me to do instead?"

"Distract me." I fisted my hands in his sweater and arched my neck toward him. "Make me forget everything but you."

"Gladly," he rumbled.

The air rushed from my lungs as he crushed me back against a tree, his mouth capturing mine and forcing me to breathe him in. All my angry thoughts turned liquid, carried away by the tide of desire.

I shivered with pleasure as the pressure of his body filled in all my curves and hollows. My hands tore at him with a desperate kind of urgency, my nails raking over his chest, his back, his neck. I wanted, *needed*, to feel him everywhere, needed the searing touch of his skin to burn through my pain.

I gasped as he broke the kiss and nipped at my lip, my senses held captive by the sharpness of his teeth in my flesh. His hand slipped beneath my pants, and he rumbled with approval at the hot wetness he found waiting between my thighs.

"Are you sufficiently distracted?" he teased as his fingers teased me, luring my pleasure to the surface.

"You can do better," I purred, my husky voice and writhing body giving away my lie.

He growled at the challenge. His fingers plunged in without warning and dragged a loud moan from my throat. His other hand clamped across my mouth as he smirked. "Careful. There's all kinds of dangerous beasts in this forest. Although..." He hooked a finger inside me to knead that hidden, sensitive spot, and my back arched as my grip on him turned bruising. "...I caught the most dangerous beast of them all."

His mouth lowered to my shoulder and scored a sizzling hot trail up the column of my throat. With every muffled cry, his fingers pushed harder, deeper, and simmering energy built in my core.

I fought the looming cliff of release with everything I had. I *wanted* the tension, the unbearable pressure, the feeling like I might implode. I relished the way my mind clouded and I felt his touch and nothing more. The pain of the buildup was so much more enticing than the pleasure of letting go— because that would mean coming back down to earth, where all my troubles lie in wait.

Luther knew it, too. Every time I clenched around him, my thighs squeezing in trembling protest, his movements would slow just long enough to let my pleasure recede, keeping me permanently wobbling on that perfect, excruciating edge.

"Distracted now?" he asked. His face was alight with a thrill I'd only ever seen from him in battle.

I pulled his hand from my mouth down to my neck, curving his fingers around my throat. His thumb brushed over my pulse where it throbbed against my skin, and his eyes flared with a predatory gleam.

"Not yet," I taunted. My hands dropped to his waist and fumbled with the clasp of his trousers. "Maybe I need to take matters into my own hands."

My fingers curled around his cock, and his grip on me twitched. His hips ground forward, urging me on.

Ceding to his control of my body in Umbros had been bliss, but demanding the same from him now was an exhilaration like no other. When his gaze turned glassy and his words devolved to quiet grunts, I felt utterly invincible. This powerful, intimidating man, this force of nature, this fearsome warrior—reduced to a panting, speechless beast by just my touch.

I smirked at my triumph, and his expression turned savage. The haze of lust cleared from his eyes, and his fingers resumed their torture, teasing me with gentle circles before pumping in deep, aggressive strokes.

Our hips rocked against each other's hands as our desire pulsed in matching rhythm. We smothered our moans in a brawl of a kiss that demanded a surrender neither of us would give. Release edged nearer, and we were both too stubborn to stop.

"I want more than your hand," I pleaded breathily.

"Not like this. Not against a tree." His tone was gruff, but his resolve wavered. "Not the first time."

My head fell back with a groan. "I grew up in a forest, Luther. All my first times were against a tree."

My breath caught as his hold on my neck slid higher, taking me by the jaw and forcing my gaze to his. "I am not the men you're used to," he snapped. "And I refuse to be just another lover to you."

I pulled his hand away, then laid a kiss, delicate and feather-light, on his scar where it plunged down his neck. "You're not just another *anything* to me."

He let out a deep, satisfied rumble. "I'll be your distraction, if that's what you need. But mark my words, Diem Bellator..." He pushed another finger inside of me, and I cried out at the exquisite fullness. "This is just a taste of what I have planned for you. Our night is coming, and when it does, I'll be the last *first time* you ever have."

His voice was rough, all fire and lust and heady promise, but the emotion behind it shone bright in his eyes. It hit me with an unexpected flash of clarity. I hadn't needed a distraction from my problems—I'd needed a reminder I wasn't facing them alone.

I'd hated Luther, I'd run from him, I'd shielded my heart and built walls that I warned him might never come down, and he'd never swayed an inch. He was steady and unyielding, the island of calm in my tumultuous sea.

"*Luther.*"

His name poured out like a breathless confession, representing so much I wanted to say but couldn't put into words. He kissed me—this one sweet and tender, full of his promise that, whatever I felt, he felt it, too.

My restraint crumbled. The pressure became a new kind of exhilaration, because I was no longer afraid of letting go.

His cock thickened in my hand as his release grew as imminent as mine. My legs began to tremble, pleasure overwhelming every sense. I buried my head in the crook of his neck as the urge to scream his name hovered on my tongue. My core was throbbing, my skin prickling, my body melting. We were close, *so close*. One more stroke, and—

"*Get the hell away from her!*"

A blur of motion flew past my face, and a harsh rush of cold air replaced the warmth of his body. I blinked in confusion as my mind floundered to make sense of the sudden change—only to find my mother clutching a blade and looking ready to kill.

"You *bastard*." Her face was red, her body quaking. "This is how you take your revenge, by defiling my daughter?"

Luther clumsily tucked himself away and straightened his clothes. "You don't know what you're talking about, Auralie. This isn't about you."

"Liar," she seethed. "I knew you were ruthless, but I never imagined you'd stoop so low."

The lingering emotion on his face rapidly froze to a hard, glacial scowl.

"Mother, stop," I begged. "I don't know what you think this is, but—"

"I'll murder you for this," she hissed. She lunged toward Luther, and I threw myself in her path.

"*Diem!*" Luther shouted, half fury, half panic. His shield shimmered into place around me a second before my mother's blade crashed against its edge.

She sucked in a breath as she realized what she'd almost done. "Diem, get away from him. He's not the man you think he is."

"Mother, please listen—"

"He wants to get back at me, and he's using you to do it."

"What kind of monster do you think I am?" Luther asked, his tone dripping with disgust.

"The kind of monster who's never had a problem threatening my family to keep me in line," she spat.

"The Blessed Mother herself couldn't keep *you* in line," he yelled back. "You always knew my threats were empty. You told me so every chance you got."

I pushed through his shield, light flaring off my skin as his magic absorbed into mine. I put my hand over hers on the knife's hilt and pushed it down. "Mother, we need to talk. There's much you don't know."

"I know enough. He's cruel. He's merciless."

I sighed. "He's neither of those things."

"He's going to hurt you. He—"

"*I love him.*"

She stopped. The knife slipped from her hand and tumbled to the ground.

"No." She shook her head. "No. You can't."

"I can, and I do."

"But... what about Henri? I thought you two..."

I flinched. "Our friendship is over."

"How? You've always been inseparable."

"It was his choice as much as mine," I said bitterly.

She balked. "That's impossible. Henri's been in love with you for years."

Her words felt like a fist to my gut. "He was in love with *mortal* Diem. We were always doomed." I shot her a scathing look. "And you were cruel to let us grow so close, knowing the truth of what I am."

Guilt flitted over her features before disappearing behind a scowl. "That doesn't have to divide you. It would be... difficult, but if you love each other—"

"We don't," I snapped. "But remember you said that when you talk to your son."

"Teller?" Her head cocked. "What does he—"

"This is about me and Luther." I set my hands on her shoulders, letting her see the truth of my words in my gaze. "Believe me, it took him a long time to earn my trust. I put him through hell and back for months, but once I saw who he really is..." My chest warmed at the depths of my affection. "He's so kind and thoughtful, and he's entirely selfless. He's more loyal to me than I deserve. He challenges me without trying to change me, and he sees me in a way no one ever has. When I'm with him, I feel safe and cherished and..." I glanced at him, surprised to find his mask down, his feelings for me laid bare on his face. "...and loved. He makes me feel *loved*." I looked back at her. "And I love him, too."

"Your daughter is everything to me, Auralie," Luther said quietly. "All that I am, it belongs to her."

Her brows dipped. She studied my face, then his, looking like she was scouring for any hint of a lie or exaggeration. She was silent for a very long time, then her shoulders fell, the fight seeming to go out of her in a rush.

"Be happy for me," I pleaded. "I finally found a man worthy of my heart."

"My sweet daughter." Her eyes closed briefly. When they reopened, they gleamed with anguish. "This is so much worse than I thought."

I frowned. "What?"

"He's not using you to get to me. He's using you to get to the throne."

"*What?*" Luther and I said in unison.

"Isn't it obvious? He's made you fall in love with him so you'll make him King Consort. He's doing whatever it takes to hold on to power."

The patronizing pity on her face set me off. I jerked out of her reach. "This is ridiculous."

"He admitted as much on the bridge in Montios. He said you stole the Crown from him."

I groaned. "By the Undying Fire, we were *joking*."

"You weren't looking at him, Diem. I saw his face light up when you offered to make him a king. That's exactly what he wants."

"It's not the throne—" Luther's jaw snapped as he cut himself off.

"You tried to fight her at the Challenging, didn't you?" she shot back. "You wanted to kill her so you could take it."

"Gods, Mother, he didn't want to kill me, he wanted to *die* for me," I said, throwing up my hands.

"I wouldn't take Diem's life even if the Blessed Mother herself demanded it," he muttered.

She let out a long, exasperated breath. "Diem, I don't doubt your feelings are real. You've always seen the best in people, and I know how convincing the Prince can be."

I laughed, harsh and bitter. "You know, there was a time when I was jealous of the work you did together. I thought you knew him even better than I did. But after all those years, you don't know him at all."

I turned my back on her and walked to his side, taking his hand. "I'm sorry," I murmured to him.

"It doesn't matter. You and I know the truth." His features were hard, but I couldn't miss the shadow of disappointment. He might never admit it, but I suspected he'd hoped to become as much a part of my family as I'd become of his. I'd seen it in the way he treated my father and Teller, and even, despite their tension, in the way he'd treated my mother.

A fiercely protective instinct flared hot in my blood. "It does matter." I glared at her over my shoulder. "This is the man I've chosen. The man I want to spend my life with." His fingers tightened around mine at my admission, and though my heart quivered with a wild, scared energy, I didn't regret it for a second. "You and Father chose to leave your past and focus on your future—well, Luther is my future. And if you won't accept him, you won't be a part of it."

She recoiled. "I am your *mother*."

Angry, vicious words fought to break free, and I ground my teeth to hold them in.

"I know we have things to work through, but we're family," she said. "Family always comes first."

My nails dug into Luther's skin as I squeezed my fraying patience into his hand and bit back my thoughts.

She crossed her arms. "I'm only trying to look out for you. It's my job to protect you."

My temper shattered.

"*And you failed!*" I shouted back.

Her face dropped. "Diem—"

I whipped to face her. "You built a house of lies around us, then you lit the fuse and walked away. When it all exploded, I had to pick up the pieces, even though I was completely falling apart. You have no idea how dark things got. The choices I had to make." Hot, angry tears sprung to my eyes at the memory of the armory attack—how I'd surrendered to my shame and welcomed a fiery end. "The choices I almost made. Choices I almost didn't come back from."

Her expression took on a horrified kind of sorrow. "I had no idea..."

"Your secrets put me in danger a hundred times over. Not just me—Teller and Father, too. If I'd known about my magic, if I'd taken the years to train... maybe I could have saved him." My voice broke. "Maybe he wouldn't be dead because of me."

"Diem," Luther said softly, looking pained. "That wasn't your fault."

"Don't," I warned him. "I know you blame yourself for it just as much as I do. So does Teller, for not being home when it happened. Father's death left scars on us all." I glared at her. "Meanwhile, *you* were off planting bombs for the Guardians."

She nodded as her own tears began to fall. "You're right. I should have been there."

"But you weren't. Teller and I lost everything. *Everything*. Father was gone, our home was gone, our lives were in chaos. All we had was each other, and I could barely give him that. I was broken. So fucking broken, in every possible way. We needed answers. We needed love and guidance. We needed our gods-damned *mother*. And you just... weren't there. So don't you dare tell me that family comes first. You put the Guardians first—and your family paid the price."

She clutched at her heart like my words had carved a bodily wound, her wet cheeks gleaming in the moonlight. "I thought I was doing the right thing. I thought I'd come home in a month, and everything would be the same." She buried her face in her hands and choked out a sob. "Gods, what have I done?"

As angry as I was, seeing her hurting brought no joy, no vindication. This wasn't a fight to be won. These were open wounds that needed cleaning, tending, and time—and even then, the scars might never fade.

Luther gently squeezed my hand. The simple gesture made all the difference, his strength soaking into me as surely as his magic had.

"You weren't there, Mother." My chin lifted. "But Luther was. He made sure I had weapons and friends and a place I could feel safe, and he asked nothing in return. He took care of me. Teller, too. Even when we had no one, we always had him."

Her bleary-eyed focus shifted to Luther, the scorn softening from her face. "Perhaps..." Her throat worked. "Perhaps I've been hasty in my judgment."

I sighed and sagged against him. "You can't imagine what he and I have been through. I owe him everything."

He laid a kiss on my temple. "You owe me nothing."

My mother took a moment to compose herself, wiping her face and taking a steadying breath. "After a lifetime of keeping secrets, openness doesn't come easy for me. It's already cost me my husband." She grimaced, another tear breaking free. "I won't let it take my daughter, too." She offered her hand. "Can you forgive me? Or at least give me a chance to make it right?"

I hesitated. "Will you give *him* a chance?"

She looked at Luther, her expression unreadable. No longer hostile— but not entirely trusting, either. "You swear your intentions toward my daughter are good? You're not using her for your own gain?"

"I swear," he said firmly. "Her happiness is my only goal."

She gave a stiff nod. "I still have questions, but I will keep an open mind. If what my daughter says is true, then it seems I owe you my gratitude."

He dipped his head low.

"From now on, we tell each other the truth," I insisted. "*All* of it."

"All of it," she echoed.

I glanced up at Luther, and I could have wept at the fragile hope in his eyes. "All of it," he agreed.

I pulled my mother into an embrace, feeling for the first time like she was really, truly back in my life. We both began to cry, then laughed through messy sniffles at our sorry states. I put an arm around her shoulders, took Luther's hand, and together we walked back to the campfire, ready to start anew.

CHAPTER
SIXTY-FOUR

"**B**e *careful.*"

I rolled my eyes, though I couldn't suppress a smile. "Mother, you've said that twenty times already this morning."

"Because I know my daughter. You've never met a danger you didn't want to run into head-first."

"Then you also know your warnings are as useless as the wind," Luther grumbled. He suddenly tensed like he was afraid he'd overstepped, but when my mother howled a laugh, he eased against me in our saddle with palpable relief.

"My magic is nearly restored," I said. "As long as Ophiucae doesn't follow us into Sophos, we'll be alright."

"And if he does, I won't let him hurt her," Luther added.

She nodded approvingly. "I'm going to hold you to that, Prince."

"Please, call me Luther."

I threw him a look, eyebrows high, but I held back my quips. Their tentative truce was more precious to me than words could say, and even my eternal love for teasing him wouldn't get me to risk it.

It hadn't come easily. We'd stayed up most of the night, sitting by the fire and sharing our truths. My mother told me everything she remembered about my birth father, as well as much more about her time both in the army and in the Guardians. In return, I told her everything that had occurred since the day she'd gone missing. We cried together over the story of my father's death, fumed together at how Vance had used me, betrayed me, then targeted me, and smiled together as I described Taran and Eleanor and the rest of my new Descended family.

To my shock, without any prompting, Luther shared his story with her, too. He told her about his mortal mother and the story of his scar, the visions Lumnos sent him and the better world he believed I was fated to lead. She interrogated him relentlessly about the evils she'd believed him guilty of, and he patiently explained the real story behind each one. Her walls began to fall as she listened in alarm at how much he'd known about the Guardians—and how much he'd done in secret to shield them from Ulther's detection.

But it was our love story that seemed to put the last nail in her suspicion. Understanding surfaced on her face as we took her through our ups and downs, the teasing and flirting, all the ways we'd saved each other, and all the times we'd nearly said goodbye. Through it all, her eyes marked Luther's every move—each clasp of my hand or stroke of my hair, each adoring smile and good-natured groan.

It would take time for their distrust to fully fade, and perhaps a close bond might never form, but by the end of the night, the three of us were smiling and making plans. When it was time to sleep, Luther boldly curled up beside me and pulled me into his arms, and she made no objection. For now, that was as great a gift as I could hope to have.

"Maybe Ophiucae won't hurt me," I said.

She and Luther exchanged a solemn glance.

"Diem," she started slowly, "you cannot let yourself forget how dangerous he is."

I stiffened. "I haven't forgotten."

"He would have killed you as a baby, had I not intervened."

"He wanted my blood. Maybe he was only going to cut me, not kill me."

"He's murdering innocent people, Diem," Luther said gently.

"I know that," I clipped, my hands clenching on the reins. "I'll do what has to be done."

An awkward silence fell between us, filled only by hoofbeats on the hard-packed soil.

"I'll do it," Luther said. "You shouldn't have to kill your own sire. When the time comes, let me be the one to take him down."

I tensed. "He can absorb magic like me. And if I'm right and he doesn't want to hurt me, I might be the only one who can get close enough to do it."

His arms tightened around me. "I'll find a way."

My heart roiled with conflict.

I knew Ophiucae had to be stopped.

Permanently. *Soon.*

But the idea of slaying my birth father—just when I'd finally found him, before we'd even had a chance to truly meet—brought a lump to my throat. I wasn't entirely confident I'd be able to follow through and strike the killing blow.

And if I was being really, *truly* honest, even if it was Luther wielding the knife, I wasn't sure I'd be able to stop myself from intervening.

Though I'd made other excuses, that was the real reason we were headed into Sophos instead of returning to the Forgotten Lands to finish what I'd started. I needed time to come to terms with this new revelation and all its consequences—but I couldn't risk more innocent lives in the interim.

"Are you sure this is a good idea?" my mother asked. "If the Crowns want you captured, why risk handing yourself over to one of them?"

"I'm not going to live as a fugitive. If the Crowns want to question me, I'll give them their answers. And if they try to kill me, they'll meet the same fate as the Fortos King. Besides, the Sophos Crown is in charge of the rituals. I need to convince them to call the Crowns to the island to finish my coronation." I glanced at her. "And *you* need to go convince the Guardians to let them."

She scowled. "Do you know how many years we've been trying to capture Coeurîle? And now I'm supposed to tell my people to give it back?"

"They don't have to leave the island, just the Kindred's Temple. And just long enough for the rituals. It's a cease-fire, not a retreat."

"If the Crowns think Diem can manipulate the rebels through you, they might be willing to leave you both alone," Luther added. "It's our only chance at avoiding an all-out war with them."

She didn't look convinced. "Isn't a war with the Crowns your goal?"

"Eventually," I agreed. "But I need to find allies and build an army. It will be easier to do that without an execution order hanging over my head."

"Or maybe you need to kill the other five Crowns and take their realms, too."

My godhood hummed eagerly at her words.

"I'm not a murderer," I mumbled, though I wasn't sure who I was trying to convince—her, my godhood, or myself. "And there are six left, not five."

Her lips pursed.

"Mother," I warned. "You promised honesty. What are you holding back?"

She blew out a sigh. "The Arboros Queen is with us—with the Guardians, I mean. She has let us operate freely in her realm for years. She helped the rebels get on and off the island the day of the attack."

"If that's true, they betrayed her. She was a prisoner like me. They chained her up—"

"A farce to cover up her involvement, I'm sure. She must have been hoping you would tell the other Crowns what you saw to throw off any suspicion."

I frowned. "Why would she help the Guardians?"

My mother smiled. "You're not the only half-mortal Crown. She and her mortal father were very close. She promised him on his deathbed she would do everything she could to help his kind."

Luther nudged my leg. "Looks like we might have just found our first ally."

Our horses slowed as the dark, hilly forest gave way to the rolling grasslands that marked the border of Sophos, Realm of Thought and Spark.

"Maybe we should escort you to the Guardian camp," I said to my mother. "I don't like you traveling alone."

"I'm not alone." She tipped her head to a patch of trees in the distance, where a flutter of movement caught my eye. She let out a series of short, high-pitched whistles. Moments later, the same sound echoed back.

I nodded reluctantly. "We'll come get you as soon as it's safe to return to Lumnos."

"In the meantime, I'll send warnings to all the cells about Ophiucae. I can't keep our members from joining him, but I can at least warn them he's got motives of his own." Her focus shifted to Luther, her eyes thinning slightly. "I'd like a word with you before I go. In private."

I sat up straighter, my defenses rising. "Anything you have to say to him, you can say to me."

"It's not what *I* have to say that I'm interested in," she said curtly. "And if you want me to trust him, then you have to trust me, as well."

With some effort, I managed to hold my tongue. We dismounted, and Luther threw me a lingering stare before following her out of earshot. I unapologetically watched their every movement, my teeth chewing nervously on my cheek while I scrutinized every gesture and expression.

The cautious cordiality she'd been giving him this morning had been replaced by a glare as hard as stone. I nearly lunged forward to interject when she jabbed her finger into his chest, but he kept his cool-headed calm, nodding repeatedly with his hands clasped loosely at his back.

She said something to him, then crossed her arms with an expectant look. Luther glanced over at me, staring so long I frowned in question. A slow smile grew on his face, then he turned away.

My heart pounded. Something about this moment felt so much more important than a casual chat. Luther talked for a long time—a *very* long time—while my mother sharply scrutinized him, her eyes jumping rapidly over his face.

It was laughably obvious now—the spy she'd been hiding inside all those years. She'd always been impossible to lie to, keenly noting details everyone else would overlook. And, though she could rival me for fearlessness and feist, she also had a nurturing warmth that could crack even the hardest heart.

If only she'd let down her guard long enough to show it to him.

I toyed anxiously with my sleeve. The one-sided conversation stretched on, and her expression didn't shift. Luther finally stopped talking, and her gaze fell to the ground, her brows deeply creased. For a minute that felt like an hour, they stood like that—unmoving, unspeaking.

Out of nowhere, my mother launched forward. Her arms wrapped around his waist, her face buried in his chest, her petite form swallowed up by his towering, muscular build. He stiffened, his eyes shooting to me in alarm as he awkwardly patted her upper back.

My curiosity surpassed my powers of restraint, and I jogged over to join them. "Is everything alright?"

My mother pulled back, her eyes red and watery, though a smile stretched across her face. "Yes. Yes, I think it will be, after all."

Luther and I shared a baffled look.

"I'll give you two a moment," he said cautiously, and my mother nodded, beaming through her sniffles. Her smile lingered on him, even when he'd walked away.

"What happened?" I asked.

She took a deep breath. "You and I are so alike, my little warrior, but there is one way in which we are as opposite as night and day." She took my hands. "You look for the best in everyone you meet, and I seek out the worst. I've spent so many years worrying that everyone I meet could be a threat."

"Luther is no threat to you," I cut in. "He would never, *ever* hurt someone I care for. He would put his life on the line to protect you or Teller or Maura."

"Yes. I think you're right."

I started. "You do?"

"He loves you. I saw it on his face the second I saw you two together in that prison. I tried telling myself it was an act, but the way he looks at you..." Her smile grew. "That kind of emotion can't be feigned."

I sucked in a breath. "And you're not upset?"

"I cannot deny it is strange for me, given our history. Trusting him completely may take me some time. But all I have ever wanted for you is a man who cherishes you as the rare treasure you are."

I smiled wryly. "I think I'm more burden on him than treasure."

"You are the most precious jewel, my darling girl. You may not recognize it, but that man clearly does." She laid a palm on my cheek. "You have my blessing. If he is your family, then he is mine, too."

My heart exploded, enflamed with a joy so bold, the morning sun seemed to bow in deference to its glow.

"He needs you," I admitted. "His mother was taken from him so quickly, and his stepmother was cruel. His father doesn't seem to care if he lives or dies. He deserves the kind of love you and Father have always given me."

She frowned thoughtfully. "I always assumed he helped the half-mortal children because he was half-mortal himself. But he was always adamant about ensuring the orphans found a good new family. I asked many times why he cared so much, and he never answered..." Her gaze touched on him. "Now I think I know."

Her chin dipped sharply, decisively, like a choice firmly and finally made.

She beckoned him over, and we all exchanged embraces and promises to stay safe. My mother mounted her horse, and Luther pressed against my back, his arms draped over my shoulders as we watched her ride away.

"You've done something I didn't think was possible until today," I said.

"Spend several weeks sleeping beside you without managing to rip your clothes off and have my way with you?" he asked dryly. "I assure you, it wasn't easy."

I grinned. "I meant changing my mother's mind." I spun in his arms to face him. "Whatever you said, it won her over. She gave us her blessing."

He tried his best to look unmoved, but a smile pulled hard at the corners of his lips. "Is that so?"

"What did you two talk about?"

"If I'm the only person to ever change her mind, I can't go sharing my secrets, now can I?"

I ducked out of his grasp and began to walk away. "I'll keep that in mind when you're ready to rip my clothes off and have your way with me."

I squeaked as he grabbed my waist and yanked me back to his side. He folded me into a savage kiss that left me panting and molten in his arms. His mouth moved to my throat, dragging his teeth along my skin. As my hand threaded into the dark locks of his hair with a whimper, I started to think he planned to *have his way* right here.

"She asked me why I love you."

"Hmm?" I mumbled, my brain drunk on lust.

"Your mother." He pulled back to look at me, smirking at my glazed-over eyes. "First, she listed all the things she'd do to my cock if I ever hurt you. You Bellator women know how to threaten a man where it hurts." He grimaced and adjusted himself, and I beamed proudly. "Then she demanded I tell her why I love you. What I love *about* you."

I hooked my arms around his neck. "And what did you say?"

His palms dropped to the curve of my ass and tugged me closer, grinding my hips into his. "I told her how stunning you look naked."

I laughed and tried to shove him away, but his hands locked together at the small of my back, keeping me caged within his arms.

He captured my laugh with a kiss that was tender and unexpectedly chaste. "Your heart," he said gruffly. "I told her I love your heart. Your kindness. Your selflessness. The lengths you'll go to help those in need. There are many things to love about you, Diem Bellator, but that remains my favorite."

My chest squeezed tight, my body too small a box to contain the world-rattling emotion exploding inside.

"You're going to ruin my reputation," I joked. "How am I supposed to scare the Crowns into standing down if you keep telling people I'm *kind*?"

He dropped another too-brief kiss on my lips, then pulled back and let me go. "You can start by stepping over that border and unlocking the final Kindred's magic."

I stared at the plaques set into the Ring Road to mark the Sophos-

Montios border. The Montios plaque seemed slightly different. Shinier. A faintly darker shade of gold.

"You really think stepping onto Sophos soil will make a difference?" I asked.

"Hard to say. You were half dead when we crossed into Umbros, and you were drugged with flameroot for all the others. This is the first time you're entering a new realm without anything holding you back."

I stepped forward until my toes grazed the border. I stared ahead at the expanse of grassy plains, the sun turning the blades a golden orange where they stretched above a blanket of fallen snow. It was surreal in its tranquility, knowing the famed city that lay beyond. Barely visible in the distance, its sky-high buildings gleamed against the pastel sky.

"Are you ready?" he asked.

My godhood seemed to understand what was about to happen. It whirled impatiently, hurling itself against my chest as if it might drag me into Sophos itself. Its eagerness was less than comforting—every time I heeded its call, it threw my life into chaos.

"I'll be here the whole time," Luther said. "Whatever happens, you won't be alone."

My racing heart slowed, and I took a deep breath.

"I'm ready."

CHAPTER

SIXTY-FIVE

The first day, all I did was *scream*.

Like all the realms, Sophos magic was two-fold in nature. Some were graced with the power of *spark*—a buzzing, electrifying current that gave power to many of its cutting-edge inventions. Others claimed the power of *thought*—an ability to memorize everything they'd ever seen, heard, or read, turning their head into a trove from which they could recall even the tiniest detail with ease.

Then there were the lucky few who inherited both—like me.

It was the former that initially rendered me frantic, trapped in an endless bolt of lightning that sent my body into rigid convulsions as I pleaded to the Kindred to make it stop.

Poor Luther was helpless, forced to stay on the Montios side of the border to keep access to his magic in case we were attacked. He hovered as close as he could, offering comforting words as my staticky hair danced and the grass around me sizzled to a blackened crisp. By the time I passed out from exhaustion, he looked as traumatized as I felt.

The second day, my mind became the greater enemy. Even the tendrils of sparking energy still snapping across my skin couldn't distract me from the throbbing pressure in my head. All my memories replayed in over-whelming clarity, the magic unlocking details I hadn't known that I ever knew.

Thankfully, the magic only seemed to enhance the memories I'd already formed, leaving all that I'd forgotten forever lost to the past.

Less thankfully, the memories I did have were too often of my lowest lows. I managed to crawl back to the Montios side, and Luther cradled me against his chest as I relived every dark moment in merciless, excruciating detail.

It wasn't until day three that I managed to scrape together enough control to resume our journey into the realm's capital of Sophos City, and even that was a hard-fought battle.

"This city never ceases to amaze me," Luther said as our horses trotted down the city's main road. "It's like stepping into another time."

I stared up at the towering buildings of metal and glass in mind-bending designs that seemed to defy the laws of the natural world. The paved streets bustled with strange machines, some carrying people that zipped impatiently around us.

Luther led us down a quiet side street, and I pulled my hood low and kept my distance as he negotiated with the owner of an inn to let us tie up our horse. As we walked away, the innkeeper stared at us both, and I became acutely aware of how obvious it was we didn't belong.

For starters, our horse was the only beast of burden in sight, and our casual, road-worn clothes were painfully out of fashion. Most residents wore smart, cleanly tailored suits in elegant fabrics, though the Descended penchant for excess came through in details like ballooning sleeves, over-sized jeweled buttons, and overcoats that trailed like billowing capes.

We were also the only two people in sight that weren't in a race to get where we were going. Our leisurely pace drew irritated looks from passersby who nearly bowled us over as they scurried past.

Though many foreign Descended and even mortals mixed among the crowds of pink-irised Sophos Descended, everywhere we walked, the rainbow of eyes lingered on us.

"It's a good thing we're not trying to hide," I said. "I'm not sure we could stick out more if we tried."

"It hardly matters. With your power, the Sophos Crown will have felt your presence by now."

I frowned up at Luther. "Why didn't you feel my presence in Lumnos before I became Queen?"

"I did. A few weeks before we met, I started to sense it—I assume that's when you stopped taking the flameroot. I thought it was one of the younger cousins whose magic was beginning to manifest. I didn't realize it was you until your last visit to the palace, when I noticed it got stronger every time you came around."

I managed a weak smile despite my wearied state. "That explains why you got so handsy with me that day."

He glowered. "More like jealousy. I saw that guard touch you, and I had to intervene before I liberated his spine from his flesh." His hand roped around my hips. "And that would be a kindness compared to what I'd do if he tried it now."

I wasn't proud of the thrill that flushed through me at his violent words —but I wasn't denying it, either.

"I wonder what those are." I pointed to a row of mammoth structures on a hill. With their grand marble pediments and intricately carved wooden panels, the buildings looked ancient amid the shiny newness of the city.

Luther cocked his head. "They're the old mortal institutions. I remember learning about them in school. The one on the left was a library, and the tall one was a university."

I stared at a pile of fallen ruins between the buildings. Bits of words and etchings were visible on the larger stones. I could feel my newly enhanced brain cataloguing every letter and symbol, permanently recording them into my memory.

"What happened there?" I asked.

His muted glance warned me I wouldn't like the answer. "It used to be a temple in the old mortal religions. The other buildings were kept in use, but that one was torn down for heresy."

My fists clenched at the wasteful loss. "They taught that in the Descended schools? Why should your kind get to learn more about mortal history than we do? It's not enough to ban us from practicing our faith, you have to hoard all knowledge of it for yourselves, too?"

He held his tongue, though muscles feathered along his jaw.

I sighed, forcing my temper down. "I'm sorry. That wasn't fair. I have no more claim over the mortals than you do."

"Yes, you do. Perhaps not by blood, but..." He gazed stormily at the temple. "You understand what it means to be mortal in a way I never will."

There was a sadness hiding there that took me by surprise. It was hard to think of someone like Luther, who had been afforded every advantage, feeling like that same privilege had taken something valuable away.

But it had. Despite the Descended's best efforts to squash it, the mortals had created a culture all our own—a vibrant one, full of music and art and rich storytelling, a close-knit community that loved and lost together, fought and died together. We found pockets of beauty and humor in our suffering, and when we couldn't find them, we *created* them as both an act of defiance and an act of survival.

It was no coincidence that the Guardians referred to each other as Brothers and Sisters—the shared trauma of our oppression had bonded the mortals in a familial way. We had our issues, as all families do, but I wouldn't trade my years among them for all the privilege in the world.

"I hope you know how much I want to make things right for the mortals, too," Luther said. "I do consider them my people, even if they do not."

"I do." I pulled his hand from my waist and laced my fingers with his. "When we get back to Lumnos, I want to show you around Mortal City. Introduce you to the people I grew up with." I smiled wickedly. "Show you all the ways I got into trouble."

His answering smile was genuinely eager. "I'd like that." He seemed to hesitate for a moment. "You could build a house there, if you want. Perhaps somewhere near your family's old home, so you can visit your father's grave whenever you like."

I froze in the middle of the walkway. Pedestrians swore at me under their breath as they darted past. "Don't I have to live at the palace?"

"You're the Crown. You don't *have* to do anything. The palace is useful for meetings and banquets, but there's no reason you can't live elsewhere." His lips hooked up. "We could have our orchard and goats right here in Emarion."

A flock of songbirds took flight in my chest, soaring and trilling their joy.

I leaned in closer. "We have more than one goat now? Our little family is growing fast."

"Well, we can't let our first goat be lonely. If we've found each other, Taran Junior needs his mate, too."

I grinned. "You named our goat after Taran?"

A mischievous spark danced in his gaze. "I think he'll be flattered."

"I think you'll have to sleep with one eye open. We'll have to get a donkey and name it Aemonn to win him back over."

Luther's head dropped back as he roared a laugh loud enough to draw looks across the road. It was a rare sight to see him so unreservedly joyous. I embraced the Sophos magic as it committed every detail to memory, grateful to know I could relive this moment any time I pleased.

"Come on." I tugged him down the road. "Let's get this over with. Suddenly, I'm dying to get home."

I pulled back my hood, letting my face warm in the sun and my milk-white curls tumble freely down my back. We'd come here to confront the Sophos Crown—no sense in hiding now.

We reached the fallen mortal temple, which was cordoned off with signs to keep away. A soft whirr and a charge in the air warned of a layer of Sophos magic protecting the site.

I let go of Luther's hand and strolled into the crackling barrier. My skin flared bright and my magic surged with new strength.

"You there," one of the guards barked. "Get out. That place is off limits."

"No, I don't think I will," I crooned.

I pulled a shield around Luther, and together we walked into the ruins. Guards ran forward to stop us, and I conjured a thick wall of white-hot light to block their path.

Luther arched a brow. "This will make the Sophos Crown see you as a threat."

"Good." I raised up on my toes and briefly pressed my lips to his. "That's exactly what I am."

He tried to pull me in, but I danced out of his reach and climbed further into the ruins. I spotted a collapsed fresco of a man leaning against a tree and crouched beside it for a closer look. Though the details had faded with time, the paint of his hair was still a vibrant, fiery red.

"I think this is the Everflame. I saw an image like it in the Umbros palace." My hand trailed over a crack that ran along the man's body, obscuring his face. "I wonder who he was."

"With that hair, he must be related to your mother," Luther joked, kneeling at my side.

A growing crowd had formed outside my wall of light to watch as the guards pummeled it with their spark magic, though their efforts had little effect.

"Did they teach you anything about the Everflame in the Descended schools?" I asked.

"Only that the mortal leaders gave the island to the Kindred as a gift. That's why depictions of the Everflame weren't banned before the war. It was meant to be a symbol of the mortals' willing submission to Descended rule."

I snorted. "They should have known better. Montios's journal mentioned there were mortals who didn't want them around even then."

He shook his head with a wondrous expression. "I can't believe you read a Kindred's diary. What else did she say?"

"She mentioned being afraid of their youngest sibling. He sounded like a brat. You'll have to remind me which brother that was." I wiggled my eyebrows and grinned. "I was *mysteriously ill* on all the days we studied the Kindred in school."

"You really hated the Kindred that much? Even Blessed Mother Lumnos?"

"Oh, *especially* Lumnos."

Luther grimaced like my words had caused him physical pain. "Do you reject the Old Gods, too?"

"The Old Gods have never taken anything from me. And they've never asked anything of me, either. They're content to sit up in the heavens and watch, and I'm content to entertain them." I stood and propped my hands on my hips. "Well? Which Kindred was it?"

"Fortos was the youngest brother—"

"I knew it. *I knew it!* I just knew he must have been a little shit to his sisters."

"—but Montios was the youngest Kindred."

I paused. "That can't be right..."

A loud roar rose from the front of the temple. I thinned my wall of light enough to see some kind of machine crafting a makeshift bridge over the barrier. A powerful aura brushed over us, and both our spines snapped straight in apprehension.

"Hello, Lumnos."

Neither male nor female, King nor Queen, the elegant Crown of Sophos defied every expectation. I'd met others like them back home in Lumnos—some who danced along the spectrum between masculine and feminine, others who were something new altogether.

"You're in my temple," they said as they emerged at the crest of the bridge.

"It's not *your* temple." I shrugged. "I didn't want to bother you, so I let myself in."

They strolled forward, their gauzy, wide-legged trousers billowing in the wind. "If you wanted a private showing, you could have requested an invitation to visit."

"You issued an edict calling for my capture. Is that not invitation enough?"

Their eyes narrowed faintly. "You've come to turn yourself in, then?"

"No. I've come to offer a trade."

"And what trade is that?"

I lifted my chin. "My Crown for my sword."

THE SOPHOS CROWN—WHOSE name I'd learned was Doriel—sat rigidly on the edge of their chair as they sipped delicately on a cup of tea. They were beautiful beyond words, with sky-high cheekbones and an effortless smoothness in the way they moved. A veil of ivory gossamer lay across their cleanly shaven head, held in place by a plain gold circlet, rather than their Crown of glimmering sparks.

"I could have you killed for coming to my realm uninvited, you know," Doriel said.

"You could certainly try. Though you might ask Ignios how that plan worked out for him. Or Umbros." My lips lifted in a smirk. "Or Fortos."

I lounged back lazily and stared up at the hand-painted ceilings adorning the library sitting room Doriel had led me to so we could speak alone. Knowing this room had been built by the mortals of old, I was having to fight hard not to turn into a gawking, awestruck rube.

Doriel's gaze trailed over me with fascination. "So you've been touring more than just my temple."

"Like I said—it's not *your* temple."

"Is the palace of Lumnos not *your* palace?"

"My palace was built by the Lumnos Crowns. That temple was stolen from the mortals."

"It was fairly given. I have the paperwork evidencing the transfer in my records."

My eyes rolled skyward. "Oh, I have no doubt some mortal king offered it up to curry favor from the Kindred, but it never belonged to them. It belonged to the people. Leaders are supposed to guard their people's treasures, not chop them up and give them away."

"I agree. That's why they were given to us for safekeeping." Doriel gestured broadly to the room. "There was a time when the continent was full of magnificent buildings just like these."

I sat up slightly. "It was?"

"We have copious records on the mortal creations. I can show them to you, if you'd like."

My fingers gripped tight to the armrest as I swallowed down my enthusiasm. "Did the Kindred destroy those buildings, too?"

"No. The mortals did. They had their own wars before the Kindred's arrival. Sadly, countless treasures were casualties of those conflicts—buildings, art, maps, books. The ruler of these lands offered them up to Blessed Father Sophos in the hopes he would protect them from meeting the same fate."

"And yet the temple did."

Doriel let out a long sigh. "It was our fourth Crown who ordered its destruction. A poor decision, I agree. Knowledge is our most valuable resource. I do not believe in erasing it."

"Just hoarding it for yourself," I muttered. "What good is safeguarding mortal treasures if the mortals aren't allowed to use them?"

They bristled. "Any mortal can request a visit, and every worthy request is granted."

"And what makes a request worthy?"

"A documented history of study and interest. Trustworthy references. No criminal activity."

"In my realm, 'study and interest' of mortal history *is* criminal activity. How is any mortal ever supposed to qualify?"

"Mortals from Lumnos have visited before. One arrived not long ago." Doriel's lips slid into a cold smile. "Regardless, that seems like a problem the Crown of *Lumnos* needs to address."

My eyes narrowed. "That's why I'm here. My Regent tells me I must complete the coronation ritual to take my throne. So..." I leaned forward, elbows resting on my knees. "What's it going to take to make that happen, Doriel?"

They sipped lightly at their tea. "There are several obstacles. Serious concerns about your legitimacy as the Lumnos Crown, to say nothing of your assistance to the rebels."

"You saw my Crown with your own eyes. And if I wasn't a Crown, I couldn't do this." I held out my palms and sent a deluge of darkness through the room. It cascaded into a sea of ebony liquid that splashed against the walls, then churned into a swirling whirlpool around our chairs.

Doriel's teacup rattled against its saucer as they lifted their feet. "Stop it," they hissed. "You'll ruin my books."

I let the magic linger a little longer—long enough for Doriel to yelp as the tide of shadows licked against their waist—then banished them with a flick.

"They're not *your* books, either." I waved a hand at the room, bone-dry and unaffected by my magic. "I would never hurt them. These books mean as much to me as they do to you."

Doriel slammed their cup down and stalked to the bookshelves, meticulously inspecting them for damage. Once satisfied I'd done no harm, they turned back in a huff. "If you're the Lumnos Crown, how do you explain what happened at the coronation? Your blood broke the heartstone, and the gems on the ritual dagger should have turned blue, not grey." They stilled, then leaned forward, their gaze thinning in scrutiny. "Just like your eyes..."

"At the time, I was as confused as you. But I think I now have an explanation." I frowned. "Or at least a partial one. If you're willing to listen."

With as little detail as I could get away with—and some creative embellishing to hide my worst misdeeds—I told Doriel the story of my last few weeks: My kidnapping by the Guardians. My flight into Ignios, then Umbros. My visit to my mother in Fortos and its King's unprovoked attack, leading to his death and my mother's escape. My confrontation with Ophiucae, and my mother's revelation about who he was to me.

For now, I left out the full truth of my spectrum of magic—and my two new Crowns.

"You're saying this man has been chained up on Coeurîle for years?" Doriel said when I finished. "And he's your father?"

"My sire," I corrected. "Andrei Bellator is my father. I've never met this man."

"How did he get on the island?"

"I was hoping you might have an answer for that. Is there anything in your archives that might shed some light?"

Doriel's eyes glazed over. They seemed to lose themself sifting through thousands of stored memories in rapid succession—all the books they'd ever read, all the records they'd ever reviewed.

My instincts poked at me to reach inside their head and take a peek. With the whole of Emarion's history at their fingertips, there was no telling the priceless information they knew. The things I could learn...

Doriel shifted their weight and stiffly shook their head. "No. Nothing I'm aware of."

My godhood snarled, the Umbros magic within me sensing the lie.

"Nothing?" I pushed. "I can't imagine the Crowns would abandon a man in their most sacred space without leaving an explanation. If anyone would know why, it would be you."

They pursed their lips. "Indeed. But I do not."

Lie.

"And his symbol—the ten-pointed star?" I had to fight an urge to touch the glowing mark concealed beneath my scarf. "The Montios Council said they asked you to research it."

Doriel's lashes fluttered as their eyes briefly lowered. "We haven't found anything yet."

Another lie.

I slumped back into my chair. I could reach into their mind and take the truth, but it might kill any hope of a truce.

"You said you've come to offer a trade," Doriel said, clearly keen to change the subject. "Your Crown for your sword?"

I nodded. "This man is dangerous. He hates the Descended and wants revenge on all of us. And he's incredibly strong. I felt his power in Montios —I might be the only person who can defeat him."

They tittered a laugh. "You are strong, I'll give you that, but even your power does not equal the Emarion Army. Now that we know where this man is hiding, the Crowns can order soldiers there to—"

"It won't work. Didn't you try that before, and the entire battalion went missing?"

"Obviously Fortos didn't send enough."

"You can send every soldier in the army. Hell, you can send every Descended in Emarion. It won't be enough to kill him. Only I can do that."

Their upper lip pulled back as they looked me over. "You're mighty confident in your own strength."

"It's not about strength. There's... something else." I hesitated. Was it was wise to reveal so many valuable secrets to a person who refused to do the same?

Did I really have a choice?

I sighed and spread my arms. "Use your magic. Attack me."

Doriel tensed. "What are you getting at?"

"Go on," I urged. "Hit me with your spark magic."

"If you're trying to provoke me into a fight by getting me to hurt you—"

I threw a note of mocking challenge in my voice. "Oh, don't worry. *You* could never hurt *me*."

My gambit worked, and wounded ego flared in their eyes. They raised their hand, and a jagged bolt of energy sparked from their palm to my heart.

I had to give it to Doriel—it hadn't been enough to kill me, but had their magic not absorbed with a tingle and a burst of light, I would have been convulsing on the floor instead of smiling calmly in my chair.

They jerked back. "Your shield... I can't see it."

"I didn't shield your magic. I absorbed it." I waved my hand. "Go on, try it again."

This time, they didn't hesitate—and they didn't hold back. The electric jolt that slammed into me next would have left me a smoking corpse.

"You're getting stronger," they breathed in awe as my aura pulsed with the newly captured magic.

I nodded. "I'm immune to magic. And Ophiucae is, too. I doubt the army will get close enough to him for their blades and arrows to do much good, either."

They looked me over like a starving tiger staring down a prime cut of meat. "You're something *new*. You have to stay here in Sophos. Let me study you, run a few tests—"

"We don't have time, Doriel. This man needs to be stopped before he kills again. He knows I'm his daughter, so I don't think he wants to hurt me. I might be the only person who can take him out."

"You would kill your own father?"

I stiffened. "He's just my sire. I have no feelings toward him."

Another lie.

Doriel assessed me for a long moment. "So you're offering yourself as an assassin in exchange for your coronation?"

"And a full pardon for these crimes I've been falsely accused of. I had no more idea about the attack on the island than you did. I'm not going to work with all of you only to have you turn on me the second he's dead."

Even though that's exactly what I plan to do to you, I thought.

"Even if I called a ritual, the other Crowns might have their own objections."

"Let them object. Montios was the only Crown who didn't complete the ritual." I shifted in my chair. "Their consent won't be a problem."

"You still need six votes for a pardon."

I carefully guarded my reaction. I controlled three Crowns—three votes. If my mother was right about the Arboros Queen, I was hopeful I could count on hers. That meant I needed Doriel's vote and one other.

Umbros and Ignios would never agree to spare me—that left only Faunos and Meros.

"I saw you and Meros talking at my coronation. You two are allies, are you not?"

"Our relationship is cordial," Doriel hedged, looking wary of my interest. "Why do you ask?"

"If you can convince the Meros King to agree, I can take care of the rest."

"And how do you expect to do that?"

"Let me worry about that. This is all I'm asking from you. Are you willing to give it?"

"There's still the matter of Coeurîle." Doriel let out a soft exhale, a touch of exhaustion on their features. "The rebels' occupation has proven harder to overcome than anticipated. The army's soldiers are already spread too thin around the continent in case of another attack. If we call them to the island for a battle, it would leave us all vulnerable."

"There won't be a battle. The Guardians will give us access to the Kindred's Temple."

Doriel sneered. "Because they answer to you?"

"Because they answer to my mother." I smiled tightly. "And she'll allow it because the Crowns are going to pardon her, too."

"*Absolutely not.* Your mother is a killer." They leapt to their feet and wagged a finger at me. "And if you think the Meros King will agree to this, you're out of your mind. His realm has been under siege by the Guardians for months."

"My mother has been trapped on the island since Forging Day. She couldn't have ordered those attacks."

"As their leader, she is responsible—"

"And what about *your* responsibility?" I snapped. "Mortals are dying on this continent every day. They're starving, freezing, being tortured and imprisoned—"

"Not in my realm," Doriel said haughtily.

"Because you exiled them all! You think that absolves you of what happens outside your borders? If you know people are dying, and you have the power to stop it but you look away, that blood is on your hands, too. And don't think I don't know what happens to the mortals you invite here to '*study*.'" I prowled forward, hissing in their face. "If my mother has to answer for her people's crimes, I'll make sure you answer for yours."

Doriel paled. "I don't know what you're talking about."

"Oh, I think you do. And so do the Guardians."

"I—we—our research…" They cleared their throat and stood taller. "The mortals in my realm are given every luxury and paid for their work. They have equal rights as any Descended. They fare better here than anywhere else in Emarion."

"Until they end up dead in some experiment."

To my surprise, Doriel looked genuinely pained. "Wisdom requires sacrifice. We are all grateful to those who volunteer—"

I waved them off with a grunt of disgust. "Defend your murders to someone else." I flopped back in my chair and crossed my arms. "You have my terms, Doriel. Take them or leave them."

"And if I leave them?"

I shrugged. "Ophiucae is coming for all the Descended eventually. I can protect my people. Can you say the same?"

Their eyes dimmed with a somber defeat. "How do I know you'll keep your word? Maybe we'll coronate you and never see you again."

Again, I hesitated. "If it will get all the Crowns to agree…" I cringed, then clenched my jaw. "I'll enter into a bonded bargain to seal the terms."

My stomach roiled, my heart regretting the words the second they left my lips. With so much at stake, putting my magic on the line could be catastrophic—especially when I still wasn't convinced I could follow through.

Doriel gazed at the floor, their brows furrowed in deep thought. "I'll consider your offer. There are matters I need to look into first. Some… research I require."

"We don't have time. If he moves his camp, we might not find him again. And if he attacks—"

"He's less than a day's ride from my city. Believe me, I'm acutely aware of the risk." Their frown carved deeper. "Give me two days. There's plenty to read in my archives while you wait."

I shot upright. "You'll give me access to your books?"

Their eyes twinkled with the triumph of knowing we each had something the other wanted. They smoothed down their jacket, then motioned for me to follow as they glided toward the door. When it opened, a wave of power crashed against my skin.

Doriel and I froze.

Luther rose from where he'd been waiting in the hallway and bowed. "My Queen." An unspoken question lay in his tone: *Did it work?*

"My Prince," I crooned back. "It seems we'll be staying a few days while Doriel makes their decision."

Doriel eyed him uneasily. "You have your magic back?"

Luther's expression was the perfect mix of coyness and warning. "Perhaps I do, perhaps I don't. Until you coronate my Queen and repair the Forging spell, I guess you'll never know."

Doriel gave us both irritated scowls. "You two could learn something about diplomacy from your Regent. Not everything needs to be a threat."

I rolled my eyes. "My Regent has to use diplomacy. He isn't scary enough to be a threat."

"He forced you to come begging for my help." They turned their nose up and strode away. "Seems he's a bigger threat than you give him credit for."

Those words were truer than I wanted to admit.

Luther and I followed Doriel to a cavernous reading room covered in bookshelves and lamp-lit tables. Towering stained glass windows painted rainbow swaths across rows of silent readers hunched over thick books and ancient-looking documents.

Doriel beckoned to a teenage boy behind a counter, who scurried to our side. "Stuart, Diem here is the new Crown of Lumnos. She'll be staying with us for a few days. I'll have my staff prepare her rooms. In the meantime, will you escort her wherever she'd like to go? She's not yet coronated —" Doriel smiled icily at me. "—but I'll grant her Crown-level access to our archives."

"Of course," Stuart gushed, then turned to me. "It would be my pleasure, Di—uh, I mean, Your Maj—uh... Quee—hmm..."

"Call me Diem," I said, my expression warming as I noticed the boy's brown irises. "And this is my Prince, Luther Corbois."

Luther offered his hand in greeting, but the boy ignored it and continued to gaze at me, moony-eyed and enamored. "Hello, Diem. Where can I take you?"

Luther growled a possessive warning. I had to bite back a grin as I subtly nudged his side. "Why don't you start by showing us your favorite places?"

"I would love to," he gasped, sounding like it was the greatest honor he'd ever received. He held out his elbow, shivering with glee when I looped my arm in his. Luther grumbled at being relegated to trail behind us.

"Tell me about yourself, Stuart," I urged him.

"I'm originally from Meros. My mother is a researcher here, and my father and I were permitted to join her. Doriel arranged a job for me in the library."

My eyebrows rose. "You call your Crown by their first name?"

"Oh, yes. Doriel insists. They said the only thing titles do is encourage an inflated ego."

I shot Luther a pointed grin over my shoulder. His answering glare was positively *scathing*.

"My mother's invitation to research was for ten years, and we've been here almost nine," Stuart went on. "We're all hoping Doriel gives us a permanent offer to stay."

My stomach dropped. If what Henri had told me about this place was true, that *permanent offer* might be a death sentence in disguise.

"But wouldn't it be nice to return home to Meros?" I pushed encouragingly. "I bet your friends there miss you terribly."

"Oh, I barely remember it. This is my home now. Besides, everyone in Meros thinks we're dead." He laughed to himself. "We'd have to go somewhere else. Umbros, maybe. Or Lumnos." He beamed at me. "You could be my Queen."

Luther growled again.

I frowned. "Why do they think you're dead?"

"Because we—oh, would you like to see the laboratory where my mother works?" He didn't wait for a response, tugging me enthusiastically toward the doors.

"Stuart, what did you mean by—" I sucked in a breath as we spilled out into the open air and another brush of the powerful aura coated my skin.

Stuart tugged me closer, leaning his face in to mine. "Diem, are you alright?"

Luther put his palm on Stuart's face and shoved him away. "Off," he snarled. "I'll escort my Queen from here."

Stuart squeaked and shrank back. Luther met my reproachful look with a possessive glare, gripping my ass in a way that communicated loud and clear he intended to do more than *escort* me. I considered scolding his coarse manners, but watching him get worked up over a mortal teen was giving me fodder to tease him for weeks to come.

And there might be the tiniest possibility that my shameless, utterly reprehensible heart was twirling at being so passionately claimed.

"Do you feel that aura?" he hummed in my ear.

"I thought it was you," I whispered back.

"No. My magic is still locked down."

I tensed. "Then who?"

"I don't know. With you and Doriel nearby, it's hard to tell where it's coming from. Close, I think."

I glanced nervously at the horizon north of the city, scouring the distant Ring Road for any sign that Ophiucae and the Guardians might have followed us, but I saw only endless fields of golden grass shimmering in the wind.

We followed Stuart to a glass-paneled dome filled with an impressive variety of plants. I perked up as I realized most were rare medicinal herbs that usually could only be grown in Arboros.

"My mother works here in the greenhouse," Stuart said. "They're trying to breed hardier versions of these plants to grow in other soils and climates. If they can do it—"

"—then more people can get access to them," I finished excitedly. "That's incredible. Is it working?"

He grinned and turned to face me, walking backward. "It is. My mother's a genius. She just created a strain of eelwood that—oh, I'm so sorry!" He spun around as he collided into the back of a towering, weapon-laden man.

The man turned. "It's alright, don't worry about—" He froze. "Your Majesty?"

"*Perthe?*" I choked out. "What are you doing in Sophos?"

He hastily saluted and bowed. "Keeping my oath. I swore to you I wouldn't leave his side."

I blinked rapidly, trying to make sense of why a member of my personal guard was dawdling in a Sophos greenhouse. "Wouldn't leave *whose* side?"

He stepped to the right, revealing a pair of Sophos Descended chatting with a young man.

My blood ran cold. Though his back was to me, I'd know that familiar auburn hair from miles away.

"Your brother, Your Majesty," Perthe said. "Teller accepted an invitation to study in Sophos."

CHAPTER
SIXTY-SIX

"*Teller?*"

"*Diem?*"

My brother and I gaped at each other in blinking, blank-faced shock.

"What are you doing here?" I asked.

"Remis sent me here to—" He paused, his eyes darting to Luther, then Stuart, then back to me. "Where is she?"

"Remis sent you?" I snapped. "I swear, when I get back, I'm going to—"

"*Where is she?*"

I jerked back at the harsh bite in his voice.

"Mother's safe. She's... with friends."

"What friends?"

I eyed the crowd beginning to form. "Let's speak in private."

"Why, so you can lie to me again?"

I fumbled helplessly for words. I'd expected him to be disappointed, even angry, but not this. My brother was glowering at me like I'd betrayed him in the worst possible way.

"Teller, I'm sorry. It wasn't safe to bring her back to the palace. I tried, I swear."

His honey-brown eyes narrowed. "Why are you here, Diem?"

"To convince the Crowns to coronate me so I can come home—and

652

bring her with me."

"Well, good luck, I guess. Maybe someday I'll find out from someone else how it went." He turned to his Descended escorts. "Let's tour a different building. I'll see this another day."

I glanced in panic at Luther, who was staring at my brother with an accusatory kind of frown.

"Is Lily here with you?" he called out.

Teller's head dipped. "No. She's in Lumnos."

I grabbed his arm. "I'll fix this. I won't let Remis exile you. As soon as I'm coronated—"

"Remis didn't exile me. I chose to leave." He pulled out of my grip. "There was nothing to stay for."

"Did you just call my sister *nothing?*" Luther asked sharply.

"No! No, that—that's not what I meant. Lily is..." His chest sank as pain flickered over his face. "She's better off. Now she can move on to someone she can spend her whole life with."

"Oh, Tel," I breathed sadly. Knowing my brother's nature, I'd worried the moment might come when he would walk away—not for himself, but for her. I'd hoped to be around to talk him out of it, but I hadn't been much of a sister to him lately. "Is that what Lily said she wants?"

His listless, heartbroken shrug answered for him. "Sometimes the best way to show your love for someone is by making the hard decision they won't."

Luther stilled. "Those are my father's words. This is his doing, isn't it? He convinced you to leave."

"Remis suggested it, but it was my decision." Teller sighed and turned away. "Do what you came here to do, Diem. Leave me out of it."

Luther and I shared another look, this one full of mutual rage. "I'm going to murder your father," I seethed.

"I'll help," he grumbled.

I set my jaw and took a deep breath, then stalked to Teller's side. "I need a moment with my brother," I barked at his escorts. "Is there somewhere private he and I can speak?"

"I don't want to talk," Teller said.

I ignored his protest, arching a brow at the two Descended. "Well? I'm a Crown. Don't leave me waiting."

They blanched in unison. "Um... there are offices in the back," one said, pointing to a row of doors. "But—"

"Perfect." I grabbed Teller's arm and hauled him away.

"What the hell, D?" he shouted. "Let me go!"

"No. If you're going to be a bratty younger brother, then I'll be a bully older sister."

I threw open the first office I came to and shoved him in. I shot a hard stare at Luther, who silently nodded and took up a post outside the door as I slammed it closed.

"You have no right," Teller snapped.

"I have every right. I'm your Queen."

"No, you're not. I'm a subject of Sophos now."

"Well I'm still your older sister, and I'm not letting you stay here."

He threw his hands up. "I make *one choice* that's not about you or Mother, and I can't even have that. Haven't I lost enough? You have to take this from me, too?"

If he'd carved my heart from my chest with his fingernails, it would have hurt less than the pain I felt at those words.

I rubbed my throat, my head hanging low. "It's not safe here, Teller."

"It's safer than Lumnos. Everyone there knows my mother is the rebel leader and my sister is the traitor Queen who broke her out. I can't go to school anymore. I can't even leave the palace. I'm a prisoner." He sighed and turned toward a window that looked out over the city. "At least in Sophos, no one knows who I am. I'm just another mortal here to study." His expression hardened. "Or I was, until that scene you just made."

I winced. "Mortals aren't as safe here as they seem. There are things about this place you don't know."

He laughed harshly. "Of course. More secrets."

"Tel, can we please just talk? I know I promised to bring Mother home, and I failed. You have every right to be angry—"

"That's not why I'm angry."

I paused. "It isn't?"

"I'm mad because you *lied*." He fixed me with a cold glare that felt nothing like the brother I knew. "Before you left, I asked you if there was anything else you were keeping from me, and you swore there wasn't."

"That was the truth. I told you everything."

"Then why did I have to find out from Remis Corbois that the Sophos Crown invited me to study here *months* ago?"

Shit. *Shit.*

The offer the Sophos representatives had made at my Ascension Ball.

"Gods... I completely forgot."

He flinched back. "You forgot? My dream comes true, the one thing

I've been working for my entire life, and you not only keep it from me, you don't even remember?" He couldn't have looked more disgusted with me if he'd tried. "Is that how little I matter to you?"

My chest squeezed tight with a crushing pressure. The air felt thicker, harder to breathe.

"You're the most important person in the world to me. I would do anything for you."

"Except tell me the truth."

I grimaced. I deserved that.

"You're right. I made a bad choice, and I let you down. I had my reasons, but..." I shook my head miserably. "None of them excuse not telling you. I'm really, really sorry."

He crossed the room and stood in front of me, folding his arms over his chest with a frown.

I was taken aback by how tall he loomed. My Descended blood made me taller than most mortal men, but Teller had outgrown me some time ago. He was so often at a desk hunched over a book, I rarely noticed it. He wasn't my baby brother anymore—his body was filling out, all the soft roundness of youth chiseling into the sharp angles of a man.

"Why didn't you tell me?" he demanded.

"I didn't trust the Sophos Crown. I was worried they were trying to use you to threaten me. They knew about you before I'd told anyone we were related."

"A lot of people knew we were related. That doesn't mean anything."

"There were other reasons. I heard... rumors." I scratched anxiously at the burning on my neck. "Mortals who come here go missing, Tel. The Sophos Descended run experiments on them, and no one ever hears from them again."

His head slowly tilted. "Who told you that?"

"Henri. He said the Guardians have—"

His loud ripple of laughter cut me off. "What would Henri know about Sophos—what would any of the Guardians know? Do you know how hard it is for mortals to get in here? If you breathe too close to someone suspected of being a rebel, they ban you for life. They only let me in because Remis is good friends with Doriel. He begged them to make an exception."

I frowned. I hadn't known *that*—and it definitely didn't ease my fears.

"The mortals here get paid so much, most of them send money back home to family," Teller explained. "Thieves realized this and started targeting anyone with relatives in Sophos, so people here began to fake their deaths. Their loved ones know they're safe, but everyone else from their home realm thinks they're dead."

"I... but... the experiments," I stammered. "I confronted Doriel about mortals dying. They admitted it was true."

"Those mortals *volunteer*. They want to do something useful with their lives, and they get paid a fortune to leave behind for their families. It's a noble choice."

I reared back. "A '*noble choice*'? They're only desperate for that money because the Descended put them in poverty to begin with. They're selling their lives away because it's a better end than dying of hunger in some dirty Mortal City back alley. That's not a choice, Tel, that's a last resort. They're exploiting desperate people, and there's nothing *noble* about it."

Teller's mouth opened, then closed, a wrinkle forming across his brow as he thought on my words. "Maybe you're right. But that doesn't make the people here murderers." I snorted in disagreement, and Teller's face turned stern and scolding. "Everything isn't so black and white, D. The results of those experiments save thousands of lives. And the money the mortals make here will keep their families out of poverty for generations. Yes, it is unfair. The *world* is unfair. The people here are just trying to do what good in it they can."

Teller's firm yet fair demeanor, his calm lack of judgment, his focus on what *was* and not what *should be*—it was all so very, very much like our father. Grief seemed to wrap its ruthless hand around my neck, choking my protests back.

Teller's tone softened. "I've met a lot of mortals here, and they're really happy. They're treated well, and they're proud of the work they do. And the Descended..." He smirked. "They're eccentric, I admit. I'm not sure most of them have ever had any fun that didn't involve a book." He cocked his head. "But they don't seem like killers. They seem like good people."

I slumped back against a desk as my resolve wobbled between condemnation and doubt. What did it mean to be a *good person* in a system built on such a fundamental *bad?* Could the best intentions and noble ends ever justify reprehensible means?

"So you told Henri I'd been invited here, but not me?" Teller asked archly.

"Henri didn't know," I mumbled, still lost in my thoughts. "Only Remis and Lil—"

I stopped too late.

"*Lily* knew?"

Shit. *Shit shit shit.*

Hurt flickered over his face, then anger, then resignation. He closed his eyes as his features pinched. "It doesn't matter. We're over now."

I stood and gripped his shoulders. "Forget what Remis said. You and Lily should be together."

"Remis might have had his own motives, but he wasn't wrong. Lily and I were always doomed. At least now she can move on." He sighed unhappily. "Even though I never will."

"It doesn't have to be like this. You two love each other. You—"

"Don't," he interrupted. "I made my choice, Diem. It's over. Let it go."

The air deflated out of me in a slow, sad exhale. I was far from done with this fight, but until it was safe for him to go home, there was no point trying to convince him.

Teller glared at me, though it was lacking all its bite. "I guess if you thought you were saving me from dying as a laboratory experiment, I'm required to forgive you."

"I've been an awful sister. I don't deserve your forgiveness." I gave a sheepish half-smile. "Maybe you'll take pity on me and give it anyway?"

He grunted. His irritated face said *absolutely not*, but I knew his peace-loving heart had already said *yes*.

"I heard you killed the Fortos King," he said.

"And his High General. Not to mention releasing most of their prisoners."

His brow furrowed. "The Crowns are going to kill you for that."

"Actually, if my plan works, they're going to pardon me. Mother, too."

"How in the world will you talk them into *that*?"

I groaned wearily. "You can't imagine how much has happened since I left, Tel. There's so much I need to tell you."

"What's that on your neck?" He squinted as he leaned in. "There's something glowing..."

I frowned and dipped my chin, realizing I'd been absently tugging at my scarf, trying to get some air into my too-tight throat. The scarf fell away, and the room flooded with an intense light.

Teller shielded his eyes. "What is that?"

I started to explain as I reached to touch it—then stilled as my fingertips brushed against blazing hot skin. It hadn't felt that intense since...

My heart plummeted.

Ophiucae was coming.

CHAPTER
SIXTY-SEVEN

I bolted to the door and threw it open.

Luther whipped to me, his eyes growing as he spotted the glowing mark at my throat and realized what it meant.

"Find Doriel," I told him. "Warn them. *Hurry.*"

"No—I'm not leaving you."

"That's an order!" I shouted.

His jaw ticked as he fought his instincts to stay at my side and protect me, but a moment later, he took off through the greenhouse.

"D, what's going on?" Teller asked.

I spun to Perthe, who had been waiting beside Luther at the door. "Take my brother and find somewhere to hide. Someone's coming— someone dangerous."

"Of course, Your Majesty. I'll keep him safe."

"*Diem,*" Teller snapped. "Who's coming?"

"My birth father." Teller recoiled, and I threw him a stricken look. "There's no time to explain. Stay with Perthe. And tell everyone you see to hide." My focus shot to Perthe. "He's coming to kill Descended. Don't take any risks—for Teller or for yourself."

He nodded sharply and saluted.

Whatever terror lay in my eyes, it scared off the last of Teller's lingering resentment. I threw my arms around his neck, and he squeezed me tightly, gripping my back like he was afraid to let go.

"If anything happens to me," I whispered, feeling his muscles tense beneath my hands, "follow the Ring Road to the Montios border. The Guardians are hiding in the trees. Tell them to take you to Mother."

When I pulled back, the blood had drained from his face, though it was firm with Bellator resolve. "We'll be fine. And so will you."

We shared a final, loaded stare, then I ran out of the greenhouse. I burst outside and nearly buckled at the wall of power that crashed against my skin—almost as potent as it had been in the Forgotten Lands.

Ophiucae was close. *Very* close.

I bolted to the top of the nearest hill and peered out across the grasslands to see a group of armed men on horseback riding our way. Though there was no glowing man among them, my gut knew it wasn't a coincidence.

I sprinted down the city streets, heart pounding, shouting warnings at every resident I passed. My voice grew more and more frantic as my efforts earned only confused stares.

Once I reached the inn where we'd tied up our horse, I used Ignios flame to burn it loose from its rope, then pulled myself into the saddle and prodded it into an urgent gallop toward the Ring Road.

I swore under my breath when I got there—a shimmering veil hung over each of the men. Wherever Ophiucae was hiding, he was using his magic to keep them safe.

I called on the stone magic of Montios, and the ground trembled as a thick wall of rock rose high to block the men's path, stretching as far as my magic would reach. It wouldn't stop them, but it would buy me precious time.

A sudden crackle ripped through the air as a bolt of lightning shot into the sky from near the library. With a tug on my reins, I raced back into town.

At the base of the library steps, Luther and Doriel were in heated debate while the Sophos Royal Guard began arriving from across the city.

"He's coming," I panted, dismounting and jogging to their side.

Doriel nodded somberly. "I can feel him. That much power..." They were forcing a brave face for their guards, but their eyes belied a hidden panic.

"The mortals working with him are just outside the city. He's shielding them, so he must be nearby."

Their eyes began to close. "I'll find him through the Forging magic."

"*No*," I shouted quickly. "Don't—when I tried that in Montios, he attacked me through it."

Their brow slowly creased. "How did you access the Forging magic in *Montios?*" Their eyes dropped to my neck. "And why do you bear his sigil?"

My hand flew to my throat, now exposed after my scarf had fallen in the greenhouse.

Shit. *Shit shit shit shit shit.*

Doriel stormed toward me in a seething rage. "You're with him, aren't you? You brought him here. You're trying to scare me so I take your deal."

Luther moved to intervene, but I raised a hand to stop him. "I swear to you Doriel, I'm not. I want to stop him before he hurts anyone else. I'll fight him here and now to prove it."

They looked me over, their delicate features gnarling in distrust.

"Think the worst of me when the battle's over," I begged. "If we're going to protect these people, we have to work together."

The crowd fell silent, awaiting Doriel's response. The sudden quiet revealed a slow, steady thump in the distance. Through the hazy canopy of grey winter clouds, a small black dot had begun to grow.

My eyes slid over Doriel's shoulder to see the Sophos gryvern—perched firmly on the ground.

Ice shot through my veins.

"Tell me that's your gryvern," Doriel said, their voice unsteady.

I already knew it wasn't. Sorae's dark rage at being imprisoned was an ever-present weight on my soul through our bond.

"That doesn't look like any gryvern I've ever seen," Luther murmured.

The dot became a silhouette: A horned reptilian head. Sprawling, red-tipped wings. A hulking leonine body with fur so dark, it was nearly black. And on its back, a grey-eyed man whose skin gleamed like moonlight.

With a Crown in the shape of a ten-pointed star hovering over his head.

"Blessed Kindred," Doriel breathed. "The lost realm. The stories are true."

The approaching gryvern let out a piercing shriek. My Faunos magic tingled, sensing its violent intentions. I shot back a pulse of calm and a plea to the creature to turn away, but my efforts were futile. The beast was as full of vicious rage as its brutal master.

I grabbed Doriel's arm. "Release Luther's magic. We need all the power we can get to shield."

They stiffened, looking between us. "This is part of your plan, isn't it? I release him, then you both attack my city."

"We don't have time for this, Doriel. That gryvern is going to be here in seconds."

"How am I supposed to trust you when—"

"*Release his magic*," I snarled, the compulsion of Umbros thought magic rippling in my tone.

Doriel's eyes glazed over. A moment later, Luther's aura tumbled across my skin.

"Did you just...?" Doriel stammered, staggering backward. "How?"

My eyes locked with Luther, his abrupt nod confirming he understood what we had to do. We both turned to the sky and lifted our palms, and a film of glimmering shadow spilled across the city center.

"Don't just stand there," I yelled at Doriel.

They jolted out of their stunned stupor. "Guards," they shouted. "Shields up!"

The gryvern arched its trajectory at the last second, shooting for the outskirts of the city. From the grasslands, the sound of falling rocks led to a rousing war cry and the patter of galloping horses.

I swore. "They broke my wall. The others will be here any minute." I turned to Doriel. "If we can get Ophiucae far enough away, his shield might fall. Can you take your gryvern and lure him out of the city?"

"Where's *your* gryvern?" they hissed.

"Chained up by my Regent because *you* refuse to coronate me," I hissed back.

Their eyes narrowed. "You're just trying to get me to leave my city to your mercy."

I grabbed Doriel by their lapels, jerking them toward me. The Sophos guards lunged forward, and Luther slid in front of us with a warning growl at them to keep away.

"If you're too scared to do it, let me take your gryvern, and you can stay here. If you don't like that either, then give me your orders, and I'll obey— but you have to do *something*. My brother is in this city, and if he dies, I'm warning you Doriel, that man up there will be the least of your problems."

They shook beneath my hands, their voice falling to a hush. "I'm not afraid for myself. My people are academics, Diem. The worst crime my guards deal with are stolen books. They're not prepared for this. Most of them don't even have weapons. I ordered some from your realm last year when the attacks began, but every shipment has been disrupted by the rebels."

I frowned. "Are there any army soldiers nearby we can call in for help?"

"They left to secure Umbros after their attack."

A howl from Ophiucae's gryvern warned of his approach—and this time, the gryvern didn't cut away. It skimmed over the gleaming shield as he leaned low and let his hand trail over its edge. His skin pulsed with light, and I gasped as I felt the tug of my magic drawing out of me. His aura swelled with a massive injection of our collective energy, laughter echoing in his wake as his gryvern swooped up toward the clouds.

"He's using our shield to get stronger," Luther ground out. "We have to get him away from here."

I released my grip on Doriel. "Listen to me. We are not letting your people die. They might not be ready, but I am. My Prince is. And you are—right?"

They swallowed, nodding. "Right."

"You and I are Crowns of Emarion. We're the most powerful Descended who roam these lands, and the Kindred have chosen us to protect these people."

Doriel's features hardened to steel. They tugged off their veil and the golden circlet, the sparkling Crown of Sophos glowing to life in its place.

They turned to their guards. "I'll take him on with Vexes. The rest of you, protect the city—and obey the Lumnos Queen's command." They shot me a dark stare. "I'm trusting you, Diem. If you betray me, you will pay dearly."

With a deep breath, they ran to their gryvern and hurriedly mounted. "Fly, Vexes," Doriel ordered, and the gryvern launched into the air.

The clatter of hoofbeats sounded from the city as the mounted rebels galloped down the main road. My insides twisted at the sight of glittering black blades in too many of their hands.

I thrust out my palms and grunted as my magic strained to reach them. *Throw them*, I begged the horses. *Trample them. Drag them from the city.*

The streets erupted into chaos as the beasts began to buck. Men went flying through glass windows and into stone walls, others tangling in their reins, fighting to stay mounted.

"Was that... *Faunos* magic?" a guard asked.

I winced at my slip. "Focus. We need to find a way to stall for time."

"How are we supposed to do that?" someone shouted. "All most of us have is our magic. They have godstone. If we can't get through their shields, they can strike us, but we can't strike them."

I stole a glance at Luther, his expression grim. The fact that neither of us was demanding the other get to safety showed what we both knew—we were this realm's best, and maybe only, hope.

"They use godstone weapons for testing in the laboratories," Stuart called out, emerging from the crowd. "There's some in the archives, too. They're locked away, but I have access."

"Stuart, it's not safe for a mortal," I warned him. "You need to take shelter."

He shook his head. "This is my home. If it's in danger, I want to help protect it."

"The godstone blades in the archives belonged to the Kindred," a guard protested. "We can't use them. They're pieces of history."

"We will be too, if we can't fight back." I pointed at a clump of guards. "You three—go with Stuart. Get anything useful you can find."

Stuart beamed proudly and took off running, the guards following behind.

I turned to the group. "Those of you who have weapons, you're with me. The rest of you, get everyone inside and barricade the doors."

The guards split off, a painfully small cadre remaining behind to fight. With quivering hands and green-faced stares, they fell into an arc behind Luther as we marched into the heart of the city.

I'd never felt closer to my father than I did in this moment. He'd led countless battalions into clashes with odds more dismal than these. It had fallen to him, as it now did to me, to find the words that would spark a fire to fuel their will to fight.

And if I chose the wrong ones, they might be the last words these guards ever heard.

"Be smart," I yelled out, recalling my father's lessons. "Remember, the weapon in your head is more important than the weapon in your hands. Outwit them, outfight them, outrun them—but above all, *outlive* them." I glared over my shoulder. "And stay the hell away from those black blades."

A chorus of grunts and thumping fists rose up in answer.

I looked at Luther. "Got it, Prince?"

His eyes cut to me, clouded with shadows, his thoughts already deep in the throes of war.

It was its own kind of weapon, that striking face of his, all pointed edges and hard, unyielding steel. He was glittering poison in a silken pouch— exquisite to behold, but lethal to endure. There was no sign of my sweet would-be goatherd who kissed my forehead and held me in the dark. This was the vicious beast who would kill for me.

Die for me.

"Understand?" I snapped again.

"Yes, my Queen." He glared at me. "Do *you?*"

I turned my focus to the street ahead, where the mortal attackers had abandoned their attempts to tame their horses and were prowling toward us in a wide, menacing line.

"Today is not our day to die, my Prince." I pulled my blade and pointed its tip at the one-armed man at the center. "I can't say the same for him."

"Vance is mine," Luther growled.

"Not if I get to him first."

"Is that a *challenge?*" His eyes gleamed with the same competitive hunger I'd seen in him that night in the Forgotten Lands forest. Though we both now craved a different kind of flesh, it set my heart pounding to the same exhilarating tune.

The sound of laughter hooked my gaze to the left. A group of oblivious teenagers had turned the corner, dumping them smack in the center of the melee. They froze, eyes going wide.

"Get them," Vance barked at his men. "Kill every Descended you see!"

Both sides launched into movement. I sent a burst of light pummeling into the mortals, then watched in horror as my magic ricocheted harmlessly away. I'd never faced a shield I couldn't easily pierce through—but I'd never faced a Descended like Ophiucae.

Though the mortals' shield held, the sheer power of my blast pushed them backward, buying us crucial time. Two Sophos guards cut off to usher the teens back to safety, and I raised a wall of shadow to ward off any pursuit.

My pent-up breath stuck in my throat at the sight of more locals spilling out of buildings to investigate the noise. On a normal day, this realm rewarded curiosity. Today, it might get them all killed.

"Run!" I shouted.

"Kill them!" Vance commanded.

As if I'd taken a club to a hornets' nest, the mortal invaders scattered with furious intent, some taking us on directly while others disappeared into buildings or down connecting roads. My chest swelled with pride as the Sophos guards set aside their fear and stormed boldly into the fight.

I lost sight of Vance as two mortals barreled down on me. With a quick glance to make sure no one was watching, I called on my Arboros magic. Roots snarled through cracks in the paved road and wound in a tangled web at their feet, sending them stumbling to their knees. I let the knotty cords grow deeper and taller into the street, forcing the mortals to turn their blades downward to hack their way out.

My godhood paced hungrily inside me, awoke by the thrill of the battle. *Fight*, its *voice* urged me on.

I happily obliged, calling on my magic to put more obstacles in their way. A tide of water to wash them back, a carpet of ice to send them sliding, a gauntlet of stone to make them climb.

It worked, but only so well. Each time, a few more escaped my reach, and as the Sophos guards advanced, it became impossible to avoid striking them, too.

Worse, some had turned their interest on me and the magic in the street none of us were supposed to have. I did my best to mask my attacks with flashes of light or shadowy shrouds, but in Sophos, even their soldiers were uncannily shrewd.

Up in the sky, Doriel was having little success. Vexes, the Sophos gryvern, was plump and petite, accustomed to a life of spoiled leisure. The fright quivering down its spine practically vibrated in the air. Not just the terror of battle—an old fear, a *remembered* fear, of a history from long ago.

My hands rose high as I channeled the Faunos magic and poured a pulse of bravery into its spirit.

"Diem, *duck!*" Luther yelled from behind me.

I obeyed without hesitation as a glittering midnight blade went slicing through the air where my throat had just been.

I fell back, heart hammering, and gawped at the mortal who'd been one second away from ending my life. He glared and raised his sword for another blow.

"Leave her," another man called out. "Look at her neck. She's been marked."

His hands flopped petulantly to his sides. "She's fighting for *them*. Why should we spare her?"

"We can't afford to lose his help. There's plenty more, find a different one to kill."

The mortal skulked off, mumbling a string of curses beneath his breath. As he turned, I spied a ten-pointed star glimmering under the shaggy hair at his nape.

All of them, I realized in stunned surprise—every single mortal bore the same glowing symbol Ophiucae had burned into my flesh.

He'd marked me.

He'd *protected* me.

Luther ran to my side and hauled me back to my feet. "Are you alright?"

My stiff, hurried nod was a glaring lie, and Luther's frown looked like he knew it.

"If Doriel doesn't make some progress soon..."

"They will," I said. "Give them a chance."

He let out a reluctant grunt, then both our heads snapped at the clink of breaking glass. Nearby, men were attempting to force their way in through the windows of a store packed with cowering faces.

We both jumped forward to stop them, but Luther outpaced me as my foot snagged and I lurched to my knees.

I looked back—and my heart stopped. Among the debris, a Sophos guard lay sprawled and bleeding on the ground. Red liquid gurgled from his lips, his pale pink eyes pleading for help. His shirt had been shredded down the center, where a ten-pointed star had been carved around a gory, jagged wound.

On reflex, I unloaded my healing magic into his skin. Blissfully, miraculously, there was no trace of godstone toxin in his blood. The guard breathed out a moan as his wound stitched closed and the star vanished from his chest.

"You... you *healed* me," he rasped.

I didn't answer. I flung a shot of wind to push back a mortal stalking toward us, then helped the guard sit up. "I'll help you find a place to hide."

"I can keep fighting," he insisted. He shoved my hand away and fumbled weakly for his weapon.

I hesitated with a grimace. The healer in me knew he should rest, but the hard truth was we needed every person we could get. I reached out a hand. "Come on, then. Let's fight."

I pretended not to notice his wobbly stance as I gazed out and spotted bodies littering the ground.

"Cover my back," I ordered.

Together, we darted through the street, crouching beside each fallen guard. I no longer bothered to conceal the truth of my magic as it flew from my palms in all directions, healing with one hand and hurling defensive attacks with the other. My heart stuttered as I found guards with godstone poison already taken root, then shattered completely with others for whom my help had come too late.

The brawl fell still at a frantic howl that dragged our focus to the sky, where Doriel had been knocked from Vexes's back and was plummeting toward the ground. Even with a pillow of wind I conjured to slow their fall, they were dropping faster than their gryvern could reach them—and faster than they could survive. All we could do was watch in horror as Doriel soared toward certain death.

A black and red blur sliced across the skyline.

My heart leapt as Doriel disappeared—then it turned to ice at their ear-splitting scream. They were caged within the talon of Ophiucae's gryvern, the creature's sharpened claw piercing through their gut.

"Diem!" Stuart's distant voice called out. "I've got the weap—"

He skidded to a stop at the sight of his Crown dangling, bleeding and helpless. "*Doriel*," he choked.

"Doriel will be fine," I lied, sprinting toward him. "What did you find?"

His trembling hands offered up a gilded, ancient-looking scabbard, while the guards with him held an armful of sheathed blades, a spear, and a quiver of black-tipped arrows.

I cringed—it wasn't enough to arm even half of our group.

"Luther?" I shouted, my heart hesitating to beat until his voice answered back. I spotted him nearby, crafting a thick, shadowy cloud around a horde of mortal men. They swung their blades in aimless arcs, slicing through each other's shields and unwittingly wounding their own as they bungled blindly in the dark.

I grabbed the scabbard, jerking as a strange pulse of energy shot through me the moment it touched my skin. I waved it at Luther. "Here, take this."

He shook his head. "You keep it. Give the rest to the guards."

I scowled. "*Luther.*"

Amusement twinkled in his eyes. "Have faith, my Queen. I've got my eyes on a different blade."

He set off down the road, where a preening Vance was strolling through the bedlam. In his hand, a familiar bejeweled handle sparkled in the light, a jarring flash of beauty among the violence and blood.

The Sword of Corbois.

I didn't even like the damn thing, but the sight of it in Vance's grip sent an inferno raging through my veins. That blade belonged to Luther—and Luther belonged to me.

"You three," I barked at Stuart's guards, "get these weapons to whoever needs them. Stuart, find me two Descended, one from Meros and one from Faunos. Brave ones." I kept the scabbard and handed my smaller blade to him. "I don't think they'll hurt you, but keep your distance."

His brow wrinkled with questions that, wisely, he didn't stop to ask. He nodded and set off running.

"*Dragonfyre,*" a guard screamed. "Take cover!"

Thick heat washed over me. Ophiucae and his gryvern tore in a low arc down the city center, Doriel still trapped in the creature's grasp—a cruel torture to make them watch their city burn. Dragonfyre flooded from the beast's open jaws, a fiery sea devouring the street in its blistering deluge.

My instincts forced my hand, casting a blanket of ice over every living being I could see. There was no time to separate friend from foe—and even if I could, I wasn't confident Ophiucae wouldn't broil his own men alive in order to win.

His grey eyes locked with mine. His gryvern hurtled nearer, and I began to raise my shield.

Fight, my godhood hissed.

Again, the scabbard tingled against my palm. Its strange, buzzing energy seemed almost like a godhood of its own, its *voice* whispering of a storied fate trapped within its gilded embrace.

A thought tickled the back of my mind.

An instinct.

A hunch.

Ophiucae's lips curled into a serpentine smile, and the mark at my throat began to throb. His gryvern was nearly on me now, sweat beading on my skin from the heat of its flames.

I raised my chin and slid the godstone sword free of its scabbard. The murmurs of its blade grew louder, the language foreign but the message clear:

Fight.

Every rational thought screamed at me to run.

But my godhood was calm. And so was I.

Without breaking Ophiucae's smoky gaze, I dropped my foot back and lifted my sword. My hair fluttered in the draft from his gryvern's wings, its inferno caressing me with a turbulent, boiling wind.

Luther yelled my name as the fire consumed me. Pale flames licked my skin, tickled my neck. They burned—*gods*, did they burn, the bone-deep intensity nearly bringing me to my knees.

And yet my body remained untouched.

The gryvern's other talon unfurled, preparing to pluck me into its grasp.

Fight.

With a cry of defiance, I punched the sword into the sky. As the gryvern soared over my head, the glittering black point pierced the soft flesh of its belly and carved a deep ravine into its ribs.

The beast shrieked and abruptly jerked skyward. Blood from its wound drizzled down, painting me in red. Its talons jerked open, and Doriel fell to the ground with a sickening thump.

I ran to their side and pushed out healing magic, grimacing at the mangled mess of bone chips and shredded organs my magic surged to repair. Relief washed over me as their eyes flew open with a gasp.

"I... I saw you from the air," they sputtered. "The ice. The roots. My... my *wound*."

I dipped my chin in a single nod to confirm the question behind their terrified stare.

"Does that mean *he* can do it all, too?"

"I don't know," I said honestly. "If he can, I haven't seen him use it."

Doriel's heart looked broken as they gazed over my shoulder. "My city —he's destroying my city."

Though the dragonfyre had done little to the glass and metal structures dominating the streets, the old mortal buildings were now engulfed in flames. I hurled water magic toward them—and swore as it splashed uselessly to the ground, the buildings too far from my reach.

"Doriel," I said, "find Stuart—he'll have two Descended with him. Take them with you and get back on your gryvern."

"He'll kill us," they said, looking hopeless. "Vexes is too slow."

"The Faunos Descended can speak to gryverns. They can't make the beast disobey him, but if they're smart, they can find ways to interfere. And the Meros Descended can use the wind to slow him down and speed you up."

The cogs in their clever mind wheeled into motion. "Yes—yes, perhaps that could work." They scrambled to their feet, whispering beneath their breath. A high-pitched trill answered from the sky.

I glanced down the street in search of Luther. Everywhere I looked, mortals and Descended were locked in combat—and not just the Sophos guards. Foreign Descended had been watching the battle unfold from their hiding spots, and several had bravely joined the fray. They had learned from my methods, working in tandem to build obstacles of vines, rock, and ice.

A part of me warmed at seeing these people put aside the differences of their realms to fight as one—and another chilled, knowing that soon, *I* might be the enemy they united to defeat.

"Luther?" I called out.

My insides turned cold as my search dropped to the bodies littering the ground.

"*Luther?*" I yelled again.

No answer came.

My faith did not come easily. I didn't put my trust in gods or Kindred, nor stars nor moon nor sun. Even the Everflame itself could not claim me as its disciple.

But Luther Corbois had asked me to have faith in *him*.

And though it ripped me apart to turn away without knowing he was safe, if there was one force in all the world I could believe in, it was my Prince.

My breath came shallow and unsteady as I grudgingly raged down the street toward the mortal buildings, slashing at insurgents along the way.

Though I aimed for sword hands and ankles to fell the mortals without taking their lives, I sensed the numbness I'd felt in Fortos regaining ground. Every splatter of warm blood left me feeling colder, emptier, more unmoved. The slice of blade through flesh felt rote, almost clinical. It felt like my humanity was fighting to keep its claim on my soul—and slowly losing. My love for Luther was the one light that refused to dim, and though it filled me with terror to think of him while he was missing, I clung to it with all my might.

Finally, I came within reach of the burning monuments. My palm curled, and the clouds darkened. With a rumble of thunder, they unleashed a torrent of heavy rain, the winds of Meros carrying the water where it was needed most. I allowed myself a slow sigh as the flames died away, the mortal buildings damaged but otherwise safe.

The earth quaked beneath me.

A blur of black, red, and silver slammed into me and knocked me to the ground, the godstone sword flying out of my reach. Before I could scream, a sharp talon curled tightly around my throat.

"When I told you to come find me, daughter, this was not what I had in mind."

CHAPTER

SIXTY-EIGHT

Ophiucae's voice wasn't just heard—it was *felt*.
It pierced my thoughts and slithered over my skin. It was nowhere and everywhere, distant and muffled yet bellowing in my ear.

It had a primal, magnetic hold on me, like my blood somehow *knew* it had come from his veins.

He leaned over his gryvern's neck to stare at me where I lay pinned in the creature's hold. The blinding starlight of his illuminated skin made him painful to look at, yet I couldn't tear my gaze away.

I could see myself in him. Not just the ice-white hair and dark grey eyes that I'd spent a lifetime explaining away, but smaller things—the bell of his nose, the slope of his cheeks. The coy smirk fixed on his lips. The way his posture oozed irreverence as his shoulders pulled lazily back.

His gryvern snapped its fangs in my face, its black-slitted eyes as wild and maddened as his.

"I'm the man who gave you life."

There was no emotion in his words, no trace of pride or fatherly love. Merely a cold introduction. A statement of fact.

"Y-yes," I stammered. "And I'm the woman who gave you freedom."

He nodded slightly. "And for that, you alone will be spared from what's to come."

"What does that mean? What's coming?"

His smile grew, no answer offered.

I struggled against his gryvern's hold. It dragged me slightly off the ground, the weight of my dangling body causing its talons to crush my ribs and choke tighter around my throat.

Ophiucae slid off its back and sauntered forward. He stared down at me, my legs flailing as I gasped for air. His upper lip twitched like he wasn't sure whether to be disgusted or amused.

"Release, Xipherus," he said.

The gryvern's talon unclenched, and I smacked down onto the road. My fear had always masqueraded as anger, and now was no exception—my answering glare was *scorching*.

Strangely, that seemed to please him.

I scrambled back to grab my fallen sword and climb to my feet. The hilt of the blade throbbed warm in my hand, a pulsing heartbeat with a toxic edge.

"The people in this city are under my protection," I snapped. "I won't let you hurt them."

"Ah, yes. I see the Crowns inside you. Three of them, in fact."

He hooked a finger and yanked it back, and the Crowns shot up through my body. They strained at my skull with excruciating force, like he might rip my head from my neck just to steal them away.

Ophiucae clicked his tongue. "How very impressive."

He wanted them. I smelled the hunger in him, saw it swirling in his eyes.

"You wish to rule these people?" he asked. "To protect them, give them a better world? Together, we can make it so."

"Not if you keep killing them," I shot back.

His smile turned colder. Harder. "There are debts that must be paid."

"I heard what happened to you. I'm sure you must be angry—"

"*Angry?* They left me to rot in a lightless room, feasting on vermin and living in filth. They tried to forget me." He laughed—a dangerous, poisonous sound. "Oh, I am so much more than angry. And I've had plenty of time to plan all the ways I'll make sure they never forget me ever again."

Icy fingers skimmed down my back.

"You want vengeance against the Descended. Believe me, that's something I understand. But these are not the people who did you wrong. You cannot punish them for—"

"*You dare tell me what I cannot do?*" he exploded. His furious roar rolled through the earth, sending buildings trembling and boulders cracking. My godhood shrank back, cowering in my chest.

His stature grew as he prowled closer. Again, the sword in my hand thrummed with an odd, restless energy. My grip on it tightened as I forced myself not to yield.

"Fire burns within you, daughter. That can be useful. But even the brightest flame can be extinguished." He raised a long finger to my throat, and the ten-pointed star burned so hot, the odor of burnt flesh singed my nose. "Perhaps you need to learn this lesson the hard way. If you—"

His threat cut short, garbled among a celebratory howl as Doriel and Vexes collided into us, sending me sprawling on my back and knocking Ophiucae and his gryvern through the air. Doriel speared a bolt of electric energy into the enemy gryvern's hide, and it tumbled to the ground with a wounded shriek.

"By the Flames," I gasped, crawling backward. "Doriel, he's going to *kill* you."

At the desperate pace they fled, they were well aware. Doriel raced from the city at impressive speed, helped by the two Descended seated behind them and casting magic at their back.

Ophiucae roared and mounted his wounded gryvern. He pressed a hand to its neck, a pale light glowing beneath his palm. The creature staggered to its feet and sprang into the air, a predatory glare mirrored on man and beast.

For a moment, I was paralyzed with equal parts excitement and horror. And then—*relief*. The plan was working. The pressure of Ophiucae's aura had already begun to ease. If Doriel could keep up the chase, we stood a chance.

But if they couldn't...

If this became Doriel's final sacrifice, I'd have to make it count.

I rushed back into the city, aiming the black blade at every shielded mortal I could find. It was getting harder and harder to remember to pull my blows. Perhaps if I were smarter, colder, more ruthless, I would have killed them all.

But these were still my people. Vance had poisoned their minds, and Ophiucae had weaponized that hate for his vengeance. These mortals were not my real enemy, and I had to hold out hope some part of them could be saved.

Between blows, my eyes combed for my missing Prince. My heart leapt at every glimpse of black hair or olive skin, only to plunge when there were no blue-grey eyes to be found.

I was so distracted by my growing unease that I nearly caught a blade as it swiped past my arm. I hissed and lunged toward its wielder—then froze.

"I know you," I said as the Sophos magic spun to life and rummaged through my memories to pluck the right one. "You're from Lumnos. You were my patient once."

"And I know you—you're Auralie's daughter," the man clipped, his hatred palpable. "How can you fight for them when your own mother is one of us?"

"I'm fighting for the mortals, too," I argued.

His brown eyes narrowed. "Are you? Because all I see is mortal blood on your blade and Descended fighting at your back."

Uncertainty tangled the words on my tongue. I looked around to see mortals fall as the Descended guards I'd armed with godstone slice through Ophiucae's shield.

Gods, was he right? Had I become the very thing I'd sworn to destroy?

A gryvern's cry rang out in the distance, and the man's shield guttered. All throughout the street, the glimmering shields around the mortals flickered, then went dark. The Descended let loose a victorious cheer.

The man staggered backward, his anger turning to alarm. "By the Flames... he's abandoned us." He looked around at the Sophos guards rushing forward with sparks swirling at their palms. "They're going to kill us all."

"*Run*," I ordered, lacing my voice with the command of Umbros magic. I turned to the street. "*Run away now, all of you. Leave this realm, and harm no one else.*"

The mortals' eyes went glassy. My will became theirs, and they were forced to obey. Their weapons rattled to the street as they began to flee.

But the Descended weren't ready to let them go. Their city had been breached, their people slain. The fear they'd carried into battle had seared away, and now, they wanted some revenge of their own.

The mortal only made it a few feet before a bolt of Sophos magic struck him in the back and he collapsed, convulsing, to the ground.

Other mortals began to fall. With no shields, no weapons, and my command to do no harm, they were completely vulnerable. If I didn't do something, I'd be trading one mass execution for another.

"They're retreating," I shouted at the guards. "Let them go."

A few Descended dropped back, but too many more continued their assault. Mortal voices rang out in agony as attacks plucked them off one by one.

In a panic, I threw out my hands and raised a shield at each mortal's back.

"What are you doing?" a Sophos guard snapped at me. "You're letting them get away."

"The battle's over. Let them go."

"So they can try again another day? You're supposed to be protecting us, not them."

I clenched my jaw and said nothing. I used to know the difference between my people and my enemy so clearly. These days, I wasn't so sure.

More mortals emerged from surrounding streets, many being chased by angry Descended now that their fallen shields had left them exposed. They took one look at the Descended-packed streets and their fleeing brethren, and their faces went ghostly pale.

"Retreat," they yelled, stumbling over each other in a dash for the Ring Road. "*Mortals, retreat!*"

"Descended, fall back," I demanded. "Let them leave. That's an order from a Crown."

The Sophos guards shot me scowls that stunk of resentment, though, to my relief, they reluctantly obeyed.

I doled out orders to secure the city, then set about wading through fallen bodies, healing who I could and whispering the Rite of Endings for the rest.

Through it all, everyone's eyes lingered on the sky. Even with the mortals retreating, we knew Ophiucae could return at any moment—and if he really wanted to destroy this city, I doubted he needed his mortal army to do it.

Doriel was still unaccounted for, as was my Prince. Both left me nervous, but the latter left me frantic. It wasn't like him to let me out of his sight for long, especially with danger so close at hand.

Every minute without him ratcheted my pulse higher and dragged my thoughts deeper into a bleak, shadowy place. What would I do, if he was gone? What would I become?

Things had changed between us these past few days. Hearing him tell me I was *enough*, even with all my limits and flaws, and knowing he would join me in anything, whether that meant leading a war or running away to a new life across the sea—my walls had turned from stone to flimsy parchment, and my heart had been falling, tumbling, *plummeting* into a love so deep no other man could ever hope to reach it.

And I didn't want them to.

I was his. Wholly, inescapably *his*.

Losing him to the godstone had nearly broken me. Losing him now would leave nothing left of me but empty, blackened earth.

"Luther?" I called out, peering in the windows of buildings the mortals had breached. "Where are you?"

I couldn't *feel* him, either. The air felt too thin, too empty. His magic had gone dark, either from distance or overuse.

Or another reason, my cruel thoughts reminded me.

"Luther, come back—I need you," I yelled, my voice going shrill at the deeper meaning beneath my words. "Has anyone seen my Prince?"

Only shaking heads and apologetic murmurs answered me back.

I ran down the main thoroughfare, the tremor in my hands growing with every empty city block. My godhood fed on my terror, building to an unbearable pressure until my ribs felt like they might crack open just to give some relief. I shot a plume of shadows and sparks into the sky, remembering how he had called me back to him when I'd gone flying in Montios.

I just hoped Luther was the only person my beacon would lure.

I waited for what felt like an eternity, and still, no sign of him came. I shouted his name louder, shriller, my voice increasingly fraught. Though the Sophos guards joined in my search, loaded stares flew behind my back when they thought I wasn't watching.

Maybe he's barricaded in somewhere, I told myself. *Or he's guarding a group of people until it's safe. Or tending wounded guards until they can heal.*

Or maybe he needs help. Maybe he's bleeding to death alone because you can't find him.

Maybe you're already too late.

"Luther?!" I screamed.

Everything about me grew wild and desperate—my voice, my eyes, my heart. The corners of my vision darkened, the gods tightening their fists around my neck. I began gasping, heaving for air.

"Luther, *please*, come back to m—"

"I'm here, my Queen."

His aura brushed against me a second before he turned a corner and came into view, dragging a body behind him using his shadow magic like a rope—and grinning with an ear-to-ear smirk.

"Where in the glaciers of hell have you been?" I snarled.

He slowed, his smile dropping at the fire in my eyes. "I went after a mortal who got away. It seemed like you had things handled here."

"I *didn't*." My voice cracked—like a whip, not a glass—pumped full of fury to cover up the fear. "I needed you. You should have been here."

A deep crease formed between his brows. His gaze fell to my hand, and he stilled. "Where did you get that?"

I stared down at the sword Stuart had brought me. I'd been so distracted, I hadn't even looked at it until now. The broadsword bore a gilded, finely carved handle and a glittering onyx blade as wide as my thigh that had been inlaid with golden scrollwork.

It was a true piece of art—and it wasn't the first time I'd seen it.

"By the Flames," I breathed, "it's the sword from our vision. The one I was holding on the battlefield."

I lifted it to study more closely. The delicate filigree on the blade seemed like a pattern—almost like words, though not in any language I recognized. The swirls and lines wove around a glassy disc embedded in the center, so dark it was nearly black yet radiating a smoky internal glow.

"Where did it come from?" Luther asked.

"The archives. The guards said it belonged to the Kindred." Its energy warmed my skin as the blade pulsed with a soft, silvery glow.

"I think it's meant to belong to you now."

I frowned. It did feel like *mine* in a way I couldn't explain. The thought of letting it go had my instincts hissing in protest.

"Looks like we both found some new *jewelry*," Luther added with a teasing lilt. He held up his weapon—not the plain blade he'd gone into battle with, but a gleaming one, capped with a jewel-encrusted hilt.

Triumph flashed in his eyes as he wiped off the bloody Sword of Corbois on his pants, then slid it into its scabbard and swung it onto his back like it had never been gone.

My heart leapt at seeing the ornate handle rising over his shoulder once more. The teasing over it, the revelation of its meaning, his offering of it at my father's grave—the sword had become part of our journey, a vital step in revealing the truth of who Luther Corbois really was.

But, glad as I was to see it restored, the red-hot adrenaline had not yet cooled in my veins.

My awestruck stare turned into a snarl. "You abandoned me in battle for a gods-damned *sword?*"

He bristled, looking wounded by my words. "Not for the sword." He raised his vine-wrapped fist and tugged the body behind him forward. "Caught this one breaking into a school."

I looked closer. The man's features were bloody and swollen, and a gag of shadow magic obscured the lower half of his face.

"He went after the younger children whose magic hasn't yet manifested. They were defenseless." Luther's fist twitched, and the dark cords clenched tighter, squeezing a gasp from the man's throat. "Fortunately, *I* am not."

He let his magic dissolve, and the man slumped to the ground, coughing as blood leaked from his lips. When he finally glared up at me, the hatred in his brown eyes was unmistakable.

"Vance," I hissed, surprised and yet not. Going after children was just what I'd expect. He might talk a bold game about self-sacrifice, but when it counted, the man was a coward to his core. "I should have let my gryvern fry you."

"And I should have let you die on the island." His focus shifted to my throat. "He marked *you?* Why would he do that?"

"Probably because he's my birth father."

"*He's* the Descended Auralie fucked?" His stunned look melted into a smile. "That should put an end to our problems recruiting the rest of the Guardians."

I crouched at his eye level. "You don't know what you're getting into with this man, Vance."

"I know he wants the Descended to bleed. That's good enough for me."

"And when he kills every Descended strong enough to defeat him, what then?" Luther snapped at him. "He's wearing a Crown, you idiot. You think he's going to hand it off to *you?*"

A flicker of something approaching an intelligent thought skimmed Vance's face before he dragged it back to a glare. "I don't need advice from you two. If you're going to kill me, get it over with."

I glanced around. We'd attracted a crowd, and they were all staring at Vance with patent bloodlust. If I didn't execute him, these book-loving pacifists might rip his limbs clean off his body themselves.

But the mortal man's accusation from earlier still haunted my thoughts. *All I see is mortal blood on your blade and Descended fighting at your back.*

Perhaps I could grudgingly accept killing in battle as a necessary evil, but slaying a wounded hostage on his knees felt like the same kind of petty revenge that had sparked this fight in the first place. Blood for blood would only end when there was no one left to kill.

I could declare Vance a prisoner of the Crowns, bound for the prison in

Fortos—but one look at the Sophos guards told me he would never make it out of this city alive.

And what good was an execution? It wouldn't stop Ophiucae and his men from continuing to kill. At best it would remove a thorn from my side, but at worst, it could turn Vance into a martyr that might ruin any chance I had at swaying the Guardians to my cause.

"Promise me, Vance," I said. "I let you go, you'll leave this man behind, and you and your followers will go back to Lumnos."

He chuckled darkly. "Sure, Sister Bellator. I promise." His toothy, bloodied grin made it *painfully* clear—to me and to everyone else—how little honesty lay in that empty vow.

My heart was torn. I desperately wanted to pull Luther aside and seek his advice, but I was still so shaken by his disappearance I could barely meet his eyes without falling apart.

All I could rely on were the same words he'd given me from the start.

Trust your instincts, my Queen—above all else, trust yourself.

If he didn't already regret saying that, this would seal it for good.

Vance flinched as I reached for him, but Luther held him still. I cupped his swollen, injured jaw—perhaps pressing a little *too* hard and savoring his grimace of pain a little *too* much—to release healing magic into his skin.

Luther had done a number on him—countless broken bones, stab wounds to the side and foot, and a thigh muscle sliced clean through. The wounds to his groin were particularly gruesome.

I gripped his face to make him meet my stare. "*Run away, Vance. Leave this realm, and don't ever come back,*" I said, lacing the command with Umbros magic. "*And stop helping Ophiucae.*"

It was unfortunately impermanent—short of erasing Vance's mind completely, the compulsion of my order would fade in a few days. Hopefully by then, he would decide to heed my warnings.

If not, as least Sophos would be ready for the next attack.

Vance's eyes went vacant. He scrambled to his feet, then set off in a rush for the Ring Road. I pulled a shield around him and used my wind to push back a few Descended who lunged forward to take justice into their own hands.

Angry mutters rumbled around me. If anyone still believed I was secretly involved in the attack, this would pour kerosene on the fire.

I didn't dare look at Luther and risk seeing his disappointment that I wasn't strong enough, brave enough to make the bloodier call. He'd risked his life to capture Vance, and I'd just let him go.

As Vance faded to a speck into the grasslands, my brow furrowed. The repetitive rhythm of his fleeing footsteps seemed to be growing louder and nearer, not further away.

Far too late, I understood why.

"*Gryvern!*" someone yelled.

The guards shouted and ran for cover, shields flickering back into place, as Luther pulled his sword and moved to my side.

"Wait," I said, squinting at the approaching form. "That's Doriel's gryvern."

Vexes let out a weak, exhausted mewl. At the last moment, its wings gave out, falling limply at its side as it crashed into the street.

The earth rumbled at the gryvern's impact, its two Descended riders tumbling to the ground. The first, thank the gods, was Doriel, bruised but otherwise unhurt. The second was a woman—unconscious, badly wounded, magic depleted—but fortunately alive. As I mended her with healing magic, her eyes cracked open to reveal two blue-green Meros irises.

The Faunos Descended who had gone with them was nowhere to be found.

I put another hand on Vexes to heal its wounds, then turned to Doriel. "What happened?"

They crouched at their gryvern's side and pulled its head into their lap, stroking along its muzzle. "Your plan was working. Then he got through my shield and knocked Brion off. We tried to get to him..." Doriel shuddered and fell quiet. Behind them, the Meros woman burst into tears.

An all-too-familiar guilt lodged in my chest.

More blood on my hands.

More corpses at my feet.

"Did Ophiucae return to Montios?" Luther asked.

Doriel's face was grave as they shook their head, their blush-colored eyes rising slowly to the sky.

My throat began to tingle.

In the distance, another gryvern approached, the man on its back a twinkling star among the clouds. His aura was far weaker than before, but even depleted, his power was staggering.

A heartbeat thundered in my ears as he drew closer. I wasn't sure whether it was mine or *his*.

Ophiucae slowed his pace, his gryvern swooping low. Its claws clicked against the pavestones as it strolled smoothly into a landing on the street.

I strolled forward and raised a shield at my back to wall off the city's guards and residents, though I left myself exposed.

"Diem," Luther warned.

I silently shook my head.

Ophiucae's smoke-dark gaze narrowed on Doriel and Vexes, then moved back to me. "Get out of my way."

I lifted my chin. I had to fight all my instincts—and the eager thrum of the golden hilt in my hands—to stop myself from raising my sword.

"I told you, these people are under my protection." My voice dropped so only he could hear. "I don't want to fight you. But I will if I must."

A chilling wrath churned in his eyes. "Where are the mortals?"

"I sent them back to your camp in Montios."

"*That is not Montios*," he thundered.

He jerked forward, palms facing me, muscles quivering down his arms. His magic crackled in the air, and I felt the violent, malicious energy that tangled through it, just as I felt his indecision as he debated my fate.

Suddenly, a puzzle piece fell into place. A realization, an innate under-standing, of the cold, empty numbness I'd been fighting since Fortos.

I gave in and embraced it, let it wash the humanity right from my bones. In Ophiucae's presence, it felt as natural as breathing. As inevitable as death.

Because it had come from *him* all along.

Those cold, steely eyes, such a mirror to my own, felt no remorse at killing, no compassion, no regret. He killed simply because he wanted to, simply because it pleased him to know that he could.

And whether I wanted it or not, some part of that lived in me, too.

Perhaps he saw it in my eyes or read it in my thoughts, but he smiled, sinister and knowing, as surely as if I'd spoken the words aloud.

"I could kill you for this," he taunted.

In the hollow abyss, I found that I didn't care. I didn't fear him, and I didn't fear death. I didn't fear anything at all.

I didn't *feel* anything at all.

"You could," I agreed.

His smile curled higher. "Perhaps I should."

His fingers twitched, his vicious magic inching menacingly close.

I blinked in surprise as a shimmering veil rose in front of me and brushed protectively against my skin, its familiar aura comforting me, encouraging me. Loving me. Reminding me who I was.

And reminding me who I had to live for.

Luther.

Ophiucae knew that, too. His eyes cut over my shoulder, and his head cocked sharply in a predatory tilt. "So my daughter has a suitor," he hissed. "Perhaps I should find out if he's worthy of your hand."

The icy numb's grip on my soul shattered.

Fear—a terror unlike I'd ever known—flooded through me, along with the grounding warmth of Luther's love.

I might lose my humanity, but I couldn't bear to lose him.

My fingers squeezed the hilt of my sword. "If you hurt him, I..."

I couldn't finish the sentence. With a man like this, my threats might only make it worse. And with Ophiucae immune to my magic, I didn't really know if I could protect Luther, if it came to that.

"*Please,*" I whispered.

Ophiucae's focus shot back to me. For an agonizingly long moment, he didn't speak. He just pinned me with those dead, shadowed eyes.

"I can be generous, daughter. I can be forgiving." His fingers curled, and the mark on my neck flared with a painful, choking heat. "But I will not be disobeyed. You have struck at me twice. Do it a third time, and my protection will end."

His hand dropped to his side, and I collapsed to my knees. His gryvern arched its neck in a howl, then fell back on its haunches and sprang into the air.

They circled the city—and then they were gone.

SIXTY-NINE

"I owe you my thanks for saving my city," Doriel said, strolling beside me. After confirming Teller was safe, I'd joined them to survey the damage and check on survivors.

"I don't deserve the credit," I said. "You risked your life to lead Ophiucae away, and your guards fought bravely here."

Their smile had a touch of pride. "I haven't had a chance to speak with them yet, but I'm happy to see our losses were few. I suspect I have you to thank for that, as well."

I held my tongue. Doriel might not be so grateful once they found out the full story of what I'd done with Vance and the surviving rebels.

"I've sent a messenger hawk to Umbros to recall the army soldiers I sent away," they said.

"Good. I'll stay until they arrive, in case Ophiucae returns."

"I was hoping you would say that." Doriel winced. "It's not an easy thing, as a Crown, to admit that I can't keep my people safe on my own."

"You know, many of your citizens joined the fight, too. I can see how much they care for this place. They were willing to die to defend it."

"Even the mortals," Luther added from a pace behind us. "When they realized the insurgents wouldn't hurt them, several came out to protect their Descended neighbors."

Our eyes met, and Luther's lips quirked up in his usual subtle, secret smile. My heart squeezed at the painful reminder that I might have never seen it again.

"There aren't many places in Emarion where mortals and Descended would fight *for* each other rather than *against* each other," I admitted. "You've done more to safeguard them than you think."

Doriel's eyebrows rose. "So you no longer believe we only bring mortals here to kill them?"

I cringed. "I owe you an apology. I spoke to my brother. I still have concerns, but I realize now there was more to the story than I knew."

"I suppose I owe you the same apology for my accusations." Their gaze ticked briefly above my head. "There's more to you than I thought, as well."

My muscles tensed. I'd forgotten to hide away my Crown after Ophiucae pulled it out of me. If anyone knew what the Crown of Lumnos was *supposed* to look like, it was Doriel.

They clasped their hands behind their back. "I'm sending messenger hawks to the Crowns this evening."

"Good idea," I said brightly, trying to mask my nerves. "We must stay on our guard for more attacks."

"The message I'm sending isn't about the attack. It's about *you*."

I stopped still. "A warning?"

"A summons." They turned to me. "To complete your coronation. With this man coming after us, it's too great a risk to let the Forging magic continue to break down. I can't promise the Crowns will agree to the pardons you seek, but you'll at least have the chance to make your case."

"And will you vote in my favor?" I asked hesitantly.

Slowly, they nodded. "I will. And I'll try to persuade Meros, as well."

"Doriel, thank you so much. Truly. I—"

"Don't thank me yet. I have one condition." Their expression hardened. "I'm going to ask you a question Diem, and if I don't believe you're telling me the truth, I'm rescinding my offer, and you'll get no vote from me. *Ever*." The tension between us struck up anew. "If I send hawks to Montios and Fortos... those messages won't reach their Kings, will they?"

My shoulders fell with a sigh. "No. They won't."

Again, their gaze rose above my head. "But their Crown will be at the ritual, won't she?"

I swallowed. Nodded. "She will."

Doriel blew out a heavy breath. "Blessed Kindred, how is this possible? *Three* Crowns. And Fortos—they've never had a Queen."

"I don't know, either. I don't even want them. I'd give all three back, if I could do it without dying."

Liar, my conscience whispered.

"I wonder..." A touch of suspicion surfaced as Doriel looked me over. "If you can absorb magic, maybe that's how you stole the Crowns, too."

"The Crowns weren't stolen," Luther cut in. "Blessed Mother Lumnos told me to serve Diem as my Queen. And I was there when Blessed Fortos spoke through the King. He acknowledged he was selecting a Queen for the first time. Blessed Montios, too—she left a message for Diem through the late King." His eyes narrowed on Doriel. "Those Crowns belong to Diem. The Kindred *chose* her."

They rubbed at their mouth, looking thoughtful. "But why? The Kindred created the nine Crowns for this very reason—to keep any one person from becoming too powerful."

"Maybe they saw what the Crowns have done to the continent, and they lost faith in the lot of you."

Doriel balked. "What have I done?"

Luther prowled closer, his menacing power rolling in waves from his skin. "I know you've got every word of scripture memorized, Doriel. Tell me, did the Blessed Kindred command the Crowns to exile the mortals—or protect them?" Doriel opened their mouth to speak, and Luther growled to cut them off. "My Queen wishes to unite. The rest of you only divide. Perhaps the Kindred have had enough of your heresy."

I pursed my lips, trying not to think about the heat sparking in my blood at my Prince coming so forcefully to my defense.

"Sophos chose not to replace Doriel as the Crown," I said, opting for diplomacy for perhaps the first time in my life. "Surely that means the Kindred want us to work together."

Doriel straightened their jacket with a huff. "Yes. Exactly. And I agreed to help you, did I not?"

"We're very grateful. Aren't we, Prince?" I shot a stern look at Luther, who glowered and folded his arms over his chest.

"I'll call a ritual to be held in two days' time," Doriel said. "You'll get word to your mother to ensure the Guardians give us access to Coeurîle?"

"I will," I lied. Tentative alliance aside, I didn't trust Doriel not to follow any message I sent. I'd just have to hope she accomplished her side of our plan on our own.

"Doriel, there's something else..." My head cocked. "Just before the battle, you made a comment about a 'lost realm.'"

Their lips pressed to a thin, pale line. "Did I?"

"And I know you've seen this symbol before," I said, tapping the mark at my neck. "I could sense your lie with my Umbros magic."

They blanched. "That information is *deeply* confidential, on the orders of the Blessed Father himself. Even the other Crowns do not know it."

"Make an exception," I pleaded. "If I'm going to defeat Ophiucae, I have to know everything."

They frowned, then glanced at the crowded streets and jerked their chin in an invitation to follow. Luther fell back as Doriel led me to a quiet nook.

"I know very little, and that's the truth," they began, their voice hushed. "All the records were destroyed. I only know what's been passed from Crown to Crown and the few details I've found in my research."

"The records of *what?*"

Their face turned solemn. "The tenth Kindred."

A wave of icy shock splashed over me. Hair prickled on my nape, all my senses on high alert, as if my body somehow knew there was a grave danger merely in *knowing* this truth.

"There was another Kindred?" I asked.

"The youngest, a brother. He had a Crown and a realm of his own in between Sophos and Montios, but he died a few years after the original Forging. The remaining nine Kindred recast the spell and allocated that land to Montios."

"The Forgotten Lands," I murmured. "That's why its Forging magic felt like it didn't belong."

Doriel nodded. "They tore down his portal at the Kindred's Temple and had all maps of the continent redrawn. Anything that referenced him was burned or rewritten. They even tried to kill his gryvern, but it escaped and went into hiding."

"Why would they do that? Why not let his Crown pass on to his heirs?"

"They believed he had no offspring to inherit his Crown." Doriel's eyes roved over me. "Apparently, they were mistaken."

I staggered back a step. "You think I come from the tenth Kindred?"

"Ophiucae clearly did. It's the only way he could have the tenth Crown and its gryvern. And his sigil, the star—the only other place I've seen it is on a carving at the Kindred's Temple where the tenth portal once stood. And if you're his daughter..."

I leaned back against a wall as my thoughts exploded in confused, directionless havoc. "The tenth Kindred... do you know his name?"

Doriel shifted uneasily. "They called him Omnos."

The name struck a bolt of lightning straight into my godhood. It jerked wildly, trembling with fear and kneeling in reverence. It ballooned to fill my body with heady, eager power, then shrunk away with a gnawing dread. The whiplash of it set my head spinning.

"You recognize the name?" Doriel asked.

"No," I said, hoarse and breathless. "But I think my godhood does."

They nodded matter-of-factly, as if my reaction confirmed it. "That must be why traces of the tenth realm remained in the Forging magic. If Ophiucae was hiding with Omnos's Crown, the recasting of the Forging spell would not have been completely successful. And that would explain why you're both so powerful, since there are only two of you." They paused. "Two that we know of."

I trembled at the possibility that there could be others like me somewhere, hiding in the shadows.

"How did Omnos die?" I asked.

"I... I'm not sure."

My Umbros magic tingled.

"*Doriel*," I warned.

They sighed. "I only have theories. There are references to the Kindred making a great personal sacrifice to protect the mortals after the Forging. The details were lost to history, but over the years, some Sophos Crowns speculated that sacrifice was Omnos."

I balked. "You think the Kindred murdered their own brother?"

"He was the only Kindred who didn't take a mate, so he never gave up his immortality like the others. He would have lived forever. And if he was immune to magic and could also steal *their* magic..." Doriel's stare cut warily to me. "I can see how that might make even the Kindred scared. Perhaps they feared what he might do once they were gone."

"If no one knew Omnos had children, how did Ophiucae end up imprisoned on Coeurîle?" I shot them a firm look. "I know you know something about that, too."

Doriel winced at being caught. "I know less than you think. Only one clue—a map of the island marking the hidden door with a note that it should never be opened for any reason. It's dated just after the Blood War —he must have been imprisoned around then."

Gods... Ophiucae hadn't just been in that cell for years. He'd been there for *centuries*.

"The Montios King and Umbros Queen were alive during the Blood War. You never asked them for details?"

"Of course I did, but Umbros refuses to speak to me. Montios refused to speak to anyone."

A blazing flash of anger tore through me. No wonder they both seemed to know about my sire—they were the ones who locked him up.

"Why didn't you tell the other Crowns?"

"I didn't think they needed to know. Even Crowns aren't permitted on Coeurîle except for rituals."

"Yes, and who could ever have predicted the *Crowns* might think themselves above the rules?" I said bitterly, drawing an irritable look from Doriel. "Did the map explain why he was imprisoned?"

"No. The Crowns must have discovered him somehow. Perhaps they also feared he would be too powerful, so they lured him to the island where he had no magic, then trapped him there in the hopes Omnos's line would die with him."

I ground my teeth, struggling to bite back my rage. Just like the half-mortal children in Lumnos, Ophiucae had been condemned to death for the sole crime of his blood.

I was beginning to sympathize more and more with his drive for vengeance at any cost.

"Is there anything else I should know?"

"No," Doriel answered, and this time, it wasn't a lie.

AS WE FINISHED WALKING the city, Luther and Doriel made a tentative peace over discussions of the battle and ways to fortify the realm in case of another attack.

I heard none of it, too adrift in my thoughts to be of any help. I could tell from their furtive looks that my uncharacteristic quiet was making them both uneasy, but neither prodded, nor did they slow when I dropped behind them, perhaps sensing I needed the space.

Omnos.

Omnos.

The name went around and around in my brain.

I'd never felt any reaction to the other Kindred's names. Resentment, perhaps, fascination at best, but nothing like *this*. This name felt like it owned me, like it was written on my flesh. It beckoned to the cold emptiness I'd felt in battle, goading it toward the surface.

My independent spirit itched to burn it off and free myself from whatever hold it had on me. But another side of me yearned to embrace it, to succumb completely and let the power of it swallow me whole.

And though that instinct terrified me, I couldn't stop wondering what might happen if I did.

"Diem?" a voice called out.

I looked up in surprise to see Stuart walking toward us. I shook my head to clear away my stormy thoughts.

"I never got a chance to thank you for what you did during the battle," I said to him. "Without your help, I'm not sure we would have survived."

He beamed so bright, he nearly glowed. "It was an honor to watch you fight. You were so brave, and so strong, and so skilled, and so... so..." His voice went breathy as he leaned in close. "So beautiful."

"And so already spoken for," Luther clipped. He might as well have been invisible—Stuart's lovestruck gaze didn't budge. Luther growled and swung an arm possessively over my shoulders. "By *me*. Her Prince."

I shrugged Luther's arm off—earning his deep, unhappy grumble—and leaned forward to set a kiss on the boy's cheek. "Thank you, Stuart. You're very handsome yourself."

Poor Stuart looked like he might pass out—and so did Luther. I wasn't sure which of them was more eager to snatch me up and run away.

"Stuart can take that sword back to the archives," Doriel offered, gesturing to my hand.

I looked down at the godstone broadsword. I hadn't let go of its humming golden hilt since I'd realized it was the same one from my visions.

"Her Majesty should keep it for now," Luther insisted. "She'll need it if Ophiucae comes back."

Doriel looked ill at the mere suggestion. "We'll find her a replacement. His mortals left several godstone blades behind."

"None that are worthy of her."

Doriel sniffed. "That sword is one of our most important artifacts from the Kindred's era. It's a priceless relic. It belongs in a museum."

"It belongs in my Queen's hand. Swords are meant to be used, not—"

"It's fine," I blurted out.

My heart sank. Though I could feel in the deepest parts of my soul that I was meant to wield this sword, I couldn't risk angering Doriel before my coronation. I'd have to find my way back to the sword another day.

I slid it into the scabbard and offered it up. As Stuart reached for it, my grip tightened on instinct. I had to clench my jaw and force each finger to uncurl before he was able to tug it away.

"I gathered everyone with godstone wounds, like you asked," Stuart said. "And the herbs and supplies you requested, too."

"You really think you can heal them?" Doriel asked. "We've been searching for a cure to godstone since the Kindred were alive."

"Not all of them," I admitted. "But I've seen my poultice work before, so it's worth a shot to try."

I didn't mention the cure-all potion from Arboros. I wanted to confront the Arboros Queen about it when I saw her at the ritual in two days, and the slow-moving toxin wouldn't turn lethal before then.

And I wasn't entirely convinced it was the Arboros potion that had really saved Luther's life.

We followed Stuart to the makeshift infirmary, where I set to work on the poultice while a handful of Sophos Descended crowded near me, scribbling notes as they watched.

At the edge of my vision, I spied Luther pull Doriel aside, heads bowed in hushed conversation. After some back and forth, Doriel waved over a few attendants. Luther began speaking to them, his expression indecipherable —not closed off as it normally was, but softer. Eager. When he stopped, they rushed off in different directions, a few throwing sly glances my way.

Luther's eyes slid to me, his lips curving up at having caught me watching him. He returned the favor and let his gaze drag slowly, greedily, down my body, bathing every inch of me in his undivided focus. I was fully clothed right down to my wrists, but the way his eyes burned with dark intention, I felt like I'd been stripped and laid bare.

My thighs squeezed as I forced my attention down to my work. *Stop drooling,* I scolded myself. *You're mad at him, remember? He ran off and left you.*

Yes, to save a bunch of schoolchildren from Vance, my conscience fired back, mocking me in my own sarcastic tone. *How dare he be so selfish?*

"Oh, shut up," I muttered.

"Did you say something?" one of the Descended chirped.

I pointed to my bowl. "I said I'm finished up."

She wrinkled her nose at the mixture. "We've tried this recipe before. It doesn't work."

"It worked once for me."

"*Once?*" she repeated. They all exchanged the same exasperated look. "One time isn't statistically significant."

"One is better than zero," I said defensively.

"If you only did it once, how do you know it was this that saved them?

It could have been any number of other factors."

Another nodded. "You have to cure it at least twice with the same treatment. That's when you know there's something there."

I scowled. Logic and procedure were never my strong suits. I was more of a *run-fast-and-wing-it* kind of girl.

They all sighed and flopped their notebooks closed, offering up empty smiles and paltry excuses to slip away.

I frowned down at my bowl. Technically, I *had* healed two patients, but the poultice I'd given Luther had never worked.

Come to think of it, the poultice I'd given Taran only worked the first time I made it, even though I'd used all the same ingredients in the second batch, right down to the water from the Ignios spring.

I used the Sophos magic to call forth my memories from the little house in Ignios where I first tended Taran's wounds, scouring each moment for a hidden clue. I watched myself prepare the herbs, just like I'd always done, then mash them into a paste, just like I'd always done. Then I cut my linen strips, just like I—

An image flashed into my head, as vivid and real as if it were playing out right before my eyes.

My palm, accidentally sliced open.

My knife, its blade edged with crimson.

My bowl, tainted with a dot of...

Blood.

An unexplainable rush took over. My eyes darted around to ensure no one was looking—only Luther, watching me as always—then I grabbed a small knife and pressed its point into my thumb. Drops of dark crimson trickled into the bowl. I hurriedly healed the wound and cleaned the blade, then stirred until it disappeared.

I waved the Descended woman back over and offered up my bowl. "I think you should try this."

She eyed it with disinterest. "You're, um... very kind, but we have, uh... other methods." She smiled, though it didn't touch her eyes. "Better ones."

"You should try *this* one," I urged. "If you check tomorrow and none of the wounds have improved, then you can try your other methods." I returned the false smile. "Your better ones."

She grudgingly took the bowl from my hands and hovered nearby, eying me like she was waiting for me to leave so she could throw it out. I crossed my arms and flashed her a patient smirk. Finally, she heaved a sigh and coaxed the others into helping her.

"What was that about?" Luther whispered from behind me. The intoxicating heat of him washed over me, and though my posture stiffened in stubborn protest, my treacherous neck arched as his lips grazed the shell of my ear. "Did you always add your blood?"

I gave the tiniest shake of my head.

"Another hunch?"

I let out a short, noncommittal hum.

His knuckles trailed the length of my spine, setting my skin shivering and yet fiery hot.

My jaw tightened. "You're distracting me."

"You're *ignoring* me."

I didn't answer.

"Very well then," he murmured. "If that's how you want to play this."

His fingers tenderly combed through my hair and brushed it away from my neck. Even my obstinate defiance couldn't stop my eyes from fluttering at the tingle of pleasure that skittered over my scalp.

"I don't mind fighting for your attention." A gasp flew from my lips as he suddenly fisted my hair, forcing my face to his. "You've always been my favorite opponent."

My traitor of a body refused to pull away, trapped in the hold of his pale blue gaze. "You fight dirty," I hissed.

Luther smirked. "For you, my love, I'll sink to *any* low."

I scowled at the blissful feeling swirling in my chest. First my body, now my heart. If my temper was a commander, its army was dropping like flies.

"Doriel's invited us to join them for dinner," he said. His eyes dropped to my lips, and my mouth went dry. Another soldier down. "Is that what you want to do?"

Yes was the only smart answer. I needed to explain my decision to Doriel to let the mortals go. I needed to probe them for more information about the other Crowns. I needed to make some allies and recruit more people to join my war.

"No," I breathed.

"Thank the Blessed Kindred." He abruptly grabbed my hand and tugged me away.

"You'll tell me if it works?" I called out to the Sophos woman, who was applying my poultice to the final patient.

But I didn't catch her answer as Luther dragged me from the building and set off into the city.

CHAPTER

SEVENTY

"Where are we going?"

"I arranged a private dinner, but it isn't ready yet," Luther said. "Doriel found our horse and had our bags sent to Teller's room so we can clean up."

"How did you know I'd say no to dinner with Doriel?"

"Because I know my Queen."

I frowned, unsure whether to swoon or be insulted.

We met up with Teller, who led us to a tall, corkscrew-shaped glass building, my dark mood temporarily forgotten as I gawked at the gravity-defying design. Inside the foyer, mortals and Descended sat on scattered couches, pouring drinks and discussing the day's dramatic events.

Teller explained that most buildings in the city were communal, with residents assigned to ensure a diverse mix. Sophos citizens were expected to embrace a love of curiosity not just in their research, but also in their private time. To encourage this, each quarter within the city held nightly events featuring music, theater, and food where neighbors could mingle and learn something new.

I hated to admit it, but this place was beginning to grow on me.

Still, it was far from perfect. Though Descended could freely come and go, the city was closed to mortals except by invitation, and with mortals prohibited from the continent's best schools, very few stood a chance at making the cut. Even in Sophos, classrooms were segregated to prevent mortal children from learning things the Crowns deemed "dangerous" for them to know.

As with any city, this place also had a seedy underbelly that its leaders refused to acknowledge. Teller admitted other mortals had warned him about venturing into dark alleys, where sex and drugs were on sale around the clock. For a mortal, losing their place here could mean losing everything —even their lives, if they had nowhere else safe to go. Many turned to mind-enhancing substances to keep up with their Descended colleagues, some ending up addicted and ruined in the process.

There was much to repair here, but also much to learn. I had to admit, the possibility of what it could become left me cautiously hopeful.

"I can't believe you live here," I said, wandering through Teller's private suite. It was nearly as luxurious as the Lumnos palace and filled with futuristic contraptions. "Convincing you to come home will be harder than I thought."

Teller groaned loudly. "Diem, I'm not—"

"We'll discuss it after I'm coronated."

"My feelings won't change then."

I shrugged. "We'll see. I'm not letting you make a decision until you've talked to Mother."

"Mother won't change my mind, either." He looked down, shoving his hands in his pockets. "I'm happy here."

"Liar."

He frowned. "I'm not lying. You see how great this place is."

"It is, and maybe you could have been happy here... *if* you'd never met Lily." Teller winced. I gave him a sympathetic look and laid a hand over his heart. "But you did, Tel. You love her. And now you're scared of how that might end, so you're running away."

"A Bellator family trait," Luther said under his breath.

Teller and I shot him matching scowls. He raised his hands in surrender.

"I'm not scared, D," Teller said. "I'm just accepting the truth. I do love Lily, but she deserves more than I can give her."

"She *deserves* to make that choice for herself," I said.

Luther's arm curled around my waist, hauling me away from my brother and up against his chest. "With all due respect, my Queen, let your brother be."

"*Thank you*," Teller grumbled.

I glowered and tried to shove Luther back, but his grip on me held firm.

He smiled warmly at my futile struggling. "When you truly love some-one, you hold on and you never let go, no matter what stands in your way. If your brother isn't willing to fight to hell and back to be with my sister, then he's right—he doesn't deserve her." His mouth dropped to mine, silencing my protests in a passionate, possessive kiss.

Teller let out a heavy, despondent sigh, but when Luther's hands began to roam across my curves, his nose wrinkled, his gloom turning to disgust. "I'll leave you two alone."

I moved to pull away, and Luther's hand clutched the back of my head, holding me in place as he branded my mouth with his tongue. He kissed me like a man with a point to prove—both to Teller and to me.

Teller groaned and kicked our bag. "Here are your things. Please don't defile my room too badly while I'm gone."

The moment the door shut behind him, Luther let me go, licking his lips with a victorious grin.

I shoved him away. "You're being an ass."

"So is your brother."

"His heart is broken. He didn't need to see that."

"I disagree." He stalked toward me. "I think he needs to see exactly what it looks like when a man loves a woman unconditionally and won't be torn away from her by any force, in life or in death."

My thoughts emptied.

Those weren't just any words.

Those were terrifyingly close to the promises Descended made at their mating ceremonies.

A promise to love, eternally and unconditionally. A promise to give your heart without reserve and be bound as one, in this life and the next.

His gleaming eyes confirmed it—the unspoken offer. After my warning to him that I might not ever want to take that step, he would never ask me outright.

But he could do this.

Let me know that his heart was ready and willing, in case mine ever was.

I desperately fumbled to hold on to my sour mood, working my face into a scowl I didn't really feel.

"I'm going to wash up," I mumbled.

I reached to grab our bag from the floor, and Luther stepped in my way. "You're angry with me."

"Of course I'm angry," I said curtly. "You were gone today when I needed you."

Liar, my conscience hissed.

Luther's eyes narrowed like he didn't believe me, either. He snatched the bag from my hand and tossed it aside, then took my hands and laid them on his face. "Show me what happened."

The note of challenge in his voice prickled my prideful nature, daring me to say no and prove myself a coward.

True to form, my temper rose to the occasion.

I clenched my jaw and slammed my eyes shut. My memories opened to him in a winding river of Sophos and Umbros magics that let him relive every detail of the attack through my eyes and my emotions. I was so drunk on my stubbornness, I didn't hold anything back, including the suffocating terror I'd felt at his disappearance—and the realizations the near-loss of him had awoken.

But as my deepest, rawest thoughts were exposed, I began to feel too vulnerable, too scared. I started to pull back, and he clutched my wrists to stop me.

"Your turn," he said darkly. "Look."

Before I fully knew what I was doing, I let myself get sucked back into the battle through his blue-grey eyes.

Blessed Kindred, she's incredible.

I was paralyzed. Transfixed.

She wielded magic like someone who'd been training with it for years. She'd only had weeks with these abilities, in some cases days, yet she wove the Kindred's gifts as if they were a single, seamless force.

True, there were signs of her inexperience. Her shapework needed refining, she was blowing through her energy reserves at far too fast a pace.

Still... even in this chaos, my Diem held her own.

And it wasn't just her magic. She was a force to behold with her blade. Her strikes were precise, her footwork deft, her timing immaculate. Wherever Andrei Bellator was, I hoped he could see the warrior his daughter had become. Her only weakness was her temper, but in moments like these where she was calm and focused, she was unstoppable.

She didn't flinch at the godstone blades sailing inches from her skin. I wasn't sure she even noticed them. It made my heart a ragged mess to watch.

I longed to carry her far away to keep her safe. If I did, she'd hate me for it. I could live with being her villain, if it kept her alive.

But she'd also hate herself. She'd blame herself for every death, and that, I couldn't bear. Even now, I could see her shift each hit, taking care never to land a killing blow.

She thought that made her weak. I wished I could make her see that it made her strong.

Damn, was she ever strong.

Too much had already been asked of her. Diem accepted each new burden with an eyeroll and a joke, but I saw the weight of it in her eyes. I felt her tremble beneath its heft when I held her in my arms.

But my Queen never crumbled.

My fearless, steadfast Queen.

It was as if she was born to do this.

Because she was, *I reminded myself.*

She might not share my trust in the Blessed Kindred, but watching her only strengthened my confidence in their judgment. Never had I been more certain that she was the one who would lead this world out of its shadows and into a new, glorious light.

If only I could make her have the same confidence in herself.

My mood soured. That lovesick little twit Stuart had showed up out of nowhere, ogling my Queen's ass when she wasn't looking, even in the middle of all-out war. I wondered how much Diem would scold me if I ripped out his eyes and saved them as a treat for Sorae.

He'd brought her godstone weapons to keep her safe, so I decided, grudgingly, to let him live.

She called my name, her voice sounding all wrong. When I called back, emotion flooded her smoky eyes and set my chest aching. She offered a blade to me, and I waved her off.

"Luther," she said, scowling at me in that way I *fucking* loved. The one that made me want to wipe it off her face in the most inappropriate ways.

"Have faith, my Queen," I teased. "I've got my eyes on a different blade."

I turned my focus down the street—to the one-armed jackass who'd almost taken me from her side.

"Vance," I growled. "You and I have unfinished business."

The piece of shit had the nerve to smile at me. Ophiucae's shield was making him too brave. He'd nearly soiled himself when I'd fought him in Arboros. If I hadn't been carrying a half-unconscious Taran and fending off ten men at once, he never would have landed that blow.

"Dragonfyre," someone shouted. "Take cover!"

My eyes went straight to Diem. My heart turned to thunder as I ran toward her—only to crash into a wall of ice. It thickened into a dome around me, trapping me in place. I slammed a burst of white-hot light against it, but Diem's magic restored every drop I melted away.

I'd never met any other Descended whose power could match mine, but with her, it wasn't even close. If my magic was a spark, hers was the gods-damned sun.

Most of the time, watching her unleash it was the most turned on I'd ever been, but when she used it like this—to protect me while putting herself at risk —that turned me into a version of myself even I was afraid of.

I screamed her name until my throat was raw as my fists slammed uselessly against the ice. The gryvern was nearly on her, and she hadn't raised her shield. Did she think she was immune to the dragonfyre, too?

...Hell, was she?

There was so much about her power we still didn't know. Her instincts were remarkable, but it would only take one mistake to lose her forever.

Blinding dragonfyre covered the street, and my heart raged at me for failing to get to her. It threatened to rip free from my chest and claw its way to her all on its own.

I couldn't see her, but I could sense her. Her magic forever called out to mine. I gripped onto that feeling of her *to tether my sanity as my magic exploded at its full strength.*

I heard the cry of a wounded gryvern just as the icy dome finally shattered. Diem was drenched in red, her sword held high above her head as she snarled like a feral beast. Her skin shimmered as bright as her sire's, mixing with the blood to cast her in a crimson halo. As she watched the gryvern flee, her lovely face was alight with rebellious triumph.

She looked... stunning. Lethal. Unconquerable.

A goddess of war.

Darkness eternal and the brightest light.

She looked like a Queen. My Queen.

Instantly, my cock was hard and ready. Forcing myself to wait—especially knowing she wanted me, too—had turned my desire for her into an insatiable monster. My baser instincts roared to strip her down and sink between her legs right here on the street.

But she deserved better than a rough, greedy fuck. She deserved to be worshipped.

I'd make sure she got both.

Tonight.

My focus landed on Vance just as he vanished down a side road. I glanced back at Diem—she looked calm. Determined. She was addressing Doriel with a commanding tone that had even the Sophos Crown nodding in submission.

I threw out shadows to suffocate scattered fires the dragonfyre had left behind, then took off in pursuit of Vance. However, the deeper I followed him into the back roads, the more it grated on me to let Diem fall so far out of my sight. There was little I feared more than not being there if she needed me.

That fear had corrupted me while I was dying from the godstone. My anger at the Kindred for taking me from her, my guilt at failing her like I'd failed my mother, my terror that Diem might sacrifice herself for me when my life was already forfeit—it had all taken its toll, and in turn, I had taken it out on Diem, Taran, and Alixe. I still had a long way to go to make things right with all three of them.

I was about to turn back when I caught a glimpse of Vance darting into a brightly colored building. I edged closer, and my stomach dropped.

A school. One for young children, judging by the toys and large print alphabets visible through the windows.

I staggered forward a step as a powerful aura slammed into my back. I recognized its malicious presence as Diem's sire. If I could feel him this strongly, he must have landed—which meant my Queen could be in danger.

I glared over my shoulder, wrestling with indecision. There was nothing I could offer against Ophiucae that Diem couldn't do herself. Though my blood boiled to admit it, I knew it was true.

And if Vance set his sights on children...

Diem would rather die than let that happen. So would I.

I snarled in frustration and burst through the schoolhouse doors. Vance had left behind dirty footprints that led me to a darkened back room. I threw up an orb of light to illuminate the shadows and found him holding a sword —my sword—against a teacher's neck as toddlers cowered, weeping, behind him.

"Hiding from battle to target children?" I sneered, disgusted.

"Kinder to kill them than let them grow up to be like you," he bit back.

"And what about that teacher?"

"What about her?"

"Did you bother looking at her eyes?"

Vance glanced at the woman—who, impressively, was spitting mad and not the least bit scared despite the blade at her throat. He swore as he noticed her oak-brown eyes.

"Doesn't matter," he snapped. "Mortals who help Descended are traitors."

My eyes ticked down to the ten-pointed star glowing on his wrist. "You're killing mortals to help a Descended. I guess that makes you a traitor, too."

His face turned an angry, flustered red. He glanced at my hip. "You're supposed to be dead."

"The Kindred had other plans. Why don't you let her go and come outside, and we'll find out if you can finish what you started."

Vance hissed a nasty laugh. "Oh, I'll finish you alright." He jerked the woman. "As soon as I finish her and these little Descended bra—"

His venom went silent as the shimmering barrier around him flickered and fell. His eyes bulged large.

Before I could strike, the woman rammed her fist into his groin. He doubled over, wheezing in pain, my sword dropping from his hand.

The children whimpered and shook, so I pulled a shadow across their eyes to block their view—I could sense where this was going.

The woman picked up my sword, then grabbed Vance by the ear, twisting it sharply. He yelped as she dragged him out, and I followed her to the street.

She shoved Vance to his knees. "How dare you attack little children?" she shouted, unleashing her rage in a flurry of kicks and slaps.

Vance curled into a ball. "Stop! They're Descended, they deserve to—ow! Stop hitting me!"

I leaned back against the schoolhouse wall and crossed my arms, unable to hide my smile.

As Vance tried to clamber to his feet, she swung my sword at his leg. Her clunky form proved she was no trained fighter, but the blade was sharp and it got the job done. Vance howled as it sank through his flesh.

"Who cares what their blood is, you spineless coward," she barked. "You're as evil a person as any Descended could be."

He reached up to grab her, and I flicked a finger to bind his arm with cords of light. She took advantage, jabbing him repeatedly while he flailed in pain on the ground.

"My Diem would like you," I told her. I cringed as her heel stomped between Vance's legs. Repeatedly. "She'd like you a lot."

She wiped the sweat from her forehead and offered me the sword. "You'll handle him from here?"

"Happily," I answered.

I took my blade, feeling a sense of victory as it finally returned to my grip. I'd never cared much for the Sword of Corbois—the day King Ulther passed it to me, appointing me as the future head of House Corbois, whatever small fondness my father had for me came to an end.

And, secretly, I agreed with Diem. It was embarrassingly gaudy.

But every now and then, I caught her staring sadly at my shoulder where its hilt used to rise. I missed the light in her eyes when she teased me for it. If wearing this tacky sword would win that back, it was worth any cost.

My eyes snapped up. A column of light and shadow rose into the sky. There were other Lumnos Descended here, but I knew on some primal level that this magic belonged to her—and it was meant for me.

I wrapped Vance into a cocoon of shadow vines and dragged him behind me. I would have preferred to kill him—ideally in a slow, exceedingly painful way—but my Queen wouldn't want that. I already knew she would set him free. There was no heart so dark that she didn't believe she could bring it back into the light.

I dreaded what this war might do to her capacity for hope. So I would do everything I could to nurture it, even if it meant sparing the life of a scumbag like Vance that my own dark heart would happily kill.

"Where are you taking me?" he asked.

"To my Queen. You can beg her for mercy."

"I'm not begging that cunt for a damn th—"

His words were interrupted by my fist smashing into his face. Selfishly, I allowed myself a few more blows, savoring the crunch of his bones beneath my knuckles and the spray of his blood on my skin.

Damn, that felt good.

"Insult her again, and even my Queen's orders won't be enough to keep me from ending you." I smacked a patch of shadow magic over his mouth to cover his gurgling response. The only way he was making it back to Diem alive was if he didn't utter another word.

I swung back to the street to resume my return.

My Queen needed me.

And I would always answer her call.

I GASPED, jerking from Luther's grasp and stumbling backward until my back pressed against the wall.

"You still think I abandoned you today?" The hurt my words had left behind darkened his tone.

I shook my head, unable to speak. I knew he loved me, but to feel first-hand the strength of his devotion and the depth of his respect...

And he'd been right about it all—how I would have felt, what I would have wanted. The whole time, he'd been exactly where I needed him to be.

As he always had been. As he always would be.

He prowled toward me. "Be angry all you want, Diem. Ignore me. Shove me away. Give me your worst. I'll take it. In fact, I *like* it. You're fucking gorgeous when you're pissed as hell. But if you're going to punish me, at least admit the real reason why."

I closed my eyes, unable to bear being so inescapably seen, so entirely known.

"I thought I'd lost you *again*," I whispered weakly. "I'm so sick of being scared, Luther. Sometimes it feels like the Kindred are taking the one thing that brings me joy and dangling it over a cliff, waiting to see how many times they can pretend to drop you before I throw myself over just to make it stop."

"If they drop me, I'll just grow wings and *fly*." He took my hand and raised it to my chest, then pressed something metallic into my palm—the pendant he'd given me, etched with the sigil of House Corbois. "I'm a phoenix, remember? I'll rise again and again. As many times as it takes to get back to your side."

My fist squeezed around the golden disc. The spark of his magic imbued inside it pulsed warm against my skin.

"Besides..." He pressed a kiss to my forehead. "I've seen you eat chocolate. I am far from the *one* thing that brings you joy."

An unexpected laugh cracked out of me. He tipped my chin up and met me with a smile.

"Can I show you something else?" he asked. "Not with magic." He took my hips, spinning me around and nudging me across the room. "You saw how incredible you are through my eyes. Now I want you to see it through yours."

He led me to an enormous mirror, my reflection on full display. My skin was caked with dried blood, my hair windblown and wild. A dark, commanding glow illuminated my eyes. Food along the road had been scarce, making my bones more prominent and my features more sharply defined.

I looked older. More serious. World-weary and jaded from all I'd seen.

I looked *so* tired—the kind of tired sleep alone couldn't fix.

But I also looked strong.

The last time I'd closely studied my full reflection had been the morning before the Challenging. That girl had been terrified and small. She'd put on a brave face, but she'd felt unworthy of the Crown on her head and incapable of fulfilling the destiny that came with it.

But the woman staring back at me now... she'd *seen* things. She'd made enemies and allies, survived battles and bloodshed and near-certain death. She'd learned to wield both her magic and her Crowns. She'd confronted Kings and Queens and bargained with the gods.

She'd fallen in love. Hopelessly, madly in love.

And she'd stopped denying who and what she was. Perhaps nothing had done more to strengthen her than that.

This woman was a survivor. She could fight. She could endure.

And she could win a war.

I still couldn't say I wanted my Crowns, but after meeting so many of the others and seeing how deeply they'd let down their people, I no longer felt unworthy. I felt inspired to prove what a Crown could be.

"Do you see her?" Luther asked. "The woman I love?"

My chin tipped up.

"I think I finally do."

CHAPTER

SEVENTY-ONE

L uther took my hand and led me into a washroom unlike any I'd seen
before. A set of glass doors opened to a small nook lined with a
mosaic of colorful clay tiles and a water-filled ceiling that made me feel
encased below the sea. The tiles lit up from behind, illuminating the
chamber in a rainbow glow that gently wavered in the undulating reflection
of the water's flow.

When he opened the doors and turned a lever, hundreds of pin-sized
spouts released a rainfall of steaming water, filling the room with a subtle,
pleasant scent that reminded me of a crisp breeze at dawn.

"Amazing," I breathed.

"Wait until you feel it. I accompanied Uncle Ulther here when I was
younger. I offered any price they wanted to build one in the Lumnos
palace."

"And they wouldn't take it?"

"Sophos inventions aren't allowed outside the realm. A handful have
been given as coronation gifts, but otherwise, they keep it all locked up
here."

I wrinkled my nose. "If you have something wonderful, why not share
it with everyone you can?"

"I've found something wonderful." He deftly unclasped my weapons
belt and let it thump to the floor. "I don't feel like sharing her, either."

The energy in the air shifted.

His hand ventured beneath the hem of my tunic and skated up the curve of my hip, bunching the fabric at my ribs.

My pulse picked up its rhythm. "I'm still mad at you."

"I'm sorry for worrying you." His lip twitched. "In my defense, you worry me every time you leave a room. And half the time you're *in* the room."

My eyes ticked to the jeweled handle peeking over his shoulder. I couldn't resist cracking a smile. "I suppose it was worth it to get back that eyesore."

His face lit up. "I knew you missed it."

My scoff turned muffled as he pulled my tunic over my head and tossed it to the ground. I fisted my hands in his sweater and tugged him closer.

"Does this mean you forgive me?" he asked.

I gave a soft, vague hum as I unhooked the baldric carrying his sword. I ran my hands across his chest, enjoying the way his muscles rippled beneath the fabric in response to my touch. My hands drifted lower and found their way to his skin.

I froze, an old apprehension winding me tight, as if he might push me away like he had in Umbros.

His smile waned.

I held his gaze, needing the reassurance I found there. "I might have to make you earn it."

I started to lift his sweater, but before I could finish, he reached over his shoulder and clutched the fabric, yanking it over his head in one smooth movement. A watery kaleidoscope of hues danced across his scar-covered skin.

"Fair enough," he said. He brushed my hair back over my shoulders, then traced the crescent-shaped scar on my collarbone. "I earned your favor once. I'll do it again."

He dropped abruptly to his knees and hooked his fingers into my waistband. With a single, firm tug, my pants slid over my hips and pooled at the floor. I gasped at being so suddenly exposed, at the warm air swirling between my thighs.

Luther unlaced my boots and gently guided my legs free of my clothes. His hands cuffed my ankles, then lazily ran up my calves to curl behind my thighs.

"I seem to remember being here once before," he said. His fingers squeezed in a reminder of the day he'd searched me for weapons at the palace. His eyes dropped, scouring my bare flesh. "I must say, the view has much improved."

My breath turned shallow as he kissed a line up my leg, each one a searing, red-hot brand.

"Do you forgive me yet?" he murmured. I squirmed, and his grip on me tightened.

"Not yet," I hummed. His lips skated up my inner thigh, and my vision went hazy, my fingers weaving into his hair. I couldn't decide whether to pull him closer or push him away. If his mouth went any higher…

Without warning, he stood and spun me around. I swayed against the lust that had dizzied my head. He unhooked my bandeau, and the strip of fabric fell to the ground, leaving me wearing only my golden pendant.

He reached for its clasp.

"Leave it," I said softly.

I couldn't see his face, but I *felt* his smile in the energy buzzing between us. I turned at the sound of rustling to see him kicking off his boots and reaching for his belt.

"You're never going to win my forgiveness if you keep stealing my fun," I scolded, swatting his hands away.

I roughly palmed the front of his pants and massaged the hard length hiding beneath the fabric, smiling to myself as his eyes went glassy.

I leaned in and set a kiss at the center of his chest where his scar was at its deepest cut. He tensed, so I let my lips linger. I kissed the scar again where it traversed his shoulder, then again on his throat, then at the corner of his lips.

Luther let out a ragged breath. His fingers swept along a thin white line on my hips. "A spar with Teller." A pink spot high on my ribs. "Thrown from a horse." An arc on my inner arm. "A violent male with a hurt ego."

His eyes darkened at that.

"You remembered," I said in surprise, recalling the day in the palace dungeon when I'd told him the tales of all my scars, hoping to prove to him that his were something to be proud of, not hide away.

"It's one of my favorite memories."

I smiled to myself and unclasped his belt, then tugged down his pants, his arousal springing free. When I kneeled to pull them down his legs, his cock twitched at my nearness. His hand curved to the nape of my neck, his grip on me flexing as he battled his darkest cravings.

Holding his stare, I mimicked him with a trail of kisses along the inside of his muscled thigh. His pupils dilated, his hand tightening on my scalp. With a groan, he slowly pulled me back up.

For a long moment, neither of us moved, both caught in the other's stare. At long last, there was nothing standing between us. No betrothals, no secrets, no incurable poisons. No wine to sleep off, no bodies to heal. No family members sleeping inches away.

Not even clothes.

Only the ever-present specter of the looming war—but I was determined not to let that rob us of whatever happiness we could still find.

He stalked toward me, forcing me to yield until the mist hit my back. "Get in the water," he demanded gruffly.

I frowned. "What about you?"

Desire smoldered in his gaze. "I want to watch."

I eased beneath the water's flow, breathing out a sigh as a thousand droplets slicked over my skin. The scalding water did wonders for the sore muscles and stiff joints that had become a constant as of late.

"By the Undying Fire," I mumbled, rolling my neck. "Tell Doriel we're moving in. I'm never leaving."

"After today, I think they might let you."

He slowly backed away and leaned against the washroom wall, watching from under hooded eyes. A mischievous fire simmered in my blood. If my Prince wanted a show, who was I to deny him?

My head dropped back as I ran my hands through my hair, moaning with pleasure at the warmth coating my scalp. The dried blood from the battle streamed down my body in rivulets of red.

Luther's throat worked.

"Soaps." He jerked his chin. "There."

I bit back my smile at seeing him reduced to single syllables. I thrilled at this game we played in private—his insistence on taking control, even though we both knew he was always at my mercy.

It was our game of cat and mouse—but both of us were lions.

"Wash yourself," he ordered.

"Yes, sir," I said, my tone taunting. I tipped a bottle into my hands, then let my palms glide along my body, lathering the sweet-smelling liquid over my skin. I started at my shoulders, then dropped my hands to caress my breasts.

A deep sound rumbled from his throat.

My eyes fell closed, and I gave myself over to the moment—the cleansing rainfall, the fragrant soaps, the exhilaration of knowing Luther was watching my every move. I skimmed over every curve, glad for the chance to pamper my body after the hell I'd put it through.

For a long time after discovering I was Descended, I'd felt like a stranger inhabiting someone else's skin. It had felt as if, overnight, my flesh was stronger, my bones harder, my blood magic-infused, yet it hadn't felt like *mine*. I'd wanted to shed it all, to let the Descended slough off and reveal the breakable, unremarkable mortal I was certain lay underneath.

That began to change at the Challenging. I'd had to accept myself, as a Queen and a Descended, to take control of my magic. Ever since, the more I learned about who I was and what I could do, the more I felt at home in my own skin. My body felt less like a costume and more like a weapon—one I could wield to accomplish whatever I wanted.

And right now, its targets were set on Luther Corbois.

My palm swept over my ribs and down the slope of my hips. His quiet grunt drew my eyes back to him. He'd taken his cock in his hand, pumping in long, slow strokes.

I bent my head out of the water. "I can do that for you if you come a little closer."

His muscles twitched at his forced restraint. "Do it to yourself. Touch yourself the way you want me to touch you."

I leaned back against the tile. My hand grazed below my navel and slipped between my thighs. My eyes stayed on his hand, watching the way he worked himself as he drank me in. I moved my fingers in time with his movements, languid at first—indulgent, relaxed, savoring the thrill of each other's attention.

Then faster. More demanding.

Each quiet grunt from him drew a breathy, greedy moan from me. His forceful pumps had me aching to have something more between my legs.

I could barely feel the water over the heat building low in my belly. His muscles tightened, my back arched, both of us barreling toward release.

"Luther," I gasped, my voice drowning in a cascade of water and ecstasy.

"Stop," he barked. "Turn around."

I was teetering on the edge, almost too far gone to obey, but the way his eyes shadowed had my fingers falling still.

"*Turn around*," he growled again.

I gave him my back and faced the wall. His magic pressed in all around me, warning me he was near. I heard the squeak of the lever, and the water stopped.

"Put your hands on the tile."

I obeyed.

"Higher. Above your head."

A rough palm splayed low on my back.

"Such a good girl."

Finally, his body curved into mine like two pieces carved for a perfect fit. My tension flooded away, along with a soft, relieved breath.

His touch was a blade of the best kind, a sword that felled the nagging beast on my heart. The smallest brush of his finger could slice through my fears and set me at ease.

And there was a hell of a lot more of him touching me now than a *finger*.

I pushed against him and rolled my hips over the hardness pressing against my ass. He hissed and gripped my waist, fingers digging into my flesh.

I stilled. Held my breath.

My body trembled in anticipation. One thrust, and I would be his, our long, torturous wait finally at its end.

Or so I thought.

He gently pushed away.

I started to turn, and his palm pressed between my shoulders to hold me in place against the wall.

"Luther." My voice was husky. Pleading. "Why—"

"I waited years for you," he began. I heard the clink of bottles and the pop of a cork pulling free. "I waited so long, I wasn't sure I'd ever find you. In truth, I'd given up hope."

"Lumnos told you I would come. You didn't believe her?"

"She told me a *Queen* would come."

"Am I not your Queen?"

"Oh, Diem." His stubble tickled my skin as he kissed the scar on my shoulder. "You are *so much* more to me than just my Queen."

My heart was a fluttering, restless dove. He poured another scented oil over me, then his thumbs kneaded into the base of my neck. My happiness melted into physical bliss as his fingers rolled down my back, working my sore, exhausted muscles until my body felt boneless.

A very un-Queen-like groan slipped out, earning his quiet laugh.

He continued his massage along my outstretched arms. Those broad, powerful hands—strong enough to kill with or without their magic—were unexpectedly tender.

"What I was really waiting for was the woman I loved. I waited, and I waited. Then I found her, and she made me wait even more." He set a kiss on my spine. "I would have waited a lifetime, if that's what it took."

Conflicting emotions tugged at my heart. Hidden admissions lay in his words—a confirmation of Taran's long-ago warning that Luther would wait out Henri's mortal life, holding on to a hope that someday, in our long Descended lives, he might get his chance.

My hands fell as I started to turn again. He grabbed my wrists and pushed them against the tile. "Behave, or you won't get your reward."

My forehead sank into the wall with a whimper. "You might be good at waiting, Luther Corbois, but I am not."

"Really?" he said dryly. "I hadn't noticed."

Again I tried to press my body into his, and again he moved away, kneeling at my legs. His fingers dug deep into my tired muscles, and I slumped against the tile, enjoying it too much to put up a fight.

"What is my reward?" I asked.

"You'll see."

I glanced down to scowl at him, and his expression stopped me still.

He looked so entirely *happy*. A happiness untouched by war and loss, unfettered by obligation or restraint. The cold, hardened mask of the Prince wasn't just lowered—it was as if it never existed at all. As if he hadn't spent a lifetime disguising his emotions so they couldn't be used against him. He looked like a man without a care in the world.

"You look *free*," I murmured.

He smiled, easy and radiant. "I am. You freed me."

I couldn't bear the distance another second. I sank to my knees and pushed my hands into his hair, tugging him into an urgent kiss. This time, he didn't fight me. His hands clutched at my back and pulled me close.

"I love you," I gasped against his lips, my eyes burning. "And I would wait a lifetime for you, too."

His eyes shone like a full winter moon. "Good. Because you have to wait a little bit longer." He reached up and flipped the lever, and a rainstorm of surging water cut off any more conversation.

He continued to kiss me as he pulled me to my feet, then to my *deep* dismay, he broke away and reached for another bottle. I stilled, panting and confused, as he combed his fingers into my hair and worked it into a lather.

Then, slowly, I began to understand.

He hadn't been able to help me in battle, and in his memories, I had felt how much that gnawed at him. But he *could* help me like this—making

710

sure my soul was calm and my body was ready for whatever the Kindred threw at us next.

My chest ached at the earnest sweetness with which he took care of me. I happily returned the favor, washing his hair once he'd cleaned mine and dragging my nails over his scalp until his eyes closed with a sigh of pleasure.

We lathered each other in soap and scrubbed away the final stains on our bodies as the love vibrating between us did the same for the stains on our souls.

It was an unexpected gift to explore his chiseled, magnificent body without the haze of lust consuming my thoughts. I traced the splintered lines of his scar, over and over, until he no longer flinched or pulled away. Then I laid my cheek against the strange, smooth place on his chest that the damage had inexplicably avoided, listening to his heartbeat as he held me in the rain.

He let himself explore me, too. His hands roamed with purpose, as if to touch me was to know me and he wanted to leave no detail left unlearned. He lingered on my scars—circling them with his hands, then again with his mouth.

Though his touch stayed innocent enough, flashes of caged desire slipped through the bars. A nip of my ear, a knead of my breast, a slow caress between my thighs. He was fighting to hold himself back, but I didn't know why, and every time I tried to goad him on, he smiled knowingly and pulled my hands away.

When it seemed like he was right on the verge of caving, he flipped the lever and the water stopped. He plucked me off my feet and tossed me over his shoulder, ignoring my squeals of protest as he carried me out.

He paused in front of the mirror and ran his hand up the back of my thigh. "Remind me to tell your brother this place has *incredible* views."

I swatted his back, which he answered with a firm smack against my bare ass. A husky gasp burst out before I could stop it.

Luther went stone still. Torturously slowly, he slid my body over his and set me on the floor. The playfulness had left his expression, his eyes now dusky with lust. "Did Her Majesty like that?"

The hot flush of blood that rushed to my cheeks gave my answer away.

"I didn't behave in there," I admitted. "Do I still get a reward, or are you going to punish me instead?"

Veins popped along his forearms. He turned away and grabbed our bag, tossing it to me. "Get dressed and you'll find out."

SEVENTY-TWO

Night had fallen over Sophos, and the city had come alive. The network of magic-powered lights illuminating the streets was a twinkling mirror of the evening stars. Strategically placed spotlights cast the architecture in bold display, while residents mingled outside to discuss the damage.

Despite the attack, the mood around town was optimistic. Casualties had been few, and the way neighbors had come together to protect each other had bonded this community in a way the easy everyday life of Sophos never could.

As Luther led me through the streets, many stopped to thank us for what we'd done. Others eyed the mark at my neck, gossip buzzing around us like a swarm of pesky flies.

For once, it didn't bother me. My focus was on my Prince.

"Where are we going now?" I asked him.

His only answer was a gleam in his eyes.

The moment we were back in public, he'd shuttered his emotions and reclaimed his usual stern reserve, but there was an excited bounce to his step. Even Stuart's appearance in our path didn't break his stride.

"Diem," Stuart called out, waving. "Have you eaten dinner? You could join m—"

"She is a Queen," Luther interrupted. "You will address her as such. And *Her Majesty*'s dinner plans are already set."

I elbowed him in the side. "Forgive my rude Prince, Stuart. Thank you for the offer, but we're off to the…" I paused, looking up expectantly at Luther. His lips pressed tight, though his eyebrows danced.

"Oh, right, the library," Stuart said.

"Library?" I repeated.

"One of my friends helped set up the surprise. Everyone's talking about it."

"*Surprise?*"

"Not much of a surprise anymore," Luther growled.

I grinned. "What's in the library?"

"My friend said—"

"Stop talking," Luther snapped at him. He glared at me. "And you, stop asking questions." He leaned in close, his hand sliding to my ass. "Or I'll have to punish you again right here on the street."

I bit my lip, my face growing hot.

Stuart frowned at him. "You really shouldn't talk to Diem like that. She is a Queen, you know."

My shield sprang up around Stuart a split second before Luther's aura shot forward in a furious, targeted pulse. I slapped a hand over Luther's mouth to muffle his snarling.

"You're very brave, Stuart," I laughed. "I think my beloved and I should be on our way."

Luther's face turned to me and softened.

Stuart shrugged. "Have a good night, Diem."

I dragged Luther forward before Stuart lost an organ. "Calm down," I said, half scolding, half mocking. "You're a handsome, powerful Descended royal. Surely you're not threatened by a mortal teen."

"Threatened?" he said incredulously. "You think I'm threa—" His eyes narrowed at the shit-eating grin on my face. "You are *absolutely* getting punished tonight."

He swooped me up into his arms, cradling me against his chest as he continued walking. I gave in and hooked my arms around his neck with a laugh, then laid my head on his shoulder, feeling irrepressibly happy.

"So you think I'm handsome," he rumbled. The faint trace of disbelief in his voice caught me by surprise. Had the man *seen* himself in a mirror?

Then again, in the vain world of the flawlessly skinned Descended, perhaps what he saw in the mirror was the problem.

"The only face I ever want to wake up to," I said truthfully.

He let out a purely male, self-satisfied grunt. "That can be arranged."

713

He carried me up the steps to the library, where one of Doriel's attendants was waiting by the door. "Everything's been prepared the way you asked, sir." She offered up a large brass key, then glanced at me and smirked, seemingly in on Luther's secret.

He set me on my feet and pocketed the key. "Do you have the other thing I asked for?"

Her cheeks pinked. She nodded and pulled out a small velvet pouch. I leaned forward to peek inside, but Luther snatched it before I had the chance. She said her goodbyes and scurried off.

His hand rose to my cheek. "Don't fight my magic," he warned.

Shadows swirled from his palm to caress my face, a cool mist against my warm skin. My godhood leapt up at its touch, aching to burst through and join with his, then sulking petulantly as I held it back.

"I think my godhood is smitten with yours," I said as his magic shrouded my vision in darkness.

"You should hear the things mine tells me to do to you." He took me by the shoulders and guided me forward. "Maybe later I'll give him what he wants."

My godhood pulsed eagerly, and Luther's low chuckle confirmed he'd felt it.

Though I walked blindly, I could sense that we'd entered the spacious center hall. Earlier, Teller had mentioned the library remained open around the clock to provide researchers unfettered access to its knowledge at all times. I wondered what the people studying now thought as they watched a Queen being led blindfolded down its aisles.

"Why are we here?" I whispered. "And why am I not allowed to see?"

I gasped as he swung me to the side and bent me over something low and firm. His palm clapped high on my thigh, the sound echoing through the vaulted hall. My shock intensified the burst of pleasure, and I had to bite down hard to stifle my moan.

"I said no more questions." His booming voice rolled like thunder through the room. He massaged the place where he'd struck me to smooth away the sting.

My face burned. First, at the thought of everyone watching. Then, at the alarming realization that I didn't entirely *hate* it.

"Isn't my reputation bad enough?" I hissed.

"We could give them something better to talk about." He pulled me upright, my back arched against his chest. My pulse quickened at the scrape of teeth down my throat. "A reason to put down their books and watch."

Apparently, they already had. The room had gone eerily silent, though it was hard to be sure over the blood pounding in my ears.

He nuzzled his cheek against mine, overwhelming me in his masculine musk. The prickle of his stubble on my flesh set my nerve endings alight.

My skin felt too-tight and deliciously sensitive. His knuckles skimmed the cliff of my cheekbones, the hollow of my throat, the swell of my breasts.

"Luther," I gasped, but it was far less protest and far more prayer.

"Tell me to stop," he said. Teasing fingertips trailed lazy rings at my navel. "If you don't like this—if you ever don't like anything I do—one word from you, and it ends."

He paused, giving me a chance to make my objection. When none came, I felt his smile against my cheek, and his fingers plunged down my center.

I grabbed his wrist, and he stilled.

But I didn't tell him to stop.

And I didn't pull his hand away.

"Are they watching?" I whispered.

"Do you want them to be?"

I tried to find an answer I could be certain of—and I failed.

Luther laughed softly. "I didn't expect that. My Queen is full of surprises." He kissed my shoulder and dropped his hands. The shadows receded from my eyes, revealing the extravagant reading room... without a person in sight.

If my life had depended on admitting whether I was relieved or disappointed, I would have been a dead woman.

"Where is everyone?"

"The roof took on damage from the dragonfyre, so Doriel closed the library until someone can make sure it's safe."

"But they're letting us in?"

"We're the someones making sure it's safe. Tomorrow when it's daylight, we'll go up and look. You can stabilize it with your stone magic, if needed. Until then..." He stepped back and tipped his head to the room. "The library is all yours, Your Majesty."

My eyes swept across the stacks of books, an endless echo of shelves packed to the brim with rare tomes. The network of lights had been shut off, so Luther had cast hundreds of glowing sparks to wash the cavernous room in soft blue Lumnos light.

This wasn't just any library. The Library of Sophos contained every book that had ever been written in Emarion. Even when the Crowns had decreed that all books on the mortal religions and histories be destroyed, a handful of copies were set aside for the archives here.

All the secrets of my people that I'd previously been deemed *unworthy* to know now lay before me, waiting to be plucked and devoured like berries on the vine.

I whimpered. "How do I stop time? One night isn't nearly enough."

"You have Sophos magic," he reminded me. "You need only look at a page to remember it forever."

My eyes went wide. I could flip through hundreds of books tonight and "read" them in my mind later. This was more than the gift of one night. This was *months* of reading material.

I spun to face him. "This is my surprise?"

He smiled faintly. "It is."

I nearly squealed. I threw myself at him and flung my arms around his neck. If I wasn't so obliteratingly overjoyed, I would have burst into tears at how much this meant to me.

That he knew me well enough to understand.

That he cared enough to make the effort.

That he was selfless enough to give me this when I knew what he really wanted.

I pulled back. "But what about our night?"

"What about it?"

"Earlier, you... in your memories, you said..." I swallowed thickly. "Tonight, I thought we might..."

"We still can, if you want. Blessed Mother knows I'm ready. But you and I have a lifetime to be together. We might only have this once." He set a brief, chaste kiss on my lips. "If finding you has taught me anything, it's that love is well worth the wait."

Something shifted in my heart.

Something foundational.

Something permanent.

"Come," he said, taking my hand. "You haven't seen the best part."

We wove through bookshelves and hallways and passed through doors with increasingly strict labels, eventually skirting past a sign reading *Crown Access Only*. We emerged into a small rotunda that seemed designed to highlight one single, extraordinary door.

The portal was cast from solid bronze and took the form of an enormous tree. It stretched from floor to ceiling with thick roots tangling into steps at its base and jagged branches spreading in a wide embrace across the domed roof. Thousands of glittering red and yellow gemstones set into the metal faintly pulsed with a subtle glow.

"The Everflame," I breathed.

Luther nodded. "The mortals who built this place claimed it's lit with embers from the Undying Fire gifted by the Old Gods. Who knows if it's true, but it's nice to imagine some part of the Everflame might have survived its destruction. A place we can still visit to pay our respects."

My eyebrows jumped. "You would honor the Old Gods? Isn't that blasphemy against Lumnos?"

His expression turned pensive as he admired the shimmering flames. "If mortals and Descended are meant to coexist, why can't the Kindred and the Old Gods? Why must we choose one and destroy the other? Why can't there be..." His brows creased. "...balance?"

Balance.

The word echoed in my ear in a *voice* both foreign and ancient. Too quick to place, but distinctly familiar.

I walked up the steps and ran my hand over the bronze trunk, the metal oddly warm despite the chilly air. My fingertips roamed along a low branch and skimmed the gemstones.

At my touch, the tree sparked to life. The jewels flared with waves of light that engulfed the room in a waltz of flickering, fiery hues. Even the bronze took on a heated shade of red.

Restore the balance, Daughter of the Forgotten.

I ripped my hand away and jerked back, Luther catching me in his arms as I stumbled down the steps. The light instantly faded from the gems.

"My godhood," I gasped. "It spoke to me."

Luther walked forward and placed his own palm against the stones. Nothing happened—no show of light, no molten bronze.

"If this place belonged to the Old Gods, why would my godhood react?" I asked.

"I'm not sure... but I think I know where we might find an answer."

He pressed a knot carved into the metal tree trunk, and thin lines of light appeared within the grooves as the door cracked open.

The room on the other side was remarkably cozy despite the ostentatiousness of its entrance. Bookshelves of varied heights and wooden pedestals bearing ancient artifacts were arranged in an arc around a central sitting area at the base of a stone hearth, complete with a low-burning fire.

On the ceiling, a sweeping mural of the Everflame reminded me of the fragments we'd seen in the rubble of the old mortal temple. The flames were flecked with veins of silver leaf, and a man with vivid red hair leaned casually at the foot of its trunk, chin tipped down and face obscured.

Blankets and cushions had been set out by the fire as well as an arrangement of food, a large wine jug, and a steaming kettle of tea.

"These are the mortal books banned by the first Crowns," Luther explained. "What little we know of the Old Gods and the ancient mortal ways lives in this room." He looked at me with a hopeful half-smile. "I thought you might want to start your exploring here."

Love.

Love.

It detonated in my chest.

It destroyed me, reduced me to bone and ash.

It rebuilt me, a bird of flame and passion.

Love, like I'd never felt. Love, like I'd never believed myself capable of feeling. Love, like I didn't think existed but in storybooks and dreams.

His eyes darted greedily over my face, savoring every speck of the joy he'd ignited. "I had the librarians pull a few books I thought you might like. They're stacked there, by the blankets. And the tea is a special blend. The researchers use it to stay awake all night studying. I guessed you might need it, since I doubt you plan on sleeping."

My hand closed around his forearm, my head reeling. "You arranged all this... for me?"

His chest puffed proudly. "Does it please you?"

Gods.

I *loved* him.

I'd known it before. I'd meant it before.

But I wasn't sure I had truly understood it until this moment.

Whatever flimsy tissue of a wall might still have been holding me back, it turned to smoke and vanished in the breeze.

A home, a marriage, a mate—I wanted it all. But only with him.

Whatever that life looked like, whether it was just the two of us growing old alone in a humble seaside cottage, or a life of obligation in a royal palace bursting with family and friends. It didn't matter, as long as the future had him in it.

I no longer dreaded what I might have to sacrifice. Luther would never demand anything of me I wasn't willing to give. If the gods did, then so be it. I'd sacrifice it all to keep him at my side.

I no longer feared giving my heart away, either. Gods, I *craved* it. I wanted to carve out half my heart and nest it inside his ribs, let it beat in rhythm with his own, keep it company, hold it in sorrow, dance with it in delight.

I wanted to wear his mark upon my skin and his ring upon my hand. And I wanted him to wear my Crown upon his head.

How had I ever doubted it? How had the choice ever been anything but clear?

One second, I was staring at him, blinking like a fool and trying to remember how to exist.

The next, I was in his arms. Mouths crashing, hands groping, legs around his waist, fingers knotted in his hair. His body going hard, mine already wet.

For months, this tension had been brewing, the pressure thick in the air like a summer storm. We'd been playing a dangerous game trying to outrun it, and now the tempest was upon us—every growl a clap of thunder, every touch a lightning strike.

I kissed him with a passion that looked more like fury. He grunted as my nails scored lines down his back, and his fingers responded in kind, roaming my flesh with his near-bruising grip. My temper rose in frustration as no touch or taste could sate my relentless need.

Clothes went flying, both of us impatient to get to skin. Luther laid me out on top of a low bookshelf, and my hips bucked as he tore the pants from my legs with so much force the fabric ripped.

"I need you," I begged.

"The books—"

"*Fuck* the books."

He flashed me a knowing, sinful smirk. "You don't like them?"

"I love them. I adore them. I want to read every one of them. I—ah... *gods,* Luther..."

My thoughts fractured as he rolled the sensitive peak of my breast between his teeth.

"Say my name again," he demanded.

"Luth—*fuck*," I gasped as he nipped harder. I raked my fingers through his hair and arched against his greedy mouth.

There was nothing gentle or delicate in the way we touched. We were frenzied, unmoored. We were rabid carnivores on a fresh kill.

I wanted him inside me. Not just between my legs—I wanted his blood coursing through my veins, his bones fused to mine to make me strong. I wanted to tear myself open and keep a piece of him hidden away inside me from this vicious world that kept trying to tear us apart. My need for him burned in my lungs, hammered in my heart, slicked between my clenching thighs.

"Pants," I huffed. "*Why* are you still wearing pants?"

"As you command, Your Majesty," he laughed against my skin.

I froze.

He instantly stopped, sensing the shift. His mouth left my body as his gaze snapped up. "What's wrong?"

I fought to force a shred of clarity into my sex-addled head and pushed myself upright. He started to pull away, and I grabbed his belt and tugged him back, spreading my legs so he could nestle between them. He watched me with a confused mix of foggy eyes and furrowed brows.

"When we're out there," I began, speaking haltingly as I panted through my lust, "we have these roles we have to play, with all their obligations and limits. And too many fucking expectations. So we wear our masks, and we play our parts: the Queen and her loyal Prince."

He frowned, not understanding. "I am your loyal Prince. And you are my Queen."

I smiled. "I know." I scraped my nails through the coarse hair dusting his jaw. A throaty rumble rolled out as he pressed closer. "But when we're alone, I want to be Diem and Luther. Equals in all things. I want you to disagree with me, yell at me, disobey me, fight me. Even, sometimes..." His eyes followed my tongue as I wet my lips. "...dominate me. Make me serve *you*."

His hands gripped harder on my thighs.

"Your fealty means the world to me, Luther. But it is not the reason I love you any more than my Crown is the reason you love me. I want more than just the Prince. And I want *us* to be more than our titles. Even if only when we're alone."

The turbulent desire in his expression tempered into a firmer, more lucid love. "Very well. When we are alone, you are not my Queen. You are my heart. And I am yours."

"Equals?" I asked.

"Equals," he agreed. He pulled me off the bookshelf so I was standing before him, then took out the velvet pouch Doriel's attendant had given him. He removed a vial of distinctive green liquid and held my gaze as he emptied its contents in his mouth, a rare gleam of mischief in his eyes.

My heart skipped a beat.

Contraceptive tonic. I'd made enough batches as a healer to recognize it anywhere. No wonder he'd been holding back in the washroom.

"So you didn't think I'd spend the whole night reading, after all," I teased.

"A wise soldier prepares for every possible battle." His eyes ran down my body as he swept away the last drop from his lips with his tongue. Just like that, I was molten all over again.

He tossed the vial aside and quickly dispensed with the rest of his clothes. My skin pebbled—maybe at the cool air, or maybe at the towering god of a man standing naked before me—and I flicked a spark of Ignios magic into the fireplace to send it roaring.

Luther prowled forward. Silhouetted by the leaping flames, he looked like a demon come to devour my flesh and fill my dreams with sin.

He stopped in front of me and caressed my face, his touch achingly light. "Answer me, my heart. How do you wish to beat?" He set a gentle kiss at the corner of my lips. "Do you prefer it soft?"

His lips lingered there as his voice turned dark and his fingers caged my neck. "Or do you prefer it rough?"

I swallowed, and his grip tightened.

"Shall I get on my knees for you?" he murmured against my mouth. "Or would you rather I force you to your knees for myself?"

The tip of his thumb pressed between my lips. My eyes blazed defiantly as I let my tongue swirl around it, then pushed it deeper into my mouth. His throat strained, veins popping along his arms.

"Should I make you beg for your release?" He took my long waves in his fist, wrapping them once around, and dragged my head back. "Or take you so many times, you scream my name loud enough to be heard in every realm?"

He pulled my body to his. "My strong, brave, beautiful heart... tell me what you want."

His eyes blazed with need as they scoured my face for my answer. Our bodies were trembling like tripwires, the tension between us lighting a dangerous fuse. I leaned up on my toes until my lips hovered a breath away.

And I whispered.

"I want to *burn*."

We detonated.

We exploded together, a bomb of lust and love, a devastating inferno that left the world raining fiery debris.

Mouths collided, tongues sparred, each of us laying claim from the inside out. We indulged on the flavor of each other's skin, tasting until we trembled, biting until we bruised.

He hauled me into his arms and crushed me against a bookshelf. The leatherbound spines dug into my flesh, and my nails repaid the favor, clawing down the granite hills of his powerful arms.

It was violent in the best kind of way—both of us allowing our most savage desires to run free, safe within the bounds of mutual trust. But there was a tenderness in it, too. He'd vowed to worship me, and Luther Corbois always kept his word.

He knelt at my feet and hooked my leg over his shoulder, then held my stare with unrelenting focus as he feasted on me to his, and my, delight.

"I've imagined this a thousand times since I knelt for you that day at the palace. I thought you'd taste like the forest." He laughed darkly, the deep rumble vibrating through every nerve. "But you taste like *fire*."

His mouth closed around my clit, and I cried out as I rocked against his face. I laced my fingers in his raven hair, loving his warmth beneath my palm. The scrape of his stubble was kerosene on my flames, each rough stroke of his jaw on my most delicate flesh sending lust scorching through my blood.

Everything we'd been through only heightened my desire. I'd seen him make Crowns tremble and warriors bleed, and I'd seen him guard the defenseless and be a hope to the lost. He was ferocity and heart in equal measures, and now he'd let them both come out to play.

He pinned my bucking hips as he devoured me with lips and teeth and tongue. Long, indulgent strokes danced with teasing flicks that left me shuddering, spots swimming in my eyes.

Pressure built, as exquisite as it was excruciating, and I pulled back, feeling like I might not survive the intense bliss of it. He nipped at me in punishment, and it nearly sent me over the edge.

Soon his fingers joined his tongue. He pumped, deep and unrelenting, stretching me around him and turning my throat raw with my moans. I pleaded for mercy, then prayed it never stopped.

He growled my name between my thighs, and I was lost. My vision splintered into a midnight sky filled with stars and flames and a mischievous silver moon. With eyes and lips shining, he worked me through each cresting wave, all the while murmuring his praise.

I went limp, nearly collapsing to the floor, and he clicked his tongue in playful disappointment. "I'm not nearly done with you yet, Bellator."

He stood and pulled me into his arms, kissing me slowly, lazily, the taste of me in his mouth. He carried me to the fire and laid me out on the blankets, then sat back on his heels, pausing for a moment to drink me in.

"Look at you," he breathed, gazing down on me like I was the only thing in the universe worth seeing.

He was a thing of beauty himself. The light from the fireplace played over his wide shoulders, the orange hues and dancing shadows enhancing the defined cut of his frame. Reflections from the silver leaf on the ceiling shimmered across his face and lit up those beloved eyes.

His scar seemed more prominent than ever, as if my affection for it had coaxed it out from its hiding place beneath his skin. I reached up and traced my fingers over its path, beginning low on his hip. His muscles flexed beneath my touch as I worked my way up the rippled planes of his torso.

"You've never asked me why I didn't have it healed away," he said, watching my hand.

"I didn't want you to think I wished you had."

A fleeting smile graced his lips at that.

"Blessed Mother Lumnos offered me a choice that night, and I accepted it. I swore to her I would serve the grey-eyed Queen and fulfill her dream of peace. I kept the scar as a symbol of that promise." His focus rose to me. "But *you* are the woman I pledged myself to. And now, this scar is for you."

He laid his hand over mine to flatten it over the scar's rippled edge. "Let all those who might try to tear us apart see this and know how far my devotion will go. I will suffer for you, bleed for you, but most of all, I will *survive* for you. My body can be carved in two, open and dying, and still I will crawl from the ruins of my flesh and fight my way back to your side. Death itself could not keep me away.

"My oath to you is written on my skin. Once, that vow was just to serve you." He brought my hand to his mouth and kissed my knuckles. "Now, it is everything."

My throat burned with emotion—not just at his passionate words, but at the precious, fragile hope that we might both survive this war, after all.

He took my other hand, and our fingers wove into knots that he pressed into the blankets on either side of my head. He hovered above me, hips nestled between my thighs. All my senses sharpened on the head of his hard arousal—nudging. Teasing.

Waiting.

He lowered his forehead to mine. "Diem Bellator, you are everything I've ever wanted. You are my joy and my salvation. You are *perfect*. And I promise you this—I will love you for as long as love exists."

He sealed his pledge with a tender kiss. My heart surged against my chest, desperate to be nearer to his.

"Tell me what you want," he whispered.

"You," I breathed. "*All* of you."

He plunged into me in a single, powerful stroke, and it felt like coming home.

I gasped his name, and he twitched inside me with a contented rumble. He waited, allowing me to adjust to the fullness, but I was greedy and impatient. I rolled my hips against him, forcing him deeper, and buried his groan in a ravenous kiss. He pulled out and sank in again and again, moving inside me in tandem with his tongue, both of them claiming me in firm, possessive strokes.

I hooked my ankles around him in a silent plea for more. His pace grew faster, his thrusts more forceful, and I bowed to the ecstasy of surrendering to his desire.

It was fitting that our first time was in Sophos, as Luther made himself a scholar of my pleasure. His eyes never left my face, always learning, always adjusting, shifting my hips just so. No mewl or whimper went unnoticed, and soon he'd found every hidden spot that sent me spiraling.

He gave me everything he'd promised. Soft and sweet, cradled in his arms and showered with kisses. Rough and relentless, my back crushed to his chest, his hand muffling my screams as he pounded into me from behind. He wielded my body like a favorite blade, gripping my flesh in his hands and carving out every last drop of bliss.

But Luther wasn't the only apex predator in the room, and I made sure he knew it.

I shoved him to his back and settled over him, seating him to the hilt. His hands reached to grab my waist, and a rope of my Lumnos light snarled around his wrists to yank them back.

He glared in protest. Shadows swirled in his palms, ready to strike back, and my pulse skipped in an excited, eager kind of fear. He wasn't someone used to losing a battle of wills *or* might.

And neither was I.

I grinned wickedly as I rocked my hips, riding his body to chase my own desire. I taunted him with my hands, running them over my breasts, between my legs, all the places he wanted to touch but couldn't. Though his scowl burrowed deeper, the sparks and shadows of his magic danced in his eyes as he watched me move. The sight of it sent me wild, and my body stiffened as release edged dangerously close.

"Don't you fucking dare," he growled. "Not without me."

"Then maybe I need to hurry you along," I purred. I slid off of him,

724

huffing out a sigh at the sudden emptiness, then laid a brief, featherlight kiss on his lips.

"Diem," he rumbled.

"Yes, my heart?" I said sweetly.

Veins rose beneath his sweat-glistened skin as he pushed at my restraints. "Let me go."

I set another kiss in the hollow of his throat. "But I'm rather enjoying this." My lips trailed down the center of his chest and over his chiseled torso. "I think you're enjoying it, too."

His skin was warm and remarkably soft despite the steel-strong core that hid beneath it. It was an odd contradiction to who he was—his stony outer facade, so cold and impenetrable, concealing the selfless heart that burned at its center.

"I'd enjoy it more if I could touch you," he gritted out.

I hummed thoughtfully, then continued my mouth's torturous path along the line of dark hair that trailed down his stomach.

He went completely still.

"Diem," he warned again, low and deadly soft.

I took his cock in my hands and swirled my tongue in teasing circles around the glistening head. He hissed, his hips jerking. The movement pushed him into my mouth, and at the salty taste of him on my lips, my thoughts clouded. I lost my focus, my magic flickering, and Luther ripped free from its grip.

His hands flew to my hair. He fisted the ivory strands, tugging my head back and forcing my gaze to his. "You're going to pay for that."

"Punish me, then," I goaded.

I dragged my tongue along him, base to tip, smiling as he twitched against my lips.

His eyes flared at the challenge. His grip on me tightened, the tingle of pain on my scalp setting my skin aflame.

This was quintessentially *us*, two warriors who craved peace but reveled in the fight. Even when we chose to submit, neither of us ever fully gave in. We were doomed to eternal battle—and I wouldn't have it any other way.

I parted my lips to let him know what I wanted.

"Wider," he demanded, and I obeyed.

His eyes lit with something fierce yet reverential as he guided me down his shaft, filling me in a new, thrilling way.

His hands and hips moved in a slow, delicious rhythm. My nails dug into his thighs in encouragement, and his thrusts became harder, deeper, faster, pushing me to my limit—then pushing me even more. I welcomed it with a soft moan that choked off as he brushed against the back of my throat.

"Fuck, Diem," he breathed, looking like a man undone. He swept a thumb across my cheek. "Do you have any idea how beautiful you are?"

I *felt* beautiful. More than I ever had in any gown or jewelry. Even on my knees, with messy hair and watery eyes, body battered from the day's attack, Luther looked at me like I was the most stunning thing he'd ever seen.

He pulled me to his base and nearly unraveled, uttering strangled psalms of worship to my name. The sound of him so out of control had me aching at my core. We were liquid fire and lust incarnate, so overfull with pleasure we might burn ourselves to ash.

He began to thicken in my mouth, and I pulled back, gasping and pleading for more. He sat up and tugged me into his lap, then sank inside me with a growl as he clutched me tight against his chest. He murmured his undying love against my neck in a rough, desperate voice, and with the Everflame watching over us, we tumbled over the cliff together, each other's names echoing through the library halls.

His godhood slipped its leash with his release, sending sizzling light and prickling darkness tumbling around us. Cords of his magic encircled my body and caressed my skin, coating me in energy that felt so overwhelmingly of *him*. My godhood pleaded to join it, and I finally let her free.

The whole of the Kindred's magic shot through the room. Fire and flowers, sparks and snowflakes, billows of wind and hoots from owls nesting outside the roof. The nips and bruises we'd left on each other healed away, and my mind opened to let him *feel* the love that bloomed inside. His magic melted into me, leaving my skin moon-bright and shimmering, and a distant harmony resonated in my ears.

He sank back onto the cushions and wrapped me in his arms. Neither of us spoke—neither of us *could* speak—so we simply breathed. Our deep pants slowly merged into a single, quiet pace, and our magic ebbed, the room left mercifully unscathed.

Eventually, Luther kissed my temple, then dragged himself away. I whimpered out a protest, and he smiled fondly and tucked a pile of cushions beneath my head and back. My eyes drooped with a long sigh, my body tired and my heart utterly content.

A few minutes later, a steaming cup of tea nestled into my hand. A plate of food appeared at my side, and a book on the history of mortal queens opened in my lap.

Luther crouched at my legs. "Get to reading."

I opened my mouth to speak, but no words existed to give life to the feeling blazing in my heart.

It didn't take long before the thrill of the books restored my energy. I tore eagerly through each one while Luther took care of me. He found warm water and cleaned me up, fussed at me to eat, tended the fire, and covered me with blankets. Then he wedged himself behind me, my back to his chest, stroking my hair as he skimmed the books I discarded.

Every now and then, I'd catch him watching me with his small, grateful smile, and the books would instantly lose their appeal. I'd pounce on him, and we'd stumble around the room, indulging in each other until we were collapsed and gasping once more.

Shortly before dawn, exhaustion caught up with us. Luther drifted to sleep, one arm draped over my hip. I shoved the books aside and curled against his chest. Against the lullaby of his heartbeat, I succumbed to dreams of the future I was finally ready to claim.

SEVENTY-THREE

"Eat," Luther demanded.

His hand appeared beneath the book my face was buried in, nudging a plate across the table.

I flipped a page. "I'm not hungry."

"I can hear your stomach growling from here."

"Fine, I *am* hungry, but I'm also Descended." I flipped a page. "Hunger won't kill me for weeks."

"*Diem*." His rumble of warning set my heart skipping. "You need to eat. They'll be here any minute to take us to Coeurîle."

I flipped a page. "Which is why I don't have time to eat. I need to read while I still can."

"You had time to stop earlier this afternoon. And at lunchtime. And several times this morning."

"That's because *you* were on the menu." I lowered my book just enough to see his eyes. "Is that what you're offering?"

His expression heated. "If I lay you out on this table, will you eat while I make you come?"

I chewed on my lip, debating my options. "Can I read while you make me come instead?"

I yelped as he plucked the book from my hands. His jaw muscles feathered with the telltale sign of his temper. "If something goes wrong on the island again, you won't have magic to rely on. Your body needs to be strong."

He had that very serious, very endearing crease between his brows that appeared every time I was doing something that might get me killed. Adorable as I found it, we'd both had enough danger lately. I needed to know he was safe, and he needed the same. I grabbed a sprig of grapes and lounged back in my chair, then gave him an adoring smile as I popped one into my mouth.

His muscles eased. He poured a cup of tea and set it beside my plate. "I don't like that we haven't heard from Doriel. I thought they would at least come by to check on the roof."

"I'm sure they're busy with the repairs from the battle." I shot him a knowing look. "And we know they're doing lots of research."

We'd learned that the hard way when a group of attendants had stopped by yesterday to collect some books at Doriel's request and let us know we could stay an extra night—and nearly walked in on us naked with me on my knees and Luther halfway down my throat.

My core burned hot at the memory. "I've had you *and* the library all to myself for a day longer than expected. I say we consider that a gift from the Old Gods and not question it." I let out a sad sigh. "I wish it didn't have to end. I know we're just hiding from our problems here, but these last two days have been some of the happiest of my life."

A fond softness fell over his features. "Of mine, as well. Going back to Lumnos will be bittersweet."

"Indeed. Though I am eager to unseat Remis, now that I finally know what I want to do as Queen."

His brows rose. "You do?"

I spread a pat of golden butter across some crusty bread, nibbling on it as I frowned in thought. "What do you think of a council to govern Lumnos, like the one they had in Montios? We could set aside half the seats for mortals and half for Descended, with me holding the tie vote."

"The Twenty Houses will say you're always going to vote on the side of the mortals."

"Good. Let that motivate them to negotiate with the mortals on plans they can both agree on."

Luther stared off thoughtfully. "It's not a bad idea. You now have three realms. If they can self-govern day-to-day matters, it would free you to focus on bigger things."

"Like murdering my birth father," I mumbled.

He hunched forward, resting his forearms on the table. "I know you don't want to do it."

I winced. "Is it that obvious?"

"No. But I know your heart. You want to find some way to redeem him. It's who you are."

My eyes fell. "Does that make me a traitor to my mother? Or all the innocent people he's killed?"

He hesitated before answering. "Hope doesn't make you a traitor... but I do think there are some people who can't be redeemed."

And you think he's one of them, I thought, though neither of us voiced it aloud.

I snatched two apples from a bowl of fruit, tossing one to him. He unsheathed a small knife from his boot, and I stared in dismay as he began to carve it into perfectly even slices without a drop of juice spilled, ever the well-heeled, sophisticated royal.

He noticed me watching him and paused. I gnawed off a massive chunk from my apple with an irreverent crunch, then wiped the juice from my lips with the back of my hand.

His eyes narrowed.

"Savage."

"Snob."

We both grinned.

"When we have our orchard, you'll have to learn how to eat apples like a mortal, or they're going to run us out of Mortal City," I teased.

He froze, his knife half-lodged in the core.

"I was thinking," I went on, "when we get back to Lumnos, let's find land near my family's old cottage, like you suggested. We can hire some mortals to build us a home. My father's friends, perhaps."

His mouth opened, but no words came out.

I smiled. I knew that feeling well.

"It doesn't have to be anything fancy. Maybe something small, or maybe..." My cheeks warmed. "Something we could grow into someday. As a family."

For a long time, Luther was still.

Then his knuckles went white. His hand slipped off the apple, sending his knife slicing across his chest. A line of red formed on his sweater.

"By the Flames," I hissed. I rushed around the table and perched on his lap, laying my palm over his chest to push healing magic into the wound.

"Gods, Luther, that was right over your heart." I shot him a playful scowl. "Be careful with that. It belongs to me now."

He stared at me, lips parted, face bloodless. His eyes were aglow, but not with his usual Lumnos light. Something warmer.

"Your Majesty?"

A pair of Doriel's attendants appeared at the door. They took one look at the food scattered among books on the library table and cringed. I wondered if risking the welfare of a book in Sophos was punishable by execution.

"The boat is waiting to take you to the island," one said. "Doriel asked that you come right away."

My gut clenched. The time had finally come.

I stood and wiped the blood from my hand. Luther looked dazed, hand gripping his chest. I frowned. "Are you alright?"

He nodded stiffly. Slowly, he rose to join me.

The attendants exchanged an awkward look. "Only the Queen is permitted to come," one said. "The Prince is to wait for Her Majesty here."

"The *hell* I am." He clutched my wrist. "No one's taking her from me."

"Luther, it's just the coronation," I soothed.

"I need to be with you. At your side." His grip tightened. "Always."

I might have laughed and baited him that one vague mention of becoming a *family* had made him lose his mind, but he looked like a man ready to draw blood if he was denied.

I pried his fingers off my arm and laced them with my own. "Why don't you escort me to the dock? Maybe Doriel will change their mind."

"Doriel was very clear," the attendant insisted. "The Prince is to stay here."

"The Prince is free to roam Sophos as he pleases, just like all Descended, is he not?" I asked curtly.

Neither attendant had an answer for that. They shot each other another look, but said nothing more as they led us through the library and down its steps.

I frowned as I looked around at the relatively deserted streets. "I thought the army soldiers were supposed to be back from Umbros by now."

"They were... delayed," one answered. "They'll be here by day's end."

"I hate to leave the realm unguarded. If we need to postpone the ritual until—"

"Doriel said it's nothing to be concerned with. Come now, we must hurry."

They shooed us into a small carriage that zipped us out of the city and through the grasslands, toward the sandy shores of the Sacred Sea.

As we rode, I forced my way through stilted small talk with the attendants while Luther gazed into the distance, brows drawn. He clutched my hand the entire time, his thumb sweeping back and forth like he needed constant reassurance I was still there.

When we arrived, Doriel was not at all pleased to see him. Their expression was clouded, and they shot their attendants a disapproving glare.

"You have to stay here," I whispered to Luther. "Doriel's upset. I can't risk angering them more. I need their support with the other Crowns."

Though it looked as if it physically pained him to give in, Luther gave a subtle nod.

I rose up and kissed him on his cheek. He leaned into my touch, curling his arm around my waist and pulling me close.

"I'll wait here until you return," he said.

"You don't have to do that. Go back to the city. Go to the library and read. Better yet, go see my brother and apologize." I shot him a hard look. "And convince him to come home with us while you're at it."

"I'm waiting *here*," he growled.

I rolled my eyes and gave him one quick, final kiss, then peeled myself out of his vice-like grip and walked down the pier toward the Sophos royal boat. As I boarded the rocking vessel, a guard grabbed my hips to steady me. Even from a distance, I heard the feral noise that tore from Luther's throat. The guard blanched and quickly pulled away.

I beamed at Doriel in greeting. "Thank you again for doing this. And thank you for letting us use the library. It's been a lovely last couple of days."

They nodded, but said nothing more.

My head cocked. "I wish we'd had a chance to speak more. I haven't seen you since the battle."

"I've been very busy."

The boat pushed off from the dock, so I looked back at Luther to wave goodbye. He looked utterly miserable as his hand pressed against his heart.

Suddenly, his expression shifted. He stared down at his palm, frowning, then looked up, his gaze sharpening on Doriel.

"Did you manage to fix the library roof?" Doriel asked.

My eyes snapped to them. "Yes, we did. It wasn't too bad, mostly aesthetic. Luckily, no books were damaged in the attack."

Doriel hummed. "Lucky, indeed."

I was forced to grab a railing to stay upright as we shot through the choppy waves. Like all boats in Sophos, this one was powered by their spark magic, designed to zip across the sea at breakneck speeds. The Crowns' boats were infused with the same power—coronation gifts from a past Sophos Crown to enable the monarchs to get to Coeurîle for rituals more quickly.

"Did your mother confirm the rebels will allow us on the island without any violence?" Doriel asked. "I took a great risk in assuring the other Crowns they would not be harmed."

My insides twisted. I had no idea what the mortals would do when we arrived. If my mother's messenger hawks hadn't made it to them—or if they decided not to honor her command—I could be leading the Crowns into a bloodbath.

Again.

I smiled brightly. "Everything's taken care of," I lied. "The Crowns will be safe. Though if they don't pardon my mother, it may be the last time we ever get through."

Doriel's lips pressed tight in silent response.

"How's your research?" I prodded. "Find anything interesting about Ophiucae or Omnos?"

Their eyes ran over me, pausing on the ten-pointed star at my throat. "When we spoke before, you offered a bonded bargain to kill him. Are you still willing to agree to that?"

I tensed and tightened my scarf to hide the mark. "After the battle, I would hope you trust me enough to keep my word."

"Even if I do, the other Crowns may not. It could go a long way for them to see that you're willing to put your magic on the line."

They reached into their jacket and pulled out a small blade. It was gilded and fanciful, as most Descended creations were. Covered in flourishes, and the gold had a hint of copper in its hue.

A beautiful weapon.

A *familiar* weapon.

Instantly, I was right back in my family's cottage on the marsh. The Sophos magic painted the scene in elaborate detail, only it wasn't the warm fire of the hearth or my parents' laughter that greeted me—it was a sea of red and the foul odor of death.

It was my father's corpse, his brown eyes fixed in an unseeing stare.

It was a blood-soaked blade in his chest, its blackwood handle inlaid with blush-colored gemstones and engraved with copper swirls.

And although the dagger in Doriel's hands had a hilt of ivory, not wood, the rest of the design was unmistakably *identical*.

Blood rushed to my head, spotting my vision.

"Is something wrong?" Doriel asked.

"Y-your knife. It's very... unusual," I stammered.

They looked mildly abashed. "Ah, yes. I know the rule—no weapons on the island except the ritual dagger. Don't worry, it won't leave the boat."

"Where did you get it?" I asked, breathless.

"It was a coronation gift. From your late King Ulther, in fact." They twisted it in their hand, the late afternoon sun glinting off the jewels. "I'm not much a fan of weapons, really, but it is a lovely p—"

"When's the last time you were in Lumnos?" I blurted out.

Doriel frowned. "It's been many years. Why?"

No Umbros magic tingle. *Not a lie.*

So Doriel wasn't there the day my father was murdered. But their representatives were—House Benette had invited them to stay after the ball.

House Benette... the same House I'd angered the day he was killed.

Shadows swirled at my palms.

"Diem?"

My eyes shot up.

"The bonded bargain?" Doriel's brows lifted. "You still want me to talk to Meros, don't you? I doubt they'll vote in your favor without my urging."

I forced myself to breathe and willed my hammering heart to quiet.

I couldn't risk making accusations. I *needed* that vote from Meros. I certainly wouldn't get support from Ignios or Umbros, and Faunos was too much of a wild card to risk my mother's fate on.

After the ritual, I could find the Sophos representatives, force my way into their minds to get the truth—and if Doriel did have a hand in my father's death, my war would start much earlier than planned.

I clenched my jaw and banished my magic. "Right. The bargain."

Doriel nicked their thumb, drawing a spot of blood, then offered the knife to me.

With shaky hands, I gripped the hilt. "You vow to do everything you can to convince the Meros King to vote for a pardon for me and my mother? And you'll recommend the other Crowns do the same?"

"I will. And you... do you swear that you didn't know about the attack on the island or the attack on my realm—and you vow to kill the man who led it?"

I nodded stiffly, then raised the blade to my palm.

And froze.

Luther was right—I didn't want to kill Ophiucae.

Andrei's murder had left a gaping hole in my heart, and though no one could ever replace him, I missed having a father in my life.

Wasn't Ophiucae my father, too—by blood, if nothing else? He had marked me with his sigil to protect me against his people's attacks, and he'd asked me to rule at his side. He had even spared the people of Sophos when he could have simply killed me and finished the job. Perhaps I was something more to him than just the woman who broke his chains.

I wanted to try to save him. I wanted a chance to understand him. Maybe even to *love* him.

My gaze locked on the blade in my hand, so similar to the one that had taken my father's life. That loss had nearly destroyed me. What would this one do to my soul—especially if I was the one who dealt the killing blow?

The knot in my gut tightened.

But maybe Luther was also right that Ophiucae couldn't be redeemed. He'd killed innocent Descended and taken their children gods knew where. His violent hatred of the Descended might be woven too deep to ever be unspooled.

And I had a duty to protect the people of Emarion—whatever the cost.

My eyes briefly closed.

War is death and misery and sacrifice. War is making choices that haunt you for the rest of your days.

I sliced the blade across my palm.

Our hands clasped, and a spark of my magic sank beneath Doriel's skin and theirs into mine. The sensation of shackles clamped tight around my wrist.

My fate was sealed.

And now, so was Ophiucae's.

CHAPTER

SEVENTY-FOUR

"How much longer are we going to wait, Sophos?" the Ignios King griped. "We can't complete a ritual with only five Crowns."

Doriel didn't answer, too busy whispering with the Meros King, their heads stooped, their eyes repeatedly darting my way.

"I have to agree with fire-for-brains here," the Faunos Queen said, leaning against her arch and boredly examining her nails. "We've waited long enough. Let's try again some other time."

"The Guardians may not let us come back another time," I said.

Ignios's orange eyes cut to me. "Why did they let us come *this* time? Let me guess—it has something to do with you?"

I shrank back into the Lumnos arch to hide from his view. My Crown had appeared on its own once I'd stepped on the island, refusing to be tucked away. Though its changes had thus far gone unnoticed, I wasn't eager to draw any more attention just yet.

"Why don't you go ask them yourself, Ignios?" Faunos ticked her head to the cluster of mortals hovering just outside the Kindred's Temple. "They look as ready for a fight as you do."

Indeed, they did. The knee-wobbling relief I'd felt when they let us through without incident had quickly turned to trepidation. They brandished their glares with as much unspoken threat as their weapons. One wrong move from either side would set this place ablaze.

"So sorry I'm late," the Arboros Queen said cheerily as she ascended the steps to the dais. "There was some, ah... delay while I was docking." She tossed polite smiles to the other Crowns but carefully avoided looking my way.

"Arboros," I called out. "I'm glad you're safe, I was—"

"It's good that we're all safe, after what happened last time," she cut in. "What a terrible incident that was. Don't you agree, Lumnos?"

Her moss-green eyes widened as she gave me a loaded stare, her head shaking almost imperceptibly.

I managed an awkward nod. Apparently, my mother was wrong—Arboros *didn't* want anyone to know I'd seen her in the Guardians' camp.

"How do we know this isn't another trap?" Ignios asked. "The mortals know our realms are unattended." He gestured to me. "She could be ambushing us like last time."

"Lumnos didn't have anything to do with that attack," Doriel finally spoke up. "She swore to it on a bonded bargain. She's innocent."

"But her mother isn't," Meros muttered. He and Doriel exchanged a tense look.

"What are you two talking so much about?" Ignios demanded. "If there's something to discuss, come out with it."

Doriel's attention slid expectantly to me. We were only missing Umbros now, but since her vote against me was a foregone conclusion—if she had even survived the attack on her realm—there was no point in delaying.

I drew in a deep breath. "Yes. Let's begin."

"We're still missing three Crowns," Arboros protested.

"We have everyone we need," I said, hoping that was true. "I asked Doriel to call this meeting because I'd like to put a matter to a vote." I shifted my weight. "I'd like to request a full pardon. For myself... and for my mother."

The Meros King scowled.

The Faunos Queen snorted and shook her head.

The Ignios King laughed loud enough to be heard from Lumnos.

"I've committed no crime against the Crowns," I rushed on. "In fact, I've committed no crime at all in any realm I'm not the Queen of."

"You killed Fortos," Ignios shot back.

Faunos snorted again. "Good for her. He was beastly—and not in the fun way."

"She also freed half his prisoners, including all the rebels." Ignios shot her a glare. "Even you can't like that, Faunos."

Her smirk faded, her yellow eyes narrowing on me. "No, I do not."

I frowned. This was not going to plan.

"Fortos attacked me unprovoked. I was defending myself. As for the prisoners..." I squirmed. "It's complicated."

A round of groans and scoffs flew up.

"He was torturing them," I hurried on. "Denying them food and water, drugging them to keep them docile, beating them and warping their bones. He was going to kill my mother without the Crowns' vote. And he was imprisoning children. I couldn't let that continue." My chin rose. "And I won't apologize for it. If Fortos has lost its humanity, it doesn't deserve our prisons."

"If what you say is true, Fortos deserved his fate," Meros said. "But there's still the matter of your mother. She's responsible for attacks that killed people in all of our realms—including yours. Surely you're not asking us to forgive *that*."

"Not to forgive—to look forward. To choose peace over vengeance. The violence between the Crowns and the Guardians has gone on long enough. You've been trying to stop them by executing them or locking them away, but every Guardian you strike down inspires five more to rise in their place. The mortals are never going to stop fighting. *Never*. And they shouldn't have to."

I cast a hard look at each of them. "Everything has been taken from the mortals—their land, their homes, their books, their wealth. Half of you exile them, others crush them under high taxes and unfair laws, and the rest of you hide your eyes and convince yourself it's not your problem to solve. But it is. How can we call ourselves caretakers of this continent if we've failed its native people? None of you—none of *us*—are without fault. None of us have done enough."

Arboros wrung her hands and spoke quietly. "But who's to say the Guardians will look forward? Umbros gave them safe harbor, and they slaughtered her people. How do we know our realms won't be next?"

Fear flashed in her eyes. She'd welcomed the Guardians even more than Umbros, and now her realm was filled with them. If the rebels were turning on their allies, she could be the most vulnerable of all.

"There is a powerful Descended man hiding in the Forgotten Lands of Montios," I said. "He is responsible for these recent attacks, not the Guardians. He has a grudge against the Crowns from the Blood War, and a small group of mortals is helping him take his revenge. My mother is...

familiar with him. If you pardon us, she will command the Guardians not to join him, and I'll..." My throat tightened. "I'll kill him myself."

Doriel stepped forward. "Two days ago, this man attacked my realm. I felt his magic—he's far stronger than any of us, perhaps even stronger than all of us combined. Without Diem, my city would not have survived. She has my vote, and I encourage you all—" They shot a sidelong glance at Meros "—to vote in her favor, too."

"Why do we need her?" Ignios asked. "If we know where he is, send in the army to get him."

"Fortos already tried," I said. "Every last soldier was killed. The army can't defeat him."

He sneered. "But *you* can?"

"Yes," I snapped. "Because he's immune to magic, and so am I."

A flutter of murmurs filled the dais.

"It's true," Doriel confirmed. "They aren't just immune—they can absorb it. Attacking them only makes them stronger."

"I *knew* something was off about you," Ignios sniped. "How is this possible?"

Doriel and I exchanged a glance. We'd agreed on the boat to keep the tenth Kindred to ourselves, but there was only so much we could hide.

"According to my research, it's a rare magic that only a few Descended have," Doriel answered carefully. "As far as we know, they're the only two alive who can do it."

"That's why I may be the only one who can do it," I said. "With his immunity, he'll easily kill anyone who comes for him. But he can't kill me."

Not exactly the truth. Though I knew my magic couldn't hurt him, he had yet to strike at me—and I had no idea what would happen if he ever did.

"This man may be the greatest threat to Emarion we've ever seen," Doriel said. "He could make the Blood War look like a skirmish. Our problems with the Guardians have to wait. We *must* defeat him first."

No one spoke. As each Crown debated their vote, a pensive quiet draped the Temple, the only sound the crackling of the nine flaming cauldrons that rose above the arches lining the godstone dais.

My eyes drifted to the opening in the perimeter of portals—a gaping hole that pointed straight for the Forgotten Lands. For *Omnos*. It was a wonder no one had guessed the truth before.

Then again, that's how the Kindred had always worked, erasing names and destroying evidence, convincing the world to forget rather than answer for their crimes. They'd obliterated one of their own as ruthlessly as they had dispensed with the Old Gods, and now it fell to me to clean up the mess they'd left behind. No matter how much it chafed at me, thanks to the bonded bargain, there was no turning back.

My resentment simmered as I watched the Crowns ponder whether my patricide would earn me forgiveness—a forgiveness I never owed to them in the first place.

A forgiveness *they* owed to *me*, and to a hundred thousand mortals and half-mortals just like me.

And to Ophiucae.

Suddenly, I couldn't help wondering if I'd made the biggest mistake of my life.

The sun had not yet set, its fiery orb perched above the horizon, but the full moon had just emerged from her slumber. Pale and bright, my ever-present and never-useful guardian, her silvery eyes spied to see what trouble I'd find myself in next.

"Well?" Doriel prodded. "Lumnos has my vote. What say the rest of you?"

Meros let out a heavy sigh. "You're sure of this, Doriel? You're certain of your plan?"

"A necessary evil, Obaneryn," Doriel answered quietly. "Whatever it takes to protect our people."

The golden beads adorning his long dreadlocks clinked as he wearily shook his head. His blue-green eyes darkened. "Aye, then. Lumnos has my vote."

My pulse grew louder in my ears. One vote. I only needed *one more vote*. If I could at least secure a pardon for my mother to ensure she wouldn't spend the rest of her life as a fugitive, all this might be worth it in the end.

"Arboros?" I asked, trying to hide the hope in my voice. I offered up a smile, friendly and conspiratorial. A smile that hinted at the dangerous secrets we shared—with just enough edge to remind her that my downfall could easily become hers, too. "Will you vote in my favor?"

She closed her eyes for a long moment. When they opened, she grimaced.

"No, I will not."

My heart stopped.

"I have made my realm a place where all are welcome. If I make the wrong decision now, many good people may pay the price. I cannot risk that, not even for..." She trailed off, looking stricken.

Not even for you and your mother.

I finally understood why she'd silenced me earlier. She wasn't trying to distance herself from the Guardians—she was distancing herself from *me*. I'd become so contagious an ally, even the simple act of voting with me could bring suspicion on her head.

She was throwing me to the wolves to save her own realm.

"I hope you understand," she murmured.

I did. I would sacrifice anything to save my people, too—including my sire.

But my hopes were shattering too fast to offer her consolation.

"Faunos?" I croaked out, feeling the hands of fate closing around my neck.

"Sorry, kitten." She gave a casual shrug, like she wasn't just sealing my doom. "Can't have the rebels thinking they can attack my realm and get away with it. Sets a bad precedent."

All the blood rushed from my head.

I didn't bother calling Ignios's name. One look at him, and he roared with spiteful laughter. "Enjoy prison, Lumnos. I'll sit front row at your execution."

"I saved your life," I hissed at him. "My Prince was about to kill you on that beach, and I called him off. I gave you mercy."

He grinned. "Let that be a lesson. Always take the kill when you get the chance."

No.

No.

This couldn't be happening.

There was no one left to vote in my favor. Like an utter fool, I'd bound myself to either kill Ophiucae or lose my magic—and now I'd have to do it with the Crowns and the army coming for my head.

"I'm sorry, Lumnos," Doriel said, looking not sorry in the least.

I shook my head frantically. "Don't you all see what you're doing? You need my help. My mother's, too. The Guardians will never let you back on this island." I stared at each of them with pleading eyes. "The Forging spell is going to break down—all your borders are going to disappear."

Doriel cocked their head. "Yes, well, about that. You see, I have a different—"

"The vote isn't over yet, Sophos."

The voice was as warm as the Ignios sands, but the sound of it sent ice through my veins.

Yrselle sauntered into the Umbros arch. "Hello, Diem. Happy to see me?"

I gripped the dark stone of my portal to keep upright. Her timing was curious, but her appearance was the true shock. She looked every inch the majestic, dangerous Queen she was in a shimmering silk jacquard gown, its voluminous skirts cascading in every direction, edged in black velvet that set off her dark eyes. An exaggerated tulle collar billowed around her head like a puff of smoke caught in perfect stillness, and a cape trimmed with diamonds as big as my thumbnail splayed behind her in a regal train. Tiny, glittering gemstones studded her bronzed decolletage and disappeared down the canyon of her plunging neckline.

"This is new," Ignios jeered. "Usually you're barely wearing any clothes at all."

The chunky baubles dangling from her ears clinked as she shrugged. "I came dressed for a coronation. *Several*, in fact." Her depthless gaze sat heavy on mine, then ticked above my head. "I see you've picked up a third since I saw you last."

Doriel stilled, glancing warily between us, while the others looked on in confusion.

"I heard what happened in your realm," I said softly. "I'm sorry, Yrselle. If I had known..."

"Then what?" One slender eyebrow arched. "Would you have stayed? Traded one last day with your lover for the lives of my Centenaries?"

My throat worked. I wouldn't do her the disrespect of lying, but I didn't know the truth.

"I warned you that if you left, my people would die," she hissed. "I should kill you for that alone."

"How did you know an attack was coming?" Ignios asked, his tone sharp with suspicion.

"I know more than you could possibly imagine, Ignios." She looked him over with an unimpressed frown. "Though you do set the bar dreadfully low."

Faunos flicked a hand dismissively. "Yes, Umbros, you and your spies know all and see all. We've heard this routine before. If you know what we're voting on, then give yours already."

"Her vote doesn't matter," Ignios argued. "Lumnos only has three votes. Without Fortos and Montios, she can't get to six."

"Diem has *five* votes," Yrselle said. "Or have you imbeciles still not looked at her Crown?"

Six pairs of eyes crept to me—or rather, to my glowing three-peaked circlet of vines, veins, and ice.

The usual cries of *this-can't-be* and *how-did-this-happen* rained down on me from the Ignios, Arboros, and Faunos arches to my right. Across the Temple, Meros gave a loaded glance to Doriel that raised the hairs on my nape.

"If you have questions, take them up with the Kindred," I said flatly. "I don't have answers. And I'm about as pleased with it as all of you are."

"If you have their Crowns... do you also have their magic?" Arboros asked.

"Theirs—and yours, as well," I confessed. "Ignios fire, Meros wind, Sophos spark." My gaze cut to Yrselle. "Umbros thought."

She nodded calmly, looking as if she'd known it all along. Looking as if she was confirming it to *me*, rather than the other way around.

The Temple fell brutally silent.

Crowns were fiercely possessive by nature. I'd felt it myself—when I'd seen the Lumnos light speckling the market hall in Umbros, some part of me had been hissing "*mine*." I'd felt the same way toward the blue-eyed staff in Zalaric's inn. Though they were technically Yrselle's subjects, their Lumnos magic had sparked a primal drive in me to claim them, to both protect them and make them kneel.

It seemed the Crowns were battling the same urges now. But I was the one and only bearer of their magic they could never force to kneel, neither by law nor by might.

And that made me a threat.

The sun was halfway to bed, its last rays gilding the tall island brush. Night was quickly arriving, and with it, changing winds. A frosty breeze kicked up the hair on my shoulders and sent it whipping like a warning shot across my face.

"Cast your vote, Umbros," Doriel said darkly.

"Please, Yrselle," I said. "You asked me how far I'm willing to go... I didn't understand then, but I do now. I'm ready to do what must be done."

"You don't deserve my vote." She spat the words, and the last of my hope crumbled. "You deserve to suffer as my people suffered. And believe me, you will." Her pitch-black eyes seemed to grow even darker. "It's not just my Centenaries they massacred, you know. They killed every Descended they could find. Tell my dear Zalaric his inn is in need of a new staff."

I flinched as an awful, poisonous guilt coated my insides. All those half-mortals Luther had saved...

"You have no idea the chain of fate you've set in motion." She smiled, but there was only anger and sadness in its curves. "Every life he takes now is on your hands. No wound I inflict will bleed you worse than that."

My eyes squeezed shut. My cowardly heart was desperate to run from the truth of her words.

Doriel pulled the ritual dagger from their coat. "Since Umbros has voted no, Diem and her mother are hereby charged as enemies of the Crowns. We'll complete the coronation ritual to restore the Forging spell, then Diem will be arrested and imprisoned."

My focus snapped to them. "What? That's not what we agreed."

"What we *agreed* is that I would give you my vote and speak in your favor. I fulfilled my side of our bargain. If you can't fulfill yours..." They trailed off, and I realized with horror just how badly I'd been duped. If the Crowns imprisoned me and killed Ophiucae before I could, the bargain would become impossible for me to fulfill, and my magic would be gone.

Both threats neutralized—permanently.

My pulse surged with mounting panic. "You can't hold me. Only Fortos has prison cells strong enough to contain a Crown, and I'm its Queen."

Doriel's lips pursed. "There are other cells we can use." Their eyes swept across the island—to a heavy godstone door laying wide open in the brush.

I stumbled backward, fighting for air. "You... you're going to do to me what they did to *him*."

"My guards told me you let his people go. You may not have planned the attack, but you clearly have sympathies for his cause. I cannot risk you killing him only to step right into his shoes." They had the gall to look mildly rueful. "I'm sorry, Diem. I have to protect my people."

Doriel stuck their fingers in their mouth and let out a loud whistle. Seconds later, a bright red flare shot into the pre-dusk sky. Clumps of soldiers appeared on the horizon near every port.

"We've been betrayed," a Guardian shouted from outside the Temple.

"Kill the Crowns," another yelled. "If we go down, they go down with us."

They raised their weapons, but just as they ran for the dais, two gryverns dove from the clouds with matching shrieks. The smaller, slower one I recognized as Vexes, the Sophos gryvern. The second I'd never seen, but from the blue-green glow building in its jaws—and the grim look on Meros's face—I could guess where it belonged.

The creatures banked into a loop over our heads and unleashed plumes of pink and turquoise dragonfyre at every mortal who came near.

Fear and fury rose in equal measures. On the island, our bonds with our gryverns went dark alongside our magic, meaning Doriel had to have coordinated this long before we left the Sophos shores.

Allowing Luther and I to stay in the library hadn't been a token of appreciation—it had been a distraction to keep us out of the way.

"What have you done?" I screamed at Doriel. "My mother swore to the Guardians that they'd be safe. They'll never trust her now. You're going to run the rebels right into his arms."

"We can handle them. Now we know where his camp is, and after the successful battle in my realm, we know how to defeat him."

"You didn't *defeat* him, you idiot, he left because of me. I told him your people were under my protection. If I hadn't, he would have wiped your realm from the gods-damned continent."

Doriel's face went a shade paler, but they raised their chin, stubbornly burying themselves in the quicksand of their choice.

I whipped around to the others. "Don't you see this is a coup? You're happy to let Sophos single-handedly take control of the army?"

Their apprehensive looks said they very much *were not*, but at least for now, none was willing to speak up on my behalf.

"An enemy of the Crowns is unfit to rule," Doriel interjected. "The Fortos Regent has stepped in to lead the Emarion Army."

"How convenient that they're answering only to you," I shot back.

The sudden sound of laughter sliced through the tension, and my furious gaze flicked to its owner. Yrselle was watching with blatant amusement, no doubt savoring my demise.

"Clever, as always, Sophos," she said between husky chuckles. "You thought of everything. Shame you showed your hand a bit too early." Her smile spread wide. "I have not yet cast my vote."

"But you said—"

"I said she doesn't deserve my vote." Her gaze cut to me. "I didn't say I wouldn't give it to her."

"You've got to be kidding," Ignios muttered. "You would pardon her after what was done to your realm?"

A storm settled over her features as she ignored him to stare me down.

"There is much I could have told you, Daughter of the Forgotten. About your father and your magic. Your fate. About Omnos."

Doriel's head snapped toward her.

"The future is so much darker now," she said. "If there is even still a future at all. Where victory was once certain..." She sighed and shook her head. "I share the blame for not telling you sooner. Blessed Father Umbros warned me that our fate hung in the balance of your choice. He urged me to trust you, Instead, I tried to force your hand. That decision cost me much. This decision will cost me *everything*."

"Get to the point," Faunos groaned. "Are you voting with her or not?"

Still, Yrselle's shadowy eyes did not leave mine. "Take the rosebane. Use my key. Heed my warnings—especially about my heir. And don't forget what you pledged to sacrifice to see your plans through."

She twirled her fingers—a seemingly idle gesture, were it not for the glint of glittering black inlaid beneath the sharpened points of her nails.

"I am giving you the thing I value most, Diem Bellator. Use it wisely." She smiled coldly and held her arms out to her sides, her voice rising. "My answer is yes. I cast my vote in Diem's fav—"

She didn't get a chance to finish before a godstone blade plunged into the hollow of her throat.

Her blood splattered across the crisp white linen robes of the dagger's bearer.

"Ignios!" Arboros screamed. "What have you done?"

Yrselle stumbled, clutching her throat and choking as red liquid dribbled from her parted lips. She swung her hand forward and just barely missed Ignios as he darted back.

"I've been wanting to do this for *years*," he said. He pulled his blade free of her neck and stabbed her again—and again, and again.

"Blessed Kindred," Doriel breathed. "Ignios, this space is *sacred!*"

Meros ripped off his tunic and revealed a hidden baldric of weapons strapped to his chest. He grabbed the longest blade and thrust its point forward. "Come anywhere near us with that thing, Ignios, and I'll paint the heartstone with your innards."

"Obaneryn," Doriel hissed. "You know weapons aren't allowed here."

Ignios fisted the fabric of Yrselle's dress to hold her upright as her body began to slump. "No need for that, Meros. I only needed to eliminate one vote, so I chose the one that's pissed me off the most. Although..." His eyes turned to me with a violent gleam.

Despite my thundering heart and shaking hands, I reached in my boot and pulled the dagger I'd hidden there. "Try me," I barked. "I dare you."

"Of course *you* brought one," Doriel huffed.

Faunos and Arboros reached beneath their skirts and drew their own blades from straps tucked high on their thighs.

Doriel threw up their arms. "Do none of you obey the rules?"

A quiet gurgle drew me back to Yrselle. Her hand was wrapped around the Ignios King's wrist. Her nails sank into his flesh, and her bright, bloody smile stretched from ear to ear.

He grunted and reared back for another blow. With one last thrust of his godstone knife into her heart, Yrselle's eyes fluttered, and she was gone.

The ground began to tremble.

The fire atop the Umbros obelisk hissed and faded with a wisp of smoke. The light illuminating the etched sigil of its realm—a skull with a chain around its throat—guttered into darkness.

Far away, a gryvern wailed in mourning.

A sharp pain pressed between my temples. The air felt hot. *Too* hot. Too heavy. Like it was crushing me in from the top of my head.

"No," I whimpered. "Please—*no.*"

The blade clattered from my hand as my knees crashed to the floor. I gripped my head and screamed.

Two beams of dark light shot through the sky.

One from the heartstone.

And one from me—the new Queen of Umbros.

CHAPTER

SEVENTY-FIVE

"I t's true... Blessed Kindred, look at her Crown—she has four of them now."

"We have to kill her, or she'll kill us and take ours, too."

"Doriel, what now? What do we do?"

"I... I don't know..."

"Fuck this. I'm going back to my realm."

The Crowns were shouting, arguing, clumping in groups, snapping out threats.

None of them dared to come near me.

I struggled to push upright through the drumbeat in my ears and the smothering weight on my head.

"Call the army in now, Sophos. Arrest her. Hurry, before she kills again."

"*You're* the one who killed Umbros, you ass."

"Sophos can't arrest her now. She just claimed the sixth vote. She and her mother are pardoned."

My eyes flew open.

Pardoned.

We were pardoned. We were *free*.

Unless my mother or I committed another crime on this island, the Crowns couldn't hold me. My mother and I could take Teller and go home.

748

We could be together as a family, mourn my father, and begin to pick up the pieces of our lives without him.

I could rule my realms in peace—and take control of the Emarion Army.

My chest shook as delirious laughter bubbled out. The other Crowns fell silent.

"You fucking traitors," I choked out between uncontrollable giggles. "You Kindred-cursed pieces of shit." I snorted loudly. "You absolute rancid, stinking *prunes*."

"I think all those Crowns have made her go mad," someone murmured.

I stood and wiped the tears streaming from my eyes. "Even your own gods know you're worthless. I got half his realm killed, and Umbros *still* thought I was a better candidate than—" I grabbed my side and doubled over into more laughter before I could finish.

"Let's retake the vote," Ignios insisted. "Sophos, Meros—one of you needs to change your decision." He raised his blade, Yrselle's blood still dripping from its edge. "Do it or else."

"Or else what, you'll kill us and give her a *fifth* Crown to vote with?" Meros snapped. "Try it, and I'll make sure she gets your Crown next, Ignios."

"Don't worry, Yrselle already took care of that," I said, tapping my wrist with a wink.

Ignios looked at my arm and frowned, his head tilting to and fro like a dog staring in a mirror. When his eyes dropped to the beads of blood on his own wrist and finally bulged in understanding, I burst out in laughter again.

He stormed to Yrselle's corpse and grabbed her hand, squinting close at her nails—then let out a shriek. "She scratched me with fucking *godstone!*"

I grinned. "She sure knew how to give one hell of a coronation gift." I rolled my neck to adjust to the added weight of the Umbros Crown, then grabbed my fallen blade. My eyes ticked to the cauldron above the Umbros arch, now relit with midnight flame.

Four Crowns—soon to be five, once the godstone did its work on Ignios. If I claimed one more, I would control every vote.

The temptation was *staggering*.

The bloodlust must have been screaming on my face, because even the confident Faunos Queen quietly edged away.

"I'm going to die," Ignios wailed. "That bitch killed me!" He scraped frantically at his wrist. "Someone cut my arm off—quick, before it gets to my heart."

"I'll do it," I chirped. *And my blade might slip and slice your throat in the process.*

He was so desperate, he actually started to walk toward me.

"Stop, Ignios, before you get yourself killed," Doriel muttered, their eyes rolling high. "Come to my realm after the ritual. My researchers have a cure."

His orange eyes bulged. "They do?"

I frowned. "They *do?*"

"And you didn't tell me?" Meros asked softly, a small crease forming on his brow.

"It's new," Doriel rushed out. "We didn't know it worked until the battle. When we tried it on the wounded, it stopped the toxin on every last one."

I fell still. "All of them? They *all* recovered?"

Ignios cackled loudly. "Hear that, Umbros?" He slammed his sandaled foot into Yrselle's corpse.

"Stop it," I hissed, feeling a sudden, strange new protectiveness over her body.

He turned to me and flashed a toothy grin, bright like pearls against his ruddy, sun-darkened skin. He held my stare as his foot connected with Yrselle's lovely, lifeless face.

Fury scorched the inside of my skin. "You know what? Fuck your coronation. Let the Forging spell rot. Let all your borders fall. I don't care." I snapped on my heel to storm from the Temple.

"Diem," Doriel said with a tone of warning. "You're going to want to stay."

"Go freeze in the glaciers of hell, Doriel. I'm getting my Prince, and we're going h—"

"*Diem!*"

I stilled mid-step.

That voice... gods, please, not *that* voice.

"I was worried something like this might happen," Doriel said. "I brought someone along to ensure your cooperation."

My head turned, and there he was—two brown eyes and a splash of auburn hair.

Flanked by a host of army soldiers with a blade pressed to his neck.

"Teller!" I screamed. "Don't you touch him. *Don't you fucking touch him!*"

"They won't. Not as long as you do as I say."

My temper exploded behind my eyes in a scarlet mist of blood and brimstone. If I'd had access to my magic, I would have razed the Temple to dust. I would have razed the whole damn island to dust.

"I'm going to destroy you," I seethed, stalking toward Doriel. "I'm going to make you—"

"Diem," Teller cried out again, his voice—that familiar, most beloved voice—now shrill with pain.

I jerked to a stop and looked out to see him on his knees, a rivulet of blood trickling down his neck.

I couldn't breathe.

"Don't take one more step," Doriel warned. "They've been ordered to kill him if you get within striking range of any Crown."

I lurched backward into the Lumnos arch, staring in horror at my bleeding brother, unable to look away.

He hadn't come easily. The two guards who held him had blood on their uniforms and still-healing bruises on their faces.

And so did Teller.

The sight of it set me ablaze.

"You have no idea the mistake you've just made," I whispered in a voice hushed but unstoppably destructive, like a loosed arrow whistling toward its mark.

"I have people to protect, and I'll use whatever means I have available to protect them. Don't deny that you would do the same."

My jaw ground tight. "Your people will die for this."

"Is that a threat?" they hissed.

"It's a *fact*. Ophiucae will strike again, and by the time you realize you need me, it will be too late."

"Well I'll know where to find you," they muttered. They glanced at the sunset. "We need to hurry, we're running out of time."

My instincts prickled. "Time for what?"

Doriel ignored me and turned their attention to the others. "My fellow Crowns, I also bring a proposal for a vote. Something that has not been done since the days of the Blessed Kindred. Rather than merely refreshing the Forging spell for the coronation... I propose we *revise* it."

Ignios grunted. "If you say you want to give yourself control of her realms, Sophos..."

"Not at all. My proposal is for this island. We must secure this Temple from rebel control."

"You can do that by working with me and my mother," I snapped.

"Even if we trusted you, your mother won't lead the Guardians forever. She's a mortal, and an older one at that. She'll be dead before we know it."

I flinched at the reminder.

"We need a permanent solution, and luckily, the Blessed Kindred provided us one." Doriel pointed to the glassy rock on the pedestal at the Temple's center. "I've been researching everything the Kindred wrote on the Forging spell. In it, they built wards around the heartstone to protect it from harm."

"So much for that," I mumbled.

Their eyes flashed to me in subtle warning. Explaining why my blood cracked the heartstone would reveal the truth about Omnos. Tempting as it was to betray Doriel in retribution, I held my tongue. Disclosing my heritage now would do me more harm than good.

"I propose we enhance those protections," they went on. "We take the heartstone's existing defenses, and we expand them to kill any person who steps foot on Coeurîle without a Crown."

"We can do that?" Faunos asked.

They nodded. "The magic that protects the heartstone is already deadly. We're simply unleashing it to its full extent."

"If the Blessed Kindred approved of that, wouldn't they have done it themselves?" Arboros asked. I found myself nodding in agreement, then wondering when I started caring what the Kindred approved of.

"They gave us the power to modify the Forging spell as long as we act unanimously. They wouldn't have done that if they didn't trust us to use it."

Faunos groaned. "I'll agree to whatever you want, if it will get this over with."

Doriel looked to Ignios, who smirked eagerly, then to Arboros, who looked pained as she lowered her eyes and nodded. They exchanged a quick look with Meros, then approached the heartstone and pulled out the ritual dagger.

It wasn't lost on me that no one confirmed my vote. The implication was clear—I would agree, or my brother would pay the price.

As Doriel shed their blood and began reciting the ritual's script, my eyes skimmed the island and paused on the Guardians being held back by the patrolling gryverns.

"There are people on the island now," I blurted out, stopping Doriel's speech. "Won't they all die if we cast this spell?"

"They'll have until sunset to leave."

"*Sunset?* Doriel, the sun's nearly gone now. That's not enough time!"

"Then you should stop interrupting me."

"The Guardians don't even have boats docked. They need at least a few days to send hawks."

"There are army vessels at the Fortos port. If the rebels give up peacefully, they'll be given safe passage to the prison."

"That's not—"

"*Back to the ritual*," they said archly with a discussion-ending glare. "As I was saying..."

Bile rose in my throat. I'd walked the mortals straight into a trap. Either certain death on the island, or torture and imprisonment on the continent.

A throat softly cleared to my right.

My gaze lifted and met two sad emerald eyes. They darted to the Guardians, then cut over her slender shoulder—toward the Arboros port.

I didn't dare show any reaction, but a gasp of relief left my lips at her offer. If I could get the rebels to the Arboros port, its Queen would get them to land.

"With this spell," Doriel began, "we bind Diem Bellator to this island. May she never again leave these shores."

A heavy *clang* resounded in my skull at the weight of those words, at their inescapable finality. There were no loopholes, no exceptions. There would be no rescue.

I was trapped.

Just like Ophiucae all those years ago.

"Furthermore," Doriel continued, "from the setting of this day's sun, may the heartstone strike dead any person who sets foot on this island, or any beast who flies over its borders, except for the nine Crowns of Emarion."

"You're even banning the gryverns?" I said bitterly.

"Well we can't have yours attacking us when we come to the island for rituals, can we?"

"Right," I muttered, looking up. "Only you and Meros get to do that."

Their jaw twitched, but they didn't respond.

I stared out at my brother through the wall of flames from the two circling gryverns, wishing with all my heart that I could push my thoughts into his head. An apology—*so many* apologies. A promise to make this right somehow. And a plea for him to fight. To survive.

One by one, each Crown stepped forward to shed their blood, and I threw every ember of my hatred into my glare. I refused to look away from the uncertain resignation of Meros, the forlorn shame of Arboros, the jaded indifference of Faunos. Only Ignios would look me in the eyes, and only because he reveled in my fury.

When my turn arrived, Doriel laid down the ritual dagger on the pedestal and stepped out of my reach. I curled my upper lip and picked it up, but as I brought the blade to my palm, my body felt as if it were fighting against itself. My hands quivered, refusing to press the edge to flesh.

"The spell only works if the blood is given willingly," Doriel reminded me. "If you can't convince yourself you want to do this—"

"Then you'll torture my innocent brother, a subject of *your* realm, who you vowed to protect?" I gritted out. "Yes, I'm aware."

They shifted on their feet, unable to meet my eyes. "We'll need your brother to ensure your cooperation for future rituals, so keeping him safe will be my highest priority. He can do whatever he pleases in my realm. Full access. I'll even put him on the selection committee for mortals invited to study, so he can address the inequities you spoke of. I'll make sure his every need is taken care of."

"How very generous. I'm sure he'll be thrilled with his golden shackles."

They sighed. "I take no pleasure in this, Diem. I am genuinely grateful for what you did in my realm. Once Ophiucae is dead and your magic is lost to the bargain, we'll recast the spell and let you go."

"Ignios will never agree to release me."

They dropped their voice. "Then we'll get a new Ignios who will."

Our gazes met. I looked for some sign of doubt in their eyes, but there was only the firm resolve of a ruler who believed this was the only way to save their realm.

Maybe this *was* for the best. I didn't want to kill Ophiucae—at least now, I wouldn't have to. And if my magic was gone, my enemies would lose their interest. My family would be safe. Luther and I could have our quiet life of irrelevance.

Isn't that what I claimed to want, to run away and leave all my problems behind?

A deep, sorrowful ache settled in my chest.

I sliced my palm before the regret could spread any further. The stones on the ritual dagger flashed a steely grey, but this time, there was no thunder, no earthquake, only the hiss of bubbling blood as it fell and melted into the stone.

A glowing orb built within the heartstone's center, illuminating its jagged, glassy peaks. A blinding pulse of light shot out in a ring and rippled over the planes of the island. My body flushed with energy as it passed over me, binding me to my fate.

"The spell is cast," Doriel announced.

I tossed the bloody dagger at their feet. "Now get my brother off this island."

"Not until you're in the cell."

"Doriel," I snarled.

"*In the cell*, Diem."

I looked out at the dark doorway in the brush. My throat squeezed shut, my lungs clawing for breath. A sudden overwhelming terror seemed to trap me, bury me, suffocate me in open air.

That cell had destroyed Ophiucae. It had turned his heart cold and gnawed at his soul until there was nothing left of it but a thirst for revenge.

And it would do the same to me. I could feel it—the hate that would fester in that lonely, unrelenting darkness.

The monster I would become.

"No," I breathed. I was ashamed of the whimper that shuddered out and the tremble that overtook me, but I was powerless to stop either. "I—I won't. I can't."

"Diem, you—"

"I don't want to become like him, Doriel. Please. *Please.*"

Their glare broke, a glint of understanding in their eyes. They stole a look at the thin orange sliver of the setting sun. "You will stay in this Temple until everyone is off the island. If you don't—"

I nodded frantically. "My brother, I know."

"Give me your weapon."

Shit. I would need that to hunt for food and build a shelter.

And to kill the other Crowns the second they came back to the island.

But more than that, I needed Teller to live.

I grabbed my dagger and threw it to the ground, then scrambled backward with my hands raised and a nervous eye on my brother's guards.

Doriel grabbed the two blades and rushed out of the Temple. They set off in a run down the path toward their dock, their gryvern flying overhead and spraying flames to keep the rebels away. Their guards fell in behind them and dragged my kicking, screaming brother in their wake.

I heard a piercing whistle, and the wall of soldiers around the island began to retreat. The other Crowns had already fled for their boats, and the Meros gryvern was no longer in sight.

I ran to the edge of the dais. "Run!" I yelled at the Guardians. "You're all in danger. You have to get off the island before the sun sets."

They stared at each other, at me, at the sun, at the receding army, unsure what to believe. A few began to walk toward me, while others stubbornly held their ground.

"Head south," I shouted, pointing for the Arboros port. "If you stay here, you'll die—*hurry!*"

Slowly, they started for the southern coast. My heart thrashed at their tentative pace, too oblivious to the invisible threat chasing them, but my attention was stolen by sounds drifting from deep within the brush—grunts, shouting, and the clash of metal-on-metal.

I squinted into the horizon, and my body locked up. Near the path to the Sophos port, the tall grass was shaking—not the slow sway of the evening breeze, but a violent disturbance that could only be man-made.

Icy fingers slithered over my skin.

Seconds later, my fears became cruelly well-founded. The grass parted, and three men broke free.

Three familiar men.

A shrill, desperate "*No!*" tore out of my throat.

Teller, Luther, and Perthe sprinted toward me at a furious pace, with Doriel and their guards in hot pursuit.

"Stop!" I screamed. I shook my head and pointed for the shore. "Go back—leave me, get off the island!"

Uncertainty passed over Teller's features. His pace slowed, but Luther was a man determined, and nothing would turn him from me.

My eyes shot to Doriel in the distance. They looked at my brother, then the sun, then their guards. They stopped running, and their gaze met mine. A heart-stopping apology settled on their face.

"Doriel, *no*," I screamed, a burning stinging at my eyes.

It wasn't enough. Doriel barked something at their guards, and they turned as a group, running for the Sophos port instead.

I flew down the Temple steps and crashed into Luther's approaching arms. His eyes were wilder than I'd ever seen them. He gripped my face in his palms, swiping away the wetness on my cheeks. "You're safe, my heart. I'm here."

"No—Luther, you have to go. The Crowns cast a spell that will kill anyone on the island once the sun sets." I tried to shove him off, but he held me firm. "Luther, please. Take Teller and run."

"Understood. Let's go." He reached to grab my hand to take me with him.

I jerked away.

He fell deathly still. "You're coming with us."

To anyone else, the growling command would seem absolute in its resolve—but I heard the fearful question that trembled underneath.

I shook my head in despair. "The spell..."

His expression hardened. "I'm not leaving you behind. If you're dying here, I'm dying at your side."

"I won't die, but you three will. You have to leave, Luther, time is running out."

"Diem—"

"*Leave*," I shrieked. I pounded my fists at his chest in an urgent frenzy. "If you love me, stop talking and *run*. Take my brother and—"

My eyes snagged on a flicker of darkness over the swaying grass, then shot to the splinter of red-orange that had nearly vanished in the sky. There were minutes left at most—maybe only seconds. The Lumnos port was at least a twenty minute walk, the Sophos port even further. Even if they ran...

Too late.

They weren't going to make it.

Luther caught me as my knees crumpled. "It's alright," he soothed. "We'll leave now."

"It's too late," I gasped, tears in freefall down my face.

I'm too late.

Everything shattered inside of me.

My most loyal guard, my baby brother, the man I loved—I was going to lose them all. They were going to die right here in front of my eyes.

All because I was too damn late.

A rift cracked through the center of my soul. It split me open with the same explosive destruction as my falling blood when it fractured the heartstone.

I no longer feared the cold, heartless monster Ophiucae had become—I welcomed it. I would embrace it with hateful glee. I would devour the world whole for all that they had taken from me. I would become a thing of vengeance and spite, I would—

Thump, thump, thump.

Luther's hand tightened on my arm.

"Blessed Kindred," he breathed.

I straightened. "Is that...?"

His eyes slid to the west, then grew wide at the sight of Sorae's outline on the horizon. "It worked. It actually worked. I didn't think..."

"*What* worked?"

He gazed at me, his features strained, like he was holding something back. Something desperately, painfully important.

"It doesn't matter," I cut in. "Go—run as fast as you can. And don't come back. The spell will kill her too if she returns after sunset."

He grabbed my jaw and crushed his lips to mine. "Stay strong, my Queen. No force in the world will keep me from you forever."

I wanted so badly to pour out the full truth of my love for him, but there were not enough words, and so very little time. I pushed him off, then looked at my brother. "Go get Mother, Tel. Then go get your girl."

His jaw flexed. "Love you, D."

I looked at Perthe. "Get my brother on that gryvern."

He nodded. "I will, Your Majesty."

I forced myself to turn my back to them, knowing one more word, one more *look*, could cost me everything. The cadence of their fading bootsteps and the howling cry of an approaching gryvern was the most beautiful music to my ears.

Sorae had come. She had known I needed her, and she had broken free of Remis's chains to get to me. It seemed utterly impossible—even if our bond had somehow overcome the island's effects, the flight from Lumnos would have taken at least an hour or two. I hadn't even known I was in danger for that long.

Wait. If she'd come to save *me*...

I whipped back around, and my heart plunged as my terror was confirmed. Sorae was spearing through the air—but her eyes were on me.

Only on me.

"Sorae, no!" I shouted.

Her talons opened wide in preparation to snatch me from the ground. I ran back up the steps to the Temple and cowered inside the Lumnos arch where she couldn't get to me. I tried to send a command through the bond, but it was suffocated by the island's oppressive force.

"Save them!" I yelled at her loud enough to bleed my throat raw. "Leave me—take *them!*"

Her golden eyes filled with conflict as her sensitive hearing picked up on my words.

"Save them, Sorae. *That's an order!*"

I could see on her face that her heart was still torn, but her body was helpless to disobey. Her wings tilted down, and her path shifted.

My heart stopped beating.

If she touched the soil, she would die.

If she missed them, they would die.

If she didn't get off the island in the next few seconds, they *all* would die.

The dark monster of vengeance waited in the wings as my fate played out on stage before my eyes.

The three men sprinted toward my gryvern, whose legs trailed dangerously close to the ground. Perthe turned his head and yelled something at Luther, who nodded. Suddenly, they grabbed my brother and launched him into the air—right into Sorae's outstretched talon, which closed tight around his waist.

Teller reached his arms down. One hand clutched fast to Perthe's wrist. The other...

Luther's fingers hooked to my brother's, but the grip was flimsy and weak. Sorae was moving too fast, Luther too slow. He began to slip.

He was going to die.

My Prince. My *heart*.

The man who'd sworn to be my equal partner in all things, who had seen me for all that I was, my light and my darkness, and not only accepted me, but cherished me. Loved me.

The man I'd given myself to, wholly and unconditionally. The man I wanted to spend my forever with. The man I wanted as my mate.

And now I'd never get the chance.

I cried out a broken, anguished sound as Teller's fingers slipped, and my Prince dropped from his grasp.

He was falling. *Dying.*

And then Teller's hand released from Perthe's wrist—and closed around Luther's.

Sorae banked up into the sky, my brother in her talon, my heart dangling from his grip.

Perthe crashed to the soil, somehow managing to stay on his feet. He staggered forward with the momentum, then slowed to a walk, then stopped.

His shoulders slowly rose and fell.

He turned to face me. Lifted his chin. Placed his fist over his chest, then sank to one knee.

Tears flowed down my face in rapids. I pressed my fist to my chest and lowered my head in a final salute to my faithful guard.

The last ray of sunlight vanished over the horizon. Another pulse of light shot from the heartstone across the island, and Perthe's body slumped to the ground.

In the distance, my gryvern kept flying.

I sank to my knees and buried my face in my hands, overcome by bittersweet sorrow and joy, liberating relief and crushing loss.

Teller had sacrificed Perthe to save Luther, perhaps as much for Lily's benefit as mine.

Oh, how that choice would weigh on him. How the guilt and second-guessing would chase him through dark thoughts, haunting him as surely as it would haunt me.

Sorae swooped in wide circles outside the island, seeming unable to tear herself from my sight. Or perhaps it was a final kindness, so I could watch as Teller and Luther climbed up her side and mounted her back.

They were safe. I dragged breath into my lungs and tried to find some shred of solace in that. My brother was alive and safe and out of Doriel's hands. Luther would help him find my mother, and they could finally go home.

And Luther was alive. The future we'd planned was not yet lost—its flame still glowed, lost in the shadows but burning strong. I had committed myself to him, to *us*, and now that I knew he was out there fighting to get to me, I would fight just as hard to find my way back to him.

And when I did, I'd tell him everything. I'd tell him that I was his and he was mine, now and always. I would tell him I wanted to be bound with him forever, in whatever life we could make in this world, and in eternity thereafter.

The very first chance I got, I would offer up my blood and tell him I was ready to be his ma—

Thwack.

A blur at the base of my vision.

A heavy pressure building inside my ribs.

A liquid warmth trailing down my chest.

Then pain.

Why was there *so much* pain?

My chin dipped as my gaze fell to my body, where the bloody point of a long, glittering black blade had erupted from my flesh.

Straight through the center of my heart.

"Doriel has their way of getting rid of problems," a low voice hissed. The sword jerked deeper. "And I have mine."

Dying feels different than I thought.

The thought floated idly through my head.

Death was supposed to be cold, wasn't it? Lonely. One's life flashing before their eyes, perhaps last-minute regrets of loves lost or choices made.

But this felt... warm.

Painful, yes. Searing agony splintered through every nerve. My heart felt like it was being shredded in half—which, by the slowing throb in my chest, it probably was.

But there was an unexpected pleasure in it, too. A peculiar rightness. A feeling like I'd just gained something I desperately wanted.

Then, the throbbing stopped, replaced by a strange kind of calm. A comforting, eternal peace.

"You were an interesting opponent, Lumnos, I'll give you that."

The blade slid out of my chest with a nauseating slurp, and my body collapsed to the ground. A boot nudged my side, knocking me on my back, and through a hazy vision veiled with shimmering gold, the smirking face of the Ignios King stared back.

"But the flames always win in the end."

To be continued...

READY FOR MORE?

The journey concludes in Burn of the Everflame, book four in the Kindred's Curse Saga, releasing Spring 2024 and available for pre-order now on Amazon.

———— ☼ ————

To get access to ARC opportunities, bonus chapters, exclusive content, and the latest news on new releases, subscribe to Penn's newsletter at

www.penncole.com/newsletter

———— ☼ ————

Want to discuss the book, trade theories on all the clues, and get exclusive sneak peeks of Burn? Join Penn's reader group, **Penn's Pals,** at

www.penncole.com/discuss

ACKNOWLEDGMENTS

If you've made it this far, THANK YOU THANK YOU THANK YOU!

Heat has been an absolute beast. It took two months to plan, eight months to write, and six months to edit (and quite possibly took you a whole month to read). I agonized over whether to split this book up or make significant cuts, but ultimately I decided to trust that you all would be up for an epic, twisty-turny journey and would stick with me for the story I believed in telling.

For me, this book is so much about Diem's growth. When we first met her in Spark, Diem was a woman in denial over just about everything, and she had no idea what she wanted. Seeing how far she has come by the end of Heat—how much she has learned to believe in herself, and how she has taken ownership of both her Crown and her heart—makes me a proud mama hen. Through it all, she has managed to hold onto her compassion and her capacity for hope and forgiveness. While some (both inside and outside of the book) might see those as faults, I think they're her biggest strengths of all.

Or at least, they *were*. It's just too bad about that godstone blade to the heart, right? RIP.

This book is also about the nuances of doing the right thing. This story has few true villains or heroes, but it does have a lot of complicated people trying to, in Diem's words, "be a *good person* in a system built on a fundamental *bad*." Whether it's their family, their people, or their realm, just about everyone in this book believes their actions are justified to protect someone else. How do you come together when both sides are convinced they are fighting the good fight? There are no easy answers, but I hope that in this book, as in life, you can try to *understand*, even if you don't *agree*.

My biggest thank you for this book goes to the members of my street team, #TeamLuther, #AAH (book four is his book to shine, I SWEAR!!), and all my Penn's Pals Discord members. Your love and support has been absolutely unreal. You keep me going when this indie author life gets tough, and I owe every bit of my success to you. Thank you for letting me be an absolute menace and loving me anyway. All of you mean the world to me.

Thank you to every single person who has been so vocal on social media about these books. I can't count the number of times I have burst into tears because I stumbled across a post in the wild of someone recommending Spark in a Facebook group or including it in a reel or sharing it with their followers. For a new indie author like me, that word-of-mouth support is everything. I am so, so grateful.

Thank you to my darling husband, who makes even Luther Corbois pale in comparison. I'd make you my King Consort any day.

Thank you to Ivy and Sheila, the best colleagues an indie author could ask for, and to all the authors of IAA and FaRoFeb who have offered up advice, support, perspective, humor, and camaraderie. The indie author community is so incredibly welcoming and open, and I am forever grateful to be part of it.

Thank you to my fantastic editor Kelly, to Maria for the lovely cover, to Stella and Vee for your gorgeous art, and to Alex for all your help with video content, your supportive texts, our all-night Zoom calls, and generally just being fabulous.

Finally, to anyone reading this: when it seems like the world wants to crush your spirit and burn you alive, never forget my little flames, pressure and heat make *diamonds*.

ABOUT THE AUTHOR

 Penn's life has taken her through many ups and downs, but her love for literature has forever been her true north. Ever since she was a child, she has been filling mountains of notebooks with elaborate worlds, feisty women, and angsty romances.

After a detour as an artist, attorney, and small business owner, she is thrilled to finally have accomplished her lifelong dream of becoming an author.

Although Penn is a Texas girl born and bred, she currently lives in France with her husband, where she can usually be found sipping wine and eating far too many pastries.

instagram.com/AuthorPennCole

twitter.com/AuthorPennCole

tiktok.com/@AuthorPennCole

goodreads.com/penncole

amazon.com/author/penncole

facebook.com/authorpenncole

Made in United States
Troutdale, OR
10/25/2023

14001168R00470